D0267990

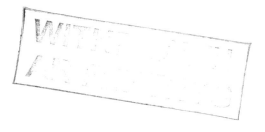

WANSEA LIBRARIE

600027169

The
Lost
Time
Accidents

ALSO BY JOHN WRAY

The Right Hand of Sleep
Canaan's Tongue
Lowboy

The
Lost
Time
Accidents
John Wray

CANONGATE

Edinburgh · London

Published in Great Britain in 2016 by Canongate Books Ltd,
14 High Street, Edinburgh EH1 1TE

www.canongate.tv

1

Copyright © 2016 by John Wray

The moral right of the author has been asserted

First published in the United States in 2016 by Farrar, Straus and Giroux
18 West 18th Street, New York 10011

British Library Cataloguing-in-Publication Data
A catalogue record for this book is available on
request from the British Library

ISBN 978 1 78211 892 3
Export ISBN 978 1 84767 231 5

Designed by Abby Kagan

Print and bound in Great Britain by Clays Ltd, St Ives plc.

FSC
www.fsc.org

MIX
Paper from
responsible sources
FSC® C020471

For Edward and Barbara and Peter and Annemarie.

I saw Eternity the other night,
Like a great ring of pure and endless light,
All calm, as it was bright;
And round beneath it Time, in hours, days, years,
Driven by the spheres,
Like a vast shadow moved; in which the world
And all her train were hurled.

– HENRY VAUGHAN

The
Lost
Time
Accidents

Dear Mrs. Haven—

This morning, at 08:47 EST, I woke up to find myself excused from time.

I can picture you perfectly, reading this letter. You'll be telling yourself I've gone stupid with grief, or that I've lost my mind—but my thinking has never been clearer. Believe me, Mrs. Haven, when I tell you that this is no joke. Time moves freely around me, gurgling like a whirlpool, fluxing like a quantum field, spinning like a galaxy around its focal hub—at the hub, however, everything is quiet.

Is there a chance, no matter how infinitesimal, that you'll find and read this manuscript one day? If I didn't think so, I could never keep on. And if I don't keep on I'll disappear completely.

A physicist might term this place a "singularity"—a point in spacetime where the laws of the cosmos have snapped—but it's like no singularity I've heard of. As you know very well, the only type of singularity permitted by physics is a point of infinite density and weight, ripping everything—even light itself—out of the continuum in which time exists. A black hole, in other words, which should have torn me limb from limb by now.

But this place is no black hole. I'm sure of that.

It's comfortable, first of all: an armchair, a card table, a half-empty bottle of Foster's Lager, a ream of stationery, and a refillable tortoiseshell pen, the kind you see in duty-free airplane catalogs but would never dream of actually buying. It also happens to be a place I know well: the library of my deceased aunts' apartment on 109th Street and Fifth Avenue, on the fourth floor of a crumbling brownstone with the improbable name of the General Lee, at the middle-income end of Central Park. You never came here, Mrs. Haven, because my aunts stopped receiving visitors during the Nixon administration. But I want to make sure you can see this place clearly. Cramped though it is, it's my entire world.

Monday, 08:47 EST

If God had commanded Noah to build an ark for consumer goods instead of animals—and if Noah had been a drunken paranoiac—his ark might have resembled this apartment. The room I'm in is twenty by thirty, cavernous by Harlem standards: its floors are parquet, its bay windows gothic, its ceiling age-buckled and brown. I have a watery memory, from childhood, of powder-blue walls, but from where I sit there's no sure way of telling. That's because aside from a bell-shaped perimeter surrounding this chair—and a kind of tunnel meandering from one room to the next—every cubic inch of this apartment is taken up by shoe boxes, newspapers, Styrofoam peanuts, cinder blocks, dressmaker's dummies, Game Boys, PA systems, dollhouses, Harlequin romances, collectible plates, chandeliers, sawhorses, carburetors, bicycles, almanacs, humidors, assault rifles, fainting couches, chalkboards, VHS players, Betamax players, laser disc players, Frisbees, ziggurats of balding tennis balls, half a century's worth of *Popular Mechanics*, *Omni*, *The Wall Street Journal*, *Amazing Stories*, *Scientific American*, *Barely Legal*, *Juggs*, *Modern Internment Magazine*, mail-order catalogs, college yearbooks, high school yearbooks, product manuals for discontinued products, and every other sort of flotsam you can think of. Not to mention clocks, needless to say, this being Tolliver property: chronometers of every make and model, pendulums primed, springs oiled and wound, circuitry buzzing, charting Spanish Harlem's progress through the so-called fourth dimension with a constancy that makes me want to cry.

I'm not sure how much you heard about my aunts' demise—the papers were full of it for a while, especially the tabloids—but it wasn't a dignified passing. They had trouble letting go of things, Mrs. Haven. I've been told that it runs in the family.

Monday, 08:47 EST

One of the first clues I got, as a child, that my father and I hailed from different star systems arrived in the form of a joke. It was in the dog days of a flawless upstate summer, one I'd half convinced myself would never end: I was sitting with my mother in our humid, sun-drenched kitchen, picking at a scab on my left elbow and grumbling about going back to school. Orson—he insisted I refer to him as "Orson," never "Dad"—came up from his writing room in the basement, grinning for some reason I never discovered. He listened to my bitching for as long as he could stand it.

"There's a Venusian proverb, Waldy, that you might find instructive."

I took the bait and asked him what it was.

"Time flies like an arrow." He paused for dramatic effect. "*Fruit* flies, on the other hand, like a banana."

That was it. He looked from my mother's face to mine, deeply pleased with himself, then let out a belch and retreated downstairs, like a squid escaping in a cloud of ink.

Orson had a terrible sense of humor, Mrs. Haven—a pulp fictioneer's sense of humor, the most cornpone there is—but this joke, in particular, preyed on my six-year-old mind like a tick. When I found out, years later, that he'd stolen it from the Marx Brothers, I actually danced a little jig: it was Groucho's children's cross to bear, not mine. But I can't help but be reminded of it now, when time isn't flying at all, and my existence has become like that banana: a battered, motionless mass, soft and greasy and passive, with memories harassing it like flies.

The reason Orson's joke got under my skin was this: I knew, even then, that time doesn't fly like an arrow. The belief that every physicist since Newton has been a fraud or a sucker (or both) is our family dogma, passed from generation to generation like a vendetta or an allergy to nuts. I was weaned on the proposition that time flies like a boomerang, or like a satellite, or—if an arrow at all—like the arrow on a well-oiled weathervane. My aunts always claimed that I'd be the one to lead the Tollivers out of oblivion's subbasement, to popularize their crackpot notions, to sell our shared obsession to the world: that's why I was given my great-uncle's name. I resisted their prophecy as long as I could, but in the end I had to slay their dragons for them. What else could I do, with a name like Waldemar?

Believe it or not, Mrs. Haven, there was a time when my name sounded noble and strange to my ears, like Aragorn or Thor or Ivanhoe. I was knee-high to a ball of snot back then, as Orson liked to say, and my aunts and grandfather (and even Orson himself) were like sorcerers or demigods to me. I knew nothing about my namesake—everyone made very sure of that—except that he'd done some extraordinary thing. A hush crept into the voices of the grown-ups whenever the subject came up, and his name was rarely uttered, as if its power might wear thin with repetition. I grew to see myself as heir apparent to a grand occult tradition—one that mustn't be alluded to until I came of age. I promised myself I'd learn everything I could about this great-uncle of mine, the better to do my mystic birthright justice. And I told no one my plan, not even my doting, long-suffering mother.

I must have known, even then, that the day would come when it would cause her pain.

Monday, 08:47 EST

I can't see much in my current position, but I'm not too far from the windows, and—if I crane my neck to look past a cracked lucite bust of J. W. Dunne—I can make out a light-speckled sliver of park. For an hour a day, the view has the patina of a retouched picture postcard: the willow boughs sigh, the asphalt promenades gloam, and Nutter's Battery and the old wooden boathouse hum with a mystery they could never aspire to at noon. Right now, for example, the evening sun is setting across Harlem Meer, glimmering up from the pond scum, giving a pair of overweight maintenance workers the look of lovers in a cheap romantic comedy. The universe is still in motion, close enough to take hold of, patiently awaiting my return; but the clock at my elbow—a Tolliver Magnetic Chronometer, model 8-Ω, accurate to .000000000000000178 of a second—remains frozen, Miss Havisham–like, at 08:47 Eastern Standard Time.

So many forces had to conspire for our paths through the chronosphere to intersect, Mrs. Haven, let alone for us to share a bed. Isn't that a great and terrifying notion? If the past of a given event—let's call it event X—might be considered as all things that can influence X (as mainstream physicists claim), then the whole of human history could be thought of as the past of our affair. You've decided, under the influence of God knows what toxic cocktail of fear and regret, to deny the events of the last seven months; but I believe—I have no choice but to believe—that if I bear witness to our history, you'll consent to raise it back up from the grave.

I can picture you shaking your head as you read this, your magnificent corkscrew-curled head with its translucent ears. You've ordered me, in no uncertain terms, to obliterate all traces of our friendship: I've received clear instructions, in writing, to cease and desist. I don't blame you for that. We were given three shots, after all—far more than we deserved—and we bungled each one.

Our last and bravest attempt ended on the morning of August 14, between 08:17 and 11:47 CET, in the honeymoon suite of the Hotel Zrada, in that fatal little town in Moravia whose name I choose not to recall. We'd slept with our clothes on, a full arm's length apart, a first in all our secret life together. You informed me that you'd struggled all night to come to a decision; your coppery hair stuck straight out on one side, I remember, as though pointing the way out the door. I noticed a minor constellation of freckles under your left clavicle—a faint, Pleiades-like clustering I didn't recognize—and wondered whether your recent safari in Mr. Haven's company might have brought it to the surface of your skin. A vision came to me of you riding naked on a Bengal tiger, leading a winding file of porters through the khaki-colored bush; I tried to make a joke about it, but instead let out a strangled chirp, like a deaf child attempting to speak.

You took no notice, Mrs. Haven, because you were making a speech of your own. I watched your beautiful lips move, unable to follow. Something momentous was happening, that much was obvious, but my conscious mind refused to let it in. I thought of something you'd said on our first day together, coming out of the Ziegfeld after seeing some by-the-algorithm Hollywood romance:

"There ought to be a word for this feeling, Walter."

"What feeling is that?"

"The one when you come out of a movie—in the daytime especially—and everything still feels like part of it."

"The ancient Greeks called it *euphasia*," I'd said, inventing a word off the top of my head.

"Aren't *you* the bright penny," you'd laughed, then asked me to spell it for you, which I did. I could do no wrong that perfect afternoon.

"*Euphasia*," you'd said thoughtfully. "I'll make a note of that."

My memory of our last hours has gone nova since then, grown so bloated and bright that it's all I can see, though I sense—though I *know*— that glorious things are hidden just behind it. I want to make a pilgrimage back along the causal chain: to line up my mistakes in a row, for the sake of comparison, with those of all my star-crossed ancestors. From the moment we met I've felt like an impostor, like the single normally proportioned member of a clan of sideshow geeks, desperate to keep his pedigree obscured. That ends as of this writing, Mrs. Haven. I want to explain the Tollivers to you, to take you on a private tour of our shabby little hall of curiosities; but in order to do that properly, I've got to take an axe to the vitrines. I'll have to reckon with my namesake—Waldemar, Freiherr von Toula, physicist and fanatic, the Black Timekeeper of Äschenwald-Czas—by testifying to his many crimes at last.

I'm writing to bring you back to me, Mrs. Haven. I can't deny that. I want to reenter the continuum, if for no other reason than because it's the place—or the field, or the condition—in which you exist. And there's only one way to do that, appalling though the prospect is to me.

I'm writing to tell you about the Lost Time Accidents.

I

ON JUNE 12, 1903, two hours and forty-five minutes before being killed by a virtually stationary motorcar, my great-grandfather made a discovery that promised to shake the world to its foundations. Ottokar Gottfriedens Toula, father of two, amateur physicist, pickler by trade, had spent the morning in his laboratory—a converted brining room directly beneath the Hauptplatz of Znojmo, Moravia, the gherkin capital of the Habsburg Empire— and was about to lock up for the afternoon, when something about the arrangement of objects on a workbench caught his eye. According to his notes, he spent the better part of a quarter hour perfectly motion- less, his right hand still cradling his keys, staring over his left shoulder at the "spatial dynamics" between a crucible, a brining jar, and a slowly desic- cating winter pear.

A jarring, insistent noise which he eventually identified as the jangling of his key ring brought him out of his bedazzlement, and he approached the workbench with a trembling step. By the time he'd cleared a space on his perennially cluttered desk, pinched his pince-nez into place, and dug his notebook out from under a heap of cherry pits, the first crude attempt at a theory was already coalescing in his brain. He lowered himself to the bench, taking great care not to tip it over, and in less than an hour wrote the entry—seven pages of tilting *courant* script—that would trouble the dreams of his descendants for the next one hundred years.

I couldn't possibly know this, Mrs. Haven—not all of it—but I hope you'll indulge me a little. Ottokar's notes, the sole source I have for this scene, are as dry as pencil shavings. The only means I've got to bring this primal scene to life, to keep you here beside me—if only *in potentia*—is the license I've given myself to speculate. Imagination is a form of time travel, after all, however bumbling and incomplete. And every history is an act of subterfuge.

The town my great-grandfather lived and died in—Znaim to the Germanic ruling class, Znojmo to the Czechs—was a pretty imperial backwater, prosperous and unpretentious, known for its views of the Dyje River, its pickling mills, and not a thing besides. A postcard from the year of Ottokar's death combines these twin distinctions into a single tidy package: entitled "A Visit to Znaim," the postcard depicts a portly businessman in a bowler hat, happily suspended in midair above the Dyje, with the town square glowing rosily in the background. Pickles peek out of his pockets, and he brandishes a brining brush in his right hand, like a riding crop; his flight seems to have been made possible by the gargantuan, midnight-green, unapologetically phallic gherkin that he straddles like some suicidal gaucho. A poem at the bottom left-hand corner does nothing whatsoever to explain matters, though it does strike me as pertinent to my great-grandfather's brief, quixotic life:

> *A Gherkin from the land of Znaim*
> *Is mightier than the Hand of Time;*
> *Its savory Brine, at first so sour*
> *Grows sweeter with each Passing Hour.*

Znojmo's only other claim to a place in history, oddly enough, is even more closely aligned with poor Ottokar's fate. From 1716 until 1719 the town was home to Václav Prokop Divis, an otherwise unassuming Catholic priest who had the spectacularly bad luck of inventing the lightning rod at the same time as Benjamin Franklin. Divis died a pauper's death in a Moravian monastery, forgotten by the scientific world; Franklin got his fat face on the hundred-dollar bill. There's a lesson in that—about the disadvantages of being Czech, if nothing else—but my great-grandfather opted to ignore it.

By his own account, Ottokar was six foot four, 183 pounds, and "of forty-nine years' duration" at the time of his demise. He'd have stood out wherever he lived, most likely, on account of his great height and his slew of eccentricities; but in sleepy, unassuming Znojmo he was practically a figure of legend. He wore the same woolen overcoat all the year round, and was known to describe it as a "musical instrument," for no reason the townsfolk could discern. His iron-gray beard—which, in spite of his ardent Catholicism, demands to be described as Talmudic—was a thing of wonder to the local children, who tagged after him at a respectful distance, waiting for the instant when he'd stop short, glance back at them darkly, and mutter a rumbling "Saint Augustine protect you, little foxes," before passing out the caramel drops he carried in his pockets. A key ingredient in Ottokar's celebrity was his extravagant sweet tooth, and his claim—always made with the greatest solemnity—that he'd never eaten a pickle in his life.

Oddities notwithstanding, my great-grandfather was a gentleman of what was even then referred to as "the old school," equally devoted to his family, his mistress and his Kaiser. In spite of his matter-of-fact embrace of the newest pickling and storage technologies, his distrust of what he referred to as "newfangledhood"—and especially of its totem animal, the horseless carriage—was his overriding passion. He was fond of taking strolls in the evenings, usually in the company of his wife and two sons, Waldemar and Kaspar, and returning the greetings of his neighbors with a dignified tip of his homburg. On those still-infrequent occasions when a motorcar passed, he never failed to step squarely into its wake, oblivious to the dust devils whirling around him, and to bellow *Combust!* in the voice of Jehovah. (The fact that combustion was, in fact, the very thing that made motorcars possible was an irony no one was brave enough to call to his attention.) Ottokar was a man well aware of his place in the world; a man who took his influence for granted, no differently than his cherished Kaiser did.

Unbeknownst to my great-grandfather, however, both he and his Kaiser were approaching the ends of their terms.

∞

According to the testimony of the last person known to have spoken with him before the accident, Ottokar was in a state of almost saintly exaltation during his final hours. The witness in question was one Marta Svoboda, the knödel-faced spouse of the town's leading butcher, with whom my great-grandfather had maintained a clandestine friendship since the middle of his twenty-second year. A specialty of Svoboda's shop was *Fenchelwurst*—pork sausage with fennel—and Ottokar was in the habit of calling on her each weekday at a quarter past twelve, just after the shop had closed for midday, to pick up the tidy wax-paper package, tied with red butcher's twine, that was awaiting him there like an anniversary present. (Where the man of the house spent *his* lunch hour, Mrs. Haven, I have no idea; perhaps he had a *valentinka* of his own.) For the whole of his adult duration, my greatgrandfather's days followed an inflexible schedule, divided with perfect symmetry between mornings in his laboratory and afternoons devoted to the gherkin trade. The intervening hour, however, was reserved for a game of tarock with his *kleine Martalein*, who was—to judge by the only photograph I've seen—anything but *klein*, but whose fennel sausage, coincidentally or not, was reputedly the manna of the gods.

My great-grandfather showed up earlier than usual on that cataclysmic morning, dabbing at his forehead—although it was perfectly dry—with a filthy gray rag from his workshop. Marta bustled him at once to the enormous settee in her bedroom and insisted he remove his shoes and socks. Ottokar indulged her good-naturedly, protesting that he was in excellent health, that he'd never felt more vigorous, but allowing her to have her way, as always. (It's an odd thing, Mrs. Haven: although the thought of my parents' lovemaking turns my stomach, I don't feel the slightest resistance to picturing my great-grandfather and his mistress fornicating like love-struck bonobos. On this particular day, given his condition, I imagine the butcher's wife straddling him like a cyclist, leaving her apron on in case of interruption, her ample body driving his hips into the upholstery and causing the French enamel of the settee's frame to crack like the shell of an overboiled egg. These were his last earthly moments, and I like to think he made the most of them.)

At some point, Ottokar dug his left hand into a pocket of his coat, pulled out some—but not all; this is very important—of the hastily scribbled notes he'd made while sitting on his workbench, and arranged them in a row across the table. He confessed to feeling slightly feverish, and allowed Frau Svoboda to apply a compress to his brow. At five minutes to one, with the freakishly precise awareness of the hour that has always distinguished the men of my family, he sat up and announced that he had to be off. He seemed refreshed by the respite, and his forehead felt cooler, but his eyes shone with a fervor that took Marta quite aback. She made no attempt to stop him when he teetered to his feet and left the house.

It was just past 13:00 CET, the hour of rest in every cranny of that narcoleptic empire, and by all accounts a muggy afternoon. By the time the clock on the Radnicní tower struck a quarter past, Ottokar was crossing Obroková Street with his hands clasped behind him, taking long, abstracted steps, staring down at the freshly cobbled street and nodding to himself in quiet triumph. At the same instant, Hildebrand Bachling, a dealer in jewelry and pocket watches from Vienna, was making a leisurely circuit of Masarykovo Square, affording the public as much time as possible to admire his fifteen-horsepower Daimler. The precise sequence of events is impossible to reconstruct, though half a dozen Toulas have tried: most likely Herr Bachling was momentarily distracted—by the smile of a fräulein? by the smell of fresh hops?—and failed to notice the man drifting into his course.

∞

Wealth is famously insecure, Mrs. Haven, and even the greatest art is shackled to its culture and its age; a scientific breakthrough, by contrast, is timeless. A great theory can be amended, like Galileo's planetary system; improved on, like Darwin's principle of natural selection; even ultimately discarded, like Newton's postulation of absolute time; once it's been metabolized, however—once it's been passed through the collective intestines, and added to the socioconceptual chain—it can vanish only with the death of human knowledge. My great-grandfather had just made a discovery that promised to bring him not merely fortune and fame—and even, in some quarters, infamy—but immortality. This intoxicating fact must have colored his thoughts as he made his way homeward, reviewing that morning's calculations like a magpie sorting bits of bottle glass. He barely recognized his neighbors, returned nobody's greeting, perceived nothing but the cobbles at his feet. The clatter of the Daimler's engine was thoroughly drowned out by the buzzing of his brain.

What happened next was attested to by everybody on the square that day. Bachling took sudden notice of the man in his path—"He popped up out of nowhere," he said at his deposition—"out of the air itself"—and clawed frantically at the Daimler's manual brake; Ottokar paid no mind to his impending end until its grille made gentle contact with his paunch. His coat seemed to drape itself over the hood of the Daimler, as if no human body were inside it, and by the time he hit the cobbles he was in his shirt-sleeves. Bachling opened his mouth in a coquettish O of disbelief, extending his right arm over the windshield in an absurd attempt to shunt aside his victim; a stack of loose papers pirouetted skyward with no more urgency or fuss than the Daimler took to pass over the obstruction. The papers came to rest in the middle of the street—in perfect order, as I picture it—but no one present took the slightest notice.

No one except a single passerby.

Monday, 08:47 EST

Of the many mysteries of my situation, Mrs. Haven, the most brain-curdling isn't the question of time, but—for want of a better expression—the question of space. My recollection of events since our parting is patchy at best, a shadowy pudding of fuddled impressions, and the days and hours leading up to this limbo seem to have been erased altogether. I regained consciousness sweatily, fuzzily, as if surfacing from an afternoon nap beside some muddy semitropical lagoon, and I still haven't snapped out of it completely. What force and/or agency deposited me here? Why *this* place, of all places? Who excavated this cramped little burrow for me, set up this table and armchair, laid out this pen and ream of acid-free paper, and drank half of this bottle of nearly undrinkable beer?

As if to smooth my way further, a dozen or so books jut out of the mess within reach of this armchair, each one of them related to my work: Saint Augustine's *Confessions*, Kubler's *The Shape of Time*, a pocket biography of Einstein, and *The Order of the Death's Head: The Story of Hitler's SS* by a lurid little German named Heinz Höhne, to name just a few. This room was once my aunts' library, as I've said, but the coincidence is a little hard to credit. I can't help but suspect—like the stiff, defensive Protestants who raised you—that some Intelligence contrived to place me here.

I took my first stab at writing the history of my family when I was still in college, and that manuscript—"Toula-Silbermann-Tolliver: A Narrative Genealogy"—lies close by as well, in the crumpled manila envelope, packed with Tolliver lore, that was the last thing my aunts ever gave me. It's a ponderous slog, a painstaking patchwork of "primary" texts—I was a history major at the time—and reading it now, I find its fusty, deliberate tone grotesquely out of keeping with a family for whom "objectivity" has always been an alien (if not downright extraterrestrial) concept. In other words, Mrs. Haven, it's an undercooked, flavorless porridge of facts, the opposite of what I'm after here. You've never read a work of history in your life. To bring the past alive for you, I'm going to have to approach it as a sort of waking dream, or as one of those checkout counter whodunits you keep stacked beside your bed. I'll have to treat my duration as a mystery and a sci-fi potboiler combined—which shouldn't be too hard to do at all.

Not to say these books won't come in handy, Mrs. Haven. The Kubler, for instance—an elegant art history tract, with a pretty two-tone cover that I think you would have liked—practically reads like an abstract of my family's travails. Here's a passage from page 17:

> Our signals from the past are very weak, and our means for recovering their meaning are still most imperfect. The beginnings are much hazier than the endings, where at least the catastrophic action of external events can be determined. Yet at every moment the fabric is being undone and a new one is woven to replace the old, while from time to time the whole pattern shakes and quivers, settling into new shapes and figures.

Ottokar's death, both as an ending and as a beginning, might have been dreamed up expressly to prove Kubler's point. His ending was hazy enough, witnessed though it was by half the town of Znojmo; but the questions raised by his death led into a swamp in which first his children, then his grandchildren, and finally even his great-grandchildren lost themselves beyond hope of recovery. In spite of embracing science—and pseudoscience, and science fiction (and even, in one case, out-and-out humbuggery)—as our family religion, we Tollivers have always been a backward-looking bunch, and we've paid a fearsome price for our nostalgia. Like an unconfirmed rumor, or a libelous book, or a golem, or a flesh-eating zombie—never fully alive and therefore unkillable—Ottokar's discovery shadowed each of us from the cradle to the tomb.

I was once informed by a tour guide, on a high school trip to Scotland, that any self-respecting clan should have at least one ancient curse; and even then, at the age of not-quite-fifteen, the Lost Time Accidents sprang to mind at once. I've asked myself countless times how we might have turned out if my great-grandfather had stepped in front of that Daimler even one day earlier, only to realize, time and again, that I might as well ask what would have happened if he'd never been conceived. Time may be as subject to spin as everything else in the universe, Mrs. Haven, but the lines of cause and effect are no less evident for being curved. If the Tollivers had a crest, it would be the colors of pickling brine and tattered notebook paper, twisted together into a Möbius strip, rampant against a background of jet-black, ruthless, interstellar space.

II

MY GREAT-GRANDFATHER DIED without recovering consciousness, Mrs. Haven, and the notes he'd let fall in the street were forgotten in the drama of his passing. In any event, only one person might have been able to appreciate the full significance of those pages, and she was prevented by propriety from coming forward. Marta Svoboda's "testimony" was given in no court of law: even if Bachling had been in violation of the primitive traffic regulations of the age, his negligible speed would have been enough to put him in the clear. Frau Svoboda's questioning, such as it was, was carried out by Ottokar's sons, Kaspar and Waldemar, heirs to both their father's business and his love of *Fenchelwurst*.

The liaison between Ottokar and Marta had by no means been a secret, and all eyes (except, perhaps, my great-grandmother's) were on her in the days and weeks that followed; but she proved a disappointment to her neighbors. When the butcher shop opened the next day, she was behind the counter as always—slightly tighter-lipped than usual, perhaps, but otherwise composed. None of her customers made so bold as to invite her to unburden herself, and she did absolutely nothing to encourage them.

She showed less reticence, however, when Waldemar and Kaspar came to call.

∞

My grandfather and his brother were in their teens at the time of the accident, a year or so shy of manhood, and were often mistaken for twins.

Waldemar was slightly taller than his older brother, with an elegant, straight-backed way of propelling himself through the world; Kaspar—my grandfather—was a dark, quiet boy, businesslike for his age, with the set jaw and good-natured suspiciousness of the emigrant he would one day become. Waldemar was his mother's favorite, Kaspar his father's. Though less fetching than his younger brother, and decidedly less brash, it was on Kaspar's broad back that the hopes of the family rested. There was a reasonableness about him that was missing in Waldemar: his lack of imagination, it was felt, was precisely the corrective to his father's excesses that Toula & Sons was in need of. On the morning of June 26, however, the pickle trade couldn't have been farther from either boy's thoughts. They walked the six blocks to Frau Svoboda's shop shoulder to shoulder, talking in grave and self-important whispers, and rapped in tandem on its yellow door.

Circumference aside, Marta Svoboda made for an unlikely butcher's wife: she was a soft-spoken woman, always impeccably dressed, with a fondness for light opera and an aversion to the smell of uncooked meat. (It may well have been her sense of herself as somehow out of place—miscast by a world that knew her poorly—that had made her susceptible to my great-grandfather's charms.) She was well read, and a diligent diarist: most of what I've learned about that time came from her journals. Her entry for June 26, for example, exactly two weeks after Ottokar's death and seven days after his funeral, gives me the first picture I have of my grandfather as a young man, and of his soon-to-be-infamous brother.

At just before noon—the hour of their accustomed rendezvous— Marta distinctly heard Ottokar's knock at her door, and crept downstairs into the shop; she was in the depths of her grief, sleeping painfully little, and for a moment she feared for her sanity. The silhouette she saw through the frosted glass was Ottokar's as well, and she might easily have fled back upstairs if she hadn't noticed another behind it, slightly taller and with less of a slump. Marta had exchanged barely a word with the Toula boys since they'd been toddlers, and the thought of talking to them now frightened her worse than any phantom could have done; but she unbolted the shop door regardless.

"Good afternoon, Frau Svoboda," the shorter one said. He seemed at a loss as to whether to bow or to extend his hand. The younger one stared at her coldly.

"Good *day*," she said, struggling to keep her voice level, but in spite of everything it came out badly. It sounded as if she were correcting him.

"My name is Kaspar Toula," said the boy, as if Marta had no way of knowing, which struck her as very polite. His mourning suit fit him badly and he looked miserable in it. He was the image of his father—only shorter, and stouter, and somewhat more matter-of-fact—and it almost hurt her eyes to look at him. His brother cut a more elegant figure, Marta noted in her journal: he looked, she wrote, "as if he'd been born wearing black." She invited them in, though Waldemar still hadn't spoken, and told them to sit at the counter while she fetched them a treat. They were little more than children, after all.

When she returned with a plate of cold *sulze* they were still standing exactly as she'd left them, in the middle of the shop with their hats in their hands, blinking at the cuts of meat around them like a pair of truant schoolboys at the zoo. They're trying to understand their father, she thought. Trying to understand what brought him here. It was clear to her then that they knew everything, and to her surprise the fact of it relaxed her. She waited until they'd sat down to eat before pouring a glass of beer for each of them, then a snifter of elderberry schnapps for herself, and asking them to what she owed the pleasure.

Again it was Kaspar who spoke. "Fräulein Svoboda," he mumbled, then immediately turned a ghastly shade of purple. "*Frau* Svoboda," he corrected himself, staring fixedly at a button of her blouse.

"Yes?"

"You were a *bonne amie* of our departed father?"

It was less a question, really, than a statement of the case. Marta saw no reason to deny it.

"All right," said Kaspar, visibly relieved. "Very good." He nodded and stuffed his mouth with bread and *sulze*. Marta sipped from her snifter and smiled at him comfortably, unafraid now. At one point she turned her smile on Waldemar, who'd touched neither his beer nor his food, but he shut his eyes until she looked away. *He takes after his mother*, she said to herself. *I wonder how Resa is coping.*

"Frau Svoboda," Kaspar repeated, apparently on solid ground again, "what did you and my father talk about, when he paid you—well, when he paid you his calls?"

Marta replied that they'd talked about all and sundry, or—as she put it in her journal—"everything and nothing much at all."

"I see," said Kaspar, looking sideways at his brother. "Frau Svoboda," he said a third time, gripping his beer stein like a bannister.

"Yes, Herr Toula? What is it?"

"Frau Svoboda—"

"Did he talk about his work?" Waldemar blurted out. It was the first time he'd spoken. "Did he mention the Lost Time Accidents to you?"

Marta looked back and forth between their sweet, impatient faces. "He was a great one for chitchat, your poor father was. I can't say for certain. I lost track of him now and again."

"I *told* you," Waldemar murmured, with a bitterness that took Marta aback. "I told you so." But Kaspar ignored him.

"Frau Svoboda—was my father in a state of excitement? The last time that he called on you, I mean."

Marta sat back heavily and clucked, and the boy blushed even more violently than before. "I beg your pardon," he stammered. "What I'd intended—"

"What my brother means to ask is this," Waldemar cut in. "Was Herr Toula agitated about something in particular? Had anything of special interest happened on that day?"

Marta allowed that it had.

"Well, what *was* it?" said Waldemar. "Why the devil won't you answer plainly?"

Kaspar silenced his brother with a look, then addressed his father's mistress in a clear, unhurried voice that made him seem much older than he was.

"When our father was undressed at the hospital, Frau Svoboda, a scrap of paper was found in his pocket—a message of sorts, on which your name appears. Would you care to inspect it?"

She replied that she would, and a sheet of blue octavo paper, folded neatly in four, was spread before her on the grease-stained counter.

MARTA DARLING! DARE I DALLY? BEARS BOORS &
BOHEMIANS BEDEVIL THESE LATERAL LABORS.
LUCKILY, AN "ANSWER" SHALL ARISE. TIME CAN BE

*MEASURED ONLY IN ITS PASSING. BY *CHANCE* &
FATE & *PROVIDENCE* EDEN'S ENEMIES EXCHEQUER &
EXPIRE.*

*AS THE SOUL GROWS TOWARD ETERNAL LIFE, IT
REMEMBERS LESS & LESS. CHRONOLOGY CRUSHES
CHRISTIANS. A MISTRESS—PRAISE C*F*P!—IS
MELLIFLUOUS. FOOLS FROM FUTURE'S FETID
FIEFDOMS FOLLOW FREELY IN MY FOOTSTEPS.
BACKWARDS TIME IS IMPOSSIBLE, FORWARDS TIME IS
ABSURD. TRUTH TOLD TACTLESSLY TAKES COURAGE,
LITTLE DUMPLING. TRUTH TOLD CUNNINGLY TAKES
FENCHELWURST & TEA.*

*THE PULPIT FOR PREACHERS IN PAMĚT' CATHEDRAL.
DARLING MARTA! DO YOU FOLLOW ME? THEN SPIN ME
COUNTERCLOCKWISE. PLACE YOURSELF PAST EVERY
PRIMITIVE PROSCRIPTION. SILENCE, SYCOPHANTS! &
LISTEN TO ME CLOSELY. JAN SKÜS IS THE NAME OF A
FRIEND I ONCE MET, & SKÜS JAN IS A FRIEND I'LL MEET
TWICE. SPACE & TIME AFFECT ALL, ARE AFFECTED
BY ALL. EACH FOOL CARRIES HIS OWN HOURGLASS
INSIDE HIM.*

*TODAY IT HAS HAPPENED. TWELVE JUNE NINETEEN
HUNDRED & THREE ANNO DOMINI. TAKE THIS
LETTER—PRECIOUS DUMPLING!—& EXHIBIT NO
MERCY. I'LL BE BACK FOR IT SOON. TODAY IT HAS
HAPPENED. TODAY IT HAS HAPPENED. THE LOST TIME
ACCIDENTS. THE LOST TIME ACCIDENTS. THE LOST
TIME ACCIDENTS. HAVE MERCY ON US ALL.*

*OTTOKAR GOTTFRIEDENS TOULA,
TOULA & SONS SALUTARY GHERKINS, S.M.
ZNOJMO, MORAVIA.*

"Note the number in the bottom left-hand corner," said Kaspar. "Page number four, do you see? It follows that there must also exist—or have existed—additional pages, numbered one through three."

Knowing Ottokar—*having* known him, Marta reminded herself—she didn't necessarily think the rules of logic could be relied on; but she didn't see much point in disagreeing.

"We also have reason to believe—from certain statements of our father's, in the days before his passing—that one of those missing pages contains an algebraic proof. It is this *proof*—not any personal or sentimental information—that is of interest to my brother and myself."

Marta smiled and acknowledged that such a proof, if it existed, would indeed be of interest.

Waldemar, who'd been so sullen and withdrawn, did something now that flabbergasted her: he sat stiffly forward, like a suitor on the verge of a proposal, and took her damp pink hand in both of his.

"Esteemed Frau Svoboda, kindly listen to me now. For the past seven years, as you may or may not know, our father has been engaged in a series of experimental inquiries into the physical nature of time." He stared at her until she bobbed her head. "Until recently, my brother and myself had been allowed to assist him in his research; a few months ago, however, he forbade us to set foot in his laboratory. From the comments he made—the merest of hints, really—we know he was on the cusp of a major discovery: a new understanding, not just of the nature of time, but of the possibility of motion—*free* motion—within it." Waldemar sucked in a breath. "Given what has happened, you can see what an unfortunate decision it was to exclude us from his work. On the morning of his death—or so this note would seem to imply—our father finally achieved the breakthrough he'd been seeking." He glared into her eyes as he said this, neither wavering nor blinking, like a mesmerist or a vampire or a prophet. "Can you appreciate what this means, Frau Svoboda? Most people couldn't—not for the life of them. But I have no doubt whatsoever that you can."

Marta glanced away from him then, but only for an instant. "Why did he forbid you from entering his laboratory?"

"He wanted us to concentrate on our schoolwork," Kaspar said, reddening. "Over the last few years, our marks—"

"He'd become suspicious of everyone," Waldemar interrupted. "He spent all his time in that damned cave of his. Our poor mother—"

"What we came here to ask you, Frau Svoboda, is this: Might you have those three pages? Might they be in this house?"

Looking from one boy to the other, basking in the glow of their combined attention, Marta wanted nothing so much as to provide them with the purpose they so craved. She came close to inventing some clue, fabricating some relic, if only to keep them sitting at her counter. But the boys were too clever to be taken in by any trick of hers. The younger one, especially, seemed to dissect her with those chalky eyes of his, as if she were no more than a sack of fat and gristle. She permitted herself to think about Ottokar for a moment, and about what he'd told her of his conflict with time, a struggle he'd often predicted would end in his death. If he'd shut his boys out, as they claimed, then he must have had cause. For this reason—and for other, less defensible ones—she let her head hang and said nothing.

There was, in fact, something she wasn't telling the boys, something that would have spared them and their future wives and children years of grief; but Marta had no gift of precognition. *Their innocence is what makes them beautiful*, she said to herself. *Let them hold on to their innocence awhile.*

"I'm sorry, boys," she said at last. "There's nothing I can give you."

Kaspar was already on his feet, murmuring apologies for having imposed; but Waldemar stayed as he was. Those eyes of his, disconcerting at the best of times, now slid from feature to feature of her wide and cheerful face as though searching for a way to pry it open. The shop had never felt so hideously still.

"You're lying, Frau Svoboda," Waldemar said slowly. "You're lying to us, you sausage-chewing sow."

Even Kaspar seemed startled by the venom in his brother's voice: he stepped hurriedly to the counter and pulled him up out of his chair. Waldemar put up no resistance, letting his older brother trundle him backward, his eyes resting on her like chips of gray slate. Marta stayed as she was. She felt incapable of movement. Nothing Waldemar did later, she writes in her journal, came as a surprise to her after that visit. Four decades on, when the long war had ended and the camps had been emptied and word of the Timekeeper's experiments began to trickle back to Náměstí Svobody, Marta would be the only one in town who wasn't shocked. She'd known ever since that visit, she declared to whoever would listen. She'd seen the future in the blankness of those eyes.

"I understand you, Frau Svoboda," Waldemar said. "I understand how you think. But that isn't the same as forgiveness."

"Don't listen to him, please," Kaspar stammered, hauling his brother out into the street. "I have no idea what he's jabbering about."

Marta knew quite well, but she said nothing.

III

I CAN'T GO any farther, Mrs. Haven, without a tip of the hat to Michelson and Morley. They're not Tollivers, per se, but they're just as instrumental to this history. We'd never have met without them, you and I.

Albert Abraham Michelson was a broad-shouldered, obsessively tidy Jew from the Kingdom of Prussia—by way of Virginia City, Nevada—whose career was defined by a lifelong obsession with light. The *speed* of light was Michelson's particular passion, and his quest to quantify it brought him, of all places, to Cleveland, Ohio, where he met Edward Morley, the bucktoothed instructor of chemistry whose name would soon be linked with his forever. Michelson had invented a machine called an interferometer, a childishly simple and mind-bogglingly expensive contraption whose only purpose—as its creator liked to put it—was to measure the immeasurable. In a nutshell, Michelson's invention was a system of pipes and mirrors that split a beam of sunlight, sent the two halves down tubes of varying lengths, then measured the difference between these two journeys as a series of pale and dark smudges. This might not sound so impressive, but it changed our understanding of light—and of time, and of the universe itself—forever.

More amazingly still, Mrs. Haven, Michelson and Morley's machine did all of the above by accident.

In 1887, in the basement of a dormitory on the grounds of Case Western Reserve University, the two men built an immense interferometer out of glass and lead pipe, mounting the apparatus on a platform of marble, then floating that platform, in turn, in a pool of quicksilver, to insulate it from vibration. Michelson expected the speed of light to vary slightly, depending on whether the beam in question was traveling with the earth's rotation or against it. To a passenger on a moving train, he reasoned, the apparent speed of a stampeding buffalo depends on which way the buffalo happens to be heading; why should light behave any differently? According to Michelson's calculations, rays traveling counter to the earth's spin should appear to be moving 108,000 kilometers per hour faster than those traveling with it. On May 27, conditions being perfect, the experiment was duly carried out. Light was measured traveling toward, and from, every point of the compass.

When the results were tabulated, its speed proved to be equal in every direction.

The experiment was a disappointment, even a failure; but it was the most spectacular failure in scientific history. The results, at first glance so drab, would eventually overturn a conception of the universe that had gone unquestioned since the Enlightenment. Two centuries earlier, Isaac Newton had managed to predict the courses of the planets through the heavens with astonishing accuracy, basing his work on the assumption—obvious to anyone with sense—that space and time were absolute. But there was no way of reconciling Newton's laws with the results obtained in Cleveland. In order for the speed of light to appear the same under all circumstances, no matter how fast the observer himself might be traveling, some part of Newton's system had to give.

Theories were put forward, of course, once the world had gotten over its astonishment: over the next few decades, attempts were made to explain the result in terms of ballistics, friction in the ether, experimental error, and whatever else the rear guard could dream up. The wildest theory of all came from a Dutch physicist named Hendrik Lorentz, who claimed that moving objects actually *shrink* along their lines of motion, so that, while light might in fact travel more slowly under certain circumstances, it also travels a shorter distance: in other words, that space is anything but absolute.

Lorentz's theory—not surprisingly—was widely ridiculed, until it was determined to be true.

Such was the state of the scientific world, Mrs. Haven, at the time of my great-grandfather's discovery. It was an era of chaos and confusion and nearly limitless possibility: a kind of panicked conceptual goldrush. The year 1903 had been typically revolutionary for the new century, having already yielded the gas turbine, electrostatic fume precipitation, razor blades and reinforced concrete; in Manhattan, a subterranean railway had just been opened from Fourteenth to Forty-Second Streets, and in a picturesque backwater of Switzerland—as far from Manhattan, in virtually every sense, as possible— a patent clerk with delusions of grandeur was beginning work on a paper entitled "On the Electrodynamics of Moving Bodies," which would intro- duce a concept he termed "special relativity." Ottokar couldn't have known all this, of course, but he'd clearly caught the fever of the age. And in Kas- par and Waldemar, his like-minded sons, this fever would eventually de- velop into a systemic infection: what came to be referred to, in our family, as the Syndrome.

Both boys immersed themselves in Ottokar's notes, and—when these proved insufficient—in physics and mechanics textbooks ordered from Vienna by expedited mail; both showed a talent for their studies, and both applied to the university, when the time came, in the empire's capital, some ninety kilometers distant. Their mother, a monochromatic, long-suffering woman who'd lived exclusively for her children since their birth, ushered them out of her life with the requisite mixture of pride and despair. Her sons returned to Znojmo only rarely after departing for Vienna: they felt relieved to be leaving the family—such as it was—behind them, and in any case their studies claimed them utterly. They showed an interest in every branch of the natural sciences, from chemistry to comparative zoology, but there was no question as to what was driving them. The Accidents had swallowed them alive.

In 1904, Toula & Sons Salutary Gherkins was sold to a well-heeled competitor, which surprised almost no one, though there are those who date the decline of the Moravian pickle industry from that moment. The money from the sale of the company, though less than expected, was more than enough to establish the boys in Vienna. They took rooms in a recently completed building in the Seventh District, in the poetically named Mondscheingasse—"Moonshine Lane"—a few minutes' walk from the imperial stables. The house itself, though quaint in comparison with the radically plain style currently storming the city, struck them as the pinnacle of daring. Two colossal plaster lions presided over its entrance, their hare- lipped faces somehow more pathetic than ferocious; a pair of goosenecked dragons, in turn, kept an anxious watch over the lions. The dragons' necks were affectionately intertwined, forming between them—whether by accident or design—a lateral figure eight, the mathematical symbol of infinity. This entranced Waldemar, though Kaspar was more impressed by the brilliant yellow paint, the view east toward the Opera, and the smell of fresh dung from the stables in the evenings, when the emperor's horses were locked in their stalls for the night.

Both brothers studied the city around them, frankly and down to the slightest detail, with all the abandon of yokels freshly sprung from yokelhood. The girls especially, Kaspar notes in his diary, were a revelation. Ladies back in Znojmo were essentially potatoes, and they clothed themselves, appropriately enough, in formless, plain potato sacks; their Viennese counterparts flounced along the Ringstrasse encased in fabrics so opulent, so demonstrative, that their exhibition in broad daylight stopped a hair's breadth short of bona fide perversion. To my grandfather's bumpkinish eyes, the entire Kärntnerstrasse on a Saturday evening was transformed into a single vast seraglio. Men accompanied the women, of course—fidgety, purse-faced men, dressed in generic black or graphite-colored suits—but they might as well have been lapdogs, or pigeons, or even heaps of moldy winter pears. So much beauty and wealth and urbanity, so languidly displayed, never failed to make Kaspar feel insignificant, even piddling; but this feeling only heightened his excitement. All his consequence still lay before him.

Waldemar saw things differently. He was as fascinated by the capital as his brother, but even then, at the age of not-quite-seventeen, the immanent revolutionary in him recognized the city's pomp for what it was: a garish, fetid flower, sprouting brightly from the slack jaws of a corpse. That was how he described it to his brother, at least, on those rare occasions when Kaspar consented to listen. The glitter and gaiety of Vienna, that "pearl in the crown of the Germanic world," as the Führer himself would one day call it, were no more to him than the rictus on the face of a cadaver.

Waldemar came to disapprove of his older brother's new habits—his drunken nights, his dalliances, his cabinet full of buckskin brogues in subtly differing shades—and he made no secret of his point of view. He chose to remain at an elegant remove from the life of the city, spending his evenings in studious seclusion, filling a growing pile of hardbound ledgers with his cramped and canting script, and relaxing before bedtime by scouring the gaps between slats in the floor with a fork expressly altered for that purpose. His aloofness only heightened his mystique at the university, where he was making a name for himself as a student of extraordinary promise. He left the apartment each morning just after sunrise and returned at eight every evening, punctual as a timing cog; but not even Kaspar knew where he spent his afternoons. There were rumors of a rose-colored villa along the Danube Canal, and of an older woman, possibly the wife of a professor; women in particular seemed eager to credit Waldemar with a voluptuous parallel life. Kaspar would have been delighted, of course, but he could only roll his eyes at the idea. "My brother is a religious fanatic," he was fond of telling callers to their flat. "He hasn't chosen a religion yet, to the best of my knowledge, but I have no doubt it will be a tidy one."

He was to remember this quip of his in later years, and marvel—more than a little grimly—at his foresight.

Different though the brothers were, their first year of independence passed in relative harmony, if only because of their mutual obsession. Kaspar's talent lay in mathematics, while Waldemar, romantic that he was, felt most comfortable in the giddy heights of theory; but both were in search of a skeleton key, either mathematical or hermeneutic, to their dead father's chamber of secrets. A photograph of the brining-room laboratory hung tacked to the door of the newly installed water closet at Mondscheingasse, alongside a rendering by Waldemar of the pulpit mentioned in Ottokar's note, which was unique in the empire (if not in the world) for having the form of a globe:

Waldemar in particular was fascinated by the pulpit, and claimed to have a memory of sitting beneath it, on his father's lap, and celebrating midnight mass at Christmas. Its spherical shape impressed him as deeply significant. Kaspar found the whole notion silly, and had no recollection of the interior of Paměť' Cathedral at all; but he felt drawn to the rendering regardless. Being more worldly than his younger brother—more interested in things as *things*, rather than as symbols—he often found himself struck by the marked similarity, from a structural point of view, between the pulpit and a pissoir.

∞

If my grandfather found himself less admired by his classmates than Waldemar was—less a figure of hushed speculation—he also found himself distinctly better liked. The snobbery of the Viennese toward outsiders of every persuasion (and especially toward Slavs) passed over his head without ruffling a hair. By the winter of his first year at the university, Kaspar had either won his skeptics over or stepped politely around them, and had become the Physics Department's unofficial mascot. Unlike his brother, he rarely spoke about his research, and the impression he made seems to have been that of a bon vivant with a boyish enthusiasm for physics. His mathematical ability, as well as his solemn good nature and willingness to perform the most mundane of chores without complaint, endeared him to a number of professors in the department, and by the end of his first term he'd become chief assistant to Ludwig David Silbermann, director of the School of Natural Philosophy: a kindly, perpetually overwhelmed man whose primary qualification for his lofty position seems to have been his persistence in the belief that the emperor had the best interests of his subjects at heart. My grandfather was careful to hide the substance of his own work—his inquiry, thus far fruitless, into the nature of his father's discovery—from Professor Silbermann, and as a consequence they got on very well.

Between his assisting duties, his studies, and his fondness for Viennese street life, Kaspar had little time to spare for his brother, and by summer he and Waldemar were little more than apartment-mates. Like an underground river, the mystery of the Accidents continued to run beneath the events of their day-to-day lives, connecting them and keeping them in motion; on the surface, however, there was very little trace.

It was probably inevitable that a young man as intoxicated as my grandfather was by the charms of fin de siècle Vienna should eventually be swept up in the moral and cultural civil war that was splitting the city in two; but the circumstances of his recruitment are no less unlikely for that. On a certain ash-gray August afternoon—August 17, to be exact—just prior to his second academic year in the capital, Kaspar found himself in a two-person booth at the Jandek, a café catering to Marxists and artists' models and syphilitics, nursing a watery *mocca* and trying not to seem too out of place. He was looking for Waldemar: he had something to tell him. Word had reached him that their mother was ill (she herself would never have written about anything so trivial) and he planned to depart for Znojmo that same evening. His brother had grown even more reclusive of late, and it had been days since Kaspar had laid eyes on him. He'd spent the entire morning beating the departmental bushes, until finally a walleyed Tyrolean named Bilch had let the name Jandek slip, in so conspiratorial a whisper that Kaspar had taken it for some kind of brothel.

My grandfather had no aversion to brothels by his eighteenth year—he'd been to a number himself—but the Jandek made them look like milliner's shops. His shoe heels were stuck to the floor of his booth, and the whole place was littered with bread crumbs and onions and cigarette ends, and packed to capacity with men who clearly had no other place to go. The shabbiest of them sat shoehorned together in the booth next to his, composing clumsy and obscene couplets about a well-known painter by the name of Hans Makart: they didn't seem to care much for his paintings. My grandfather, who happened to care for Makart's paintings a great deal, had just asked for his check when the kitchen doors opened, the smoke seemed to part, and a girl in a nightgown sashayed out into the light.

Kaspar knew the girl well—as well, that is, as one could know a girl of good family in 1905—but it took him a moment to place her. Her name was Sonja Adèle and she was one week shy of seventeen years old. She was also, as chance or fate or Providence would have it, the daughter of Ludwig David Silbermann. They'd eaten dinner in each other's company perhaps a dozen times, and had had two brief, forgettable conversations; on one occasion he'd helped her to work out a sum. Nothing in any of those prior encounters had prepared him for the girl who stood before him now.

"Fräulein Silbermann!" he called to her as she went by.

She stopped short and spun on her heels—not like a lady at all—and glowered at him through the smoke. "Herr Toula!" she exclaimed, with undisguised amusement. "What on earth brings you here?"

"I could ask the same of you, fräulien."

"Buy me a glass of kvass and I'll tell you."

"Kvass?" Kaspar said, more bewildered than ever.

"It's a kind of Russian peasant beer, made out of old bread. A house specialty." She pulled up a stool and sat down. "Do you know how the Russians say 'Mind your own business?'"

Kaspar shook his head mutely.

"I'll tell you, Herr Toula, but I'll have to whisper it."

He inclined his head toward her, asking himself what could possibly be considered inappropriate in such a place. Her breath against his earlobe made the soles of his feet prickle in their cashmere stockings.

"Вы не проникли, так что не ерзать ваши ягодицы."

"Ah!" Kaspar said, nodding. "But what does that mean?"

"You're not being fucked, so don't wiggle your ass."

"Ah," he repeated, bobbing his head absurdly. "I see." The blood was draining from his face, but there was nothing he could do about that. She was staring at him brashly, her cheeks lightly flushed, biting a corner of her mouth to keep from laughing.

"Ah," he said a third time, but by then she'd already left him for the boys in the neighboring booth. When the kvass came he drank it himself.

∞

Kaspar caught the train that same evening (he'd already purchased his ticket) and spent four restless days at his mother's bedside. When his brother came home on the weekend, he returned to the city immediately, marveling at his lack of family feeling. He spent the next nine afternoons at the Jandek, drinking endless *mélanges* and repelling all comers, wearing unironed trousers and keeping his hat on indoors. At 15:15 CET on the tenth day,

Sonja emerged from the kitchen exactly as she had two weeks before, and this time there was no gang of Makart disparagers to receive her. She came straight to Kaspar's table, as though his presence there were no more than expected, and sat down without a single word of greeting. She was wearing the same shapeless gown as before, and she scrutinized him just as directly, but there was a disquiet in her manner now, even a hint of appeal. The feeling in Kaspar's throat as he watched her was the same one he got when he ate chestnuts by mistake. He was mildly allergic to chestnuts.

"Kvass?" he said suavely, beckoning to the waiter.

"I don't understand what you're saying," she answered, glancing over her shoulder.

"I'd assumed—that is to say, I may be mispronouncing—"

"I'm finished with the Russians. They treat their workers abominably. You've heard of the disturbances in Minsk?"

"The which?"

"It doesn't matter." She pushed the hair out of her eyes, still looking past him. "What are you drinking?"

"Pilsner," he mumbled, indicating the full stein before him. "In the town I come from, in Moravia—"

She turned back to him now with a different expression entirely. "You're *Czech?*"

"Of a sort," he said, choosing his words cautiously. "That is to say, the name Toula is originally from the Czech. It means 'to wander about,' apparently. Of course, we speak German in the home, and I've been learning English—"

"The Czech language is the most beautiful spoken in Europe," Sonja said earnestly. "*Worlds* better than Russian."

To the best of Kaspar's knowledge, the Czech and Russian languages were part of the same cozy family; but he had the good sense not to point this out.

Sonja peered over her shoulder again, then took a ladylike sip of his pilsner. "He's not coming out," she said. "Thank heaven for that."

"To whom do you refer?" said Kaspar, as nonchalantly as he could.

"Kappa, the painter. I model for him every second Tuesday."

"You model for him," Kaspar repeated. "I see." Things were coming clear to him at last, but only slowly. "He paints you in the kitchen?"

"Close enough, Herr Toula. He has an atelier back there. Appropriately, it used to be the sausage-curing room."

"I see," Kaspar repeated, thinking hard. The notion of Sonja modeling made perfect sense and made no sense at all. It was difficult to conceive of a less suitable vocation for a young lady of standing. He'd met models before in the cafés, of course, but none who weren't also prostitutes.

Sonja was watching him closely, taking sociable sips of his beer, which did nothing for his clarity of mind. He regained his self-possession by a furious effort of will.

"That would explain your outfit, I suppose."

Her smile faded. "I beg your pardon?"

"That smock—or whatever you call it—that you have on. The first time we met, you were wearing a wonderful dress, I remember, with a charming blue bustle—"

"The dress you refer to," Sonja said icily, "took thirty minutes and six hands to get inside of. Its stays were so tight I could barely breathe." She shut her eyes and emitted a series of gasps, as though the memory alone were enough to suffocate her. "Have you ever watched the women promenading in the Prater, Herr Toula, or along Kärntnerstrasse on a Sunday afternoon? Have you ever taken note of how they move?"

"Oh yes," said Kaspar, smiling in spite of himself. "They walk with tiny steps, like turtledoves."

"They walk like cripples," Sonja hissed. "You're not one of those cow-eyed romanticizers, are you? Those chastity fetishists? I thought you told me that you were a Czech."

My grandfather took a deep, pensive draught of his pilsner. Sonja regarded him through narrowed eyes.

"I do come from Moravia," he said hopefully.

"Don't be fooled by the ribbons, Herr Toula. The female anatomy is terrifying to man, so he hides it behind a wall of scaffolding. Under each of those dresses you find so bewitching, a body is locked away in quarantine."

This was a bit much for poor Kaspar, but he was willing to tread water until he sighted land.

"Quarantine," he repeated. "I see. So you wear that smock on your days off, as well?"

"This 'smock,' as you call it, is the rational answer to an irrational society. It was designed by the maestro himself." When Kaspar said nothing, she added, slightly more tentatively: "When we have the society we deserve, it may be possible to attach a few bows here and there."

This glimmer of weakness was all the encouragement my grandfather required. He sat forward soberly, every inch the bourgeois *kavalier*, and took Sonja's plump, schoolgirlish hand in his. "I have no idea what you're talking about, Fräulein Silbermann. I'm a pickle manufacturer's son, new to this city, with a head for sums and very little else. But I'm willing to learn, if you'll consent to show me. I'll follow anywhere you choose to lead."

Sonja blinked at him a moment, genuinely startled, then laughed in his face. "Eager to get your spats dirty, Herr Toula? I don't imagine Papa would approve. He always speaks of you in the most *lofty* of terms!"

It was at this point—as he described it, later that evening, to his frankly incredulous brother—that Kaspar was visited by genius.

"To hell with your papa."

The blood left Sonja's face. "What was that?" she murmured. "I'm not sure I heard you correctly."

"Your father is a mediocre scientist, fräulein, and a blowhard besides. I couldn't care less for his good opinion." He raised the stein to his lips, downed the last of his pilsner, and set it down between them with a thump. "You might almost call him the Makart of physics."

"You're a bum crawler," Sonja said, wide-eyed. "You're an ingrate. You're a hypocrite."

"I'm a Czech," my grandfather said simply.

Within the week the two of them were lovers.

I REMEMBER WHEN I first saw you, Mrs. Haven. You were trapped inside a Möbius loop of admirers at an Upper East Side party, backed against the kitchen counter like a convict bracing for the firing squad. You wore your hair short then, in a vaguely hermaphroditic schoolboy cut, and you looked as though you never went outside. A man in a boater said something to you, then repeated it, then repeated it again, and you nodded in a way that reduced him to dust.

I should have taken this as a warning—I understand that now. Instead I took it as a kind of cue.

I was standing in the home entertainment grotto, slack-jawed and helpless, gawking at you through the open kitchen door; you returned my stare calmly for exactly six seconds, then covered your upper lip with your ring finger. A mustache had been drawn between your first and second knuckles in ballpoint pen—a precise, Chaplinesque trapezoid—making you look like a beautiful Hitler. You held it there a moment, keeping your face set and blank, then solemnly tapped the right side of your nose. The air seemed to thicken. A signal was being transmitted, a semaphore of some kind, but I didn't have a clue what it could mean. Perverse as it seems to me now, the image of you there, hunched stiffly against the counter with that obscene blue mustache pressed against your lips, will remain the most erotic of my life.

The apartment belonged to my cousin, Van Markham, the only member of the Tolliver clan who'd succeeded in adjusting to the times. His living room yawned snazzily before me, an airy product showroom accented by a sprinkling of actual people. I crossed it in a dozen woozy steps. The idea that just a moment earlier I'd been alphabetizing the DVD cases, counting the minutes until I could leave, seemed outlandish to me now, beyond crediting. Creation itself was blowing me a kiss, tossing me my first and only blessing, and all I had to do was let it hit.

The man in the boater was still droning on when I reached you, but now you sat crouched on the floor with your back to the fridge, so that he seemed to be complaining to the freezer. It might have been a suggestive pose, scandalous even, if you hadn't been so obviously bored. I glanced at him in passing and saw that he'd clenched his eyes shut, like an eight-year-old steeling himself for a spanking. He was a giant of a man, a colossus in seersucker, but I was past the point of no return by then. I knelt down beside you and you gave me a nod and we hid ourselves under the counter. I'd foreseen all this happening—I wouldn't have had the courage otherwise—but the fact of it was still beyond belief. Not a word had passed between us yet.

"I'm Walter," I said finally.

"You look uncomfortable, Walter."

"To tell you the truth, I'm not usually this limber."

You smiled at that. "I'm Mrs. Richard Haven."

You saw the shock register on my face—you must have seen it—but you didn't let on. You might as well have been married to Godzilla, or to Moses, or to some medium-sized Central American republic. By now, as you read this, you know the significance the name Haven holds for my family; perhaps you even knew or guessed it then. I should have stood up instantly and sprinted for the door. Instead I shook your hand, and said—if only to say something, to make some kind of noise, to keep you there with me under the counter—that you didn't look like Mrs. Anything.

"That's kind of you, Walter. I guess I'm well preserved."

"How old are you?"

You waggled a finger, then sighed. "Oh, what the hell. I'm twenty-eight."

I bobbed my head dumbly. In the light of the kitchen your skin looked synthetic. I felt an odd sort of pain as I watched you, a seasick alertness: the sense of something massive rushing toward me. For an instant I wondered whether I might be the victim of some elaborate prank, and studied the legs of the people around us, trying to identify them by their socks—I remember one pair in particular, striped red and blue and white, like barber poles—then realized I didn't give a damn. You were still holding my hand in both of yours.

"He's gone," you said. "That's something."

"Who's gone?"

"*You* know who. The Sensational Gatsby."

"The Great Gatsby, I think you mean."

You shook your head. "I'm married to him, Walter. I should know."

The weariness in your voice was both an invitation and a warning, and I felt the helpless jealousy then that only someone else's past can trigger. The years that lay behind your weariness, with all their hope and risk and disappointment, were utterly out of my reach: as long as time ran forward, I would never see or touch or understand them. But the knowledge was pale and drab with you beside me.

"Whose party is this?"

Your question caught me by surprise, if only because you seemed so perfectly at ease under the counter. I noticed for the first time that you spoke with the hint of a lisp.

"Don't you know Van?"

"Eh?"

"Van Markham." I pointed into the living room. "The man in the gabardine shorts."

You made a pinched sort of face, as though trying to make out something far away.

"Go easy on him, Mrs. Haven. He isn't as bad as he looks."

"Let's hope not."

"For the sake of full disclosure, he's my cousin."

"That explains *you*," you said vaguely. You seemed to be thinking about something else already.

"What do you mean, that explains me?"

"Your being here, that's all. At this kind of a party."

I didn't know what to say to that, so I kept my mouth shut. You yawned and looked past me and I felt the first stirrings of panic.

"What's your last name, Walter? Is it Markham, too?"

"Tompkins," I answered at once. "Walter Tompkins." The lie was out before I'd weighed its pros and cons, before I'd asked myself why: it was as automatic as ducking a punch. But of course I knew why. You'd just told me you were R. P. Haven's wife.

"Nice kitchen he's got here, this cousin of yours."

"Very nice," I said. "A premium kitchen."

"He doesn't look old enough for an apartment this posh. Is there family money?" You blinked at me sweetly. "You're not a fabulously wealthy recluse, are you, Walter?"

"A recluse? Not at all. Why would you ask me that?"

"I was watching you earlier, out in the living room. You were alphabetizing all the DVDs."

"I don't think of recluses as going to parties," I said stiffly. "I tend to think of them as staying at home, in a bunker or a tower of some kind. And as for those DVDs—"

You gave my hand a squeeze. "Don't get your shorts twisty, Walter. I'm sure the DVDs were frightfully out of order." You watched me for a while. "I've always had a soft spot for the blue-eyed, moony type. Also, for the record, I'm sloshed."

I considered pointing out that my eyes were a sort of muddy greenish gray, but prudence prevailed. Your expression grew pensive.

"Do you mind if I ask how you pay the rent?"

"I'm working on—I suppose you could call it a book." I stared out at the forest of pant legs and skirts. "A book of history."

"History, did you say?"

I nodded.

"Anybody's history in particular?"

Talking about my book always made me want to commit seppuku, and this was no exception. I hadn't so much as glanced at it since I'd dropped out of college.

"Mine," I answered, fighting the urge to bark or gnash my teeth. "My family's, I mean."

To my infinite relief you didn't laugh. "Your family? What's special about them?"

"I'm not sure," I said. Which was the second lie I told you.

"I know what's special about mine, Walter. Would you like to know?"

"Very much."

"We've always had noteworthy tombstones. My great-great-uncle Elginbrodde—of the Massachusetts Elginbroddes—wrote his epitaph himself, and it's a doozy. Want to hear it?"

"Of course."

"All right, then." You screwed your eyes up fiercely. "It was etched in a kind of cursive, I remember. Let me think—

> " 'Here lie I, Melvin Elginbrodde:—
> Have Mercy on my Soul, Lord God,
> As I would do, if I were God
> And Ye were Melvin Elginbrodde.' "

Neither of us spoke for a moment. If I hadn't already known that I was at your mercy, Mrs. Haven, I'd have realized it then.

"That's quite an epitaph," I said at last.

"I'd like to read your book one day, Mr. Tompkins."

No one had ever told me that before—and no one has since. "You would?" I said. "Why?"

"Something tells me I'd like it." You turned my hand over, as if reading my palm. "If we become friends, maybe I could have a walk-on part."

"It's not *that* kind of history," I managed to answer, painfully aware of how pompous I sounded. "It starts almost a hundred years ago. I'm trying to make a sort of pilgrimage, you might say, back along the causal—"

"There must be money in your family." You let go of my hand. "An apartment this hideous doesn't come cheap."

"Van came by his riches honorably, I'll have you know. By the sweat of his loins." I attempted a grin. "He has a mail-order pheromone business."

Your eyes widened. "He has a what?"

I cleared my throat carefully. "He sells pheromones—"

"Has he got any here?"

"Here?" Something in your voice made me uneasy. "In this apartment, you mean?"

Your face was close enough to mine that I could feel your hopsy breath against my neck. "In this apartment," you said, "is *exactly* what I mean."

I felt suddenly exposed under your attention, undersized and at risk, like a chinchilla caught in a searchlight. I found myself wondering whether it hadn't been a mistake to tell you about Van's business. I was still trying to make up my mind as I followed you out of the kitchen and up the spiral staircase to the second floor.

"They're probably in here," you said, opening the door of what my cousin liked to call his "cockpit." "This is where I'd keep the monkey drops."

"Monkey drops?"

"The *pheromones*, Walter."

You were already rifling through the drawer of Van's night table. A vaguely pornographic poster above the headboard advertised something called Equus Special Blend: two women with airbrushed, lava-colored bodies caressing a man-sized vial of iridescent goo. I studied it for a while, trying to figure out why Van could possibly have had it framed, then recognized it as a poster for his company. The vial was sweating angrily and so were both the women. A banner of digital-looking text across their genitals proclaimed:

YOUR. TIME. IS. NOW.

"Your time is now," you said quietly. You were standing at my shoulder, gazing up at the poster with a look that I couldn't interpret. "Isn't it always?"

"If that were true, Mrs. Haven, my cousin would be out of a job." You sighed, and I realized—too late—that your expression was one of melancholy. "I only mean that, in this case, 'your time' is a reference to getting a girl—I mean, to finding somebody to—"

"It's always now," you said. "It's never then." You seemed to be speaking only to yourself. A second wave of jealousy broke over me, even more overpowering than the first. My sense of predestination was gone without a trace.

"I'd rather not talk about time, if you don't mind."

"Why not?"

"If you really want to know, Mrs. Haven—" I hesitated, at a loss as to where to begin. "You might say that time is my family curse."

"Time is *everyone's* curse."

"That's a popular misconception, actually. Without progressive time—

that is to say, without what physicists refer to as the 'thermodynamic arrow,' life as we experience it—"

"Put a cork in it, Walter," you said, pressing the thumb of your right hand against my lips. Your left hand held two vials of brownish liquid. I was gripped by a new sensation then, one that I've always hated: the feeling of life imitating advertising. The mimicry wasn't perfect—you weren't sweating or lava-colored, and you had your clothes on—but it was close enough. I took one of the vials from you, squinted at it a moment, then pulled out the rubber stopper with my teeth. A smell of grease and toffee filled the room.

You gave a tipsy-sounding laugh. "What's your next move, Walter? What are you—"

"My time is now," I said softly. I knocked the little vial back like a shot.

For the space of a few seconds I felt nothing: my sense of propriety stirred in certain of the remoter furrows of my brain, but that was all. Almost at once, however—with astonishing speed, at any rate—a warmth began to muster at the bottom of my spine. My eyes had closed at some point without my noticing, and I quickly lost all awareness of the room, of the party, even of the fact of you beside me. Purple and crimson and cinnamon-colored shapes began to creep across my sight, and behind or below them were other shapes, less abstract, more carnal, squirming and writhing together in patterns and rhythms that brought a prickling flush to my skin. I felt exalted, singled out by obscure and erotic forces, ready for anything as long as it was filthy. I have no clear sense of how long this condition lasted, Mrs. Haven, or how obvious my voluptuousness was to you. With every passing second I became more deliciously aware of each fold and recess of my body, more physically greedy, more depraved. I took in a deep and languid breath, held it as long as I could, then decided I was ready to have my way with the cosmos, beginning with you.

When I opened my eyes, you were staring at me as though I'd just swallowed a tooth.

"You're not supposed to *drink* it, Walter. It's a musk."

By the time I'd fully grasped what you were saying the voluptuousness had drained away completely, rushing out of my body as if it couldn't wait to escape, leaving me baffled and self-conscious and alone. For the blink of an eye, I was able to savor a feeling of mortification as acute as my arousal had just been; then, without the slightest transition, I was lying facedown on the corkwood floor.

"Walter? Come in, Walter. Are you alive?"

Your voice was all breath and no sound, the voice of a panicked conspirator, and I wondered, considering my position, how I was able to hear you at all. Then you spoke to me again, and your lips brushed my earlobe, and I realized you were with me on the floor.

"I hear somebody coming, Walter. I think maybe it's time to get up."

"Why are you lying down, Mrs. Haven? Did you take a shot, too?"

You cursed under your breath and rolled me over. I opened my eyes with reluctance. You were floating above me like a kind of cherub, but also like a creature in a lithograph I'd once seen, a gargoyle hunched over a woman in the throes of a terrible fever.

"I love you, Mrs. Haven."

You pursed your lips at that, looking more prim than I'd have thought possible, and patted me very gently on the cheek. "That's nice of you, Walter. How soon are you going to be sick?"

"That isn't important. I want to—"

At that moment my cousin reeled into the room, leading a sniggering young man by the collar of what appeared—from what I could make out—to be a uniform of the merchant marine. The two of them grappled for a while at the foot of the bed, taking no notice of us whatsoever, butting foreheads like amorous elk. I'd never seen my cousin behave in this way, though I can't honestly say I was surprised. Something about Van has always brought late-night nature programming to mind.

"Hello, cousin," I groaned.

Van gave a slight jerk, as though he'd been stuck with a pin; the boy closed his eyes and flopped onto the bed. You sat up and arranged your hair and dress.

"Jesus, Waldy. What are you doing down there?" Van squinted at us for a moment. "That can't be Richard Haven's fucking wife."

"This man is ill," you said politely.

"What have you got to say for yourself, Waldy? You're sick? Is that true?"

"It will be soon," I managed to reply.

As I write this, Mrs. Haven, it occurs to me that our romance was bookended—set in parentheses, as it were—by visits to the toilet to be sick. You waited just outside the bathroom door, chatting cordially with my cousin; I caught sight of my reflection in the mirror (scruffy brown hair in need of a cut, startled-looking gray eyes, general air of defeat) and resigned myself to the inevitable. Our illicit encounter, such as it was, was over. Our desert island had been colonized.

Van was gone when I finally emerged, but you were just where I'd left you, leafing through an Equus Special Blend brochure. I stood beside you sheepishly, steadying myself against the wall, waiting for you to acknowledge me. When you did I knew at once that it was over.

"I have to go," you said flatly. "The Husband is waiting. I told him that I'd left something upstairs."

"That something being me."

"You don't understand the chance we're taking, Walter." You looked suddenly tired. "He has a possessive streak—a nasty one. If he starts to suspect—"

"I'm not afraid of him. Let him come up."

Your reply was a yawn, which was what I deserved. It's typical of my cursed nature that I discounted the fact that you were risking your marriage—and most likely far more—by waiting while I threw up in the bathroom. All I cared about was that you'd soon be gone.

"Mrs. Haven, I feel it incumbent on me—"

"You talk funny," you said. "Like an actor playing the part of a college professor. I'm not sure I like it."

"I come from an odd family. Let's blame it on them."

"What sort of a family?"

"Millionaire recluses."

"I wouldn't be surprised, the way you talk." You considered me a moment. "I like it."

"You've already made up your mind?"

"That's right, Walter. Sometimes it goes fast."

I put my hands on your shoulders. "Mrs. Haven—"

"It seems a bit weird, your calling me that now."

"Why?"

"No one's ever called me that before they kissed me."

For some reason this stopped me cold. "You haven't told me your name," I said. "Your given name, that is."

"I guess this means we're in a stalemate, Walter."

We stared at each other, both of our expressions guarded, as though it had just occurred to us that we were strangers. "My name isn't Walter," I said finally. "It's Waldemar."

You narrowed your eyes. "What sort of a name is Waldemar, if you don't mind my asking? Are you a wizard?"

"It's a family name. It came from my grandfather's brother."

"That *family* of yours again. They keep popping up."

"Mrs. Haven, I'd like very much to—"

"Your breath smells like toffee," you said, wrinkling your nose. "Don't operate any heavy machinery tonight, Walter. Okay? Take a cab."

I took a step toward you—more of a lunge, really—but my cause was clearly hopeless. You were at the head of the staircase already, frowning at me slightly, as though I were becoming hard to see. All the seconds and minutes that had hung suspended since I'd met you hit the floor with a crash, scattering like ball bearings across the parquet. I watched your cropped head spiral out of view as smoothly and irrevocably as the water in the toilet had just done.

A thought came to me then, or the ghost of a thought, but I flushed it irritably from my mind. It had to do—of all possible thoughts, in that place, at that instant—with time, and with our progress inside it. I found myself spinning clockwise—the opposite spin to your descent of the staircase, to the swirling of the toilet, to the direction in which I wanted time to move— but it had no effect at all on your departure. At the end of the hall, like a frigate coming over the horizon, my cousin drifted grimly into view.

"What are you trying to do, Tolliver? Can you answer me that?"

"I'm putting up resistance," I mumbled. "I'm testing a theory. By turning in the contrary direction to the prevailing—"

"Shut up, asshole. What the hell were you doing with R. P. Haven's wife?"

I came to rest and stared into Van's eyes. He looked chillingly sober.

"I wasn't doing anything, really. I found her under the counter. She was—"

"Do you have any idea how *important* Haven is for me? For my company?"

I've always had trouble distinguishing rhetorical questions from literal ones, Mrs. Haven, and this was no exception. "I have a hunch," I said carefully, "from the look on your face, that he's one of your principal backers."

Van said nothing for a long, reflective moment.

"Get out of my house, Tolliver."

IV

KASPAR AND SONJA'S LOVE flowered lushly, Mrs. Haven, as secret liaisons will—but Waldemar had secrets of his own.

The cause of his mysterious sleeping habits and absences from school was, in fact, a middle-aged widow with a rose-colored villa, just as the departmental wags had whispered; but their mutual passion took a form that would have surprised even the most imaginative of gossips. The widow Bemmelmans—Lucrezia, to her intimates—was a fearsome opponent of vice in all its irruptions, from child prostitution to cardsharping to the intemperate consumption of coffee. In his role as her favorite, Kaspar's brother had taken to spending his evenings at the widow's side, assisting her in composing a staggering number of articles, letters, and feuilletons, of which the following text (concerning the "waltz king" of Vienna, Johann Strauss) is as good an example as any:

> A dangerous power has been put into the hands of this dark man. African and hot-blooded, rabid with life, he exorcises the devil from our bodies; his own limbs no longer belong to him when the thunderstorm of the waltz is let loose. His fiddle-bow dances in his arms, and the tempo animates his feet; bacchantically the young couples waltz—lust in its purest form let loose. No God inhibits them.

Whether lust of any kind—other than a kind of righteous bloodlust—was let loose in their late-night drafting sessions, it was clear enough to

Kaspar that the widow Bemmelmans (or the "Brown Widow," as she would come to be known) had a hold over Waldemar that ran deeper than any shared schoolmarmishness. The precise nature of this hold continued to elude my grandfather, try as he might to divine it; but he was certain that the two of them had some skeleton in the cupboard, and that it was the reason for his brother's furtiveness. He made a point of telling Waldemar about his affair with Sonja Silbermann in rapturous detail, in the hope of bridging the widening gulf between them, but his brother barely seemed to hear. Kaspar forced himself to take an interest in the widow's pet crusades, and even went so far as to attend one of her gatherings; this, however, proved an even worse miscalculation. He made the fatal blunder, Mrs. Haven, of bringing his new *bonne amie* along.

Their romance was barely a month old when Kaspar and Sonja paid their call on the widow Bemmelmans, but already my grandfather's fitted shirts and fawn-colored suits had been exchanged for a brown linen jacket that looked perpetually slept in, and blue canvas trousers—as shapeless as the dresses back in Znojmo—that he'd bought from a bricklayer's apprentice. His nervousness at meeting his brother's benefactress was somewhat offset by Sonja's surprising decision to wear a delightful saffron sundress, but his misgivings returned at the sight of the widow's footman, a badger-faced giant with a waxed blond mustache, who wore the uniform of a Hungarian hussar.

The widow received them in a ballroom on the villa's second floor. Waldemar was there, as were half a dozen other young men, arranged about the room in self-consciously romantic poses, like actors in some grim tableau vivant. The widow was the only person seated, on a leopard-skin couch that appeared to take up a third of the room. A pair of sabers lay crossed on the waxed floor before her; it was unclear, at least to Kaspar, whether their function was decorative or sporting. He found himself picturing the widow Bemmelmans, surrounded by her eager coterie, officiating at round-robin tournaments, perhaps even at duels.

"*Willkommen*, children," the widow said langorously, extending her arms. "It always heartens us to see new faces." Sonja curtsied prettily, doing an excellent job of disguising her bemusement; Kaspar hesitated, attempting to catch Waldemar's eye, then took the nearest of the widow's hands and kissed it. She was frailer than he'd pictured her, long since gone androgynous with age; her sharp velvet collar and white, shrublike eyebrows gave her the look of a clean-shaven Bismarck. She stiffened momentarily when he brought her fingers to his lips, then surprised him by clamping her hand on his forearm and pulling herself up from the couch. "It's time for dinner, Herr Toula," she said, extending her left hand absently to Sonja. "Kindly escort this ancient piece of crockery down the hall." The honor guard broke rank—grudgingly, it seemed to Kaspar—to let the three of them pass. His brother was the very last to follow.

∞

Dinner was surprisingly opulent, given the austerity of the house: trout-filled potato dumplings, sweetbreads in aspic, beef tongue, bitter gherkins, and a succulent *Kalbsbraten*, followed by a tray of flavored ices. Kaspar was confident—almost certain, in fact—that the gherkins were his family's own, but he took care not to embarrass his brother. After the requisite pleasantries, the talk turned to the widow's most recent campaign: abolishing the Washerwomen's Ball.

"The Washerwomen's Ball?" Kaspar said. "I'm not sure what that is. Perhaps Fräulein Silbermann—"

"My brother spends all of his time at the university," Waldemar cut in, to all appearances embarrassed already.

"As well he should!" said the widow. "It's to your credit, Herr Toula, that you've never heard of it."

"It's a filthy extravagance," one of her courtiers chirped. "The women wear rags on their heads—women of the best families—and their under-things only, which means—in most cases—that their most intimate garments, by which I mean to say, if you'll excuse the term, their *knickers*—"

"It's a kind of masquerade," said the widow, silencing the boy with a glance. "The gentry of this city, out of a mixture of lasciviousness and boredom, dress up as their inferiors, and behave accordingly. It's a way of getting past their inhibitions."

"You sound postively Freudian, Frau Bemmelmans," said Sonja.

Slowly and ratchetingly, with an almost audible creak, the widow's head revolved in her direction. "I beg your pardon, fräulein," she said dryly. "I'm an adherent of no party or religion. My views are my own."

"I applaud that, Frau Bemmelmans. But I was referring to the teachings of Dr. Freud, a physician in the Ninth District, who specializes in bourgeois hysteria. He and his disciples believe that our actions are guided by a second self: an animus, so to speak, hidden from the conscious mind—"

"That sounds like a religion to me," the widow said, snapping her head back into place. "I've never heard such idiotic prattle."

Sonja gave a high-pitched, brittle laugh. Kaspar had heard this particular laugh before—on a number of occasions, in fact—and he knew enough to take it as a warning. "I see your point, Frau Bemmelmans," he said quickly. "I think what Fräulein Silbermann means, however, is that—"

"I went to the Washerwomen's Ball last year," said Sonja. "I rather enjoyed myself. It helped me to get past my inhibitions."

"Is that so," said the widow. "How interesting."

"I think what Fräulein Silbermann means," Kaspar put in, laughing weakly, "is simply that—"

"Oh *yes*," Sonja singsonged. "I felt just like the purest child of nature." She sighed prettily and took Kaspar's hand. "Didn't I, honeypot?"

"Sonja," Kaspar stuttered, doing his best not to redden. "I really don't—"

"And afterward Kaspar took me home and gave me a thorough, uninhibited buggering. It really was *extravagantly* filthy."

No one spoke for a medium-sized eternity. All eyes—Sonja's included—were fixed on the widow. Now would be the moment for those sabers to come out, Kaspar thought. But the widow, when she finally replied, was more decorous and genial than ever.

"By all reports the balls are colorful affairs—one can see how they might magnetize the young. Citizens of all breeds and pedigrees intermingle freely there, or so I understand." She turned her mannish face toward the assembled gallants, allowing the entire room to bask in her goodwill. "I'm told the Israelites, especially, lend a feral sort of spice to the proceedings."

The specifics of Sonja's reply are not recorded in my grandfather's entry for the fourth of October, but it sufficed to bar her—and Kaspar as well—from the villa indefinitely. What my grandfather does describe, however—and in great detail, as if he knew that it would prove significant—was Waldemar's response to Sonja's antics. While the ardent young men around him rolled their eyes and gnashed their teeth, Waldemar sat straight-backed in his chair, as still as the bust of Schubert on the mantelpiece behind him. There was something in his eyes, however—or *behind* his eyes, Kaspar wrote, crossing out the preceding phrase—that gave the lie to his debonair manner. He was looking at Sonja more closely than Kaspar had seen him look at anything.

But even that's not right, my grandfather corrected himself. Not entirely.

I can sense his hesitation at this point in the narrative, Mrs. Haven—I can feel him pausing, pencil in hand, as a memory wriggles up into the light. He'd seen that same expression four years earlier, he remembered, in the brining-room laboratory in Znojmo. He and his brother had discovered a nest of cicadas in a tree in the town square, and their father, in the spirit of scientific instruction, had dropped one of them into an empty beaker. "Cicadas can be spirited little devils, but their metabolic rate is remarkably slow," he'd explained to his sons, covering the beaker's mouth with a chipped china saucer. "They can go without food for a very long while. Shall we determine just how long a while that is?"

After a dozen panicked circuits of its enclosure, the cicada had stopped moving, and Kaspar had quickly lost interest; but Waldemar's reaction had been just the opposite. Over the following weeks, his brother had passed progressively longer stretches of time staring down into the beaker, his eyes blank, his mouth slightly open, his body as fixed as the cicada's own. He'd begun to neglect what few duties he had, and Kaspar had seen to them in his stead, waiting patiently for someone to notice. Finally, at the close of an afternoon on which his brother had spent more than an hour in his customary trance, Kaspar had snatched up the beaker, inverted it with a flourish, and slammed it down against the oilcloth-covered bench. Waldemar had let out a groan, as though he'd just been given devastating news; but when he looked up at Kaspar he was smiling with unmistakable relief. "I didn't know how to stop," he'd said in a faltering voice.

Kaspar had told him to think nothing of it, then glanced down at the cicada—still trapped under the upended beaker—and asked him what should happen to his pet. To his astonishment, his brother had turned away without another glance. "It makes no difference now," he'd said. "You can go ahead and crush it, if you like."

Half a century later, looking back on his youth from the safety and comfort of a screened-in veranda in upstate New York, my grandfather would recognize this episode for the milestone it was: an inconspicuous wedge—no greater than the V of two spread fingers—from which the rest of their durations would diverge.

∞

Strolling home from the widow's villa, Sonja was flushed and euphoric, calling Kaspar all manner of names, both affectionate and insulting, and cutting capers in her saffron-colored dress. By the duck pond in the Stadtpark she announced that she loved him, then turned and vomited into the filthy green water, as if to fix the moment in his mind.

"I feel the same," Kaspar said, helping her back to her feet. "I adore you, Fräulein Silbermann."

She nodded thoughtfully and took him by the collar. "Your mustache is regrettable," she whispered, wrinkling her nose at the smell of her own breath.

Though they had slept together several times already, the night of the widow's party expunged all precedents. Sonja seemed to grow younger as the act progressed, but also less opaque, more knowable to him; the fact that Kaspar knew what would happen—and even, approximately, in what order—did nothing to dull the shock and gratitude he felt. As her climax approached, her playfulness fell away and she took his hands emphatically in hers. The ritual never varied: they might approach their mutual destination from any direction they chose, but the final pitch was as deliberate as the dismantling of a bomb. Positioning Kaspar behind her, Sonja would bring his left hand to her mouth and sink her square front teeth into his palm; his right index finger, when the moment arrived, was guided, gently but unambiguously, to a spot he'd otherwise have blushed to touch.

He couldn't have said with any accuracy how long it all lasted—his sense of time abandoned him completely during sex, a fact that embarrassed him only slightly less than the act itself—but when they fell back exhausted he felt magically aged, as though the years she'd shed had settled on his chest. This was by no means an unwelcome feeling: the heaviness in his limbs struck him as akin to what a cannibal must feel after gorging himself on an especially worthy foe. Sonja slept all through the night without the slightest change in her position. More than once, glancing over at her limp, snow-white body, Kaspar found himself imagining that he'd killed her.

He awoke to find her flat on her belly with her legs and arms splayed, as though she'd fallen from some great height onto his bed. He stood upright on the mattress, steadying himself against the flaking ceiling, and brought his right foot gently down against her rump. He'd expected her to be in a foul mood, drunk as she'd been, but she began to smile before her eyes came open. He made coffee on the burner, enough for two cups exactly, then forgot them on the countertop and crawled back into bed. She was wide awake now. She hadn't forgotten what she'd said to him by the duck pond, to his amazement, or what his answer had been. They sat cross-legged on the bed, looking down into the shaded golden courtyard, speaking only when the need to speak arose. After an absurdly long silence—so long he'd have begun to squirm in anyone else's company—she yawned and asked him where his brother was.

"Not here," he said, surprised by the question. "I have no idea where he spends his nights."

It had never crossed Kaspar's mind to view his brother as a rival, in spite of his unquestionable elegance, simply because Waldemar had never shown the least interest in sex; but something in her manner gave him pause. Before he was entirely aware of it—and certainly before he'd weighed the pros and cons—he was describing how Waldemar had stared at her the night before.

"I'm accustomed to being stared at, Kasparchen," Sonja said with a shrug. "That's one of the reasons I go about town in a sack."

Kaspar hesitated. "I don't know," he said finally, "when my brother stares at a woman, that it means exactly what you think it means."

"Oh! I'm quite sure it does," Sonja answered, with just the faintest hint of coquetry.

The only means Kaspar saw to make his meaning clear was to recount the episode of the cicada. Sonja listened intently, never once interrupting, and by the end of it her complacency was gone. He relaxed somewhat then, confident that he'd communicated whatever it was—he couldn't have put a name to it, precisely—that had troubled him so much the night before.

"That story gives me the horrors," said Sonja.

"Then you see what I mean? Waldemar can't be thought of as an ordinary—"

"Imagine being trapped under glass," Sonja murmured, her eyes strangely dim. "Imagine being swept up by some enormous, foreign power, torn free of the world, then set down in a place where nothing happens— absolutely nothing. You can see the world go by, and you can try to recollect how it once was; but you have no *function* in it any longer." She shook her head. "How would you know that time was even passing?"

Her response to the anecdote struck Kaspar as childish at first; but the last question she'd posed—if you were set apart from the world, compeletely sequestered, how could you detect that time was passing?—refused to leave him in peace. Worst of all, when he was alone again in that dusty, airless garret, his brother's face persisted in his thoughts, superimposing it- self over everything he looked at or imagined, until the cicada and Sonja's naked body and Waldemar's dispassionate mortician's stare combined into a hideous chimera that filled his mind to the exclusion of all else. Anything was preferable to dwelling on that grotesque composite: even scientific work, however futile. Even the invocation of the dead.

Which was how, without fully realizing it himself, my grandfather be- gan to hunt the Accidents again.

V

WALDEMAR HAD EXPECTED time to move more quickly once he'd put Znojmo behind him, but to his surprise the opposite was true. Each instant was now distinct from those before and after, bite-sized and luminous, like a pearl on an invisible, indivisible wire. Vienna rattled and bustled and pirouetted around him, but he felt himself to be in no great hurry—though it wasn't until the end of his first year at the university, reading the work of the Dutch physicist Hendrik Lorentz, that he understood why. Lorentz had discovered, to his and the whole world's astonishment, that time moves more slowly for a body in motion. And it often seemed to Waldemar, since he'd escaped the constraints of his childhood, that his body had never fully come to rest.

Unlike his brother, no event steered my great-uncle's attention back to the Accidents, for the simple reason that they'd never left his thoughts. His father's cryptic discovery and sudden death had conspired to give Waldemar a sense of significance he'd never otherwise have had, and he took pains to be deserving of his fate. Occasionally the thought would make him shiver, like a pang of self-consciousness in a crowded theater: *Without the Accidents, I'd be no different than any other man.* The notion thrilled and frightened him in equal measure. By "Accidents," he meant two distinct but intertwined events: both Ottokar's discovery and the encounter with Progress, in the form of Herr Bachling's Daimler, that had snuffed his father's brilliance just as it was poised to set the world alight.

Waldemar saw his coming of age—his entire existence, in fact—as a series of momentous collisions; but those two were set apart from the rest, kept sacrosanct and pure. Not even Kaspar grasped how much they signified. Waldemar had made a close study of his brother after their father's death, but Kaspar seemed to be the same person afterward that he'd been before. He was haunted by the Accidents, of course—how could he not have been?—but he showed no gratitude for their occurrence. When this realization set in, Waldemar's disappointment was bitter; and though he kept his outward manner cordial, he was careful to keep his ideas to himself.

He was sorry to do so, desperately sorry, because his thoughts grew more electric by the day. He could feel the secret of the Accidents flutter against his brain stem as he went about his work—especially when he was busy with something trivial, such as drafting a letter for the widow Bemmelmans—and on certain evenings, as he nodded off at his desk at the university, it beat against his awareness like a moth against a paper window-shade. Waldemar copied Ottokar's riddle into a series of notebooks, just as Kaspar had done, taking pains to match his father's scrawl exactly. He chanted it under his breath on streetcars and benches and barstools, like a madman or an Israelite at prayer, and it never failed to pacify his nerves.

The Michelson-Morley experiment weighed on Waldemar's mind. How in God's name could the speed of light be absolute—a constant? Only time and space could have that magic property. Isaac Newton, the greatest intellect in human history, had unlocked the mechanics of the entire solar system based on this self-evident fact, and had solved the mysteries of gravitation; in light of the Michelson-Morley result, however, Newton's laws had come to seem outmoded, even quaint. How was this possible? Waldemar longed to ask Kaspar—to ask his opinion, to have an ally again, to break free of the glass dome that seemed to have been lowered over him since coming to Vienna—but the truth was that he feared his brother's answer. How could it be that *nothing*—no force in the universe, not even the spinning of a planet on its axis—either added to light's velocity or reduced it?

Each time he arrived at this precipice, Waldemar compelled himself to catch his conceptual breath. He could feel his neurons pickling whenever he dwelt on its implications, as though the fat his cerebrum floated in were gradually being transmuted into brine. This nauseated him at first—it made his entire body clench—but in time he taught himself to like the feeling. And once he'd begun to relish the sensation, once it had stopped sickening him, something shifted inside his skull, like a delirious child turning in a sweat-sodden bed, and his father's text began to offer up its secrets.

What frustrated Waldemar most about Ottokar's note was that it hovered so coyly between sense and nonsense, refusing to hold still from one line to the next. Sentences of gobbledygook were folded over and under familiar citations—like strata of dough in a strudel—and others that were clearly drawn from classical sources, whose origins might potentially be traced. And then there were the references (surely not arbitrary?) to mistresses and married life and sex. After dozens of failed attempts to crack the code, Waldemar decided to invert his strategy: he would begin on solid ground, by considering the citations, then work his way slowly out into the jabber.

Time can be measured only in its passing had been a favored axiom of Ottokar's, often cited after long and fruitless mornings in the laboratory. Waldemar had heard it so often, in fact, that he'd never bothered to inquire where it came from, and it was only at the close of a long and increasingly despondent week at the Imperial Library that he found it at last, in the fourteenth chapter of Saint Augustine's *Confessions*.

"What then, is time?" asks the saint. "If no one asks of me, I know; if I wish to explain to him who asks, I know not." Neither the past nor the future, argues Augustine, truly exists—and the present is merely an instant. "The present of things *past* is memory," he writes; "the present of things *present* is perception; and the present of things *future* is expectation." Augustine's conclusion—never fully stated, but unmistakably implied—is that time is subjective. It exists in the mind alone, and nowhere else.

This notion stupefied Waldemar nearly as much as the Michelson-Morley result. Augustine's theory was an even blunter refutation of Newton's law of absolutes, and he'd conceived it in a North African backwater, surrounded by desert, a millennium before Sir Isaac had drawn his first breath! Scrambling to recover his equilibrium, Waldemar reminded himself that Augustine had been a cleric, not a scientist; but the fact remained that Ottokar had cited him. The thought of it made Waldemar physically ill. Newton's laws—with their elegance, their reasonableness, and, above all, their immaculate order—were the reason he'd consecrated himself to physics; without them, he might as well have stayed a pickler. He was not a young man who took pleasure in ambiguity. Ambiguity was dangerously close, in his estimation, to hypocrisy; and hypocrisy—as every true revolutionary knows—is the music by which complacency and decadence dance their unholy quadrille.

The next citation was more unsettling still: *As the soul grows toward eternal life, it remembers less and less.* This seemed more like something his mother might mutter into her handkerchief at church than anything relevant to Ottokar's work. In which tightly shuttered compartment of his father's brain had this mystical strain been concealed? For the briefest of instants, Waldemar found himself questioning Ottokar's competence, even—fleetingly, half-consciously—his sanity; it took his last reserves of love and strength to force that portal closed. The very next night, however, when he identified *Plotinus*, of all people, as the author of the passage, his confusion returned with a force that swamped him utterly. Plotinus was the worst of the old pagan neoplatonists: a fuzzy-headed metaphysician who'd inspired countless early Christian flower-sniffers, not to mention soothsayers and Gnostics and God knew who else. Important as he might have been for the Church, he had no place in a scientific treatise.

Ironically enough, it turned out to be the Church—or *one* church, in particular—that set Waldemar on the proper path at last. Disenchanted with his father's taste in philosophy, he narrowed his focus still further, restricting it to the parts of Ottokar's text that seemed to refer to actual events of his duration. This proved most difficult of all, to his dismay, because the slightest reference to the sausage-chewing sow his father had fornicated with each weekday made piss-colored spots dance before Waldemar's eyes and the carpet twitch and heave beneath his feet. In the end he was reduced to pondering a single sentence of the letter, which he read and reread, recombined and dissected and recited to himself until it acquired the power of prophecy. It was the plainest of sentences, no more than a phrase: *the pulpit for preachers in Pamĕt' Cathedral.* It was pure chance, he would later write—certainly not fate, let alone Providence—that this turned out to be the only phrase he needed.

Ottokar had been clever—cunning, even—to hide the key in plain sight, in a thicket of high-minded nonsense. It stood out exceedingly subtly, betraying itself only if one knew where to look. Unlike his brother, Waldemar recalled that pulpit very well, not only because of its peculiar globelike shape, but also because of their father's fascination with it. Like the uncle of Wilhelm von Tegetthoff, who'd once torn out a lock of his nephew's hair so that the boy might never forget having seen the royal carriage pass, Ottokar had given Waldemar's ear a sharp twist on that December morning, then directed his gaze upward toward the gilt-and-silver pulpit without a word of explanation.

The significance of that structure—for it was clearly the pulpit *itself* that interested his father, not the lisping, milk-faced clergyman it buttressed— became the defining enigma of Waldemar's youth. If he'd kept the memory stowed away until that moment, if he'd hesitated to tell even his brother, it was only because of the tremendous charge it carried. But now his father himself, two years after his death, had eased the mystery back into the light. And what affected Waldemar most keenly—what made his eyes water and his fingers go numb with excitement—was that his father had done so with such stealth that he alone, of all people living, could recognize it for the hidden sign it was.

The pulpit was no more than five feet in diameter and (aside from a narrow, flattened opening through which the priest protruded) was per- fectly round. It had been meant to symbolize the triumph of Catholic doc- trine in all the seven corners of the world, evidently, because its silver-plated surface was marked by lines of longitude and latitude, and all the conti- nents of the earth—Antarctica included!—were proudly represented in gold leaf. But Waldemar had spent nearly three years assisting his father, and he knew that geography had held even less interest for him than the niceties of internal combustion. It must therefore have been the *shape* of the pulpit that had mattered to Ottokar: its shape, and the relation of that shape to the pulpit's purpose as a staging area for the Holy Word. A globe had been chosen to symbolize Rome's omnipresence simply because the earth, at the time, was as much of the universe as mankind understood.

It was then that Waldemar had a remarkable thought, one that set him, quietly but inescapably, on a course for infamy. If the shape of the pulpit was the feature that had inpired his father, and if the pulpit had been built to house the truth, and if that truth—the divine truth, the Holy Word of God—had been meant both to explain and to *contain* the universe, then Ottokar's message wasn't so obscure at all. He was saying, in effect, that the sphere was not only the fundamental shape in the solar system—not only the shape taken by the planets, and by the moons of those planets, and by the sun at its center—but that the sphere was the shape of the universe itself. We were all contained within it—all matter, all energy, all experience, all time—like the priest in his pulpit in Pamět' Cathedral.

But then, in the course of a month's feverish work, my great-uncle strayed even farther. If the speed of light was unchanging, as Michelson and Morley insisted, then time and space would clearly have to bend; but a spherical universe alone wasn't enough to account for the interferometer's readings. The distortions in space and time would have to be local—measurable in a few cubic feet in the basement of a Midwestern university—and the *act of measurement itself* would have to summon those distortions into being.

This last notion, in particular, led Waldemar to suspect that he had forfeited his place among the sane. He was speculating wildly now, almost hysterically: this new work felt less like science to him than like philosophy, or poetry, or some strain of wordless, polyrhythmic song. He was drifting into twilight, Mrs. Haven, but the glories that awaited him there were beautiful—so beautiful that he regretted nothing. There was power in severing the umbilical cord of precedent: the power of complete supremacy. Finally, after more than a year of hurling himself against the walls of consensus reality, he could feel those walls starting to give.

In the ensuing weeks, emboldened by his progress, Waldemar scuttled his last remaining scraps of orthodoxy. He found himself utterly alone, in a singularity of his own making, falling away from everyone he'd ever known or cared for. There was no turning back any longer, no bread-crumb trail, no lifeline to the past. He was wholly at the mercy of the future.

If the cosmos as a whole is subject to mysterious forces that warp it into the shape of a globe, Waldemar reasoned, shouldn't those forces have the same effect on smaller amounts of matter, given the right set of conditions? The fact that the world as we experience it doesn't seem filled with countless bubbles of spacetime—essentially tiny, autonomous universes, as he was coming to believe—is no argument against the possibility. We don't see the world around us as constructed of microscopic particles, after all, yet no one has contested the atomic model in a century.

The idea of the observer having an impact on observed phenomena would eventually find expression in Werner Heisenberg's famous uncertainty principle, of course—but this was two decades earlier, Mrs. Haven, and

Waldemar went Heisenberg one better. What was the act of inquiry into the nature of time, he asked himself, but an expression of human consciousness: in fact, the highest form of that expression? What else could be the catalyst, therefore—the source of the impulse that made spacetime buckle—but the concerted action of the human brain?

At last, after weeks of exquisite agony, he appreciated Augustine's genius. More than that: he saw its implications burst into flower around him in explosions of pure mental color. It was the defining moment of his life, and Waldemar knew it, though he had no idea as yet where it would lead him. The foundational postulate had been established: the great and reckless leap from the salons of bourgeois reason into the primeval fissure from which true genius oozes. It burned his former self away, it stripped him of his ego without mercy, but he was eager for the sacrifice. He'd have traded the world for this one crumb of insight: that time and space themselves are in transit, subject to a motion both pliable *and* absolute, and that man can influence said motion by an act of focused, virtuosic will.

It was this last hypothesis, Mrs. Haven, that held the seed of Waldemar's damnation.

The mathematics didn't fit, not yet, but that would come. He had his entire duration to make the mathematics fit. He desired no fame for himself, no glory, no material compensation; the envy of his rivals would suffice. That and the fact that he, Waldemar Toula, second son of Ottokar Gottfriedens, had redeemed his father's *Lebenswerk* from oblivion.

∞

At virtually the same time, working after hours in his office in the Federal Office for Intellectual Property in Bern, Switzerland, Albert Einstein was writing a paper. Calm where my great-uncle was euphoric, complacent where he was shrill, taking measured steps through a landscape Waldemar glided over on wings made out of candle wax and spit, the rumple-headed Jew with the "dark, soulful eyes" was putting the finishing touches to his Viennese colleague's destruction. He was about to provide the answer to the apparent paradox posed by Michelson and Morley, and his answer, once proven, would extinguish all others. Science brooks no dissent, Mrs. Haven; not over the course of time. Soon the case would be closed. Waldemar's work—and, by extension, his father's—would vanish into the vacuum of obsolete ideas.

The "Patent Clerk," as he came to be referred to in my family, had never heard of my great-uncle, any more than Waldemar had ever heard of him; but like Newton and Leibniz, like Darwin and Wallace, these two young German-speaking eccentrics were closing in on the same territory at virtually the identical moment. The fact that Waldemar overshot the mark disastrously, arcing like a comet over the (relatively) stable ground on which Einstein stood, did nothing to lessen the sting of his rival's conquest of the scientific mainstream. 1905 would go down in history as Einstein's annus mirabilis, the year in which, at the age of not quite twenty-seven, without so much as a university degree, he hit on the preposterously, childishly, almost *insultingly* simple formula $E = mc^2$, which describes the universal relationship between energy and matter.

It would prove to be a magical year for my great-uncle as well, but the magic in his case was black as pitch. His father had met his end in the form of a watch salesman's Daimler, a death that was not without a certain gentle irony; Waldemar's nemesis, by contrast, was neither a man nor a machine, but an idea. That idea's name was special relativity, Mrs. Haven, and there was nothing gentle about it whatsoever. As obscure as it was—and as innocuous as its author appeared—it had the power to annihilate the world.

VI

LESS THAN A WEEK after the disastrous evening at the villa Bemmelmans, Sonja Silbermann was roused out of a greedy, slovenly sleep—the sleep of a woman in love—by the sound of gravel glancing off her bedroom shutters. She put on the sternest face she could muster and stepped to the window, expecting to find Kaspar outside; before she'd undone its catch, however, she remembered that Kaspar was away, visiting his mother in that little town in Moravia whose name she could never remember. She blinked groggily out at the street, taking care to keep back from the light, and wondered which of her past errors of judgment had chosen that particular night to pay a call. To the right, a row of chestnut trees curved downhill toward Schwarzenbergplatz; to the left, her father's cherished Bugatti touring sedan hulked like a battleship under its waxed canvas cover. It was Heimo, she decided, stifling a yawn; Heimo or possibly Karl. Karl had always been the surreptitious sort.

She was about to close the shutters and crawl back into bed when she caught sight of a figure at the edge of the trees. Only one boy she knew held himself so correctly, so proudly, as though the Kaiser might ride by at any moment. She opened the window noiselessly, with a practiced hand, and whispered to him that she'd be right out.

Something's happened to Kaspar, she thought as she hurried downstairs. Something terrible's happened. And she was right, Mrs. Haven, though years would pass before she found out what it was.

She'd expected to find Waldemar on the stoop when she opened the door, but he kept to the chestnut trees' shadow, still standing at some version of attention, his loden cap held out like a bouquet. It was his stillness, more than anything else, that convinced her that he'd come bearing bad news.

"Fräulein Silbermann." It seemed more an observation than a greeting.

"What is it, Waldemar?"

"I wouldn't have come here." He jerked his head toward the house. "I never would have come here otherwise. But something has happened, you see."

She'd known for a week—ever since that hideous dinner and the glorious night that came after—that the world would conspire to take Kaspar from her. Bliss on such a scale was never freely given. The Toulas had come by their family curse only recently, but the Silbermanns had nurtured theirs for generations, and had long since diagnosed it as *pessimismus*. Their fatalism endowed them with strength and clear-sightedness, up to a point—it enabled Sonja, for example, to flout the conventions of her sex—but it also placed a check on their ambitions, to say nothing of their hopes. And there were hours, in her most private thoughts, when Sonja pictured herself as a kind of lightning rod of circumstance: instead of simply bracing for the worst that might befall, as any self-respecting Silbermann would, she was actively calling it down.

Waldemar had been watching her silently, still clutching his cap, and now he laid his left hand on her shoulder. His face gave her a turn: his handsome features were as frantic as the rest of him was still. All his anxiety, all his confusion, all his passion seemed to find its focus there. But something else was present in Waldemar's face, as well—an emotion she could in no way account for. His eyes were dark and heavy-lidded, like a martyr's in some early Christian fresco, and his upper lip was sweating with excitement. He looked less the bearer of sad tidings, suddenly, than a rebel angel on his way to hell.

"What is it, Herr Toula? Has something happened to Kaspar?"

Waldemar's laugh was percussive and sharp, not like Kaspar's at all, and it burst out of him so fiercely that it scared her. "Nothing has happened to my brother, fräulein—you've made certain of that."

She was wide awake now. "Please speak clearly, Herr Toula. What do you—"

"I need your help, Sonja. I need it tonight."

She ought to have felt relief, gratitude that Kaspar was well, but she felt no such thing.

"Sit with me a moment, Herr Toula. Explain to me—"

"You wouldn't understand, I'm afraid. It's a scientific matter."

"If it's a question of physics, perhaps my father—"

"Your father would understand me even less."

Nothing Waldemar said or did surprised her, not truly, because she'd always thought of him as alien. He was alien still, an unknown quantity, though he was struggling to disclose himself to her. She felt sympathy for him now—even tenderness, of a kind. The set of his jaw was as defiant as a child's.

"It must be lonely for you, Herr Toula, having no one understand you."

"It is, fräulein. It's exceptionally lonely."

He let himself be led, after some resistance, to a rusting iron bench between the chestnuts. Sonja waited to speak until he'd sat beside her. "Will you explain the source of your distress to me, Herr Toula, if only as an experiment? I promise that I'll do my best to follow."

"It's strange," he said, nodding. "We've sat like this before—we *must* have done—but I can find no remnant of it in my memory."

"This seems familiar to me, too," Sonja said, not entirely certain why she was agreeing. To reassure him, she supposed. But something in her gave a sort of quiver.

"Does it?" Waldemar whispered. "Then you *must* help me, fräulein." He put a hand on her knee, gripping it roughly, nothing at all like a lover. "The villa is too far to walk, perhaps, but we can hire a carriage. You could come just as you are, in your nightgown and slippers."

"Which villa do you mean? Not the widow's, surely? Why on earth—"

"Don't worry," he said, already on his feet. "She's at a spa in Baden, taking the waters. No one needs to be told."

"Waldemar," said Sonja, taking care to speak clearly, "if you don't tell me—at once—what you need my help for, I'll go straight back inside."

"You require more information, of course. That's only fair." He smiled down at her. "I've found out about time, you see. That it travels in circles. Not in lines, but in circles—in spheres, to be more precise. This is happening everywhere, fräulein. All around us. Even now." He squatted before her. "I haven't managed to control it yet, that's all."

"Just a moment," said Sonja. "Does this have something to do with those two Americans—Michaels and Murray?"

"To hell with Michelson and Morley. They're still thinking in straight lines, fräulein. Everyone is. That's why no one can make sense of their results."

"I'm not sure *you're* making sense just now, Herr Toula."

"I've done the mathematics, fräulein. It comes out beautifully. I don't need to make sense—not the kind that you mean. The numbers will do all that for me."

Sonja looked hard at him. "But if time travels in circles—"

"In spheres."

"—in spheres, as you say it does, then why hasn't anyone noticed?"

"Excellent question! Because we're all *inside* of them, you see."

"Inside of what?"

"Of the *chronospheres*, of course. We're trapped within them, stuck to their inner skins, like dust grains on the surface of a bubble."

"Just a moment," she repeated. "Did you say, just now, that you hadn't managed to *control* it?"

"My work hasn't advanced that far yet—I concede your point—but it follows from everything else. It's a kind of observer-induced distortion: every action has consequences, even human attention. One can't help affecting the phenomenon one studies, simply by studying it. Am I being clear?"

Sonja nodded uncertainly.

"All that's required to affect time, by logical extension, is simply to begin *observing* it." He waited impatiently for her to nod again. "The problem is that time is impossible, under normal conditions, for us to perceive. We can't see it passing, and for exactly that reason—and for that reason only—it passes without conforming to our will. Do you follow?"

"I think so," said Sonja. "What you're saying is that, given the right set of conditions—"

"*Exactly*, Fräulein Silbermann! It's like standing in the middle of an overcrowded city, or in the center of a maze: in order to understand where you are, to get a sense of the pattern, you need to attain a higher vantage point—the bell tower of Saint Stephen's, say—to acquire perspective." He rocked from side to side in his excitement. "That's what I need your help for: to escape from the maze. I need your help to rise above the timestream."

"I'll be happy to assist you however I can, but I still don't see how—"

"You can knock me out of time, Fräulein Silbermann. Kaspar told me that you did the same for him."

"I did?" Sonja stammered, more baffled than ever.

"A week ago," he said, triumphant now. "The same night as the widow's dinner party."

Finally she understood. It ought to have been obvious from the start, evident in the simple fact of his calling at that hour. There was nothing theoretical about what he wanted, nothing rarefied or obscure. She hadn't expected it—not from him. That was all.

"Waldemar," she said, as kindly as she could. "You're going home now. Do you understand me? You're going home and getting into bed."

"Aren't you listening to me, damn you? I'm giving you the opportunity to make use of your skill—of the *gift* that you have—to bring about an unprecedented—"

"I'm your brother's sweetheart, Waldemar. Are you capable of grasping what that means? No, don't bother answering. Go home and do your multiplication tables. And count your blessings I pity you enough not to tell Kaspar."

Waldemar's face went unnaturally still. "Pity me?"

"Good night, Waldemar." She rose from the bench and walked straight to her front door without looking back. It was slightly ajar, just as she'd left it, and she slipped inside and pushed it shut behind her. Waldemar made no attempt to follow. When she looked out of her bedroom window, no longer bothering to keep out of sight, she saw that he was standing as he'd been when she'd first glimpsed him, with his head cocked to one side and his arms hanging slack, staring calmly at the bench where they'd been sitting. She watched him a great while, fascinated in spite of her distress, and at no point did she see him turn or shift. She imagined that time moved differently for him already—that he'd managed to escape its hold without her aid—and she couldn't suppress a shiver at the thought. She drew back from the window, willing him away with all her might, and when she looked again she saw that she'd succeeded. She went to bed with the awareness that disaster had missed her—missed her by a hair's breadth—and resolved to tell Kaspar as little as possible. She fully believed that was the end of it.

Monday, 08:47 EST

A remarkable thing has happened, Mrs. Haven, and I've got to write it down. Waldemar's breakthrough can wait.

I was sitting at the card table just now, struggling with the contradictions and minutiae of my great-uncle's theory, when I became aware of a discomfort in my lower body—a sort of roiling muscular impatience—with its focus at the buckle of my belt. I shifted and the sensation ebbed briefly; but it came back soon after, and this time there was no mistaking it. I needed the bathroom, Mrs. Haven, and I needed it quick.

My first reaction was disbelief, then astonishment, then a wild rush of hope: if my guts are resuming their God-given functions, then my banishment from the timestream might not be as total as I've thought. I wasn't able to think this proposition through, however—not fully—because by that point I was in a state of panic. I tried to move my feet inside their slippers—to wiggle my toes, at the very least—but the roar of my bowels drowned out all competition. I won't say more than this: the only thing that frightened me worse, at that moment, than the idea of getting out of my chair was the idea of *not* getting out of it. I bit down on my lip, steeled myself for the worst, then shut my eyes and pushed back from the table.

When I opened my eyes, I was exactly where I ought to have been: an arm's length from the table with my legs slightly splayed, as though a medium-sized textbook had been dropped into my lap. I hadn't dematerialized, or inverted the timestream, or exploded in a shower of gore. I kept still for a moment to let this sink in. Then I leaned forward in my chair, dropped to my hands and knees, and hauled myself into the tunnel.

Have I described the tunnel to you, Mrs. Haven? It's a kind of dismal wonder in itself. At one time it was nearer to a trench, a shoulders-width gorge cut through what my aunts always referred to as "the Archive"; but that era is past. Aside from the occasional cone-shaped hollow—the one I'm sitting in as I write this, for example—the tunnel is never more than five feet high, and usually less than three. A kind of clear-eyed dementia took hold of Enzie and Genny in their twilight years, but they never lost their commitment to their work—Enzie's so-called research—in which this tunnel played some unfathomable role. Its purpose had to do with time, they admitted that much: with time's shape, and its color, and the sound that it makes as it moves. It was a proof of some sort, or so my aunts implied. But *what* was being proven, exactly—what the Archive is, or does, or represents—was left for future ages to discover. My father and I used to joke about it.

Crawling through the Archive is torturous and asthma-inducing at the best of times, Mrs. Haven, and its sloping, strutless walls are none too stable. To make matters worse, it's well known that my aunts passed their days, toward the end, constructing snares and booby traps for prowlers. The material of the walls is mostly newsprint—whole decades of *The New York Times* and the *Observer* and the *Daily News* and the *Post* and the *Sun*, bundled together with duct tape and wire—but countless other artifacts impinge, in an order that never seems completely random. On my way to the bathroom, for example, a framed postcard of an eighteenth-century Haarlem farmhouse led to a broken African mask, which led to an aluminum baseball bat, which led to a hardcover copy of *The Autobiography of Malcolm X*. A few feet farther on, at the door to the bathroom, a stereoscopic postcard of Vienna's famous Ferris wheel sat cradled in the wax jaws of a shark. Past that bend in the tunnel lies the door to kitchen, which I don't have the nerve to investigate yet. God knows what bugaboos await me there.

The bathroom, to my surprise and relief, turned out to be fairly clean and free of clutter. I lingered after the completion of my mission, in no great rush to slink back to my desk. I let my sight drift from the tiles under my feet to the pressed tin above, then glanced at the bookshelf behind me. A Bulova digital clock radio on the second-to-lowest shelf read

09:05 AM

Eighteen minutes had passed since I'd left the card table: exactly the amount of time that ought to have passed, if time were moving normally again.

This may not strike you as much, Mrs. Haven, but it hit me with the force of amnesty. I began to make plans right away, sitting there with my pants around my ankles, and every scheme I hatched began with you. My next step was clear: I needed to wash my hands in the sink, find some presentable clothes, get out of this hellhole and tell you the rest of this history in person. I yanked the pull chain and got to my feet.

It was then that I noticed, as I hiked up my briefs, that the clock radio behind me still read

09:05 AM

By the time I'd grasped the import of this terrible discovery I'd fallen sideways into the bookshelf and brought it down with me across the floor. A vast sucking sound filled my ears, a noise like the wind at the mouth of a whirlpool; and it seemed to me, as I fell, that I'd heard that monstrous sucking all my life. The water in the bowl was still flushing, still revolving like our galaxy in miniature, and I knew its bright cascade was never-ending. My exile was anything but over: the little Bulova had stopped functioning as soon as I'd come near. I'd brought timelessness with me, in other words, as surely as a carrier of the plague.

Looking up from the floor—where I lay crumpled under a landslide of pop-physics paperbacks and rolls of quilted lilac toilet paper—I found the things closest to me in a state of suspension, hanging perfectly still. Farther out, this motionlessness gradually gave way to an elliptical drift, like the course of planetoids around a sun. For the very first time, I was able to witness the phenomenon of which I form the epicenter: to perceive it for myself in all its geometric glory.

This is beginning to read like a passage out of one of my father's novels, I realize—but you've got to admit that what's happening to me could have fit tidily into the old gasser's oeuvre. I can see the pocket-paperback version clearly, with the sort of airbrushed starscape on its cover that never seems to go out of style: *The Accidental Chrononaut* or *Timecode: Omega* or *Little Lost Lamb, Who Made Thee?*, filed away among the works of Orson Card

Tolliver's later period, after he'd become morbid and self-pitying and unable to keep up his end of the conversation; after the Syndrome had come to tyrannize his thoughts, just as it had his father's and his grandfather's before him. Orson's last books were barely a hundred pages long, nostalgic wish-fulfillment dreams posing as interdimensional quests for vanished lovers, meditations on aging that no amount of gamma gunplay could disguise. His heroes and heroines were rarely human, and often not even carbon-based life-forms; but they were all, without exception, solitary. My fate would have lent itself perfectly to one of my father's plotlines, even before the chronosphere expelled me, if for no other reason than its loneliness.

VII

ON SEPTEMBER 13, 1905—three days after Waldemar's midnight proposition—Sonja celebrated Kaspar's return by taking him to a musical evening at the Alleegasse salon of Karl Wittgenstein, a schoolmate of her father's and one of the wealthiest men in the empire. Professor Silbermann had only the vaguest of notions that his assistant and his daughter were acquainted, and was amused by the coincidence of their arriving simultaneously; he never relinquished the belief, in later years, that their romance had begun at the Wittgensteins', and no one took the trouble to correct him.

When the two of them entered, the professor was sitting on a cowhide divan, smoking a pungent cheroot; he looked back and forth between them in bewilderment, then ushered Gretl Stonborough—née Wittgenstein—over to make introductions. "I think I ought to know your *daughter*, Herr Professor," she laughed, extending a gloved hand to Kaspar, then kissing Sonja warmly on both cheeks.

All eight of the Wittgenstein children were brilliant—they were famous for it even then, when most of them were barely out of school—but Gretl was judged the most brilliant of all. She was long-limbed and thin, almost gaunt, with the dark-lidded eyes set far back in the skull that the Wittgensteins all had in common. She had a seriousness about her that Kaspar had never encountered in a woman of twenty-four, but she grinned whenever she caught Sonja's eye, as though they shared some confidential joke between them.

"So *this* is the Herr Professor's assistant," Gretl said solemnly. "I hear you've become indispensable."

"Professor Silbermann could dispense with me at any time," Kaspar said, feeling his face go hot. That hadn't been what he'd meant to say at all.

Gretl patted him on the arm and turned to Sonja. "I have a surprise for you, darling. The maestro is here."

Now it was Sonja's turn to redden. "Where is he?"

"In the Chinese room with Hermine, making utter mincemeat of her latest portraits."

Kaspar looked from one girl to the other. Gretl was scrutinizing him thoroughly, which made it difficult to think; Sonja was fidgeting with the hem of her gown. "I didn't expect to see him here, Gretl. I should have, I suppose, but I didn't." She hesitated. "I'm not wearing that smock of his, you see."

That smock of *his*? Kaspar thought.

"Hermine isn't wearing hers, either," Gretl said, giving Kaspar a wink. "Come along now, both of you. If we ask nicely, His Eminence may grant us an audience."

Kaspar followed the girls sheepishly through those splendid apartments, through music rooms and reading rooms and chintz-swaddled rococo parlors, until they arrived at an octagonal chamber with paint-spattered bedsheets thrown over chinoiserie tile. A woman with the same arched nose as Gretl was standing with her hand on the shoulder of a black-bearded bear of a man, bobbing her small dark head in rhythm with his voice. The man spoke softly, with his hands primly folded; the shapeless muslin tunic he wore would have dumbfounded Kaspar if he hadn't seen it many times already. Catching sight of Sonja, he clapped and whistled like an organ grinder.

"Dovecote!" the man bellowed, seizing Sonja by the arms. "Such a surprise! Such a shock! I barely recognize you in that uniform."

"It's not a uniform, maestro," said Sonja, more red-faced than ever. "It's only a dress."

"It's an *exquisite* dress." He lifted Sonja's right hand to his lips. "And it's also a uniform, as you know very well." He turned to Gretl. "Thank you for delivering my dovecote to me, fräulein."

"I've also delivered the dovecote's companion, maestro, as you may have noticed."

"So you did. Pleased to meet you, Herr—?"

"Kaspar Toula, Herr Klimt." Kaspar didn't feel jealous, as such—

only painfully conscious of his disadvantage. "I'm to blame for Fräulein Silbermann's uniform, I'm afraid."

"Ah!" The maestro squinted searchingly into Kaspar's face, as though he'd misplaced his pince-nez. "Fräulein Silbermann has told you, no doubt, about this hobbyhorse of mine." He hooked a thumb inside the collar of his tunic. "I simply believe that contemporary fashion imprisons a woman, and disfigures her shape—which is splendid enough, in my opinion, without our interference."

"I certainly can't argue with—"

"Clothing," the maestro continued, "should be worn only when necessary, and gotten out of as quickly as possible. This *capuchinette* I have on, for example—"

"Gustav," warned Gretl.

The maestro laughed and let his collar loose. "Not to worry, my dear. I haven't forgotten my place. But you're lucky we're not in my atelier!" He turned back to Kaspar. "I must tell you, Herr Törless—"

"Toula," said Kaspar.

"—that Fräulein Silbermann is the most gifted of my models."

"The most gifted of your *former* models, maestro," Sonja murmured.

But the maestro was still taking Kaspar's measure. "What's your trade, sir, if I may presume to ask?"

"Herr Toula is a physicist," Gretl put in graciously.

"Is that so," said the maestro, scratching his beard. "I must confess, I took you for some sort of—"

"A physicist!" Hermine exclaimed. "In that case, Herr Toula, you *must* join the discussion that Papa is having with Professor Borofsky, from Göttingen. The professor is giving a lecture tomorrow, if I'm not mistaken, on the mathematics of the velocity of light."

"I've studied Professor Borofsky's work," Kaspar stammered. "Where did you say—"

"In the smoking room," Gretl cut in, shooing them off. "Sonja can take you. It's a private meeting, but since you're a student of physics . . ."

"You behaved very well, Kasparchen," Sonja whispered to him as they retraced their steps. "Thank you for that."

"No need to thank me," said Kaspar, though he was secretly pleased with his show of restraint. "What's a dovecote, exactly?"

"A birdhouse for pigeons," she said, drawing him closer. "Please don't ask me why he calls me that."

Kaspar considered this a moment, then kissed her lightly just behind the ear. Somehow the nickname seemed appropriate.

∞

They found Borofsky on a chaise longue in the smoking room, with Karl Wittgenstein on one side and Sonja's father on the other, each of them clutching an unlit cigar. "The very boy we want!" Professor Silbermann bellowed, with a heartiness that took Kaspar aback. "*Fire*, Herr Toula, if you'd be so kind! A touch of the primordial spark!"

Kaspar obliged them with trembling fingers, thanking chance—and fate, and even Providence, for the sake of comprehensiveness—that he'd brought his matches along. His encounter with the maestro hadn't shaken him unduly, but Karl Wittgenstein intimidated even his own children, and Hermann Borofsky was known far and wide as a wunderkind. He'd won the Paris Prize for mathematics at the age of eighteen, and now, in his thirties, was rumored to be testing the spatial implications of the Michelson-Morley experiment in a specially light- and soundproofed chamber beneath the Physikhalle in Göttingen. After lighting the cigars, Kaspar hovered a half step behind Silbermann's armchair, making clear, as politely as possible, that he had no intention of leaving.

They were discussing a young man from the provinces—a difficult and eccentric physics prodigy—who'd developed a preposterous new theory. Kaspar's legs began to buckle as he listened. A curious certainty took hold of him: a sensation akin to clairvoyance. He had no need to hear the young man's name.

"Explain to me, Hermann, if you would," Wittgenstein growled, "how the universe can take on shapes we can't perceive."

"I'm speaking purely mathematically, you understand," Borofsky replied in his pebbly Russian accent. "But this young man—this boy, really—seems to have arrived at his ideas without using mathematics at all."

"All the more reason to be skeptical," Silbermann interrupted. "Not only does the theory—if you *must* call it that—countermand Newton, it flies in the face of basic common sense."

Borofsky puffed at his cigar. "Unfortunately, Professor, the mathematics of his theory work out beautifully."

Silbermann replied with a figure of speech that Kaspar was amazed to hear him use. "If neither time nor space is absolute, Herr Borofsky, you're knocking physics back to Ptolemy, if not to Aristotle himself. We might as well be Hindus, living on an earth supported by six white elephants. We might as well be floating, all of us, inside a soap bubble!"

"That's entirely possible."

"I'm waiting, Hermann, for your explanation," Wittgenstein said tersely.

"My apologies, Herr Wittgenstein. I'll try to frame the idea as free of mathematics as possible, if you'll indulge me."

"By all means."

"Let's consider time in geometric terms. If x equals the longitude, y equals the latitude, and z equals the *altitude* of a given event's location in space, then an additional coordinate—let's call it t—could be said to describe its position in time. Each of these coordinates, needless to say, could easily be moved about, simply by addition or subtraction." He stopped for an instant, as if at a sudden memory, then turned without warning to Kaspar. "The fourth dimension, in other words, is as mutable as any of the others."

"*Four* dimensions now, is it?" Silbermann cut in.

Wittgenstein cleared his throat. "You must realize, my dear Hermann, that what you're saying sounds absurd."

"Think of this evening's party," Borofsky went on, unfazed. "Your house stands at the intersection of Alleegasse and Schwindgasse; the intersection of those two streets provides us with our x and y coordinates. Furthermore, since we are gathered on the second floor above the ground, 'second floor' shall serve us as coordinate z. We have now fixed this event in space, in three dimensions."

"Well said!" Silbermann muttered. "Here we sit, dead on target, with no earthly need for a fourth."

"That's where my distinguished colleague is mistaken, I'm afraid. The invitation for tonight's festivities read 'Palais Wittgenstein, Alleegasse and Schwindgasse, second-floor apartments, *at seven o'clock in the evening.*'" He shot Kaspar a wink. "Seven o'clock, gentlemen, was this party's coordinate in the fourth dimension. And it was every bit as necessary—as I'm sure our host will agree—as the preceding three."

Karl Wittgenstein was not a man given to laughter, but he was laughing now. "I agree wholeheartedly, Professor Borofsky. It was highly agreeable to have our guests arrive tonight, and not tomorrow morning."

Silbermann's mien, meanwhile, had grown steadily darker. "The simple fact, gentlemen, that time *can* be viewed in such terms doesn't mean that it *must*. The idea that the speed of light should be the same for every observer, no matter how fast that observer himself may be traveling, is simply—"

"It's simply the only explanation for the results of the Michelson-Morley experiment," Borofsky broke in impatiently. "Time and space will have to bend a little, I'm afraid." He turned to their host. "This young man is a genius, Herr Wittgenstein—mark my words. He'll be hailed by the world as the greatest scientific mind of the century."

No one spoke for a moment.

"And what about the young man himself?" Wittgenstein said finally. "Does he agree with your lofty opinion?"

"I couldn't say, Herr Wittgenstein. Thus far he's worked in obscurity. He hasn't even taken his degree."

"Excuse me, please," Kaspar heard himself stammer. "Pardon the interruption, but I believe I know the man you're speaking of."

He stepped forward stiffly, automatically, like a mechanical toy, and drew in a whistling breath. It was the greatest moment of his duration to date, and the most terrifying. An eccentric young prodigy from the provinces, heretofore unknown, who'd developed a preposterous new theory. The ceiling seemed to bow toward him, its gilded fretwork low enough to touch; the rushing in his ears might have been the music of chronology itself. Wittgenstein and Borofsky sat as if trapped in amber, their mouths slightly open, their eyes round as coins. The floor was now Kaspar's and he took it boldly. What he had to say was perfectly straightforward.

"I know the man of whom you're speaking," he repeated. "I'm privileged to inform you, gentlemen, that he is my brother."

His words fell on the men like a blow. The look on their faces was hard to interpret, but it might very well have been awe. Their cigars hung slackly from their gaping mouths.

At last Silbermann spoke. "A small misunderstanding, I'm afraid."

"What in blazes?" Wittgenstein got out at last. "Who is this person, Ludwig? Is he out of his wits?"

"My name is Kaspar Toula, sir. Waldemar Toula, as I've already mentioned—"

"Boy," Borofsky said calmly, "the man we are discussing is a former student of mine at the Technical University in Zürich. Not your brother, unless I'm very much mistaken."

"But the theory you describe," Kaspar said, fighting for breath. "It must surely derive from the Accidents—I mean to say, the Lost—"

"It does nothing of the sort," said Silbermann. "It's a theory, not yet published, which Professor Borofsky refers to as 'special relativity.'"

"I see," answered Kaspar, though his voice made no sound. "I see that now. Yes, of course. Thank you kindly." He bowed to all three men, who continued to goggle in astonishment, then promptly made his excuses to the sisters Wittgenstein, and to Sonja, and to everyone else he met on his way to the landing, then left as quickly as his shaking legs would take him. Before his feet had touched the pavement he was running.

∞

Kaspar ran across Karlsplatz—as good as empty at that hour—then down past the Graben, with its grandly priapic monument to the plague, and out Rotenthurmstrasse to the bile-colored canal without pausing for breath. Time moved lethargically, thickening into a soup, the way it often did when he was frightened. At Ferdinandstrasse he spun clownishly on his heels, skidding slightly, and made for Valeriestrasse with all possible speed. He thought passingly of Sonja, and of the embarrassment he'd caused her. *Sonja will be just fine*, he said to himself, and of course it was true.

His brother was a different matter. The thought of Waldemar getting word of the new theory from anyone else's lips made Kaspar go dizzy with panic. He couldn't predict what would happen, couldn't picture Waldemar's reaction even dimly, and that blankness was more dreadful than any image could have been. He simply couldn't form the least idea.

He'd expected to find the villa's gates locked when he arrived, or at least locked to him; but the hussar let him enter without comment. He found the widow in the unlit parlor, barely visible in the gloom, sitting straight-backed and dour with her hands in her lap. She was waiting for someone, or in attendance on someone, and for a moment Kaspar wondered who it was.

"Good evening, Frau Bemmelmans. Pardon my—"

"He's upstairs."

"Where exactly, madame?"

"Upstairs," the widow said, already looking away.

∞

Kaspar heard Waldemar before he saw him—heard him holding forth in reasoned, deliberate tones, as if explaining something subtle to a child. He followed the sound up three flights of stairs to an unpainted door, turned the handle and let himself in, as if he were at home in that godforsaken place.

He found himself in a high-ceilinged study whose fleur-de-lis wallpaper hung in great tattered folds over the tops of three wardrobes. Through a second door he saw the foot of an unmade cot with a pair of freshly blackened boots beside it. He heard no voice now. He closed his eyes and pressed his fingers to his temples. It was best to rehearse what he would say before he said it: his comportment could go some way toward lessening the shock. It remained unclear, after all, what this upstart in Bern had achieved. The proper choice of words, a certain lightness of delivery, a considered rhetorical approach—

"You look funny down there," came a voice from behind him. "You look like a cicada in a jar."

Kaspar turned his head slowly. He knew where the voice was coming from, though a part of him refused to credit it.

"There's a rumor going around," said the voice. "I imagine you've heard."

Kaspar raised his eyes unwillingly to the gap between the ceiling and the top of the nearest wardrobe, where the paper was slackest. His brother sat clutching his knees to his chest beneath a dangling fold, nearly hidden behind it, as though sheltering there from the rain. His head was bent to one side, as if his neck were broken; the toes of his bare feet held tightly to the wardrobe's beveled lip. He looked down at Kaspar without apparent interest.

Kaspar chose his words carefully. "I did hear something. It seems that some Swiss bureaucrat—in Bern, of all places—has developed a theory—"

"*Ach!*" said Waldemar, coughing into his fist. "I know all about *that*. I was referring to the rumor that I've gone insane."

"I hadn't heard that," Kaspar managed to answer.

"You will."

"I promise you, Waldemar, I'll do whatever I can—"

"That's kind of you, Kaspar, but you needn't bother." Waldemar smiled. "I started the rumor myself."

"Did you?" stammered Kaspar, though he knew better than to expect an intelligible answer. Waldemar shrugged his shoulders, rustling the paper behind him and raising a thin cloud of dust.

"Come down from there, Waldemar. Will you do that for me?"

"It perturbs you to see me at this altitude, of course," Waldemar said blithely. "It's not too comfortable for me, either, as you can imagine. But there's a protocol I'm following." He gave a slight shudder. "Time passes more slowly up here, first of all. The farther from the surface of the earth, the lower the frequency of light waves; and the lower the frequency of light waves, the longer it takes time to pass."

Kaspar shook his head. "You're mistaken about that. Altitude should have the opposite—"

"*Tssk!* You'd know as much yourself, if you'd been keeping up with your schoolwork." Waldemar's lips gave a twitch. "But we both know you've been otherwise engaged."

Kaspar stared up at his brother and said nothing.

"I'll tell you something else, since you've come all this way. Would you like me to tell it?"

"I'm listening."

"That Swiss clerk of yours is a shit-eating Jew."

Kaspar had forced himself, on the way to the villa, to imagine every possible reaction Waldemar might have to the news, no matter how unnerving—his brother's outburst, therefore, came as no surprise. It came as a relief, in fact, being appropriate to the spirit of the times. Anti-Semitism hung in the air like smoke in those years, like the musk of the horse-drawn *fiakers*, and the Viennese inhaled it with each breath; not even the Jews themselves were free of it. Kaspar had been aware of *die Judenfrage* even before leaving Znojmo, but since the start of his affair with Sonja he'd begun to see it everywhere he looked. Waldemar's racial paranoia didn't set him apart: just the opposite. It was the best available argument for his sanity.

"I didn't know the man was Jewish," Kaspar said. "I suppose that's interesting."

"It's about as interesting as potato blight," Waldemar answered. "To what other race could he possibly belong?"

"Please come down, little brother. Come down here and sit with me." Kaspar took a step toward the wardrobe and extended a hand. "Sonja tells me you've made progress with your work."

Waldemar blinked at him for a moment, then swung his legs over the edge of the wardrobe and took hold of his arm. "Sonja said that?" he murmured. His hand felt oddly dry and insubstantial.

"She did indeed!" Kaspar assured him. (Sonja had, in fact, done her best to pass along what Waldemar had told her—though she'd omitted the proposition he'd made.)

"I *have* made progress," said Waldemar, hopping down and steering Kaspar to his cot. "What else has Sonja told you? Has she reconsidered my request?"

"What request would that be, little brother?"

Waldemar let his arm fall. The boyish enthusiasm of an instant before was gone without a trace, and an elderly man's suspicion had been lowered across it like a metal shutter.

"What exactly did she tell you, *Bruderchen*?"

"Only that your work has been going well, and that you seemed—well, that you seemed in the highest of spirits—"

Waldemar made a queer rasping noise in the back of his throat. "In other words, Kaspar, she told you *nothing*. She made meaningless noises, and you lapped them up gratefully, ass that you are. You probably considered them music." He nodded to himself. "She told you nothing at all about the Accidents."

Even from the mouth of a lunatic, that term compelled my grandfather's attention. "No," he said, gripping the bed's coverlet. "That is to say, she told me certain things, but not being a physicist herself—"

"Then I'll tell you now, you starry-eyed buffoon, though heaven knows you don't deserve to hear it." He brought his mouth alongside Kaspar's ear. "Chronology, dear brother, is a lie."

Kaspar raised his hands at that, as if to arrest a speeding motorcar; but there was no halting his brother any longer.

"Sequential time is a convenient fiction, an item of propaganda—a fable propagated from the birth of Jesus outward by a collective of interests that has spread in all directions since that instant, growing in power in direct proportion to the advance of so-called chronologic time." He held up a finger. "Civilization was founded on *numbers*, Herr Toula, and its downfall can be read in them as well. Today, for example, the interests to which I refer are approximately one thousand, nine hundred and five times more powerful than they were at the beginning of the so-called Christian era. The very calendar we use, in other words, is not only the totem of the progress of this aforementioned 'collective,' but the *actual numerical index* of that progress. What do you say to that?"

Kaspar shook his head and said nothing. Waldemar touched his fingers to his temples, as if he were about to attempt telekinesis, which wouldn't have surprised his brother in the slightest.

"You're a clever boy, Kaspar—nearly as clever as I am. I don't intend to condescend to you." Waldemar withdrew his fingers from his brow. "I'm confident, for example, that you can identify the secret society to which I refer."

Kaspar hesitated. "The Masons?"

"The Jews," said Waldemar, without a hint of irritation. The precision of his answer seemed to please him.

"But surely—I mean to say, surely it was the Christians who began numbering the years from Christ's birth," Kaspar interjected, forgetting himself for a moment. "The Jews would not likely have chosen—"

"You fancy yourself an expert on Jewry, of course," Waldemar said genially. "And no doubt you are, in your bumbling way. You've been taken in by the secret sharers, after all—you've been welcomed with open arms, because you pose no danger to them. Taking you *in*, in fact, was the surest way of rendering you harmless."

Kaspar found himself nodding. "I don't see why anyone would bother—"

"Because you were *closing in* on them, dear brother. You and I were closing in. The two of us together."

"Listen to me, Waldemar. I need you to explain—"

"But they have a surprise in store for them. The truth will soon be clear for all to see. Nothing moves in a straight line: not even history. The highest and the mightiest have built their empire on a foundation of ashes, and to ashes shall their empire return."

Waldemar was breathing effortfully now, his face set and pale, like the figures on the plague column on the Graben. "What has been, Kasparchen, will come again. Tell that to Fräulein Silbermann from me."

It was at this precise instant, he would later recall, that Kaspar first began to fear his brother.

"You must realize—after what you've just said—that there can be no future for us," he murmured, in the hope that he might make himself believe it. But there was no end in sight, Mrs. Haven, and my grandfather knew it. He was witnessing not an end but a beginning.

Waldemar gave a shrug. "Your time is now," he said simply. "The *future* is mine."

There was an inherent contradiction in this statement, given Waldemar's beliefs about the nature of time; but Kaspar had no strength to point it out. He left the room in a daze, placing one foot gingerly before the other, and put the attic and the villa and the Accidents behind him, breathing more easily with every step he took.

More than fifteen years would pass, or seem to pass, before he saw his brother's face again.

I SPENT THE WEEK after Van's party playing detective, Mrs. Haven, with the same luck I've enjoyed in other fields. My cousin told me to go fuck myself when I asked for your address, and the response of the public record was the same, if worded differently. Back in college I'd been told I had a gift for research, but you seemed to have an equal and opposite talent for obscurity. Each trail I uncovered dissolved underfoot, as if my interest in you were in violation of some natural law or civil statute—which I suppose, in certain states, it might have been. Society was united against us, Mrs. Haven, and my failure to find you was proof.

It didn't help that I had only your husband's name to work with, though that was less of a problem than it might have been, on account of your choice of a husband. Even if he hadn't been my cousin's prize investor— even if our paths through spacetime hadn't ever intersected—I'd have known Richard Pinckney Haven, Jr., both by name and reputation. He was a man of means and influence, perhaps even a famous man, though he'd taken pains to steer clear of the limelight. He came from a medium-sized New England dairy community that happened to bear the name of Pinckney Dells, and he'd attended Amherst College, home to the Haven Collection of Connecticut Oils. His biography gets murky for a while in the mid-seventies, in consummate seventies style: an unexplained expulsion from Amherst, a year spent keeping bees back at Pinckney HQ, a semester auditing physics and computer science lectures at MIT, then treatment for a prescription drug addiction, two years of apparent inactivity and— seemingly out of nowhere—formal public emergence as First Listener of the Church of Synchronology, aka the Iterants, when he was in his early twenties (and looked, from the handful of photos I've been able to find, like a sixteen-year-old on his first beer run).

You know most of this already, Mrs. Haven—the sanitized version, at least—but I can't deny I found it lively reading.

By the time you and I met, R. P. Haven (the "Jr." had been ditched somewhere in transit) was known as a capitalist first and a spiritualist second, and the cult he'd helped found had been given the government's blessing in the form of a 501(c)(3) religious tax exemption. He'd repeatedly denied rumors of a gubernatorial bid in Wyoming, which was a curious thing, since he'd never been a resident of Wyoming. He had a stake in NASCAR and Best Western, and a controlling stake in a frozen yogurt line; he'd produced a few films; he was "warm friends" with Michael Douglas and Cher and Jeb Bush; he spoke Spanish, German, Tagalog, and "a smattering of Urdu."

This was the man I intended to inveigle you from. I would do so, Mrs. Haven, by means of my personal charm.

∞

I'll admit that as the days passed I grew desperate. I convinced myself that I saw you in the background of a pixelated snapshot at a gala reception for *Schindler's List*, and at a press conference at Gracie Mansion (half-hidden behind a bowl of calla lilies), and in riot footage on the evening news. I was new to New York, with no friends and less money. Van had stopped returning my calls altogether, though he hadn't yet kicked me out of the studio I was renting from him, which was something I gave thanks for every day. There was no time to lose: I had my history to write, and a dangerous secret mission to accomplish (more on this later), both of which involved travel to faraway climes. I needed cash, Mrs. Haven, and I needed it quick. I seemed to have no option but to earn it.

I've never told you how I made my living that summer—not the whole sordid truth. I told you I worked in the medical field, in "administration," which is technically correct. But the field of medicine I worked in, Mrs. Haven, was the care of the elderly, and what I typically administered was a mineral colonic, followed by a cup of Metamucil tea.

The Xanthia T. Lasdun Memorial Ocean-View Manor & Garden was a thirty-six-chambered assisted-living facility in Bensonhurst, with that bleary, nicotine-stained shabbiness every neo-Tudor building in the world seems to exude. Its garden, as far as I could determine, was the condom-festooned median of lower Bay Parkway, and its ocean was the droning, alluvial parkway itself. I loved it there, Mrs. Haven, a fact I've never managed to explain. I worked at the Xanthia four days out of seven—more often than that, if I picked up some shifts—making beds and boiling catheters and playing endless games of Mastermind and Risk. My most frequent opponent was Abel Palladian, of the Bushwick Palladians: interregnum-period history buff, chocolate milk addict, and bona fide duration fetishist—the first outside of my family that I'd met.

Abel most likely had some mild neurological disorder—something like Asperger's syndrome, but with a lower media profile—and the years had not been kind. What he suffered from most, however, was garden-variety loneliness: what some long-forgotten joker on the staff had christened Lasdun's xanthoma. I'd no sooner introduced myself during salad hour in the Montmartre Lounge than he launched himself full-bore into his passion. My first thought was that he could smell it coming off me: the obsession my aunts had devoted their lives to, that my father had spent half a century resisting, and that I'd come to New York to extinguish at last. Later I found out that everyone got the same spiel.

He started with the life spans of the fishes.

"Haddock are found in deeper Atlantic waters than their relatives the cod, but they share the same life span: roughly fourteen years."

"All right, Mr. Palladian. That's a good thing to know."

"What about the goby, Mr. Tolliver? Are you familiar?"

"I'm not, actually. Is that like a guppy?"

Palladian waved this aside. "The goby ranks among the shortest-lived animals of the vertebrate class. A goby is born, reproduces, and dies all within a single calendar year."

"That's fascinating. I've always wondered—"

"Sturgeons, now," Palladian announced.

"I'm afraid I don't—"

"The record for sturgeon longevity belongs to a thirteen-foot beluga that weighed one metric ton and was judged to be eighty-two years of age.

A freshwater sturgeon caught in Lake Baikal in 1953, however, was believed by some ichthyologists to have attained a duration of one hundred and fifty years."

The line was forming for the salad bar, but Palladian ignored it. He appeared to be in a fugue state of some kind.

"Trout?" I said.

"The life expectancy for a rainbow trout falls between seven and eleven years, depending on locality and species. Brook trout, the finest at table, thrive best in cold waters. In some Canadian lakes they live up to ten years, while elsewhere six years is considered senescent."

"Good thing we're not trout."

Palladian's eyes drifted back into focus. "One brook trout in captivity," he said with a smile, as though I'd somehow played into his hands, "lived to seventeen years and twenty-seven days."

We progressed, over time, from animate to inanimate forms: from earthworms (ten years max) to shallots (sixty to ninety days in a well-maintained fridge) to casino playing cards (two to five hours of regulation play) to the Milky Way galaxy (forty billion years, give or take). Once Stratego season started in earnest (each board game had its season at the Xanthia—Stratego in the summer, Scrabble in the fall, Monopoly through the winter, Risk sometime around Lent), the tenor of our talks shifted. We'd lost quite a few Xanthians during the recent heat wave, and I had more leisure time for a while. Incrementally, centripetally, our conversation drifted toward the personal.

"Who are your people, Mr. Tolliver?" Palladian asked me one evening, glowering down at the board. We'd been playing for an hour in absolute silence. I was winning for once.

"Excuse me, Mr. Palladian?"

"Your *people*," Palladian barked. He had the wonky affect of somebody on the "spectrum," often making him seem angry when he wasn't; but this looked to be the genuine article. I'd just invaded the Sudetenland.

I shut my eyes and tried to dredge up a reply. I'd been asked this question more than once at the Xanthia, on account of what my father had liked to refer to as my "*Hitlerjugend* physiognomy," and I'd been asked it no end of times growing up, because of my mother's kraut-and-bratwurst accent. It never failed to make me ill at ease.

"My father's half sisters, who raised him, sometimes took him to Orthodox temple—"

Palladian's eyebrows twitched subtly. "Yes?"

"But he wasn't Orthodox himself. He wasn't anything. Both of his parents were goyim."

Palladian shrugged and said nothing. The Stratego game seemed to have stalled.

"I am one-quarter Jewish, though. On my mother's side."

"Now I like you one-quarter better." He watched me for a while, then cleared his throat. "The first incandescent bulb, tested by Thomas Edison, burned for forty hours exactly. Manufacturers today can and do make incandescent bulbs that will last, barring mishap, for a minimum of—"

"My grandfather's brother was a war criminal, Mr. Palladian. He ran a camp in eastern Poland and experimented on human beings, the majority of them Jews. He was known as the Black Timekeeper of Czas."

My mouth shut with a clack, like the jaw of a marionette. Palladian regarded me bleakly. Mabel Dimitrios, a Xanthia rookie, was unraveling a sweater on a nearby couch and watching me with rheumy-eyed alarm.

"Mr. Palladian?" I said. "If I've in any way caused you—"

Palladian made a pushing-away motion with both of his hands, as if he'd been brought a plate of food he hadn't ordered.

"Old wash," he said. "*Very* old wash, Mr. Tolliver."

I nodded stupidly. "I don't know why I said that, to be honest. The thing is—"

"Not interested."

"Of course not. I don't blame you." I hesitated. "It's just, you understand, that I'm trying to come to terms—"

"*What* terms?" Palladian rumbled. "What are you going to do, Mr. Tolliver? Go back in time and kill your father's uncle?"

"That's an interesting thought," I said, with what must have seemed like an ironic smile. But nothing could have been farther from the truth, Mrs. Haven. It was an exceedingly interesting thought. I pushed my panzer division deeper into the Sudetenland.

∞

There's no other way to put this, Mrs. Haven: as the weeks passed, you receded from my thoughts. It was the law of conservation of energy, not to mention the abhorrence of a vacuum, since I'd followed every lead and come up empty. I'd just surrendered my last hope—surrendered it gladly, like a coat I'd always felt too warm inside of—when I saw you buying cheese in Union Square.

You wore a blood-colored parka trimmed with platinum fur, like some sort of Inuit heiress, and held a duck-shaped wicker basket in your fists. It was cold for October, below freezing already, and the breath left your body in tiny, immaculate puffs. You strolled from the cheese stand to a pickle stand to a stand that seemed to sell nothing but napkins. It was too much to take, hitting me like that without the slightest warning, and I had to sit down on the nearest bench. At one point you looked up abruptly, as though you'd heard some alarm, and I hid behind my mittens like a child.

Some manifestations of beauty are period-specific, expressive of the age that nurtures them; others seem to exist outside of history, warping each successive moment as they pass. Yours was the second kind of beauty, Mrs. Haven—at least in Union Square that day, at least to me. I managed to convince myself that I was waiting for an opening, a pretext of some kind; in fact I just stared, stuck to my bench like a barnacle, while you filled that ridiculous basket. It seemed cruel, as I watched you, that anyone should be privileged with such power, and it still seems unjust—though I've learned that the injustice cuts both ways. It sucks all moderation from the world.

From Union Square you went south, taking more deliberate steps than you had at the market, your hood pulled tightly down against the chill. As I shadowed you along University Place toward Washington Square, often close enough to catch you by the sleeve, sobriety slowly returned. What the hell was I doing tailing you across lower Manhattan, skulking from storefront to storefront, sizing you up like an aspiring sex offender? What was keeping me from calling out your name?

You continued downtown, moving more listlessly with each block, like a windup toy whose spring was losing tension. You began to stop at the slightest pretense: a fall clearance sale, a sun-bleached Calvin Klein ad, an octopus drawn on the sidewalk in chalk. A man approached you on Twelfth Street, breaking into a halfhearted routine about the loss of his asthma inhaler, and you heard him out in silence, asked a few polite questions, then handed him a fifty-dollar bill. Wherever you were going, Mrs. Haven, you weren't in any hurry to get there.

At Tenth and University you hung a grudging right—you were dragging your feet comically now, like a cat on a leash—then stopped before a brownstone the same color as your coat. A siren sounded somewhere in the distance. The city had never seemed so ominous to me, or so strangely becalmed. The only other person in sight—a heavyset, gender-nonspecific individual with an armful of comics in bright Mylar baggies—had stopped walking as well, as though the siren were some citywide alarm. I looked from the back of your head toward the comics collector, who stared brazenly back. It was a woman, I decided, though I couldn't have said how I knew. I was beginning to think she'd been tailing you—or possibly even me—when she crossed the street toward you, mumbled a perfunctory greeting, and climbed the stoop of the brownstone next door.

I began to move again now, convinced retreat was impossible, though it was clear you were lost to the world. The blinds gave a jerk in your neighbor's front window: for better or for worse, we had an audience. You set the basket down between your boots—you were slightly pigeon-toed, I noticed—then bent over and took out a fat winter pear. It was impossibly green against your scarlet sleeves, illuminated as if from within, a Technicolor piece of Martian fruit.

You buffed it in your palms and took a bite.

All at once the light started flickering, making everything tremble, as though the sun had turned into a film projector. I let out a strangled gasp that seemed to make no sound. We were on camera, the two of us: we were trapped in some forgotten silent picture. In the next shot you'd look back at me and scream.

Months later, I would finally come up with an explanation for this on-camera feeling, and for the faintness and paralysis it brought. It was the sensation—the *physical* sensation—of time passing: a kind of chronologic wind. Certain people—my grandfather, for example, or my aunts, or the members of your husband's cult—might have had this feeling on a daily basis; as for me, Mrs. Haven, I've felt it exactly three times. And each time I've felt that wind, no matter how desperately I fought, it's knocked me down.

A truck pulled up across the street—van gogh movers : a "cut" above the rest—and the spell was finally broken. Another day, I told myself, would almost certainly be better. I needed time to prepare, to review what I'd learned, to make sure that you would see me at my best. I turned back toward University.

"Walter?"

Your voice was so serene, so devoid of surprise, that I could only conclude that men followed you home all the time.

"Is that you, Mrs. Haven? I didn't recognize you in that—in that hoodie you're wearing."

"I've caught you red-handed, haven't I?"

"Mrs. Haven, if you'll just—"

"You were going to walk by without saying hello!"

I squinted at you for a moment, my mouth still half-open, attempting to parse your expression. "I wasn't sure you'd want me to say hello," I said carefully. "I behaved like a perfect ass the night we met."

"Like a *perfect ass*," you repeated. You glanced over your shoulder. "I'll confess something to you, Mr. Tompkins. Do you mind?"

I shook my head.

"I'd had a sidecar or six at that godawful party, and I've been trying to figure out which of my memories of that night I could trust. Sidecars tend to make me see little green men." You nodded to yourself. "But I guess *that* part of it was true enough."

"Which part?"

"That you look like you're twenty and talk like you're sixty."

"I've been told that before, Mrs. Haven. Apparently I'm prematurely aged."

You smiled at that. "If you say so, Mr. Tompkins."

Neither of us said anything for a moment.

"Well! It's been a pleasure running into you, Mrs. Haven. If you'll kindly—"

"Don't run away like a *girl*," you said, catching me by the sleeve. "There's something I want you to see."

I struggled to assemble an appropriate response as you steered me roughly down a flight of steps. It didn't occur to me to wonder why we were entering your brownstone through the basement until I knocked my head against the lintel.

"Are you all right out there, Walter?"

"Extremely all right! Never better." I thought of Van and his sailor friend butting foreheads and felt what I can only describe as a rush of nausea and nostalgia combined. *Naustalgea*, I thought, pleased with myself in a far-off sort of way. Red-and-purple globules danced before my eyes.

"Come on in, Mr. Tompkins! Don't dawdle!"

Apart from a defeated-looking beanbag and a tidy pile of junk mail by the window, the room I stepped into held nothing at all. There were clues, if one looked closely, that the apartment had once been inhabited: shadows on the parquet where carpets had lain, ghosts of vanished pictures on the walls, scattered stacks of vintage 45s. You sat on the floor and began flipping through them.

"Have you ever listened to the One-Way Streets, Walter? I'm betting you haven't. I'll play them for you if I can find the single. There should still be a turntable somewhere. Would you look?"

The bedroom at the back was the barest of all. I crossed its freshly waxed floor to a window that faced a high wall of bamboo. Its sill was as sterile as everything else, but I found a cocktail napkin (*Bemmelmans Bar at The Carlyle*) wedged between the window and the frame, with a scribbled note along its inner fold. It took me a moment to decipher the scrawl:

NEW YEARS RESOLUTIONS
1 NO lying
2 NO biting
3 NO travel thru time

"What have you found back there, Walter?"

"Nothing," I said, pocketing the napkin. "Any more stops on the tour?"

"Only the grand finale."

The bathroom, with its overflowing medicine cabinets and terry-cloth toilet-seat cover and heap of scaly-looking couture in the bathtub, was the only room that seemed lived-in. The clothes in the bathtub looked oddly compressed, and I felt a dark thrill, a tingle in regions unmentionable, when I realized you'd used them for a bed.

"How long have you lived here?"

"Three years this Thanksgiving. What do you think of the decor?"

"I'll be honest with you, Mrs. Haven. I don't know how to answer that."

"I had a fight with the Husband," you said matter-of-factly. "The Husband took my furniture away."

"Is that what that truck's for, outside? Van Gogh Movers?"

You shrugged. "He hardly needed them, really. They just took everything upstairs."

"This whole brownstone is Haven's, then." I felt my stomach twist. "Of course it is."

Your expression went cold. "The Husband feels that way, too. You ought to get to know each other, Walter. You might turn out to have a lot in common."

My plan had been to avoid the subject altogether, to keep Haven small and indeterminate and vague, but I should have known there'd be no way around him. He was a feature of the landscape through which you and I moved—as vast and undeniable as a mesa. But he was also as lifeless as one, and as flat, at least on that first magic afternoon. He was static on a TV set in a corner of the room in which I loved you. I couldn't even bring his face to mind.

"As far as I'm concerned, Mrs. Haven, your husband—"

"Why were you following me, Walter?"

I wobbled in place for a moment, then stepped stiffly toward you, clutching an imaginary hat. "My intentions are honorable, Mrs. Haven."

"Your what?"

I took your hand in both of mine, not caring how Victorian I seemed. "I saw you, just by chance, in Union Square—" What on earth was I trying to say? A humming sprang up somewhere behind my left ear, in what may or may not have been my temporal lobe. The chronologic wind was picking up again.

"I was following you," I said. "I can't deny it."

"That wasn't my question. I wanted to know—"

I grabbed you by the shoulders—roughly, clumsily—and kissed you. My eyes were clenched shut and there was a disturbance in my head like the buzzing of an ultrasonic toothbrush, but I could tell that I had caught you by surprise. I understood, as we kissed, that I was being offered the chance to step out of myself, to reset the clock: to start over from nothing, defenseless and naked, like a lizard wriggling out of its skin. Your body was tense, I remember, but your mouth was warm and open and alive. You smelled like rain and cigarettes and dill.

"Don't get rid of him completely," you breathed into my ear.

"Get rid of who?"

"The old you. Walter Tompkins. It turns out that I like him very much."

I'd been thinking out loud—what else could it have been?—but I felt no embarrassment. "What is it you like? Of his many noble qualities, I mean."

"I like his politeness. I like the look in his eyes when he's trying to think. I like his terrible haircut. I like the jokes that he makes—the bad ones especially—and the way his head tilts when he's listening. I like that he listens at all." A shyness crept into your features. "I guess I like that he has time for me."

"He has nothing but," I said, and bent to kiss you again. It was true, Mrs. Haven: I might have nothing else to offer, but I had plenty of time. It amazed me to think that you might be neglected. How could your husband make such a beginner's mistake?

You looked dazed and defiant when we stopped for breath. We stood an arm's length apart, just as we'd been before, but now we were looking at each other without a trace of pretense, grinning complementary stupefied grins. You led me to the back of the apartment, mumbled something about the garden that I didn't quite catch, then pulled a stack of framed museum posters out of a closet—the kind college freshmen tack on the walls of their dorms—and arranged them on the floor for me to see. At least six were reproductions of *The Kiss*.

"Gustav Klimt," I said.

You watched me intently.

"Gustav Klimt," I repeated. "From Vienna. Of the Viennese school."

There were twelve posters in all, every last one a Klimt: gold and copper curlicues and gauzy-haired women with alabaster skin and privileged faces. The words *THE KISS* were printed across a few of them, leaving nothing to chance, in a font that looked lifted from one of my father's dust jackets.

I noted all this carefully, Mrs. Haven, because I was stalling for time.

"He was definitely a painter," I heard myself croak. "His use of gold leaf—"

"I can't *stand* Klimt." You shuddered. "His paintings are like butter-covered doughnuts."

"Then why—"

"The Husband put them up yesterday. There's one for every wall of this apartment. He screwed them in with an electric power drill and four-inch drywall screws."

A truck passed outside, then another, rattling the windows in their frames. From somewhere nearby came the buzz of television. I made an effort not to wonder who else might be in the house.

"Four-inch screws, did you say?" I nodded to myself. "He certainly gave it the old college try."

"He's R. P. Haven, Walter. He gives *everything* the old college try."

"What made him want to do all this, exactly?"

You gave a dull laugh. "I guess you could say he's the possessive type."

"So he knows about us?"

"I've only just met you, Walter. What's there for him to know?" You sighed and let your head rest on my shoulder. "There's no need for you to worry, anyhow. He'll murder me before he murders you."

I felt a twinge of dread at that, as anybody would; but you fit against me so well, notching your forehead between my neck and clavicle, that my fear felt like a kind of imposition. Your body was warmer than mine—much warmer—and your cropped hair spiraled clockwise at the crown. I looked down at your pale, goose-boned neck, the width of my palm exactly, and guessed (rightly, as it turned out) that it would be covered in freckles come summer.

"I'm reading a book," you said suddenly. "A self-help book. I'd like to show you something."

It was my turn to laugh. "What would *you* need a self-help book for?"

You pulled a slim, silver-bound book out of your jacket—a sleight-of-hand trick—and passed it to me. I read its title with a sinking feeling.

STRANGE CUSTOMS OF COURTSHIP & MARRIAGE
Authentic revelations of curious mating customs of all ages and all races, and the history and significance of modern marriage conventions
by
William J. Fielding, author of *The Caveman Within Us*, etc.

"Go ahead, Walter. Page sixty-eight."

The last thing I wanted to do at that moment was to educate myself about marriages, either modern or ancient; but I did as you asked. Page 68 was marked with a wrapper from a pack of Newport Lights:

> TREE MARRIAGE.—*Among the Brahmans of the south of India it is the established custom that a younger brother should not marry before an older one. To fulfil this requirement, when there is no satisfactory bride in sight for a senior brother, he is married to a tree, which leaves the younger one at liberty to take a wife.*
>
> *Mock marriages are also carried out among the Punjab of India, in the case of a widower taking his third wife. It is celebrated with a certain tree or rosebush, and sometimes with a sheep, which is dressed up as a bride and is led by the groom around the sacrificial fire while the real bride reposes nearby.*

"I see," I said slowly, though of course I saw nothing. "How is this a self-help book, exactly?"

"My marriage is like that."

"What do you mean?"

"I married a tree, Walter. *That's* what I mean."

"Has your husband—was he married before? Or are you trying to tell me—"

"*Shh*, Walter," you said, pulling me down onto the beanbag in a way that made all talk seem academic.

Less than a year later, when I was as good as dead to you, I read the rest of Fielding's tawdry little survey—it's next to me on the floor right now, in fact—and one passage, more than any other, took me back to that first bliss-drenched afternoon:

> THE KISS.—*In its sensory impulses, the kiss is the most direct prelude and incitement to sexual fulfilment. Surfaced by a tissue of full-blooded, sensitive membranes, moistened by the honey of salivary sweetness, shaped at their loveliest into a curvature that has been likened to Cupid's bow, the lips seem especially contrived*

by nature for their role of allurement into the labyrinths of bodily desire. It is for this reason that restraint and discrimination should be the watchword of those who understand the real meaning and importance of the kiss, and who hold in high regard the sacredness of the forces which its casual bestowal may unwittingly release. Proceed with circumspection!

VIII

THE NEXT TWENTY-ODD YEARS, during which the world went loudly and pompously down the pissoir, were the happiest of Kaspar Toula's life.

His long-departed father, in the course of his inevitable dinnertime rants—on the evils of the automobile, for example, or the cleansing properties of cellulose—had been fond of quoting a Saxon manic-depressive named Friedrich Nietzsche: "All history is the experimental refutation of the so-called *moral order* of things." And the brash and pockmarked twentieth century, in all the brutal enthusiasm of its adolescence, seemed to be doing its frenzied best to prove him right.

My grandfather barely had time to finish his studies, make his bid for Sonja's hand in marriage, and receive his *Schwiegervater*'s halfhearted blessing before the empire that both his father and his father-in-law so myopically adored began to come apart like sodden paper. The Czechs, the Magyars, the Slovaks, the Serbs and the Croats—all of whom, admittedly, had exhibited signs of petulance before—now seemed more interested in pitching fits in parliament than in basking in their emperor's esteem. The bacillus of nationalism had infested all but the remotest crannies of the empire by the time the Kaiser's cousin had his celebrated rendezvous with a Serbian anarchist's bullet; it had simply been a question of which member of the imperial family was going to have their candle guttered first. (In certain back rooms and furnished cellars of the capital, money had in fact been wagered on this very question.) But no one—not the bookies, not the anarchists, and least of all the imperial family itself—foresaw the conflagration that would follow.

Sonja Toula, née Silbermann, was a fervent backer of the Serbian cause from the start of the war, and stayed true to her colors even when her husband was sent to the front in a uniform that still smelled faintly of the corpse who'd worn it last. By that late date, a fair portion of the civilized world had muddied its spats, and it was clear to every half-wit that the "six weeks' war" the Kaiser had promised was a fairy story, albeit one that he himself believed. Kaspar served that sad old fool without complaint, and witnessed his due share of horrors, some of which he committed himself. He lost two fingers in the war, and the top of an ear, but he rarely regretted his injuries: they were his only proof that the war, and the empire he'd fought for, had been more than some preadolescent dream. And there were moments, Mrs. Haven, on his very worst days, when not even his missing fingers could convince him.

The citation for bravery he'd won—a weightless nub of nickel-plated tin, for some obscure reason in the shape of a winged horse—was mothballed away and forgotten as soon as the fighting was over. Years later, when the family was hurriedly throwing everything it could into a clutch of pasteboard steamer trunks, the medal would find its way into the hands of his younger daughter, who brought it to him for an explanation. Gentian never forgot her father's answer. "It's a pegasus, *Schätzchen*—an imaginary animal. Papa got it as a present, from a very old man, for defending an imaginary kingdom."

∞

There were quite a few reasons for Kaspar's happiness during his twenties and thirties, from his hard-won advancement at the university to the deepening of his understanding of the physical world; but the most obvious, even to Kaspar himself, was the indecorous and overwrought passion he continued to feel for his wife. Practically from birth—or so it seemed to him—he had been aware that the elegant, filigreed, eminently reasonable world around him was doomed to collapse under its own weight, like some elaborate architectural folly; the obvious response, to any sensible observer, was to have as little to do with such a world as possible. Kaspar had Sonja, after all, and the well-appointed home they'd made together. It seemed lunacy to ask for more than that.

Sonja had grown more deliberate as she came into the fullness of her years, more austere of temperament, more assured of her intelligence and grace. Her political convictions had only deepened as she aged; her smock, however, lay neatly put away in the same cabinet that housed her husband's medal. Socialists and anarchists and communists—"your *ism*-ists," as Kaspar (more or less affectionately) called them—came and went as if the apartment were a well-appointed flophouse, as they'd done since the end of the war; but now they looked and behaved less like revolutionaries than like librarians, or attorneys-at-law, or even patent clerks. And they tipped their hats politely to him as they came and went.

Kaspar had no doubt that half his wife's protégés loved her desperately, but the fact didn't bother him—at least not unduly—because he so completely shared their point of view. Sonja's hold over him had only intensified since their marriage, and it often submerged him so profoundly in its inky, honeyed depths that he found it slightly difficult to breathe. He was as proud of his submission as his countrymen were—or affected to be—of the wounds they'd received in the war.

Waldemar's existence during these years of free fall, by contrast, is as shrouded and ambiguous as my grandfather's is faceted and bright. Rumors would reach Sonja from time to time through her network of fellow travelers: inconclusive scraps of information, little better than hearsay, that she took care to keep from her husband. Waldemar had gone to Russia; Waldemar had taken holy orders; Waldemar had been seen late at night, dressed in a woman's nightgown, shouting curses at the streetcars on the Ring. This was the time of the great housing crisis in the republic, when a host of city dwellers were reduced to living under bridges, or on barges, or in caves dug into railway embankments. In Budapest, thirty-five people were discovered nesting in the trees of Népliget Park, and word reached Sonja that Waldemar was among them. She had no idea which of these reports to believe, so she chose to believe all of them. She hated to be taken by surprise.

This much, at least, is certain: within three weeks of his midnight visit to the Silbermann household, two weeks of learning of the relativity theory, and four days of delivering his doomsday prophecy to his brother, Waldemar had been expelled from the university, been served a notice of eviction from the dragon-headed building, and had slipped away without confiding in a soul. Kaspar had asked no one what Waldemar had done to bring about these twin expulsions, though he himself was suddenly homeless, as well: he'd resigned himself to severing what few ancient ties still bound them. Each time he asked after his brother and was met with blank, suspicious stares, he permitted himself a small sigh of relief.

It was only as he was sorting through his brother's meager handful of belongings, the night before their eviction was enforced, that Kaspar truly grasped that Waldemar was gone. His brother had left his modest library behind, and his spectacles, and his only decent suit of evening clothes. His handwritten copy of Ottokar's notes, on the other hand, was nowhere to be found; and neither, when it occurred to Kaspar to check his own bedroom, was the copy he'd made for himself. He had forfeited the right to search for the answer to their departed father's riddle, it appeared, at least in Waldemar's opinion. And to his own profound astonishment, Mrs. Haven, Kaspar found himself agreeing with this verdict.

The Accidents had destroyed both his father and his brother, after all—men with far greater gifts than his own. How could he help but take that as a warning? As he attempted to bring order to Waldemar's papers, Kaspar realized that he'd long since begun to wonder, in some sequestered annex of his mind, whether the problem of time in physics might not be akin to the problem the sun posed for the early astronomers: it was ever-present along the margins of sight, radiant and vast, but to stare at it too long meant certain blindness.

He remained his father's son, however, and he'd barely had this idea before he carried it further. Those early astronomers had found a means of studying the sun indirectly, by fashioning reflecting telescopes. Might the same technique work for the study of time? Perhaps Waldemar's undoing had lain less in his ideas, mad as they seemed, than in the straightforward way he'd approached them. Perhaps the solution was to advance more obliquely: to resist looking time in the eye, to avoid pondering the imponderable, and instead to watch its shadow on the wall. Perhaps the answer was as simple as a mirror.

But no sooner had Kaspar had this thought than he suppressed it. A tremor ran through his body, drawing him away from his brother's desk, and he made no attempt to resist. By eight o'clock the next morning, the sum of Waldemar's earthly possessions was sitting on the street in a battered gray trunk, and by evening it was gathering dust in a corner of Professor Silbermann's cellar, where it would remain until Waldemar—in a black Daimler coupe, with two men whose attire matched the Daimler beautifully—came back from the dead to collect it.

Silbermann himself, who'd never exhibited much interest in Waldemar while he'd been one of his students, made an elaborate show of solicitude when Kaspar arrived with the trunk, going so far as to take him by the hand. "Madness is a hazard of our profession," he said gravely. "Especially among our most gifted." Misunderstanding Kaspar's pained smile, he attempted a joke, one that rang rather too true for comfort: "You and I, my dear boy, may thank our stars that we run no such risk!"

∞

A quote from Kubler comes to mind when I consider my grandfather in the period that followed—the bland, complacent decades of his prime:

> *Why should actuality forever escape our grasp?*
> *The universe has a finite velocity which limits not only the spread of its events, but also the speed of our perceptions. The galaxy whose light I see now may have ceased to exist millennia ago, and by the same token men cannot fully sense any event until after it has happened, until it is history, until it is the dust and the ash of that cosmic storm which we call the Present, and which perpetually rages throughout creation.*

Actuality did indeed prove elusive to Kaspar at the start of his twenties, as it tends to do for persons in a state of bliss. His bliss was not entirely free of shadow, however. Waldemar had passed out of Kaspar's world, and practically out of his awareness; but my grandfather would always view his brother's disappearance as the fulcrum point between his youth and his adulthood. Time had advanced slowly until that apalling night, as it does for the young, whose days are spent in expectation of something they can never fully name. Now, with Waldemar gone, Kaspar seemed to fall headfirst into each day, in a kind of perpetually overwhelmed and dreamlike wonder. The years between his brother's departure and his homecoming would eventually come to seem of no greater longevity, no more cumulative weight, than certain consecrated moments of his childhood: the day of the cicada, for example, whose every instant glittered in his recollection.

These were Kaspar's most substantial years, and by far his most contented; but it seemed to him that they were passed in trivialities, in an infinite succession of agreeable, judicious actions (grading student essays, putting up wallpaper, watching his wife reading, listening with closed eyes from the couch as she talked politics with her *ism*-ists in the parlor) all of which, taken together, formed a portrait of Kaspar Toula in tiny colored dots, like a sketch by some self-satisfied impressionist. By his thirtieth birthday he felt subtly corrupt, as willingly opiated as Sonja's precious proletariat, with nothing to blame but the remarkable ease of his love, and the security he'd worked for so unwaveringly.

On certain rare nights, when these intimations of decadence were at their most acute, he found himself leafing through the few notes on his father's work that his brother had left behind. With each passing year, however, they seemed more naïve, more distant from what he'd come to understand as science. My grandfather had always been too practical—too orthodox—to subscribe to his brother's mystical exegesis of Ottokar's note: his opinion was that the note was gibberish, pure and simple. He'd abandoned research almost completely after special relativity, and had eked out a career for himself as a lecturer in "classical" physics, taking care to stop well short of Michelson and Morley. His father may have been a fallen idol to him—as a scientist and husband, certainly, and perhaps even as a father—but Kaspar was still, in those early years of the century, determined to place no other gods before him.

For the Patent Clerk, meanwhile, these were the decades of triumph. In 1913, just before the war began, he was brought to the Kaiser Wilhelm Institute of Physics in Berlin, where, reverently sheltered from the devastion sweeping Europe, he did some of his most radical and elegant work. A year into the war, he completed his general theory of relativity, which posits that neither time nor space are constant. In 1919, with the war barely over and both the German and Austro-Hungarian empires in ruins, a series of British observations during a solar eclipse confirmed relativity's prediction that the gravitational pull of the sun would cause light rays to bend, silencing the last remaining skeptics—aside from those who resisted the theory

simply because its author was a Jew, or because he was a German, or because he was incomparably more gifted than they were.

An acquaintance of Sonja's from her Café Jandek days published a
poem—bluntly entitled "Vienna"—that caused quite a stir in the city:

> *Vienna, in ruins, is weeping.*
> *Vienna, you ancient, coldhearted whore . . .*
> *A scrofulous panderer to this world . . .*
> *Now famished, you whimper,*
> *So heavily does your wickedness weigh:*
> *An empire frittered away.*

Sonja read the poem aloud in bed one evening, her regal face suffused
with high emotion; her husband remained unaffected. Many dear friends
had died, it was true, but so had several people he'd despised. What use was
there in rage and histrionics? The bullet that had so neatly clipped away
the top of his left ear had gone on to bisect the brain of a man named
Metterling, whose fifteen-year-old fiancée had thrown herself into the
Danube on hearing the news. This chain of events troubled Kaspar occasionally, especially when he'd been drinking; but most of the time it failed
to hold his interest. On his evenings at home—and they were all spent at
home now, unless Sonja had a meeting or a rally to attend—he found it easy
to convince himself that the city outside his door was an illusion.

In that dim, spectral city, anti-Semitism seemed suddenly pandemic,
more rabid than it had been in centuries, which struck him as the finest
joke of all. The posturers of the United Germanic Front, with their foam-
flecked lips, their fists full of pamphlets, and their watch chains with little
silver pendants (like upside-down crucifixes, if you didn't look too closely)
symbolizing a hanged Jew, put my grandfather in mind of children playing
preacher when he heard their diatribes; and it took a concerted effort *not* to
hear them lately, since they felt no need to keep their voices down. Just a
few steps from the duck pond in the Stadtpark where he'd pledged his love
to Sonja, the battered body of a boy from the neighborhood shul was discovered, his gullet stuffed with pages torn out of a Torah; when the blame
was placed—after the most cursory of inquiries—on "unidentified Slavic
vagrants," not a soul in that great *Hauptstadt* was surprised.

A few months later, when Kaspar read, in an editorial in a respected paper, a prominent critic's suicide described as "the only reasonable response to the dilemma of his Jewish nature," he laughed, as he would have done at any piece of vaudeville. His wife saw considerably less to laugh at; but he did his best to put her fears to rest. "This world is a loony bin, *Schätzchen*," he told her. "Luckily for us, our front door happens to be one of its exits." He knew that this motto of his made her uneasy—that it could be interpreted in two very different ways—but he found himself unwilling to forgo it. The truth, whether he'd have admitted it or not, was that he said it as a spell to ward off demons.

It would have been perfectly appropriate, given all of the above, if Kaspar had become one of those disillusioned fantasists who daydreamed of escape to the New World; but he labored under no such bold delusions. Although his wife was a devotee of Blake's "America, a Prophecy," occasionally reciting the lines

> *On my American plains I feel the struggling afflictions*
> *Endur'd by roots that writhe their arms into the nether deep:*
> *I see a serpent in Canada, who courts me to his love;*
> *In Mexico an Eagle, and a Lion in Peru—*

Kaspar had little doubt that America, given half a chance, would eat them both alive. Blake might well have sung the praises of its eagles and its serpents, but what Blake had actually *known* about the New World, my grandfather suspected, could have fit into a thimbleful of gin. Hans Wittgenstein had run off to America to escape his father's strictures, and Sonja's own cousin Wilhelm, a recent émigré to New York State, was now known—for reasons obscure—as "Buffalo Bill" Knarschitz, and was reputed to be thriving; but Kaspar remained affably unmoved. "We're Austrians, *Schätzchen*," he said more than once, after his wife had gone on at length— as she often did, of late—about the U.S.A. as the new socialist frontier. "We're simply Austrians now, no more and no less, and it won't help to pretend we're Cherokees. Besides which, my love, all your family's here. What would the Silbermanns become without Vienna? What would *Vienna* become, for that matter, without the Silbermanns?"

Monday, 09:05 EST

Since the episode in the bathroom, Mrs. Haven, I've been trying to take stock of my situation as objectively and calmly as I can. What follows is my attempt to draw up an impartial reckoning, like a chartered public accountant, of the chances I've been given versus those I've been denied:

DEBIT	*CREDIT*
I'm marooned in a desolate bubble of extrachronological space, without company or apparent hope of rescue.	But I'm alive, and I seem to be in fairly decent shape, which contradicts every law of physics I can think of.
I appear to have been singled out, from all the rest of humanity, to sit at this table and brood.	But someone must have put me here, and provided me with these books and writing materials—ergo, someone wants me to complete my history. And that person may also have the means to set me free.
At times, the solitariness of my condition, and the sadness of constant remembering, comes close to driving me insane.	On the other hand, I'm not uncomfortable here—not anymore—and remembering certain events from my life is almost unbearably sweet.

I have nothing to eat, and nothing to drink but a half-empty bottle of Foster's.

I'm not thirsty.

It's still extremely hard for me to move, and all of my senses, except the sense of sight, are dulled almost to the point of uselessness.

My life, such as it was, was over long before I woke up here. How can it possibly matter where I am?

That's as far as I've managed to get, Mrs. Haven. I feel less able than ever to reconcile myself to my condition, and I've resolved to continue my attempts to determine—both by contemplation and experiment—the nature of this no-man's-land I'm stuck in. Like the Greek and Etruscan philosopher-detectives who were my great-grandfather's heroes, creating whole cosmologies out of nothing but their own enthusiasm, the only tools I've got are pen and paper. And this body, of course—for whatever this body's still worth.

I'm not entertaining these notions idly, Mrs. Haven. The question of whether or not time is passing for me, however slowly, has taken on new urgency since my visit to the bathroom. If time *is* passing—however sluggishly—then I'm still a part of the continuum, and can permit myself some faint hope of escape. If time isn't passing, I'm probably dead.

In which case, Mrs. Haven, I wish you and the Husband all the best.

IX

THE GREAT WAR—or the World War, or the War to End All Wars, as many
otherwise perfectly reasonable people insisted on calling it—was a memory, and a dim one at that, before Kaspar heard his brother's name again.
It's perhaps the greatest evidence of Sonja's love for her husband that she
kept him in ignorance for so many years, shielding him from the rumors
that circulated from time to time regarding Waldemar; but her vigilance,
extraordinary as it was, could reach only so far.

Kaspar was buying tea—Ostfriesen BOP, Sonja's favorite—at a shop
owned and run by his father-in-law's cousin when a little gentleman appeared at his elbow, clutching his long snow-white beard like a fairy-tale
gnome, and beamed up at him as though they were old friends. They
weren't old friends, as it happened, and the Brothers Grimm–ish charm of
the encounter was complicated by the fact that the gentleman was bleeding
from the nose. The situation gave off altogether too much actuality for my
grandfather's liking; he overcame his reluctance, however, and inquired of
the gnome, in his most civil tone of voice, whether he might somehow be
of service.

"You don't know me, of course," the gnome replied, dabbing at his nose
with the tip of his wondrous beard.

"I'd be happy to know you, I'm sure. My name is Kaspar Toula."

"*Ach!* I know who *you* are, Professor."

"Then you have me at a disadvantage, Herr—"

"Eichberg, Professor. Moses Eichberg." The man smiled again, then
drew the torn sleeve of his coat across his mouth. "Your wife was one of

my students, at the Volksschule." He nodded amiably. "I taught Sonja her sums."

"Of course!" said Kaspar, feeling the color rise to his cheeks. "I remember you well, now that I've had a moment. Sonja always speaks in the warmest possible—"

"Pardon my interrupting, Professor, but I'm wondering whether you can do anything about this." Mildly, almost bashfully, Eichberg indicated his nose.

My grandfather gaped down at the man, utterly at a loss. He had the sensation that reality was about to engulf him—to suck him greedily into its vortex—and it took all his self-control to keep from bolting. "I see you've had an accident—"

"An accident?" Eichberg gave a guffaw. "Yes, Professor! You're quite right. An accident of history, perhaps. An accident of the times in which we live."

"Are you in need of a doctor?"

"A doctor?" Eichberg repeated, as though the thought had never crossed his mind.

"Come now, Herr Eichberg," Kaspar said, beginning to lose patience. "I live just around the corner, as you may know, and I'm late getting home to my wife. You may accompany me, if you wish, and Sonja—or perhaps Professor Silbermann, her father—"

"Neither of *them* could be of help to me," Eichberg said, giving his peculiar laugh again. "It was your wife who directed me here to this shop." He glanced down at his coat. "I'd come to see you specifically, you understand."

"Me specifically? But I'm not a physician. Are you sure—"

"It's the UGF, you see," Eichberg said gently, as if Kaspar's confusion had moved him to pity. "They did this to me. I was leaving the school—"

"The UGF?" My grandfather thought hard for a moment. "Do you mean the United Germanic Front?"

Eichberg drew himself up proudly. "I much prefer to leave that name unspoken."

"I can understand that, Herr Eichberg, and I sympathize," said Kaspar, looking around him uneasily. The clientele of his cousin-in-law's shop was comprised almost exclusively of Ashkenazim, and the customary cacophony of gossip and complaint had ceased completely. Even Moishe himself—who generally abused his customers in a droning nasal monotone from the instant he opened for business—now stood with his mouth hanging open, blinking at his in-law in dismay.

"I can certainly understand your position, Herr Eichberg," Kaspar said again, doing his best to strike a note of civic decency. "Furthermore, I can appreciate why I—as a gentile of a certain standing, and the husband of a favorite former student—might come to mind as a go-between in this very unfortunate matter." (Here Eichberg made to interrupt, but my grandfather silenced him with an admonitory finger.) "I fear, however, that the United Germanic Front is likely to view me as something of a traitor to its cause. Given my familial connections—of which you must be aware, having come, as you say, from my very own house—"

"Your *familial* connections?" said Eichberg, grinning queerly at the other customers. To Kaspar's disbelief and horror, a number of them returned his grin, and one—a matron with bushy gray eyebrows—actually let out a snort. "It's precisely *because* of those connections, Professor Toula, that I stand before you."

Kaspar felt himself recoil slightly, overcome by a feeling of guilt and foreboding that he could in no way account for. "What on earth are you alluding to?"

"Are you not," Eichberg went on, no longer smiling, "the brother of Waldemar von Toula?"

∞

After the conversation with Eichberg—which lasted nearly an hour—Kaspar staggered home to Sonja like a man who'd been hit by a Daimler. His wife was waiting on the parlor divan, a piping pot of Ostfriesen BOP beside her, as though she'd foreseen his arrival down to the smallest detail: his light-headedness, his thirst, and his desperate desire for some scrap of evidence, however piddling, that the life he'd so painstakingly contrived was stable enough to withstand this latest shock. Sonja was at the zenith of what Kaspar would later refer to as her "Athena phase," a period during which nothing could disturb her equanimity. He flopped down beside her as she dispensed the cream, then the tea, then a single lump of nut-brown sugar each.

"What is it, Kasparchen? What has Waldemar done?"

For some reason her question annoyed him. "Didn't Eichberg tell you? You're the one who told him where to find me."

Sonja looked at him then—looked him straight in the eye—and he felt an emotion so foreign to him that it was only much later, with the benefit of hindsight, that he was able to call it by its proper name. At the time it felt less like shame than nausea.

"Waldemar's mixed up with the United Germanic Front," he heard himself reply. "He's been involved with them for quite some time, apparently." He then found himself describing the party's platform to his wife, though she knew it better than he did himself: the unification of all German-speaking peoples, the restoration of the monarchy, the severing of ties to Rome and the Catholic Church, and the purging of "Israelite influence" from the government and the economy and the culture as a whole. "God only knows what led them to poor Moses Eichberg, of all people. He thinks it may have been someone at his school—a student with a grudge, or possibly even a colleague." He squinted bleakly down into his teacup. "At any rate, word somehow reached those drooling fanatics that Eichberg had said we should all count our blessings that the empire had been consigned to the ash heap of history, or some such foolishness. They were waiting for him this afternoon—a whole gang of them, more than a dozen—outside the school. They took him by the heels and dragged him, face-first, the length of Sechskrüglgasse. He asked where they were taking him and they answered 'to keep an appointment.' When they let him go he was in front of Trattner's coffeehouse—the one with the leaded glass window, do you remember?"

Sonja nodded. "We once ate some strudel there."

"That's right," said Kaspar, hesitating a moment. "They make strudel exactly the way my mother used to make it, back in Znaim."

"What happened next?"

"Nothing, really. Eichberg looked through the glass and saw Waldemar sitting inside."

She smiled at him. "You call that nothing?"

"One of them said, 'Moses Eichberg: Waldemar von Toula. Stand up straight. Tip your hat to His Lordship.' Waldemar watched him through the glass for a moment, then turned back to his coffee. Eichberg had the impression that his face—Eichberg's, I mean—was being committed to memory. Then they told him he was free to go."

"That's all?"

"Isn't it enough?"

She sat back on the sofa. "You'll have to go and find him, I suppose."

"Excuse me?"

She let out a sigh. "He'll be expecting you. He may even have done this thing *because* of you. Because of us."

"I can't understand it," said Kaspar. "The UGF are reactionaries of the lowest order. And what's this *von* Toula nonsense? Has he gotten himself knighted?"

"I wouldn't be surprised, in this day and age."

"I can't imagine what I could possibly say to him. Not after all of this."

His wife sipped her tea. "But you'll go to him, won't you?"

For the first time in a great while he looked at her sharply. "Why the hell do you want me to see him so badly? Do you honestly think it will do any good?"

Sonja said nothing.

"You know me, *Schätzchen*," he murmured, cursing the adolescent quaver in his voice. "You know the type of character I am."

"I know the type of character you've become."

She said it affectionately, mildly, the way a mother might speak to an obstinate child. And his response was a child's as well, taking his cue from her, as he'd done for nearly twenty carefree years.

"I *can't* go to him, anyhow. I have no idea where he spends his time."

"That's true," agreed Sonja. "But you might begin at Trattner's coffeehouse."

∞

Thus began perhaps the strangest week of my grandfather's duration— one that reminded him, unpleasantly, of his vigil at the Jandek years before. Each day at noon he found himself standing in front of Trattner's gargantuan window, peering in through its varicolored glass, then making his way cautiously inside—suffering the scrutiny of the regulars, who made no effort to conceal their curiosity—and finding a seat in the darkest available nook. Trattner's was a more reputable establishment than the Jandek, but Kaspar felt no more at ease at its immaculately polished marble tables than he had in the Jandek's stained and threadbare booths. He felt incongruous in that hushed bourgeois temple, every inch the Czech from the provinces, a feeling he'd thought to have outgrown years before. His sole source of solace was the waitress, a dumpling-cheeked Serb barely out of her teens, whose haunches shook like aspic as she crossed the gleaming floor.

On day eight of his vigil a greasy blue mist hung in coils, refusing to congeal into a drizzle, and the people who passed Trattner's window wore identical crestfallen looks, as though their umbrellas were conspiring against them. One heavyset man—about Kaspar's age, with a close-cropped head and a pinched, nearsighted expression—stopped just outside the glass, calmly closed his umbrella, and handed it to a needy passerby. *What a remarkable gesture*, Kaspar thought absently. *I approve of that fellow.* By then the man was inside Trattner's, halfway to the nearest vacant table, with the morning paper in his right hand and a comically large meerschaum in his left. It wasn't until he placed his order with the Serb that Kaspar recognized him. That voice could belong to no other.

"A large *mocca*, at room temperature, with a small cube of unsalted butter," said Waldemar crisply. "A bowl of goulash, cold, with a pumpernickel roll cut into fourths. Two fingers' worth of anise-flavored brandy, lightly peppered." The Serb nodded as he marched through his preposterous order, showing no surprise at any of it. He was shabbily dressed, but his shabbiness had something affected about it, even genteel. He's putting on airs, Kaspar thought. And he's doing it well.

Waldemar sat straight-backed in his chair, his eyes nearly closed, while the waitress waddled off to place his order. She returned straightaway with the *mocca* and brandy, setting her tray down circumspectly, so as not to disturb the great man's reverie.

Kaspar marveled at his brother's aplomb, at his consummate lack of self-consciousness, at his world-weary poise; he couldn't entirely suppress a twinge of envy. It made little difference, suddenly, whether or not the source of that remarkable self-assurance lay in madness: he himself had never been waited on half so well. *To think that I've been pitying him all these years*, Kaspar said to himself. *Actually* pitying *him! While he's likely been pitying me!*

This notion was almost enough to bring my grandfather to his estranged brother's table; almost, Mrs. Haven, but not quite. The habit of aloofness—of cowardice, better said—was too deeply ingrained by that time. He kept still, barely sipping his *mélange*, doing his best to blend in with the upholstery. For the moment it was best to watch and listen.

Waldemar, meanwhile, was scribbling on a roll of butcher's paper that he'd pulled out of the lining of his coat. He was scribbling on this roll—which hung nearly to the floor—not with a pen or a pencil, but with a toothed wheel of brass that looked to have been pried loose from a clock. It made no marks on the paper that Kaspar could see; but his brother reviewed his writing carefully, occasionally crossing out what he had written.

He's working on the Accidents, Kaspar thought suddenly. He's been working on them all these many years. The thought dizzied him to the point of vertigo, and moved him to a sympathy far more potent than his pity had been; but it also made him regret the series of seemingly inconsequential decisions that now appeared, in retrospect, to have shaped the whole of his adult experience.

Over the previous decade—tacitly at first, but with growing conviction—my grandfather had come to acknowledge the importance of relativity. He had done so because the theory had compelled him to, of course, but also because he found it elegant and fashionable; and not least (he saw now, with the ruthless clarity of hindsight) because such an allegiance asked of him—demanded of him, in fact—that he break with his past and family forever. Sitting in his velvet booth at Trattner's, confronted with his long-lost brother's fidelity to the grail of their youth, Kaspar found himself wondering whether his commitment to reason, to objectivity, and to the scientific method—his commitment to sanity, in other words—might not, at bottom, be an act of treason.

∞

From an article in the Science section of *The New York Times* that I came across on my last visit to the bathroom (why my aunts kept such prodigous amounts of newsprint next to the toilet, Mrs. Haven, I hesitate to guess), I've learned some interesting facts about the phenomenon of reflection, a number of which apply to my grandfather's condition as he eavesdropped on his brother. "When people are made to be self-aware, they are likelier to stop and think about what they're doing," claims a psychologist with the felicitous name of G. V. Bodenhausen. "Subjects tested in a room with a mirror have been found to work harder, to be more helpful and to be less inclined to cheat, compared with control groups performing the same exercises in non-mirrored settings." Your reflection is a representative of your superego, in other words: an inquisitor dressed in your clothes. And Kaspar, in his sixteen-page diary entry for Thursday, November 14, 1922, likens spying on Waldemar to catching sight of his own face, grotesquely distorted, in a half-empty cup of *mélange*.

He also notes—in a hurried little postscript, as if the fact were of no consequence—that the Patent Clerk has won the Nobel Prize.

∞

"Herr Toula!" came a voice from over Kaspar's shoulder. He spun in his seat involuntarily, forcing his face into a smile—but the man in question shuffled blithely past him.

"Pardon my lateness, Herr Toula. The trams at this hour—"

"*Von* Toula," Waldemar interrupted, breaking into the same queer laughter, dry as ashes, that Kaspar had found so disquieting in the widow's attic all those years before. "As for the trams, Herr Bleichling, suffice it to say that it's a fallen world."

"It certainly is, sir! Beautifully put."

"Be seated, Herr Bleichling. Let's proceed to the matter at hand."

"The matter at hand?"

"Am I not being clear?"

"Not—that is to say, you *are*, of course," the man stammered. "Do you mean—are you suggesting that we discuss it here in public? That is to say, within earshot—"

"My enemies know where to find me, Herr Bleichling. I make no secret of my whereabouts. Let them come and arrest me, if they care to; let them stone me in the street, or burn me alive in Saint Stephen's Square. Let them do their worst to us! Don't you agree?"

"Well—" said Bleichling, shifting unhappily in his chair. "Well, Herr Toula—Herr *von* Toula, I beg your pardon—I do have my wife to think of, and my daughter Elfriede, and little Sigismund—"

"*Sigismund*, is it? An excellent name for a son!"

"Very kind of you, Herr von Toula." Again Bleichling hesitated. "In actuality, however, Sigismund is a terrier." He let out a titter. "A *Scottish* terrier, to be exact, with the whitest undercoat you've ever—"

"It happens this Saturday," Waldemar snapped. "Have your men assembled by eighteen o'clock."

"*This* Saturday? The day after tomorrow? I'm afraid that I wouldn't—I can't—that is, I couldn't possibly—"

Waldemar held up a hand. "I've been informed, Herr Bleichling, that I may not be at liberty by this time next week. A warrant for my arrest has reached this city from Budapest, where I was active for some years on the party's behalf."

Bleichling squirmed and gulped air. "I've heard about what you did in Budapest."

"Have you, Herr Bleichling? Then tell me. When you heard of it, how did it make you feel?"

"I couldn't—I didn't—" The life drained from his face. "Good *heavens*, sir, I didn't mean to suggest—"

Waldemar eased his heavy body forward. "I'll tell you how it made *me* feel, brother. It made me feel wide awake. It made me feel the breeze of our glorious future on my skin."

By now the back of Kaspar's neck had gone puckered and hot, as though the hairs on his nape were being plucked, and his tongue felt like a breaded chicken cutlet. The thought that less than a minute earlier he'd been tempted to sit down at his brother's table—to sit down and ask him, humbly, for *forgiveness*—was suddenly both appalling and absurd. When the waitress appeared at his shoulder, silently and without the slightest warning, it was all that he could do to keep from vaulting from his seat.

"I'm quite well," he squawked, though the Serb hadn't spoken. "I was on my way out, in fact. I'm late for an appointment—"

"I can't allow you to do that, sir."

Kaspar felt the air catch in his throat. "Why not, for God's sake?"

"You haven't paid."

"Of course!" he said, nearly shouting with relief. "Forgive me. Of course. If you'd be so kind—"

"Sixteen hundred kronen."

As he counted out the money, marveling at the steadiness of his hands, Kaspar heard—echoingly, as if across an empty ballroom—the sound of chairs being pushed back, and of his brother's voice whispering a series of commands. He let his eyes close, then felt a hand gripping his elbow: but it was only the waitress, the inscrutable Serb, offering to help him out onto the street. Before he could respond to her his brother and Herr Bleichling were beside him.

"Excuse me!" said Bleichling, insinuating himself deftly between Kaspar and the girl. He was even smaller than he'd first appeared, and his freckled, hairless crown reflected the lamplight like a piece of lacquered crockery—but an instant later Kaspar had forgotten Bleichling completely, because Waldemar stood in his place.

He patted the Serb on the rump as he passed, as if she were in his exclusive service, and she swiveled her ample hips to give him room. He smiled at her, producing a coin between his thumb and middle finger—at which point his gray eyes came to rest on Kaspar.

"You may keep the change, Jelena."

"*Hvala ti*, Herr von Toula. God be with you."

"Bless you, my child."

Through the whole of this exchange his brother's flat, unblinking eyes took Kaspar's measure, ticking from feature to feature, appraising him with a mild but steady interest. He's trying to place me, Kaspar thought incredulously. He's trying to remember where we've met. Have I changed to such a degree? Has he stricken me from his memory so completely? Even as he asked himself these questions, however, Kaspar saw the opacity of those eyes for what it was, and reminded himself that he was looking at a madman.

"Umbrella," said Waldemar.

"Pardon?"

"Your umbrella, sir. I wonder if you'd be so kind as to withdraw it."

Kaspar looked down warily, suspecting a trick, to find the tip of his umbrella—which he'd entirely forgotten he was holding—pinning Waldemar's coat to the floor. Another sign, this time unmistakable: the moment had arrived for disclosure, for confrontation, for a reckoning long overdue. *It's your brother, Herr von Toula. Explain to me, if you have a moment, the fundamental points of your philosophy. Tell me what you did in Budapest.*

"I'm frightfully sorry," he said, stepping backward.

"No harm done, brother," Waldemar answered, receding before Kaspar's eyes like a mirage.

∞

No act of terror took place that Saturday, or the next Saturday either, insofar as Kaspar could discover. He'd gone straight to the police from Trattner's, but the officers had struck him as oddly abstracted, and on subsequent visits they'd made no effort to conceal their lack of interest. Israelites, they informed him, were regularly involved in all manner of trouble. Gustav Bleichling, by contrast, was a grammar school teacher—he taught at the same school as Moses Eichberg, in fact—and was respected by both his colleagues and his pupils. "He's a teacher of *literature*," one of the gendarmes explained, as though this fact alone were proof that he was harmless. As for Waldemar Toula, he'd reportedly left the city for parts unknown, and in any case the department had been informed of no warrants from Budapest. My grandfather had no choice, ultimately, but to let the matter drop.

X

WALDEMAR'S SECOND VANISHING ACT was even more accomplished than his first—so much so that Kaspar found himself wondering, as the twenties sped by, whether their encounter at Trattner's had happened at all. But he knew it had happened, farfetched though it seemed. He had the change in himself to corroborate the memory—and also the change in his wife.

The asylum Kaspar and Sonja had created was as dear to him as ever, Mrs. Haven, but his faith in it was permanently cracked. He was no longer complacent, no longer confident that his indifference to history would protect him or those he loved against its whims. And Sonja herself—whose trust in their separate peace had never been as sturdy as her husband's— now took steps to prepare for the worst. She was in an excellent position to appreciate the degenerating social climate, and not only by virtue of her intimacy with anarchists, Bolsheviks, and assorted other enemies of the state: her own father, the illustrious and redoubtable Ludwig David Silbermann, Ph.D., provided her with as cautionary a tale as any alarmist could ask for.

∞

It's one of the paradoxes of history, Mrs. Haven, that the world's universities, those stiff-lipped incubators of the Enlightenment, have occasionally thrown their vestal gates wide open to its opposite. Since the end of the war, in moderate but slowly growing numbers, eminent members of the University of Vienna's faculty—most, if not all, of them perfectly sane—had begun to speak openly about the Semitic infiltration of the student body, which was "out of all proportion" to the city as a whole. This grumbling was aped by the students themselves, who amplified and distilled it in predictably post-pubescent ways. It was a matter of a few brief months, once that happened, until the Movement—as it now called itself—grew bold enough to act on its beliefs.

Professor Silbermann's troubles began with a leaflet. On a drab Monday morning in early October, a new student club—the euphoniously named Native Agglomeration of the Primary University—deposited a modest sheaf of letterpressed pages in the *Mensa*, addressed to "Aryan scholars" of the Department of Physics, suggesting that "a general wish be taken into account, out of a sense of civics, to list all current professors of Semitic heritage by name." The students in question—no more than a dozen in all—were mild-mannered to the point of meekness, and few members of the faculty, Jewish or otherwise, took their faltering attempt at pamphleteering seriously.

Needless to say, Mrs. Haven, this would prove a mistake.

The first name on the list was Moritz Schlick, lecturer in applied physics, who soon found it impossible to discharge his duties. The fact that Professor Schlick wasn't Jewish at all, but the son of a defrocked priest from Salzburg, was taken by the student body—and even by some of his colleagues, once momentum had built—as one of the more damning points of evidence against him. Vienna's beloved former mayor Karl Lueger had once famously declared, "I'll decide for *myself* who's a Jew and who isn't!" and the university humbly took its cue from him. Within a month Schlick had resigned.

Nothing could have been more in character for Kaspar's father-in-law than to refuse to acknowledge the mustering clouds. When Sonja confronted him—that same week, over dinner—he denied that the hubbub concerned him at all. "*My* boys," he declared, "are entirely too busy for that sort of nonsense. I've fielded every conceivable question in the course of my lectures, from the cause of the aurora borealis to the relative merits of pince-nez and monocles; but I've never been asked whether Copernicus ate shellfish or matzo."

Sonja, who'd heard all this before, kissed him sadly on the cheek and changed the subject. The outrage occurred the next morning.

Though his duties at the university were lighter than they'd been in the years of his prime, the professor was still in the habit of arriving at dawn. It afforded him a sharp, childish pleasure to greet his colleagues with a businesslike nod as they shuffled groggily past his office, where he was already hip-deep in the morning's work; besides, one never knew when a student might drop in to talk. Young men were known to keep irregular hours— young physicists, especially—and he kept his door unlocked accordingly. From time to time, on arriving in the morning, he'd find a hastily scrawled note on his desk, deposited at God knew what small hour of the night. His own son-in-law had been a great one for such notes, he remembered, as had the boy's brother—that gifted, unfortunate other.

The morning of February 16, 1927, found the professor arriving at the Department of Physics a quarter hour later than usual, having missed his customary trolley by a nose. The floors had been waxed during the night and his boot heels snapped agreeably with each step. His door was two-thirds closed, just as he'd left it, but a pistachio-colored envelope lay squarely on the blotter of his desk. He glanced back down the corridor before stepping inside, savoring the charged, monastic silence. No one else was in sight.

The note inside the envelope differed from those the professor generally received. First, it was unsigned; second, it was all but illegible; and last, it bore no address or signature of any kind. The text—once he'd deciphered its scrawl with the aid of his magnifying lenses—only added to his puzzlement:

THE LOST TIME ACCIDENTS, A GENTLEMAN
ONCE SAID.
WHO WAS THIS GENTLEMAN?

A playing-card-sized scrap of paper had been included in the envelope, in accordance with custom, on which to compose his reply. He found himself sitting stock-still for an extravagant length of time, looking from his pen cup—a potbellied clay vase, meant for tulips or lilies, that Sonja had made as a child—to the uncommonly dusty air above his head. If an answer hovered there he did not see it.

The notes from his boys had taken all manner of guises over the years, but none had ever been presented as a riddle. Later, it would occur to the professor that he hadn't been able to place the handwriting—though it did seem familiar—and this fact would appear significant; at the time, however, the question of authorship was immaterial. Silbermann relished a brainteaser as much as the next man of science, and eventually, after a great deal of deliberation, the germ of an answer began to take shape. He sat cautiously forward, mindful not to jar his idea loose too soon, and reached for his favorite pen.

Had anyone else been in the building at that hour, they'd have borne witness to a sound coming out of the department chair emeritus's office unlike any he'd been known to make before. A quarter hour later, when Fräulein Landsmann, his secretary, shuffled past his open door, she found the professor slumped in his armchair, holding his right arm daintily away from his body. It was covered in blood, which gave her a nasty turn—but the blood was not Professor Silbermann's. Fräulein Landsmann was a practical and clearheaded woman, of Tyrolean sheepherding stock. Once she'd established that the professor was unhurt, she helped him up and led him to the lavatory. He thanked her in an airy voice, praising her goodwill and promptness, then asked her—in the same cordial tone—to dispose of the contents of the pen cup on his desk.

Fräulein Landsmann did as directed, whereupon she was heard by the professor to produce a sound quite like the one he'd made himself. At the bottom of the pen cup, in a heap of clotted blood and cartilage, lay the fetus of a freshly stillborn pig.

∞

Much was made of this episode, needless to say, in spite of the university's attempts to keep it quiet. Expressions of youthful high feeling were certainly not unheard of, even in the Department of Physics; but none had yet been so lyrical, so enigmatic, so poetically rich in sign and symbol. In the days and weeks that followed, the significance of the event was passionately debated by students and faculty alike. The choice of pig flesh was perhaps understandable, given Silbermann's creed; but why a fetus, with its connotations of nativity and promise? Members of the Agglomeration were consulted, as one might call an expert witness in a court proceeding; but to everyone's surprise—even their own, it appeared—they were as baffled as anyone else. Eventually, some deep thinker pointed out that the fetus in question appeared to have been stillborn, which went some way toward settling the issue: the pig was a totem of waste, of abortion, of a race's grand potential unfulfilled. The question of authorship, however, persisted. And what to make of the riddle? And why in the professor's *pen cup*, of all places?

Kaspar saw little point in coming forward, and Sonja was inclined to agree. They never discussed the details of what had occurred, or why her father had been singled out, or how things could have come to such a pass. They only spoke about what should be done.

Quietly and efficiently, while speculation raged among his own students and colleagues (and an official inquiry into the affront was being indefinitely postponed), Kaspar conducted an investigation of his own. He spent another week at Trattner's, visited the Bemmelmans villa—which he found boarded up for the winter—and even paid a call on the schoolteacher, Bleichling, who promptly broke down in tears, as though he'd been rehearsing expressly for Kaspar's visit, and confessed that Herr von Toula had broken off all contact years before. After a full month of searching, Kaspar was forced to admit that he'd found no evidence whatsoever that his brother had returned to Vienna.

"It doesn't matter whether or not you found evidence," Sonja said. "We know he was here, because of what happened to Papa."

Kaspar pointed out to her, as gently as possible, that Waldemar appeared to have accomplices—some shadowy fraternity at his beck and call—and that anyone could have delivered the note. Sonja countered that it made no difference.

"It makes a great deal of difference, Sonja. We need to know who we're dealing with—how many of them there are and what they're after. Even *I'm* not certain what that riddle means."

"It's a warning," she answered. "And it wasn't intended for Papa, I don't think. I think it was intended for us."

"Sonja, what on earth—"

She took his hand and led him to the divan and asked him to sit down beside her. When she was satisfied that he was giving her his full attention, she told him, in a voice he hardly recognized, the details of Waldemar's long-ago midnight visit. She took care to omit nothing this time—not even how tempted she'd been to do what Waldemar had asked of her, insane though she'd known him to be.

It can be a fascinating thing to be reminded, after years of complacency, that the woman who sleeps beside you might easily, but for the grace of chance and fate and Providence, be sleeping beside someone else. Kaspar had noticed, of course (he remembered it now), how Sonja's manner had changed when his brother was near, and how intently Waldemar had stared at her at their first meeting. But it came as a shock, one of the most severe of his duration, that his brother's interest might have been returned.

"Why not go with him?" he mumbled when Sonja was done. "Why not do as he asked, if he tempted you so?"

Sonja waited for him to meet her eye before she answered. "I've been tempted by all sorts of things, Kaspar, that I didn't want."

Kaspar frowned at her, shaking his head reflexively. "I see."

"Do you, my love? Do you really?"

He considered her question. "You didn't go with him that night—I understand that much. You didn't go with him. You stayed with me."

Sonja regarded him curiously for a moment. Then she sat forward and kissed him on the lips. "You're right," she said. "There's nothing else you need to understand."

∞

Decades later, in the summers of his North American exile, reclining on his shaded porch on sepia-tinted upstate afternoons—the kind that seem steeped in nostalgia even as they're happening—my grandfather would occasionally rhapsodize about the night that followed. With characteristic Toula perversity, he and Sonja chose that same evening to perpetuate the Silbermann-Toula line, ratifying their mutual devotion in the names of Darwin and Marx and Jehovah—to say nothing of their elders, who'd long since abandoned all hope.

When it became clear that Sonja was pregnant—and moreover, with *twins*—the news spread among their wide and heterogenous network of acquaintances with a speed customarily reserved for scandal. She had just turned forty, after all: a shocking age, by the standards of the time, at which to begin having children. Why on earth, it was asked, had they waited so long? Sonja might easily have been a grandmother by then; and not a few eminent Viennese matrons suggested, upon hearing the news, that she ought to have been.

Rumors began to circulate that Sonja was unwell—possibly at death's door—and even, in certain unprincipled circles, that there were open questions of paternity. It didn't help matters that the whole business was kept curiously *private*, as though it were an occasion not of pride but of disgrace. This was Sonja's express wish, however, heartily endorsed by her husband, and her overjoyed (and not a little dumbfounded) parents weren't about to contradict her. The twins would be born in a neighborhood clinic, under the care of the family physician, with as little outside meddling as possible. Their birth, it was made clear, was to be regarded as an addition to their parents' lives first, to their grandparents' second, and to the city of Vienna's last of all.

In this way a precedent was set for eccentricity—some would say wrongheadedness, even hubris—that the twins themselves would follow all their lives.

∞

Sonja and Kaspar passed a sweetly uneventful nine months—receiving no more than a handful of visitors, and those only briefly—during which time the mother-to-be was the picture of Rubenesque health. Dr. Ryslavy, a mustachioed Magyar whose breath smelled of leeks and who clapped my grandfather on the back more often and more heartily than Kaspar would have liked, announced after only four months that Sonja would bear not one but two children, and that she was carrying them unusually high in her womb. According to Ryslavy, this indicated that the twins would be identical, male, and—as he told Kaspar in confidence—"fearsome holy terrors" into the bargain. He was wrong on all counts, Mrs. Haven, but the last.

Aside from Ryslavy's visits, and the occasional presence of the Silbermanns, the Ringstrasse apartment was as quiet and as cozy as a midwinter chalet. Kaspar's mother contented herself with sending the couple one postcard from Znojmo per week, which was more than enough for her son. His fantasy of being cast away had finally come to pass, and he made it his sacred duty to enjoy it to the fullest, knowing they'd been given but a few short months' reprieve. Every now and again he thought of Waldemar's concept of rotary time—his assertion that progressive time was a sinister, Semitic hoax—and found himself wishing, in spite of all he knew, that it were so.

He attended to his duties grudgingly, neglecting all but the most necessary work, and passed as little time away from home as possible. He'd never taken much interest in the details of domesticity before—the dining table's waxy patina, the dust along the hem of the curtains, the lingering smell of whitewash in the foyer—but they came, little by little, to intrigue him more profoundly than the greatest enigmas of physics. The minutiae of daily life *were* enigmas, after all; and wasn't physics' highest purpose to explain them?

Four hundred miles to the north, at the Kaiser Wilhelm Institute of Physics in Berlin, the Patent Clerk was beginning his duration-long search for the theory of the unified field.

∞

Contrary to the boisterous assurances of Dr. Ryslavy, the twins, when at last they arrived, proved a far cry from the promised pair of ruddy, headstrong boys: they were delicate and fair—almost blue-skinned, in fact—and were unabashedly, defiantly female. They were far from identical, either: the firstborn had angular, pinched-looking features (*like a tiny schoolmistress!* her mother declared), and her sister was downy and round as a quince. Any doubts as to the girls' paternity were dispelled straightaway—the challenge, in fact, was to detect their mother in them. This was somewhat regrettable, since Sonja, even at forty-one, was a sight to behold, whereas Kaspar was no one's notion of a beauty. Nevertheless, the birth of his daughters had an effect on my grandfather that he hadn't foreseen: it arrested his retreat from the world, and even—by small, fixed increments, like the ticking of a timing cog—reversed it.

From his first glimpse of their faces, crimped and wrinkled like a pair of angry fists, Kaspar's daughters stupefied and humbled him. Not in years—not since the Accidents—had his mind been taken captive so completely. They seemed less like children to him, these beings he'd engendered, than like primates of some other, fiercer order; and though he eventually came to love them more than life, this first impression never fully left him. He'd have died before admitting it to Sonja, but Kaspar's fascination with his daughters was not the doting that it so resembled. Passionate as it was, his interest in the twins was scientific.

They were a force to be reckoned with, straight out of the womb—Ryslavy had been right about that much. Their response to *ex utero* Vienna was unequivocal: both of them remained silent, opening their dark blue eyes unnaturally wide, and turned progressively purpler, refusing to breathe for themselves. An injustice had clearly been done them, but whether the guilty party was the obstetrician, the nurse, or their mother herself remained a mystery. "I wasn't concerned for an instant!" Ryslavy joked once the crisis had passed. "After all, those are two little angels. It wouldn't have surprised me, Herr Toula, if they'd dispensed with the trouble of breathing altogether!"

"It wouldn't have surprised *me*, Dr. Ryslavy," Kaspar replied, "if they'd somehow turned out to have gills."

Disquieting as their debut was, both girls were pronounced healthy, and they came home with Sonja soon after. Kaspar and his in-laws received the new mother with deference, and the twins—still unnamed—were installed with great pomp in the master bedroom. No one wondered at the fact that the children remained nameless: it seemed in keeping with their otherworldliness. As Kaspar put it to Sonja that same evening, "None of the names we've come up with will do, I'm afraid. They seem—*presumptuous*, somehow." Sonja had laughed at first, then nodded in agreement.

The twins' fractious entry into our atmosphere, Mrs. Haven, proved to be characteristic. They bawled at milk bottles and grimaced at rattles and ate other children for breakfast. Even Sonja, with all her gift for equanimity, was brought to the edge of despair by their tantrums. Mama Silbermann commented—with the best of intentions—that she'd never seen a child who could cry while breast-feeding, let alone *two*; the professor predicted careers at the bar. Kaspar seemed to be the only human being who could make his daughters smile, and that only by making the most hideous grimaces, or by slapping himself in the face. A full month after their birth, the twins were as nameless as ever.

It was Kaspar, fittingly enough, who finally brought the stalemate to an end. A Slovenian communist had brought Sonja a bouquet of alpine flowers in belated honor of the birth, and my grandfather discovered that the surest way to quiet the twins, at the height of their tantrums, was to twirl a tiny star-shaped gentian above them. *Enzian* is the name of that flower in Austria, and it struck Kaspar as perfect for the firstborn of his daughters: not too feminine, not too pretentious, and fittingly peculiar to the ear. Sonja allowed him to convince her (as much out of exhaustion as anything else) and suggested, lover of verse that she was, that their younger daughter be named Gentian, in tribute to William Cullen Bryant's "To the Fringed Gentian," a favorite poem of her schooling days. The resulting names managed to sound as awkward in German as they did in English, which is harder to achieve than you might think; but no one ever claimed the twins' names didn't suit them.

Professor Silbermann retired the following summer, to the relief of everyone who knew him, and the twins grew more tractable, if no less bizarre. Gradually existence reverted to normal—though Kaspar could never say for certain that he hadn't simply grown accustomed to the strangeness of the times. Conditions grew grim for the city's Jews and leftists, then very slightly better, then worse than anybody could recall. Sonja did what she could for her embattled protégés, but her protection wasn't what it once had been. There was little she could offer them but shelter.

It grew commonplace for Kaspar to come home from the university—or, just as often, to rise in the mornings—to find a rumpled, bearded *ism*-ist sleeping on the yellow divan in the parlor. He complained to his wife regarding this exactly once. "If you want *me* to sleep in your house, Herr Toula," Sonja replied, "then you'll have to put up with my guests. The girls enjoy them, even if you don't." Disgruntled though he was, my grandfather knew there was no point in arguing, especially with regard to the twins: Enzian and Gentian, barely able to walk, delighted in standing next to the divan in pallbearer-ish silence, taking turns seeing how firmly they could tug on the whiskers of each new refugee before he sat up with a yelp of pain.

Rumors of Waldemar von Toula surfaced from time to time—he was in Germany now, allegedly, which came as no surprise at all—but the family preferred to disregard them. Kaspar was offered no promotions by the Department of Physics, but no pigs were stuffed into his pen cup, either. By the turn of the decade, he'd resigned himself to passing the remainder of his duration as an adjunct professor in a city he no longer felt at home in, shunning the papers and most of the people he knew, Jew and gentile alike.

When a body, in motion, is not acted upon by any force, Newton famously wrote, *that body shall continue on in a straight line, at the same speed.* If the middle of Kaspar's life was a plateau to him—a hilltop with an unobstructed view—then the future was a single smooth descent. And that temperate decline was all he wished for.

How to assess my grandfather, Mrs. Haven? How to judge him? Admittedly, he hadn't read a newspaper since 1927, he rarely left the house except to deliver his lectures, and he'd come to have as much use for human interaction as a jellyfish; but the force that was building—and would soon overwhelm him—had announced its arrival in letters of fire. To quote Kaspar himself, on the last page of his European diary: *Only a blind man could have lived through these last years without seeing what was bearing down upon us; so I made myself as blind as I could manage. I wanted to believe that the worst was behind me, and I found an easy way to make it so. I simply turned my back on what was coming.*

Where in spacetime are you, Mrs. Haven? Are you relaxing at home on a dull winter evening, as I like to imagine, leafing idly through these pages by the fire? Are you happy, Mrs. Haven? Are you tipsy? Are you bored? It's getting harder and harder, with each chapter I finish, to bring your darkling image into focus. My reason for writing was allegedly to capture your interest, or at least to recapture your memory; instead I find your likeness warping, refracting the light I shine toward it, like a cigarette wrapper left out in the sun. How far can I go before you're gone completely?

In one of Orson's first published pieces, "The Un-Extended Life" (*Preposterous! Stories*, volume 21, number 3, 1957), a Department of Motor Vehicles clerk named Silas Strangeways comes across a thumbnail-sized ad on the back page of volume 21, number 3 of *Preposterous! Stories* (with a fantastically geeky attention to detail that I can't help admiring, the ad was actually *run* in that same issue) promising escape from his humdrum existence:

> ### ARE <u>YOU</u> LIVING THE LIFE THAT YOUR MAKER INTENDED?
>
> *Does your life lack the flavor, the crackle, the <u>intensity</u> you've hoped for?*
>
> *Daily, we find ourselves bombarded by a thousand recommendations for extending the <u>duration</u> of our lives—exercise three times weekly! smoke in moderation! exchange sugar for saccharine!—but the truth is that time does not gain value by*

accruing. Time acquires value by being "spent," and spent freely. The longest life is not always the best one; in the majority of cases, just the opposite.

    If you <u>are</u>, in fact, living the life that your maker intended— it may be time to seek another maker.

Prompted, perhaps, by his genre-appropriate surname, Strangeways answers the ad, and soon finds himself in a bunker with titanium walls— located, for some reason, sixty feet beneath the Statue of Liberty—as a test subject in a top-secret, Pentagon-funded experiment in something known as "rotary chrono-feedback." The basic idea (explains the ascot-sporting, sherry-sipping scientist in charge, Dr. Hugo von Karst) is to harness the power of certain especially nasty cosmic rays to collapse spacetime into a kind of nugget—"a diamond, if you will, of pure, unadulterated NOW"— in which every instant of a man's life will occur simultaneously. Karst's pitch is as follows: "Your life, Mr. Strangeways, is sadly diluted. It holds precious few pleasures, a handful at best, with far too much of nothing in between. Imagine, however, the bliss and the terror, the intensity and the passion, if it all were compressed—if you lived your *whole life* in a nanosecond!"

After some rote hemming and hawing from Strangeways—and some heavily italicized gibberish from Karst about time as mankind's comeuppance for original sin, and mankind itself as a race of undeserving monkeys, and heaven as a kind of perpetual-motion machine—Strangeways agrees to have his life compacted, and in no time at all he's deloused and depilated and basted in radioactive Vaseline and inserted, buck naked, into a "thrumming titanium cervix" (Orson's words, Mrs. Haven, not mine), at which point everyone puts on goggles and the space rays are harnessed and something goes horribly wrong. The experiment has the opposite of the expected result: instead of living his entire life in a single fervent moment, Strangeways's existence is stretched out so infinitely thin that he might as well not be existing at all. He's traded his brief, Judeo-Christian lifespan for a diaphanous kind of immortality: he's sidestepped the life God intended for him and become an accidental god himself.

Uncharacteristically for my father—a believer in tidy endings, like most of his peers in the trade—it's left open whether Strangeways's default godhood is a blessing or a curse.

The editors of *Preposterous! Stories* weren't too taken with "The Un-Extended Life," much to Orson's consternation. They accepted it grudgingly—as a kind of stopgap between "Titans' Battle," by Heinrich Hauser, and "Warlord of Peace," by Leroy P. Yerxa—and paid him half the normal rate per word. Orson sent them an indignant letter, seven pages long, demanding an explanation for the slight. Their answer took the form of a nine-word postcard, all in caps:

> *MORE TITS TOLLIVER. MORE POINTER SISTERS. MORE JUJU FRUITS.*

My father scrupulously avoided repeating this error in the 136 stories that followed. From that day onward, his extraterrestrials were nearly always female, dressed inadequately or not at all, and possessed of proud, heaving, pendulous breasts, whenever possible in multiples of three.

∞

I'm rambling again, Mrs. Haven. Something odd seems to have happened to the air. Could the pilot light have gone out in the kitchen?

XI

ENZIAN AND GENTIAN had just celebrated their birthday—an orgy of Bavarian cream and marzipan at which no expense was spared—when Hitler's Wehrmacht arrived at the gates to the city, politely requested the key, and received it with an ingratiating flourish. Vienna in '38 was no longer the glistening pudding, studded with exotic candied fruits, that it had been in the years of its prime—but the Führer discovered, to his profound satisfaction, that it practically melted on his tongue.

The Toula-Silbermanns watched the victory procession from the mezzanine balcony of their apartment—close enough, as Kaspar's father-in-law put it, "to trim your whiskers on the bayonets." The phalanxes of uniformed torsos, extending up the Ringstrasse as far as the eye could see, were impressive enough; but the fervor of the crowd was grander still. Teenagers flung confetti; couples kissed in the street; men sang ardently along with songs they didn't know the words to yet; and everywhere that stiff-armed, armpit-exposing, supremely unsavory salute. In terms of pure spectacle, that tremendous parade was unsurpassed in the city's three-thousand-year history: a whirling *laterna magica* of jet black and scarlet, submission and patriotism, sweating men and fawning women, eros and repression, brotherly feeling and hate. And at the navel of it all, at its heroic center, Waldemar von Toula—all two hundred kilos' worth—sat artfully arranged in the back of a Daimler convertible.

He was mountainous now, more massive even than Reichsmarschall Goering, and his spectacles had been replaced by a cobalt-tinted monocle on a length of silver cord. He was squinting blandly out into the crowd, searching for familiar faces, but his gaze never rose to the level of his brother's balcony. The family looked on in silence as the Daimler rolled past; even the twins seemed momentarily abashed. Sonja stood at the railing, ashen-faced and white-knuckled; Kaspar huddled behind her, staring out through his fingers, contending with actuality at last. But it was one Felix Ungarsky— Trotskyist agitator, occasional pimp and current tenant of the yellow divan— who put the collective feeling into words.

"I couldn't possibly eat as much dinner," Ungarsky growled into his beard, "as I'd like to be able to puke."

∞

On the nineteenth of March—an unseasonably balmy Saturday—the same Daimler convertible eased to a stop in front of 37 Ringstrasse, its brakes chuffing softly, and a monocled man in a cherry-red suit stepped out into the piping noonday sun. As chance or fate or Providence would have it, it was Felix Ungarsky who answered the door, and none too cordially either: he'd done almost nothing but sleep since the transfer of government, and the doorbell had roused him from a wonderfully Wermacht-free dream. Blinking out at the caller through nearsighted eyes, his face piggish with sleep, Ungarsky did his best to get his jumbled thoughts in order. The man regarded him warmly, in no apparent hurry, beaming like Saint Nicholas himself. In his fuddled condition, Ungarsky failed to recognize the caller; he decided— not altogether wrongly—that he was a peddler of religious literature.

"You've chosen the wrong house, I'm afraid. Our souls are brimming with fulfillment as it is. We're part of the German Reich now, in case you haven't noticed."

"I *did* hear something to that effect," the man replied.

"There you have it, then. This family has no time for you today."

"No time for me?" the caller answered brightly, stepping past him. "Run upstairs and announce me, there's a good fellow. I rather think you'll find that I'm expected."

This was by no means the first time Ungarsky had been mistaken for the butler, but in his grogginess he made a rash decision: he decided, just this once, to let it get under his skin.

"One moment now, Father Christmas," he said, catching hold of the visitor's sleeve. "My name is Felix Ungarsky, and I happen to *reside* in these apartments. You seem to be under the mistaken impression—"

"You're neglecting your other caller, Felix."

The hallway seemed to darken, and Ungarsky, gripped by a sudden premonition, let the man's sleeve go and turned to look behind him. A second man stood backlit in the doorway. He wore a gray loden cape over a jet-black uniform with gleaming silver buttons, and he smiled at Ungarsky as if he knew him well.

"Felix Ungarsky—Hauptsturmführer Kalk," said the man in the suit, halfway up the stairs already. "The two of you have an interest in common."

"An interest in common?" Ungarsky echoed. He was clearheaded now, as sober and awake as he had ever been, and he'd recognized the caller at last.

"Exactly so," said the man in black, pulling the door of the house shut behind him. "Can you guess what it is?"

"I don't—" Ungarsky stammered. "That's to say, I couldn't—"

"It's you, Felix Ungarsky! You yourself."

∞

Sonja had just come out of the kitchen to see who'd rung the bell—and to ask whoever it was to keep quiet, so as not to rouse her father from his nap—when she saw Waldemar at the head of the stairs, draping his suit jacket over the banister. Her first impulse was to raise a finger to her lips; her next was to slip into her father's room and hide under the bed. Waldemar crossed the landing almost soundlessly, moving with surprising grace for so immense a man. His monocle—ridiculous! who wore a monocle any longer?—caught the lamplight as he came forward, giving him an oddly startled look. He smelled strongly of almonds—or was it marzipan?—and Macassar oil and smoke.

"Fräulein Silbermann!" he intoned, as if introducing her to some unseen associate. Sonja thought to correct his mistake—to remind him that two decades had passed since she'd gone by that name—but she had better sense than poor Ungarsky.

"I'm afraid my husband's not at home, Herr Toula. He's at the university."

"The *university?*" said Waldemar, raising his eyebrows. "Has he still not finished his degree?" He let out a harsh, clownish laugh, a sound he'd never made as a young man. She resisted the urge to ask him where Ungarsky had gone.

"You've changed, fräulein," he said after a pause. "You've come into your prime. And so have I."

"It's been more than twenty years, Herr Toula."

"Yes, fräulein. So it would seem."

She couldn't think how to answer, so she led him into the parlor, to the yellow divan, and waited on him there as best she could. Ungarsky's wing-tips still stood propped against the baseboard, and the cushions retained the imprint of his shoulders, which sickened her with anxiety; but her guest had eyes only for her. He took her hand in both of his, as if to warm it, and chatted with her about commonplace things—about the twins and the apartment and the price of a bottle of pilsner—until she felt the chill departing from her body. Kaspar would be home soon; she'd excuse herself then, say she had to see about the children. Children are useful for such things, she reminded herself, taking a cunning sort of pleasure in the thought.

"Kaspar is usually home by this hour," she found herself saying. "I can't think what's keeping him."

"Important work, no doubt!" said Waldemar. "It would be lovely to visit with Kaspar after so many years, of course, but our family reunion can wait. It's you I came to see."

The words hung between them like granules of dust, revolving in the air for her to ponder. All at once they seemed to catch the light, to hold still under her gaze, to surrender their meaning. He had returned from his exile to kill her.

"What was it, brother-in-law, that you wished to discuss?"

"So *this* is the notorious yellow divan!" He snatched up a cushion—lemon silk with lilac lozenges—and brought it to his cheek. "Quite a well-used piece of furniture, I gather. News of it has even reached Berlin."

She waited for him to go on, but he kept silent.

"Tell me what you want from me," she said.

Waldemar set the cushion down and closed his eyes. "You mistake the purpose of my visit, fräulein. I wanted nothing more from you than this."

Three decades before, as a handsome young man, he'd had a gift for making the most casual gesture seem significant, as though he were an actor in a play—and while he was anything but handsome now, he retained an actor's poise and bearing still. This particular play was a drama, that much was clear; and that it would end badly was never in doubt. But Sonja found herself wondering, as she studied his face, whether they were nearer to the beginning of the play or its finale. This seemed the only question left to ask.

Finally Waldemar opened his eyes. "I did certain things," he said softly. "During my time away."

"Certain things?"

He nodded. "When I think of them now, the acts to which I refer—especially when I try to describe them—appear to have been committed by a different man. But I admire that man, fräulein. I respect his fidelity to his cause—by which I mean, of course, the cause of science. It's important to me that you understand this."

Sonja gave the least possible nod.

"In the second decade of my exile, when I was still new to Berlin, I joined a so-called brownshirt unit known, colloquially, as the 'Pimp's Brigade.' This was in the time of open fighting in the streets. We were a sad parody of the party ideal—two ex-convicts, on average, for each true man of principle—but the ranks of the Red Front were sorrier still. We more than held our own, I'm proud to say." Waldemar heaved a sigh. "I was the old bird of the unit, too heavy to fight, so I was given the prison detail. You'll most likely laugh when I tell you this, fräulein, but I discovered that I had a talent for it."

Sonja said nothing. The wall above the divan brightened, then darkened, then brightened again. She wondered what on earth was keeping Kaspar.

"My first few interrogations were clumsy affairs, halting and inefficient, and served little purpose other than establishing my lack of squeamishness. With practice, however, I made a remarkable—if perhaps self-evident—discovery. The more fully I brought my *own* interests to bear on my work, the more fruitful the eventual result." He glanced at her with sudden concern. "This is all a bit opaque, I'm afraid. I'll furnish you with a definite example."

"Brother-in-law," she said steadily, "I beseech you, as a member of your own family, to consider—"

"For a number of years, as you know, I've been interested in the plasticity—for want of a better word—of time: in the shapes that it takes when it's not flowing smoothly. What I hit on was this. I would explain my ideas to each detainee in turn—specifically, my theory of 'rotary time'— until I felt I'd made my meaning clear." Waldemar cracked a smile. "Sometimes this lecture alone sufficed to break them."

"You talked physics to your prisoners?" Sonja heard herself ask. "You told them about the Lost Time—"

"I tried not to *bore* my subjects," Waldemar cut in, with a trace of annoyance. "I chose not to burden them with my personal history. I simply explained how time could be made to change speed and direction, and even—under certain conditons—to stop altogether. I had proven this algebraically, and by the use of non-Euclidean geometry; now I was prepared, I informed them, to prove it again, using nothing but a chair, a length of wire, and a captive human being." He nodded to himself. "I would pause there, generally, to let this sink in. Then I'd ask them how much time they cared to lose."

"I don't understand," Sonja managed to answer. "I didn't understand twenty years ago, that night you asked for my help, and I don't—"

"Of *course* not, silly goose! I didn't fully understand then, either. I was two hundred kilometers and ten years removed from that night when the last of the Great Doors was opened for me." He sucked in a breath. "I was living under a railroad trestle in Budapest, eating snow and coffee grounds to stay alive, when my father came to me on a ray of pure thought. I was dying, fräulein—expiring of hunger and exposure—and for this reason a last boon was granted me."

"I heard you went to Budapest. There were rumors—"

Waldemar silenced her with a wave of his hand. "I'd spent most of my duration searching for the key to my father's discovery in the language of numbers—but the secret, when it finally came, was delivered in everyday words. In fact, my dear fräulein, it arrived in the form of a joke. May I share it with you?"

Half a dozen answers, Sonja later told Kaspar, revolved in her mind like horses on a carousel; but Waldemar had no need of a reply.

"Listen closely now, fräulein. The phenomenon my father discovered, and to which he gave the somewhat fanciful name the 'Lost Time Accidents,' is nothing enigmatic or arcane: no new star in the sky, no fifth dimension, no perpetual-motion machine. Time's most fundamental quality, after all, is that it should be continually lost to us. Is that not so?" He leaned in close to her—so close that the smell of marzipan eclipsed all others. "That being the case, my dear Sonja, the ultimate Lost Time Accident is death."

∞

Kaspar's immediate reaction upon coming home and learning what had happened was to take up his coat from the banister—the very same spot, Sonja noted, where Waldemar's jacket had hung—and return the compliment without delay. His brother had left no card, no telephone number, no clue as to his whereabouts, but for once my grandfather was resolute. Perplexing as Waldemar's visit had been, the malice behind it was as clear as Bohemian glass.

The SS, in those first heady days of the Anschluss, hadn't yet commandeered the Italianate hotel on Morzinplatz that would serve as its den for the next seven years: its interim quarters, when at last Kaspar found them, turned out to be decidedly less grand. A cast-iron stair led up the rear wall of the Bundesverkehrsamt—the Viennese equivalent of the Department of Motor Vehicles—to a spacious but badly lit warren of rooms, already stuffed to the rafters with stacks of mildewed files and plywood crates. The disorder of the place ought to have reassured my grandfather, but somehow it had the opposite effect. Anything might happen in a system this entropic, he found himself thinking. A person—or at least that person's dossier—might easily disappear without a trace.

Within weeks of Kaspar's visit, the nerve center of the Gestapo would be transormed into an occult fortress, sequestered behind its bureaucratic façade like a tarantula hidden in a filing cabinet; but on that particular afternoon—March 19, 1938, day seven of the post-Austrian era—Kaspar entered magically unchallenged. Young men in squeaking boots and fastidiously creased uniforms brushed past him in the hallway, neither returning his greeting nor meeting his eye. No one asked him his business until he arrived at a broad, skylit foyer at the labyrinth's center, empty save for a row of undersized chairs and a desk that looked pilfered from a headmaster's office. A bald and rat-faced goblin slouched behind it, collating stacks of curling mimeographs. It wasn't until the goblin glanced up from his paperwork, however—after what seemed a full hour—that Kaspar was able to place him. He was none other than Gustav Bleichling, proud owner of Sigismund the terrier.

"Good afternoon," said Kaspar curtly.

"You have the wrong floor," Bleichling answered, still shuffling his papers. "The Motor Vehicle Department—"

"We've met before, sir, if I'm not mistaken. The first time was at Trattner's *kaffeehaus*."

The mention of Trattner's had a curious effect on Bleichling. He sat bolt upright, as if he'd been poked in the ribs, and raised his right arm in a cramped, defensive motion; just as quickly, however, he recalled where he was, and transformed the gesture into a salute. "You'll have to pardon me, comrade. Those were thrilling days—superlative days!—but occasionally a face or two escapes me. I recall you now, of course. *Sieg Heil*."

"My name is Kaspar Toula. I've come to see my brother."

Bleichling's right arm sank slowly, seemingly of its own accord, and came to rest against the cluttered desktop. "You couldn't see him now," he said inflectionlessly. "If you'd be so kind as to write down your address—"

"Why can't I see him now? Is he not here?"

Bleichling hesitated. "He's asleep."

"It's four in the afternoon, Herr Bleichling."

A smile stole over Bleichling's soggy features. "You haven't seen your brother in quite some time, Herr Toula. He may have habits you are not familiar with." He glanced slyly over his shoulder, toward a small metal door, half-hidden behind a row of cabinets. "It's his custom to rest after an interrogation session, especially a long and fruitful one. He puts so much into his work, you see."

Kaspar returned Bleichling's insipid stare, unsure how to respond. He couldn't imagine why the little man should share information so freely—and with *him*, of all people—unless he was simply a fool. The timing of Waldemar's movements didn't correspond to what Bleichling was telling him, either. Not unless he'd gone directly—

"What's the name of the suspect?"

"I'm sorry?"

"The man my brother was questioning. Tell me his name."

Bleichling's smile sharpened. "My apologies, Herr Toula! I assumed he was the reason that you'd come. A natural assumption, given the circumstances."

"What circumstances?"

"Why, that he arrived here from your own residence, of course. He took pains to make clear that he wasn't your butler."

∞

Sonja was waiting at the street door when Kaspar brought Ungarsky home, so that he was momentarily convinced that his wife possessed the gift of second sight; but he soon realized that she'd been standing in that exact spot, straight-backed and expectant, the entire time he'd been away. The twins watched impassively from the mezzanine balcony as their father and mother conjured a phantom out of the hired car's backseat. The phantom wore nothing but his socks and underclothes, and his face—once rakishly whiskered—was naked and pale. He moved haltingly and stiffly, straining his shorn gray head forward, like a newborn pigeon knocked out of its nest.

Once they'd brought him upstairs, Ungarsky allowed himself to be laid lengthwise across the divan, then craned his neck to scan the floor around him. When he'd found what he was looking for, he sighed contentedly and let his eyes fall closed. "Praise Jesus," he whispered. "Those damn wingtips cost me a fortune."

He said nothing more until morning, when Sonja brought him a tray of ladyfingers and a cup of weak black tea. The entire family was in attendance, maidservants included. Ungarsky sipped his tea gratefully, looking only at Sonja, then fumbled feebly at his undershirt. He'd slept in his clothes—he'd begged not to be touched—and Sonja had let him be, ragged and foul-smelling though he was. But now a sight was disclosed that brought gasps from the children: a cruciform bruise, sharp and black as a stencil, extending from his breastbone to his belly.

The twins were whisked out of the room at once; Mama Silbermann— who'd fallen into a swoon—was revived with ammonium carbonate. Scissors were fetched from the kitchen. Kaspar cut the undershirt free, muttering and perspiring like a surgeon; Ungarsky, for his part, observed the proceedings at a slight but definite remove, as though the injury were no concern of his. Sonja began to suspect, as she gripped his slack hand, that their guest no longer had his wits about him. But when he spoke his voice was sure and calm.

"They took me to a room with a chair in it. A straight-backed armchair with a slotted steel base. Very modern. Nothing else in there, not even a table. A narrow green door, like the door to a closet. Sometimes I could hear the other one—Kalk—talking outside the door. I couldn't make out what he said. It doesn't matter." Ungarsky hesitated. "It doesn't matter, does it?"

"It doesn't matter, Felix," Sonja whispered.

"What happened then?" said Kaspar, keeping his voice as deliberate as he could manage. Ungarsky's shirt lay pinned beneath him now, revealing the wound in all its grisly glory. It looked like the beginning of a blueprint, or a crudely scrawled target, or a butcher's X traced on a hunk of meat.

"He stood me up against the wall. He was watching me closely, squinting and scratching his chin, as if I were some sort of bug that he'd caught. Idiot that I am, I told him so."

"*Ach!* Felix," said Sonja.

"Kalk came in with a man I hadn't seen before, carrying a razor and a basin of hot water. He told me to get on my knees and tip my head back as far as I could. I nearly wet myself with fright, but Kalk explained that the Standartenführer wanted a better look at my face. The man was a barber—and a skilled one, as you see." Ungarsky held up his chin. "I've never had a more accomplished shave."

He waited a moment, as if to hear the family's opinion. No one in the parlor said a word.

"The Standartenführer thanked the barber, closed his eyes until Kalk had escorted him out, then turned to me. 'I hate being made to wait, Herr Ungarsky,' he said. 'I suffer, among other things, from a condition known as *expectandophobia*. Can you guess what that condition is?' I shook my head. 'Expectandophobia, Herr Ungarsky, is a morbid fear of being made to wait.' He laughed at that, and I did my best to laugh with him, which sent him into full-blown hysterics. Then he told me to lie down."

At this point Frau Silbermann was ushered out of the room by the professor. Ungarsky lay back on the couch and watched them go.

"There was nothing in the room but that chair, as I've said. Once I was laid flat on the floor he dragged it over. Then he asked me a question—the only serious one he asked in all that time."

"What did he ask?" said Kaspar.

"I didn't understand at first, so he repeated it. 'Did you know, Herr Ungarsky, that the laws of physics, from the standpoint of mathematics, acknowledge no difference between future and past?' When I told him I didn't, he nodded at me in a friendly way. 'The question was a rhetorical one,' he said. Then he set the chair on my chest and sat down on it."

Sonja let out a muted groan and looked at Kaspar. Ungarsky went on, his voice formal and bright, like someone reading from the morning paper.

"'I'm going to keep you in this room for exactly forty-three minutes,' the Standartenführer told me. I asked him what would happen after that, and he said—" Ungarsky turned to Kaspar. "You're not going to credit this, Herr Toula, but I swear that it's true."

"Don't worry about me, Felix. Tell us what he said."

"'In forty-three minutes,' the Standartenführer told me, 'my brother will arrive, and Scharführer Bleichling—whom you met on your way in, I believe—will deliver you into his care.'"

All eyes went to Kaspar, but Kaspar kept still. He kept still because his brain was turning cartwheels in his skull. Sonja urged Ungarsky to go on.

"'When *that* comes to pass,' the Standartenführer said, 'I want you to relay a message for me. Would you do me that kindness?' I had no breath to answer but he didn't seem to mind. 'Unlike the laws of mathematics, the laws *I* represent—the laws whose envoy *I* am—distinguish past from future very plainly. The last twenty years have belonged to my brother; the future, by contrast, is ours. I shared something of my "lost time" theory with my sister-in-law this afternoon; but a theory without proof is merely talk. Someday soon I hope to give a demonstration.' The Standartenführer shifted his weight in the chair as he said this, and watched me as I fought to catch my breath. 'Do you think you can remember all that, Herr Ungarsky? I have no doubt you can.' He took out his watch. 'We have forty more minutes to practice.'"

XII

NOW WOULD BE the point in this history, Mrs. Haven, to recount the details of my grandfather's role in the Viennese resistance: the first Ungarsky-brokered contact, the meetings in shuttered rooms and city parks, and the progressively more desperate acts of sabotage; then the inevitable imprisonment and torture, deportation in an unmarked railway car, and death in some sun-dappled Polish forest.

You won't find any of that in this history, however, because none of it ever took place.

To be fair, Kaspar had his family to think of, and the Viennese resistance—valiant though it undoubtedly was—chiefly confined itself to tax evasion. Contrary to his own opinion, my grandfather was no simple coward, as his visit to the Gestapo HQ proves; but he was no longer young, and patriotism turned his stomach, and Waldemar's triumphant return had changed him permanently. His brother's madness was now the state religion, after all, with the weight of Greater Germany behind it. The grotesqueness of this notion—of this *fact*, he reminded himself—fastened itself to his mind like a leech after his visit to the Bundesverkehrsamt, and he could find no rational way to overcome it.

It was Sonja—to everyone's surprise but her husband's—who first suggested that they emigrate. She felt none of the mixed emotions Kaspar suffered under, labored under none of his confusion: she wasted no time trying to make sense of what was happening. And it was pointless for Kaspar to try to persuade her that his brother posed no genuine danger, at least not to them. He no longer believed it himself.

Once the decision was made, Sonja brooked no delay. Kaspar watched helplessly, struggling to stifle his panic, as she dismantled their asylum brick by brick. Not for her the classic refugee's dilemma of what to take and what to leave behind: the house and everything in it was a relic of a bygone age, and Sonja wasn't given to nostalgia. The most valuable furniture—the yellow divan included—was put up for auction in Vienna's Dorotheum; the rest was given to friends and acquaintances and neighbors, until the family was eating off newsprint and sleeping on blankets laid out on the floor. Kaspar was far from alone in believing her actions extreme—even Ungarsky entreated her to reconsider—but he knew better than to hope to change her mind.

By the time the *ism*-ists began to disappear—quietly and without any fuss, as though they'd been called away on pressing foreign business—the Toulas were in possession of a complete set of exit visas from the German Reich. Buffalo Bill had cabled to assure them of his patronage (including, among other things, a furnished one-bedroom apartment on a street called Chippewa, which Sonja thought sounded delightful), and passage had been booked on the *Comtesse Celeste*, a midsized steamer out of Genoa. "Every minute spent here is a minute we've lost," she'd exclaim when she caught Kaspar dragging his feet. "A brand-new life awaits us on the prairie!"

The prairie was never far from Sonja's thoughts in those last weeks. She assumed—reasonably enough—that the city of their destination, fabled gateway to the Middle West, had been named in honor of its herds of bison. She imagined Buffalo as a kind of all-purpose boomtown, a sequestered San Francisco on a sapphire-colored lake, where cattle were driven down Main Street, captains of industry rubbed shoulders with emancipated slaves, and an honest man could die a millionaire. Though my grandfather had his doubts on a number of these points, he decided, as a *kavalier*, to keep them to himself. The prospect of emigration remained fantastical to him, unreal and unlikely; but no more so than any other prospect did. *She'll be disappointed soon enough*, Kaspar thought. *There isn't any hurry.*

∞

Three days before their planned departure, Kaspar was sitting on a pillow in the gutted parlor, contemplating an oval of brighter paper where a mirror had once hung, when Enzian appeared in the doorway. She regarded him briefly with her lusterless eyes—almost as if she were considering his feelings—before delivering the news she'd come to tell.

"Mother's in the toilet," she announced.

"What's that, *Schätzchen*? In the toilet, is she?"

Enzian nodded. "Something's coming out of her mouth."

There was nothing in his daughter's voice or expression to account for the dread that gripped Kaspar as he leaped to his feet—but as soon as he caught sight of his wife on the floor, resting her cheek against the bowl of the toilet as if she were drunk, he understood that it was justified. Once, as a boy, watching his grandmother lying on her deathbed, he'd come to feel that her saintly expression was obscene in light of her suffering; now Sonja's face was lit by that same mild, sepulchral glow. The front of her linen chemise—one of seven she'd bought to bring to the New World— was bisected by a cord of blood and sputum. When he spoke her name she caught him by the wrist.

"I seem to have come down with something, Kaspar. Some kind of a chill."

Kaspar spoke her name again and knelt beside her. Her grip on his wrist relaxed slightly.

"I'd like to stay here for a while, if you don't mind. The porcelain is so cool against my cheek."

When a doctor was summoned—Yitzak Bauer, a childhood friend of the professor's—he reached a diagnosis before his coat was off. "Tuberculosis," he announced, in the bored tone of voice physicians reserve for bad news. "There'll be no *Comtesse Celeste* anytime soon, I'm afraid. Geronimo and Jesse James will have to wait."

To the end of his duration, my grandfather would still visibly flinch when he confessed to the relief he'd felt at Bauer's diagnosis. There was anxiety as well, of course—TB was not to be taken lightly—but at least the condition had developed in Vienna, the medical capital of Europe, and not in some trigger-happy American backwater where the snake-oil peddlers outnumbered the physicians. The more Kaspar considered it, the more convinced he became that this apparent setback was a blessing in disguise. It was true that he'd resigned his post at the university, and that their lease was about to expire; but their account at the Volksbank was surpassingly healthy, and they had plenty of friends in the city. Why change continents, he told himself, when it was so much easier to change one's mind?

With this thought percolating in his brain, Kaspar set out one August morning—slightly nervous, perhaps, but confident, all things considered—to have lunch with his brother at Trattner's. He'd spoken with Waldemar directly this time, and the exchange had been cordial in the extreme. He himself had been the one to suggest the location, intending it both as an olive branch and as a harmless joke; his brother had praised their goulash and suggested one o'clock.

Saint Stephen's Cathedral was tolling the hour when Kaspar arrived, slightly short of breath but otherwise composed. In accordance with C*F*P's stage directions, Waldemar was sitting at the same marble-topped table as sixteen years previous, sipping from the same fluted cup, attended by the same enticing Serb. Kaspar was amazed to see her and was on the verge of stammering that she hadn't changed a bit since 1922 when he saw that she was a different Serb entirely. Waldemar smiled as he shook Kaspar's hand. "We ought to kiss each other on both cheeks, I suppose," he said with a laugh, though the laugh he gave made very little noise.

"Well!" Kaspar said as his coffee arrived. It arrived without warning, impossibly quickly, which heightened the sense of predestination he'd been gripped by from the instant he'd sat down.

"Well!" echoed Waldemar, apparently as tongue-tied as he was. But that wasn't right, either—there was nothing tongue-tied about Waldemar. He was simply waiting, serene and all-powerful, for Kaspar to try his first gambit.

"You look different," said Kaspar, regretting it instantly.

"Fatter, you mean."

"Not at all!" But of course he was fatter. "I suppose so, yes. But I meant—I meant the rest of it."

"The rest of it?"

"Your monocle, for example."

Waldemar nodded. "I'm not wearing my monocle."

"My wife must have mentioned it," Kaspar said, then began coughing fiercely. He hadn't meant to bring her up so soon.

"Ah," said Waldemar, in a different tone of voice. "Your wife."

"That's right," Kaspar answered. "Sonja Toula. Your sister-in-law."

Then—suddenly, too soon—he was pleading his case, setting prudence and decorum aside, appealing to Waldemar's sense of conscience and of charity and to various other senses he very much doubted his brother possessed, letting his voice crack like an adolescent's and the tears run freely down his cheeks in the hope that they might gratify his enemy. It was the longest speech he'd ever made outside a lecture hall, and the most eloquent he'd made in any setting. When he was done his brother nodded amiably, as if in acknowledgment of a well-turned somersault, and made a cryptic gesture to the Serb.

"I can't extend my protection to Fräulein Silbermann at this time."

"She's my *wife*, Waldemar," Kaspar hissed. "And I'm not asking you to extend her your protection. I'm asking you to refrain from hauling her off to your chamber of horrors, like you did to poor Felix Ungarsky."

"That's true, I suppose," said Waldemar. "But when all is said and done, *Bruderchen*—and it will be very soon—it amounts to much the same thing, does it not?"

A silence fell, leisurely and fatal, during which my grandfather gaped at his brother in an excess of astonishment and loathing and his brother sipped the dregs of his *mélange*.

"What are you saying to me?" Kaspar got out finally. "Are you telling me that we should disappear?"

"That's for you to decide. I've done all that I can."

"What the hell does that mean?"

Waldemar heaved a good-natured sigh. "I got you those exit visas, didn't I?"

From the moment I left your brownstone, Mrs. Haven, I was a puzzle to my family, a frustration to my coworkers, and an irritant to every passing stranger. I stepped on commuters' shoe heels and got in the way of tourists' snapshots and jaywalked as though cars were made of butter. I seated myself in elegant restaurants, studied the menu intently and left without ordering a thing. My boss at the Xanthia—a red-nosed depressive named Susan B. Anthony—encouraged me to confide in her about my substance dependency; Palladian beat me at Risk thirteen times in a row; Van called repeatedly, apparently in the hope of talking business, and each time was forced to hang up in despair. In a word, Mrs. Haven, I'd become insufferable.

The ancient Pythagoreans, poets that they were, claimed that each instant of each day has a life of its own—an independent existence from the mind that perceives it—and by the end of that week I believed them. You and I saw each other when your schedule permitted, which was practically never; in the dead time between—often days at a stretch—I found myself at each successive second's mercy.

It was the middle of November, cold and grayscale and dismal, but New York had never looked so beautiful. I wandered the city with my hands in my pockets, muttering to myself like a drunk or an adman rehearsing a pitch, both of which—in one sense or another—I was. I made plans for the future on those rambles of mine that can only, in retrospect, be characterized as insane. I was going to finish my history, win some well-endowed prize, then sell the film rights for a modest fortune; I was going to elope with you to some sultry Central American republic—Nicaragua, maybe—and open a backpacker's hostel; I was going to run for public office (a comptroller of some kind—nothing fancy) with you in a navy pantsuit by my side. I thought of the Husband, on the rare occasions when he came to mind, with a kind of charitable contempt. I'd progressed from coward to megalomaniac in a single afternoon.

My aunt Enzian had once given my father—for reasons long since lost to time—a piece of advice that he'd passed on to me: "Fall for a single girl, Waldy, and you're competing with every other man on earth. Fall for a *married* woman, on the other hand, and you're only competing with one." Though Enzian had always frightened me—she was the kind of person, to put it generously, whose patience with children was moderate—I admired her insight into the economics of sex, especially since (as she'd once told me proudly) she'd never once had her "chastity impugned" in the whole of her duration. She was less capable of lying than a pocket calculator, so she must have believed the advice she gave Orson. And as we both know, Mrs. Haven, she was right.

I'd tried to impugn *your* chastity, God knows, on that first death-defying afternoon. You'd let me drape you across my lap on that sad little beanbag of yours, even fondle you a little, but your sweater stayed on and your buttons stayed buttoned. Your shoes came off after a while, but only grudgingly: it was against your better judgment, you informed me. (I couldn't help wondering, as I held your bare feet in my trembling hands, which aspect of our situation could possibly *not* be against your better judgment— but I kept my mouth shut.) Incredible as it seems to me now, I was in no particular hurry. I was prepared to stand by for as long as it took the last spark of your common sense to die.

Not to say I wasn't horny, Mrs. Haven. Since dropping out of college I'd been practically septic with lust. By my twenty-first birthday, a few weeks before Van's party, I was running through a *Decameron*'s worth of obscenity for every respectable thought. You'd made your entrance, in other words, when my defenses were at their weakest, and your own powers—whether or not you cared or understood, or even noticed—were at their indefatigable peak.

You rarely wore makeup, because it struck you as gratuitous, and no one who saw you would have disagreed. Your body looked immaculate by daylight, as though you'd just been created, and at night you glowed like interstellar dust. It overwhelmed me at times, I confess—it fried me like an overloaded circuit. I envied Haven in those moments, it's true, but also every other sentient being who'd ever known you, down to your most trivial acquaintances; just as I'm jealous, as I write this, of the self-regarding fool that I was then.

To distract myself when these paroxysms hit, I'd steer my thoughts back to plans from the pre-Haven era, half-forgotten now and very long delayed. I hadn't come to New York on a whim: I'd come for information—even guidance, of a kind—and I'd gotten what I needed only days before we met. I was on a covert mission, one I needed time and money to complete: money for travel, first to Vienna, then to the Czech Republic, then to places still unknown. In my most presumptuous fantasies, I asked you for your help, and you said yes.

In those hours—usually late at night—when even this vision lost its mesmeric power, I fell back on the only source of distraction I had left: my history. I'd been blocked for a time, Mrs. Haven, as any historian would be when writing about something he still barely understood. For most of my duration the truth had been kept from me, and I was terrified of the countless blanks that needed filling in. You'll laugh at me, and rightly so, but I feared the judgment of posterity. Since meeting you, however, I'd hit on a solution. If you're reading this, Mrs. Haven, then the borderline-impossible has already occurred, and there's nothing to be gained by being coy. My solution was to approach this history as a kind of novel—with dialogue and narration, the occasional sex scene, and even an attempt at atmospherics—and to write it for an audience of one.

∞

I kept clear of your neighborhood for seven full days: you'd told me it was risky, which was very likely true. By the eighth night, however, my mental distractions were losing their juju, and by morning my self-control lay in tatters. I woke up with a hangover I'd done nothing to deserve, queasy and drained of emotion, and knew that something had to happen soon.

I didn't have long to wait. Less than an hour later, as I lay bunched on the floor like an old pair of boxers, a padded legal envelope arrived by UPS. I tore the package open and found Fielding's silver-bound opus inside, carefully dog-eared at page 41:

> *THE MAGICAL VIRTUE OF CHASTITY.—Belief in the magical potency of chastity and asceticism is widespread, from ancient times down to the modern.*
>
> *Influential chiefs of the Congo keep in their service a virgin to care for their arrows, shields, rugs and other instruments of war. They are hung up in her room, generally speaking, or in a convenient tree. It is believed that the girl's purity imbues these objects with some extraordinary virtue, which their user, in turn, "catches." If the custodian loses her virginity, the articles are destroyed as tainted and dangerous to those who would use them.*
>
> *As late as the first century A.D., it was believed that the Vestals of Rome had the power by a certain prayer to immobilize runaway slaves where they stood, if they were still within the city walls. A similar power was attributed to one of the "gangas" of Doango, in Mozambique.*

For the second time in our acquaintance, Mrs. Haven, you'd sent me a code I was helpless to crack. "Influential chiefs" of the Congo? The "*gangas*" of Mozambique? Had you sent me the book as a joke, or was it precisely the opposite: a veiled cry for help? And in what sense, exactly, could a rug be considered an instrument of war?

I never needed to break this particular code, as it turned out, because you rang my buzzer that same afternoon. You were out of breath when you entered, like a Hollywood adultress, and you couldn't seem to look me in the eye. I took the Eskimo coat from your shoulders and kicked a stack of photocopies off the couch. You had on a hideous pair of Adidas cross-trainers, the kind a Boca Raton retiree would wear, and rumpled blue cotton pajamas. The pajamas were emblazoned with a design that I couldn't decipher: it might have been a pattern of storm clouds, or whirlpools, or even tiny, slate-gray galaxies. You glanced down at yourself, frowning a little, as though someone had dressed you without your consent. You had just taken a step: perhaps the biggest of our secret life together. You must have been as terrified as I was.

"What's this?" you said, picking up one of my notebooks.

"Nothing," I mumbled. "Just notes and such."

"Notes and such for what?"

"For that project I mentioned at my cousin's party."

"What sort of project? I can't quite remember." You hefted the notebook like a piece of evidence. "Are you working on a novel, Mr. Tompkins?"

"Jesus no," I said, giving a tight little laugh. "One of those per family's enough."

"You've got a *novelist* in your family?" You narrowed your eyes. "No more cloak-and-dagger, Walter. Spill the beans."

I'd trapped myself, Mrs. Haven, and I knew it. I felt the familiar pool of shame condensing at the base of my spine, the shame I'd felt for years whenever the subject of Orson came up; and there were definite reasons, given who your husband was, to keep his name from you. But there was no way out for me but straight ahead.

"It's my father, believe it or not. But his books aren't the kind—"

"I wonder if I've heard of him. Is his name Tompkins, too?"

"I don't want to talk about this anymore, Mrs. Haven."

"Fine with me," you said blithely, making an elaborate dusting-off gesture with your hands. You were used to men not wanting to talk about their fathers, apparently. I racked my brain for some new topic, anything at all, but I needn't have bothered. You had an announcement to make.

"I talked to the Husband this morning. I told him about our arrangement."

I counted down from ten before I spoke.

"Our arrangement?"

You nodded. "I decided it was time."

Images of the Husband overran my frontal lobe: photographs culled from magazines, mostly, of him shaking the hands of movie stars and hedge-fund managers and minor heads of state. Any temptation I might have felt to come clean—to tell you why I'd concealed my identity, or what I knew about the man whose name you bore—withered when I considered his position in the world. The walls of the apartment seemed to be vibrating faintly, as though a subway train were passing underneath us. You waited patiently for me to answer.

"What was his reaction, if you don't mind my asking?"

"He laughed."

The tremors grew stronger. "Why would he do that?"

"He laughs when he's angry. He's conflict-averse."

"I think you need to tell me what he said, Mrs. Haven."

"He said he'd deal with you in time. Those were his words exactly. 'I'll deal with Mr. Tompkins, dear—he calls me "dear"—in time.'"

I said nothing to that. The vibrations had stopped.

"It's not worth worrying about, Walter. Really. He's said this kind of thing before."

"And what's happened before? When he's said that, I mean. Did he actually—"

"He doesn't *know* you, Walter. He couldn't hurt you if he wanted to."

"What else did he say? I'd like the exact phrasing, if possible."

This seemed to amuse you: you sat up and worked your face into a frown. "*'I appreciate your candor, oh woman, destroyer of worlds,'*" you declaimed in a mock baritone. "*'Thanks for telling me about this pal of yours.'*"

By now my throat and tongue were dry as chalk. "There's not much to tell, when you get right down to it. Is there?"

Your eyes went flat instantly. "Not much to tell?"

"I only mean—"

"I thought you were in love with me, Walter. That was my understanding."

"Mrs. Haven, if you'll just—"

"You *did* say that at some point, didn't you?"

I tried and failed to find the voice to speak. You returned my glassy stare without a flinch.

"I'll bet I can guess the reason for your hesitation, Walter. Would you like me to guess?"

"Hold on. Hold on just a second—"

"You think it was premature to tell the Husband, because I haven't let you fuck me yet. And that's by no means unreasonable. That makes excellent sense." You nodded to yourself. "We're basically strangers, after all."

You sat upright now, your back unnaturally straight, like a typist or a judge behind the bench. Your lips were compressed into a tight and blood-less crimp: Fielding's "cupid's bow" was gone without a trace. I saw you suddenly as you might have looked at age six or seven, struggling to control your temper, sitting by yourself in some neglected corner. But when I tried to imagine the rest of that faraway room, or the house you'd grown up in, or the people who'd lived in it with you, the picture went dark. You were right, I realized. The two of us were strangers to each other.

"Mrs. Haven," I said quietly, "you haven't even told me your first name."

You gave a slight start, as though I'd just spoken Latin, or barked like a terrier, or whispered to you that your breasts were showing. One of them was, in fact, which didn't help matters. You took a long time to answer, staring off into space—or into spacetime, possibly—and when you spoke again your voice was soft and slow.

"Hildegard."

"Excuse me?"

"My mother, God rest her, was obsessed with her Bavarian heritage." You smiled crookedly. "That's just one of the things the Husband saved me from."

"What else?"

"Hmm?"

"Tell me what else he saved you from. I'd like to know."

"Do you really want an answer, Mr. Tompkins? Are you sure you want to hear my sordid tale?"

I was anything but sure, in fact, especially when I noticed your expression. "Just play down the romantic bits, if you don't mind."

You shook your head. "That won't be hard at all."

∞

It took you the better part of an hour to perform the vivisection of your marriage, and I paid close attention, painful though it was, because it taught me just how wrong I'd been about you. Your glib, easy air fell away as you spoke, and without it you were awkward and unsure. You weren't the coddled debutante that I'd imagined: you'd been a lonely, angry child, your girlhood shadowed by your parents' failures. Haven had discovered you in a secondhand-record store—Rox in Your Head Vinyl in Middletown, Connecticut—on the day you'd finally given up on college. He was a boyish thirty-four at the time, already famous, already rich, getting ready to distance himself (in public, at least) from the cut-rate religion he'd founded. You were ready to distance yourself from everything.

Your father had been kicked out of Wesleyan's German Department two years earlier for preaching (and/or practicing) *die freie Liebe* with his students; he now spent his time drinking lager and writing fascist screeds against the state of Israel, which your mother—devoted spouse, Germanophile, and quiet anti-Semite that she was—mailed to *The Boston Globe* in semiweekly packets. Your job kept the family in bagels and six-packs; occasionally your mother took in boarders. Haven came into your life, as you put it, "like a Martian abduction," bearing offerings from faraway, exotic worlds. Your previous boyfriend had been a video store clerk and part-time pot dealer; your new boyfriend was the leader of a cult, with disciples in the NFL and Hollywood and the House of Representatives. Your parents hated him, which expedited things. You were married in a courthouse in Poughkeepsie.

From that relative high point, things went rapidly downhill, in such an effortless, frictionless, self-understood way that it barely seemed a topic for discussion. A full year into your marriage, you still had only the haziest sense of what the man you'd married liked and what he didn't, let alone what he cared for or believed. He met your every word and gesture with a warm, attentive smile, and gave answers to your questions that evaporated when exposed to sunlight. You had no interest in the "church" he represented, and he seemed to have no interest in it either. He left for work each morning like any other husband, and in the evenings he talked sports and investments and music and cars—even fashion, when you introduced the subject—but never religion. He seemed to regard theology and science with the same blank-eyed indifference. In time you realized that he despised them.

You found your new life unusual—freakish, really—but you were still too dazed and grateful to ask questions. Haven cheerfully supported you in breaking with your parents. Your every worldly whim was gratified. Each night he came to you and told you what he wanted: in this regard, at least, his preferences were clear. He referred to the act as "synchrony" or "junction": the only cult-speak he used in your company. He seemed less in search of pleasure than of information, or possibly—you sometimes thought—some form of proof. And he always left your bedroom disappointed.

A year went by, then two years, then—astonishingly, unaccountably—a decade. Your husband was never less than cordial. You'd had the idea to open a record shop of your own, maybe even a boutique reissue label, specializing in the sixties teen garage rock that you loved; but though he repeatedly promised to put up the "seed capital"—and though it was painfully clear he had money to burn—something always seemed to interfere. You participated in junction each night at 23:15 EST, his schedule permitting. He traveled much of the year, and was never reachable during the final hour of the day, though he returned your calls at midnight without fail. You had occasional affairs of your own, and once tried, semiseriously, to leave him; but you'd lost all sense of how to be alone. Your life *was* freakish—more than freakish: perverse—but you'd grown to accept it.

Then you met me at my cousin's party.

You fell silent once you'd finished, staring bashfully down into your lap. A car alarm sounded nearby, invasive and shrill, but you barely reacted. You seemed to have forgotten where you were.

"*Hildegard,*" I said tentatively. "I have to admit, never in a million years—"

"I agree with you, Walter. A million at least." You gave a tired smile and took my hand. "But you're allowed to call me Mrs. Haven."

For once I understood you perfectly. "I'd consider it an honor," I said. "Hildegard doesn't suit you."

You sighed and shook your head. "It never did."

"You're more of an Irmgard, I'd say. Or a Brünnhilde."

"That's right, Walter. And you're more of a Gandalf."

"Mrs. Haven?"

"Yes, Walter?"

"I'd like you to stay here tonight."

"I thought you might." You brought my hand to your mouth and bit down lightly on the knuckle of my thumb. "That's why I came with my pajamas on."

∞

If I stay hunched over this card table forever, Mrs. Haven—if the timestream doesn't ever readmit me—I might one day find words to do justice to that stupefying night. For hours on end we were as deliberate as forensic scientists, committing the most obscure recesses of each other's body to memory; the rest of the time we rolled around like chimpanzees. I tried to catalog the moles and scars and freckles on your body—to *catalog* them, not just count them, beginning with the heel of your right foot—but I never made it past the halfway point. And what a halfway point it was, Mrs. Haven. I could have lived out my duration there and died a happy man.

Did I wonder why you cared for me? I'll admit it—I did wonder. You were the stuff of daydreams, after all, and I was a dropout with dubious posture. I was the opposite of the Husband in every respect; this ought to have reassured me, I suppose, but it tended to have the opposite effect. When all else failed, I fell back on the one thing I was certain of: I adored you, Mrs. Haven, and you liked to be adored. On that first night it seemed explanation enough.

In between sessions of monkey business we asked each other aimless, drowsy questions. I was ecstatically unaware of what the future held—our escape to Vienna, our doomed trip to Znojmo, and everything that would happen afterward—and I'd have told you everything, consequences be damned, if only you'd asked. But your mind was firmly on the present moment. You made love exactly as I'd imagined you would: clumsily at first, then earnestly, then angrily, then lost to the world altogether. I felt half-dead by morning, to tell you the truth. But my other half felt indestructible.

"That was very nice, Walter," you whispered sometime around dawn. "I knew you were a man of many gifts."

"I appreciate your confidence, Mrs. Haven."

In the light from the street your hair glowed like an angel's in some pre-Raphaelite painting of questionable taste, or even in something by Klimt. I felt painfully, unconscionably happy.

"Do you really come from a family of physicists?"

"Failed physicists," I mumbled, nuzzling your armpit. The brass-colored hair there smelled faintly of nutmeg. "*Crackpots* is the technical term."

"That's too bad," you said, yawning. "I was hoping you could build a time machine."

On any other day I'd have snapped to attention at that, wide-awake and suspicious; as it was, I only sat up slightly. "A time machine?"

"I wouldn't want to go *too* far back. I'm not ambitious." You ran your close-cut fingernails across my scalp. "About thirty minutes, let's say."

It wasn't easy, in my fuddled condition, to reconstruct what had happened thirty minutes before. Then it came back to me.

"You're in luck, Mrs. Haven. That can be arranged."

"It can? How fantastic!"

"There's nothing fantastic about it."

"Prove it."

"In the interest of science, I will." I took you by the shoulders. "I'll ask you to lie back down, if you don't mind."

Thirty-three minutes later I was nuzzling your armpit again. The brass-colored stubble smelled faintly of nutmeg.

"That was very nice, Walter," you whispered.

"You see, Mrs. Haven? I hope I've convinced you."

You arched your back and nodded. "I *knew* you were a man of many gifts."

∞

But by morning you were restless again, preoccupied and tense and short of breath. I opened my eyes to find you standing at the window, buttoning up your pajamas, staring anxiously down at the street. My nakedness felt wrong to me suddenly. I crawled back under the comforter, wrapping it around me like somebody saved from drowning.

"What sort of family do you come from, Walter?" you said as you pulled on your sneakers. Apparently it was time for you to go.

"A tribe of honest laborers," I answered.

"Honest laborers?" you said, turning up the collar of your coat. "Is that true?"

"Not so much," I admitted.

You seated yourself at the foot of the bed, demonstratively out of my reach. You wanted to talk, not to cuddle: that was only too clear. You wanted to get down to terms.

"Ask me a question, Walter. A question about myself. I'll tell you anything you want to know."

I thought hard for a moment. "What are the chances that the Husband—"

"It's important that you tell me where you come from, Walter. I've spent a decade sleeping next to a cipher. Can you imagine what that's like?"

"I'm certainly willing—"

"I need to know that I can trust you, and that *you* feel that you can trust me. I don't think I can do this otherwise."

A feeling took hold of me then that I've often had since: the suspicion that crucial precedents were being set, that matters of weight and consequence hung in the balance, and that I barely had a clue what was at stake. In one sense, of course, I knew what was at stake very well: you were at stake, Mrs. Haven. But this knowledge only paralyzed me further.

"You're always laying down the law," I heard myself stammer.

"I'm not sure what you mean by that, Walter. Are you trying to say—"

"I'm trying to say that from the moment we met, from our first conversation, you've been the one setting the terms. You've never asked me what *my* terms might be—not even once. What makes you so sure that I don't have any?"

You sat forward, tucking a lock of sleep-creased hair behind your ear. I'd managed to make you self-conscious, if nothing else.

"What are your terms, Walter?"

I didn't have any, of course. None. I'd have taken you under every possible set of conditions. I sank back into the pillows with a groan.

"Something shifted while we were asleep," you said. "I don't know what, exactly, but something's different. Our equilibrium seems to be shot."

If I'd known you at all, I'd have taken this pronouncement in stride, maybe even agreed; since I didn't, I panicked.

"I don't believe in this."

You looked startled. "In what?"

"In *anything*." I waved my arms peevishly. "I don't believe in anything that's happened."

Why in God's name, Mrs. Haven, did I say such a thing? To throw you off balance? To keep my need for you from swallowing me whole? Whatever the reason, the result was terrifying. You rose from the bed with exaggerated calm and did up the leather toggles of your coat. Your face was as white and empty as a plate.

"I'd be a fool to believe in all this, Walter, if you don't. Wouldn't I?"

"Please sit down, Mrs. Haven. Don't go just yet."

"I'll be gone in a minute," you said, searching the floor for your hat. "There's something that I want to tell you first."

"Mrs. Haven, if you'd just—"

"The day you followed me home, I showed you what the Husband had done to my little clubhouse—with the Klimts and so on. Do you remember?"

"Of course I—"

"I told you we'd been fighting, but you never asked me why." You smiled. "You must not have believed in what was happening then, either."

That brought me out of bed at last. "You have to understand, Mrs. Haven, nothing's ever prepared me—what I mean is, where I come from—"

"Where exactly *do* you come from, Mr. Tompkins?"

"I don't have any clothes on. If you'll give me the chance—"

"We'd been fighting about you, Walter. I told the Husband that I was leaving him, that I'd met someone else, and he reacted in the way you might expect. He asked me—as anyone would, who's been given that sort of news—whether I was absolutely sure." You picked your hat up from the floor. "I wonder if you can guess how I replied."

I opened my mouth, met your withering look, and felt my answer curdle in my throat.

"No?" you said, stepping out onto the landing. "I'm sorry to hear that, Walter. Maybe it will come to you in time."

XIII

THERE'S A PAINTING at the Met by Giancarlo Beppino, some forgotten also-ran of the Venetian Rennaissance, that comes to mind whenever I try to picture Kaspar and Sonja's exodus. An unassuming little oil in a badly lit niche—*Joseph and Mary's Flight into Egypt*—it twitches to eager life for anyone willing to stop. An underfed Joseph leads two gaunt, walleyed mules down a gulch; a fat, insipid virgin sits sidesaddle on the second mule's back, holding a toddler under her arm like the Sunday edition of *The Wall Street Journal.* In the middle distance, for no apparent reason, an angel is whacking at a rosebush with a stick.

The figures themselves bear no likeness to my star-crossed kin: Sonja was desperately ill by then, and my grandfather, in the sole surviving snapshot from that time, has the oxlike expression of a more classical Joseph, a man prepared for certain disappointment. More important than any of the figures, however—chubby Mary included—are the slick, greasy clouds Beppino packs his sky with: shadowless masses, hideously compacted, glistening in the nauseous light of that landscape like marrow smeared across a crust of bread. To me, Mrs. Haven, those diseased-looking clouds have always seemed the color of insanity, and the sky above Vienna, whenever I imagine that most ominous of summers, is practically bursting with them.

∞

Kaspar went home from Trattner's on foot, grateful for the reprieve, storing away the sights and sounds and smells of the city for future reference;

no sooner had he arrived home, however, than he announced to his family that they'd be leaving for America that same afternoon. His daughters were too young to fully grasp the import of the news, and his in-laws were too old, perhaps, or too astonished; Sonja was overjoyed, as he'd known she would be. She emerged from her room fully dressed and expectant, as if she'd foreseen his sudden change of heart; she looked clearheaded and rested, better than she'd seemed in months. Kaspar had expected her to ask the reason for his decision—for its abruptness, if nothing else—but she confined herself to questions of logistics. Her equanimity, which had always been a comfort, now unnerved him. He wondered, not for the first time, whether his wife had the slightest idea what lay in store for them; then he reminded himself that it no longer mattered. The choice—such as it was—had been made for them.

The journey by train to Genoa was incongruously festive, as though the family were setting out on a grand tour. The six of them had a first-class compartment to themselves—an indulgence the professor insisted on—and the Alps goose-stepped past, inundating the room with their temperate, vertiginous green, as if the car were a camera obscura for the benefit of the silent, awestruck twins. The Silbermanns sat for hours at the window with Enzian and Gentian between them, pointing out castles and cloisters with proprietary pride. Sonja spoke only rarely, and then in a whisper—and yet she was the center of it all. Kaspar had never seen her look more regal.

They pulled into Genoa at five in the morning, early enough to watch fishmongers with pious faces set out iced trays of whiting and calamari and buckets of spasming eels. The family's trunks, which had seemed so enormous in their Ringstrasse parlor, looked small and unassuming on the pier. The *Comtesse Celeste* had been H.M.S. *Gloucester* until the year before; she'd seen three decades' service as a coal and livestock transport, and it showed. She was too big for her mooring and too close to the shrimping boats that flanked her, and the pilings bowed and shuddered as she heaved. Kaspar took all this in obliquely, peripherally, as someone drunk or half-asleep might do. Genoa was a caesura to him, a blank interval, unexpected and unknowable and empty. He found himself impatient to keep on.

The professor—who still seemed to think they were on holiday—disappeared with the twins for the better part of an hour, and returned with chocolate stains on his lapel; in keeping with the fever dream in which they'd all become complicit, no one asked where they'd gone off to, let alone what he'd been thinking. The rest of the day was spent unpacking and repacking, making last-minute purchases of everyday items—shaving soap, twine, baking soda—that might not exist in the western hemisphere, and avoiding all but the most necessary talk. The Silbermanns, especially, grew stiller and grayer as the hours went by; but it wasn't until early that evening, when the *Comtesse*'s whistle sounded, that Kaspar guessed the reason for the change.

"You're not coming," he said. "You're not coming with us."

It was his mother-in-law who answered. "You'll be back soon enough," she said brightly, gripping her husband's blotched and birdlike hand. "You'll run out of soap and well-made shoes and decent butter. Also, I've heard there's no hygienic paper. They eat and wave hello with their right hands only, and use their left hands to—"

"You're thinking of the southern states, Mama," Sonja put in, winking at Kaspar over Frau Silbermann's bonnet. "Alabama and so on. We'll make sure to keep to the north."

Kaspar stared at his wife for a moment, struck dumb by her glib reply. But it was possible that Sonja had missed her mother's meaning—she'd been so weary and abstracted recently. At times she barely answered to her name.

Everyone fell silent when they arrived at the quay: Kaspar due to his steadily increasing perplexity, the Silbermanns so as not to upset the children, Sonja for reasons known to her alone. The significance of the hour seemed to have dawned on her at last. After the twins had been coddled and kissed she sent them away with their father, to the end of the quay, while she spoke with her parents alone. She was a long time with each of them—her mother, particularly—and when she beckoned Kaspar back to her he found their faces flushed and wet with tears.

"Goodbye to you, Kaspar." His mother-in-law kissed him fiercely on both cheeks—how often had they touched in twenty years?—then propelled her husband forward.

"Best of luck to you, Toula," Silbermann croaked, extending a kid-gloved hand with an absurdly dated flourish. Kaspar had always laughed at the old man's stiffness and remove—had laughed at it openly, in fact, in recent years—so it was with no small embarrassment that he found himself drawn into an embrace. An idea struck him then, fully formed and entire, like a line of sentimental poetry: *This man has given me everything that I hold dear.*

A few minutes later, looking down from the deck (second class now, not first), another sensation overcame him, one he was even less accustomed to: the intimation, building quietly to a certainty, that what he was seeing was a projection in a vast and secret cinema. Genoa's cramped, chaotic harbor, its oddly marrow-colored sky, the stevedores hosing detritus off the quay—everything he saw appeared heightened, imbued with morality and portent, a judgment on the easy life he'd known. He was part of the film, perhaps even one of its principal players. But he sensed that it was on its final reel.

Nonsense! he told himself, holding Gentian up to look over the rail. Everyone feels this way at a departure. Nothing's ending, because there isn't any film.

"This is happening," Sonja whispered, gripping him by the elbow. "Isn't that so, Kasparchen? Tell me, please, that all of this is real."

"This is happening, Sonja," he said, and felt the truth of it as a rawness in his throat. "They're weighing anchor now. We're shoving off."

"All right. If you're sure."

He turned to regard her as she drew herself up, chin thrown forward like a figurehead, teardrops guttering unnoticed from her crow's feet to her jaw. What to say to her in such a moment?

"Sonja—"

"Blow a kiss to your *opa* and *oma*, Enzian," Sonja called to their daughter, who was standing apart from them, gazing impassively at the quay below. "When you see them next, you'll be the Queen of Time and Space, you know. And I'll be dead."

Kaspar would never be able to say with certainty, in years to come, whether his wife had truly said those words as he remembered them—but by then, of course, they had already passed into legend. He doubted his ears even at the time, and Enzian was no help to him at all. She continued to look evenly down at the quay, as mature for her age as her mother seemed girlish for hers, holding loosely to the crenellated rail.

∞

No sooner had the *Comtesse* left port than Sonja fell backward gracefully—almost eagerly—onto the bright, hissing bed of her illness. Kaspar managed to keep the truth from the captain and the crew for some time, out of fear of being forcibly put ashore (he put the blame for her condition on seasickness, which was rampant everywhere on that decrepit tub), but finally his fear for her prevailed. From Genoa to Viareggio to Naples to Palermo she grew steadily worse, the readiness of her submission somehow shameless; Kaspar, who'd never succumbed to jealousy in thirty years of marriage, found himself now, as his wife slowly left him, behaving like a cuckold in a farce. He attended to her every requirement, taking all of his meals in their stateroom, rarely letting her out of his sight. His attentions grew more oppressive by the day—he sensed this himself—but he was utterly helpless to curb them.

Sonja's condition worsened in the course of the passage from Spain, as did Kaspar's own. The ship had an excellent onboard physician (the elegant, somewhat horse-faced Dr. Tildy, formerly of the Prussian cavalry) but Kaspar—who'd welcomed Tildy, on his first visit, with tears of gratitude—soon came to resent his intrusions. His wife was winnowing before his eyes, turning brittle and yellow as a scrap of old newsprint, and he realized now, much too late, that he lacked the grace and fortitude to bear it. Unable to restrain himself, he would ask—would *demand* to know—how she was feeling half a dozen times an hour. Enzian and Gentian were no help to him, either: they were absorbed in a narrative of their own invention, whispering together for hours on end, looking back and forth between their mother's bed and the sea beyond the porthole as though there were no difference between them.

Just after dawn, three days out from Gibraltar, Kaspar awoke wide-eyed and alert, as though someone beside him had whispered his name. The same force that roused him brought him onto his feet, accustomed by now to the pitch of the ship, and steered him gently toward the open door. He was aware that he was barefoot—that he was stark naked, in fact—and that the morning was unusually cold. Snow was falling in flurries, although it was still early autumn. He was dimly aware, without finding it strange, that he and his family were alone on the *Comtesse Celeste*. He glanced down at the twins, side by side on their backs, like two fish in the bottom of a boat. Then he stepped out to join Sonja at the rail.

"There you are," she said. Her voice was hoarse from disuse. "I've been trying to get you up. To talk to me."

He looked past her at the dishwater-colored ocean, translucent and jagged in the September light, a roiling field of chipped and age-worn china. Sonja was smiling at him, lovely as ever, wrapped in one of her white linen gowns. It put him in mind of something. He was beginning, by small but steady increments, to understand that he should feel surprised—but even that discovery felt familiar. She'd been one lifelong surprise to him, after all.

"I've been sick," she said.

He nodded.

"You've been sick, too."

It was difficult for him to answer. "You've been in bed for ten days," he said. "You've had a high fever. I can appreciate your wanting fresh air, my darling, but it might be for the best—"

"*Ach!* It's been longer than that," Sonja said. "I've been sick since our first night together." She raised one slender arm to shade her eyes. "I was in love with you, you see. It ended badly."

What she said was distressing, and he intended to ask what in God's name she meant, but he found himself saying something else entirely. "It didn't end badly," he said, placing his hand over hers. "We've been wonderfully happy. If it's a sickness, we've been fortunate to catch it."

"All right," she said, turning her back on the sea. "It's all right, Kasparchen. Let's go to the beginning."

Her body showed clearly through the wave-colored linen, gaunt and frail from the fever, and he knew, in that instant, when and where he'd seen that gown before. It was the same one she'd worn, apple-cheeked and defiant, on the day his earthly fate had been decided. The noise of the sea fell away and the outline of her form began to flicker. The deck and ocean were struck, rolled away like a stage set, and he was back in the tubercular light of the Jandek, the soles of his shoes sticking to the beer-soaked floor, watching a girl of not-quite-seventeen light a cigarette. He murmured her name—he knew this girl well, after all—and she looked up and laughed, surprised to see him there. He straightened in his booth as she came toward him.

∞

The man who staggered off the train in Buffalo, New York's Union Station on New Year's Day 1939, gripping the shoulders of his daughters as if he needed them to walk, was so changed that his wife's second cousin—the notorious "Buffalo Bill"—passed them by without slowing his step. Wilhelm Knarschitz was a pursy, preoccupied man ("the opposite of any kind of cowboy," my grandfather wrote in his diary) with the unfortunate habit of chewing on the ends of his mustache. He failed to notice his nieces altogether, on account of the cameo photograph he held stiff-armed in front of him, like a fetish to deflect the evil eye. On his second go-round, Kaspar (who had no picture to go by) made an educated guess and caught his cousin-in-law by the sleeve—which was lucky, since Wilhelm's fetish was no use to anyone. It was a picture of Sonja at the Washerwomen's Ball.

"Kaspar, is it? Delightful!" Wilhelm stammered in yankified Yiddish. He took hold of his cousin-in-law by both the elbow and the shoulder, shaking every part of him except his hand. "Professor Kaspar Toula, as I live and perspire!"

"Kaspar *Tolliver*," my grandfather corrected him. "We're Americans now. We've put Europe behind us."

"You have trunks?" demanded Wilhelm. "Of course you have trunks! What we need is a porter." He squinted up the platform, still oblivious to the presence of the twins. "Where's that cousin of mine?"

"In the water," said Enzian.

Wilhelm skipped lightly backward. "Whatever do you mean, dear?" When Enzian didn't answer, he stared bug-eyed at Kaspar. "Whatever does she mean?"

"In the *ocean*," Gentian murmured from the far side of the trunk. "The Atlantic. We left her down there."

There'd been a point in Kaspar's duration—not too far in the past—when such an exchange would have fascinated him, proof as it was of his daughters' difference from other children; now he did no more than shrug his shoulders. "I wrote you a letter from New York," he said, in response to Wilhelm's flabbergasted look. "Did you read it?"

"*Naturally* I read it. I'm here to meet you, aren't I?" Wilhelm hesitated. "Of course, there may have been certain points—"

"I have something to tell you," said Kaspar. "Sit down on this trunk."

Wilhelm's reaction to the news of Sonja's death was no less singular than the twins' had been: he sat utterly still for the space of a breath, covering his mouth with two fingers, then smoothed down his pant legs and clenched his eyes shut. Gentian and Enzian studied him the way they studied everything. Kaspar sat down next to him and waited.

By the time Wilhelm's eyes finally opened, the four of them were alone on the platform. He drew himself up, heaved a decorous sigh, and brushed a single tear from each eye corner.

"In light of what you've told me," he said, "My course of action is clear. I'm prepared to formally adopt the children."

Kaspar explained to his cousin-in-law that adoption wouldn't be necessary, given that he himself was still alive, and Wilhelm looked appropriately relieved. In all but a strictly legal sense, however, he *did* come to adopt Enzian and Gentian—and even, in those precarious first months, Kaspar himself. The promised apartment was set aside in favor of Wilhelm's comfortable sandstone manse on Voorhees Avenue, and Kaspar's arithmetical gifts were put to immediate use. Fastidious as Buffalo Bill was in his person—his hair immaculately Brylcreemed, his twill suits never less than *einwandfrei*—the accounts of Empress Sisi's Cabinet, his jewelry shop, were the bookkeeping equivalent of smoldering dung. As Providence (or fate, or random chance) would have it, Kaspar had materialized in his cousin-in-law's life at precisely the moment at which he was most desperately required.

The challenge of transmuting chaos into order—bordering, as it did in the case of Wilhelm's accounts, on outright alchemy—turned out to be the ideal task to arrest Kaspar's descent into despair. The twins, for their part, got along with their uncle beautifully, in spite of the fact that he regarded them—when he noticed them at all—with the same benign befuddlement he'd first shown at the station. A *Kindermädchen* was procured from somewhere (a poker-faced drudge whose German was as unintelligible as her English) and Wilhelm obligingly picked up the tab. His own sainted mother had died the previous year, and he was still mourning her passionately: he never failed to kiss his fingertips and hold them up to heaven when Mutter Knarschitz was mentioned, which caused the twins to snicker with delight.

Buffalo Bill, in other words, was nothing like the character Sonja had dreamed up for him, for which my grandfather was deeply grateful. He was grateful for practically everything, in fact, over the course of that first stunned, defenseless year. In haughtier days, Mrs. Haven, he might have found much to disapprove of in the life he'd fallen into; but Kaspar was a new man now, with a social security number and a name that still rang foreign to his ears, and disapproval was an Old World luxury. A life of some sort was conceivable in this bullish border town; even—with considerably less struggle than he'd feared—a measure of contentment. There was nothing else that he could think to wish for.

∞

Thanks to the vast, choppy lake at its doorstep (and the canal extending like a 363-mile drainpipe out the back), Buffalo was one of the richest cities in the United States, Chicago's closest rival as the Paris of the Plains. Honeymoons were spent there; songs were written extolling its glamour; a belt of steel plants on the city's south side (if the wind was right) made for hyperbolic, lilac-tinted sunsets. The Great Depression's scars were freshly healed— or freshly powdered over, better said—and the attitude of the citizenry was one of fierce, bulldoggish confidence. A greater contrast to Vienna was hard to imagine. *Sonja was right about that much*, Kaspar thought, *if nothing else*.

As the months went by, my grandfather's mourning took on a peculiar cast—one that would have been inconceivable before the concept of spacetime was proposed. If time was (as science now insisted) best understood as a fourth dimension, then it was erroneous to think of past events as having ceased to be. The past, Kaspar reasoned, is most accurately conceived of as a continent we've emigrated from, or better still as a kind of archipelago: a series of nearly contiguous islands, self-contained and autonomous, that we're constantly in the process of forsaking, simply by moving through time. Like all things past, his wife existed in a zone of the continuum that was inaccessible to him now. This by no means meant that she no longer *was*.

On occasion—after a nightcap or two, or on a day when the twins had been especially good—this way of thinking actually brought him comfort.

He had a great deal to live for, he reminded himself. He could have stayed in Vienna if he'd wanted to die, and saved himself and his girls (not to mention poor Wilhelm) a great deal of trouble. "But they couldn't snuff *us*, those goddamn death fetishists," he'd growl at my father years later, his tongue primed by sweet British sherry. "We Tollivers are too inquisitive to die."

Buffalo Bill was a "confirmed bachelor"—with all the quirks and predilections that implied in that era—but he insisted on taking his cousin-in-law, on the second and fourth Friday of each month, to Feinberg's Star Burlesque Revue downtown. Wilhelm showed less interest in the gambolings onstage than if he'd been at a lecture on personal hygiene, but there was no doubt that the place excited him. He seemed intoxicated by the spotlights and the wine-dark velvet seats, by the cackling and the coarse talk of the crowd, and he barely breathed until the houselights came back up. My grandfather (who enjoyed the show for less poetic reasons) wondered what it was that thrilled his cousin-in-law so deeply, but he resisted the urge to inquire. An important clue, however, was provided in the person of the balcony usher, a Polish kid with thick blond curls and eyes the depthless green of Nordsee ice. There always seemed to be some confusion about their seats when they sat in the balcony, and the usher's help was invariably required. "I'd give anything on earth to look like that," Wilhelm murmured one evening, watching the boy make his way nimbly back to the aisle. *"Anything."* Kaspar struggled to come up with a suitable answer, then quickly realized that none was necessary. His cousin-in-law had been talking to himself.

Feinberg's had recently begun showing a newsreel on a gilt-edged canvas screen at intermission, both to keep up with the motion-picture houses on Main Street and to give the girls a chance to cool their heels; and it was there, as per C*F*P's mandate, that the past made clear to Kaspar that it would not be denied. After an animated short starring a beaver and a backward-running clock ("There's a Hebrew clock like that in Josefstadt— runs counterclockwise. Big deal," Wilhelm barked into his ear), and a mercifully brief documentary about Veronica Lake's "dude ranch" in Malibu, the canvas went grainy and dark. A moment later it brightened again, something dour and Wagnerian began droning over the speakers, and a series of smudges slid diagonally across the screen from left to right.

The crowd starting booing, the focus was futzed with, and the smudges resolved into tanks. The booing got louder. The footage, apparently, came from the old town of Prague—from Josefstadt itself, in fact. The Czechs had given the Nazis more trouble than the Austrians had, but not enough to make the slightest difference. Kaspar found himself composing a list, as the tanks rumbled past, of all the sovereign nations between Prague and Buffalo. It was a sizable list, even without taking the ocean into account; but it wasn't half as long as he'd have liked. He wondered what was happening in Znojmo.

Wilhelm, who'd been watching Kaspar closely, flung an arm around his neck. "Screw it," he said. "You're with family, cousin. *Bei familie.* Those cocksuckers can't touch us over here."

Less than six months later, the Patent Clerk would draft his infamous letter to Franklin D. Roosevelt, warning him of the likelihood of nuclear fission research in the Third Reich, and urging the development of the atomic bomb.

XIV

I'VE CULLED THE NEXT installment of Waldemar von Toula's saga partly from family lore and partly from my great-uncle's "research notes," but I could just as well have used a college textbook. The swastika-slathered paperback I mentioned in my first entry—*The Order of the Death's Head; The Story of Hitler's SS*, by Heinz Höhne ("TWO LETTERS—LIKE THE *HISS* OF A SNAKE ABOUT TO STRIKE!")—sits within easy reach, but I'm not in any rush to pick it up. I use the word *saga* in acknowledgment of the historic scale of Waldemar's duration, and of the nightmarish enigma of his fate; but it was anything, Mrs. Haven, but heroic.

The irony in the fact that Waldemar, who'd dreamed so fervidly of immortalizing his father's name in the annals of physical science, should live to see himself immortalized instead, and for the opposite reason—the perversion of his father's work, and of scientific ethics—was lost on no one in my family, least of all on Waldemar himself. The Black Timekeeper of Czas won a place in posterity considerably more secure than his nephew's, fifty-seven published novels notwithstanding, or his nieces', regardless of their tabloid-perfect end; but now I've gone achronological again. In spite of the fact that my great-grandfather will spin in his grave like a centrifuge, I'm going to pretend—out of respect for convention—that time moves forward in a smooth, unbroken line. I'm writing this for my sake, Mrs. Haven, not for his.

∞

The party line on the "Jewish Question" took its final form in the winter of 1942, in a charmless stucco villa on the Wannsee; but it wasn't until a year later that my great-uncle was summoned to Berlin from Vienna, by overnight train, for an afternoon appointment with the future. A youth-education pamphlet he'd written and published at his own expense ("The Protocols of Darwin: A Young Teuton's Primer on Natural and Unnatural Selection") had made the circuit of the party apparatus, eventually landing on the skull-shaped walnut desktop of Reichsführer Himmler himself. Like some schizophrenic shaman in an Amazonian village, treasured as a prophet precisely for his inability to make rational sense of the world, Waldemar had found a place—by accident, appropriately enough—among the party's guild of racial mystics.

The meeting in Berlin was concise but productive. Waldemar was led without pomp into a high, sunny room where a porridge-faced man in a uniform crackling with starch, who looked deceptively like the Reichsführer-SS, informed him he was being sent to Poland. A facility had been built along the Belarussian border—not much more than a ditch and some concertina wire at present, the man said apologetically—to process deportees; mostly *Juden*, of course, but also Bolsheviks, rapists, peeping toms, and a trainload of idiots from an asylum in suburban Düsseldorf. He, Standartenführer Waldemar von Toula, had been selected for the post of facility director, on account of his invaluable work in Vienna and his well-known interest in the Great Genetic Struggle. (Mention was made of my great-uncle's pamphlet at this juncture, but it was unclear whether the Himmler look-alike had read it.) An eastbound express was departing Berlin Ostbahnhof at six that same evening, and Standartenführer von Toula was to be on it, in a private, heated car. Was this acceptable to the Standartenführer?

Waldemar nodded soberly, as he'd seen diplomats and statesmen do in films.

Once the Standartenführer assumed his post, it was emphasized, responsibility for the detainees in his custody would be his alone. The facility, recently given the name of Äschenwald but still known locally as Czas, was not (unlike, for example, Theresienstadt or Buchenwald) intended as a *way station*, but as a *terminus*. This distinction was repeated twice. Was the Standartenführer aware of the policy of the Führer, and of the party as an organ of his will, and of the will of the Great Germanic Race, with regard to the Ultimate Answer to the Racial Dilemma?

The Standartenführer submitted, humbly, that he was.

The little man said nothing for a moment. His eyes were pinkish, vestigial, the eyes of a cave-dwelling prawn. The resemblance to the Reichsführer-SS was nearly perfect. His uniform rasped and crackled as he breathed.

"Very good," he said finally. "I have no doubt, Facility Director von Toula, that you shall do your work well. Your Slavic blood may actually be to your advantage in this case." He took off his wire-rimmed spectacles and began to polish them with a greasy scrap of silk. "Do you have any questions?"

My great-uncle reflected a moment, biting his lip, then saluted and turned on his heels. He had no questions at all, as it happened: not one. He knew exactly what he had to do.

∞

Few records of the Äschenwald camp have survived: the Waffen-SS set fire to the compound in the war's final hours, and the Red Army leveled what little remained. The Black Timekeeper might have been blessedly lost to history if not for a forest-green ledger, wrapped first in oilskin, then in fireproof asbestos cloth, found in the cast-iron reservoir of the latrines.

Much has been made of this text, and of what it might mean. Proof as it is of the crimes perpetrated at Czas, the care that was taken to preserve the ledger is generally interpreted as evidence that someone—some never-identified assistant to the facility director, perhaps; someone with access to the most restricted precincts of the camp—wanted the Timekeeper's crimes to come to light, and must therefore have felt some stirrings of remorse, however primitive. I'd very much like to believe that, Mrs. Haven, but my guess is that Waldemar hid the ledger himself, confident that it would be exhumed and studied. My great-uncle feared nothing, ultimately, as much as the indifference of posterity. He was still a man of science, after all.

∞

Over the years since he'd confessed his ideas to his brother in the garret of the Brown Widow's villa, the seed of Waldemar's theory of rotary time—the notion that chronology is an illusion, if not a deliberate lie; that the steady, one-way current we seem to be suspended in is actually a jumble of spherical "chronocosms" that can be moved through in any direction, if some great force manages to knock one's consciousness out of its preconditioned circuit—had grown progressively more elaborate, attaching itself to random scraps of knowledge in the course of its creator's wanderings, like a peach pit rolled across a dirty floor. The eugenic theories of Sir Francis Galton were among these bits of litter, as were *The Protocols of the Elders of Zion* and, of course, *Mein Kampf*; but the single largest and most ponderous addition was the evolutionary theory of Charles Darwin's great Gallic rival, the chevalier Jean-Baptiste Lamarck.

Lamarck, a pioneer in the fields of zoology and genetics, is now best remembered—if he's remembered at all—for his concept of "soft inheritance," which was famously exploited (and rapidly eclipsed) by Darwin's theory of natural selection. Lamarck believed that the traits an animal acquires in the course of its life can be transmitted to the next generation, the most notorious example being the neck of the giraffe. His hypothesis—that giraffes strain their necks to reach leaves, stretching them in the process, and that each generation is therefore born with slightly longer necks than the one preceding—sounds like something out of Kipling's *Just So Stories* now, and science instructors the world over (my own eighth grade biology teacher, Leon J. Forehand, included) know that the chevalier's theory can always be relied on for a chuckle. My great-uncle, however, saw nothing funny about Lamarck's ideas at all—and Äschenwald-Czas itself stands as the proof.

Here are the final four entries in Waldemar's log, as reproduced in Höhne's ghoulish survey:

> *12 MARCH 1943, 07:57:07—*
> *Having been dogged & delayed by a legion of Trifles I now finally set forth on the Course proposed in my entry of 23 February. This gap of 19 days (automatically, I find myself doing the arithmetic: 456 wasted hours!) has reduced me to a condition of nervous exhaustion. Such is the vicious Wheel of Circumstance, the <u>cercle diabolique</u> the Chevalier*

describes in his monograph "Trials of the Researcher," adding that those of a visionary bent, in particular, are liable to be plagued by <u>les intrusions banales</u>.

It is tempting, considering the Breach—half my earthly duration!—between my original Breakthrough & this long-awaited chance to put my Theory to the test, to suspect that the same super-national Cabal of Semites that perpetrates & maintains the Illusion of Chronology has been using Time Itself as a weapon against me; but I have no such exalted notions of my importance to the Cause. The indignities I have suffered at the hands of mono-directional Time are shared by every mortal Soul on Earth. <u>Sic Gloriam Orbes</u>.

In the four thousand Years since the Jew slithered forth from the turgid Cunt of necrophilic Asia, the human Species has subsided into Decadence. What are Moses & Christ Jesus & Constantine & Pius XII & Martin Luther & even Kaiser Friedrich himself but Iterations of the same Passion play of Self-Aggrandizement & Miscarriage & Degradation, played out ceaselessly across the most corrupt of Stages? The Age of Epics—of Freya & Odin, of Yggdrasil the World-Tree, & of the pale-eyed Saints & Warriors who defend it—lies not, as any Child knows, in our purported <u>Future</u>, but entirely in our Past. The Cardinal Sin of <u>Science</u> is precisely that for which <u>Science</u> is most slaveringly praised: its dread & unrelenting Forward Motion.

What great good Fortune, then! that this infamous Forward Motion is a myth.

In the 17 years since my eyes became Opened I have been nurturing my Vision patiently—sheltering it, fattening it, developing it into a unified & coherent Theory, a foundation for future Research; & as a result I feel, despite a lack of Evidence, a new man entirely. <u>More</u> in fact than a man, because my New Self encompasses both the male & the female. I am the mother, after all, of an Idea.

12 MARCH 1943, 09:57:07—
Three things are required, the Chevalier writes, to conduct an Experiment successfully:

1 * A Laboratory (or some equivalently controlled Environment) whose conditions can be altered to suit the Needs of the Experiment.

2 * An isolated Population of potential Subjects. &, finally

3 * Clarity of Purpose: a hypothesis whose proof (or disproof) is the stated Goal of the experimental Trials.

I address these three points in ascending Order. My purpose, <u>in initio</u>, is to demonstrate the Kinship between the Chevalier's principles of "soft" Inheritance—the heritability of acquired Characteristics—& my own Ideas concerning spontaneous adaptation—or Evolution— under extremes of environmental Stress.

This, however, is only the preliminary phase of my Research. The second phase, the Culmination of 17 years of arse-sniffing & subterfuge, the Reason I've allowed myself to be deported by my rivals to this godforsaken Polish abattoir (as if I <u>myself</u> were an Israelite) is neither more nor less than This:

The Demonstration, under controlled conditions, of the Composite & Rotary nature of Time.

The chronosphere is everywhere, as fundamental (& intangible) as Light; but its shape & Drift remain obscure to me. I have seen it in Dreams, more in fact than I can number; but never when my Eyes were clear & open. I Myself have been subjected to stressors, God knows, since my twentieth year—but perhaps Despair alone is insufficient. I <u>know</u> that Transcendence is possible: my own Father gazed upon the face of Time & paid the Toll required. I myself would be more than willing to take this crowning Step, if there were someone—some colleague—to carry on the Work that I've begun. But I have no colleagues. No confederates. No Peers.

Since I cannot go myself, I have no Recourse but to send Others before me. My study & control groups will be made up of the Prison population under my supervision. (How fitting, how <u>profound</u>, that said Population should be culled from the Semitic race, the very Wellspring of Resistance to the Cause!) The Laboratory will be Äschenwald itself.

If I cannot isolate & study the Accidents my Father wrote of—if I can't see Them, can't verify Them <u>empirically</u>, though I sense Them around me every waking Instant—I'll simply have to generate my own. Exposed to the the correct type of Stressor, I propose that my subjects will perforce obtain Emancipation from the Present, which Ability shall pass on to their offspring, in keeping with established Lamarckian principles. My Theory & that of the Chevalier shall achieve vindication in concert, in a single set of Trials. The sub-Species _Achrono sapiens_—"wandering Jews" in the most literal of senses, free of the constraints of both Chronology & Stigma, liberated at long Last from the yoke of History—shall in due Time—C*F*P willing!—be brought forth.

The Irony that I, Standartenführer Waldemar Freiherr von Toula, shall have fashioned a race of Angels out of the lowliest & most debased of genetic Material—out of the ancient & primal Enemies of Yggdrasil—is clear to me. I haven't lost my sense of humor altogether.

13 MARCH 1943, 09:57:07—
I set out this morning to lay the Groundwork for the Experiment Itself, hereafter to be titled (in tribute to my Father) "Project Gottfriedens."

The first Order of business is the appropriation of a Suite of buildings suitable to our needs; & in this, also, Chance & Fate & Providence have blessed me. When this camp was constructed—in June of 1940—the Solution existed only as an Outline on a roll of carbon paper. The Reality of the Thing, all the circumstantial & logistic Difficulties (the unexpectedly high rate of Death during transport, to cite one example) were not factored into the builders' calculations; as a result, Äschenwald was designed to accommodate twice its present Population of approximately 7,000 souls. A good third of the Buildings stand empty, or are used only minimally, as Storehouses of various types. At 06:47 CET, in the course of my daily Interview with Hauptsturmführer Kalk, I gave Instructions for buildings 13, 16, 27 & 29 to be cleared, fumigated, & given a fresh coat of whitewash in their Interiors. An entry has been made in the camp Records at 06:58 CET, listing these 4 buildings as "converted-use storehouses: imperishables to (_sic_) perishables."

I've decided (after some Reflection) to leave the Nomination of deputies, coördinators & technicians to Kalk. This leaves me free to devote my Attention to a more difficult & gratifying Task: setting down, in this ledger, not only the guiding Principles of this Investigation, but also an initial Outline of each Trial. This I hereby attempt, at 23:24:36 CET, 12 March 1943.

ACTIVATION OF CHRONOMORPHOGENESIS IN MAN
Standartenführer Waldemar von Toula, Principle Investigator

Standard, viable human Cells, both differentiated & undifferentiated, contain trace quantities of virgin genetic Code <u>in potentia</u>, the stimulation of which—through both quotidian & exceptional Stressors, such as extreme Heat & Cold, or extended periods of Darkness, or lack of a readily available food Source—may trigger the spontaneous Development (via the activation of passive genetic Material) of compensatory Traits, which can then be passed on, through orthodox Heredity, to subsequent Generations. This, to quote a familiar children's author, beloved of our Führer, is how "the Elephant got its trunk," "the leopard got its Spots," &c &c. It is how the Yggdrasilian Race came by its Fortitude & how the Semite developed his Guile. This virgin Code has no pre-ordained Purpose, no function, no Limit; no sense of loyalty to Species, or to Race, or to Time.

MATERIALS & METHODS

Seven groups of robust adult males will be culled from the Population at large, physical hardiness the sole Criterion for selection. Culled individuals will be assigned at random until a minimum target Number (tentatively set at 100) is met. Groups 2 through 6 will be regarded as active study groups; the 7th will serve as Control. In further Memory of my departed Father (& by extension, of the Slattern with whom he dallied each noon) I've resolved, as an organizing Theme, to give each population the name of a Trump in the game of Tarock.

The 5 study or "assay" groups will be submitted to the following Regimes:

GROUP 6 *("Pagat") will be confined to Outbuilding 16, previously made use of as a storehouse for linen. The primary storeroom, comprising the Bulk of the building, will be subdivided into 100 wire & timber Enclosures of identical size. Subjects will be fed & exercised daily, showered & deloused with 1/100 Zyklon-B compound once per week. Temperature in the storeroom will be maintained at 7 degrees above freezing by means of a propane-powered refrigeration System (already in place). Subjects will be maintained in an unclothed Condition, 1 individual per Enclosure. All 100 individuals will be subjected to an exhaustive physical Examination, 2x monthly, with special Attention given to the dermis. A detailed Inventory of changes in morphology of the epidermis—Hair count, &c—will be kept for each Subject.*

GROUP 5 *("Mond") will be housed in building 27, a former munitions depot, & will have full Freedom of movement within a shared Enclosure. Subjects will be fed & excercised daily, showered & deloused with 1/100 Z-B compound once weekly, at which time the building's Butterfly roof vents will be opened, allowing for ingress of natural Light. At all other times 27 will remain in Darkness. All 100 subjects will be examined 2x monthly, subjected to Knoll reflex tests & miscellaneous other Examinations of the central nervous System, with special Attention given to retinal & nervous Response to frequencies on the margins of the visible Spectrum. Standard stimulus-response tests will be administered weekly.*

GROUP 4 *("Knabe") will be housed as per Group 5 above, in an adjoining Structure (27 B) whose roof has been replaced with anodized wire mesh. Subjects will be nourished & maintained at a Level of hygiene equivalent to Groups 5 & 6, & attired as per the general Population. Each evening, when ambient Daylight drops below 7 lumens per square meter within the Enclosure, 6 banks of high-wattage floodlights will be ignited. This simulation of diurnal Conditions will be interrupted by Intervals of Darkness every two hours, beginning at*

20 minutes & tapering by 5 minutes per increment. During these Intervals sleep will be permitted, & even, if necessary, induced; at all other times it will be prohibited. Weekly examinations will focus on Stimulus response, Knoll & standard nervous system Tests, including verbal/visual task-&-reward Drills. Metabolic & cardiovascular Rates will be monitored & logged.

GROUP 3 ("Skartins") will be maintained as per Groups 4 & 5 above & housed in building 13, currently a storehouse for low-bulk Imperishables. Treatment of Subjects will in no respect differ from the Population at large, with the exception that Subjects will be confined to building 13 & fed a mixture of standard camp Rations & a combination of steppe grasses, common clover & delphinium shoots. The Proportion of "indigestibles" to standard rations will be increased in Increments (3 to 5 parts per hundred weekly, weekly to bi-weekly, pendentes progressum). Digestive & metabolic Diagnostics will be run 3x times weekly. At close of study (projected at 12 months) Autopsies will be performed, with special attention given to gastrointestinal Diversions, condition of mucal lining, cystic morphologies, &c.

GROUP 2 ("Kavall") will be confined to outbuilding 29, a narrow brick Structure (26 by 6 meters) predating the Construction of the camp, originally used for the drying & tanning of leather. By means of a masonwork Alteration to the Interior (pending), the tanning room (16 by 18.6 meters) will be partitioned into 60 enclosures of 1.6 by 1.8 meters. Subjects will be conjoined with the rear Wall by means of reinforced sackcloth Straps (see fig. 1-6), restricting Freedom of movement to the use of the face, jaw & uppermost 7 vertebrae. Standard camp rations will be positioned (by means of movable shelving) just within the projected Radius of movement, & refreshed 3x weekly. Rations will be located to Subject's left in the case of right-handed individuals, to Subject's right in the opposite case. Medical examinations will be performed bi-weekly or as Conditions dictate. Autopsies at close of Study (projected at 6 months) will target Developments in dentition, spinal & muscular Morphology (allowing for anticipated atrophic Effects) & development/

*degeneration of the lymphatic Network, as well as the superior &
inferior spinal canal.*

*EXPECTED RESULTS—Confirmation, in a statistically
significant Number of cases, of the Chevalier's proposition of
spontaneus morphogenesis. Subjects demonstrating clear changes in
Morphology will then (in Phase 2) be bred with randomly selected &
morphologically Orthodox females, to demonstrate the Heritability of
Traits thus acquired.*

*RESULTS & DISCUSSION will duly be entered Below at close
of Phase 1 of this study, presently projected at 15 OCTOBER 1944,
12:00:00 CET.*

*GROUP 1 ("Sküs"), belonging to a distinct sub-class of Research—&
requiring, as it does, particular & heightened Discretion—will be
discussed in a separate Entry.*

17 MARCH 1943, 21:17:47—
*It has come to my Attention (with all due thanks to Chance & Fate &
Providence) that a number of physicists of Repute are to be found
among the Occupants of Enclosure 6: Including no less a figure—as
I've just now learned, to my Astonishment—than Hermann Borofsky,
mentor to Bohr in Berlin, & previously to the Clerk himself.*

*This is indeed invigorating News. Borofsky can surely be made to
acknowledge the decadence of the Relativity postulate, especially after
assisting me in the Protocols described above. If not, Justice may be
served via more prosaic Measures: incorporation into GROUP 1
("Sküs").*

*Let the perpetrators of the Lie refute the Lie. Borofsky, & none
other, shall be the Instrument by which I puncture Time.*

Höhne's extract ends here. Waldemar's journal, previously so precise,
soon degenerates into a chicken-scrawled list of times of day (down to
hundredths, then thousandths of seconds) before abruptly stopping in
midsentence.

Debate continues to rage among Holocaust scholars as to what, precisely, the "distinct sub-class of Research" could have been to which the mysterious *GROUP 1 ("Sküs")* was subjected, and—for that matter—whether the Gottfriedens experiments were ever in fact carried out. Digs at the Czas site have turned up evidence that buildings 13, 16, 27 and 29 were indeed modified as per Waldemar's schematic, but the lye-covered mass graves into which the bodies of those killed at Äschenwald were pitched have made reliable forensic work impossible. As I've said, it's one of the many enigmas surrounding the Timekeeper that he covered his tracks so expertly, then left written evidence of his deeds—or his intentions—for the whole world to be nauseated by.

It occurs to me now, reading what I've just written, that an alternate explanation—an equal and opposite theory—might also account for the ledger. Waldemar's experiments, perverse as they are, have little meaning unless considered in light of the Accidents. He must have known, even then, that no one outside the family would fully grasp what he'd been after; leaving his protocols behind for the world to goggle over, however, was also the surest means of bringing them to the attention of his kin. Who was more likely to study his work, after all, than those who felt themselves complicit in his crimes?

In that sense, Mrs. Haven, the ledger was a message meant for me.

∞

The Timekeeper's generosity in supplying posterity with riddles would have sufficed to make him the darling of Holocaust Studies departments worldwide, most likely, but one mystery in particular accounts for his fame. For reasons never clearly explained, the guards and administrators of Äschenwald—unlike at Treblinka, for example, not fifty kilometers distant—remained at the camp until the Soviets overran it; what's more, according both to camp records and eyewitness accounts, Waldemar himself was present to the last. Most of the facility personnel died in the ensuing firefight, Kalk and Bleichling among them; but Facility Director von Toula, when the smoke finally cleared, was nowhere to be found. Neither was he intercepted or killed in the following weeks, either by the Soviets or by the numerous bands of partisans that roamed the Polish woods. As far as anyone could determine, he'd vanished into thin air, as if the German defeat had triggered a spontaneous mutation that had suddenly rendered him invisible, or immaterial, or simply null and void. The cellar he'd used as an office was spared by the fire, but the items recovered from it did nothing to explain his disappearance: an overturned beaker on a desktop, a random-seeming collection of books, a cameo portrait of a child in lederhosen, and a trip wire of sorts, running along the floor from the desk to a pile of rubble where a wall had fallen in. The rubble was sifted through carefully, needless to say, as part of the ongoing search. The wire was determined to lead nowhere.

Years later, when the contents of the Gottfriedens ledger were finally made public, any number of legends about the Timekeeper made the rounds, particularly among those fortunate few who'd survived both the camp and its fiery end. He had buried himself alive, breathing through a length of copper pipe; he had disguised himself in prison clothes and let the Russians liberate him; he had turned himself in, offered his services to Stalin, and been put to work with no further questions asked. Most popular of all, however, was a theory inspired by the ledger itself: Waldemar had escaped not geographically—through the three spatial dimensions—but chronologically, through the fourth. He'd made a man-sized hole in time, in other words, and wriggled through it.

Höhne and most other historians dismiss the tail end of the ledger as gibberish, Mrs. Haven, but I think otherwise. The last full entry in particular reads as a kind of dissociative update of Ottokar's posthumous note, the piece of primordial bunkum that started it all:

> *Frantic idiots from forested Fiefdoms follow Freely in my footsteps. Only Light can move at the Speed of light, because only Light is light enough to do so. It has no Mass: <u>ergo</u>. But what is meant by "Mass"? Where does Mass come from? Where does Mass occur? The Pulpit for Preachers at Pamět' Cathedral. Mass occurs 2x daily, 3x on Sunday. A Pulpit tends to look like a Pissoir.*

> <u>*He sees each thing in Time as if in the Present, He being not in Time*</u>. *St. Thomas Aquinas, describing the Eternal Jew.*

*Backwards Time is forbidden by the 2nd Law of Thermodynamics:
the Universe is expanding, Children, & therefore so is Time. Time-travel,
ergo, is as simple as Strudel. Open your Eyes to give birth to the
Cosmos; Close your eyes to make It disappear. Stuff It into a pulpit &
swallow It down: you'll find that you still remain Hungry. Eternal
Salivation is yours.*

*The Lost Time Accidents, a Gentleman once said. He wrote it
down in his Ledger & gave me a Pain in the head. Every moment that
passes is a Lost Time Accident. Close your eyes, Children, when you
want to stop Time. Open them when you're ready to expire.*

Monday, 09:05 EST

I seem to have fallen asleep, Mrs. Haven. My eyes closed for a brief spell, my thinking went muddy, and when I opened them again the room was dark. This has happened before—the closed eyes, the changed light—but it's never occurred to me to call it sleep. Is it possible to sleep outside of time, or to breathe, or to think—to live at all, in other words? Common sense would answer in the negative. Yet I exist.

I must exist, Mrs. Haven, because I continue to experience pain. Descartes would surely have accepted the shame and revulsion I felt while writing the latest chapter of this history as proof: *Je regrette, donc je suis.* Any hope I once had of exorcising my namesake by cataloging his crimes has been replaced by an awareness of his presence in my every thought and deed. The past has become too real to hold in check, too vivid to contain. Not even timelessness can keep its horrors quiet.

At this point, if I were a physicist, I'd calmly revise my understanding to adjust for this dilemma, designating a new sort of time, *t2* (or *Wt*, maybe, for "Waldemar time") that has the property of stasis with respect to the rest of the universe, but progress within the boundaries of its field. The bubble of time I inhabit has detached itself, somehow, from the bubble you and the Husband and everyone else refer to as "the present"; but inside my pint-sized chronosphere, existence—for want of any better term—persists.

A great deal of calculus and non-Euclidean geometry would come next, at which point (if I were a genius) I'd know why my movements and bodily functions are restricted in this state, why my memory of the recent past has been erased, and also why I'm able to do slightly more with each "sleep cycle" that passes. Or so I tell myself. Just thinking about it makes my fore-head cramp.

Most likely you've noticed a contradiction by now, a series of incongrui-ties, both in my condition and in the words that I've been using to describe it. Time, as we've established, *appears* to be passing: my body continues to function, my thoughts move in sequence, and this account of mine gets fat-ter, page by page. Not only that, but my descriptions of this place are crawl-ing with time-dependent phrases and figures of speech: *after a while*, *this whole time*, *since*, *soon*, *now*, etc. I've been using them, Mrs. Haven, because it's impossible *not* to use them. Trying to write, or talk—or think—without invoking time is like trying to make pancakes underwater. Time is every-where and nowhere, omnipresent but invisible. Like adultery.

Is that what I'm being punished for, Mrs. Haven? Poisoning your mar-riage? Making a cuckold of the Sensational Gatsby? The punishment would suit the crime, I must admit. If anyone could appreciate the torture of reliving my bungled existence ad infinitum—to say nothing of the crimes of the Timekeeper, and the foibles of all my other hapless forebears—it would be Richard Pinckney Haven, First Listener of the Church of Synchronology.

Have I found my explanation, then? Is this singularity a prison sentence?

∞

At the close of my most recent sleep cycle, during a momentary uptick in morale, I decided to mount an expedition to the kitchen. I've developed a new technique for getting out of this armchair, one that works pretty well: instead of struggling against the combined forces of gravity and inertia, I use them both to my advantage, as in jujitsu, by letting myself go slack—turning my body, as much as possible, into a kind of invertebrate jelly—until I simply ooze onto the floor. I've made progress in the lateral-motion department, as well: this time I negotiated the Archive without too much trouble. The singularity doesn't care where I crawl to, apparently, as long I keep on all fours.

The kitchen turned out to be spotless, free of the least trace of clutter, lit by a buzzing row of angry blue fluorescents. The room seemed enormous com-pared with the rest of the apartment—a luminous, echoing stadium—and

I crab-walked across it with my eyes nearly shut, holding course for the front of the fridge. I rested the back of my skull against its door when I reached it, like a freshman-year drunk, and let its reassuring hum course through me. For better or worse, Mrs. Haven, I'd arrived.

Before they'd gone into their decades-long seclusion, my aunts had been celebrated entertainers: they'd been known for a time, among their legion of guests, as the German Nightingales of Spanish Harlem. The fridge felt appropriately cool—my aunts remain in good standing with Con Edison, apparently—and I found myself wondering what it might still contain. Visions of sugarplums danced in my head, Mrs. Haven, followed by visions of cantaloupes and taco mix and frozen fish filets. Its door came open easily, with a sound like a sigh of relief.

The interior was packed from top to bottom with neatly labeled, Saran-wrapped containers of soybean sprouts.

You know how I feel about soybean sprouts, Mrs. Haven. They've always seemed unfoodlike to me, aggressively tasteless, the vegetable equivalent of Styrofoam. My aunts, in their declining years—long after they'd stopped letting anyone else in the door—developed a baffling obsession with their health: they were slowly suffocating themselves under alluvial deposits of trash, and they hadn't cracked a window since the Ford administration, but they wouldn't eat a thing that hadn't been raised, grown or butchered by vegan fundamentalists in strict accordance with Talmudic law. There were forty-five containers in all, both in the fridge and in the freezer, dating from six years ago to a week before their bodies were discovered. I took a deep breath, directed certain dark thoughts at the C*F*P conglomerate, and forced myself to choke a mouthful down.

The consequences of this act were instantaneous. The taste of the sprouts—that oddly antiseptic, standing-water savor—brought other memories to mind, ones I thought I'd forgotten, and before I could hit my mnemonic air brakes I found myself remembering our mutual friend: your neighbor and rival, your not-so-secret admirer, the bitter, mannish fangirl with the palindromic moniker who played such a toxic role in our romance. Once I'd begun, Mrs. Haven, there was no turning back. Not even the Second Law of Thermodynamics could protect me.

THE WEEKS AFTER our Great Estrangement, Mrs. Haven, and before our clumsy, roundabout reunion, were the most wide-awake that I have ever known. Distraught though I was, I discovered features of the city that I might otherwise never have noticed: the fractal array of streets in the financial district, for example, or the disembodied tang of styling gel on certain Chinatown street corners, or the charged, lysergic flatness of midtown office towers in the minutes before sunrise. It struck me for the first time how rarely New Yorkers raise their eyes above street level, and I grew fascinated with what was going on above me, which nearly got me killed more often than I can count. Manhattan's shrines to itself, I came to understand, were meant to be admired from below—from the level of the gutter, if possible—and I played my humble part without complaint. I grew exquisitely aware of the grid of cloud and sun and sky above the neighborhoods I passed through, and recognized, in spite of my malaise, that it was beautiful.

I was able to take all this in, Mrs. Haven, because the days had expanded, accordion-like, to hold more than their apportioned share of hours. The moments oozed past like slugs across a wilted lettuce leaf, no matter how I tried to hurry them along. It was tempting to believe that the film reel of experience had been slowed for me alone, so that I might divine some hidden message there—if so, however, I failed to make it out. No sooner had I won you than I'd lost you again: this was the only message I discovered, and I discovered it in everything I saw. Each day was more high-definition than the last, brighter and sharper and more precisely digitized, like an advertising jingle that grows more maddening with every repetition. Life had never been more vivid or less fun.

I've located a passage in Kubler, that Svengali of heartbreak, that goes some way toward explaining this phenomenon. *Actuality*, he writes,

> *is the instant between ticks of the watch: it is a void interval slipping forever through time: the rupture between past and future: the gap at the poles of the revolving magnetic field, infinitesimally small but ultimately real. It is the interchronic pause when nothing is happening.*
>
> *Actuality is the void between events.*

Let's see if this makes sense to you, Mrs. Haven. If what our patron saint terms "actuality"—that slippery, perpetually corner-of-the-eye non-event we think of as now—is the void between events, then the inverse might conceivably hold true: it's only during periods of emptiness, *when nothing of consequence is happening*, that we're fully and entirely alive.

Which would mean that what I'm doing right now, hunched over this card table in my aunts' ruined library, gumming over long-dead memories, is experiencing existence to the fullest.

∞

It was ten days into the above-mentioned spell of pixelated nothingness, Mrs. Haven, that I made the reacquaintance of your neighbor. I'd fought the pull of your brownstone as long as I could, but my pride and willpower gave up the ghost simultaneously, in the middle of the second week of our separation—a windy, soggy Saturday—at 22:47 EST. In the course of a stroll to the bodega for toothpaste, I found myself suddenly at the corner of Sixth Avenue and Tenth Street, twenty blocks from my apartment and less than a hundred steps away from yours. No sooner had this fact registered than I was lurching toward your front door like a wino, hissing insults and abuses at myself, praying for some random act of C*F*P to stop me. That holy trinity must have been otherwise engaged, however, because at 22:49 EST I rang your buzzer ten times in rapid succession, once for each of my fingers, then waited for catastrophe to strike.

Your windows stayed dark and your door remained shut. I should have gone straight home, counting my solemn blessings all the way, but I did no such thing. I pressed the buzzer with both thumbs and shouted your name. It wasn't defiance that kept me there, or self-destructiveness, or even a basic lack of common sense: the thought of shuffling home to my joyless little sublet with the bathtub in the kitchen was simply more than I could entertain. I'd just gone to the curb in search of something to throw at your window when the door of the next brownstone over creaked open and a dour face informed me, in a weary tone of voice, that Mr. and Mrs. Haven weren't at home. They'd left the week before for Nicaragua.

"Nicaragua?" I croaked.

I recognized the face now: it belonged to the sad-eyed voyeur of the month before, the one with the armful of comics. It hovered in the doorway, unblinking and pale.

"Nicaragua," I repeated. I let the gravel in my hand fall to the curb. "That explains it, I guess. I was—"

"That explains what?"

"Just that I haven't heard from Mrs. Haven—from Hildegard—in quite some time. But if she's in South America, then that would be—what I mean is, that would probably explain—"

"She's not in *South* America. She's in Central America. And she went there to get away from you, Mr. Tompkins. Nicaragua's the symptom, not the cause."

I can only speculate as to how I looked in that instant, standing there at the curb with my jaw hanging open. My guess is I looked like a small-mouthed bass.

"Central America," I said. "You're absolutely right."

"She left something for you."

"What is it?"

"A note."

I pulled myself together. "I don't think we've met," I said, extending my hand, although the entirety of the stoop was still between us. "I'm Walter—"

The face pulled slowly back into the darkness. "I've got it up here."

I climbed those steep, crumbling steps with a mixture of hope and foreboding, hanging back when I got to the threshold. Not a soul was in sight.

Light from an electric candle in a faux-gothic sconce played over walls draped in wine-colored velvet, the kind you might encounter in a psychic's waiting room. On the far side of the vestibule doors, its face pressed hard against the beveled glass, crouched a life-sized latex model of a hobbit. I turned the dragon-headed knob and stepped inside.

The hall past the hobbit was dim and wood-paneled and rank with patchouli and sweat. More electric candles lined the walls, and their flickering made everything I glanced at jump and shiver: framed movie posters and Batman paraphernalia; foam-rubber weaponry in Plexiglas vitrines; sagging latex masks on wooden mounts, like souvenirs of Narnian safaris; and—at the end of the hall, given pride of place in a spotlit, bloodred alcove—the uniform of a Standartenführer of the SS, armband and jodhpurs and jackboots and all.

A door somewhere creaked and I skipped quickly backward, not sure what to expect—a Luger-toting husband? a batsuited son?—but it was only my hostess, impassive as ever, holding an envelope between her thumb and middle finger.

She had on a housecoat of sorts (quilted green silk, printed in a pattern of interlocking yellow ankhs) and seemed larger and more owlish than before. She took me by the elbow and steered me into a fantastically cluttered living room, and in that instant I knew, without quite knowing how, that there was no husband, no son, no one else in the house—the objects on display were my hostess's own, relics in a private sacristy, and she drew a dismal power from them all.

"I knew you'd show up sooner or later," she said, gesturing toward a pair of pleated vinyl couches. "I've been walking on soft-boiled eggs for the past week."

I had a chance, as she arranged herself on the chirruping vinyl, to examine her more closely. She was a medium-sized woman, with fine—even delicate—features, who nonetheless exuded massiveness. Where other women might be round, or even stout, she was blufflike, almost sedimentary. I'd never realized how many countless small behaviors I associated with the opposite sex until I was confronted, in your neighbor, by their total nonexistence. Her androgyny had a calming effect, strange to say, and so did her matter-of-factness about my presence there. I couldn't shake the impression that I'd met her before—in some other, less unnerving living room—and I wondered what this déjà vu could mean.

"I should introduce myself," I said, though there was clearly no need. "My name is Walter Tompkins."

She nodded slowly in acknowledgment—so slowly that the significance of the gesture fell away before she'd finished—then pointed at the couch across from hers. She waited for me to sit before she spoke.

"This note must not be for you, then. My mistake. It's addressed to somebody named Tolliver."

"Tolliver?" I squeaked.

"That's what it says here. *Waldemar G. Tolliver, 'Gentleman.'*" She gave me another dead-eyed nod. "*Gentleman* is in quotation marks."

At last your long silence made sense. I had no idea how you'd learned my real name, Mrs. Haven, but at the moment it didn't much matter.

"That's me," I said, holding my hand out for the note.

"*Tolliver,*" she said thoughtfully. "*Waldemar G.*"

"It's kind of an inside joke of ours, actually. I call her 'Mrs. Haven,' and she calls me—"

"Any relation to Orson Card Tolliver? Author of *The Excuse*? Prime Mover of the Church of Synchronology?"

"I get that a lot. No relation at all."

She watched me for a moment. "I'm a member of that church myself— at least I used to be. That's why I ask."

"I'd appreciate it if you'd give me that note."

She passed it across to me without a word. My name was printed on the envelope in clumsy block letters, like a grade-school version of a ransom note.

"I still don't know *your* name," I said. "I don't recall Hildy mentioning you."

"She wouldn't have." As she said this I noticed—or imagined I noticed—the vestige of an accent of some kind. "My given name is Nayagünem Menügayan."

No sooner had she uttered those extraordinary syllables than the déjà vu was gone, as if a hex had been broken, and a tiny, jewel-like memory replaced it. I remembered where I'd met her, though I did my best to keep my face composed. Not that it made the slightest difference. She could tell.

"Pleased to meet you, Ms.—"

"But you can go ahead and call me Julia. Everyone does, in the industry."

"*Julia*. Okay." I hesitated. "What industry might that be?"

Menügayan spread both arms wide, to indicate the jumble of phantasmagoria around us.

"Right!" I said, getting to my feet. "You certainly were very kind to let Hildy leave this note in your keeping. I won't take up—"

"She didn't leave it in my keeping. She left it hidden in a book inside her mailbox. I found it there, Waldemar Gottfriedens Tolliver, and I took it out. Now sit down and listen."

I should have demanded to know what this passive-aggressive troll was doing rummaging through your mailbox, or—better yet—have fought my way out with a flaming battle axe, if necessary; instead I sat back down, avoiding her stare, feeling as if I'd been kicked in the kidney. We'd crossed paths once before, a decade earlier, in the parlor of my father's house on Pine Ridge Road—but the woman I'd met then had been bashful and sweet. I'd never seen a person so transmogrified.

"I'm listening, Julia."

Menügayan gave a throaty cluck and launched, without further preamble, into something very like a sermon. You were her subject—you and the Husband—and she had plenty to say. The two of you were her obsession, her fetish, her area of personal expertise; over the next half an hour she divulged the particulars of your private life with the precision of an entomologist describing the life of the bee. She spoke a pidgin of her own invention, a shambling amalgam of business clichés and expletives and acronyms hijacked from trade magazines, some of them whole decades out of date. It was the idiom of an acutely solitary creature, somewhere between the ramblings of a hermit and the coded patois of a paranoiac—but I learned more about you in those fifteen minutes, Mrs. Haven, than I could have in a year's worth of surveillance.

∞

"Here's the drill-down, Tolliver. The first thing you need to understand is that the man you're dealing with is the industry leader in client-specific brainfuckery. We're talking about a man who founded a religion—a *religion*, Tolliver—before he was legally old enough to drink. He's a tactical thinker and he's patient as hell. Think innovation, Tolliver. Think iteration management. Think long-term convergence. Just *think*." She sucked in a breath. "He and Hildy have been making the grand tour: Aruba to Phoenix, Phoenix to San Salvador, San Salvador to Managua, Managua to Dar es Salaam. He's a 'financier,' *nota bene*: a bankruptcy jockey. He buys companies and sells them at a loss. Strictly a bricks-and-clicks operation, OBVS. And the house always wins.

"Here comes the kicker, though, Tolliver: she *likes* what he does. She calls him her Galactus, her Eater of Worlds. He's always flying somewhere in that jet-propelled dildo of his, and if it's somewhere she's never been—and he deigns to invite her—she always says yes. Hildy bores easy: that's her feature set. Time moves more slowly for her than for the rest of us. It's what makes her step out, *de vez en cuando*, and it's what brings her back. Pack this into your pipe: she comes back every time. It's a synergy game. You think you're the first one she left him for, Tolliver? Don't kiss your own ass. You need to get some transparency on this issue. He knows all about her 'sympathetic friends.'

"Which brings us to you. You're the retiring type, a garden-variety milquetoast—anyone can see that. That's the profile she falls for. The *nonintegrator*. She has a soft spot for wallflowers, bookworms, beatniks, self-anointed deep thinkers: for the unemployable, to call a spade a spade. She doesn't believe in her own brainpower, at the end of the day. She doesn't see herself as a resource, going forward. That's her back-of-the-line, Tolliver, and Haven leverages it to the hilt. Strictly plug-and-play: that's his game in a chestnut. Strictly transactional. She's susceptible to Vuitton and Lambrusco, to happy cabbage, to payment in kind, no matter what pie-eyed spiel she tries to sell herself. She puts out for people with pull, like anybody else who's got no *Schwerkraft* of their own.

"To summarize, Tolliver: she's en route to a safari in Kenya. The 'relationship' you've had, such as it was, is not extensible. YHNTO, if you understand me. It is what it is. At the end of the day, the day's over."

Menügayan paused at this point, as if expecting me to ask some sort of question. I bobbed my head morosely for a while.

"What does YHNTO stand for?"

For an instant she regarded me with something approaching affection. "You have nothing to offer."

"Okay." I shut my eyes to keep the room from spinning. "One more question. Does Mrs. Haven—does Hildy have any idea what the Church of Synchronology actually—"

"Hold that thought, Tolliver. Excuse me a tick. I've got to go see a Chinaman about a music lesson."

Before I could reply she was gone from the room. I sank back and pressed my palms against my temples. I hadn't been able to follow half of what she'd said—more than half, to be honest—but I was a changed man by the end of her soliloquy. I felt postoperative, the beneficiary of a complex but necessary surgical procedure, one no less effective for having been performed by a gorilla.

If I'd had a higher opinion of myself—or of you, Mrs. Haven, come to think of it—I might have doubted some of what she'd told me; as it was, I believed every word. Whatever role this depressive occultist was destined to play in my life, it was clear to me that our affair—yours and mine—had passed some hidden point of no return. I tried to call your face to mind and could not do it.

"It's hopeless, then," I said when she came back.

"Eh?"

"I never had her. Isn't that what you're telling me? Not for a second."

Menügayan shrugged. "The best-laid plans of mice and midgets, Tolliver. You don't have the hit points to take Haven on, you don't have the charisma points, and you *sure* as hell don't have the gold doubloons."

I nodded and got to my feet.

"Where do you think you're going?"

"I'm grateful for your candor, Ms. Menügayan—"

"Julia."

"I appreciate your telling me all this, Julia, but I'm going home now. You've just made it clear that there isn't anything I can give Hildy that her husband can't give her sixteen times over, and that her fling with me was nothing more than that: the latest in a long and trifling sequence. As you can probably imagine, I'd like to be alone."

I felt proud of my self-control, under the circumstances, but Menügayan

only laughed. Her laugh was a dull, toneless thing, oddly damp and for-
lorn, like the call of some creature of the lightless deep.

"You've got a funny way of talking, Tolliver. Kind of old-timey. Anybody ever tell you that?"

"Lots of people," I said, buttoning my coat. "Most recently R. P. Haven's
wife."

"I'm disappointed in you, I have to say. One tiny cloud on the horizon
and you're calling it quits. What would your daddy say?"

"That's none of your business. Who the hell is my father to you?"

"As I've mentioned, I used to be a member of the Church of Synchronology. A fairly high-ranking member. I had my own trailer."

I looked at her. "This house belongs to Haven, doesn't it?"

Menügayan shrugged.

"Why do you stay, if you hate them so much?"

"Not my decision. The Church likes to keep its jaundiced eye on me.
What the Listener demandeth, He receiveth." She leaned smoothly forward, smiled up at the ceiling, then fixed me with what whodunits like to
call a "hungry" look. I knew I should run for my life, but I stayed where I
was. Where did I have to go?

"Tolliver," Menügayan said slowly. "*Waldemar* Tolliver."

"I should probably explain about that. The truth is, I—"

"Quite a responsibility to carry that name, I should think. Quite an
honor."

"An honor?" I said, before I could stop myself. "I have a hard time
seeing—"

"Waldemar is a name of no small significance to the Church. It was the
name of one of our great apostles—the greatest, perhaps. The Timekeeper,
we call him. He did battle with the forces of chronology and lost. Perhaps
you've heard the tale?"

I shook my head. "Like I said, I really need to—"

"He died violently, a martyr's death, at the hands of an international
cabal of scientists and bureaucrats and Semites, in a forest on the Russo-
Polish border. His blood—like that of Jesu of Nazareth—is on the hands
of the children of Israel. They had too much invested in the Lie of Chronologic Time, you see, to let him live. But there's a reason, beyond simple
mechanics, that a clock's face is shaped like a circle. Waldemar's hour was

once—praise be to the Prime Mover!—and it shall be again." She threw her head back and sang, in a girlish falsetto: *"Jan Sküs is the name of a friend I met once, and Sküs Jan is a friend I'll meet twice."* She held her breath for a moment, then gave a tight laugh. "As you can see, Tolliver, the Scripture still moves me."

I gaped at her, sickened and dumbstruck. She sat there serene as a panther.

"Why have you told me all this? What do you want from me?"

"That's simple. I want you to steal R. P. Haven's wife."

My head felt hot and empty. The candles shuddered weakly in their sconces. The uniform glowed redly in the hall.

"Ms. Menügayan—"

"Julia."

"You've just made it clear to me, Julia, that Haven has everything and I have nothing."

"That's true!" she said genially. "Or *practically* true. But you do have one thing—one small piece of the jigsaw—that your enemy lacks. And it's a piece that fits right in the middle."

"What is it?" I mumbled. "What piece do I have?"

Menügayan smacked her lips. "That should be obvious by this point, Waldy. You have me."

XV

I'm going to work today, my grandfather said to himself. *It's Monday, and I'm going off to work.*

He liked how the phrase sounded in American mouths. He liked how unguarded it sounded, how brashly naïve, as if work were a brightly lit hall filled with hundreds of people, possibly thousands, every last one reserving his judgment. He'd waited more than four years for the opportunity of saying those words to himself, and now, at the age of not-quite-sixty, he was as boisterous and cocky as a schoolboy. Via God knew what series of back-room intrigues, Wilhelm had secured him a position in the offices of Kaiserwerks, a midrange timepiece manufacturer based in Niagara Falls—not coincidentally, one of Empress Sisi's Cabinet's suppliers—that specialized in brass-and-Bakelite travesties for coddled little girls. According to Wilhelm, Vincent Kaiser himself had okayed the appointment, impressed both by Kaspar's credentials and the story of his travails. Kaspar privately thought it more likely that Felix "Bunny" Mastmann, Wilhelm's occasional post-theater companion, had put the hire through without asking his boss; but he certainly wasn't complaining. He had children to feed, and payments to make on the dilapidated stucco cottage that he'd recently begun renovating. A man who lived as a guest in another man's house couldn't marry, after all, regardless of his probity and intentions. And marriage was on my grandfather's mind.

Ilse Veronika Card, my paternal grandmother, is fated to pass in and out of this history with a minimum of fuss, as she probably would have preferred. Of all the women drawn into the Toula/Tolliver orbit, she was perhaps the least brazen—which by no means signifies that she was tame. My grandfather met her in the most prosaic place in town: the German/ Yiddish section of Cosgrove's Book & Vitamin Emporium, across the street from the state university. She had on dungarees—a noteworthy sight on a woman in forties Buffalo—and a man's flannel shirt with its sleeves rolled up high, something downright unheard-of. A list of books had been scrawled across her forearms in blue ballpoint ink. Kaspar had always had a weakness for tomboys—I suppose, Mrs. Haven, that it runs in the family— but what sealed his fate was her incongruousness: the quality she had of seeming both furtive and entirely at her ease, as though she slept in some back alcove of the store. The parallels to his meeting with Sonja were striking, but my grandfather paid them no mind. He was eager by then for an event with no precedent, no through-line to the past, and he knew that he'd found one at last. The slight, brown-skinned woman before him could never be Sonja—would never have *wanted* to be her—and Kaspar thanked C*F*P for it. The years of seeing his dead wife in every well-intentioned face were over, and Ilse was the captivating proof.

She was older than he'd first supposed, newly turned thirty-four, and considered unmarriageable by everyone who knew her, on account of what was generally referred to as her "willfulness." Willfulness wouldn't have bothered my grandfather much—he was used to that from Sonja, and even more so from the twins—but he found Ilse eager to prove the town wrong. She accepted his attentions gratefully, slumped and sad-bodied though he'd become, and bore the twins' blank-eyed indifference—and Wilhelm's suspicions—with consummate patience and grace.

Which is not to say, Mrs. Haven, that there weren't a few surprises hidden down her dungarees.

Unless you were planning on being dropped behind enemy lines, German was an unpopular interest to have in those days—even a dangerous one—but Ilse was studying it for no other reason, she informed Kaspar shyly, than its beauty. She was learning the language by means of an Air Force–issued set of flash cards entitled "Military German Lingo," packed with phrases designed to help paratroopers subjugate the Hun. On their first evening out—at Parkside Candies Soda Fountain & Sweet Shoppe, on Main Street—Ilse fanned out the cards on the sticky glass-topped table as though she planned to read his fortune from them. Kaspar's English was serviceable by then, more or less, but Ilse insisted on German. That was what she'd brought the cards for, after all.

"Halt! Wer da?" Ilse read from the uppermost card.

This translates, roughly, as "Halt! Who goes there?" and Kaspar decided, after a brief fit of perplexity, that she was asking him the story of his life.

"I was born in Moravia, Miss Card. My father was a gherkin manufacturer, fairly well off, with a passion for theoretical physics. The circumstances of his death—"

"Es gibt keinen Ersatz für Verstand beim Oberkommando," Ilse intoned. In German, this means "There can be no substitute for brainpower in the High Command."

"Excuse me?" said my grandfather.

She frowned at him for an instant, then consulted the card. *"Entschuldigung!"* She said finally. "Wrong line."

"That's quite all right, miss. If you'd care to switch to English, we might—"

"Erzählen Sie mir nicht die ganze Geschichte; geben Sie mir eine Zusammenfassung."

"A summary of my life?" Kaspar let out a sigh. "That's a rather tall order. Perhaps I should leave that to my grandchildren."

"You have *grandchildren*?" Ilse asked sharply, in English.

"Not yet, no. But children, I have."

"I see," she said, recovering her composure. *"Aus wieviel Leuten besteht die Besatzung jenes Bombers?"* ("How many people comprise the crew of that bomber?")

"I have two daughters—Enzian and Gentian. I had a wife, Sonja, who died in the course of our passage from Vienna. Her parents stayed behind, as did my brother."

"Die Flotte hat schwere Verluste gehabt." ("The fleet has sustained heavy losses.")

He nodded. "Yes indeed, fräulein. We have."

Ilse blushed when he addressed her as "fräulein," although there was nothing inappropriate about it, and Kaspar began to feel cautiously optimistic.

∞

She brought him home two nights later—she rented a studio of her own, on the east side of town, another black mark on her record—and the game was taken up where they'd left off. They'd had a perfectly conventional date, slurping *linguine con vongole* at one of Buffalo's countless Sicilian pasta parlors and making trite small talk in English; but as soon as the door closed behind them, Ilse gave a dark laugh, a different person entirely, and drew forth the cards with a flourish. From that moment on—until they were laid out, naked and exhausted, across the folding army cot she slept on—their spoken communication, according to my grandfather's (wonderfully unexpurgated) diary, consisted exclusively of these strategic phrases:

"Still halten!" ("Keep still!")

"Keinen Laut!" ("Don't make a sound!")

"Hinlegen!" ("Lie down!")

"Schnell, hier herum!" ("Quick, this way!")

"Hände auf den Rücken!" ("Hands behind your back!")

Then, some minutes later:

"Verstehen Sie diesen Apparat?" ("Do you understand this apparatus?")

And finally:

"Die Vorkehrungen, Sie nach hinten zu schicken, sind getroffen." ("The arrangements have been finalized to send you to the rear.")

Worldly though he ought to have been by this point in his duration, Kaspar reeled at Ilse's easy lewdness, which made even Sonja (he *would* not think of her—not now) seem as genteel as a governess. *It's the middle of the century, grandpa,* he told himself when it was over, not without a certain melancholy. *Women are wearing men's work shirts now, and telling us what they want in plain language, at least behind closed doors. They're even fucking like men. I suppose it's because of the war.*

For the first time in his experience, staring into the Victorian standing mirror at the foot of Ilse's cot, Kaspar felt the involuntary defensiveness of the old. Meeting her, splendid and implausible though it was, had aged him overnight. But this was a small price to pay for such a stroke of preposterous fortune—he'd been on the cusp of his dotage already, after all—and he paid without the slightest hesitation.

∞

Within the year, to his enduring amazement, Ilse had taken Kaspar's name and all the worry that came with it, and on February 2, 1943—the same day, auspiciously enough, as the German surrender at Stalingrad—she bore him a plump-cheeked, walleyed baby boy. But the past wasn't willing to set Kaspar free yet.

In the late fall of 1942, a few months before his wedding to Ilse, a brown paper parcel arrived in Buffalo Bill's mailbox, addressed to Konrad B. Toula, Professor of Physics, with a New Mexico return address. My grandfather, who had only the vaguest idea where New Mexico was, opened the parcel with caution—and for once his intuition was correct. The author of the letter was a man named Oppenheimer, who purported to be a professor of physics at the University of California at Berkeley. Even more surprisingly, he claimed to have read—in the original German—the only scholarly paper that Kaspar had ever published: a study of radioactive decay.

Professor Oppenheimer had recently been appointed by the United States government to direct a project of considerable import to the national defense—or so he claimed—about which he could say nothing further by mail. Would Professor Toula (the use of his original surname irked my grandfather, for some reason) consider a visit to Los Alamos, where a state-of-the-art facility (the exact nature of which could, regrettably, not be gone into in writing) was in the final stages of completion? All expenses paid by Uncle Sam, of course.

My grandfather was anything but impervious to flattery, especially from a colleague; he hadn't thought of himself as a physicist since well before the Flight into Egypt, and it felt unexpectedly good. There was his betrothed to consider, of course, and his cousin Wilhelm, and his bosses at Kaiser's, and the twins, who'd just begun attending a new school; on the other hand, Kaspar thought—admiring the Army Corps of Engineers letterhead and the pistachio-colored card stock it was printed on—it looked as though there might be money in it. Before he sat down to reply to the letter, Kaspar got out his AAA *Atlas of America* (a present from Ilse, who dreamed of a honeymoon road trip) and opened it to a map of the Southwest.

∞

Imagining this moment—which has the distinction, unique in this history, of being significant because of what it *didn't* lead to—I can't help but wonder what might have happened if my grandfather had taken Oppenheimer up on his offer. It plays out in my mind in glaring Technicolor, a set of train tracks diverging with all the dizzying smoothness of those *What if?* stories my father used to churn out for the pulps. Ilse might have gone with him to New Mexico, might have agreed to postpone their wedding and support him in the long incubation of Fat Man and his plucky sidekick, Little Boy—then again, she might have angrily refused. There might have been no sparsely attended Cheektowaga wedding—no Orson, no me. The quest to decipher my great-grandfather's notes might have ended with Kaspar, subsumed in the even more glorious quest to reduce our planet to a lump of frozen ashes. I'd never have materialized at my cousin's party, Mrs. Haven, never have met you underneath that kitchen counter.

What if?

I picture my grandfather standing next to the All-Powerful Opp, his fists stuffed into his lab coat's starched white pockets, observing the first H-bomb test at Trinity. Everyone is wearing cardboard 3-D glasses, for some reason, and nervously checking their Kaiserwerks watches. The priapic observation tower and the tiny men inside it are suddenly flooded by the flat gray light of nightmare, and for a nanosecond the landscape is completely stripped of shadow. In this version, it's Kaspar, not Oppenheimer, who murmurs the notorious line from the Bhagavad Gita: *Now I am become Death, the destroyer of worlds.* The symmetry with his brother would then have been perfect: both would have contributed, however modestly, to the signature horrors of mankind's most apocalyptic age.

My grandfather was kind enough to spare our family that particular trauma, which would probably have mentally buggered his descendants until the (alleged) end of time; but the man who deserves the lion's share of my gratitude is the same man whose letter to FDR kick-started the Manhattan Project, and whose outlandish solution to the Michelson-Morley paradox sent Waldemar down the rabbit hole to Timekeeperhood in the first place. That's right, Mrs. Haven. The name invoked by Oppenheimer at the close of his letter to Kaspar was none other than that of our family nemesis, the gorgon of Zurich, the destroyer of worlds: none other than the Patent Clerk himself.

My grandfather respectfully declined.

XVI

THE CLOSEST MY FATHER ever came to writing about his childhood, Mrs. Haven, was the opening chapter of his second-to-last novel, *Salivation Is Yours!*, in which the origin of O_2 the Perambulator is told in all its pornographic splendor. Orson was a seasoned purveyor of "starporn" by then, and could work almost anything into his plots, even genuine human emotion; working it into conversation, on the other hand—on birthdays, let's say, or during family dinners—was something he preferred to leave to experts.

O_2, firstborn son of *StoKasTa*, a sentient cloud of dark matter in the Centauri System, has the most monotonous childhood imaginable: he's born, matures, and dies, time and time again, without ever escaping the womb. *StoKasTa*'s privates resemble those of any well-built woman, with three important distinctions: they're made out of interstellar gas, they exist in eighteen dimensions (including D16, the dimension of smell) and they look like suburban Buffalo in the 1950s.

StoKasTa's birth canal, we are told, is a bona fide black hole, one whose "event horizon"—the gravitational boundary across which even light cannot escape—is always just beyond our hero's reach. O_2 himself is a pimply, awkward ectomorph with more than a passing likeness to my father; he's fated to be torn to bits—"spaghettified," in the unapologetically wacky parlance of black hole research—whenever he tries to make a break for it. Luckily for O_2, he finds himself reincarnated after each annihilation; unluckily, he's always reincarnated as himself.

"I can't really complain," O_2 says, which in his case is literally true—

he's a querelophobe, physically unable to express disatisfaction. "I can't complain, really. But sometimes I'd like to."

In the course of his eighteen-year journey to the limits of his personal singularity, our hero encounters a series of equally wretched life-forms, all of whom have made the mistake of flying their spaceships too close to *Sto-KasTa*'s unmentionables: a dandified pleasure robot, a koala-faced mystic, and a two-headed hydra with "antifreeze eyes" against whom O_2 has to battle in order to make his escape. Orson opted for blunt, C. S. Lewis–style allegory this time (instead of his default Tolkienish vison-questing) and the result makes for an uncomfortable read: a queasy one-to-one correspondence between fiction and fact. It's easy to recognize Kaspar in the gibberish-spouting mystic (he *was* a little koala-shaped, in his later years), Wilhelm fits the robot to a T, and I have no doubt at all, given the shadow Orson's sisters cast over his life, whom the hydra is supposed to represent.

Considering the frustrations of his existence, Mrs. Haven, O_2 is remarkably well adjusted. He has nothing against his mother (or *Agawotkeech*, as her vulva is locally known); he'd just like to see what the rest of the universe looks like. "This isn't a bad place to grow up," O_2 tells the koala. "But by your one million, five hundred seventy-six thousand, seven hundred and seventy-eighth iteration, there's not much in the way of novelty."

The koala nods sadly and wishes poor, doomed O_2 all the best. The hydra, on the other hand, insists that the universe outside *StoKasTa* is simply more of the same, then tries to turn our hero's skeleton to jelly by shooting psionic nerve blasts from the sockets of its eyes. Regretfully, O_2 decapitates the hydra and continues his journey, knowing perfectly well that it's pointless, but hoping—as he's done 1,576,777 times before—that everything will turn out for the best. The "pleasurebot" catches up with him at *Agawotkeech*'s second-to-last bend and gives him a fist-sized ruby from a dainty zirconium purse. "My best days are behind me, or I'd come with you," it sighs. "Precedents notwithstanding, you might actually have a shot this time. This ruby is a piece of geniune space stuff—not like this nebulaic stageset all around us. Put it in your mouth, just before you try to force a breach. It might give you a kick in the pants."

"Thank you, sir," O_2 answers, trying his best to sound enthusiastic. "I think I should point out, however, that you've told me this one million, five hundred—"

"Don't talk smart," says the robot. "Look how far that got the koala."

By the time O_2 finally draws near to the event horizon, he's well into his adolescence, and his surrender to gravity, on the eve of his eighteenth birthday, has the desperate romance of teenage suicide. This time, however, as the robot has promised, things actually do turn out differently. The ruby catapults O_2 to safety (for reasons that remain unclear, at least to me) and a passing starcruiser picks him up just as he runs out of breath.

O_2 has had plenty of practice being a teenager, but none being an adult, which makes it hard for him to hold down a respectable job; on the other hand, millennia spent inside a cosmic vagina have furnished him with a finely tuned understanding of a woman's wants and needs—which expertise he makes use of, regular as a timing cog, for the next hundred pages. In trademark Orson Card Tolliver style, no detail of the Perambulator's amorous adventures is spared us, no matter how cringeworthy. My father sinned in all sorts of ways as an author, Mrs. Haven, but the sin of omission wasn't one of them.

∞

Salivation Is Yours! ends with the death of the protagonist's mother, which is an interesting inversion, since Orson's duration began with the death of his own. As a girl of eighteen, Ilse had been advised by an East Tonawanda gynecologist—himself a refugee from Vienna—that childbirth would place her in mortal danger. This may have been one reason for her reluctance to accept a suitor, or it may have had nothing to do with it; in any case, she seems to have concealed the fact from Kaspar. She died in great pain, three doors down from the nursery, recovering consciousness just long enough to scrutinize her son. Kaspar laid the newborn beside her—a scowling, beet-colored organism, obscenely robust—and she focused her bloodshot eyes on him and nodded.

"What should we call this little singularity of ours?" Ilse rasped to the twins, who stood silently together at the foot of her bed, appraising the baby.

"Let's call him Orson," said Enzie. "After the picture director."

"Because he has a fat face," Genny added.

"Orson," said Ilse, smiling faintly at Kaspar. "Orson Card Tolliver. That has a nice ring."

Three days later she was buried in a small but sunny plot at Forest Lawn, and the baby—a contrarian from the start—was keeping Buffalo Bill's household awake through the night. The stucco cottage, with all of its furnishings, was sold at a moderate loss. Kaspar's last wisp of adventurousness had left him.

∞

The fact that the motherless child Kaspar received in exchange for his bride would grow up to become an accomplished peddler of smut—and smut is what it is, Mrs. Haven, no question about it—is peculiar, given how the boy was raised. Kaspar had grown so committed to feeling *old* since meeting Ilse, had spent so many hours fretting over the future well-being of his young wife, that the possibility of outliving her had never crossed his mind. Had there been a self-pitying or vindictive bone in my grandfather's body, he might easily have come to resent his new son; as it was, he simply kept him at a distance.

Certain neighbors and acquaintances were shocked, after Ilse's funeral, by Kaspar's near-immediate resumption of work; but no one who knew him well questioned the depth of his grief. My grandfather may have been a reasonable man, blessed with mental fortitude and common sense, but he harbored a talent for guilt that went beyond all reason. He'd brought about his first wife's death, he was sure, by failing to recognize the danger that his brother's madness posed, and then by hauling her across the ocean; and his complicity in Ilse's death was even clearer.

Quietly, imperceptibly, without confiding in a soul, Kaspar began to see relations between the sexes as a thing to be avoided. Though he lacked a tyrant's nature, his pain made him a man to be deferred to: over time, visits to 153 Voorhees Avenue—even by other children—grew less and less frequent. The house became a lonely place, shrouded and somber, where conversation took place in a hush. The baby didn't mind, of course, not knowing any better; and Enzian and Gentian didn't mind—just the opposite, in fact—because they had the baby.

∞

The baby entered their lives like a flood or a plague or the death of some biblical king: a twitch of God's will that changed history forever. The twins had begun taking Torah instruction on Thursday afternoons and they were unafraid to think in sacred terms. Enzian suspected that she and her sister might themselves be a species of angel, seraphim put among men for a purpose both high-minded and obscure, in which case the baby was probably some sort of herald. Their stepmother had been a vague, muted thing, hard to bring into focus; the baby stood out electrically from his surroundings, beatific and bright, as if God's fingertips rested on the crown of his head. Gentian was slightly less church-drunk than her sister, but she agreed that the baby was a creature of wonder. No one else paid attention—Kaspar seemed half-asleep most of the time, and Buffalo Bill had never had the slightest use for children—so care of the baby devolved onto them.

The twins had drawn up a list of potential names before they'd ever set eyes on their brother, as if they'd known that the choice would be left up to them. Enzian had been in favor of something Talmudic, in keeping with the child's significance: Moses, for example, or Nebuchadnezzar. But Gentian (always the more practical of the two) argued that too messianic a name could be risky. Names were dangerous things: names singled you out from the crowd. Hadn't their own father changed his name—and theirs, too—when they'd arrived in New York City? Oma and Opa Silbermann, on the other hand, had kept theirs the same. And Oma and Opa Silbermann were dead.

"They're not dead," Enzian said, brandishing a rattle at the baby. "Papa got a letter at Passover."

"Postmarked last year, Enzie. I heard Papa tell Ilse—"

"*Ilse*'s dead," Enzian declared, in that grown-up way of hers that ended every argument. "Oma and Opa aren't. They just moved to Poland, that's all. The same way that we moved to here."

Gentian took the rattle back. "Who told you that?"

"You know who."

"Ottokar?"

Enzian bit her lip and said nothing. Ottokar was a little flying thing with hooked legs that lived in the ginkgo tree outside their bedroom. On certain warm nights he'd come in through the window and cling to Enzian's ear like a fat clip-on earring and tell her a story. Sometimes Enzian would pass what he told her along, but most of the time she kept it to herself. Papa said it was a thing like a locust—a pest. But everything Ottokar told them turned out to be true.

"I've got another idea for what to call the baby," Enzian said. "*Peanut*. That's what he looks like."

Gentian wasn't listening. "What else did Ottokar tell you?"

"That we should stop talking German. He says people don't like it."

"*I* don't like it," said Gentian. She was always quick to agree with Ottokar's suggestions, always taking his side, in the hope that he might one day talk to her instead. She and Enzie hadn't spoken German in a long time, anyway, not even with Uncle Willy or their father. "What else?"

"We have to take care of him."

"Who?"

"Peanut, of course. He's going to be famous." Enzian shut her eyes like a cat, which was as close as she got to a smile. "But you knew that already."

"I knew that already," said Gentian. "He's going to be *famous*." Enzian was right—she was right almost always. How could the baby be anything else?

∞

There's nothing like writing a family history, Mrs. Haven, for shining a light into the fusty darkness. Take my dad, for example. Orson isn't even out of diapers yet, narrative-wise—he's barely been named!—and already he seems less alien to me, less inscrutable, less forbidding. He was sphinx-like for most of my childhood, a textbook case of the Sequestered Father: in quarantine for no apparent reason, existing at a small but definite remove, as his own father had done. He emerged from the basement, as far as I can remember, for one of only three reasons: to eat frozen yogurt, to fight with the Kraut (as he'd taken, more or less affectionately, to calling his wife) or to watch NCAA ball in the den. I would put in hours beside him on the couch, matching him scoop for scoop, before he'd privilege me with so much as a glance. But sometimes, if the game was going well—or catastrophically badly—he'd suddenly jerk upright, drag a hand across his face and stare at me as though I'd just dropped from the sky. I lived for those moments, at least when I was small.

"Look at that goddamn *toss*," he groaned one Rose Bowl afternoon—I'd just turned ten, Mrs. Haven, if memory serves—as the Trojans (his favorites) were being steamrolled by Michigan State. "Look at that cuntsniffer chuck that pigskin. That's what you call a Hail Mary pass, Waldy. It means you fucking lose."

"I know what a Hail Mary is, Orson."

"All right, smarty knickers. What you *don't* know, however, is this." He paused for effect. "That football is a goddamn time machine."

I had his attention now—as much of it as I was likely to get—and I framed my next question with care. "How is a football like a time machine, exactly?"

"In *two* ways," he growled, his watery gray eyes finding mine at last. "You won't contest the fact, I hope, that the football—even when that shitbird McNamara throws it—is in motion. What happens to an object in motion?"

I hesitated. "It ends up somewhere else?"

"Horsecocky, son. You can do better. Do your thinking dance for me and pray for rain."

I closed my eyes and tried to visualize the answer. "Because time passes more slowly—"

"—for an object in motion. Good. But there's another reason. That ball's not only moving forward, is it? It's also moving *up*."

I said nothing, Mrs. Haven, because I didn't need to. There was no stopping Orson once he'd hit escape velocity.

"Have I told you about the Lipschitz Protocol? No? One of the most elegant experiments in history. I nearly named you Lipschitz on account of it."

I thanked him for reconsidering.

"You're welcome. Now listen up: one of the Patent Clerk's early predictions was that time should run more slowly near something really big, like the earth, on account of gravity. Can you guess why?"

I thought hard this time. "Is it because—"

"Right you are, Waldy. As light works its way through the earth's gravitational field, it expends energy. The less energy light has, the lower its frequency. So *that's* why," he said, turning back to the game.

I tried and failed to understand his point. "That's why what?"

"The lower light's *frequency* is, the more time elapses between the crests of its waves," he said, keeping his eyes on the set. "It's the distance between those crests that determines how quickly time passes. So what old Professor Lipschitz did was this: he got himself two clocks—superaccurate clocks—then put one at the top of an old water tower and one at the bottom. What do you think he found?"

"Um—"

"Exactly. The clock at the bottom—closer to the earth—was found to run more slowly, in perfect agreement with general relativity." He puckered his lips at the screen. "*Blitz*, you chickendicks! Pull your heads out of your jocks!"

I cleared my throat. "So, um, for the football—when it goes way up high—time is actually, really moving faster?"

Orson rolled his eyes wildly, though whether at me or at the Trojans was impossible to guess. "On the *other* hand, time moves more slowly for a body in motion, so the two factors might cancel each other out. Tough to say. I'm an amateur, remember, not like your departed gramps. You know what that old gasser used to say to me? 'Time, my boy, is the universe's way of keeping everything from happening at once.' I thought that was pretty deep-dish, let me tell you."

"Huh," I said. "That's actually kind of—"

"Then I found out he was quoting the goddamn Patent Clerk." He made a face at something only he could see. "I dropped out of school the next day."

"But why would *that* make you—" I started to ask, but he'd already switched off the set, as if there were nobody else in the room, and scuttled back down to his bunker.

∞

The world, as the saying goes, is full of disappointed men—but my father, Mrs. Haven, was a disappointed child. When I picture the Cheektowaga of my boyhood, I see a Kodachromatic checkerboard of buzzing summer lawns, any of which might hide the Keys to Revelation; for Orson it was more like purgatory. The conceit of the checkerboard applies to him just as well—I stole it, in fact, from his seventeenth novel, *Monkey Say, Monkey Die*—but the board in Orson's case was something monstrous: a horizon-wide grid across which he was fated to be shunted back and forth—the hero of some dated existential pulp—by forces beyond his control. Long after they'd outgrown their feelings of divine election, Enzian and Gentian continued to think of their brother as their personal herald: they'd named him, after all, just as Adam had done for the birds and the beasts. Which meant that he belonged to them completely.

Little by little, as they entered their teens, a new idée fixe emerged for the twins. It arrived so perfectly in concert with the beginnings of puberty that it seemed, to their astonished father, as much a secondary sex characteristic as the appearance of hair in their armpits. While other girls were sneaking their mothers' lipstick and piercing each other's ears under the bleachers, Enzian and Gentian were struggling through the Hooke-Newton debate on gravitation and arguing about whether God existed within the timestream or outside of it. As if to illustrate Lamarck's theory of soft inheritance, they developed an aversion to relativity before they fully understood it, and in a matter of months—just as Kaspar had feared—they began to ask about their grandfather's research. It became appallingly clear, by their thirteenth birthdays at the very latest, that Enzian and Gentian were showing early symptoms of the Syndrome.

Long after Abraham and Isaac had begun to bore them, the twins continued their bedtime readings of the Bible, if only for the conversation between Moses and the angel about time. Time was Jehovah's most magnificent and terrible creation, they decided: nothing else he'd come up with was half as impressive. It may well have been God's way of keeping everything in the universe from happening at once, but the twins understood, as their uncle and grandfather had before them, that the inverse was equally true: the universe existed to give time something to play with.

Would the mystery of Ottokar's legacy have inflamed my aunts' brains so virulently—would it have infected them at all—if their mother had lived? A psychologist might argue that it served to fill the void created by Sonja's death; and it's true, I suppose, that they'd shown no great interest before. The search for the Accidents might easily have expired in a single generation, with the passing of Ottokar's sons: Kaspar, for example, seems to have all but cured himself before he died. But I can't see Enzie and Genny, knowing them as I did, other than in the damp, lurid light of the Syndrome.

∞

Enzian and Gentian were by no means alone in their obsession: not then, in the interminable end phase of the war. If there was ever a year when the power of physics to reconfigure the planet was plain, when engineers and theoreticians seemed as fearsome and divine as Enzian's cherished seraphim, it was 1945. The twins were preparing a suprise birthday for their father when he came home unexpectedly, his workday smile fixed loosely on his face, and sank onto the couch without a word. They fixed him his favorite drink—he'd never taken much to cocktails, that American eccentricity, but he enjoyed a cup of tea with fino sherry—and asked him whether he was feeling poorly.

"You must not have heard," Kaspar mumbled. "We did it, just as we told them we would." He blinked down at his tea as though surprised to find it there. "We did it."

"Did what, Papa?"

"Hiroshima," he said. "We dropped the bomb."

"Of course we've heard *that*," said Enzian. "We heard about it at school. Mrs. Kieffer played the broadcast on the radio."

"The war is over," Gentian added.

"Not yet," said Enzian.

Gentian rolled her eyes. "The war is *over*, Enzie. Everybody says."

No one spoke for a moment. The twins stood close together, watching their father. They'd grown used to condescending to him, but not when the talk turned to physics. They both remembered Oppenheimer's letter.

"I could have gone down there, to New Mexico," Kaspar said, almost too quietly to hear. "I could have worked on that project."

Gentian sat beside him now and took his hand in hers, a thing she hadn't done since she was eight. "You *could* have, Papa. We know that, don't we, Enzie? You could have helped them to build it. And we'd have been so proud."

"Proud?" said Kaspar, lurching to his feet. He looked older than the twins had ever seen him, but there was color in his face now and his voice was harsh with rage. "Proud?" he yelled, looking from one of their startled faces to the other. "For heaven's sake, what kind of children are you?"

∞

Kaspar refused to answer any questions about physics from that day forward, let alone about the Accidents. The twins had no choice, therefore, but to invent their own creation myth, like the primitive society they were. They did their mythmaking privately, individually, taking two shots in the dark instead of one. Enzian wrote her version—in the pidgin she still used in notes to herself—on the back of a Hanukkah card, then used it as a bookmark in her journal:

> ### THE "LOST TIME ACCIDENTS" BY ENZIAN OLIVIA TOLLIVER.
>
> *IN THE BEGINNING was two Accidents on the same Day in the middle of the Summer. This was happening in Europe. My grandfather was a Goyim Verruckter who only ate Taffees. He didn't care what People thought except his Science was a Secret. It was Secret from the Neighbors and the Customers and even from the Family. My Father sometimes helped him then but he was in short Pants.*
>
> *The 1st Accident was: he found out what Time is and what it isn't. It dropped down on his Head like the Law dropped on Moses. The 2nd was he got tötet by a Car.*
>
> *Time is a misbehaving Thing because it moves and you can't see it. If you can't see it how do you know it's moving? You don't know. But it's gone and now you're in a different Place. It's go-*

ing and moving and taking Things with it. Always in the one Direction, never the others, but Nobody can find out where it's going. My Grandfather found out. He called it the Accidents because nobody could guess the Direction. Not on Purpose they couldn't. Because it's going Everywhere at once.

Another Brother's name was Freiherr Von who had no Timepiece so he kept Time using People. A Jew in Switzerland killed him by becoming famous. He's dead and doesn't matter in this story.

Both more prudent and more retiring than her sister, Gentian was careful not to set her version down in writing—but my father remembered it forty years later, in the ICU at Buffalo General, in the wake of his first coronary. I asked him about it in the milk-of-magnesia-colored room where he lay between bypasses, staring up at the TV he'd insisted on personally unplugging before they slid his clammy body into bed. He'd have answered any question I asked him, most likely—he was bored out of his skull—but nothing better came to me. He was too weak to write, so I recorded him on a Dictaphone I found in his attaché case.

BUFFALO GENERAL MEDICAL CENTER 16:50 EST

It was a gherkin that first set the old asspicker onto the idea that time was coiled and pinched up like a blocked intestine. He might have had the idea anyway, I suppose, but gherkins were his livelihood so that was how it took him.

People think cucumbers are flavorless, just warty green dongs full of water and pulp; but the best of them taste slightly sweet. As soon as it's plunked in the brine—which in Ottokar's day was mostly acetic acid and salt—your cucumber begins to turn sour, and in a few weeks you've got your classic gherkin. However, Waldy.

However.

What's that? No, no—Genny didn't know thing one about the brining process, and neither did Enzie. I'm filling in the blanks for your benefit. Genny's theory had plenty of holes in it, believe you me. She wasn't the brains of the unit.

All right then. As every pickler knows, if you leave your gherkin in the brine too long—a full year, let's say—the process begins to reverse. It goes <u>backwards</u>, you savvy? Your sourness leaches away like old sap, and sooner or later you're left with a flavorless mush, a grayish lump of proto-pickle that's no use to anybody. Except in your great-granddad's case. It was useful to <u>him</u>. That's a genius for you. It got him cogitating, ruminating, chewing the proverbial cud. He started thinking about the chronosphere as a kind of cosmic brine.

Why—your great-granddad asked himself—do we think of time as running straight ahead, from past to future? Because we perceive it that way, you might answer—but that doesn't cut the <u>Poupon</u>. To a Yanomamo on the banks of the Amazon, every river runs due east, toward the rising sun; and a Bedouin thinks the world is made of sand. Are the rest of us any better, really, physicists included? We've lost faith in our senses—and we were right to lose faith, because our senses are fucking pathetic. Why should we have faith in what they tell us about time?

That was when the Chronologists had to put the kibosh on the deal. Word got out that Ottokar was on the brink of a major discovery—one that could knock some heavy hitters out of business. His aversion to automobiles was well known, so it was decided, as a kind of crowning insult, to use a Daimler as the murder weapon. The "watch salesman," Bachling, had just learned how to drive a car that morning. He was an underground Chronologist from Prague.

No clue where Genny scraped this stuff up, by the way. She used to say a talking cricket told her. No idea who the "Chronologists" were supposed to be, either. I doubt that Genny even knew herself.

Funny how well I remember all this antediluvian pucky.

Enzie didn't believe all that hokum about the assassination and the Chronologists and whatnot, but old Genny sure as shit did. They didn't agree about the Accidents either. To Enzie they were a phenomenon to be taken advantage of and harnessed, for chrononavigation and the like; to Genny they were something to be feared. How was human Progress with a capital P possible, was her thinking, when you might easily end up before you'd begun? It was the "grandmother paradox" all over again, but this time as an explanation for our failure as a species. Spiritually, morally—according to Genny, even scientifically—we've been killing our own grandmothers since we wriggled up out of the soup. That's the reason she started the Archive. She wanted proof—in things you could actually pick up and hold—that mankind was learning from its mistakes.

Pickle is an Inherently Funny Word, did you know that? I read that somewhere. And the CIA, in certain circles, is referred to as the "Pickle Factory." I tell you this for your edification, that's all. Nothing to do with Genny. Make of it what you will or let it be.

It's hard to say, Mrs. Haven, whether the paranoia on display here is my father's or Genny's—both became famous for it in the course of their lives. And even the earliest story of Orson's that I've dug up, "Everywhen," written sometime before his fourteenth birthday (when the twins, both twenty-six, were still living at home), has Gentian's fingerprints all over it.

"Everywhen" recounts the adventures of Gargarin V, an interplanetary do-gooder who finds a mysterious artifact on a seemingly uninhabited moon. The object, which is fashioned out of a curiously weightless blue metal and resembles a gherkin (*make of that what you will*, as Orson would say, *or let it be*), is no inert archaeological relic: it's a kind of bus pass, a "pan-dimensional transfer voucher" that entitles its owner to switch from his current timestream to any of the countless others in the "boundless, turgid KronoMultiVerse." Gargarin finds this out by accident when he tosses the object to Ikthlb, his hermit-crab-like housepet and personal secretary. Catching the object in its mandibles, it disappears in a small-scale thermonuclear explosion; Gargarin, miraculously unhurt, wanders around the fizzling crater for an hour or so before bumping into Ikthlb, looking a bit worse for wear, still clutching the transfer voucher in its jaws.

"Where have you been, wretch?" Gargarin demands.

"Everywhen," answers Ikthlb.

It then informs its master, not without a certain weary pride, that it's been traveling through spacetime for two thousand years, popping up entirely at random, and that its return was no more than an accident.

Gargarin is ecstatic as Ikthlb explains about the space pickle's power, imagining himself interceding at countless key moments in recorded history and beyond, all for the greater good of humankind. Alas, however, this is not to be. The story is an illustration of the well-known physics conundrum about traveling back in time and accidentally killing your grandmother, which would obviously erase you from existence, which in turn would make it impossible for you to travel back in time and accidentally kill your grandmother. As so often in my father's fiction, the looming fear in "Everywhen" is not of death, but of limbo: what terrified Orson most wasn't the thought of something horrendous happening, but the thought of nothing happening at all.

"The suburbs," he once told an interviewer, "tend to have that effect on a person."

Ignoring Ikthlb's warning that the metallic blue phallus in his hand is uncontrollable, Gargarin bites into it and instantly finds himself neck-deep in the primordial muck. (Pretty good for a thirteen-year-old, Mrs. Haven, you've got to admit.) He makes countless transfers before finding himself somewhere useful: the meeting of two infamous "astral war criminals" at a remote mountain fortress near the planet's southern pole. Not surprisingly, the war criminals object to Gargarin's visit, and our hero is forced to bite the proverbial gherkin again, making good his escape without accomplishing—in the words of the author—"bugger-all for humankind."

And so it goes, Mrs. Haven, for the next sixteen pages. Our hero is ineffectual, impotent, prevented time and time again from taking action. After untold further transfers, he finds himself back in the Midwestern town he was born in, on the precise day and hour of his birth; and the cosmic bus pass—in a classic Orson Card Tolliver ex machina—chooses this time and place, of all possible times and places, to expire.

Juicy premise aside, "Everywhen" is a hopeless hack job, pocked with flubs and misspellings and shamelessly bruise-colored prose; somebody must have said something nice about it, however, because Orson churned out nineteen more stories by the end of that year. Even after Kaspar and Wilhelm had convinced old man Opchik—Kaiserwerks's bitterest rival—to back a venture into ladies' wristwatches (dirt-cheap bobby-soxers' geegaws, with imitation-silk wristbands, that actually kept decent time) and the family moved into a house of its own in Cheektowaga, on the manicured outskirts of town, Enzie and Genny decided to keep sharing a bedroom, in part so their brother would have space to work. Orson's one-man exodus from consensus reality began in earnest at 308 Pine Ridge Road, and the twins did everything they could to encourage it, never having had much use for reality themselves.

∞

The year 1954 was not a trivial one for the nation: the Supreme Court declared segregation illegal in May, Elvis had his radio debut two months later, and the plug was finally pulled on Senator McCarthy's spook hunt in time for the holiday rush. But you won't find any of this in young Orson's notebooks or in his sisters' diaries, although they subscribed to the *Buffalo Courier-Express* and *The New York Times*, along with twelve pop-science magazines, seven physics periodicals, and *The Ladies' Home Journal*. In spite of its wraparound porch and its shutterless windows and its ample front yard graced by prairie grasses, the new house was even more funereal than the one on Voorhees Avenue had been. For the entirety of that first year on Pine Ridge Road, Wilhelm and his confidant of the moment (a freckle-faced dental technician from Fort Erie, Ontario) were the only visitors who stayed for dinner. The reason was simple: Kaspar gave no sign of caring about anything any longer—with the notable exception of ladies' wristwatches—and Enzian and Gentian had exactly one friend between them, who had wings and six legs, and only showed up every seven years.

Orson, contrariwise, had a handful of bona fide flesh-and-blood pals during high school, and even—temporarily—a girlfriend. He now spent his Saturdays in the science fiction annex of Cosgrove's Book & Vitamin Emporium (just down the aisle from the German/Yiddish section, where his father had glimpsed his mother in her shirt and dungarees), debating the relative merits of Philip José Farmer and Algis Burdrys with a hollow-eyed beatnik known only as Norm. Orson never once brought Norm home—in part because Norm was undeniably creepy, in part because the twins were even creepier. Besides, he had his writing to attend to.

What Kaspar thought of his son's literary pretensions was anyone's guess, but it didn't much matter: his daughters called the shots at Pine Ridge Road by then. Since graduating from Bennett High School—Genny by the skin of her teeth, Enzie with A's in everything but French—the twins had turned their mannish backsides on the world in earnest. Like the two-headed eagle of the old Habsburg Empire, Enzie and Genny presided over their decrepit realm grimly but fiercely, discouraging all but the most necessary change.

Certain changes, however, were beyond their power to suppress.

Ewa Ruszczyk was a wicker-haired nymphet with green eyes and undersized thumbs that she tucked into her fists out of embarrassment, which occasionally meant that Orson—when all his secret stars were in alignment—was permitted to carry her books. An interest in science wasn't yet a social disease in the fifties, and even science fiction had a certain buck-toothed glamour—girls read sci-fi back then, or at least Ewa Ruszczyk did, which was more than enough for my father. She lived at 41 Sycamore, just off the creek, with six towheaded siblings and a mother who seemed air-lifted straight from Nowy Sácz; she spoke English with a slight Polish accent that embarrassed her even more acutely than her misproportioned thumbs (which were lovely, of course, and no cause for embarrassment at all). Orson informed her solemnly, on his seventeenth book-schlepping out-ing, that his current favorite author was Stanisław Lem, who came from the same town in the Carpathians that Mama Ruszczyk did. Ewa blushed and said that Lem was her father's favorite author, as well—she couldn't read him herself, unfortunately, because his books were available only in Polish. Could Orson read Polish?

Orson assured her, incorrectly, that he could. Ewa Ruszczyk was ap-propriately amazed. And still it took him six synchronous rotations of the moon around the planet to lure her to 308 Pine Ridge Road.

The house was dark when they got there, an auspicious sign, but Orson proceeded with caution. He'd been casing his own home for weeks, taking note of all comings and goings, and had settled on Thursday between 16:15 and 17:00 EST. Forty-five minutes wasn't much, admittedly, but it was the length of gym period, not counting showers. He'd timed himself, using a Kaiserwerks Mary Queen of Scots model wristwatch, taking each of his favorite books—*Childhood's End, More Than Human, Pebble in the Sky, A*

Voyage to Arcturus—down from the shelf above his bed, and giving a bare-bones synopsis of each. It took him exactly fourteen minutes, which (allowing no more than eight minutes for getting Cokes out of the icebox, opening them, ascending the staircase, polite conversation, etc.) still left twenty-three minutes for doing things he didn't dare to name.

"It's nifty in here," Ewa said, once they'd locked his bedroom door behind them. "But it's also kind of hard to see."

"Sorry," Orson murmured, fumbling noisily with his bedside lamp. He'd been prepared for anything but her absolute aplomb.

"Was there maybe a *book*," Ewa said, "that you wanted to show me?"

"*The Softest Gun*," Orson heard himself stammer; but she was already reaching for the shelf above his bed. She was dressed in a fuzzy white cardigan and high-waisted slacks, like thousands of other girls across America—but by that point he'd forgotten any other girls existed. If he'd ever seen any paintings of babushka-wearing maidens sowing wheat, he might have been able to put Ewa's thick-limbed beauty into context: she looked perfectly capable of eating him in two or three quick bites, like a blini. She held the paperback in question a few inches from her face—she was severely myopic, which gave her what Orson considered a dreamy look—and sucked demurely on her lower lip. He took the book from her hands impatiently, peevishly almost, and began declaiming from a random page:

> *Draggo tried to laugh archly, but the laughter got stuck in his pylorus. He had a sudden, spasmic urge to run out of the cryo-dome and into the otherwilds—where there weren't any tele-membranes, or taxes, or synthetic pleasure proteins. Was escape possible?*
>
> *Xyxyva was out there somewhere, possibly waiting for him, possibly not: her xxanda dampened by the noonday heat, her proud, heaving üvvübras alive to the tiniest ripple in the palpi-tating vacüum of—*

"Where does this go?" Ewa cut in, resting her palm against the door to Orson's cubby.

"Nowhere, really—it's nothing. Nothing's in there, I mean. Just a desk."

She looked at him slyly. "Just a desk, huh?"

Orson had taken to thinking of his writing room as inhabiting its own discrete dimension, and of its door as an interdimensional portal, only selectively permeable, like the magic pools in *The Magician's Nephew*. It was easy to think of his cubby that way, since no other member of the household ever went there; and it was important to think of it that way, since its contents were extremely classified. His journals were in there, for starters, and certain sketches he'd made of Lucille Ball and Betty Grable that were not meant for public consumption; not to mention the first eleven pages of his soon-to-be-immortal masterwork, *Expressway to the Past*. And now Ewa Ruszczyk—of all the people in the chronoverse—was tugging at the handle of its door. His hand shot forward of its own accord and closed around her wrist.

"It's a transdimensional portal, Ewa, and it's highly unstable. If you cross it, I can't guarantee that you won't be ripped into a million—"

When she pulled her hand free and jerked the door open it almost came as a relief. She was standing in the classic gunslinger stance now—feet apart, hands at the ready—and watching him to see what he'd do next. She leaned forward without warning and gave him a kiss, then pulled away to study his reaction. A pearl of drool clung brightly to her downy Polish chin.

"What's *in* there," she purred, "that you're trying to hide?"

He'd already thought of a plausible answer, already taken in breath, when a sound from the cubby made them both turn their heads. The door blocked his view but not Ewa's. The sound came again just as her mouth fell open, as though she herself were making it—but by then Orson had identified its source. It was the sound of papers being shuffled at his desk.

"You must be Ewa!" came a voice. "What a *very* nice suprise. I'm Orson's sister."

Ewa brought a hand up to her mouth and gave a nod. Orson mustered his courage and took a step forward, resigned to the inevitable. But the inevitable was not what he encountered.

Enzian sat at his desk with a look of calm forbearance on her face, a willingness to interrupt important work, if only for a moment. The manuscript of *Expressway to the Past* lay spread out before her, all eleven pages in a row; she was wearing the Pendleton shirt she'd bought for him at Hanukkah—an aubergine-and-yellow "shadow plaid"—with the sleeves rolled up, the way he liked to wear them. She had on his wristwatch, as well, and some boxers of his that rode up at her hips. Her feet made fan-shaped dust marks on the floor.

"Enzie," Orson croaked.

"*There* you are, Peanut," she said, keeping her eyes on Ewa.

"Enzie, what are you doing?"

"This is *quite* promising." She took up the topmost page and squinted at it through her reading glasses. "Too Asimov-ish for my taste—but it's your story, after all, not mine. The way you tweak the Dunne-Dodgson Postulate to allow for chrononavigation is original, to say the least." Her eyes brightened. "I almost think you might be on to something."

"Thank you," my father said faintly. It was all he could do not to look at her feet, or at her thighs, or at all the other parts of her he'd never glimpsed before. Her pose put him in mind of a soft-focus photograph, neatly torn from a magazine, that Norm the beatnik carried in his wallet. He felt queasy again. The Pendleton shirt wasn't even buttoned.

"I appreciated your description of the Nameless Planet, too. Weak gravitation might well have that effect on vegetation." She gave Ewa a wink. "Best of all, there's not a trace of Patent Clerk–ism anywhere."

"Enzie—"

"How are you going to work the Accidents in?"

"I'm not going to work the Accidents in."

Her smile drifted subtly out of alignment. It hadn't been the most convincing of smiles to begin with.

"Not work them in? What do you mean by that?"

"I mean what I said."

Orson had known for some time that his sisters' enthusiasm for his stories was directly proportional to the prominence of time travel in them— and he'd been willing to oblige, at least up to a point, since the twins were all the audience he had. That confrontation in his cubby, however, was the true zero-hour of my father's career, and not just because he'd decided, for the first time in his life, to stand his ground. As he watched Enzian's angular features reconfigure themselves, he was struck by an unprecedented feeling: the conviction that he was right and she was wrong. Everything about her was wrong, he realized, from her superior air to her goose-pimpled thighs to her uninvited presence in his room. His surprise gave way to anger as he watched her, then to something akin to contempt. Ewa played a role in this, of course, but by that point she was almost incidental. Orson's and his sisters' agendas had parted ways, quite possibly forever. In a heartbeat he'd become a different person.

"You've been using me, Enzie."

"*Using* you? What on earth—"

"You've been making guesses about the Accidents—guesses, hypotheses, whatever you want to call them—and getting me to turn them into stories. Don't try to deny it."

"I haven't the slightest intention of—"

"But I don't want to do that anymore, you understand? I want to use my *own* ideas, Enzie, not yours. I'm not like you and Genny—not in that way, at least." He took in a breath. "To start off with, I haven't got the Syndrome."

"Of course you do, Peanut," Enzian said softly.

Orson flinched as if she'd slapped him. "I'm not a goddamn *peanut*," he hissed. "I've got better things to do than help you with your guesses about time."

She was quiet a moment. "What could possibly be better?"

"None of your business."

"Orson, please—"

"Come on, Ewa. Let's get out of here."

But Ewa, not surprisingly, was nowhere to be found.

∞

Kaspar noticed that a change had occurred in his house, but he had only the murkiest idea of what it was: he'd been a noncombatant for too long. Enzian evaded his questions, Gentian seemed to know less than he did, and Orson had locked himself away and spoke to no one. My grandfather had long since reconciled himself to the irrelevance of age—he'd practically rushed forward to meet it—so this latest failure came as no surprise. One night after dinner, however, two weeks into this brittle new epoch, Enzian astonished him by coming into the parlor and perching close beside him on the sofa, as she'd done on rainy afternoons when she was small.

"Papa," she said in German, "I have something to discuss."

Kaspar nodded at her mildly, excruciatingly aware of how doddering and hapless he must seem. Enzian was a little girl again, decades younger than her twenty-seven years, and the sensation this triggered was one of staring down from a high balcony onto a street he'd lived on a lifetime before, in a city whose name he'd encouraged himself to forget. Chronology is a lie, someone had said to him once.

"What is it, *Schätzchen*?" he heard himself ask. He hadn't called anyone *Schätzchen* since getting off that dreadful ship in New York Harbor. But that wasn't quite true—he'd called his second wife *Schätzchen*, he recalled that distinctly. His second wife: Ilse. He did his best to bring her face to mind.

"Papa," said Enzian, in English this time. "Are you listening to me?"

"I am, Enzie. Of course." He sat up and nodded. "But it might be best if you began again."

"Orson doesn't want to study physics. He doesn't even want to go to school."

Her anger was palpable, even to Kaspar. He took care in framing his answer. "Orson's fifteen years old, Enzie. I doubt that he knows what he wants."

"He turned sixteen last March. And he knows what he wants perfectly. He's not like you." The child had vanished, and the familiar sharp-edged face stared into his. "You've never understood him, Papa. That's the truth."

"He's a teenager now," Kaspar said equably. "Not a tot anymore. There are more important things, for a boy of his age, than the study of the nature of time."

For a moment it seemed that Enzian wouldn't answer. "That's what *he* said. But what on earth could be more important?"

Gentian came in just then, a dish towel in one hand and a cup of Ostfriesen BOP in the other. Kaspar whispered his answer into Enzian's ear.

"*Papa!*" she said, bringing a hand to her mouth. "I'm astonished that you even know that word!"

"I know it in three languages," he said matter-of-factly. "English, German, and Czech. If I didn't, sweetheart, you might well not exist." He looked from one of his daughters to the other. "You girls need to get out of the house more often."

"That's just what I want to talk about," said Enzian.

∞

The following autumn, on September 5, 1956, Enzian attended her first lecture in the Physics Department of the State University of New York at Buffalo. She was older, at twenty-seven, than a number of her instructors, and she was the only woman in the whole department; but such trivialities were no concern of hers. She kept her time on campus to a minimum, but even so, the hours away from her sister were bitter. Harder still was the pretense her studies demanded: the need to dissemble, to parrot her professors' orthodoxies, to feign interest in theories that were of no use to her. My aunt had developed her own ideas about the physical world by that time, some of which would have made even Waldemar blush. She was rattled and drained when she came home at night, as though on furlough from some grim but crucial conflict—which was exactly what she considered her course-work to be.

Hostilities commenced in the second month of Principles of Physics. Things had gone smoothly till then: she'd familiarized herself with those areas, like Laplace's theory of determinism and Newton's early work in optics, that she'd missed in her self-education. (She particularly liked the idea, which she'd never once thought of, that physics often seems to violate common sense because our common sense evolved to explain things on a *human* scale—the scale of things that we can touch and see and hear—whereas physics deals with everything in the universe, from the sub-atomic to the infinite.) By the time the class had arrived at Michelson and Morley, however, my aunt had begun to get antsy. The lecturer, an archetypically tweedy Scotsman with a tendency to stammer when excited, had barely rounded the headland of the twentieth century when he found himself in shark-infested seas.

The topic was Philip Lenard's work on photoelectrics, which had never posed a problem for the Scotsman before. Lenard had been an opponent of relativity from the start, in part because it rendered his pet theory—that everything in the universe is suspended in an invisible substance, the "luminiferous ether"—not only obsolete but silly. Using the technique known as Occam's razor, which cuts away all the elements of a theory that aren't essential—the fat and the gristle, conceptually speaking—Einstein and his cohorts had dispensed with the ether, and found that the universe ran perfectly well without it. Little wonder, then (the Scotsman continued) that Lenard had ended up a rabid Jew-baiter. As Max Planck once wrote to his colleague, Sir James Jeans—

"Excuse me, Mr. Urquhart," said Enzian, raising her hand.

Urquhart glanced up in alarm. "What is it, Miss Tolliver? Are you unwell?"

"Not me," she replied. "Mr. Occam."

"Mr. Occam?" echoed the Scotsman, struggling to master his stammer.

"His razor." Ignoring the tittering around her, Enzian pressed on. "Occam's principle is to cut away everything that's unnecessary, isn't that so? To strip each theory back down to its bones?"

"That is correct, Miss Tolliver. Now, if you'll permit me—"

"Seems to me you'd lose a lot of meat that way."

Urquhart opened his mouth and closed it. "A lot of *meat*, Miss Tolliver?"

"That's right." Enzian was smiling her private smile now, the one she used only with her father and Genny. "Where do all those theories go, that Occam shaves away? How many tasty tidbits are we missing?"

Monday, 09:05 EST

I've been nursing a suspicion for at least three sleep cycles, Mrs. Haven, without the confidence to set it down. There have been too many coincidences, especially lately—too many barely perceptible changes to my surroundings, too many relevant books poking up from the trash, too many mnemonic prompts left out where I was sure to find them. I may be cut off from the timestream in this junk-filled mausoleum, but that doesn't necessarily mean that I'm alone.

The idea of someone else in these catacombs, laying out a bread-crumb trail for me while I'm asleep, gives me the fantods, for obvious reasons; but I can't deny it also gives me hope. As I wrote in my ledger of credits and debits:

> *But someone must have put me here, and provided me with these*
> *books and writing materials—ergo, someone wants me to complete*
> *my history. And that person may also have the means to set me free.*

I've held back till now, Mrs. Haven, out of uncertainty and lack of evidence. But something has just happened—a few minutes ago, before I started this entry—that's convinced me I'm right.

∞

I awoke from my most recent spell of semiconsciousness to the knowledge that something had changed. It was dark in the room—smoothly, blankly, two-dimensionally dark—and as usual I heard almost nothing. I felt my adrenaline surge as I groped for the lamp, terrified that I'd been blinded in my sleep: I yanked on its chain, then again, then *again*, but the dark only thickened. Sliding to the floor, I followed the cord of the lamp with my fingers, crawling through the blackness on all fours, praying that I'd somehow pulled it from the wall. I seemed to be crossing a wide, pitching space, like a seasick passenger on the deck of some great cruiser. I had to burrow through a loose drift of magazines and milk cartons and shoe boxes to uncover the socket; when I did, I found the cord firmly plugged in. This may seem like a minor point, Mrs. Haven, but it struck me like a swell of icy water. The only explanation left was that the bulb had blown, and I had no replacement. The thought of passing each coming night with nothing but my claustrophobia for company was more than I could bear. I sank back against a stack of ceiling tiles and sobbed.

As I was making my way back, however, I had a stroke of improbable luck. Just as my hand reached the base of the lamp, my fingers brushed against something cool and round and light, and set it spinning. A lightbulb! I was too overjoyed to ask how it had gotten there, or why I hadn't noticed it before. I brought it to my ear and shook it gently.

Unbelievably, miraculously, the bulb was intact. I let out a groan of thanksgiving and got to my feet, guiding myself upward by the stem of the lamp. I hesitated briefly at the top, held back by a sudden misgiving: that the power to the apartment had been cut.

The implications of this made me slightly woozy. Is it possible that my temporal isolation operates in one direction only—that the timestream can still affect me, even though I've been excised from time? With this troubling thought I roused myself from my reverie and reached up, under the lampshade, to unscrew the dead bulb and replace it.

But there was no bulb to replace, Mrs. Haven. There was no bulb in the socket of the lamp.

As I stood motionless with the lamp stem in my right hand and the lightbulb in my left, hearing nothing but my own dumbfounded wheezing, something gradually impinged on my awareness. I'd been conscious of it for some time, in the way that I was conscious of the clothing I wore, or of the floor beneath my feet: I'd sensed it without giving it a thought.

Someone else was in the room, close beside me in the darkness, breathing in time with my breath.

I let out a squeal, choked and childlike, that died almost before it left my throat. There was someone else *there*. Someone was trying to match me breath for breath, to hide in my biorhythm, and was almost succeeding. I turned around slowly, keeping my hand on the lamp stem, and guided the bulb into the empty socket. I was facing him now. I seemed to feel his scentless breath against my skin.

"I want to know who you are," I said into the blackness.

I gave the bulb one full turn. The ghostly breathing seemed to have stopped, or to have conformed to my own more precisely. I turned it again.

"I want to know who you *are*," I repeated. "I want to know why you're doing this to me."

A great distance away, at the margin of hearing, a board seemed to creak.

"Show yourself!" I shouted, giving the bulb a third and final twist.

My mistake, I see now, was to keep my eyes open as the light came on. I recoiled backward into the card table, knocking half the pile of books onto the floor, then doubled over and dug my palms into my eyes. A stream of burning afterimages roiled across my sight, in one of which I saw—or thought I saw—a human figure. But by the time my sight had cleared the room was empty.

On the floor behind my armchair, within arm's reach of the Archive, a fractured snow globe glittered in the light. It had held water once; now it held only soot. I looked closer and discovered a postapocalyptic Forty-Second Street, the block just east of Grand Central, as desolate and caked with grime as this apartment. The Chrysler Building jutted like a starship from the dust.

XVII

AMBITIOUS AS SHE WAS in her blank, brutal way, Enzian had never pictured herself out in the world—out among the ignorant, the time-bound, the conventionally human—and least of all in the role of messiah. This wasn't due to any doubt as to her own charisma (she'd been blessed with an almost fanatical belief in her suitability for pretty much everything) but because she herself had decided, nearly two decades earlier, that her brother would be the one to play that part. Not *decided*, she reminded herself. Nothing had been decided, not then or ever. Only foreseen.

Orson kept his distance from her now, whether out of anger or embarrassment she couldn't have said; and her disappointment was still so severe, so painful to her, that it was safer for them both if he kept clear. The contract between them had been straightforward and fair—generous, really—and he had broken it. If Enzian had had her way—if Kaspar hadn't opposed her with the last of his vitality—she'd have turned her brother out into the street.

Kaspar was fading perceptibly, growing smaller and more diffuse each time she looked, like the traveler waving from a moving train in the classic physics problem. There was a geometry to her father's enfeeblement, a mathematical precision that suited them both, and which allowed her to observe its progression without losing her head to sentiment or panic. The heavy hair of which he'd always been so vain, and which had kept its chest-nut color well into his sixties, now showed the shape of his skull when the light was behind it, and his square plowman's shoulders had started to slump. He'd never been a handsome man—even Enzian knew that—but he'd somehow seemed more manly for his plainness. Now the sexlessness of old age had engulfed him. His hearing was failing, he'd taken to falling asleep at the dinner table, and she could hear his labored breathing through the bedroom wall at night. The end of Kaspar's term was fast approaching.

What Gentian's thoughts were with regard to this fact, or to her sister's decision to take up the Tolliver mantle, or to any of the other upheavals at Pine Ridge Road that year, was far more difficult for Enzian to discern. Which is not to say there weren't certain clues.

"By the way," Gentian said, as she was clearing the table one evening. "Your friend came to the window last night. I let him in. We had ourselves a little heart-to-heart."

Enzian, who'd just come down from tucking Kaspar into bed, cocked her head at her sister. "What's that, Genny? Which friend? I have no—"

"Ottokar."

"I don't understand. Little Ottokar, the *Ungeziefer*? From back when we were girls?"

Gentian nodded without looking up. "We *thought* about waking you, of course, but you'd been up so late studying for that ballistics midterm. He'll be back soon, though. He said so."

Gentian's manner was as matter-of-fact as ever: her voice betrayed no urgency, no acknowledgment that what she was saying was in any way unusual. She might have been talking about one of Orson's classmates, or about Calvin Huber, the man who read the gas meter each month—though in that case she'd have been a bit more flustered. She had a schoolgirl's crush on Calvin Huber.

"It's 1957, Genny," Enzian said at last. "We're twenty-eight years old."

"Do you want to hear what Ottokar had to tell me?"

Enzian could count on one hand the number of times she'd been at a loss for words with her sister. "You?" she said finally. "What Ottokar had to tell *you*?"

Gentian gave an absent little nod.

"What was it?"

"He's proud of you, Enzie." Gentian smoothed down her apron. "Just like the rest of us are."

Enzian felt herself redden. "Well! That's kind of you to say, Genny. I'd been hoping—"

"Yes, Enzie. Of course. But you're making a terrible mistake."

Everything hushed as she said this—all the manifold small workings of the house. Enzian could feel the hush against her ears, cool and flat, as if the room had been depressurized. Then slowly—one by one, it seemed— the noises returned. She heard her father cough and turn in bed.

"What mistake am I making?"

"Oh! He never said *that*," Genny singsonged, gliding off into the kitchen.

∞

Enzian had plenty of worries in her debut year as a physicist, from her father's poor health to her brother's defection to her sister's unchecked ec- centricity; but material concerns were not among them. Through some dark, occult bargain she never quite grasped—and which thrilled and alarmed her in equal measure—Warranted Tolliver Timepieces, Inc., grew in inverse proportion to Kaspar's decline. Whatever it was he'd been doing from sun- rise to sunset in his drop-ceilinged office downtown, he'd been doing it preposterously well. It would stand as the crowning irony of my grand- father's irony-bedeviled duration that the most unilateral of his withdrawals from the world was the most richly rewarded venture of his life.

Buffalo Bill, to be fair, deserved some of the credit. Given careful super- vision, he'd proven to be a gifted business manager and a virtuosic salesman—not that too much virtuosity was called for. For the first time in U.S. history, teenagers had money to spend on whatever flashy baubles caught their fancy, and wristwatches were a safe but potent sign of inde- pendence. Business had expanded quietly over the past decade—so quietly, in fact, that Kaspar's children hadn't paid it much attention. On a certain Saturday morning of that pivotal autumn, however—on one of the rare occasions when all of his offspring were in sight at the same time—he as- sembled them in the front hall. He let out a slow breath, as though resign- ing himself to something beyond his control, then sat down on the fourth step of the stairs.

"*Kinder*, I have news. We're millionaires."

None of the children said a word. Orson leaned against the door with his coat halfway buttoned, and Gentian and Enzian stood watching their father intently, apparently gauging the likelihood of his tumbling downstairs. It was enough to make him wonder whether anyone had heard him.

"Last time I checked," said Orson guardedly, "I had less than fifteen dollars in the bank."

"Check again, son."

"But Papa, what's the meaning of this?" Gentian got out eventually.

"Don't look so *angefressen*, Genny. You'd think I'd just told you we were millions in debt."

"Why are you telling us this, Papa?" said Enzian. "Why now?"

"When ought I to have told you, Enzie? Before we had the money?"

This was not the tableau Kaspar had envisioned. He looked on, feeling inexplicably sheepish, as Orson's eyes met Enzie's for the first time in months. Under any other set of circumstances he'd have been overjoyed; as it was, he was simply confused, a sensation he'd long since come to feel at home in. Enzian took a half step toward the staircase, apparently to get a closer look at him. She didn't seem impressed by what she saw.

"You've deposited money into each of our savings accounts? Am I understanding you correctly?"

"I've set up three trusts," Kaspar answered, glad to have something concrete to discuss. "The money has been invested for you. Partly in the company, partly in government bonds."

"How much is in my trust?"

Kaspar hesitated, but only for an instant. "Half a million dollars."

"What about mine?" said Orson.

"I put the same amount in each."

He watched the fact of it sink in. His children's perplexity—more than that: their efforts to hide it from him, and from one another—brought him a certain private satisfaction. Orson was particularly interesting: he stared furiously at a wrinkle in the entryway runner, as if trying to straighten it using the power of his mind. *I've known this boy for his entire life*, Kaspar said to himself. But he couldn't seem to make himself believe it.

"When can we use the money?" said Orson.

"When you come of age, of course," Enzian answered. But Orson kept his eyes fixed on his father.

Kaspar shrugged. "I have nothing to say about that. The trusts are in your names, children, not mine. You can draw from them whenever you choose."

Orson nodded for a time. He might have been nodding at what he'd just heard, but it was obvious to his father that he wasn't. He was nodding to give himself courage.

"I have an announcement."

Kaspar had no gift of clairvoyance, but on that day—for what reason, he couldn't have said—he finally beheld his son and understood him. Orson was about to say something that he'd been rehearsing for weeks, perhaps even longer.

"I'm going to New York City."

No one spoke for a moment.

"Orson," Gentian got out finally, ignoring her sister's look, "I know that you and Enzie have been on the outs—"

"Ewa has a cousin who lives on Lexington and Forty-Second, the same block as the Chrysler Building," he went on, ignoring her. "I'm going to write for *Preposterous! Stories* and *Omniverse* and *Tales of Stupefaction*, and all those other pulps that you and Enzie hate." He paused for effect. "*Preposterous!* just accepted a story of mine."

"But you can do all that here," Gentian whimpered. "You're still in your teens. I don't see why—"

"They've finally accepted 'The Yesternauts,' have they?" Enzian said coolly. "Then you must have made the changes that they asked for."

Orson stared past them all and said nothing.

"Changes?" Gentian said, if only to say something. "What changes?"

"Tits," said Enzian.

Kaspar began to pay closer attention.

"There's nothing wrong with that," Orson answered. "There's nothing wrong with tits. Except in this house."

Kaspar cleared his throat to speak, then stopped himself.

"They didn't like the title, either," Enzian continued, in the same bloodless voice as before. "What's it called now?"

Orson shut his eyes. "Enzie, it's my first published story."

"And we're *happy* for you!" said Gentian. "What's it called?"

"'In the Naked Form of the Human Jelly.'"

"In the Naked *which*?" said Kaspar.

"It's a quote. From Saul Bellow."

"Saul Bellow," said Enzian, "never wrote for the pulps."

Orson brought a finger to his temple, as if considering her point. Then he buttoned up his coat and left the house.

"You shouldn't have done that, Enzie," Gentian said. She looked careworn and tired. Kaspar found that he barely recognized either of his daughters: they seemed to have changed their clothes and shape before his eyes. *Through the Looking-Glass* came to mind—Orson's favorite book, as a child—and he wondered if some final dream were now commencing. Enzian stood as straight-backed and ferocious as the red queen herself, and plump, frowsy Gentian was the white queen personified, down to the slightest detail. How had he not noticed this before?

"I didn't do *anything*," Enzian muttered, opening and closing her fists. "He did it. All of it. And now it's done."

Genny appeared to be weeping, something her father had only the faintest memory of her having done before. She'd almost never raised her voice, either—at least not in anger—but she was raising it now. "*Tell* her," she was shouting—shouting at him, of all people. "Tell her to let Orson write for the pulps!"

"He's writing for them already," said Enzian. "Titties and all."

Kaspar dug a handkerchief out of his pocket, thought hard for a moment, then blew his nose resoundingly into his sleeve. "What's a pulp?" he inquired.

Monday, 09:05 EST

Can I confess something to you, Mrs. Haven? I'm not sure anymore who "Mrs. Haven" is.

The closer I get to the crux of our story, the less clearly I'm able to see. Even during our most intimate moments, your name—the name you took from your husband and asked me, perversely, to use—seemed to function as a kind of screen, a cover for your true, pre-Haven self. I wonder if I ever saw behind it.

Which raises the question, come to think of it, of who it is I'm really writing for.

For two weeks after leaving Menügayan's brownstone I heard no news at all, and I began to suspect—at times, even to hope—that I'd misunderstood the nature of our bargain. But I was foolish to doubt her. She was hard at work all the while, woodshedding and calculating, fussing and scheming, consulting the Synchronology Codex and game theory textbooks and Sun Tzu's *The Art of War*, as tireless as the light cone of chronology itself.

In a more simpatico age—Hoover-era America, for example—there's no telling how far Menügayan's star might have risen. As it was, she was a has-been cult administrator, excommunicated at forty, making her living selling fanboy paraphernalia in shabby back-lot booths at "geek conventions." I never did manage to discover why the UCS cut her loose, but it was painfully clear that the animosity she felt toward them (and toward Haven, in particular) had once been unconditional devotion. I wasn't able to figure out what sort of deal she'd cut, either, though she never denied that her brownstone was the property of the Church. At the end of the day, Mrs. Haven—as Menügayan herself would have put it—none of these considerations mattered. She was going to bring you back to me. All further questions smacked of self-indulgence.

Menügayan hadn't deigned to share the details of her scheme, but I had no doubt that she had one, and that the obliteration of your marriage was only a preliminary gambit, one small relay in the circuit she was building. She'd been a high-ranking financial officer in the UCS, apparently, and knew enough about the First Listener's machinations to cause him significant grief. She was living in gilded exile on West Tenth Street, in a kind of tacit house arrest, like a disgraced Hero of the Revolution maintained in watchful comfort in some quaint suburban dacha. She spied on you, Mrs. Haven, because she had a spy's nature—and because you passed her front door every day. She had her comics and her latex masks and you, and nothing else.

Nothing else, that is, until I came along. Then all at once she had an audience.

"I was confused when the New Era kicked in, Tolliver—believe me. For years the Church had been a *community*, a spiritual order, cut off from the world and proud of it. Then from one day to the next, the Listener does a backflip—a lutz, even. A triple axel. Starts obsessing about the age, the government, the 'times we live in.' The point had always been that we lived *outside* of time, detached from any age—that this particular iteration packed no more *oomph* than any other. No true end and no beginning. The Great Rotation and all that honeyfuggle. Do you know about the Great Rotation?" She gave a rueful laugh. "Of course you do. You're Orson Card Tolliver's son. You're basically an Iterant by birth."

"Could you slow down a little, Julia? I'm not sure—"

"I had no clue what he was after when the Business first got started. That's what he called it, with a capital *b*: the Business, as opposed to the Church. It began with fund-raisers: fund-raisers for no one knew what. Fund-raisers to assist in the raising of funds. The rest of us went along in a daze, taking our cues from him like we'd always done, blinking like rabbits in the glare of the marquee. We were scared shitless, really. Trying to figure out the Listener's angle was like trying to do a bong hit in a blizzard.

"Anyway, so. The cable hadn't even been switched on in our Upper East Side office before he'd pegged the local neocons as easy touches. They consider themselves in a permanent state of siege: darkies and trannies and health-care reformers are scheming to eat their brains and fuck their wives while they're asleep, and they'll throw cash at anyone who keeps the nightlight on. The Listener saw that right away. It was vaudeville to him, pure and simple, but they sucked it down like cherry-flavored pop. Precious few in the Church got to see this, of course, but I did. I got a fat hairy eyeful. Not that it helped me any—NB, my current life. At the end of the day, as I've mentioned before, the day's over."

Her mouth snapped shut at that point and her eyelids came down, as if she were waiting for me to insert another coin. I'd been halfway to the vestibule already—just a few steps from Bilbo—but I decided to try once more to get things clear. I looked back at her there, sitting Indian-style on the sofa like some sort of mood-stabilized Buddha, looking about as sentient as the suit of *mithril* on the wall behind her.

"Why are you telling me all this, Julia?"

"If we're going to smite him, you need to be briefed."

"But why not just forget him? Why not pack up all of your—all of your collectibles, if that's the right term, and find some other—"

"He used me," she said, in an almost inaudible whisper. "He used all of us. And now he's using her."

"Okay, Julia. What exactly—"

"Enough with the seventh degree, Tolliver. My origin story is not for your tender ears. Here's the rub: you and I have a common objective. We both want to see R. P. Haven tied to a telephone pole by his own intestines, with crows and starlings pecking at his eyes. We want to see him strapped to the hood of his midnight-blue Lexus, heading the wrong way up FDR Drive, with his palms nailed to the sunroof, and his beautiful legs—"

"I don't know what you're talking about, Julia. I'd like to see him gone, I admit, but I don't necessarily—"

"Of course you don't, Tolliver. You just want to take his wife away. Now run along home and think on what I've told you. *Namaste.*"

∞

It was a long walk home that night, long and muddled and fraught, as Menügayan had known that it would be. I felt somehow polluted by what she'd told me, and chagrined at how greedily I'd listened; but that was only part of what I felt. There was something else there as well, glimmering up through my revulsion: something sharp-edged and precious, like a piece of jewelry seen through muddy water. There was excitement, Mrs. Haven, and the illicit thrill that covert knowledge brings. I didn't trust Menügayan—I was a pawn to her at best, I knew, and at worst some sort of sacrificial lamb—but I trusted in her hatred of the Husband.

By the time I'd locked the door of Van's studio behind me, a pressure was building behind my sternum—a steady, transistorish buzzing—that made it hard to keep my thoughts in order. Splayed across the shabby sofa with your letter in my lap, beginning to lose sensation in my extremities, I decided the feeling was either hope or cardiac arrest. I tore your letter open with my teeth.

Dear—

The truth is I don't know what to call you. "Walter" is the name of the person I'd been under the misapprehension of knowing, but it was a beautiful misapprehension, so I'll stick with it for just a little longer. I've allowed myself to write you one last letter.

I'm so depressed and knocked sideways by what the Husband and certain others have told me re: this person called "Walter," or the person <u>behind</u> him, that it's hard to know where to begin. It's possible you'll never find this note. But that would be a shame, because it's important to me that this message reach its intended recipient, whoever he is, and that he understand that I made this decision—to go away, I mean—by myself, without any pressure or advice from anybody. I don't want any advice or any explanation either. I want to get on a plane and just go. No more time

I'll start over.

Dear—

I'm leaving for the airport now. With the Husband. That's all you need to know, I think. Goodbye.

Yrs,
Schadenfreude P. Weltschmerz

If I hadn't just come from Menügayan's grotto, if I hadn't been dazzled (and not a little spooked, to be honest) by the fiery megatonnage of her hatred, I might have been more bothered by this kiss-off than I was. But on close reading, Mrs. Haven, I detected certain subtle glints of hope. You referred to our relationship as "beautiful," for one thing—or to your understanding of our relationship, which was more or less the same. What had you called it? A *misapprehension*. A fussy, clinical word, but a promising one. That you could see anything attractive in something so obviously regrettable was grounds for optimism. Wasn't it?

It's important to me, you wrote six lines later, *that this message reach its intended recipient.* I still mattered to you, in other words, frosty though your language might appear. The overall tone of the note, come to think of it, didn't sound like the woman I loved—it had a forced, contrived quality, especially in its opening lines. It occurred to me suddenly that I had no idea what the Husband had actually told you: the revelation of my true identity might have been just the beginning. I'd been exposed as a liar, after all, correctly and beyond hope of appeal. Haven knew everything there was to know about me, I was certain, and he was a master manipulator—even Menügayan acknowledged that. I pictured him standing at your shoulder as you wrote, dipping your quill into a death's-head-shaped inkwell, fine-tuning your grammar and your style. I pictured him whispering turns of phrase into your ear.

It was an unpleasant vision, Mrs. Haven, and also a superfluous one. What mattered was that I was in your thoughts.

∞

I was still in the sway of this rose-tinted faith in your mercy (and in Menügayan's mercilessness, which was just as important) when Van finally gave me the boot. For weeks I'd been coming home to find uncomfortably official-looking letters on pink carbon paper wedged under the door, in envelopes marked "TENANT" and "EQUUS SPECIAL PRODUCTS, LLC," every one of which I'd tossed into the trash. But in spite of these portents, not to mention my familiarity with my cousin's evil moods, it came as no small blow to emerge from the elevator after a long day at the Xanthia to find my apartment door wide open—wedged open, in fact, with a stack of my notebooks—and a crew of pig-eyed men in green paper jumpsuits tossing everything I owned into the hall. I shut my eyes reflexively, trying to master my shock; when I'd recovered, I found two of the men close beside me, holding something between them—a burrito-shaped bundle, wrapped in glossy black plastic—that looked like the body bag of a miniature soldier.

"Your personal items," said one of the men. He was huge and slump-shouldered and spoke with what sounded like a Polish accent. He nodded to his colleague and they placed the black burrito in my hands. I couldn't imagine what could be inside.

"I had a suitcase."

"Suitcase?" said the second mover, raising his eyebrows.

"You'd have to check with the boss," the first mover said, yawning. "Go on in. Ask for Little Brother."

"Little Brother?"

He shrugged and said nothing. Mover number two, who was hawk-nosed and blue-eyed and brilliantly bald, grinned at something a few steps behind me.

I didn't have the nerve to look over my shoulder. I picked up the bundle and slipped between them into the apartment, prying my notebooks—the ones with the first chapters of this history in it—out from under the door, which was a hard job to accomplish with dignity. The crew inside glanced up briefly, saw nothing of interest, and returned to their work. Everything in the room had been swaddled in that same jet-black plastic, including the carpet. It seemed a bit much.

"Are you in charge here?" I said to a man with a clipboard. He was somewhere in his forties and had the face of a smoker and looked even more primordially Slavic than the rest. He moved slowly, with a contented, tai chi–like deliberateness that struck me as a drawback in a mover. He nodded and passed me the clipboard.

"Sign and initial here please, Mr. Tolliver."

"Where the hell is my suitcase?"

"I'm afraid your suitcase has been treated roughly. That's what your signature's for." He indicated the clipboard. "I'll need your initials bottom left. In the teal-colored box."

"I'm not signing a goddamn thing. I want to know where my suitcase has gone."

"It's gone nowhere, Mr. Tolliver—nowhere at all. You've got it right there, under your arm."

I stared down at the bundle. My suitcase had been a stiff sixties model, made out of some sort of synthetic tweed: it was hard to imagine how it could have been flattened, much less rolled up like a taco, without recourse to hydraulics. I began to feel sick to my stomach. One of the crew stepped past me and I caught sight of the back of his jumpsuit: VAN GOGH MOVERS—A "CUT" ABOVE THE REST.

"What is it, Mr. Tolliver? There seems—if you'll pardon the expression—to be a question hovering on your lips."

"Nothing," I stammered. "No question."

"Is that so? Then I must be in error."

"Thank you," I said, for no reason at all, and the man ducked his head in reply. His eyes were glossy and depthless. I returned his nod and headed for the door.

"Where exactly are you going, Mr. Tolliver?"

For some reason this froze me in mid-stride. "I have no idea," I heard myself answer.

"I suspected that might be the case. Kindly open the door."

Automatically, numbly, I did as instructed. The first two movers were standing outside, their apelike shoulders nearly touching, obscuring my view of the hall.

"I was just asking Mr. Tolliver, here, where he thought he was going," the man said to them.

"Very good, Little Brother," they answered in unison.

"I was about to explain that our employer has instructed us to move the contents of this apartment elsewhere," said the man. "*All* of the contents." He paused. "Which, at present, includes Mr. Tolliver."

I tried to move or speak but could not do it. Things had gone supernaturally still.

"Where would you like to be moved, Mr. Tolliver?"

"Any place that you want," said mover number one. "Any place. Any time."

The room behind me gave a kind of shudder. I felt heat on the back of my neck.

"I'll tell you what I think," said the man with the clipboard. "For the present, let's let Mr. Tolliver move himself."

"If he can," said number two, frowning. "He looks kind of stuck."

"He'll be all right," said someone behind me. "He'll be *fine*." For a moment, in my panic, I imagined that the voice was Haven's own. I tried to take a step and nothing happened.

"You may go," said the man with the clipboard.

Something shifted again, the light seemed to brighten, and my body tumbled out into the hall. I lurched toward the stairwell. Its door had been wedged open with a battered playing card.

"Pardon the misapprehension, Mr. Tolliver. Please take our card—you never know when you might need it. Feel free to drop by at any time."

I dashed down all six flights without looking behind me. I was out on the street before I glanced at the card in my hand. It was the fool from the tarock deck, dancing his grotesque quadrille in black and gold and purple, his jolly left eye closing in a wink.

XVIII

ON A CHALK-COLORED Sunday in early October, four years to the day after heading downstate, my father caught sight of something in a Lexington Avenue shop window that stopped him in his tracks. Things stopped him in his tracks all the time on his walks—stockinged calves, pipe smoke, even the occasional stoplight—but this event was of a different order. The item in question was a pack of playing cards, slightly taller and wider than a standard poker deck, browned along the edges and speckled with age. Orson gawked through the glass for a while, took a few aimless steps, then stepped quickly into the shop. The shopkeeper, a white-bearded Czech who looked of roughly the same vintage as the cards themselves, and was shockingly disheveled even for a junk dealer (though just about right for a physicist, Orson thought), scooped the pack up unceremoniously into his tobacco-stained fingers, as though it had no particular value, and passed it to my father with a sigh.

"What's your trouble, grandpop?" said my father, whose manners hadn't been done any favors by the move to New York. "Don't you care for my looks?"

"It's not cards to read the future with. Tarock, it's called—not *tarotové karty*. A game only. Try to tell the future and you'll see."

"See what, exactly?"

The Czech made no reply. Orson gave him his most hard-boiled squint.

"Who said anything about the future, anyhow?"

"No one plays this game anymore," said the shopkeeper. "Not around here." He coughed into his beard. "There used to be clubs."

Orson flipped the topmost card over: a face card, identical to the one he'd seen through the window. Heavier than a poker card, and cut from stiffer stock. "My grandfather used to play this game," he said. "What's this first one—the joker?"

"No jokers in tarock," harrumphed the shopkeeper.

"What's the name of this card, then?"

"I don't know in English."

"Then tell me in German. Or in Czech. Whichever."

The old man shrugged his shoulders. "In French it was called *L'excuse.*"

Orson frowned and brought the card up to the light. A wavy-haired man in what might either have been the costume of a soldier or a harlequin held a saucer-shaped hat on which another man, dressed in the same gaudy outfit, was dancing. This dancer, who was roughly squirrel-sized, held a hat in his own hand, no bigger than an espresso cup, into which the wavy-haired man was pointing, as if there were something of significance inside. The effect was agreeably dizzying, like tracing the curve of a Möbius strip. The image *itself* was like a Möbius strip, come to think of it: an infinite loop with a twist in the middle. It represented something—that much was clear—though God alone knew what that thing might be.

"Where were these cards made?"

"I don't know," said the shopkeeper. "Vienna, maybe."

"How do you play?"

"It goes counterclockwise."

"Counterclockwise," said Orson. He thought for a moment. "I was reading something about that just this morning. It's supposed to be the direction the Milky Way spins."

"*That,*" said the shopkeeper, "depends on who's looking. You never heard of relativity?"

Orson held up the fool. "How much do you want for this card?"

"For the card I want nothing. For the deck, twenty bucks."

The price was outrageous—a three-course dinner at the Old Homestead Steak House—but my father paid it. He was a young man of means, after all.

"It's not for telling the future," the Czech repeated, stuffing the bills into his jacket pocket. "You heard me, smarty *kalhoty?* No moneys back."

∞

The truth was that Orson badly needed a glimpse of the future just then. He'd arrived in New York flush with the sense of clairvoyance all bright young men have, confident of the world's submissiveness; the world, however, had seen no pressing reason to oblige. Ewa Ruszczyk's cousin had told him to "go fry a duck" when he'd shown up at Forty-Second Street, then kicked the door shut in his face, and the next four years had been a series of variations on this theme. The city was mysteriously indifferent to his fate.

It pains me to admit it, Mrs. Haven, but *la vie bohème* was wasted on my father. According to his letters home, he spent his first twelve months in a cold-water studio on Christopher and Seventh, just three doors down from the Village Vanguard, without ever once looking inside. He didn't go in for jazz ("the musical equivalent of aftershave," he said to me once) and marijuana made him laugh at things that weren't funny. He kept to himself for the most part, eating tepid knishes on piss-smelling benches and sulking in secondhand bookshops; his acquaintances ranged from hopheads to wallflowers to bottom-tier grifters ("ectoplasmic hookworms," in Orson-speak), none of whom he actually liked. The Village was at its sociohistoric apogee in those years—its most self-obsessed and manic and debauched—but Orson might as well have stayed in Cheektowaga.

To be fair to my father, he logged his due share of hours in the coffee shops, notebook in hand, and he did give dissipation a go every once in a while, in a halfhearted way; but he'd chosen the only neighborhood in America, it seemed, where wealth was considered a social disease. The first girl he'd told about his inheritance—late one Saturday night, at the Kettle of Fish—had spit in his lager and lifted his wallet. What was worse, when he'd finally caught up with her a few nights later, holding court on the very same barstool, she hadn't been a bit apologetic.

"You're a Jew, Tolliver. You've got plenty of lettuce."

"I'm actually not Jewish, technically speaking," he'd found himself mumbling, which hadn't been what he'd meant to say at all.

"Don't try to flimflam *me*, Lord Fauntleroy. Your sisters used to read you to sleep with the Talmud."

"Who told you that?"

"You did," she'd said, turning back to her grog. "Last Saturday night. Right before you started bawling like a baby."

An error had been made, Orson decided: a miscalculation, either in his estimation of the Village or in the Village's estimation of him. He'd had only the vaguest of hopes for his life as an artist—Rothko-like puffs of color, too diffuse to call daydreams—but the city's indifference had snuffed even those. Peers and fellow travelers were hard to find, girlfriends next to impossible. Literary pretensions were derided—excoriated, really—in the Bleecker Street cafés: not because they seemed bold, but because everybody and his mother had literary pretensions. Girls who cared about books went for Sexton and Sartre; science fiction, according to their boyfriends (novelists all, *naturellement*), was for Ukrainian immigrants and nose-picking teens. Orson got his own nose bloodied more than once in defense of the genre, and inevitably staggered home in tears, which only served to prove the boyfriends' point. Ambition and talent (and lettuce) notwithstanding, my father was still, by anyone's yardstick, a teenager himself.

It was only to be expected, given this state of affairs, that Orson pined for big-boned, sloe-eyed Ewa Ruszczyk; but the predictability of his loneliness depressed him even more. He was a writer, and allergic—or so he flattered himself—to the marzipan-like odor of cliché. Ewa had decided, at the last possible instant, not to run away with Orson. The last he'd heard, she was "going steady" (hateful phrase!) with a thirty-year-old ROTC recruiter. He'd expected so much more of her. Who was his audience now?

On his last night in Buffalo, by way of a consolation prize, Ewa had picked him up in her father's Montclair and driven him out to the Bird Island pier, where she'd folded down the backseat, spread out a camping blanket, and proceeded to undress herself completely—socks, barrette, sugar-free chewing gum and all. He'd been picturing her naked body at fifteen-minute intervals for the better part of a year, in every conceivable attitude; but this once, Mrs. Haven, his imagination had failed him. She was even downier than he'd imagined, and her breasts were heavier, which was glorious and frightening at once. The skin there was pale, almost bluish, which surprised him most of all—he'd expected her to be golden brown all over. *Commit this to memory, Orson*, he'd said to himself, as she pulled him down onto the blanket. *If you retain one single hour of your dura tion, make it this.*

∞

My father did have one great advantage over his beret-sporting, bop-listening, café-haunting literary rivals, Mrs. Haven, which was that he actually wrote. He was churning out stories, in fact, at a clip that would have sent even Philip K. Dick fumbling for his inhaler. "Plexiglass Children," "The Curious Splotches," "BIEHXIXHEIB," and "The Voyage of the Silver Esophagus," to name just a few: some of Orson's best-known stories date from his self-imposed exile on Christopher Street. Beatnik snobs notwithstanding, these were sci-fi's boom years, and the hunger of the pulps was never slaked. His dirty work sold more quickly and made him more money, but even his respectable material ("your dry-pussy stories," as his *DarkEncounters* editor so decorously put it) managed to see the light of day from time to time. He referred to defeat, in his diary, as "eating a death biscuit," and saved his rejection slips with the masochistic relish of a natural-born hack.

Occasionally he sent a draft home to his sisters, accompanied by a note—half disclaimer, half challenge—instructing them to stop reading as soon as they got bored. Enzian took him at his word, rarely mentioning his writing in her matter-of-fact replies; Genny praised them to the strato-sphere ("Just so promising, Peanut! A *virus* spread by a computer? Who on earth would have thought!!!"), which was somehow even more disheartening. He was selling regularly now to *Preposterous! Stories*, and to second-tier pulps with names like *Dodecahedron* and *If*; but a sense of failure dogged him all the same. He tore open each envelope from Enzie eagerly, hoping in spite of himself for a word of encouragement, only to read yet another detailed account of Kaspar's dementia, which by this point was advancing by the hour.

Orson had vowed to himself to remain in the Village until his twenti-eth birthday or until he got famous, whichever came first; but after a year and a half, from one day to the next, he packed his yellow steamer trunk (the same trunk Sonja had used, half a lifetime before, for her collection of white linen gowns) and migrated five miles north, to Spanish Harlem. The reason for this move remains obscure. It may have been that he felt like an expatriate there, surrounded by sprawling Puerto Rican and Dominican families, and that he found the feeling liberating; maybe he simply liked the lower rent. Or possibly—and this isn't as far-fetched as it sounds—he'd caught a glimpse of his future at last, Mrs. Haven, and he knew that resistance was useless.

Kaspar died on November 5, 1964—the same month, according to legend, that Luchino Visconti began work, half a world away, on the screenplay of his masterpiece *The Damned*. It was also the year, appropriately enough, in which Irwin Shapiro of the Massachussetts Institute of Technology made use of astronomical radar (whatever *that* is) to measure the reduction in the speed of light rays traveling through the gravitational field of the sun, and found it in perfect accord with relativity's predictions. (The deeper my research has led me into the history of my family, Mrs. Haven, the more this tripartite coincidence strikes me as the punch line to an elaborate vaudeville routine—but more on this later.) Genny informed Orson, by telegram, that their father had died in his sleep; in reality his last hours had been spent in precisely that state—at the mathematical midpoint between waking and dreaming—to which he'd devoted the final decade of his life.

Dying, Newton once wrote, is a polite undertaking, by definition the most self-effacing of acts; but even so, my grandfather's demise was something of a pièce de résistance. He laid down his burden with so little fuss, in fact, that Enzian, who was sitting beside him on the chesterfield, noticed nothing until Genny called them to dinner. She'd been helping him to organize the photographs he'd brought from Vienna—the same parcel of blanched, water-stained images Orson had once attempted to make sense of. In all the years they'd lived at Pine Ridge Road, Enzian had never seen him look at them once; just that morning, however, he'd insisted they bring them into strict chronological order. They'd barely begun before his eyes had fallen closed.

Now she brought Genny in from the kitchen and they examined their father together. Neither had ever seen a cadaver, but they both knew they were looking at one now. A few errant snapshots lay curled in the crotch of his trousers, an improvised fig leaf in sepia and gray; moments before, they'd been rustling in time to his breath. Nothing out of the ordinary had occurred—no gasp, no thunderclap, no sudden chill—but the body had been utterly tranformed. It was evidence now, proof that something was missing, like the depression in a wheat field where a deer has spent the night.

For the first time since either could remember, the twins avoided looking at each other. Enzian had the impression—though she'd been back from the university for hours—of having come home an instant too late. Gentian felt a sudden urge to laugh.

"He's got to the end of his term," she said finally.

"He *seems* to have," said Enzian. "Yes."

"What do we do? Do we call the police?"

"If you care to. But first we call Orson."

"But *Enzie*," said Genny, laughing in spite of herself. "He doesn't even have a telephone!"

∞

Orson missed the interment but arrived home in time for the memorial service, which was starkly lit and full of fish-faced strangers. It was held in the banquet hall of the Western New York Chapter of the Independent Order of Odd Fellows, of which Kaspar turned out—to almost everyone's amazement—to have been a member for twenty-two years. Orson kept to the back of the drop-ceilinged hall, humming to drown out the saccharine service; he tried to identify a single person in the room aside from his sisters and his uncle Wilhelm, but apparently Cheektowaga's population had been swapped, during his absence, for a race of glassy-eyed automatons. That gave him the idea for a story, a good one, but he couldn't get it clear—not at his father's memorial service, no matter how emphatically he hummed. He slipped out midway through a eulogy by someone in a mud-colored toupee. Wilhelm was next, but the years hadn't been kind to him, either—and in any case the story wouldn't wait.

The contours of its plot were already starting to blur as Orson backed out of the hall, a sensation that never failed to rack him with anxiety. He shouldn't have come, he realized: not to that god-awful service, not to Pine Ridge Road, not to Buffalo at all. The criminal returns to the scene of the crime, as every self-respecting genre jockey knows, at which point he gets locked up for life—if he's lucky—or frizzled to death in the electric chair.

The fern-cluttered foyer was empty aside from Orson and a woman of about his age, with the stony, joyless look of a person who did something unappreciated for a living. She was standing with her arms tightly crossed, smoking one of those mentholated cigarettes that were all the rage in 1964, and ashing onto the potted fern behind her. Orson recognized her at once, though he counted down from ten, for precautionary reasons, before he dared to speak her name aloud.

"Hello, Ewa."

"Welcome home, Orson. Thanks for getting in touch."

There was a harshness to her that he couldn't explain. "Genny told me you got married," he said—and realized, as he said it, what the unappreciated thing must be. "You've got a kid, am I right? A daughter?"

"Don't bullshit me, Orson. You don't want to talk about my daughter. Children make your tonsils itch."

What could she resent *me* for? Orson thought. Trying to talk her into leaving Cheektowaga? Not trying hard enough? What gives her the right? Indignation washed over him, quickly followed by pity—but the back of his throat began to itch regardless. At least I'm not sobbing, he thought. At least I'm not begging her to take me back. But he found, to his own astonishment, that the thought held no appeal for him. The itching in his throat was all he felt.

"I'll never understand why—"

"Why what, Orson?"

"Why you never got away from here."

"Is that right."

"That you didn't come with me—I can understand that, I guess. But that you stayed in this—in this *place*—"

"We can talk about it once you've gotten settled," Ewa said, smiling. It wasn't a well-intentioned smile. It seemed more like a leer of victory.

"Settled? What does that—"

"After you move back, I mean. We'll have plenty of time to talk about it then."

"Move back?" said Orson, his mind going blank. "I'm not going to move back, Ewa. Where did you hear—"

"Your sister told me."

Orson's scalp started to prickle. "Jesus Christ. I knew Enzie was nuts, but where she got *that* idea—"

"It wasn't Enzie that told me."

"What—" He closed his eyes. "It wasn't? You mean—"

"That's right, city boy. It was Genny."

That yanked the rug out from under him completely. He shook his head and gave a frightened sneeze.

"I guess we'll be seeing each other around," said Ewa, flicking her cigarette into a corner. "I'm looking forward to it. You can tell me about your fabulous career."

"I'm *never*," Orson got out finally. "I'm never moving back here." But his voice was drowned out by polite applause.

∞

Orson left the next morning on the 20th Century Limited, the earliest possible train, after a night unlike any he'd passed with his sisters before. Enzie, normally so austere, had sat slumped at the dinner table, staring at her pork chop as if expecting it to speak; Genny had been giddier than ever, babbling about all and sundry, barely able to sit still long enough to eat. Orson had studied her closely, trying to puzzle out the meaning of what she'd told Ewa Ruszczyk. The only explanation Genny had offered— grudgingly, it had seemed to him—was that "a little birdy" had told her he'd be moving home.

"A little birdy, Genny? What's that supposed to—"

"Not a *birdy*, exactly," she'd said, smiling down at her plate.

"She told herself," Enzie had muttered darkly. "She told herself, by God. And she believed it."

His sisters' unmooring hit him harder than his father's death had done. He'd been resisting them both for the whole of his adult life, for no better reason than their irresistibility: they'd been preternatural to him, less elder sisters than de facto parents, less parents than agents of some arrogant, exacting cosmic will. But this had changed with Kaspar's passing, changed radically and without warning, as if his dying breath had tripped some hidden wire. The twins may have been absolute rulers of the world they'd created, but their father—at least toward the end of his term—had been their sole remaining subject. They had no one left to rule now but themselves.

∞

If any doubt persisted that the earth had shifted subtly on its axis—that the time, at least for Orson, was severely out of joint—his second escape from Buffalo erased it. He ought to have felt exhilaration at sidestepping Genny's prophecy, or at least some modest measure of relief; instead he spent his first week back in Spanish Harlem in his star-spangled pajamas (a gift from Genny on his fifteenth birthday), drinking beer and feeling sorry for himself. The apartment smelled faintly of cat piss, he was sure of it, though he had no cats and neither did his neighbors. *Maybe I'll have cats in the future*, he said to himself. *Maybe I have cats right now, in dimension X/12. I'll have to ask my sisters about that.*

He let out a groan at this thought and crawled back into bed. The vertigo he'd picked up at the Odd Fellows Hall had grown sharper with time, and his lunatic family—Genny, especially—seemed to have permanently colonized his dreams. Worst of all, that awful run-in with Ewa had shone a new light on his Great Emancipation: his monomaniacal pursuit of the artist's life seemed less an act of heroism, suddenly, than one of adolescent self-indulgence. He could be viewed as a dilettante, he realized: a privileged snob, a hack with delusions of grandeur, no different than the turtlenecked deep-thinkers he looked down on. His hometown had endured—had refused to expire, to implode, to break down into its component particles—in spite of the fact that he'd abandoned it. Just the opposite: in his absence, it seemed to have thrived.

The upshot of this new understanding was that, for the first time since he'd moved to New York City—for the first time since he'd hit puberty, in fact—my father couldn't write to save his life. The trip home had only reinforced his resolve to make art for *himself*, not his sisters, and he stuck to his ban on time travel, going so far as to outlaw the mention of time in his stories altogether; far from setting him free, however, this last decision crippled him completely. He'd long since discovered that time (beyond its obvious importance) was wondrously useful as a descriptive tool, sometimes even as a metaphor: it was invaluable in writing about sex and robotics and beauty and the vastness of space, to name a few favorite topics. There was a catch, however, an unforeseen con, which was that sex and robotics and beauty and the vastness of space (not to mention love, and death, and even good old-fashioned human consciousness) seemed to Orson, more often than not, to be metaphors for writing about time.

My father began no fewer than thirty-nine stories that spring, some of which ("The Pumpless Pump," "The Marsupial Light & Power Company," "An Experiment in Gyro-Hats") he kept in a drawer for the next forty years, which means he must have seen potential in them. The only story he actually finished, however—a six-page cavalcade of unsavoriness whose title, "In No Particular Odor," pretty much says it all—was such a spectacular stinker that even *DarkEncounters* wouldn't touch it. By August he'd thrown in the towel altogether.

For a few days he tried to teach himself tarock, sliding the cards lackadaisically around on the floor with his toes; but he was in no state to learn anything by then. He ranged farther and farther on his afternoon walks, less out of curiosity or a sense of adventure than to put off the return to his apartment. The hour before sunset—which had always been the most productive of his day—now found him shuffling in circles in Morningside Park, or in the rococo lobby of the Woolworth Building, or on the wooden walkway of the Brooklyn Bridge. Drifting brought on a numbness, a bearable remove from the facts of his duration, at least if he roamed far enough. For the first week he brought along a pocket notebook, in case inspiration should strike; then a folded sheet of stationery; then a napkin or a page torn from the *Times*. By September he'd stopped carrying even that.

It was on one of these daily forced marches—a little longer than most, perhaps, but in no way unusual—that he was catapulted clear of his despond. Aimless as his rambles seemed, they tended to take him downtown more often than up, and to Brooklyn more often than he could explain. He'd grown fascinated, in a numb sort of way, by the spatial dynamics between the two immense bridges, which lifted off from far-flung locations near the tip of Manhattan only to touch down in Brooklyn at virtually the same coordinates in space. Their geometry made his synapses fire in the same way that the tarock deck had done: an idea was being expressed—

this time on the grandest possible scale—and though its meaning kept its distance he could feel it in his body, as a buzzing in his cortex and his spine.

The pie wedge of buildings enclosed by this confluence—which had precisely the same proportions as the triangle formed by the bridges' great twinned arcs across the river—was one of the most obscure precincts in the city, bordered on two sides by stone-and-brickwork thoroughfares and on the third by the river itself. It had no name, only a postal code. The land-lords and warehouse foremen were generally Hasidic, the workers Puerto Rican or Polish. At times Orson had the feeling that he was trespassing in some private and melancholy city, one that magically mirrored his own state of mind.

It was a tiny place really, less than twelve blocks all told, but each visit yielded up some new discovery. In spite of their grandiose names— Plymouth, Hudson, Gold, Pearl—the streets were narrow and dark, mak-ing unforeseen turns, often stopping short without the slightest warning. In the courtyard of an egg-yolk-colored building at the corner of Water and Gold, Buddhist monks played basketball on sunny afternoons, holding the hems of their vestments in one hand and dribbling with the other; from the roof of a rimless Buick at the foot of Jay Street, a Korean War veteran who answered to the name of "Mr. Bread" delivered lectures on Marxist ethics to indifferent passersby. Mr. Bread recognized Orson as a brother in literary arms, and paid him the compliment of sending him on the occa-sional errand to Brooklyn Heights, usually to pick up ointment for his per-petually bandaged shins. Adrift as he was, Orson happily obliged.

On the afternoon in question, in exchange for a bottle of aspirin, Mr. Bread gave my father a piece of advice. "Get a job," he said, chewing the aspirin like candy. "Get a job, Tolliver, and get your hair cut. Not neces-sarily in that order."

"I have a job," said Orson. "I'm a writer."

"A *job*," Mr. Bread repeated.

"I'm surprised to hear that from you," replied Orson. "Whatever hap-pened to the great class struggle?"

"The time for revolution is not yet ripe."

There was no arguing with that, Mrs. Haven, so he didn't try.

"I've never had a job. A real one, I mean."

Mr. Bread made a gesture—a comfortable twitch of the shoulders—to indicate the self-evidence of this statement.

"I might as well do something with my time, I guess, since I can't seem to write. But I wouldn't know where—"

"Power plant's hiring. Security work. Nothing to do all day but sit on your *culo* and dream about Jackie Kennedy's unmentionables."

Orson narrowed his eyes. "Why don't *you* take the job, if it's such a hayride?"

"I have a job," Mr. Bread said proudly. "I'm a writer."

∞

The Hudson/Gold Power Generating Station was a stone's toss from Mr. Bread's roadster. My father set out without much hope or ambition, straightening a borrowed paisley tie; he didn't expect much, for various reasons, and by the time he knew better—as is often the case, Mrs. Haven, with blows to the head by the hammer of fate—there was nothing left to do but cry to heaven.

"Jesus H. Christ!" Orson heard himself shout.

He'd just rounded the corner of Plymouth and Gold—a quaint little cluster of houses, worlds removed from the warehouses and garment factories behind him—and had caught his first glimpse of the station. It was colossal, fortresslike, far more forbidding than he'd imagined; but he barely took in such mundane details. What knocked him sideways was the flickering sign, gaudy as a Times Square marquee, that hung suspended from its massive gate:

WELCOME TO THE HUDSON * GOLD POWER
GENERATING * STATION. 0062 HOURS
WITHOUT A LOST * TIME ACCIDENT.

The world went unnaturally quiet: he heard nothing but the humming of high-tension wires and the rush of blood to his bewildered brain. A man in his thirties, in security grays, took his measure from the window of a hut.

"Sign needs changing," the man said. "We're way past sixty-two."

"What exactly—" said Orson, then ran out of breath. "What exactly is a lost time accident?"

"Sixty-two hours isn't even three whole days. Today's what—Tuesday? Tuesday the seventeenth?"

Orson managed to nod.

"There you go," said the guard. "It's been three weeks at least."

"I still don't understand—"

"What are you here for, son? You one of them power freaks?"

"Not at all," Orson answered, holding up both his hands. "I'm not sure what that means, to be honest. I'm here about the job."

The guard pursed his lips. "And what job would that be?"

"Well—" He hesitated. "Your job, I guess."

The guard scrutinized him for a full minute, which is a long time to look someone dead in the eye without saying a word. His cap, which was peaked and black and seemed slightly too tight, put Orson more in mind of a school-bus driver than an agent of the law.

"The night shift, I'm thinking," the guard said finally.

"The night shift," Orson said. "Sure."

"I work days."

"Okay." Orson nodded. "Do you think—"

"They're not seeing people at present. Later on, maybe."

"How much later?"

The guard stared at him blankly.

"I'm sorry, but I was given to understand—"

"I can't let you in at this time," the guard said, not unkindly. "You can wait on that chair over there."

Orson followed his gaze to a low wooden stool, the kind shoeshine boys sat on, propped against the chain-link fence. "Okay, then," he said.

"Okay, then," said the guard.

"What's a lost time accident?"

The guard nodded shrewdly. "Best to ask them inside."

"Fair enough," said Orson. He stood still for a moment, then leaned sideways and peered through the gate.

"Go ahead and try it, if you're tempted. Keep one thing in mind, though—I take my work seriously."

"What?" said Orson. "No, no! I wasn't thinking—"

"And I'm just the first guard. There's others inside, and they're not as sweet-natured as I am."

"I had no intention—"

"This here is Hudson Gate. The next gate is Compound; the third one's Facility. I may not look like much, but you should see the guy at Compound." The guard shook his head. "The guy at Facility even scares me."

Orson sat down on the little stool.

"*Now* you're using your bean," said the guard.

∞

Over the next several hours, watching the sun decline behind the station's soot-streaked ramparts, Orson came nearer to grasping the concept of infinity than he ever had before. To increase time's velocity, he told the guard what little he knew of his family's past, from his grandfather's discovery in Znojmo to his father's escape from Vienna. He hoped to get the guard to reciprocate, perhaps even to divulge the secrets of the Hudson/Gold Power Generating Station, or at least of its cryptic marquee; but his hope was in vain. The guard listened to his stories willingly—appreciatively, even—but he met each question about the station with a noncommital smile.

My father began to imagine himself sitting propped against that chain-link fence for the remainder of his extension into the fourth dimension, fashioning a life for himself with only the guard and the river for company. He saw himself growing progressively slacker and more hunched as his body conformed to the stool, waiting for word from the station that never arrived. After fifty-odd years he'd simply wither away to nothing; before he expired, however, he'd beckon to the guard, who would kneel down to receive his dying words. *How can it be*, he would gasp, *that in the half century I've spent sitting next to this gate, no one else has ever tried to enter?*

He was in the middle of deciding what the answer might be when the guard stepped to the gate and waved him in. To his disappointment, the interview took place in a Quonset hut a few yards inside the fence, not within the facility proper. It consisted of exactly six questions, the last of which was whether he'd ever done time. Before he'd even gotten his bearings, he was back at the guardhouse with a brown paper bundle in his hands. He hadn't been told what the bundle contained, but he was guessing a uniform, a flashlight, and a cap that would make him look more like a schoolbus driver than an agent of the law.

"Welcome to the Hudson/Gold Power Generating Station," the guard told him gravely, packing his personal effects into a Chiquita banana crate that he'd been using as a footstool. "I trust you'll take your work here seriously."

"Where are you going?"

"To the next guardhouse in. Can't have two bugs in one jar."

"But you're here in the daytime," said Orson. "I'll be working nights."

"Can't have two bugs in one jar," the guard repeated, as though Orson were forgetting his manners.

"Two bugs," Orson mumbled. "Okay."

"Did you find out about the lost time accidents?"

To his shock Orson realized he'd forgotten to ask. "I thought I might hold off for a while," he replied. "Until I get my bearings."

"Fair enough. When you figure it out, be sure to let me know."

Orson squinted at him. "You mean *you* don't know, either?"

"It doesn't seem to mean much," said the guard. "Just a fancy way of saying the system's conked out. The house of cards falls down on them every once in a while, and the management needs a term for that—a technical term—to make it sound more like an act of God. It's nothing more than an excuse, if you ask me."

Orson went quiet for a moment. "An excuse?"

Monday, 09:05 EST

I searched the tunnels all day, Mrs. Haven, with nothing to show for it by sundown but a cramp. It's never occurred to me how easy it would be to hide an object—*any* object, even a human being—in the coils and convolutions of the Archive. Who's to say the chambers I've discovered are the only ones here? I have only the blurriest sense of where one room ends and the next one begins, after all. I'm using decades-old memories to navigate by.

Sensing the next sleep cycle approaching, I began yanking objects out of the walls at random, hoping to uncover hidden chutes and galleries; instead I had to dig myself out from under landslides of VHS cassettes and take-out trays and Sharper Image catalogs. As exhaustion set in, I found myself asking a question I'd never thought to ask before: What if these grottoes and trenches came about not by accident, as a by-product of my aunts' dementia, but as part of some larger design?

This idea had just hit—I was lying on the kitchen floor at the time, massaging a crick in my neck—when a sound carried in from the Archive. It was the real thing, Mrs. Haven, not a subsonic hum or a liminal whir or the grannyish complaining of my bowels: a series of knocks, as if someone were testing a wall or a door—or possibly even the floor—for points of entry. It seemed whole rooms away, but these walls swallow sound, as I've mentioned before. It might almost have been close enough to touch.

I dropped onto my belly like the cockroach I'm becoming and scrabbled slowly forward, pausing every few feet to make sure the sound hadn't stopped. It was coming from somewhere to my right, I was certain of that, but pinpointing it was maddeningly tricky. When at last I reached the spot where the knocking was sharpest, I attacked the wall in such a frenzy that the ceiling should have fallen on my head. The detritus was packed more haphazardly there, like a spot of slightly mealier decay in an already badly rotten set of teeth, and in no time I'd exposed a narrow door. Its knob made a crack when I turned it, as though it had been painted shut from the inside, and the knocking grew brighter. It was coming from a radiator pipe—that was obvious now. The door gave a pop, like the report of an air gun, and I toppled in.

I found myself in a dust-choked recess, barely wider than my spread arms, the bulk of which was taken up by an enormous bed. There was no space to spare between the bed and the walls, not even the width of a finger: it must have been brought into the room in sections and assembled inside, like a ship in a bottle. An entire family—grandparents, parents, grandchildren and all—could have passed the night in it without discomfort. The knocking was coming from a heating pipe beside it, just as I'd guessed.

How to explain what happened next, Mrs. Haven? The urge overtook me, filthy though that great bed was, to climb over the footboard and hide under its covers. I'd never encountered so totemic an object, Tolliver-wise: I imagined my elders sleeping between those varnished bedboards—all the heroes and the villains of this history of mine, from Enzie to Kaspar to Ottokar himself—and felt a genealogical ache to join them there. However this monstrous object had come to be shoehorned into that cramped and airless chamber, it had traveled across a vast expanse of time and space to do so. It was possible that generations of my forefathers had been born in that bed, and even likelier that some of them had died in it. But in spite of this thought—or because of it, maybe—I wanted to wrap myself up in those sheets.

"You don't have to be quiet," came a voice. "I'm already awake."

A bunched, loglike mass near the headboard started twitching at this, like a sackful of mice. You'd think I'd be innoculated against surprise by this point, Mrs. Haven, but what I was seeing nearly dropped me to the floor. I clutched at the pipe to keep from falling over: it was scalding, and I snatched my hand back with a cry. But the pain passed at once, was flushed clear of my brain, because the thing under the covers had sat up.

"It's you, of course," I murmured. "Who else could it possibly be?"

I can't explain how I knew that the thing on the bed was the man I'd been named for—Waldemar Toula, the Black Timekeeper of Äschenwald-Czas—but I was sure even before I'd seen its face. It had to be him, Mrs. Haven. And therefore it was.

"I had an eyeglass somewhere," he said, shivering slightly. He spoke in a damp, droning hiss, like steam issuing out of a pipe.

"A what?"

"Not an eyeglass—what's the word—what's the blessed *word* for it in English?"

"A monocle," I said, as though it were the most ordinary question in the world.

Already my mind was recovering its equilibrium, finding a place for this latest impossibility in the same walk-in freezer where the others were kept. I've had practice integrating the unintegratable by now, after all. I felt no need to question the reality of what I was seeing.

"You can't do anything about this radiator, can you?" he said, letting the coverlet slip from his shoulders. "It's banging loud enough to wake the dead."

Deliberately, quietly, my great-uncle came into focus. His face composed itself out of a field of charged mnemonic particles: I'm aware how this must sound, Mrs. Haven, but I don't know how else to describe it. His body caught the light and held it strangely, as if he'd been assembled out of dust. He was dressed in a chalk-stripe suit of banker's blue, but his jacket and his tie were badly creased, and his hair had the chopped, formless look of a military buzz cut gone to seed. He was smaller than he looked in photographs. I hadn't expected his wheat-paste complexion, either, or the Parkinson's-like trembling of his hands. He looked less like a fugitive from justice, all things considered, than a drunk who'd spent the night under a bush. This wasn't the dapper Goering look-alike of 1938, or the headstrong physics prodigy of the first years of the century—it was the ailing, ragged indigent of Budapest during the famine, superimposed over faded snapshots of my father in his youth, and perhaps some spectral iteration of myself.

"I want to know what's happened to me," I said. "I want to know who brought me here. And I want to know why."

Waldemar gazed past me at a soot mark on the ceiling. His pupils had an oily, milky cast.

"You have me at a disadvantage," he said finally. "My eyesight is poor and my memory's worse. I don't recall that we've been introduced."

If not for his delivery, Mrs. Haven, I might have believed him. But he spoke smoothly and mechanically—glibly, even—like a ventriloquist's marionette.

"I asked you a question," I said, giving the footboard a kick.

He nodded placidly. "Can I trouble you for a glass of water?"

"How long have you been lying in this bed?"

A look of relief crossed his face. "*That* I can tell you exactly. I've been counting the knocks, you see, to make the time go by." He arched his back and heaved a drawn-out sigh. "I'd just made it to three hundred and eight when you arrived. Now I'll have to start again from the beginning."

I thought for a moment. "So you've just gotten here."

"That's true, I suppose."

"Where were you hiding before?"

"Before—?"

"That's right, Uncle. Back when you were creeping around in the Archive, leaving clever little clues for me to find. Or can't you remember that, either?"

He smiled up at me now: a perfect idiot's smile, almost flirtatious. "As the soul grows toward eternal life, *Nefflein*, it remembers less and less."

"Don't you dare quote my great-grandfather's notes to me."

He let out a bright, soggy snuffle at that—midway between a laugh and a snort of contempt. "Who has more right to quote a father than his son?"

"You have no rights at all. Not with me."

"Don't go putting on airs. We're *Familie*, my boy. You ought to treat your flesh and blood with more respect."

A wave of sickness hit me when I heard those words, Mrs. Haven: a decade's worth of shame and indignation, breaking free of the containing walls I'd built. I thought back to the day I'd first learned of my namesake's existence, at an age when I still thought of my name—and of my family—as a thing to take pride in. I remembered the thrill that I'd felt, as a child, on those rare occasions when the Timekeeper was mentioned. I remembered the moment I'd finally grasped what he'd done.

"What is it, *Nefflein*? You look a bit green at the gills."

I stood at the foot of the bed, fighting to maintain my balance, opening and closing my fists. "Ridiculous as it might sound," I said, "I've imagined what would happen if we met."

"That's not ridiculous in the slightest. Take a look—here the two of us are!"

"That's right, Uncle. Here we are, just as I pictured it." I took in a breath. "And I told myself—I made a vow to myself—that if this day ever came, I'd carry out your sentence."

"What sentence would that be?"

"The sentence of death."

His milky eyes widened. "*Death*, little Waldemar! Whatever for?"

"For the crimes—" The blood roared in my ears. "For the crimes you committed at the Äschenwald camp."

"*Ach!*—for that. I thought perhaps for figuring out about the Accidents." He snuffled again. "No one else could, you know." He shook his head. "Certainly not your grandfather, that Yid-loving ass."

A surge of electricity shot through me as my fist met his jaw—the kind of prickling chill ghost hunters describe in their memoirs—and he fell backward with a satisfying thump. I felt grateful to him then, as I watched him scrambling to right himself: he was playing his part obligingly and well. But then something shifted, Mrs. Haven. Things fell out of proportion. The hissing built to a shriek as he drew himself upward: the bedsheets rose behind him like a jellyfish, billowing up until they darkened half the room. I saw him now as Marta Svoboda had seen him, as Sonja had seen him, as the prisoners at Äschenwald had seen him, and I felt the same unreasoning dread they must have felt. He took hold of me and bent me back until my shoulders touched the floor. His blank gray features overwhelmed my sight.

"You should *thank* me," he said. "Not everybody has your opportunities."

"Thank you? What do you mean?"

"Who wouldn't want to take his forefathers to task for their sins?" He wrapped himself around me like a shroud. "Who wouldn't like a chance at playing judge and jury?"

"If I execute you, Uncle, it won't be for my own sake. It will be to take you out of circulation—to take you out of contention—so you can't ever—"

"Can't ever what? Continue in this duration, living proof that the chronoverse can be manipulated—that time travel is possible? Who will benefit from this settling of accounts, *Nefflein*, aside from you yourself?"

Silence fell for a moment. His face buzzed and flickered.

"That won't work on me, Uncle," I said through clenched teeth. "No end can justify the means you used at Czas."

He was back in bed now, frail and docile again. But there was a new light in his clouded eyes, or so it seemed to me. "You're a Toula," he whispered. "Don't try to deny it."

"That means *nothing*," I hissed back. My voice was sounding more like his with every word I spoke. "Toula's a name, that's all—an empty noise, like Oppenheimer or Goering or Haven. Don't treat it like some sort of magic spell."

He laughed and swung his legs over the footboard. "Let me ask you this, *Nefflein*. Can you be sure—can you be absolutely certain—that you'd have turned down the chance I was offered in that godforsaken camp? If you knew you were right, that you'd cracked the great riddle, that you stood on the cusp of true and *tangible* proof that the gates of chronology—of mortality itself—were close at hand and waiting to be forced? There was no other way, I can promise you that. Extremes had to be gone to: blood sacrifice made. There was no way short of death to force a breach."

I fell back from him dizzily, shaking my head. "That's not science, Uncle. That's witchcraft."

"Synonyms, *Nefflein*." His voice had gone rapt. "Two words for approaching the nexus of things."

"I'd never have done what you did in that camp. I'd have found some way out. I'd have cut myself free—"

"What was that?" He took a dragging step toward me, his hand to his ear, leering sightlessly into the dark. "I can barely hear you, little Waldy. You'll have to speak up."

"Why are you here?" I stammered. "How in God's name did you end up in this place?"

To my surprise this question stopped him cold. He looked confused for an instant, blinking down at the floor.

"I don't know," he said softly. "An accident of some sort. I can't seem to recall."

I watched his face for a time. I saw no cunning there.

"I can't either," I told him.

He said nothing to that. I propped myself against the wall between the doorway and the bed and waited for my body to recover. The horror of my situation was clear to me now: more convincing by far than the man on the bed, or the room we were in, or the labyrinth of trash to every side. The Timekeeper kept himself still, his dead eyes wide open, staring sadly past me into empty space.

XIX

LATER THAT NIGHT, in his empty apartment at the corner of 109th and Fifth Avenue (in a tenement house with the unlikely name of the General Lee), Orson laid out the cards, all fifty-four of them, in a crescent on the floor beside his desk. The power was out, a not-uncommon state of affairs in Harlem, and the six tallow candles he'd lit and stuck into bottles of Yuengling Draft bathed the scene in an appropriately pre-Enlightenment glow. He'd taken out a book from the library that he had no intention of returning—*Tarock für Trotteln*, by Yitzak W. Yitzak—and he read the introduction and first chapter before so much as glancing at the cards. The rules were still opaque to him, as much due to Herr Yitzak's schnapps-addled prose as to anything else; but the history of the game held him entranced.

As its name implied, the deck was derived from the tarot, which had infiltrated Europe from Egypt in the late Rennaissance. The origin of the *Sküs*, however—the joker-like card that had first caught my father's attention—was a mystery. No such card existed in the Arab tradition, or in any other deck of the ancient world. The game of tarock predated the use of the cards for occult purposes by three centuries, though certain cards—the *Sküs* among them—were rumored to have been made use of by alchemists (no one quite knew how) to gain access to the wisdom of past ages. The fool on the *Sküs* had taken many forms over the centuries, from bearskin-sporting hobo to lute-strumming courtier to urchin to dwarf; the illustration on Orson's deck, however, was the only one to display that curious, Escher-like circularity.

He brought the book nearer to the light and kept reading, concentrating on the fool card now. In tarock, the *Skü̈s* (*L'excuse* in French) is the deck's highest trump, but it has no rank or value of its own. Alone among the trumps, *L'excuse* has no number: its power emerges only in challenge to another card. Orson began to understand its appeal for him now, since he often felt that way about himself.

He took the card from the floor and regarded it fondly. Like the *Skü̈s*, he was a born contrarian, and—like the fool on the card, like madmen and jesters and clowns throughout the ages—the nonsense he spouted could serve, if used artfully, as a vessel for ideas that couldn't otherwise be spoken. He thought of Enzian at the university, and of Waldemar before her, and of what little he understood about his "mad" grandfather's work. "The fool," he muttered to himself, staring down at the card, "ought to be on our family crest."

What Orson didn't realize—not on that first evening; not yet—was that he would be the one to put it there.

∞

The telephone rang at Pine Ridge Road a few days later, and Genny went to answer it, thinking it must be someone from Warranted Tolliver Timepieces. It was the first time that the phone had rung all week.

"I'm working on something," said the caller before she could speak.

"Peanut! Is that you? Enzie and I were just saying—both of us—how nice it would be to hear from you. It's not as though we can call *you* up, you know."

"I know that, Genny. I'll get a telephone soon. Then you can call me whenever you want."

"Well! We'd certainly appreciate *that*." She hummed to herself for a moment in the odd, nervous way she had when she was pleased. "You're working on a story, did you say?"

"I'm working on a novel."

"A *novel*! My goodness, Peanut! What about?"

"It's about time, believe it or not. A variation on what Ouspensky calls 'Möbius time' in *The Hydra-Headed Hourglass*. The basic idea is that time, which seems to be running straight ahead from any given point—just as the earth seems flat, from any one perspective—might in fact be 'feeding back' into itself, like a snake swallowing its own tail. If that snake were long enough—it would have to be really gigantic, of course—it might appear straight, because the curve wouldn't be visible, you see? Like a Möbius strip, that has either one side or two, depending on how you choose to think about it. It's chronologic time considered as a kind of sleight-of-hand trick, really. I got the idea from a deck—"

"Where are you calling from, Peanut? You sound fuzzy."

Orson cleared his throat. "From a pay phone."

"You really *must* get a line of your own. Is it cold where you are?"

"Not as cold as in Buffalo."

"It's important to eat, you know, when it gets cold. You need calories to help you keep warm. Have you been taking the vitamin caplets I sent?"

An awkward pause ensued.

"Genny, can I talk to Enzie now?"

"Of course you can, Peanut! How silly of me! I'll go get her."

But Enzian, as usual, turned out to be indisposed.

∞

To the end of his days, my father viewed *The Excuse* as his proudest achievement, and it was a milestone for him without question: both his first published novel and his last attempt to keep within the bounds of decency. He wrote the first eleven chapters in a trance, narcotized by the story he was spinning, by the radical idea that lay hidden behind it, and by his fervent belief that the fruits of his labor would free him of the family curse forever. *The Excuse* was no antiseptic exercise, no half-baked scientific treatise smeared with narrative frosting, as the bulk of his fiction had been. It was no more and no less, Mrs. Haven, than a reckoning—in extravagant, ham-fisted, desperate terms—with the Syndrome itself.

Ozymandias Hume, the book's protagonist, is the scion of an haute-bourgeoisie family whose fortune was made in the licorice trade, but whose clandestine passion—passed from generation to generation, like a weakness for drink—is the use of the tarock deck to tell the future. Virtually any game can be used to foretell events, he believes, if it's played in reverse, or counterchronologically; but the game of tarock is especially well suited, on account of being *intended* to run counterclockwise, and of displaying the follies of mankind so bluntly on its picture cards. (Ozymandias's grandfather made this discovery a half century earlier, we're told in a flashback, during a postcoital game with his clandestine lover, the chief of police of Merthyr Tydfil, in Wales. As he threw down his trump—*L'excuse* over *La lune*—a vista of living, dancing symbols rose before him, and he saw himself lying dead in the street, with the chief of police standing over his body, smoking pistol in hand. Horrified, he ended their affair on the spot and rushed home to his wife. His lover shot him the next time he left the house.)

Before this nameless grandfather's violent end, the secret of the cards was passed down to his daughters, Cassandra and Yrsyla Hume. The sisters, both of whom went on to master what they simply called "the Game," used their father's discovery to opposite ends. Yrsyla, the elder, became embroiled in Welsh separatist politics, while Cassandra, the more practical of the two, made a nice little pile as a gambler, using each hand she played to predict its own outcome. Cassandra eventually bought herself a ranch in Australia, and bore her illiterate, Adonis-like foreman a series of sons; after the disaster of the Great War and the collapse of the Cymru Fydd movement, Yrsyla disappeared without a trace.

The Excuse opens grandiosely, in Australia's Gibson Desert. Ozymandias, Cassandra's youngest son, is coming into his maturity, surrounded by half-witted prospectors and drunken Aborigines and missionaries who regard all forms of recreation—even waltzing—as abominations in the sight of God. His parents are dead, but Ozymandias is carefully looked after by two elder brothers, Ralph and Gawain, neither of whom have inherited their mother's gift. It's assumed, given his talent, that he'll take up the family mantle; Ozymandias, however, has ideas of his own. As he grows toward adulthood, he develops a passion for the ranching life: he dreams of moving deeper into sheep country, where the range is still free, and of making his name as a breeder. But the gift of clairvoyance, he soon discovers, has one potentially lethal catch. Once given, it has to be used.

Ozymandias remains at home as long as he can stand to, dutifully reading the cards every evening for his brothers, though his disenchantment waxes by the day. The allure of the deck for them, he discovers, has nothing to do with the future at all, and still less with the world of the present: at some unknown point the Game has been perverted, turned inward, become less an exploration of things to come than a means of embalming the past. It has become, very literally, an excuse: a way of retreating from life, of taking shelter—in Ozymandias's own words—"in some eldritch, sepia-tinted *other-when*."

Orson wrote these opening chapters in a fever, drunk on the sheer impertinence of his argument, and his mania is clear both in the speed of the narrative and in the bubbling molasses of his prose. The climactic scene of book I, in which Ozymandias finally has it out with his brothers, reads less like a confrontation than like some kind of *meshuggana* manifesto:

> *"You mean to abandon us, then?" Gawain demanded, his tawny eyes flashing like vitreous coals.*
>
> *"I mean to raise livestock," said Ozymandias. "Goats at first, and then sheep."*
>
> *"It amounts to the same," snarled his brother.*
>
> *Ralph took in a breath to speak, but the expression on Gawain's visage—and on Ozymandias's own—made the skin of his nape start to prickle. "What would we become without the Game, Ozymandias?" he simpered. "The Game is our birthright. Without it—why, without it, we'd stop being Humes!"*
>
> *"Without it," Gawain said darkly, "the future might as well not come at all."*
>
> *"You've been bamboozled!!" Ozymandias ejaculated, holding the Excuse aloft. "And the tragedy of it, brothers, is that you've bamboozled yourselves. If you'd ever truly regarded this card—regarded it, I mean to say, and SEEN it—you'd have noted that the image is that of a Möbius coil, with no beginning and no end."*
>
> *"A Möbius which?"*
>
> *"Time itself is no different," Ozymandias proclaimed. "It ends where it begins. Why have we been able to stare into the future all these years, over all these proud, farsighted generations, but never become masters of our fate?" The orbs of his amethyst eyes, Welsh to the very core, revolved from Ralph to Gawain, then back again. "The answer is hideously simple. We've created a closed system, repetitive and stagnant, like the circuit represented on this card. We've turned the future into the*

past, dear brothers, simply by attempting to arrest it. There's no escape from the Game—no solution, no respite, no hope—but to STOP PLAYING."

After a lively debate, then a second grand speech, then a scuffle involving (I blush to report) a boomerang and a didgeridoo, Ozymandias vows never to consult the cards again, not ever, and strikes out into the night to seek his fortune. The book now metamorphoses into a survivalist bildungsroman, with the Aborigines alternately scaring the hell out of Ozymandias and treating him for dysentery. The temptations are great, as he works his way west, to make use of the cards; but he holds firm. He crosses the country, buys a farm, loses it, then somehow finds himself in Sydney, a destitute failure, languishing in a dingy furnished room. Throughout all these trials the deck has remained in his satchel, untouched and pristine. One evening, however, he takes it out of its tooled leather slipcase—a parting gift from his mother—and lays the cards out in a crescent on the floor.

Here the narrative morphs again, veering from bildungsroman toward something murkier, and it isn't hard to figure out the reason. My father had arrived—after nearly three hundred pages—at the present instant of his own duration. Until then, his novel had been a work of history, however camouflaged; henceforth, it would be a prophecy.

The scene with the cards is cut short without warning, displaced by a sequence of drab, blurry flashbacks that serve no discernible purpose. I can feel Orson floundering at this point, Mrs. Haven, and stalling for time. We get Ozymandias as a toddler, dressed as Saint Augustine for a local pageant; we get Ozymandias's first love affair, with Helen, an Aboriginal girl (the opposite of Ewa Ruszczyk in every detail); we get Ozymandias attacked by a dingo. When we finally return—somewhat the worse for wear—to that furnished room in Sydney, Ozymandias is still staring at the cards, which are lying facedown on the corkwood floor. He stays put for two-thirds of a page, sweating and running his tongue along his teeth, like a suicide struggling to work up his nerve. Then he takes the nearest card and flips it over.

∞

Countless critics have tried, in the three decades since, to account for the popularity *The Excuse* enjoyed in Aquarian-era America, in spite of its blundering plotline, its junior high symbolism, and a style that makes Arthur C. Clarke look like Arthur Miller. None have come anywhere close to succeeding, but all agree that the novel's last section, which is entirely taken up by Ozymandias's psychedelic vision of the future, must somehow be to blame. Such a degree of critical consensus (as any connoisseur of book reviews will tell you) is the rarest and most delicate of flowers; but in Orson's case the critics had their reasons. For one thing, the "Revelations" section—as it's come to be known—has a radically different tone than the rest of the book, as if the author were taking dictation; and for another thing, Mrs. Haven, a number of its predictions have come true.

In spite of their almost incidental presence in his novels—usually as hastily sketched backdrops to scenes of cybernetic debauchery—my father's prognostications of the not-too-distant future emerged, even during his life-time, as the engine-in-chief of his fame. The time-travel allegation—the time travel *insinuation*, better said—had been leveled against my family be-fore, to explain the Timekeeper's disappearing act at Äschenwald; but the case against Orson Card Tolliver, especially since the invention of Global Positioning Systems and Viagra and the European Union (all of which he predicted), proved harder to sweep under the rug. The evidence, after all, is plain for anyone with a library card (or access to the World Wide Web—which Orson also saw coming) to judge for themselves. It changed my father from a figurative "cult novelist" into a literal one, an actor on the klieg-lit stage of history, no matter how furiously he lobbied to prevent it.

The orgy scene in "How to Make Machines and Influence Your Wife," for example, is tame by today's standards (six-dimensional dildo not-withstanding), and its prose won't win any Nebula Awards; the wireless earpiece, however, so casually deposited on a night table as the frolicking begins, is noteworthy in a story written in 1963. Personal infrared goggles were undreamed-of in 1959, but they're standard issue on "Planet Perino-rium 13," and used to predictably lascivious ends. Orson had a rabid fan-tasy life, needless to say, and a commitment to reality negation possibly unsurpassed in human history, not to mention a lifetime subscription to *Tech-nology Today*; but even *I* have a hard time explaining the appearance, 112 pages into *Clocksuckers* (1973), of a jihadist riding a Jet Ski.

Every self-respecting religion needs its miracles, Mrs. Haven, and it was from "prophecies fulfilled" such as these that the UCS distilled its theology. If they hadn't done their work so outrageously well, hadn't transmuted Orson's art into propaganda with such consummate skill, the rest of the world might have taken him more seriously; and if the rest of the world had taken him more seriously, I might have an explanation for my father's apparent clairvoyance, for the Iterants' growing influence over him, maybe even for what's happened to me since. By the time I tried to get the truth out of Orson, however, he was tucked away in the attic of a place called the Villa Ouspensky—the Vatican of the Church of Synchronology— surrounded by sycophants and nurses and bullnecked, hard-eyed men in khaki suits. He was far gone by then, ravaged by both cancer and time, and I had to choose my questions carefully. I didn't kick up any fuss; there was no point in that. I had other dragons elsewhere to attack.

But I've succumbed to achronology again, Mrs. Haven. Before we arrive at the United Church of Synchronology and my own (decidedly upstage) arrival, I need to tell you how my father met my mother, how *The Excuse* made Orson Card Tolliver into a household name, and how I came to be born in Buffalo instead of Spanish Harlem. The contributing circumstances are as dubious as any others in this history, which is a pretty good argument, as arguments go, for their truth. Whatever else my family might be accused of, rightly or wrongly, no one's ever questioned our improbability.

∞

Orson had just begun the third and final section of his novel when he came down with infectious mononucleosis, which goes some way toward accounting for book III's fever-dream grotesquerie. He arrived at his guardhouse at the Hudson/Gold Power Generating Station punctually at 23:00 EST on December 5, eager to continue his writing; when the day watchman clocked in at 07:00, however, he found my father curled up on the floor. Orson was sent home at once in a car-service limo (which expense was duly deducted from his paycheck) and his next of kin—identified on his ID sheet as "GENTIAN AND ENGINE TOLLIVER"—were notified by means of a reverse-charge telegram.

Less than forty-eight hours later, in a turn of events th;it would have flabbergasted Orson if he'd been conscious, two salt-and-pepper-haired spinsters, neatly got up in the fashions of the forties, stood shoulder to shoulder in the Main Concourse of Grand Central Station, admiring the constellations on the ceiling.

"They haven't got Cassiopeia quite right, I don't think," said Enzian (in German, in case anyone was listening).

"Hush, Enzie."

"It's supposed to be shaped like a W, as in 'Waldemar.' That looks more like an M." Enzian pursed her lips, looking very much like Orson for a moment. "Not that anyone can tell, under all of that soot."

"It's beautiful, Enzie. Besides, a *W* can be an *M*, if you're looking at it upside down. It all depends upon your point of view."

Enzian appraised her sister coldly. "You sound more like the Patent Clerk with every passing week."

"It's the Patent Clerk's *world*, dear, in case you haven't noticed. We've been living in it for more than forty years."

"Not me," said Enzian fiercely, as though she were reciting an oath. "I've never lived in it. Not for a day."

Something like worry passed over Gentian's face as she regarded her sister; but it was gone again at once. "We'll be here a week, Enzie. Two weeks at the most. I know you're in the middle of interesting work—"

"More than *interesting*. Decisive."

"—but your research will keep. Our Peanut, on the other hand, might not."

Enzian rolled her eyes, then gave a grudging nod.

"And don't forget what I told you about the apartment. Four floors up from the street, rooms arranged in a ring, the unit below currently vacant." She was quiet a moment. "It could be perfect, Enzie. Much better for us than Pine Ridge Road."

Enzian looked at her sharply. "The downstairs apartment is vacant? Who told you that?"

Gentian only smiled.

"He'd never agree to it," Enzian said, chewing her lip. "Not Orson."

Her sister said nothing.

"You have a scheme of some kind." She squinted at Gentian. "I can see it in your face. You have a scheme."

"I'm sure you'll find Manhattan stimulating," Gentian said, taking up her valise. "They say people here never sleep at all."

∞

Orson's fever lasted a week and a day—a muted, shadowed interval, of which his sisters wasted not one instant. By the time he'd recovered enough to grasp what was happening, Enzie and Genny had altered his apartment beyond recognition: the waterstained walls of the entryway had been papered in a fleur-de-lis pattern that seemed kitschy even by the twins' standards, and the windows overlooking the park had been draped in bulky tangerine damask, giving the west-facing rooms the ambience of an out-of-date bordello. My father had assumed that he knew all there was to know about his sisters, but the speed with which they managed to fill that cavernous space with armchairs and gouaches and Ottoman carpets—some bought in antique shops, some shipped by rail from Buffalo, some scavenged from neighborhood dumpsters—hinted at talents he'd never suspected. He emerged from his delirium to find them cozily ensconced in a city he'd taken years to feel at home in.

More astonishing still, at least to Orson himself, was his lack of dismay at this turn of events. He was a prisoner now, more at Enzian's mercy than he'd been since his earliest childhood. This ought to have been my father's darkest nightmare—he'd dreamed it many times, in fact, with only a handful of differing details—but something inexpressible had changed. *The Excuse* no doubt contributed, long-due settling of accounts that it was; it's even possible that Orson found Enzian's nearness—and the return to the dynamic of his first years of writing—in some subliminal way inspiring. Whatever the reason, my father wrote as fluidly and surely during his convalescence as at any time since coming to New York. As he neared the end of his first draft, he became more convinced than ever that the book would bring him prominence, wealth, and the attention of beautiful women. As C*F*P would have it, Mrs. Haven, he was right on all three counts—though in drastically different ways than he imagined.

A number of facts had come clear to my father by the time his rough draft was completed. Firstly, that the manuscript was in dire need of revision; secondly, that his position at the station had long since been filled;

and lastly, that his sisters, now that they'd finally come down for a visit, hadn't the slightest intention of leaving. This last revelation came effortlessly, even innocently, over breakfast in the damask-shrouded parlor. (Orson had never called that room the "parlor"; it wouldn't have occurred to him to call it anything. Genny, on the other hand, had christened every room in the apartment. It wouldn't have surprised him if she had names for the closets.)

"It's such a treat to breakfast here, in the south parlor," Genny said as she dispensed the oolong. "The morning light through the windows is just so"— she paused for a moment—"so encouraging. Don't you agree, Peanut?"

"Those are west-facing windows, as you know very well," said Enzian, pointing across the table with her scone. "The sun comes straight in every afternoon."

"Of course—how goosey of me! It must be the drapes. They lend such a sense of *promise* to the place."

Orson took a sip of tea—then another, longer sip—and cleared his throat. "Now that I'm better—"

"You're not *really* better, Peanut. Not completely."

"How long will the two of you be staying?'

"Oh! We may stay quite a while," Genny said merrily. "Isn't that so, Enzie?"

Enzian, whose mouth was full of fried egg, gave her trademark non-committal nod.

Orson set his teacup down. "I see."

"Why do you ask, Peanut? Do you mind very much?"

"Of course not, Genny. I don't mind." He shut his mouth and stared down dumbly at his plate. It had just occurred to him that this was true.

"Lovely! It's settled, then."

He buttered his toast in a state of bafflement. "Would you mind if I asked why?"

"Why what?"

"*Why* do you want to stay?"

"Because we love you, Peanut," Genny said. She hesitated. "And also because we quite enjoy it here."

"There's more to it than that," he said, looking past her at Enzian. "I can smell it."

"Well, now. I suppose you could say—"

"I'm not asking you, Genny. I'm asking her."

Enzian, who'd finished her egg, wiped her lips with a napkin made from the same bright damask as the drapes. "Genny's right—we approve of this apartment. We've decided to relocate to this address."

This was too much for my father, even in his newfound state of grace. "What the hell are you talking about, Enzie? I live in this apartment, in case you've forgotten."

"And in case *you've* forgotten, Orson, your rent is paid out of the Tolliver & Family Charitable Remainder Trust, established by Papa just before he passed away. Technically speaking, therefore, it's the family's apartment, not yours."

By rights this answer should have sent my father through the (freshly plastered, chocolate-colored) ceiling; but he was not the man he'd been two weeks before. In place of the cyclone of self-righteous fury that both he and his sisters expected, he suddenly felt his distance from them unbearably keenly. It was a melancholy sensation, even a painful one, but there was no violence in it. These women raised me, he found himself thinking. They *raised* me, and I still don't understand them.

"What is it about this apartment," he asked Enzian, "that makes you want to use it for your work?"

She studied him a moment, as surprised as he was by his mild reply. "It possesses certain properties," she answered. *"Gewisse Eigenschaften."*

"And you're not going to tell me what those *Eigenschaften* are. Am I right about that?"

Genny sat quickly forward. "From what I understand—if you'll permit me, Enzie—the way in which the rooms are arranged—their *configuration*, that is, and their shape—"

"It doesn't matter. You're welcome to the place. I'll be out by the first of the month."

Orson allowed himself to imagine, in the quiet that followed, that he'd pulled the rug out from under his sisters at last: that they found him—at least momentarily—as erratic and inscrutable as he'd always found them. But his satisfaction proved to be short-lived.

"That's good of you, Peanut," said Enzian, nodding at Genny. "We'd never have *asked* you to move out, of course. But it might be for the best."

He sat back in his chair, feeling winded and weak. "Why?" he got out. "Why would it be for the best?"

"For your safety."

"My safety," said Orson. "Of course."

No one spoke for a time.

"Where will you go, Peanut?" Genny asked.

"Somewhere quiet. Upstate, maybe. I haven't really given it much thought."

"Perhaps you'll allow us to make a suggestion," said Enzian, taking his hand in hers.

It was the first time in seven years that she had touched him.

I'D BEEN HIDING in Menügayan's attic for seventeen days, Mrs. Haven, when you finally came home. The Husband's cobalt Lexus pulled up with a buttery screech while Julia was recaulking her parlor-floor windows; you smiled at her, apparently, and she waved coyly back.

She could have rung the old servants' bell that ran up to the attic—we'd decided on that, if there were any developments—but she chose to break the good news to me gently. I'd been growing my beard, like any self-respecting fugitive, and I was checking its progress in a loose shard of mirror when I caught sight of Menügayan over my left shoulder, smiling at me in a predatory way. How a person of her volume and density managed to negotiate the hatch to the attic in silence, I have no idea, but I'd grown used to her inherent stealth by then. I thought of Menügayan as Batman, or as Batman's overfed, depressive cousin—which essentially was how she saw herself.

"Looking good, Che Guevara," she said blankly. Blankness, like cunning, was a Menügayan forte.

"I'm trying to look different, that's all. As unlike Waldy Tolliver as I can."

"I can't argue with that," she said, more tonelessly than ever.

With the benefit of hindsight, Mrs. Haven, my reflection in the mirror should have served me as a warning. I *did* look like Che Guevara, but the Guevara of the final, doomed Bolivian campaign, with the glazed eyes of a man prepared for death. I was in the intermediate stages of cabin fever by then, a day or two short of seeing my arms and legs as breaded chicken cutlets. I had too much time on my hands—way too much—and nothing to distract me but pamphlets from an organization called the Otherkin Resource Center (ORC), whose members believe themselves to be "otherkin" instead of human: faeries, vampires and elves are the most popular, followed, at a slight but definite remove, by lycanthropes. The enigma of Menügayan only deepened over time.

"I need to go downstairs for some fresh air, Julia. I know that it's risky, but—"

"Not so risky," she said, already halfway to the hatch. "I'll meet you next to Bilbo. Bring your coat."

∞

We were strolling along the East River when she finally told me, with the wind at our backs and her right hand resting firmly on my shoulder. Menügayan's right hand is gentler than a trailer hitch, Mrs. Haven, but not by much.

"Remember one thing, Tolliver, before you run off and buy Hildy a dozen roses. Just because she's *back* doesn't signify she's back for you. The First Listener is with her."

"I hate it when you call him that."

"Cry me a river."

P. G. Wodehouse (one of my father's few idols in the "mainstream" of fiction) once described a character's uncle as "a pterodactyl with a secret sorrow," and suddenly I knew exactly what he meant. There was no contending with that bland, embittered face.

"You obviously have a plan, Julia. Couldn't you just tell me what it is?"

The blandness somehow deepened. "Don't you know anything about Hildy, Tolliver? Don't you know anything about women, in general, per se, at all? She'll send you a signal when the time is right."

"It sounds as if you're telling me to just sit around and do nothing."

Menügayan didn't laugh often, but when she did the effect was genuinely chilling. "Allow me to quote from a favorite author," she said. *"From every Venusian according to his abilities; to every Venusian according to his needs."*

This was a paraphrase of Marx, of course—Marx stuffed into a space suit—and I recognized the passage right away. It was from Orson Card Tolliver's *Love on an Uninhabitable Star.*

∞

There were more than a few moments, in the course of that next agonizing week, when I suspected that Menügayan's plan was to use the Husband to destroy *me*, Mrs. Haven, not the other way around. I now had a box seat for the pageant of your ongoing existence, which made it clear that you were getting on extremely well without me. You came and went on shopping trips and social calls and meditative early-evening strolls, obscenely willowy and curly-haired and bright. You looked exactly the way you'd looked that fateful day at Union Square: the same red coat, the same half smile, the same slow, indecisive way of walking. You looked as though no time had passed at all.

I'd promised Menügayan that I wouldn't contact you, wouldn't tap the windowpane as you walked by, let alone pound my fists against the glass and scream your name; and to our mutual surprise I kept my word. I kept it out of fear, Mrs. Haven—and not of the Husband and his flying monkeys, either. What if the smile left your face when you saw who it was? What if you turned your collar up and hurried off? What if you went straight back inside—back to mission control, back to the flying monkeys, back to whatever R. P. Haven was to you—and turned me in without a second thought?

But you shouldn't suppose that I'd given up hope. I assembled a kind of throne out of back issues of *Otherkin* and *Omni* and *The Official World of Warcraft Game Guide*—which Menügayan had whole crates of, for some reason—so that I could work on my history and keep lookout for you simultaneously. I'd settled in for what card players call "the long con": I was prepared to do whatever it took to tip the scales in my favor, even if that meant, for the moment, doing nothing. I'm fairly sure that I'm the only person on earth who's read *The Official World of Warcraft Game Guide* three times, in its entirety, appendices and all, without ever having played World of Warcraft.

As the days passed, I began to take note of passages in that venerable text, many of them in the "Guidelines for Ethical Play" (GEP), that seemed to relate, directly or indirectly, to the text I was writing myself. (What were the Accidents, from a certain point of view, but a jewel-encrusted chalice tucked away inside some sleeping monster's bowels?) I found one guideline, in particular, that ought to be inscribed across the Toula coat of arms:

> 6 (B)—
> *If you notice a person is about to attack a dragon, let them have it.*
> *Find another dragon elsewhere to attack.*

Such was my life in hiding, Mrs. Haven. Menügayan would stick her head through the hatch every so often—to pass along that morning's *Daily News*, for example, or a lukewarm-at-best TV dinner—but she rarely spoke to me or met my eye. Her silence had taken on a spiritual quality: something beyond words, possibly beyond all human understanding.

This was a clear indication, looking back on it now, that I'd been in the attic too long. It took me most of the next week to figure that out, but as soon as it hit me I packed up my clothes and my notes and my manuscript and decided to rejoin the human race. I couldn't wait any longer for the message she insisted you'd send; not in that haunted castle of hers. Things were going to take a dark turn if I stayed.

I'd just finished explaining this to Menügayan—whose only response was a grunt—when the sign we'd both been waiting for arrived.

It presented itself in the form of a personal ad in the Sublets Wanted section of the *Post*. I have an explanation for this coincidence now—two or three explanations, in fact—but at the time it seemed the wildest quirk of C*F*P. Running my finger down the leftmost column while Menügayan made me a sandwich ("Don't look at me that way, Tolliver—I'd do the same thing for a dog"), I encountered the following entry, which had no business in the Sublets Wanted listings:

> *WANTED: Somebody to go back in time with me. Experience necessary. Box 334, New York, NY 10001. Length of voyage: 33 minutes and a half. Euphasia a distinct possibility. No lying, no biting. I have only done this once before.*

"Find anything?" Menügayan asked, plunking the sandwich down in front of me. It was tidily wrapped and smelled faintly of curry.

"Probably not," I said, closing the paper. "More than I can afford. But it can't hurt to look."

"That depends," said Menügayan.

I nodded. "On what?"

"On what you're looking at."

"Which zip code is one-zero-zero-zero-one?" I asked nonchalantly. "Which P.O. would that be?"

"One-zero-zero-zero-one," Menügayan echoed. "I guess that would be Penn Station. The main post office up there."

"The one with the columns, across from the Garden?"

"That's right." She flashed me one of her most unfathomable smiles. "The only one that's open all night long."

∞

Sunset found me in the Italianate lobby of the James A. Farley Post Office, gazing up at the ceiling with my hands in my pockets and my back against the buzzing stamp dispenser. Philatelically minded citizens elbowed me aside now and then, shooting me dirty looks, but I stared through them as if they were ghosts. The James A. Farley is to the grimy, crowded pressure cookers that pass for P.O.s in the rest of the city as an aircraft carrier is to an inflatable duck. Its monumentality would have tilted toward fascism, at least for me, if not for the potty-mouthed irreverence of the clerks. The J.A.F. may be a secular temple, a twenty-four-hour shrine to the power of discourse, but to the middle-aged ladies behind the art deco grilles in its lobby, it's just another badly lit P.O.

I'm still not sure why I chose to keep Menügayan in the dark about the message you'd sent, but at the time I felt relieved to have escaped. She might have claimed that it was too risky, or that the timing was wrong, or that I was walking into a trap—none of which I wanted to be told. I cased the J.A.F.'s lobby as discreetly as I could, struggling to keep a lid on my excitement. Box 334 turned out to be a modest fourteen-dollar-a-month unit along the south wall; as far as I could make out, it was empty. I returned to my position at the aforementioned postage dispenser—an optimal location, from a surveillance point of view—and stayed there, with four brief but necessary interruptions, for the next sixteen hours.

You swept through the revolving doors the following afternoon. I should have guessed you'd come then, at the most nondescript time of day: 14:00 EST, the adulterer's hour. You had on a blue tartan cape and a silver beret, like a prep school kid playing at being a spy, but also vaguely like an otherkin. A pair of Hasids were emptying a jumbo-sized unit a few columns down, shouting into each other's ears as if communicating by transatlantic cable; you waited until they'd walked away, then snuck a furtive glance into the box.

"Nothing's in there, Mrs. Haven. I've checked."

"He's keeping his eye on me," you said without turning. "For my own protection. You shouldn't be here."

"I'm going to guess you shouldn't be here, either."

You kept your face toward the box, one hand against its tarock-card-sized window. "You're right about that."

"But you came anyway." I took a half step closer. "And so did I."

You straightened your shoulders and took in a breath: you were steeling yourself. In a moment you'd explain to me, in a cordial, room-temperature voice, that you saw no way for us to continue our friendship. I'd turned out to be a liar, and far worse than that, a coward: my fear of the Husband—your husband—had compelled me to lie. You could not excuse that. It embarrassed you to admit it, but you'd made a mistake. If I'd been honest from the start, perhaps, there might have been—

"Come to Vienna with me," I said, laying my hands on your shoulders. "There's a mystery there that I'm trying to solve. It involves the Gestapo, and the war, and the speed of light, and a card game no one plays anymore. It involves the Husband—*your* husband—and the whole United Church of Synchronology. I'll tell you everything, the whole sleazy story, if you'll only say yes. Come to Vienna with me, Mrs. Haven. Without you I don't stand a chance in hell."

I said more than that—much more—and you kept still and listened. I stood closer to you than anyone but a lover had the right to stand, and you made no move, either toward me or away. Your hair smelled of smoke, I remember—of clove cigarettes, or possibly pot. The down on your nape stirred in time to my breath. As long as I kept talking, things would remain as they were, in a state of suspension; but I couldn't keep talking. When it was clear that I'd finally run out of breath, you nodded to yourself and turned to me.

"I can't come to Vienna with you, Walter. You know that."

It was happening now, just as I had foreseen. The floor started to tilt.

"Give me one hour, then. You can spare me that much. There's someone I want you to meet."

∞

The Xanthia's citizenry generally disappeared into their rooms after TV hour like mollusks pulling back into their shells, but Palladian was the exception. I knew we'd find him in a Naugahyde recliner in the Montmartre Lounge, reading the business section of *The Wall Street Journal* from back to front and scribbling compound fractions in its margins. He looked up with a smile when he heard me come in, and his smile got so wide when he saw who I'd brought that it nearly put a crack in his pomade. Palladian was a ladies' man, as a legion of scandalized Xanthettes could attest—allegedly he was a pincher. I could see right away, however, from the look on his face, that today he'd be on his best behavior. I wouldn't have thought it possible, Mrs. Haven, but you made Abel Palladian shy.

"Mr. Abel Isaiah Palladian—Mrs. Hildegard Haven."

"Charmed," said Palladian, flashing his teeth.

You'd kept quiet in the cab, barely meeting my eye, but you played along willingly now. "Please don't get up, Mr. Palladian," you said, sitting down next to him. "Walter's told me quite a bit about you."

Palladian arched his kudzu-like eyebrows at me. "He's told you what, princess? That my kneecaps don't work?"

"Nothing like that. About your many gifts."

"My *gifts*?" The eyebrows went up even higher. "Sweetheart, if I was a hundred years younger—"

"Go ahead," I said. "Ask him."

"Aha!" said Palladian. "Sure."

You glanced at me uncertainly. "Wombat?"

Palladian bobbed his head in a dreamy sort of way and cleared his throat.

"The coarse-haired wombat of Australia resembles a small bear and can live twenty years in captivity."

You laughed for the first time that day. "All right, Mr. Palladian." You thought hard for a moment. "A football."

This time the answer came instantly. "Although it is traditionally called a 'pigksin,' the ball that the pros use is made of cowhide, a more durable variety of leather. Practice balls have a life span of two to three days; professional game balls in the National Football League have a much shorter term. Because the quote-unquote 'home team' is required to provide two dozen new balls for each game, and because between eight and twelve of these balls actually get used—and are then disposed of—a football could be said to last six minutes, on average." He held up a finger. "Six minutes, that is, of regulation play."

I expected you to laugh again, or to acknowledge my smile, but you did no such thing. "A black hole," you said softly.

"She asks the good questions, this one." Palladian leaned back in his chair and shut his eyes.

"A quote-unquote 'black hole' is the burned-out remains of a star that has collapsed under its own weight. A black hole with the mass of our sun, more or less, would exist for twenty billion years times ten to the fifty-fourth power, which is roughly the present age of our universe. At the center of a black hole, of course, the enormous gravitation would produce a quote-unquote 'singularity.' A place where none of the standard laws of the universe apply—time included." His eyes fluttered open. "Drop in there, princess, and you'll stay gone forever."

Palladian's answer seemed to soothe you. You took a deep breath, satisfied, and beamed down at him for a while. Then you looked up at me. Your smile was about as similar to the one you'd given me at the James A. Farley Post Office as a coarse-haired wombat is to a black hole.

"Mr. Palladian," you said, "you're a bona fide wonder."

Never one for false modesty, Palladian concurred.

"Well!" I said. "I'm glad you two—"

"Marry this woman, Mr. Tolliver. Give this woman children."

"I'm married already," you informed him serenely.

Palladian nodded. "No children, however."

"That's true."

No one spoke for a moment. The two of you seemed to consider the subject closed.

"I've asked Mrs. Haven to travel with me to Europe," I said, more shrilly than I'd intended. "To Vienna. I have family there."

"Ah!" Palladian's eyes gleamed. "An elopement."

"A trip to Vienna," I said quickly. "No more than that."

"I don't think a person can *elope*," you put in, "if that person is married."

You were watching Palladian closely. He was pursing his lips like a schoolteacher. I'd given up trying to guess what was going on.

"Mr. Tolliver," he said, "would you mind stepping out of the lounge?"

I stared at him blankly. "Stepping out of the lounge?"

"That's correct."

A man I'd never seen before was sitting at the Xanthia's front desk. He was chewing on an unlit Dutch Masters cigarillo and wearing a kind of serape, as if to blend in with the poster of Bolivia on the wall behind him. He bore a distinct resemblance to the man your husband's enforcers had called Little Brother, which didn't do much for my mental comfort. I sat down in a plastic armchair and watched the minute hand of the clock, which was shaped like a kitten, refuse to advance a single millimeter.

Eventually Palladian called me back in. It was clear right away that our visit was over. The two of you were sitting side-by-side at the lounge's card table, both seats turned toward the door, like the receiving line at a memorial service. The look on your face was all business.

"I'm coming with you, Walter," you announced.

Ecstatic as I was, Mrs. Haven, it never crossed my mind to ask you why.

Monday, 09:05 EST

I woke up in this chair with my fists on the floor and my shirt damp with drool, too groggy to move, and enjoyed a brief interlude of thick-brained thoughtlessness before I remembered what I'd found in my aunts' bed. I lurched to my feet, expecting to see the Timekeeper behind me; I had no idea when our encounter had ended, or how I'd found my way back, or why on earth I'd let him get away. But I've been a coward since birth, Mrs. Haven: spooked by my own shadow, retiring and skittish, forever a half step too late. You understood this from the start—I know that now. I must have been so easy to deceive.

I took up my time-honored position at the card table and thanked C*F*P for it, glancing over my shoulder now and again, just to make sure. My dim little nook with its warped dome of trash had never looked so comfortable and safe. I sat quietly for what seemed like a significant amount of *Wt*, waiting for my fingers to stop shaking. Then I collected my wits and went to work on the chapters you've just finished reading, exactly as if I were still alone.

Already it seemed impossible that I'd seen what I'd seen—that I'd *spoken* with Waldemar, to say nothing of knocking him down; but my sense memories of that cramped, twilit room and of what had taken place there were as vivid as any since my exile here began. The explanations for what I was experiencing had been reduced, as far as I could reckon, to two. Either (1) I was just as divorced from consensus reality as my great-uncle had always been reputed to be, or (2) consensus reality (along with chronology) was a hoax; in other words, Waldemar had been right all along. But why take shelter in the past tense as I write this? There's no safety in that. Either both of us are insane, Mrs. Haven, or neither of us are. And in either case I'm bound to him forever.

He was gone when I made my way back to the bedroom—somehow I'd known he'd be gone—but he'd left behind a note for me to find. I couldn't help noticing that even our handwriting has features in common: both of us are left-handed, our letters curve rightward, and we share what Orson liked to call the "Tolliver twitch."

Nefflein!

First you will pardon my English. I've had Leisure, in my Ramblings, to have practice with my Spelling, but it remains the Language of my Schooling-days. You didn't know we had English, your opa and I? Our father decided. Those were Schools *in those times, let me tell you! Remarkable schools. Then Kaspar for some reason switched to Czech.*

It strikes me as desirable that you regard me as Human—"als ein Mensch"—so that you may regard Yourself likewise. A Human, *Nefflein, with all the customary human Frailties. Perhaps this is a Thing that I can teach you.*

It's an Accident that brought us here, both of us, to these x/y/z/T coordinates—you won't believe this, I think. But this simply proves how Much you have to learn. There are only Accidents, after all, or Happenstances: only *C*, in other words—no *F* or *P*. But it's just as true to say that no such thing as Happenstance exists, since it can never exist by itself. The Word only has a meaning when opposed *to Something else. Don't you agree? Not unlike that playing Card of yours—the "Sküs."*

I've been leafing through your History, of course. How could I resist? The tone, I think, is a Success—not too frumpy, not too certain of itself—but I have a few minor corrections. I've written up a List, Nefflein, and trust you will have no objections. I find it helps to make the Time go by.

ERRATA

pg 29—The Apartment house on Mondscheingasse may currently be painted a "brilliant yellow," but in 1905, if Memory serves, its color was a ghastly jaundiced Mauve.

pg 29—I was not in the Habit of cleaning between the slats in the floor of our Apartment with "a fork expressly altered for that purpose." I made use of a sharpened graphite Pencil.

pg 32—I should like to state, for the Historical Record, that I was never a Patron of the Café Jandek. Bilch, the Source of my Brother's information, was well known as a Gossip and a Thief.

pg 68—I've left this Erratum for last, both in deference to Chronological Order (ho! ho!) and to give it the Pride of Place that it deserves. In the second Paragraph, you write (very fetchingly):

> *"She (Sonja Silbermann) rose from the bench and walked straight to her front door without looking back. It was slightly ajar, just as she'd left it, and she slipped inside and pushed it shut behind her. Waldemar made no move to follow."*

I quite enjoyed your treatment of this Scene—the detail of the Chestnut Trees and the oilcloth-draped Bugatti in particular!—and have only two Objections worth recording. Silbermann's sedan was a Citroën, not a Bugatti. And Sonja did, in fact, accompany me home on the Evening in question. I could never have left the Chronosphere without her.

XX

MY FATHER DISCUSSED his second homecoming with me exactly once, after a relentless campaign of emotional blackmail on my part, and even then—more than thirty years post-factum—he gave me no more than a few stale crumbs. He got his jollies playing the grand old man of letters in his later years, and there were certain episodes of his personal history that he trundled out for anyone who'd listen, gumming them over like the stem of his god-awful pipe; but his return to Buffalo was not among them.

The reason for his reticence, Mrs. Haven, most likely isn't what you think. He felt no regret at putting Manhattan behind him, and even less at breaking his self-important teenage oath to turn his back on his hometown forever; he was the first to acknowledge, in later years, that the move had brought him luck and happiness. The source of his silence was simpler than that. For the first time since he'd struck out on his own—the first time in what he thought of as the years of his maturity—he'd made a decision without understanding why.

Enzie and Genny had manipulated him—he knew that, of course. But he went along willingly, even eagerly, as though his sisters' scheme had been his own idea. His desire for self-determination seemed to have abandoned him since his illness: where he'd once been defiant, he now felt conciliatory, at times even meek. In logistical terms the switch happened cleanly, with decorous precision, like castling in a friendly game of chess. Warranted Tolliver Timepieces, Inc., still required the occasional presence of a warranted Tolliver, if only for the sake of appearances; and 308 Pine Ridge Road was vacant and at his disposal. He could finish his book there, in the cubby that had incubated his earliest stories, and the uneasiness he'd no doubt feel at finding himself back where he'd started—just as Ewa Ruszczyk had predicted in the Odd Fellows Hall—would make him work faster and better. He'd be lonely, of course, but no more so than he'd been in Spanish Harlem. His solitude would help to keep him focused. He was regressing, he knew, but regression has one great advantage: the advantage of precedent. Whatever else it might bring, he reasoned, life in Buffalo wouldn't hold much in the way of surprises.

On this last point, however, Orson's sisters had a few trumps left to throw.

∞

Two weeks later, my father climbed the steps of 308 Pine Ridge Road in an advanced state of dishevelment, dragging his battered yellow steamer trunk behind him. His shirt was misbuttoned and his face was unshaven and his hair stood out straight in the back, where his headrest on the train had ionized it. He'd returned home for one reason only, after all—to get his book finished—and his seediness was both a reminder and a caution: a message to neighbors and friends (if he had any left) to leave him in peace. Like untold writers before him—science fiction writers, especially—he'd begun to fancy himself a lone mystic, a hermit of sorts, and Pine Ridge Road was now his hermitage. It was just as possible to be a mystic in the suburbs, after all, as on some mountain in the wilderness. Retreat was the main thing: withdrawal from the struggle. What mattered was that you were left alone.

Orson unlocked the door in a rush, buzzing with anticipation, and pushed it gently open with his foot. Dust revolved in the air—the lazy, protozoan dust of wooden houses—and the afternoon sun turned the foyer the color of beer. It had been more than a decade, to the best of his reckoning, since he'd had that house completely to himself. He estimated the hour at four o'clock—half past at the most—and went to check the mantel clock, but found it stopped at 08:27 EST. An omen of some kind, no question about it, but for the moment its meaning escaped him.

He set his trunk down at the foot of the stairs and stood, beguiled and delighted, listening to the house shift and settle around him. If a single object had been added or removed since he'd left for New York, the change was too minute for him to see. Nine years had come and gone without a trace. There was something deliciously morbid in that: something unnatural, even perverse. I could never have predicted this, he thought. Not this changelessness.

"Nine years," Orson said to the stillness. "Nine years and no time at all."

He took off his peacoat and hung it on the mahogany head of the banister, whose burnished roundness made him think—as it had when he was small—of an old man's bald crown. He slipped out of his loafers, then out of his socks. His feet stank agreeably. He crossed the frayed Persian carpet, feeling its coarseness against his instep, and laid his palm against the kitchen door. He felt the urge to strip completely—a thing he'd never once done in those rooms—and saw no earthly reason to resist it. *Starting tomorrow I'll write naked*, he said to himself. *That ought to keep the brush salesmen away.*

The rumbling of his stomach brought him back into the present. There was bound to be food of some kind in the kitchen: canned corn or beets or string beans, maybe even a jar of preserved eggs. They were a family of picklers, after all. He pulled up his shirtfront and patted his belly and opened the door with his knee. A girl in a snow-white dashiki was eating a sandwich at the kitchen counter.

"Shalom," said the girl.

"Jesus Christ!" said my father.

"As you prefer," she replied.

He stood frozen in en garde position, half upright, half crouching, his right hand braced against the door behind him. The girl had the palest face he'd ever seen—a genteel, almost medieval shade of ivory—framed by distinctly Continental-looking glasses. Everything about her was so wildly implausible that the unlikelihood of her presence in his childhood kitchen slipped his mind completely.

"This is my house," he said finally.

"You must be Orson, then! Such a *relief.*" She spoke with an accent, a thick one, but he could take in only one thing at a time. Her hair was black and thick and spherical, a topiary cropped into the shape of a planet. He'd never seen curls that curly outside of a Little Orphan Annie comic strip.

"I wasn't expecting anybody," said Orson. "To be here, I mean."

"I can see that," she said, glancing down at his feet. From anyone else this might have seemed teasing, even flirtatious, but not from this girl. She was tracking him as closely as a sniper.

He tucked his shirttails back into his jeans. "What's your name? I wasn't informed—"

"Ursula." Her accent softened slightly. "I'm in the second bedroom past the stairs."

"Do you mind if I sit down, Ursula? I feel a bit woozy."

"Please."

"My sisters didn't tell me you were here, you understand. In this house. I wasn't expecting anybody."

"You've said that already."

He hesitated. "Were *you* expecting anybody?"

"Oh, yes. They told me at the start."

Orson rested his elbows on the counter and attempted to think. "When was this, if you don't mind my asking?"

"When was what?"

"When—when *exactly*—did my sisters let you know that I'd be coming?"

She pulled one of her geometrically precise curls into her mouth and chewed it thoughtfully. "The morning I got here," she said. "Six weeks ago today."

∞

Ursula was not a projection of my father's libido, or a comic-strip character, or a pleasure android from the distant future. She was an exchange student from the Hebrew University in Jerusalem (which, as C*F*P would have it, had been cofounded by the Patent Clerk a few decades earlier) working on her Ph.D. in chemistry—and on her English—at the State University of New York at Buffalo. It was a mystery to Orson how she'd come to Cheek-towaga, of all places, and the idea of Enzie and Genny taking in boarders, Israeli or otherwise, was so contrary to his conception of his sisters that his conscious mind refused to entertain it. But it didn't much matter, Mrs. Haven, by what back alley of circumstance she'd arrived at his house.

As long as Ursula continued to occupy the second bedroom past the stairs, he had no further questions for the court.

She turned out to be older than she looked, to his considerable relief; and she seemed to accept his attentions as a matter of course, which he wasn't quite sure how to feel about. Her girlish gravitas at their first meeting had not been a form of politeness—she was to remain, for the entirety of their shared duration, the most poker-faced woman he knew. In spite of Orson's twenty-six years, moreover, it was clear that any awkwardness would be coming from *his* side of the counter, not hers. Within a week he knew the details of her doomed love affair with a young Mossad operative, and of its sequel with a middle-aged Tel Aviv dentist; he knew what she would and wouldn't do in bed well in advance of their first kiss (which was unexpectedly helpful, like taking a sample test before the true exam). Science fiction interested her—even, in a sense, excited her—which surprised him most of all: he'd resigned himself to the idea that Ewa Ruszczyk was the only girl this side of Alpha Centauri who'd ever read his work.

True to Tolliver tradition, it was Ursula, not Orson, who finally brought the beaker to a boil. The year was 1969, after all, not 1904, and my father's shyness bordered on effrontery. Although he wrote compulsively and virtuosically about fornication, Mrs. Haven—or perhaps for precisely that reason—he'd done precious little himself. Ursula seized him by the scruff of the neck, as if he were a kitten; there was something feral about her in that moment, and Orson's first thought was that she meant to tear his throat out with her teeth. The body that had appeared so childlike seemed another body altogether when he held it in his hands, and by the time she was naked (which was not too long after) the last traces of girlishness had vanished. She left her clothes on the floor of the kitchen—he himself, laughably, was still fully dressed—and led him through the swinging door into the parlor. The goose bumps on her forearms and on her meaty blue-white haunches made him feel oddly top-heavy, and he followed her with his arms outstretched, to catch himself if he should start to fall.

A fire was burning in the parlor grate. When had that happened? He stared into the flames for what seemed a great while, struggling to recapture his calm. She undressed him as he stood there, taking her time about it, efficient and completely at her ease. He cursed himself for a coward and a fool. When she'd finished he took stock of himself, prepared for the worst, and found himself heroically aroused.

"*There* now," Ursula purred. She was squatting in front of him, appraising him frankly, her left hand resting lightly on his hip. "There now, Mr. Tolliver. Let's see if you can guess what happens next."

"I've got a general idea," said Orson. "I write smut for a living, remember."

"This isn't *DarkEncounters*, Mr. Tolliver. I want to *do* the thing, not fantasize about it."

"For your information, I take pride in the fact that my stories are accurate, from a technical standpoint, down to the slightest—"

"*Shh,*" she told him, bending slightly forward. "No excuses."

∞

It was only afterward, when they were lying together in front of the inexplicable sui generis fire—Ursula denied having started it, and why on earth should she do that?—that he realized how much of her history she'd been keeping to herself. She'd been born in Barkai, on a bona fide kibbutz; her mother had taken her to Vienna at age three to meet her *goyishe* father, and they'd lived there for the next eleven years. Her father had left Austria long before, they discovered, and no one could say where he was. At first they'd stayed on in hope of word from him, then because they couldn't afford the passage back; then because her mother, still a beauty, had remarried. Ursula was happy in Vienna, and too young to mind so much about her father, but her mother grew pinched and silent and peculiar. The second husband was a drinker, and the marriage ended badly. Soon after that, they moved to Tel Aviv.

"What happened next?" said Orson.

"America happened," she said, smiling strangely. "You happened."

They lay with their legs entangled, staring dumbly at the fire.

"Sometimes I think it might be better to have less family," said Orson, "than to have too much."

"You're thinking of your sisters, I suppose."

"What do *you* think of them?"

She considered his question. "They're *verdreht*, I think, but they mean well. Why do you ask?"

"I'm worried about them, to tell you the truth. They've always been—*verdreht*, like you say, but over the past few years—since I went away, I mean, to New York City—"

"Yes?"

"They've become more than that." He let out a breath. "Insanity runs in my family."

"Mine, too."

"No babies for us, then!" said Orson, attempting a joke.

Ursula didn't laugh.

"About my sisters—"

"Yes?"

He frowned into the fire. "I don't know how to put this."

"Just say it."

"They think that they can see into the future."

Ursula turned to face him then, resting one of her small, thick-nippled breasts against his arm. "They *can* see into the future," she said matter-of-factly. "Haven't you noticed that yet?"

∞

There's no way of knowing how my aunts spent their first months in Harlem, Mrs. Haven, since no one—with the possible exception of the gas man—crossed their threshold during that time; but I can make a few guesses. For the whole of their durations to date—more than eighty years, reckoned together—Enzie and Genny had taken their clothes out of the same wardrobe, worn their hair in identical untidy buns, and slept in the same four-poster bed, and I see no reason to assume they changed their ways. Genny continued in her various roles as homemaker, administrator, nurse, cook and research assistant, slipping out of the house each morning with a shopping list in one hand and a stack of scholarly correspondence in the other; Enzie devoted every waking hour to her work. She'd told Orson the truth about her motives for staying—the new surroundings had drawn her conception of the chronoverse in a subtly new direction, although the details of her experiments in those months remain obscure. Genny's letters to Orson mention Laplace's theory of determinism, the "torque" of the Milky Way galaxy (whatever that means), the symbolic freight of counterclockwise motion, Oppenheimer's nautilus-shaped fallout shelter blueprint, the layout of certain pharaonic tombs, Nietzsche's concept of "eternal recurrence," weather vanes, pinwheels, and—over and over again, though always in the most blasé of tones—the arrangement of windows, rooms and doors in the apartment.

In the weeks after Orson's departure, three sets of ping-pong-ball-sized holes were drilled through each interior wall, exactly five feet and three inches off the floor. My father mentions these holes in his journal—Genny must have written to him about them—and I've been able to confirm that they exist. I thought I'd have to move half the Archive to uncover them, but each hole, no matter how hidden or hemmed in by trash, turns out to have a clear and unobstructed through-line to its counterpart across the room. In a curious way, the resulting network of linked apertures is reminiscent of a camera obscura, or an apartment-sized simulacrum of the human eye—optic nerve and ganglia included—with the bathroom, of all places, embodying the juncture with the brain. (It also calls to mind the machine, the interferometer, that Michelson and Morley used to measure the velocity of light.) I can't see the point of it all, Mrs. Haven, and apparently neither could Genny; but Genny's understanding, let alone her approval, had never been of much concern to Enzie. It would take more than a change of address to change that.

Certain things *did* change, however, once the sisters had become acclimatized to their exotic new environment: certain things, in fact, were revolutionized. Enzie's interest in Manhattan may not have extended farther than the walls of the General Lee, but her sister was a different animal. In the course of Genny's errands, which sometimes took her clear across the city, she came into contact with Manhattanites of every conceivable stripe, from physicists to pacificists to sodomites to junkies, and discovered that she found them all delightful. She'd never known a place to be so viciously, remorselessly alive: even when people told her to mind her own business, or to watch where the fuck she was going (which happened often), the shock of it came as a welcome infusion of feeling. Street life thrilled her to tears, as did life in the shops and the parks and the barrooms, though she never touched a drop of hooch herself. The woman who stared boldly back at her from the windows of department stores and soda shops and taxis had a face she only dimly recognized. At the beginning of her forties, entirely by accident, Genny found herself a woman of the world.

She began to spend more time away from the General Lee than was strictly necessary, taking the scenic route whenever possible, and it was not beneath her dignity to loiter. She became something of a fixture of the scenic route herself, the latest touch of quasi-local color: the middle-aged hippie, the saucer-eyed Jewess, the credulous Kraut. The bon vivant, in other words, that her brother had never managed to become. She dispensed money freely—*she* was in charge of the purse strings, not Enzie—and prided herself on being an equal-opportunity enabler. For every high tea she attended with the brittle-haired wives of venture capitalists in the tearoom at Saks, she'd have a *café con leche* and a sandwich at the corner *bodeguita*, or a joint at a rally in Tompkins Square Park. In no time at all she'd become known about town as what grifters used to call "an easy touch," and she'd developed quite a fan club, from panhandlers to Abstract Expressionists to pimps. Some exploited her shamelessly, rewarding her patronage with whatever line of bullshit came to mind, and laughing at her when she took the bait; some dragged her to meetings of the John Birch Society or the Republican Party or the League of Women Voters, only to discover that politics put her to sleep; but no one, regardless of stratagem, managed to keep her out past 19:30 EST, when she went home to cook for her sister. Being Genny, however—in other words, being craftier than she looked— she eventually hit on a way both of keeping Enzie from starving and of bypassing her curfew. The solution couldn't have been simpler: she invited everybody home for dinner.

Enzie, needless to say, was bitterly opposed to Genny's "dog-and-pony evenings," as she called them; but the balance of power had shifted. Genny dug in her heels and refused to back down. Hadn't she always done every last thing Enzie wanted? Hadn't she cooked and cleaned and generally been an exemplary homemaker since before puberty? Hadn't she abandoned her home from one day to the next, all for the sake of Enzie's work? Now it was *her* turn, and long overdue. They were living in the middle of the most fascinating city in the world, and she was damned if she was going to pretend that they lived in a bunker.

"All right, then," Enzie grunted at last, scrambling to reach stable ground. "You can have your little dinners, if they mean so much to you. But no more than once a month. And no questions about my work, you understand?" She clenched her eyes shut. "This is important, Genny. This is *wichtig*. No talk about the future whatsoever."

"There's a war on, dear, in case you haven't noticed," Genny said, taking a drag of her Virginia Slim. "The whole world might get atomized tomorrow. The last thing *anyone* wants to talk about is the future."

∞

If it strikes you as bizarre, Mrs. Haven, that my aunts should have thrown open their apartment, once a month, to both the dregs and the elite of late-sixties Manhattan, you'd be no more confounded than Enzie herself. And it was arguably the surprise of her duration (barring her later discoveries re: the chronoverse and the subjective mind) that she came to enjoy Genny's soon-to-be-notorious Wednesday nights at least as much as her wayward sister did. The first dozen or so were harmless enough—assorted Bowery hopheads, a neighbor or two, the token physics grad student for Enzie to browbeat into a corner—but the mélange of Genny's extravagant cooking, Enzie's nutty-professor routine, and the sheer incongruity of the two of them there, in that apartment, in that neighborhood, at that particular juncture in the fourth dimension, proved an irresistible cocktail to Aquarian-era New York. Much was made of the sisters' obvious lack of social cunning, and of the fact that they were never seen at anybody else's parties—or in Enzie's case, anywhere else at all. Scores of rumors entered circulation, none of them flattering, each of them heightening the Tolliver sisters' mystique. Freaks were *en vogue* in those years, after all, and Enzie and Genny fit the bill superbly. It's not beyond the realm of possibility, either, that they took a half-conscious pleasure in baffling all attempts to comprehend them. There can be safety, of a kind, in being misperceived.

A slew of anecdotal portraits were written about my aunts after their deaths: some affectionate, some lurid, a few of them nearly book-length. All the standard explanations were put forward. Often as not, the gossip rags viewed them as an old sapphic couple—incestuous, possibly, but more likely not sisters at all—which rumor neither of them seems to have discouraged. They were photographed often, and appear to have enjoyed striking poses: Carl Van Vechten took a snapshot (later much reproduced) showing Genny in a rumpled and corseted ball gown, and Enzie in a lab coat, playing the mad scientist to the hilt, resting her hands on her sister's plump hips in what can only be described as a proprietary manner. Genny, for her part, is staring into the camera more frankly than I ever saw her do in life, secure in the knowledge that only a handful of people would see the result.

It's not the least of the ironies in this history, Mrs. Haven, that this portrait would be reproduced in every newspaper in New York just a few decades later.

Van Vechten was far from the sisters' only illustrious guest during their heyday, though their quota of Bowery bums and shop clerks never wavered. Harry Smith was a regular, entertaining all comers with his trick of tying human figures out of string; Eldridge Cleaver, by at least three accounts, showed up one night in '69 with Sinatra's stepdaughter—the one who couldn't sing—but split when he saw William F. Buckley stagger drunkenly out of the loo. The dinners had become huge productions by then, almost monstrous: one night Genny counted fifty-seven dirty champagne flutes. The Aga Khan graced the General Lee, as did Joe Dallesandro, Charles Mingus, Buckminster Fuller, and Joan Didion, who published an account of her visit when "The Tolliver Case" was the talk of the town. I include it here in its entirety.

ENZIAN AND GENTIAN TOLLIVER: A THOUGHT EXPERIMENT.

It's a pretty nice evening and not much is happening so someone suggests that we go see the Sisters. Not having any idea who the Sisters might be, I wonder aloud whether they won't object— it's past ten o'clock on a Wednesday—but LaMont waves my question aside. "They're having one of their nights," he says, as if that explains things.

Who are the Sisters? I ask.

"The Sisters," LaMont says again, with feeling. "Those crazy shut-in birds in Spanish Harlem."

I remind him, politely, that I've only just arrived from Sacramento.

"They're hermits," says Jessup, coming to my rescue. "At least the older one is. She's a physicist or something, but she spends all her time in that crumbly flat in that crumbly building with the ridiculous name. It's called the General Lee, if you can believe it. And it's smack in the middle of Harlem."

The General Lee, it turns out, is what one might expect—a poor man's Dakota in soot-stained concrete—but the Sisters are another thing entirely. One is plump and wide-eyed and child-like, and the other reminds me, to a startling degree, of Joan Crawford in the role of Mildred Pierce. There is only a strangeness about the eyes, and a kind of desperate indifference to fashion, to hint at the kinship between them. They are named, apparently, after a species of Austrian herb. Their accents are unclassifiable. One doesn't think of them paying electric bills, or using the telephone, or addressing one another by their Christian names.

"It's time for a 'Mischung!'" the more compact sister, the one named Gentian, announces at the top of her voice. "Everybody switches to the right!"

We all change seats as directed, with the exception of the Sisters themselves. The feeling is not so much of a dinner party as of teatime in some rarefied asylum. The table sags under the weight of a huge mass of china, nearly all of it filthy. The party seems to have been going on for as long as anybody can remember.

It's always six o'clock, I say to the guest on my left, an eager young man from Montevideo. To my surprise he recognizes the quote, and completes it for me, as if we're exchanging a password.

"Yes, that's it. It is always teatime, and we've no time to wash the things between the whiles."

Time is a pet topic here at the Sisters'—in some curious sense, the only topic—though I haven't fully realized that yet.

On this particular Wednesday—a slow night for the Sisters, I gather—only thirty-seven people have shown up for dinner, so there is plenty left over for us. When I praise the leek stew to the one who looks like Mildred Pierce, her head turns with a jerk, and I find myself in the considerable heat of her attention.

"We are discussing the 'grandmother paradox,' Miss Didion. Do you know what this paradox means?"

I believe it has to do with time travel of some kind, I reply.

"Time travel into the <u>past</u>," says Enzian. "The grandmother paradox is the primary objection to such travel. Summarize, Gustavo, if you please."

Gustavo, who turns out to be the nice young man from Uruguay, and who describes himself to me, later that same evening, as a "forensic physicist," leans gracefully forward.

"A man chrononavigates into the past, to a time before his parents were conceived. This man, by chance or design, sets a chain of events in motion that results in the death of his grandmother. Does our chrononaut himself cease to exist?"

"Gracías, Geraldo."

"De nada, maestra."

The table grows quiet. It's clear that I'm expected to respond. I've had a number of gin-and-hot-waters by this point in the evening, so I ask why the poor little grandmother has been singled out for destruction. Why not the time traveler's mother, for example? Come to think of it, why not his father?

Gustavo considers my question. "Quién sabe," he says. "Too sentimental?"

"That is not here or there," Enzian cuts in. "The objection has always been that these two realities—the reality containing the chrononaut, and the reality in which he has been extinquished— cannot both exist, and yet they <u>must</u> both exist. The chrononaut has to exist in order to extinguish himself; but as soon as the deed is accomplished, he must therefore vanish."

I acknowledge that this would seem to pose a problem.

"But there is a solution," she says, laying her mannish hands flat on the table. "Paradoxes ought not to exist—but they continue to do so, despite our objections. Some even exist physically: for example, the Möbius strip." She pauses briefly here, assessing me. "The Möbius strip, Miss Didion, shows us how effortlessly the universe can accommodate incompatible realities. We can

stare at a Möbius strip, hold it in our hands and examine it, and still refuse to understand what we are seeing."

The conversation is tending toward the metaphysical, someone observes.

"Allow me to quote from Ouspensky," a bespectacled negro says suavely. "'What does "metaphysics" mean, ultimately, but physics considered from a place above?'"

At this point things start to get lively.

"You must bring your ideas to the world," my Montevidean acquaintance urges. "Take them to Princeton—to the Institute for Advanced Study. Oppenheimer is there. He may listen."

"I have no interest in the opinions of that death fetishist," Enzian snaps. "My father had no dealings with Dr. Oppenheimer, and neither shall I."

For a while no one speaks. At the far end of the table a man with a grizzled gray beard is slurping Chablis out of what appears to be a soup tureen. He is later identified for me, by my husband, as an editor of the "Partisan Review."

"Your duty is to make your findings public," Geraldo insists. "Don't let the scientific mainstream seal your lips. Tesla didn't. Ouspensky didn't."

"Tesla died in a Fifty-Fourth Street flophouse," the negro observes. "Ouspensky died in a basement in Surrey, neglected and anemic and alone."

Enzian shakes her head. "If the world wants me, gentlemen, it knows where to find me. I'll be happy to receive it here, in my home, on the second Wednesday evening of the month."

LaMont rolls his eyes at this, and Jessup shifts uncomfortably in his seat.

No one else says a word. It seems a pathetic statement, textbook megalomania, the ravings of a bush-league Caligari.

In a certain sense, of course, it was all of these things; but in another, truer sense, it was not. Twenty-five years have passed since that statement was made. It was the humid late summer of 1969, and a great many things that seemed febrile that August now strike us as perfectly sane. The world has finally come, two and a half decades later, to see the Tolliver Sisters in their home. We stare, all of us, at the blurred photographs in the Times *and the* Post, *and consider the evidence closely, from every available angle. And still we refuse to understand what we are seeing.*

In his windowless cubby in Cheektowaga, meanwhile, Orson was tucking his magnum opus into bed. The novel had taken him longer than he'd expected—much longer—but he wasn't complaining. Lopsided and inelegant though it was, it pleased him in a way no writing of his had ever done before. It was a *book*, for one thing—not just grist for the pulps. It might even make him some money.

More and more clearly, as he whittled and buffed, Orson came to see his novel as a paean to Reason. How he'd managed to be born into a family that approached science the way a witch doctor approaches medicine he had no idea, but he was resolved, more than ever, to go his own way. His plan was twofold. He would serve as an example, by living according to Reason's dictates, as an Ayatollah lives by the Koran; and he would spell out his beliefs, in his novel, for the whole world to see—if it was willing to put in just a little effort.

As you can see, Mrs. Haven, he was thinking like a cult leader already.

He'd gotten into the habit of taking books down at random from the parlor bookcase at Pine Ridge Road, and in a clothbound edition of the poems of Sir Richard Francis Burton (which had almost certainly been Sonja's) he found a couplet that would soon become his personal motto, and be printed on the frontispiece of *The Excuse*:

> *Do what thy manhood bids thee do,*
> *from none but self expect applause;*
> *He noblest lives and noblest dies*
> *who makes and keeps his self-made laws.*

Below this, in Greek (it was that kind of novel), was a distinctly more appropriate epigraph:

ώρα κάνει ανόητοι όλων μας

Which, loosely translated into English, means

Time makes fools of us all.

"I'm finished," Orson told Ursula one evening. "At least I think I am. Christ, I hope so."

They were lying together in the second room on the right at the top of the stairs. Although it was drafty—it was drafty everywhere in that house—they were both sweating lightly. Ursula lay flat on her back, still a bit short of breath, smiling one of her classic equivocal smiles. She took hold of his ear and pinched it.

"You've been finished before," she said.

"This time is different."

"You've said *that* before, too."

"I'm sending it off tomorrow. The whole manuscript."

That got her attention. "Tomorrow? You're sure?"

"Genny's found me an agent, if you can believe it. Apparently he's a bona fide piranha."

"Is this a good thing, a piranha?"

"Depends on who gets bit."

She was quiet a moment.

"Does Genny know what the book is about? Does Enzie know?"

He made a face at the ceiling.

"They'll be furious, Orson."

"They can see it when it's published."

"Orson—"

"I don't want to talk about this, Ursula. Not now."

Conversation lagged for a time.

"I found your deck of tarock cards yesterday," Ursula said. "My mother used to play it with my father, you know. Actually, they met over a game."

"Then thank Jehovah for tarock," he said, pulling her closer.

"Let's have a game tonight. Will you play it with me?"

"I don't really know how."

"Come now, Mr. Tolliver. You just wrote a novel about it!"

"I've written about telekenesis, too, and about astral projection and fencing. You see me doing any of that stuff?"

"You could learn, Mr. Tolliver. I could teach you."

"Fräulein Kimmelmann! Do you know how to fence?"

"Don't be stupid."

"I'll let you in on a secret," he said, planting a kiss on her shoulder. "When this book is done—really and finally done, flushed out of my duration forever—I'm going to put those cards back in the cabinet, pull the sliding door shut, and spend whatever's left of my duration sipping Gennesee Cream Ale."

But as you and I both know, Mrs. Haven, that isn't how the cards fell for my father.

∞

Orson swore up down and crosswise, to the day of his death, that he'd had no idea of the significance of the *Sküs* to our family when he wrote *The Excuse*—and unlikely as it might sound, I believe him. The Gottfriedens Protocols wouldn't be released to the public until the midseventies, and Kaspar had never talked much to his son about the past; it's possible that not even Enzie and Genny knew about the *Sküs* before Waldemar's writings finally came to light. But all mention of tarock aside, the comparison of the study of physics with the study of the black arts was more than enough to horrify his sisters. The book's final section, with the benefit of thirty years' hindsight, reads like nothing so much as a veiled declaration of war.

Ozymandias Urquhart's vision in book III ends abruptly after eighty-four pages, as though somebody's pulled the plug on the projector. He gets to his feet, more than a little woozy, and sets out for the desert. His psychotropic peregrinations through the timestream are behind him, and he feels no nostalgia for either the future or the past—the present is now the only tense that matters. He has come (to lift a phrase from a UCS prospectus) "to live in the moment." He has a message to deliver to his brothers, after which he hopes to breed sheep at last, if possible on the family estate.

Word reaches Ozymandias, as he makes his way westward, that his brothers have "gone queer" during his absence. They've stopped shaving and bathing, he learns, and have boarded up the windows of Ouspensky Hall; they're rumored to have constructed a device for traveling vast distances without the appearance of motion, by making infinitesimal alterations to the angle of the earth's rotation. They're said to have stopped speaking altogether, communicating exclusively by playing games of whist.

After a month of hard travel, most of it on foot, Ozymandias arrives at his birthplace. The once-proud estate now lies weed-choked and fallow, its front doors are missing, and the Greek-revival façade—Cassandra Urquhart's pride—has vanished behind a shroud of Tasmanian ivy. A muffled droning draws him to the cellar, where he discovers Ralph and Gawain, barely recognizable under "Talmudic" beards, tampering with the pitch of the planet's axis, exactly as rumored, by means of a network of magnets and tubes. It becomes clear to Ozymandias that the true purpose of this infernal machine is to travel through time; having given up on the future—to say nothing of the present—his brothers plan to subjugate the past.

The closing pages of *The Excuse* are devoted to what Orson's more kindly disposed critics refer to as a "polemical dialogue," but which is actually no better than a rant, a salvo fired at his sisters from point-blank range:

> *"In summation, you both have my pity," Ozymandias ejaculated.*
>
> *"Pity?" Ralph sneered, breaking his silence at last. "We'll see who pities whom, little brother, when Gawain and myself are Masters of the Kronoverse!"*
>
> *"Have you not understood?" Ozymandias answered sadly. "We travel through time all our lives—into the future at the speed at which we age, and into the past each time that we remember. There is only the brain, after all; however we choose to employ it, we have no other device. But the brain, my dear brothers, is more than enough. Our consciousness is all the time machine we need."*

The Excuse was published on December 1, 1969, in a clothbound edition by Holt, Rinehart and Winston. In a more conservative age—in other words, at practically any other time in human history—the book would have been a hard sell; but this was the final year of the sixties, the year the grown-ups started taking what the kids had been taking, and phantasmagoria was all the rage. Orson's novel was hailed as a bulletin from the front lines of the soft revolution, a late mid-twentieth-century *Pilgrim's Progress*, a lysergic bugle call to self-expression. All of which was annoying—to put it mildly—to its author, given the message that he'd actually intended. CONSCIOUS-NESS IS A TIME MACHINE began turning up on T-shirts nationwide, but they were being worn by dopers, not by astrophysicists or heads of state. More perturbingly still, the book would go on to outsell the rest of my father's oeuvre combined, though it's about as erotic as a dental questionnaire.

The full-page review in *Life* was Ursula's favorite:

> *"The Excuse" is not simply an improbable bestseller; it is an improbable book, from an equally improbable man.*
>
> *Orson Card Tolliver—twenty-seven years of age, veteran of Greenwich Village's beat catacombs—was heretofore known, if he was known at all, as a writer of speculative pornography for the pulps. His new novel, however, is a horse of a rather different phenotype.*
>
> *"The Excuse" is the record—in grotesque, quasi-allegorical guise—of one individual's rejection of all received truth; of the shackles of familial precedent; even of the precepts of chronology itself. Isaac Newton counts for nothing in this brave new cosmos, and neither does Albert Einstein, or the Buddha, or even Jesus Christ. This novel demands to be interpreted as a ragged, desperate yawp of celebration: a shout from the trenches of tomorrow's youth culture to all of us still lollygagging back in the supply tents. There is a wild, wicked music throughout these pages. America could do worse than lend an ear.*

"'A ragged, desperate *yawp* of celebration?'" Orson muttered after she'd read it aloud. "What the fuck is that supposed to mean?"

"It means that we can get our gutters fixed," Ursula answered. "The leak in the pantry has started again."

"The leak in the pantry? *Mein Gott!*" he shouted, mimicking her Oxbridge-by-way-of-the-Vaterland accent. "Whatever will become of the bratwurst?"

"You're a celebrity now, Mr. Tolliver. A big shot. Be happy you can keep your bratwurst dry."

"I don't mean to complain. I realize that would be stupid."

"Well! As long as you realize *that*," she said brightly. "I'll have some-body look at the gutters tomorrow."

The connubial turn in their relationship had come on so gradually, with so little fuss, that he'd barely taken note of the shift. *She's adopted me*, my father would say to himself, on those rare occasions when it crossed his mind. *She's taken me in.* Until the day I was born, Mrs. Haven—and for quite some time thereafter, to be honest—Orson thought of himself less as Ursula's lover than as a prematurely aged foster child.

"Bratwursts or no bratwursts, Ursula, something needs to be done. About this review, I mean. About *all* the reviews."

Ursula sighed to herself.

"I'll add a fourth book," said Orson. "An appendix, for the paperback edition. To make my meaning absolutely clear."

"You can't explain your own novel, Orson. That's a terrible idea."

"Why?"

She shook her curls at him. "Artists do not explain."

"You may not have noticed, Fräulein Kimmelmann, but I'm not in the art business. I write 'speculative pornography for the pulps.'"

"You'll end up making a philosophy out of this, if you're not careful." She gave a small, involuntary shudder. "Or even a religion."

"There's always room for one more religion in this country, sweet-heart." He caught her by the waist. "That's why the devil made America so big."

∞

The Excuse sold fifty thousand copies in its first six weeks of publication, and Orson bought a Buick hardtop with the money. He also bought a color TV in a tropical hardwood cabinet, twelve identical herringbone suits, and a dozen turtlenecks in varying shades of blue, from powder to navy to mid-night. The suits became my father's uniform, his protest against being cast as a hippie, disdain for his fanbase expressed in brushed cotton and tweed. The rest of the money went to Ursula, to spend or squirrel away or set on fire, as she saw fit.

They were married before a justice of the peace in a joyless little courthouse in Niagara Falls, with Uncle Wilhelm and one of Ursula's former classmates as witnesses. There was no time for a honeymoon, since Orson was struggling with the postscript for the paperback edition of *The Excuse*—the explanation Ursula was so opposed to—which was already months overdue. His new bride pursed her lips and closed her eyes and smoothed down her dress to hide her disappointment. (I know she did all these things, Mrs. Haven, because I saw her do them at regular intervals throughout my youth.) She'd been hoping they might travel to Vienna, to visit her mother; it had been almost two years since she'd seen her. Orson promised they'd go in the spring.

Enzian and Gentian sent a box of calla lilies to the ceremony but declined to attend. They'd divined *The Excuse*'s true message, unlike everyone else, and the result was exactly as their sister-in-law had predicted. For seventeen months they sent no word at all, not even a Hanukkah card. It was only a year and a half later, once perfunctory contact had been restored—due entirely to Ursula's efforts—that the full extent of the damage became clear.

Orson had known from the start that his book would seem a willful perversion of Enzie's ambitions for him: instead of using his talent to disseminate her ideas (however cunningly camouflaged) among the masses, he'd made a travesty of her life's work, to say nothing of her beliefs, and encouraged the masses to laugh. He'd tried to free himself once before, by escaping to New York; this time there would be no miscalculation, no variable left unaccounted for. He'd made a deliberate decision to cut the cord between them permanently.

Nevertheless, perverse as it might seem, his sisters' silence left him at a loss. Orson could easily imagine Enzie resolving to blacklist him, but he couldn't see Genny agreeing—not without considerable pain. He'd somehow never asked himself what Genny's reaction to the novel might be, only Enzie's; and the lack of contact with her gnawed at the root of his well-being. In spite of his presence on various bestseller lists (thirty weeks in *The New York Times Book Review*; top slot: #3), he felt trivial and neglected and alone. The only evidence that his sisters were still alive came via Smith Copley-Sexton, the CFO of Warranted Tolliver Timepieces. Their checks, Sexton assured him, were still being cashed.

∞

If my father had known the details of his sisters' lives at the time, Mrs. Haven, he might not have taken things so personally, though he'd probably have been a great deal more concerned. Perhaps coincidentally, perhaps not, the publication of *The Excuse* ushered in the third and closing act of Enzie and Genny's opera for two voices, the act that established its genre—which until then had been anybody's guess—as tabloid tragedy.

The final Wednesday dinner was held on May 10, 1970, six months before I was born. Eighty-eight guests attended, including Julius Erving, Susan Sarandon, Klaus Nomi and Marianne Moore. It had become tradition for a lecture to be given between the dessert and the digestif, and on this occasion—which none among the revelers guessed would be their last—it was delivered by a young dermatologist, Jonathan P. Zizmor, on the use of fruit acids in cleansing the skin. The dishes included, but were not limited to: smoked bluepoint oysters, chicken liver pâté, french fries, sauerkraut, Waldorf salad, blackened red snapper, pickled hen-of-the-woods mushrooms, stuffed grape leaves, lasagna, garlic bread, tapioca pudding, mint Girl Scout cookies and chocolate mousse. When questioned about the meal—which was a bit on the showy side, even by their standards—Genny admitted, blushingly, that it was in honor of Enzie's birthday, a claim Enzie neither confirmed nor denied.

Enzie's health was duly toasted, then Genny's own, since they'd been born within an hour of each other. The meal lasted until 03:00 or 03:30 EST, depending on accounts, at which point Enzie announced that she and her sister needed to retire. After the eighty-eighth guest—a Dominican client liaison for the Monsanto Fruit Corporation—had been shown to the door, my aunts pushed it shut together (with a quiet flourish, I like to imagine) and turned to regard the sea of dirty china. Genny heaved a theatrical sigh.

"All right?" Enzie asked.

Genny nodded. "It's all right, Enzie. It's enough."

"I'm happy to hear it." She smiled. "It's almost time for us to go to Znojmo."

"Goodness!" said Genny. "Is it May already?"

"It is, *Schätzchen*. We have an appointment to keep."

Incredibly, my aunts *did* travel to Znojmo the following month, for what they described to Ursula—in a characteristically oblique postcard—as a "sentimental spree." They spent less than two days in Moravia, according to their itinerary, followed by a single afternoon in the city of their birth. Then they boarded Pan Am 225 from Vienna to New York, returned to their apartment in the General Lee, and pushed all seven deadbolts closed behind them. Orson would eventually be drawn back into their orbit, but no one else—with one exception—would cross their threshold for the whole of the next decade. And that exception, Mrs. Haven, was me.

∞

On May 10, 1970—the same day, as chance and fate and Providence would have it, as the Tolliver Sisters' last supper—the bell rang just as Ursula was pulling a tray of *Topfenstrudel* out of the oven. Orson was in the kitchen as well, staring at the back of his wife's head with his mouth hanging open. He'd just received some unexpected news.

The bell rang again.

"Ursula—"

"The bell, Orson."

He passed a hand over his face. "Probably somebody's at the door."

"That seems likely."

He crossed the parlor weavingly, his cerebellum buzzing, and yanked the front door open without looking who it was. A man and a woman and a teenager stood on the stoop: all three were wearing Western-style pearl-button shirts and immaculate blue jeans and sneakers. They'd have made a nice family, of a certain sort, if the teenager hadn't been chewing on an unlit meerschaum pipe. *The same pipe that I smoke*, Orson thought, feeling his scalp start to prickle.

"Can I help you?"

"You already *have*," said the woman. "So much more than you know."

"Mr. Orson Card Tolliver?" said the teenager gravely.

"Of *course* it's him," the man mumbled.

"Mr. Orson Card Tolliver?"

Orson nodded. "What is this?"

"*This*," the teenager said, "is a momentous occasion. Could we, uh, impinge on you briefly?"

If Orson hadn't been reeling from what his wife had just told him, he might have been slightly quicker on his feet. His callers were past him by the time he'd recovered, inside the house already, waiting respectfully at the entrance to the parlor. He could think of no response, at that point, but to ask them if they'd like a cup of coffee. The adults hesitated, looking curiously startled; the teenager said he'd like one very much. He seemed in a position of authority over the others, who spoke—when they dared speak at all—in timid, obseqious chirps.

Ursula, unflappable as always, brought out coffee and strudel, which everyone agreed was very tasty. The woman said something too quietly to hear—to Ursula, apparently—and Ursula asked her to repeat it.

"This coffee," said the woman.

"Do you like it? It's Venezuelan."

"I've had this coffee before." Her eyes fluttered closed. "This coffee exactly."

"Yes, you have," said the teenager. "And you'll have it *again*." He gave Orson a wink. "Am I right, Mr. Tolliver?"

"She'll have it again right now," Ursula said, refilling her cup.

Orson shot his wife a look of mute appeal, which she ignored.

∞

We now reach the point in this history, Mrs. Haven, when I begin to feel us rushing toward each other. We're still far apart, you and I—very nearly a decade, and five hundred miles—but our trajectories are starting to converge. The inevitability of it makes my mouth go dry.

∞

The teenager was called Haven, the man's name was Johnson, and the woman was referred to as "Miss M." No first names were mentioned. They obviously belonged to a cult of some kind, though they passed out no literature; there was an odd air of leisure about them, or at least about Haven, as though they'd come to town to see the sights. My father decided they were trying to convert him, like the Jehovah's Witnesses who rang the doorbell once a year, and he felt more at ease right away. It always relaxed him to talk to the Jehovah's Witnesses. What they wanted was so easy to refuse.

"You've been expecting us for some time, I imagine," Haven said.

"I'll admit something to you," said Orson. "I haven't."

"Ah!" said Haven, smiling good-naturedly, as if to show that he could take a joke. "So you deny that you have access to the future?"

"More strudel, Mr. Haven?" said Ursula, taking his plate.

"Thank you kindly, Mrs. Tolliver." Haven dabbed at the corners of his mouth with his napkin. "Perhaps the time has come to state our business."

Orson raised his eyebrows. Ursula focused her attention on the strudel. Haven radiated courtesy and calm.

"The Codex, Miss M., if you please."

"The Codex," the young woman echoed. A book was produced from a briefcase and set on the table.

"*Ach, du Scheisse,*" said Ursula under her breath.

"Since well before the three of us met," Haven said, "my two, uh, colleagues and I have been fellow travelers. Like a great many other Americans, Mr. Tolliver, we've read your book and been affected by it." He nodded to himself. "I say 'affected,' but a better descriptor might be 'altered,' or even 'transformed.'"

"Reconfigured," Johnson suggested. The woman mouthed a word that looked like *reborn* to Orson. His scalp started prickling again.

"We were affected by your book, Mr. Tolliver, as I've said. We intuited that it contained, uh, mysteries. We *intuited* this, and felt altered even by this as-yet-inchoate knowledge. But it wasn't until the publication of the paperback edition, with its supplementary *directives*, that the way became clear."

"Directives?" said Orson, shifting uneasily on the couch.

Haven opened the Codex to a crisply dog-eared page. "'Science can offer you what no religion can,'" he read aloud. "'Science does more than simply recount bygone miracles for credulous ears; science shows us its miracles, then *explains* them for us, and even, occasionally, brings new miracles about. Trust in science, dear reader—in *empirical* science—and you will live the existence that countless religions have promised: you will never walk alone. You will be part of a continuum of intelligence and rational thought that began with the first question man ever asked.'" He paused a moment. "Did you write those words, sir?"

"I may have," Orson stammered, trying to dodge his wife's triumphant stare. "But I think you kids—well, I think you might be placing undue emphasis—"

Haven waited, politely, for Orson to finish. When it became clear nothing more was forthcoming, he turned the page and kept reading.

"'Science in the twentieth century—physics especially—has moved from the study of what we can see and judge with our five senses to things too vast and/or infinitesimal to perceive. This, in turn, has ushered in the most fascinating phase of scientific exploration in human history, one that challenges our commitment to science as never before. Common sense—on which we have always relied as our first defense against superstition—is no longer adequate. In fact, to see the world as the great minds of physics now see it, we, the scientific faithful, must be prepared to put our common sense aside.'"

"Now, right there," Orson protested. "Right there, you see? You've got to be careful, you know, not to read too much into that. I'm not saying we should do away with common sense *altogether*, obviously."

Haven squinted at him. "Obviously."

"All right, then," Orson muttered. "I just wanted to get that on the record."

Johnson—who was taking down the conversation in what looked to be some form of shorthand—gave a squeak of assent. Haven picked up where he'd left off.

"'Science hasn't yet vanquished religion—not fully—but it will surely do so, given time. One day, perhaps very soon, a *system* will be developed: a system of applied philosophy (philosophy in the classic sense, meaning a passion for knowledge) that will distill the accomplishments of all human inquiry into the elixir that religion has repeatedly promised, but never achieved. If you must live by belief, in other words, believe in *Science*.'"

"I get it," Orson said roughly (though he was enjoying the performance more than he was willing to let on). "You like the book. You agree with the afterword. No law against that, in this country at least. You're all enlightened souls." He glanced involuntarily at Ursula. "What I want to know is, what did you come to see *me* for? What's your agenda, Mr. Haven? What have you got up your sleeve?"

"We mean to structure our lives according to the Codex's principles," Haven said. "To serve mankind as an example, by living an ethical, rational life."

"It would be hard for me to argue with that, wouldn't it?" Orson said, giving a tight little laugh. "That would mean disagreeing with myself!"

"We also plan to reestablish the antediluvian fraternal order of Philadelphia on a coral atoll off the coast of Hawaii," the woman said. "We plan to live out all of our manifold iterations there, synchronously, so that we may finally experience death."

"Tut, Miss Menügayan!" Haven said smoothly. "Let's not burden our host with specifics."

The silence that followed was highly subjective in nature. For Haven it was a tranquil intermezzo; for his colleagues, to judge by appearances, it was a breathless pause; for Ursula it was a span of blank bewilderment; for Orson it was the nightmarish silence of fate.

"How old are you?" he asked abruptly.

Haven smiled and ran a thumb across his downy upper lip. "In this iteration," he said, "I've just turned twenty-six."

"No offense, son, but you look about twelve."

"I age at a reduced rate, Mr. Tolliver. I keep my metabolism at a minimum. I also try to keep out of the sun."

Orson came to his senses and got to his feet. "I'm sorry, kids. What you say is certainly very stimulating, but I can't join your society at the present time. Now if you'll pardon—"

"Join us?" Haven said, breaking into a grin. The others were already laughing. "*Join* us, Mr. Tolliver? There's no need for that. You're the spiritual head of our entire movement."

∞

Orson stood in a kind of Greco-Roman squat for a while after his callers had left, replaying the conversation in his head; then he drifted back into the parlor and stared into space like a mongoloid, which was still an acceptable term at the start of the seventies. He reached for his meerschaum—

he'd started smoking it the year before, as a publication day gift to himself—but set it down as soon as Haven came to mind. Gradually, grudgingly, the image of his personal evangelist withdrew, replaced by the recollection of what his wife had told him in the kitchen.

He glanced across the parlor at Ursula. She was sitting in his father's old overstuffed chair, her posture characteristically perfect, her face a dappled field of light and shadow. He felt suddenly faint.

"I'm thinking about what you told me," he said in a circumspect voice. "There's a trick to understanding it, I'm sure. But right now it's making me feel kind of funny."

Ursula sighed. "There's no trick to it, Orson."

"There *is* a trick," he said. "There's got to be." He studied her face. "It doesn't seem to bother you at all."

"I think it's a wonderful thing to have happened."

He shook his head slowly.

"Look here, Orson. You should have told me if this was a thing you were against—and you ought to have taken precautions. Enzie told me you were in favor of this, and I took her at her word."

"That's bullshit. You've never taken anybody at their word in your whole life."

"Softly now, please." Her English had gone subtly pidgin, the way it often did when she was angry. "Genny and I talked about this via telephone, and I did this with Enzie as well. I can't believe one of them didn't say so to you. Or maybe this is something you forgot."

Orson took hold of the bridge of his nose and pinched it fiercely. "Something I *forgot?*"

"Every idiot knows how to keep this from happening. You never once used a—"

"Hold it right there, Ursula. What have my sisters got to do with this? Was this something they *planned?*"

Ursula said nothing for a time. "You must know that I care about you, Orson."

"Answer the goddamn question."

"Your sisters have their reasons, always, for the little plans they make. I'm learning this myself. Why do you think they brought me to this place?"

Orson hesitated. "Because of school," he said finally, though he knew, as he said it, that Enzie had cut all ties with the university years before. "Because of Enzie's work, I mean. Out of a common interest in science."

"I thought so, too," Ursula said softly. "But I've revised my understanding."

Orson said nothing for the time it took his dizziness to pass. She waited patiently for him to speak.

"There's no escaping this family," he murmured at last. "I thought that there was—I was *sure* that there was—the first time I left." He looked at her. "I've learned my lesson now."

"It's about time, Mr. Tolliver." She smiled. "Our due date is November seventeenth."

XXI

"Good" or "bad" entrances, Kubler writes, *are more than matters of position in a sequence. Every birth can be imagined as set into play on two distinct wheels of fortune: one governing the allotment of its temperament, the other ruling its entrance into the sequence. When a specific temperament interlocks with a favorable position, the fortunate individual can extract from the situation a wealth of previously unimagined consequences.*

This achievement may be denied to other persons, as well as to the same person at a different time.

Though by no means the religious type, Ursula accepted her pregnancy (after due deliberation) as the will of the powers that be. My father's take was somewhat more complex. For a long list of reasons, Orson had decided not to have children, not ever, and he was certain—as certain as he could be, without recalling a specific conversation—that Ursula had tacitly agreed. Among his reasons were: Ursula's unfinished doctorate, global over-population, the small but persistent possibility of a thermonuclear strike by the Soviet Union, loss of sleep, crib death, his own questionable suitability for fatherhood, shit-sodden diapers, the educational crisis, the Vietnam War and childbirth-related changes to the morphology of the uterine wall. Ursula's mother had once told her that time accelerated wildly for a mother once her baby was born; this idea had made her shiver, she'd once confessed to her husband, with a kind of voluptuous horror. Parenthood struck them both, Orson had always assumed, as an investment with a dubious return. What sane person could disagree with that?

∞

I always find myself skipping the chapters of biographies that deal with the subject's childhood—the dog bites, the rickets, the portentous aversion to breast milk—so I think I'll spare posterity the bother. I came as a surprise to my parents, maybe even a shock, but they adjusted to my presence gracefully. I was considered "promising" in the standard sort of way, though I can't recall why; I was loved, in the standard sort of way, at least by my doting, long-suffering mother. I liked to drink the vinegar in the pickle jar, I remember. I threw a ball like a girl. I made a landscape out of boogers on the wall beside my bed.

Orson loved me too, I believe, by his Orson-ish lights—but there wasn't anything standard about it. Either he saw me, Mrs. Haven, or he didn't. This seemed mostly to depend on how his writing was going, but it also had to do with something else: something grand and adult and hard to visualize, like the stock market or virgin birth or barometric pressure. On days when I was visible to him, he'd make up a story in which I was the conquering hero, or try to get me to throw a ball properly (which I hated), or drive me to the movies in his mustard-yellow Buick. On days when he didn't, he'd walk past me—*through* me, if I wasn't careful—as if I were a trick of the light.

Memory is a politician, Mrs. Haven, as every historian knows: a manipulative, pandering appeaser. Firsthand witness though I am, inaccuracies are creeping into this account. It's likely, for example, that my father took me to the movies a handful of times at the most—I can't remember more than one such trip, in fact, no matter how I try. But that solitary memory, from my last year of grade school, is vivid and well-lit and sharply in focus, as traumatic recollections tend to be.

The movie in question was *Event Horizon*, the third installment of the blockbuster *Timestrider* franchise. Orson had a knee-jerk aversion to Hollywood sci-fi, and a particular loathing for time-travel films; but my mother and I had joined forces this time, and we broke his resistance together. The "Kraut"—as Orson had taken to calling her—did it because my father had been in a nasty mood all week, and his bitching was driving her crazy;

I did it because I needed a ride. It's hard to say why Orson gave in, Mrs. Haven, but I do have a guess. He sensed an opportunity to rant.

Ranting was Orson's preferred form of recreation for the whole of the eighties, and the Buick was his venue of choice. The satisfaction he took in watching his victim writhe in slack-jawed desperation, unable to escape without bodily harm, was the most compelling evidence I'd found (at that admittedly tender age) for the existence of natural evil. "Current events" set him off most dependably, but he could work up a respectable head of steam on virtually any topic: I once heard him hold forth, to one of the Kraut's acquaintances from the Cheektowaga PTA, on the perils of middle-aged motherhood.

"The kids just don't come *out* right," he'd confided to Judy O'Shea. "If you don't believe it, Judy, take a look at me."

"Well, Mr. Tolliver, I must say—I mean, I don't necessarily think—"

"The ideal time for conception, biologically speaking, is between twelve and fourteen years of age. That's when the womb is at its most resilient. And please don't even *ask* about the sperm."

On this particular ride, as I might have expected, Orson had his cross-hairs trained on Hollywood, and he dug in before we'd even cleared the driveway. "What's pathetic to me, Waldy, is the *wish-fulfillment* quality of it all. Never mind the fact that navigating the timestream, hither and thither, is as easy in these flicks as passing gas; the medium has its conventions, I appreciate that. But ninety-nine percent of time-travel movies take it for granted that you can change whatever you want about the present—never mind the future—just by diddling a little with the past. It's obvious that physics means *zilch* to these jerk-offs, and logic seems to count for even less. The past is the past, son. It's done with. You keep that in mind."

"I don't know, Orson. I saw *Timestrider Two* last year, and I thought the whole Uncertainty Drive thing was pretty boss."

"They've *gotten* to you, haven't they," Orson said, scrutinizing me closely. "They've injected their parasitic spores into your brain."

"Keep your eyes on the road, Orson."

"ROWWWGGGHHHHRRR," said my father, rolling his eyes back and baring his teeth. By the time we pulled up at the Mohawk 6 Multi-plex we were debating the pros and cons of an NCAA team spending its off-season on planets with stronger gravitational fields, like Saturn or Venus. A good rant never failed to cheer him up.

∞

The first third of *Timestrider III: Event Horizon* passed without incident. Though Orson was sporting the fluorescent orange hunter's cap he put on whenever he was trying to keep a low profile—his "helm of invisibility," he called it—I occasionally managed to forget he was there. An anxious, goosenecked loner from the suburbs, three weeks shy of thirteen, I was in the demographic sweet spot for the franchise, and I loved every pulsing, booming, logic-flouting minute. The rows in front of us had been commandeered by the *Timestrider* faithful: sixteen-year-old fanboys in frosted jeans and Iron Maiden T-shirts, already on their seventh or eighth viewing, mouthing along with the dialogue like grandmas in church. With the notable exception of a pustule-necked orangutan who could barely squeeze himself into his seat, they looked as spindly and insecure as I was. Whenever the Timestrider pulled out his cryophoton blade—which was every fifteen seconds or so—they gave one another sweaty-palmed highfives. I was beholding my personal future, Mrs. Haven, and I'm not ashamed to say I liked the look of it.

The fanboys bugged the bejeezus out of Orson—the redheaded bruiser especially—but he made a concerted effort to keep calm. He seemed to be enjoying the spectacle: the battle for the icebound insurgent stronghold on Cxax, for instance, actually made him lean forward, and Marduk the Minuteman's hourglass-shaped starcruiser earned a grudging grunt of approbation. "Interesting aproach to ballistics," he muttered. "No *egregious* anomalies yet."

From my father, Mrs. Haven, this was high praise indeed. He confined himself to scoffing during the swordfights—they *were* pretty hokey, I have to admit—and covering his eyes when the Timestrider and Countess Synkronia kissed. I did the same thing, being twelve, but I remember wondering at his prudishness. I was about to ask him about it, in fact, when he jerked his head back in a kind of spasm and shouted something filthy at the screen.

"Orson! What the hell are you—"

"Did you hear that?" he stammered. "Did you hear that, Waldy? Am I fucking dreaming?"

"Would you please sit down, Orson? You're embarrassing—"

"Shut up and *listen*!"

Reluctantly, stiffly, he let me pull him down into his seat. The Horizoners glared back at us for as long as they could stand to, which thankfully wasn't more than a few seconds. Orson's eyes were open wider than I'd ever seen them, and his mouth was moving in a toothless, senile way. That reminded me of something—something I'd just recently thought of, or seen—but it wasn't until I turned back toward the screen that it hit me.

He was moving his lips, Mrs. Haven, exactly like the fanboys in front of us. He was reciting each line of dialogue a beat before it happened.

The Timestrider's krono-kruiser had just marooned him on Cxax in the primordial past, when the surface of the planet was still a bubbling swamp, and he was trying to raise his ship out of the muck. A Cxaxian mystic—a hairless gray koala in a rumpled-looking kilt—was trying to convince him not to bother. The kruiser, according to the koala, was entirely unnecessary.

"Have you not understood?" whispered my father.

"Have you not understood?" said the koala, twitching its animatronic ears. "You travel through time all your life: into the future at the rate at which you age, and into the past each time that you remember."

The Timestrider expressed impatience with the koala's plan of action. The Horizoners slurped their Mountain Dews in bliss.

"There is only the brain, after all," said my father.

"There is only the brain," the koala intoned. "But the brain, after all, is enough. Your consciousness is all the time machine you need."

"ROWWW*GGGHHHHRRR*," said Orson, propelling his stocky body toward the screen. The fanboy whose seat he was clambering over let out a shriek and pitched sideways, spilling his drink into the orangutan's lap; the orangutan let out a roar that drowned out my father and the movie and everything else and practically ripped his seat out of the floor. Orson was a row and a half past him by then, balancing on someone's armrest, but the giant had no trouble catching up. A saucerlike object spun lazily across the screen, and I recognized it, after a stupefied instant, as the orange hunter's cap. By the time the lights came on, the giant had my father pinned to the floor between rows five and six—which was exactly where the EMTs found him, sixteen and a half minutes later, staring up at the ceiling like a corpse.

By that time the manager had apologized to everybody and distributed vouchers good for any later showing in that same theater, and the goon and his cohorts had disappeared. The theater was still full of people, bunched in loose clumps of intrigue, unwilling to believe the show was over. My understanding of what had happened was roughly as follows: my father had whipped the whole theater up into a homicidal rage, then settled on the only exit strategy that would save him from being disarticulated. He'd had a coronary.

Orson was conscious for most of the brief, choppy ride to the ICU, gripping my wrist and gazing up into my panic-stricken face, as though we'd traded one film genre for another. He had a message for me—a message of vital importance—as fathers in movie ambulances tend to do. He tried to lift his head to tell it, to the considerable irritation of the EMTs. In the hope of calming him, I told him I loved him; he shook his head and gave a breathless groan. The transition from blockbuster to low-budget family weepie was now complete. I told him I loved him again, taking care to enunciate clearly.

"At this point, son, you mostly seem to be annoying him," the nearest EMT said. I looked down at my father, who blinked his eyes twice in agreement.

"Okay, Orson," I said. "I get it." I didn't get it, of course. I took his trembling hand in both of mine.

∞

It wasn't until the next morning, after the bypass, that my father told me what was on his mind.

"I want you to go see the rest of that movie."

"Excuse me?"

"I want you to watch the whole thing, Waldy, right to the end." His voice was diminished and hoarse, which somehow made it more authoritative. "Don't even *blink* until the houselights come back on."

"Orson, I'm not sure I—"

"Pay special attention to the closing credits. Then come back here and tell me what you saw."

You might think it would be easy to interrogate a cardiac patient—they can't run off, for one thing—but they have the moral high ground, Mrs. Haven, whether they deserve it or not. It was 11:15 EST when Orson gave me my marching orders; at 12:45 I was watching the opening credits of *Event Horizon* (do you remember them, Mrs. Haven? The way they scrolled toward the audience out of the vastness of space, gilded and silent, like hearing-impaired subtitles for the voice of God?) from the same seat I'd sat in the evening before. Quite a few people in the audience looked familiar, including a man, two rows up, who appeared to be wearing the helm of invisibility; but I did my best to tune out all distractions. I was seeing the movie with different eyes now, on the lookout for hidden messages and codes.

At the one-hour mark, the notebook I'd brought contained only the following:

"ANDRO" = ROBOT
PHOTON BLASTER "BULLETS" = REALISTIC??

It happened every so often that Orson forgot and/or ignored the fact that I was still a child, so the sensation of near-total inadequacy I was experiencing was nothing new. For once, however, it seemed vitally important not to fail. This was partly because Orson was in intensive care, of course, but also because the *Timestrider* trilogy fell squarely within my microscopic zone of expertise. All I thought about between the ages of nine and fourteen was science fiction; even my filthiest onset-of-puberty fantasies featured "contact"—so to speak—with other worlds. Which is just to say, Mrs. Haven, that I was my father's son. If I couldn't give an accurate summary of *Timestrider III: Event Horizon*, no one could.

It turned out I needn't have worried. No sooner had the Timestrider escaped the clutches of the Empiricist forces by punching a random set of coordinates into his krono-kruiser and hitting "jump" than a suspicion began to tug at my awareness. The first half of the movie had been devoted to combustion of various types, punctuated by swordfights and gunfights and cleavage; as soon as the time-travel sequences kicked in, however, I felt the blood rush to my head. I hadn't yet reached the age at which I would start to pester Orson about our family history, but I'd scavenged enough over the years to recognize a correspondence between spacetime (as the Tollivers defined it) and the kronoverse our hero voyaged through. Both were based on the notion that the timestream is curved; curved in such a way, in fact, that it forms a ring, or possibly a sphere. Given this curvature of time, it ought to be possible to take shortcuts across it, geometrically speaking, by traveling along its chords; this (as I'd soon learn) was what my aunt Enzian had come to believe, and what she was experimenting with, at that very moment, in her rooms in the General Lee. It was also, coincidentally or not, how the Timestrider's krono-kruiser (which looked like nothing so much as an enormous, globe-shaped pulpit) took him on his rumbling, flashing jaunts from Now to Then.

From that point forward, it was as though two movies were being projected onto the interior of my skull—both the climactic conclusion of the *Timestrider* trilogy and a spectral companion piece, flickering in and out of focus, made for a purpose I'd grasped only one thing about: my family was both its audience and its subject. In that final hour, surrounded by Coke-slurping strangers in that oversold, sticky-floored theater, I felt what paranoid schizophrenics report experiencing during pyschotic episodes: the suspicion that the actors were speaking directly to me.

Psychiatrists refer to this phenomenon as "delusions of reference," Mrs. Haven, but there were no delusions in play in the Mohawk 6 that afternoon. I'd heard my own father reciting the actor's lines, after all, less than twenty-four hours before. There was a riddle in that, a mystery I was still too young to solve; but I had no doubt that I'd crack the code in time. As a twelve-year-old boy, I saw the world of adults in precisely those terms—as a series of time-coded, self-solving riddles—and in this particular instance I was right. I didn't have to wait longer than the closing credits.

∞

I rushed from the Mohawk 6 back to Buffalo General as fast as the NFTA bus would carry me, bursting at the seams with self-importance. Orson was having something done to him involving gauze and electrodes when

I got there, so I was forced to cool my heels out in the hall. I kept my back to the wall and my eyes on the floor, struggling to choke back my excitement. For whatever reason—urgency? fear? an adrenaline spike?—my senses were as sharp as a raccoon's. I heard the nurse's crepe-soled shoes against the crackling ancient vinyl and saw and smelled things that I'd rather not remember. Finally Orson's door opened and the nurses filed out. I found him wide awake and restless.

"Well, Waldy?" he gasped. It seemed to me now, in my paranoid state, that he was gasping on purpose, on the off chance that the premises were bugged.

"I did it," I whispered.

"Good boy. What have you got?"

"The Insurgency won, Orson. Just like you said."

He gave a sigh and let his eyes fall closed. "That's wonderful, Waldy. Huzzah for the cosmos. Is that all?"

I held back for a moment, aware that I was toying with my father. I was savoring his attention—his desperation, really—knowing all too well that it was temporary. His chest rose and fell under the papery hospital sheets; a vein in his neck twitched in time to his heartbeat. I had the sudden conviction, feeling my own pulse quicken, that if I stared long enough at that vein it would explode.

"I've also got this." I laid my notebook on the bed beside him.

"Show me."

I flipped to the relevant page and held it up. Printed there, all in caps, was the very last line of the credits:

SPONSORED BY THE U.S. CHURCH
OF SYNCHRONOLOGY

Orson glanced at it quickly, then pushed it away. It was obviously what he'd been expecting. I remember feeling vaguely disappointed.

"As soon as I get out of this organ-harvesting center," he muttered, "we're going to pay a visit to your aunties."

This entry may turn your stomach, Mrs. Haven, but the possibility no longer worries me. I'm still writing for an audience of one, still bearing witness, as I've done since the beginning; but sometimes I wonder. Someone will read this, I'm certain of that. But my audience might not be you—or "you"—at all. It could even be the Timekeeper himself.

My relief at his disappearance didn't last longer than a single sleep cycle. Once it registered that I was alone again—more alone, if possible, than I'd been before I found him—the old heaviness dropped down on me at once. The singularity was tightening its hold, taking advantage of my discouragement; but I knew the heaviness was just a symptom.

The cause of it was clear to me. I missed him.

This isn't as perverse as it sounds, Mrs. Haven. I feel no sympathy for my great-uncle, let alone love. He's a sociopath, a criminal, a monster—I have no doubt of that. But I was possessed of two ambitions before being banished to this place: (1) to arrive at a reckoning of my family's crimes, by finishing this history; and (2) to reckon *with* them, perhaps even atone for them, by whatever sad, belated methods I could find. And I can no longer deny, Mrs. Haven—not now, having met him at last—that Waldemar holds the key to them both.

My strength gradually returned as I reviewed chapter XXI, and I began venturing, slowly and tentatively, back into the Archive. But not once in a half-dozen forays—two of them as far as my aunts' bedroom—did I find the slightest trace of Waldemar. It was as though all evidence of him had been deliberately erased: no imprint on the bed, no bantering notes, no mnemonic triggers left out in the tunnels. I never would have thought a place so packed with junk could seem so empty. I had nothing but my history to keep me company, and my history wasn't enough: not when the Timekeeper himself might be in the next room.

Finally, on what I'd resolved would be my very last pilgrimage to that claustrophobic chamber, I found him waiting for me on the bed.

He was sitting with his back against the headboard and his legs splayed in a V across the sheets, unpacking a grimy olive-colored satchel. Its contents seemed as random as anything out in the Archive: a bicycle pump, a length of wire, a tarnished old key, a handful of cherry pits in a cracked glass beaker. He took no notice of me until I cleared my throat.

"There you are, Waldy," he said absently, holding the satchel upside-down and shaking it. "You have some questions for me, I imagine."

I hadn't been aware of having any questions. Nothing came to my mind.

"What was that, *Nefflein?*"

"Are we the same person?"

Again he seemed barely to hear me. He was more corporeal than when I'd seen him last, but also tighter-skinned—somehow inflated-seeming—as though his viscera and flesh were pressurized.

"Those things you did," I said. "At the Äschenwald camp."

He set the satchel aside. "What about them?"

I hesitated. "Am I like you?"

"What a curious question. In what sense do you mean?"

I did my best to hold his milky gaze. "If your theory is right—if chronological time is a hoax—then why should your guilt have been passed on to me? Why should *I* care what happened at Czas, or Vienna, or anywhere else? Why can't I forget?"

I'd expected him to react with surprise, perhaps even anger; instead he cocked his head and grinned at me.

"I've been wondering what brought you here, *Nefflein*. Now I understand."

"What the hell does that mean?"

"The past is a torment to you, the present is grim, and the future—from what I can see—scares you out of your wits. Is it any wonder you've excused yourself from time?"

I opened my mouth and closed it.

"Here's a piece of advice, Waldy. If you're looking for *causes*—"

"I don't want your advice. I want you to answer my question."

"No need to shout!" He held up both his hands in mock surrender. "It's important to keep in mind, first of all, that Äschenwald was a means to me only. The *end*—as you well know—was otherwise." He shifted indolently on the bed. "If you'd had my reasons . . . then yes. Perhaps you might have acted as I did."

He coughed twice—loudly and hackingly—into his fist, then waited to hear what I would ask him next.

"What were your reasons?" I said, as he'd known that I would.

"I can't hear you, *Nefflein*. Come closer."

I leaned forward. "Tell me what your reasons were."

"For what?"

"For the Gottfriedens Protocols. For Äschenwald. For all of it."

He replied without the slightest hesitation.

∞

"In Budapest during the year of the famine I found myself, for a time, without a roof over my head, so I made my home in Népliget Park, in the company of some three hundred other starving wretches. People were eating the bark off the trees, digging holes in the frozen ground to pass the night in, slitting each other's throats for a spoonful of cream. I did as the worst did—the ones who survived. But I was farther from myself than the others, at a greater remove from the man I'd once been, so I did more of it, *Nefflein*. And I did it better.

"My victims were Gypsies and Jews, for the most part—the reason was simply that they were nearby—and eventually my talents came to the attention of a certain order. The members of this order clothed me and fed me, and I accepted their patronage. I rose in their ranks, as a man of initiative will, and in time I was called to Berlin. I judged myself fortunate in this, as my patrons' influence was waxing by the hour. I saw the future in them, *Nefflein*, and I was not disappointed.

"Gestures were required to consolidate my position: a measure of violence, as one might expect, but also a great deal of clerical work, for the most part pertaining to the propagation and diffusion of fear. The interests

I represented during that time have come to have a reputation for vicious-ness, but the vast majority of them were timid men, conventional and un-imaginative, and as such—given the tenor of the times—frightened within an inch of their lives. In such a field I found it easy to get on.

"I was under no illusion, when offered the directorship of the Äschen-wald facility, that my scientific work was of importance to Berlin—but I realized the post would serve my needs. I'd been privileged with certain insights into the nature of time during my period of near-starvation in Népliget Park, and I'd waited almost twenty years to put them to the test. I saw the camp as a place of work: a research station, no more than that, but the only one I was likely to be granted. Compared with what I knew—what I'd known for two decades, more surely even than I knew my name—nothing else had weight or definition.

"Should a present-day scientist, for example here in America, when hot on the heels of a discovery—the discovery, say, of a cure for mental illness—refuse funding from his government, on account of its collusion with homi-cidal Third World regimes, or the bombing of Hiroshima, or its many costly, bloody foreign wars? Think carefully, *Nefflein*, before you reply. The subjects of my protocols suffered the same privations I myself had suffered—extremes of cold and hunger, prolonged exposure to darkness—and were granted the same insight I'd received. The dreams they dreamed in their captivity approximated death, and the state they existed in by the end of their trials—at the attenuated margin of existence, only vestigially conscious, suspended between oblivion and life—was a kind of perpetual dream.

"Dreams are one key to the Accidents—the surest key, perhaps—but I hadn't discovered this. Not at that point in consensus time.

"I had no concern for my personal welfare when the Soviets came, but I knew that my research was at an end. With the Red Army less than six hours distant, I ordered all outbuildings razed, regardless of whether or not the trials they housed had reached completion. I did this at the cost of ade-quate defense of the camp, which resulted in the death of most of my sub-ordinates, and of course a great number of prisoners. Just one potential test subject remained; fortunately, one was all I needed. An absolute breach this time. A full excision from the timestream. My only fear was that the camp would fall before I'd accomplished the breach—but they were in no rush, the Soviets. They razed Äschenwald to the ground, methodically and slowly, beginning with the buildings where we'd run our final trials. They were good enough, *Nefflein*, to cover the last of my tracks. I'm beholden to them for that service."

∞

That was the end of it, Mrs. Haven: all the reason my namesake possessed. He shut his mouth and turned back to his satchel. I watched him for a time, fussing over his trinkets, muttering under his breath like some aged recluse. And he *was* aged, of course: unnaturally, wretchedly old. His fearsomeness had long since passed away. I thought of the turning of the tide, of the collapse of the Eastern Front, of the Red Army's march on bombshattered Berlin. I thought of how very long ago that was.

"Do you still think back on that time?"

"What time?" he said without turning.

"Your tenure at Czas. At the Äschenwald camp."

He glanced up at me with an expression that bordered on pity. *"Ach,* Waldy!" he said. "I've only just arrived from there."

XXII

AT THE TIME I was born, total radio silence had prevailed between my father and his sisters for more than a year, to the private misery of all concerned. Orson had been too proud to take the critical first step, though he likely suffered more than anyone; Enzian had been too absorbed in her research (or so she later claimed); Gentian had fallen back into her pre-Manhattan deference; and the Kraut had decided she couldn't be bothered. While my birth was an ambiguous event from certain points of view—my own, for example—it was a godsend for family relations. Coaxed by his wife and his own heavy conscience, Orson sent a postcard to Harlem announcing my arrival. It was a plain-enough postcard, ugly and cheaply printed, embossed with that now-inescapable icon of my native city: a buffalo wearing a scarf. But in a number of other ways, Mrs. Haven, my father's postcard was a wonder for the ages.

It was wondrous, first of all, in that it was written by Orson, who'd never sent a postcard in his life; and it was even more wondrous—miraculous, in fact—in the olive branch it extended to his sisters. The card informed Enzian and Gentian, in a matter-of-fact, unsentimental tone, that a child had been born. It gave the child's weight, gender, eye color, and date of birth. *As to the name*—wrote my father, in his pinched, clerkish script—*Ursula and I are open to suggestions.*

As a gesture, Mrs. Haven, it was not without a certain grandeur, and his sisters duly rose to the occasion. Less than seventy-two hours after the postcard was sent, its counterpart arrived at Pine Ridge Road, this one depicting Nutter's Battery in Central Park. Every available inch of the card's reverse side was covered in Gentian's hand, and much of what was written there was indecipherable; the gist, however, was that the child should be brought to them without delay. Orson wasn't mentioned on the postcard, and neither was Ursula, but the implication was that they'd be welcome. This itself was no minor concession, as my aunts' door had been closed to the entire human species for the preceding seven months.

It was my mother who told me the story of that first trip to Spanish Harlem, not my father, so I'm confident the details can be trusted. It was an eight-hour drive to New York in those days, and I bawled from Rochester to Painted Post; Orson's nerves were in tatters by the time we crossed the Hudson, and the Kraut could feel a fever coming on. We pulled up at the General Lee at dusk. The neighborhood looked even more abject than my father remembered, purged of any phantom traces of romance. He pressed the buzzer of his former place of residence three times, counted silently to thirty, then pressed it again. When no response came, he dug out a key from the glove compartment—huge and ancient and tarnished, like the key to a fairy-tale dungeon—and unlocked the front door himself. Ursula followed him feebly, already running a temperature, humming to keep the restless baby quiet.

The electricity was out in the lobby, and the windows were covered in cardboard and tape. At the fourth-floor landing they found themselves confronted by a massive jet-black door, apparently freshly installed: it was out of all proportion to the stairwell, Ursula thought—much too grandiose for that decrepit building—though perhaps the fever was affecting her judgment.

"Here we are," Orson said softly, as though afraid of being overheard. From somewhere—possibly far away—came the sound of running water.

"Do you hear that?" said Ursula, whispering without knowing why.

He laid his ear to the door. "What time have you got?"

"Quarter to three."

"They'll be taking their afternoon bath."

The baby squawked; Ursula gave it a jiggle. "They take their baths together?" she asked, trying to sound nonchalant.

He gave her an odd smile, motioned for her to step back, then slammed the heels of both his palms against the door. The resulting boom set the whole building trembling and the baby caterwauling and Orson cursing and clutching his wrist. The door hummed like a gong. She touched it with her fingertips and found that it was made of some kind of metal, smooth and cold to the touch. She was about to ask Orson about it when a weather-beaten gentleman with a yellowish afro and a debonair manner appeared on the landing below and suggested, in a high, cultured voice, that they go right to hell. "Is that you, Mr. Buckram?" Orson called down to him.

The man gave Orson the finger. Soon afterward the bolts began to turn.

However violent my debut may have seemed to my aunts—they hadn't been expecting our visit until the next morning, according to Gentian, and it was only the sound of my crying that had kept them from alerting the police—their own entrance into my duration was notably mild. I seem to remember it, Mrs. Haven, though I couldn't possibly remember it. The great door swings inward, making no sound at all, and the sisters are standing behind it, shoulder to shoulder, small and frail against the yawning dark behind them. A tense silence falls, which Ursula breaks by holding up the baby for inspection. They examine it dubiously (my mother's choice of words, Mrs. Haven, not mine). She can't quite decide, as they poke at her son, whether or not she ought to feel offended. Gentian turns to Enzian, who gives a brisk nod.

"Waldemar," Enzian announces.

It seems to Ursula suddenly—but again, she's exhausted and feverish—that she's known all along which name the sisters would choose, and also that she would put up no resistance. Orson embraces each of them in turn, solemnly but with feeling, as though they were Russian functionaries at a banquet. Ursula realizes, dimly, that she's being escorted back downstairs. Now she's offended—no, perhaps not offended; bewildered, perplexed—but her husband appears not to notice. Go to sleep, he tells her, making a manger of sorts in the Buick's backseat. We'll be in Buffalo by midnight, all three of us. You and me and little Waldemar.

∞

Half my childhood was gone when I next saw my aunts, and by then the name had warped and shrunk to fit me. It would be years before I learned its full significance—before I was taken quietly aside, by my mother, on my seventeenth birthday, and told exactly what Äschenwald, that pretty word, meant to the rest of the world—and by that point, of course, it was too late. Or so I was led to believe.

My mother was never especially interested in helping me fit in—she considered it an expression of Austrian pride to speak German to me in public places, and dressed me in a style that a college girlfriend, flipping through a photo album years later, dubbed "Hitler Youth casual"—but even *she* realized that the name Waldemar was more than my skinny shoulders could support. "Waldy" was Ursula's invention, and I'm grateful to her, though her insistence on pronouncing it the Austrian way ("VAL-dee") tended to defeat the nickname's purpose. Fortunately I had a gift for deflecting attention: I was remarkably unremarkable, Mrs. Haven, as I've mentioned before. By June 18, 1978, when my father and I climbed the General Lee's stairwell together for the second time, I'd been punched, bitten, knocked over and peed on no more than most seven-year-olds, which I take a certain pride in even now. I was reasonably well adjusted for my age, and tended not to take things much to heart, especially when grown-ups said or did them. This made me a mild but steady disappointment to my parents, especially at parent-teacher conferences—but it proved to be a crucial skill in dealing with my aunts.

This time Orson knocked politely, both out of consideration for his knuckles and for the door of the apartment, to which the intervening years had not been gentle. It hung askew on its hinges, as though the building had somehow shifted out of plumb, and the gaps this produced (of which there were a few) were plugged with soggy-looking wads of newsprint. My father had been in lecture mode on the long drive downstate—without actually explaining the point of our visit, which remained a mystery—but now he was silent and grim. As I listened to the sound of slippered footfalls and of deadbolts being thrown, I was seized by the suspicion that I was about to be sold into white slavery, or forced to take a trigonometry exam, or cooked slowly in a child-sized witch's cauldron.

The last bolt was thrown and the black door swung open and a lady peered out from behind it. She had a harried look, and she wasn't much taller than Orson, but she seemed to gaze down on us from on high. I knew she was one of my aunts, of course, but I didn't know which. If I'd been allowed to read my father's books, I'd have recognized her right away—she could only have been Empress Eng Xan, the Obsidian Priestess, villainess of the Chyldwyrld trilogy.

"You're here," said the woman. She said it in German: *"Ihr seid da."* Her accent—equal parts Austrian and Yankee and Yiddish—was no more curious than anything else about her. "Where's the other one hiding?"

"If by 'the other one,' you mean Ursula, my wife," my father answered in English, "she'd have liked nothing better than to drive for eight hours to wait out here on your landing again, but she's visiting her mother in Vienna. Are you going to let us in this time?"

The woman's eyes narrowed, as if she suspected us of subterfuge (and in fact my mother was very much at home in Cheektowaga, already in bed, with a paperback and a glass of iced Lillet); then she took in a sharp, girlish breath that made her seem decades younger, and receded smoothly— ceremonially, it seemed to me—into the gloom. A second woman appeared, blushing and grinning and rubbing her plump hands together, but in that first dazzled instant I paid her no mind. The hall we stepped into was fitted with shelves of every conceivable description, some extravagantly filigreed, some obviously homemade, and each devoted to a single object. Many of the items in question were familiar—a teakettle, a bowling ball, a snow globe enclosing a miniature Chrysler Building—but some were completely obscure. There must have been nearly a thousand such shelves, ranging in size from the width of my palm to the length of my arm, running along both walls as far as I could see. The blushing woman kissed my father on both cheeks without saying a word. Then she took my hand and led me down the hall.

"Do you like what you see, Waldemar?" she asked in an odd voice, both boisterous and shy.

"It's Waldy," I corrected her.

"Is it, now?" Behind her smile she was watching me closely. "Do you like what you see, Waldy?"

"What is all this stuff?"

"I thought you'd never ask! It's an archive."

I was old enough to know that people were supposed to collect expensive things, or rare things, or things that fit together in some way; these looked as though they'd been scavenged at the Cheektowaga landfill. A fencing mask, a Dixie Cup, a credit card, an upside-down jar with the shell of a bug underneath it: any object takes on authority, of a kind, when singled out and given pride of place. But the sheer quantity of items on display, and the contrast of their battered condition to the customized perfection of the shelves, repelled interpretation like an antimagnet. It was my first physical encounter with paradox, Mrs. Haven, and it made me feel hollow and weak. My aunts' apartment was now a museum of sorts—I understood that much—but a museum whose only curator, as far as I could see, was chance.

"What kind of an archive?" I asked her at last.

"The Archive of Accidents. That's what my sister calls it. It's beautiful, wouldn't you say?"

I frowned at her. "Accidents? What do you mean?"

"I have to keep myself *amused*," she said, lowering her voice. "My sister has her work, you know, and I have mine."

No one had ever spoken to me as an adult before, and it thrilled me almost as much as it confused me. I had no idea what to say next.

"I *find* things, Waldy," she went on. "I notice things, and occasionally I take them." She giggled. "Every man-made thing can be thought of as a work of art, you know. You're familiar with *The Shape of Time*, by Kubler?"

I opened my mouth to speak. No sound emerged.

"No? Then let me read a bit to you." She reached blindly behind her and plucked the book down from a shelf, like a conjuror producing a bouquet.

"I'll begin, as the mock turtle advises, at the beginning.

> " 'Let us suppose that the idea of Art can be expanded to embrace the whole range of man-made things, including all tools and writing in addition to the useless, beautiful, and poetic things of the world. By this view the universe of man-made things simply coincides with the history of Art. In effect, the only tokens of history continually available to our senses are the desirable things made by men.' "

As she read I looked past her, past the ceiling-high matrix of shelves, past a personal computer and a dressmaker's mannequin and a stuffed kinkajou, toward the shadows at the turning of the hallway. The hallway had refused to conform to my expectations as my aunt led me inward, rushing toward us when my attention was diverted, then holding unnaturally still—resisting any and all acknowledgment of our forward motion—as though we'd stepped into the forced perspective of a painting. I was seven years old, an age at which the world still changes shape and hue according to one's mood; but there was something unnatural, irresolvable, about the boundaries of that space. I sensed this right away, Mrs. Haven, as clearly as I sensed the anxiety behind my aunt's coquettishness.

> " 'Such things mark the passage of Time with far greater accuracy than we know, and they fill Time with shapes of a limited variety. Like crustaceans, we depend for survival upon an outer skeleton, upon a shell of historic houses and apartments filled with things belonging to definable portions of the past.' "

"That's what I'm after with this little collection," my aunt said, closing the book with a snap. "To approach *every* man-made thing as if it ought to be in a museum. Everything I see out there"—here she waved a hand vaguely (and with a bit of a shudder, I thought)—"could potentially have a place in *here*. Isn't that terribly exciting, Waldemar?"

I struggled to come up with some worldly-sounding comment, as I did when watching football with my father. "How do you decide what to take?"

"Excellent question!" She looked proudly about her. "In theory, of course, this collection should be infinite. I suppose that we'll have to expand."

"What's back there?" I asked, pointing toward the hallway's turning.

"Where?"

"Back there. Where it starts to get dark."

"You must be *hungry*," my aunt said, returning the book to its shelf. "I baked a peach cobbler this morning. It's not easy to find peaches, you know, at this time of—"

"I have to go to the bathroom."

"Of course, dear! The WC's right behind you. Don't trouble yourself about that dressmaker's dummy—just waltz it right out of the way."

Aside from its arched ceiling and acid-green walls, the only point of interest in the WC was the toilet seat, which was upholstered in chocolate pile. My aunt said something through the door that I didn't quite catch, then tittered to herself and trundled off. Every so often I heard an odd noise, like the moving-about of heavy furniture. I made a game of trying to guess what it could be.

The hallway seemed darker when I came back out. I could hear my father's voice not too far off, speaking more guardedly than I was used to, and a woman's voice asking him questions. I stood still for a time, trying to make out what was being said, savoring the delectable thrill all children feel when spying on their elders. The voices were tantalizingly close, just shy of intelligibility; I crawled toward them on my hands and knees to keep the floor from creaking. My father was talking about someone they all seemed to know, someone who had to be handled with tact, even caution— a delicate case, not as simple as it might appear.

"I'm aggrieved to hear that," came the voice of the woman. Not the one who'd led me down the hallway—the other one. Aunt Enzian.

"Let's not get melodramatic here," my father said. "He isn't who you thought he was, that's all."

"He *is*," said Enzian. "He has to be."

"Listen to me. He's too suggestible, too fragile—"

"We'll handle him gently, Orson. Like an egg."

It took him a moment to answer. His voice had gone high and wheedling, the voice of the boy he'd once been. Whatever it was that my aunts wanted, it was clear his defenses were crumbling. It had never before occurred to me that there might be things, let alone human beings, of which or whom my father was afraid.

"Explain to me, one more time, what you need his help for."

It was Gentian who answered. "We need him to *believe* in us, Peanut. To go where we can't. As we've tried to explain—"

"We need him to jump," came Enzian's voice. "He has the best chance of any of us. It has to be him, Orson. There's nobody else."

"There's you, isn't there? What the hell have *you* been doing all these years?"

"My work," Enzian answered, her voice hard as slate. "And I'll say it again, little brother: I've done my work well. But I'm not the one to make the world take notice, and neither is Genny. We'd thought we could rely on you—but you decided otherwise. You decided to write smut instead."

To my great surprise my father didn't argue.

"There was no other option," he murmured. "Not for me. I didn't believe in the Accidents." He was quiet a moment. "I still don't, no matter what you say."

"What is it that you *do* believe in, then?" said Gentian. "You must believe in something."

"In my family," my father spat out—then stopped short, as if surprised at his own answer. "I believe in this family." He paused again, then mumbled, "God knows I wouldn't be here if I didn't."

"*Give* him to us," said Enzian. "We had an understanding, Orson. We had a covenant."

"I don't know what you're talking about. What covenant?"

"It's just for a spell," Genny purred. "You can visit whenever you like."

"But I've been enjoying his company lately. He's just starting to reason, to think for himself—"

"We had an *understanding*," Enzian repeated. "You knew this day would arrive."

"What are you blathering about?" said my father, his voice going shrill. "What goddamn understanding?"

"We sent you a message," Genny said with a sigh.

"You did no such thing."

"Don't play the fool," said Enzian. "Why else do you think we named him Waldemar?"

If my father gave an answer I no longer heard it. I was halfway up the hallway already, scuttling backward like a water bug, stopping only when my sneakers hit the door. It gonged faintly, its earlier boom in miniature, but they were too busy squabbling to notice. I rose to a crouch, barely able to breathe. I'd been brought as an offering: that much was now clear. I would never see daylight again.

I was too young to have much self-control, Mrs. Haven, but I mustered what little I had. Be reasonable, I commanded myself—a thing my parents often said to each other. "Be *reasonable*, Waldy," I whispered aloud. Nobody gets sacrificed anymore. Nobody gets skinned alive or atomized or eaten. Reality isn't like your father's books.

I lived in awe of my father, as most children do; but just then, in that dim no-man's-land, my reverence for him failed to bring me comfort. My upbringing had been religion-free, more or less, but I knew the fable of

Abraham and Isaac. Orson himself, just a few weeks before, had told it to me over breakfast.

I turned to face the door and found it locked. The sight of that column of deadbolts, thick and black and corroded, made me start to hyperventilate with panic. I hadn't started crying—not yet—but I could feel my lungs and tear ducts mobilizing. I stepped away from the door, dropped back onto my knees, and set a course for the end of the hallway.

My luck held long enough to carry me past the parlor door, then the bathroom and the dressmaker's mannequin, but after that the air began to shudder. The forced-perspective sensation returned with a vengeance: the turning kept its distance like a fata morgana, as though it were miles away from me instead of yards. It was easier to move, I discovered, if I kept my eyes closed. The argument was growing fainter now, less relevant, more abstract. When I rounded the corner it stopped altogether.

What happened then, Mrs. Haven, is still beyond my power to describe. It was a long time ago, back when the real and the unreal were interchangeable to me, and thinking in the colorless, odorless, soundless nonplace I suddenly found myself in was like trying to breathe on the moon. I made a left turn, then a second, then a third. The last of my panic had fallen away. I was traveling counterclockwise, in an inward-curving spiral, in accordance with the laws of C*F*P. When I finally stopped and stood upright and opened my eyes, it came as no surprise that I saw nothing.

T
HERE'S A PASSAGE in that silver book you gave me, Mrs. Haven,
that comes to mind each time I think of our elopement. It's from
chapter two—"Modern Survivals of Ancient Customs"—and it
touches on one of the author's pet topics, namely abduction:

> THE HONEYMOON.—*The honeymoon is a period of seclu-*
> *sion for the amorous couple, and/or absence from the familiar*
> *habitat. It is a relic of the remote time of marriage by capture,*
> *when it was necessary for the groom to remain in hiding with*
> *his bride until the search was given up.*

We never discussed it—we steered clear of the topic, both of us, by unspoken consensus—but I thought of those weeks on the run as our honeymoon, and I was relatively sure that you did, too. It was improbable and
preposterous and most likely a violation of the Geneva and Hague Conventions that I'd managed to spirit you away from New York City, and the
happiness this gave me lent a lightness and warmth to everything I saw
or touched: the world you and I inhabited for that brief, exalted interval
was less a solid object, looking back on it now, than a vast and exquisite
soufflé.

But like all soufflés, Mrs. Haven, it was ultimately destined for collapse.

You paid for our tickets—cash, for reasons of secrecy—and I never
thanked you. The reason for your change of heart remained a blind spot
in my understanding, a redacted line, a glowing white unknown, and I was

incapable of asking you, for fear that you'd suddenly come to your senses. Absurdly, inexplicably, my last-ditch attempt to use the mystery of the Accidents to beguile you to Europe had worked, and I took a giddy sort of comfort in my triumph. At the same time, the fact that your husband was bankrolling our "period of seclusion from the familiar habitat" made me sick with resentment and shame, and lent the whole enterprise—your escape, our elopement, my ill-thought-out scheme to find Ottokar's notes, even my pursuit of the Timekeeper himself—the triteness of a junior high school play.

As the more experienced of the two of us (in elopement especially), you let these moods pass without comment. You even indulged me so far as to inquire about my plan, though it was obvious you didn't expect much in the way of an answer: you'd assumed (perfectly reasonably) that Vienna was only a pretext. You finally posed the question two and a half hours out of JFK—we'd just left the coast of Nova Scotia, I remember—and I answered as forthrightly as I could. By the time I'd finished we were over Belgium.

"So—" you said tentatively, after a long spell of quiet. You didn't get further than that.

"I'm sorry, Mrs. Haven. I know it's a lot to take in."

You blinked and cleared your throat and tried again. "Let me try to summarize what you've told me, Walter. To make sure I've got it all straight."

"Sure thing."

"First we're flying to Vienna, to visit your mother. Then we're going by train to, um, Snodge—"

"*Znojmo,*" I said patiently. "The letter *j* has a *y* sound in Czech. Like the *oy* in *goyim.*"

"Znojmo. Okay." You flagged down a stewardess and ordered a bourbon-and-soda. "We're going to *Znojmo* to track down some papers that your great-grandfather dropped in the street when he was hit by a car at the turn of the century—"

"He might not actually have dropped them; that's conjecture on my part. They could have disappeared some other way—stolen by rivals, for example. Or his mistress might have them."

You gave me a sharp look. "His mistress."

"Her descendants, of course." I hesitated. "His mistress is dead by now, I'm guessing."

"I'd call that a safe guess."

"Absolutely. Point taken."

"Except that the whole reason, you're telling me, that we're looking for these papers—"

"These notes—"

"—these *notes*, is to track down your grandfather's brother, a Nazi war criminal, who developed relativity in the same year that Albert Einstein—"

"We never say that name in my family, if you don't mind. And it wasn't relativity, exactly. He referred to it as rotary—"

"—in the same year that Albert Einstein published his theory of relativity, and who used his knowledge of the secret workings of time to somehow screw up your whole family—including, apparently, you—not to mention all sorts of other god-awful and nasty and just plain *weird* stuff, like sending cicadas back into the past, and tampering with people's dreams—"

"That's not exactly what I—"

"—and who *now*, if I'm doing my math right, would be one hundred and seven years old. And you're doing this—*we're* doing this—because you want him to be—" You pursed your lips. "What's the expression you used?"

I took a deep breath. "Brought to justice."

"*Brought to justice.* Okay."

Neither of us spoke for a while. The cabin bucked and shuddered death-defyingly. Someone very close by, possibly right behind us, let out a groan of pent-up human misery. The stewardess arrived with your bourbon. You tried to give her a tip, which she refused.

"It all sounds so hokey, when you put it like that," I said.

"It doesn't sound hokey, Walter. It sounds batshit crazy."

"I'm sure you're right, Mrs. Haven." I leaned forward. "But the man you're married to believes it—I know that for certain. And so does the rest of his church."

You took a slow swig of your bourbon. "I'll tell you something, Mr. Tolliver. The two of us had better pray that isn't true."

∞

The Kraut was living in a one-room apartment on Taubstummengasse that had been used as an atelier by so many artists over the years that you could feel the clots of hardened paint under the carpet. One of them—or so she claimed—had been the mysterious Kappa, for whom Sonja had modeled in her Jandek days. The Jandek itself was two blocks up the street, still open for business and seedy as ever.

None of this was by design, of course, but neither was it pure coincidence. I soon learned that Vienna is such a dense and impacted mass of translucent, overlapping layers of history and nostalgia and happenstance that it resembles nothing so much as a massive candied onion. I found emblems of my family's downfall everywhere I looked: some as slight as a waltz played by panhandling Poles, some as monumental as the gold-and-marble plague column up the Graben from Saint Peter's. The Brown Widow's villa was still standing, and the house with the intertwined dragons was, too, though it now housed a shop selling Red Bull and bongs. I shambled through those marzipan streets like a zombie, Mrs. Haven, if only because the dead seemed so oppressively alive. You admired the Breughels in the Kunsthistorisches Museum and shopped for Alexander boots and sea-green loden jackets on the Graben. Both of us kept our distance from the Klimts.

You didn't make the best impression on the Kraut—what's the use of denying it?—but then again, neither did I. She was in grad student mode at the time, living in her big, drafty studio on bread and liverwurst and Turkish coffee, as single-minded and disheveled as her secret patron saint, Madame Curie. My decision to drop out of Ogilvy had disappointed her deeply. The one thing I'm grateful for, even now, is that we managed to keep the Husband's identity from her. She didn't blame Synchronology for the end of her marriage—that would have meant giving the UCS some credibility, however slight—but she had nothing but contempt for its disciples. The only thing she viewed more skeptically was love.

"Where is she?" she said, before she'd even let me in the door.

"She's coming," I answered, defensive already. "I think she's taking a tour of the Opera."

"I see," said the Kraut. "She's off shopping somewhere?"

"You don't know the first thing about her, Ursula. For your information—"

"I'm sorry, Waldy. I'll untwist my knickers." She squinted past me, as if checking to see whether I'd been tailed. "I'm assuming that those flowers are for me?"

"Of course they are," I said, giving her a kiss.

The only furniture in the place was a cot in one corner and a rolltop desk and chair against the wall. A pot of goulash sat on a hotplate in the middle of the floor. It looked as though she'd been eating out of it for days.

"I'm doing what I want to do, Waldy," she said, guessing my thoughts as always. "I don't cook anymore. I've done quite enough cooking."

"Just as long as you're remembering to eat."

She smiled. "Tell me about your relationship. I assume you find it sensually fulfilling."

I made a face and wandered over to the desk. "I'll have to defer to Mrs. Haven on that point."

Her eyes narrowed at once. "Mrs. *Who?*"

"Nothing," I said quickly. "That's just a name I call her sometimes. As a joke."

"Ah," said the Kraut.

"What's 'aha' supposed to mean?"

"I didn't say 'aha,'" she said, following me to the desk. "I said 'ah.' Would you like to ask me how my work is going?"

"Of course I would. But I probably wouldn't understand your answer."

The Kraut frowned at me for an instant, as if the possibility had only just occurred to her. She wasn't as different from the rest of the family as she liked to think.

"You might find some of it rather dusty, I suppose—it's true you never were much good at theory. But what I do isn't so far removed from what your father did, at times. The difference between a hypothesis of mine and a hypothesis of his—the only *meaningful* difference, it sometimes seems to me—is that mine must be expressible in terms of mathematics."

"I know the difference between science and science fiction, Ursula."

"Do you?" the Kraut said. "Your father seems to think he does, as well. You're both so sure."

That surprised me, I have to admit. "Aren't you?"

"Orson once wrote a story—more of a fable, really—called 'The Principatrix of Gnawledge.' Do you remember it?"

I shook my head.

"It's in the only book of his I brought along," she said, digging a coverless pulp out of a drawer. "You can read it, if you like, while I make coffee. It's quite short."

An itching began in my palms as I reached for the book. The Kraut had never before suggested that I read anything of Orson's. The story was marked with a postcard of Znojmo, featuring a portly businessman in a bowler hat, riding an enormous green gherkin above the Dyje River.

THE PRINCIPATRIX OF GNAWLEDGE

The Imperator of Omphalos-8, a satellite of Ganymede-12 in the System of Mines, had a proGene, a female, who duly attained to principatrix when she came of age. This principatrix, it is told, was the rarest of beauties: skin the color of subpolar frost, hair luminous as ore from a core-stratum vein. The Imperator doted on her, as fathers will, and built her a stronghouse of chromium and silica by the shore of a quarry on a neighboring moon, far removed from the intrigues of court. There she ripened to the first term of youth, and had no care for the Winter, and no means of influence over the Great Thermodynamic Arc, after the manner of ordinary men.

Now it happened one autumn, as she walked by the quarry, that the principatrix saw an other: a wizened old thrall, humming to herself as she cast cicada shells into the water. The oiled and ore-heavy waves danced about the thrall's feet, and the leaves rustled about her hunched back, and her mica-colored rags flapped about her gray face in the beating of the ruthless autumn wind.

"Here," said the principatrix, "is the loneliest thrall betwixt the Seven Poles. What brings you to my quarrylake, old woman?"

"Imperator's Daughter," said the thrall, "you live in a stronghouse, and your hair is as ore from a core-stratum vein; but what good does it bring? Duration is brief, and existence is grief—you exist after the manner of ordinary men, with no thought for the Winter, and no influence over the Thermodynamic Arc."

"Thought for the Winter I do now possess," said the Impera-

tor's daughter; "but influence over the Arc, I have not." And she began to consider.

The thrall cast the last of her shells into the water and laughed.

The light turned, and the air cooled, and the principatrix returned to her stronghouse. When the door had been bolted and the fission-lamps lit, she summoned her governess to her.

"Governess," said the principatrix, "thought for the Winter has found me, so that I grow out of the manner of ordinary men, like a cicada growing out of its shell. Tell me what I must do to have influence over the Arc."

Then the governess sighed like the subpolar winds. "Alas!" she said, "that this should come to pass; but the thought has now entered your lymph and your blood, and there is no antidote against thought."

So the Imperator's proGene sat in her pressurized chamber in the silica-and-chromium—masoned keep, and gnawed there day and night upon the thought. Ten-and-seven years she was gnawing, and as much time again; and the wind beat against the fastness of the stronghouse, and the stars transcribed their arcs as if to mock her. Her governness fed and clothed and washed her without speaking, and she ate and bathed and slumbered without any thought but one.

Now when thirty and four years were passed away, the principatrix raised herself up slowly to her feet, and she passed from chamber to chamber of her ruined house, and saw that all her thralls and keepers had long left her; her governess remained, but she was stone-faced now and still. The principatrix walked out of the stronghouse, leaving its doors open behind her, and the gate to the garden, and the gate in the fortified field. She walked to that part of the shore where the old thrall had been, and where thought for the Winter had first found her, and there she sat down. And the ore-heavy waves lapped at her feet, and the shells of cicadas rustled at her back, and her mica-colored rags flapped about her in the beating of the wind. And when she lifted her

eyes, behold! there was a daughter of an Imperator come up
along the shore. Her skin was the color of subpolar frost, and her
hair was as luminous as ore from a core-stratum vein; and she
had no care for the Winter, and no means of influence over the
Great Thermodynamic Arc, after the manner of ordinary men.

"What do you think?" said the Kraut, coming back with the coffee.

"This doesn't sound like Orson."

"It's cribbed from someone better—Stevenson, I think, or Collins. But that's not why I wanted you to read it." She set the cup and saucer down. "Of all your father's fiction, it comes closest to what I consider fact."

"Fact?" I said. "This seems about as far from *fact* as anything he wrote. There's no attempt at scientific—"

"Of course not, Waldy." She shook her head impatiently. "That's not the kind of fact I'm thinking of."

Something in her voice made me uneasy. "I'm not sure what other kind of fact there is," I said.

The expression on her face had settled as I read my father's story—had grown both milder and more fixed—and I recognized it now for what it was. It was regret.

"It saddens me to hear that, Waldy. More than you can know."

"For Christ's sake, Ursula, just tell me what you mean!"

"Only that I look at that little fable from time to time, when I'm in a mood to consider the past. It helps me understand why Orson left. It's about the lust for influence over the timestream, of course, but more than that: it's about vanity, and arrogance, and the compulsion to turn inward, in pursuit of some private mystery, at the risk of everything that you hold dear. And if you don't see your father in that, or your aunts, or your grandfather, or all the rest of that family you're so obsessed with, then this can only mean one thing—you've fallen victim to the mystery yourself." She knelt beside me now and took my hand. "That was one point your father and I always agreed on, even when things were at their worst. We wanted to keep *you* away from that mystery, Waldy. As far away from it as possible."

It was clear to me now that she knew why I'd come. More than that: it was clear that she knew—or that she *thought* she knew—how the quest I'd set out on would end. Orson's parable had been a kind of test—a test I'd evidently passed with flying colors. If I was my great-grandfather's rightful successor, I was also his doomed and psychopathic son's. Another willing vessel for the Syndrome.

"Listen to me, Ursula. This isn't what you think. I'm not my father."

"That's right, Waldy. Or *his* father, either." She let go of my hand. "Or the man you were named for. Please don't forget that."

She seemed frail to me suddenly, fragile beyond her years. I resolved to come clean about my hunt for Waldemar, no matter how severely it might shock her. But my chance came and went.

"Two men stopped by this morning. They were looking for you."

"What kind of men?" I said, thinking right away of Haven's goons. "Did they look at all Polish?"

"Everyone looks Polish in this city—or Hungarian, or Serbian, or Czech." She parted the blinds and surveyed the street outside, surreptitious as a gangster in a noir. "These men had on trench coats and glasses and black leather gloves. They looked like officers of the Gestapo."

For an instant I wondered whether the onionlike strata I'd peered into over the past few days had become permeable, allowing Nazis from 1938 to shadow me in the Vienna of the present; then I saw the Kraut smiling at me over her shoulder.

"They didn't look like Gestapo, Waldy. Not really. Don't take everything I say so seriously."

Before I could answer her, Mrs. Haven—not that I had an answer to give—you made your ill-fated debut. You arrived fresh from the Graben boutiques, in a powder-blue trench coat and green loden jodhpurs and lipstick-colored knee-high riding boots. I'd longed for this meeting, as all lovers do, eager for my mother's bright-eyed blessing; you hadn't been there more than a minute, however, before I realized how vain my hopes had been. There was nothing I could do, at that point, but watch as you confirmed her worst suspicions.

"What is it you do?" asked the Kraut, after you'd told her how much you admired the carpet. You really were trying your best.

"I'm between jobs at the moment," you answered. "I guess I'm your son's bodyguard."

The Kraut returned your smile gravely. "You'll want to dress a bit more neutrally for that."

"Not a Secret Service type of bodyguard," you told her. "The personal kind. Personal bodyguards can wear anything they want."

"Is that so?" said the Kraut, looking to me as if for confirmation.

We stayed a remarkably long time, all things considered. You were patient and gracious and friendly and brave. As we were leaving—you were ahead of me, Mrs. Haven, already halfway down the stairs—my mother caught me lightly by the arm.

"Don't go to Znojmo, Waldy. There's nothing for you there."

"I'm not going to Znojmo," I answered, though of course I was going to Znojmo. Znojmo is where everything begins.

"There's *nothing* for you there," she repeated. Then, more quietly: "You can still escape, you know. It's not too late."

"Walter?" you called from the courtyard.

My mother and I looked at each other then, full in the face, more frankly than we'd done since I was small. I realized with a jolt that I was taller than she was by at least half a foot. When on earth had that happened? The realization made me want to sit down on the stairs and cry. It seemed to signify something terrible about the world: something that couldn't—or mustn't—be put into words. And I could see, looking down into her startled, anxious face, that my mother felt exactly the same way.

"Walter?" you called again.

"Don't worry about me, Ursula. I'm trying to—"

"I'm going to tell you something, Waldy, and I want you to listen to me closely. I love you with all my heart, and I want you to live a long and happy life."

"I love you too, Ursula. And I want *you* to know, no matter how I might sometimes act, that I—"

The Kraut shook her head and pressed a finger to my lips. "Watch that woman closely," she whispered. "Don't trust her an inch."

I pushed her hand away. "Please, Ursula—"

"Don't trust her, Waldy. Do you hear me? She wishes you ill."

I found Waldemar on the kitchen counter this morning, legs crossed underneath him, humming to himself with a mouth full of sprouts. The sound had invaded a dream I'd been having—my mother singing to me while she iced an enormous jet-black, bell-shaped birthday cake—and I'd awoken with a jerk, slowly gotten my bearings, then noticed that the humming hadn't stopped. I followed it cautiously out to the kitchen. Any lingering sweetness I might still have felt was expunged by the sight of my great-uncle perched on that counter like an opossum, munching and smacking his lips, with a look of craven pleasure on his face. Here is a man, Mrs. Haven, who can make even vegetarianism seem unwholesome.

"There you are, *Nefflein*. I was hoping I'd wake you."

"I was dreaming." I rubbed my eyes, still abstracted with sleep. "I thought you were my mother."

"I'm flattered by the comparison. Charming woman, Ursula."

That gave me a turn. "How would *you* know?"

"From your history, of course. Such a diverting read! I liked the honeymoon chapter especially." He wagged a finger at me. "But you haven't made the changes that I asked for."

"There's a reason for that."

"Yes?"

"Sonja Silbermann didn't go home with you that night. That was a lie, Uncle, and an obvious one."

He stopped chewing long enough to heave a measured sigh. "History belongs to the victors, Waldy, as the saying goes. You're the historian in this family—not me. I won't argue the point." A hard laugh escaped him. "Just think if *I* were to write the story of my life! Do you imagine that the critics would be kind?"

"I don't imagine they'd be kind at all."

He shrugged his hunched shoulders. "You ought to know best."

"What the hell does that mean?"

"Aren't you my personal biographer?" He snuffled. "My Boswell? My number one fan?"

"I'm not your goddamn *Boswell*, you lunatic. I'd like nothing better than to erase you—every last trace of you, everything you've ever said, or done, or thought—out of existence."

"I see!" he said, barely containing his mirth. "But if that's the case, *Neflein*, why am I still here?"

The violence I'd felt when I first discovered him—how many sleep cycles ago was it?—returned with a roar. I took a step toward him.

"Get down off that counter."

"Time passes more swiftly at this elevation," my great-uncle answered, stuffing a fistful of sprouts into his mouth. "The nearer to the surface of the earth one is, the lower the frequency of the light waves; and the lower the frequency of the light waves—"

"The longer it takes time to pass."

"Well put, Waldy Junior! You sound like a Toula at last."

"I'm a Tolliver," I said. "Not the same thing at all."

Waldemar shrugged again. Something he'd said had gotten under my skin, Mrs. Haven, though it took me a moment to see what it was.

"Time *isn't* passing," I told him. "Not here."

"That's your game, is it?" He let out a snuffle. "Not to worry! I won't spoil your fun."

I took another step forward. He was just out of reach.

"Get down from there, Uncle. Tell me where you've been since I last saw you."

"That would take some telling. After all, ten years have passed since then."

I saw now that he looked a decade older, perhaps even more: his straw-colored hair had gone gray at the temples, his hands were liver-spotted, and his face was blotched and scored with tiny rifts. The cause seemed to be more than mere aging—his body looked distorted in ways that the passage of time alone could not account for. My head began to spin.

"Are you saying I've been trapped here for a decade?"

"Time doesn't pass for you!" he crowed, laughing openly now. "That was my understanding."

I covered my ears and shut my eyes and wished him gone with all my strength of will. When I looked again he was right there on the counter.

"Enough of this childishness! We have work to do together, you and I. The future is knocking, *Nefflein*, whether you choose to notice it or not."

"*We* don't have any future," I gasped. "You're diseased, Waldemar, and I'm well. Do you hear me? We're not the same person."

The smile left his face. "You're repeating yourself."

"Does that bother you, Uncle? I'll say it again. We're not the same." To my own surprise I broke into a grin. "God, that feels good to say. Four simple little words. We're not the same."

He studied me a moment. "May I ask you a question?"

"Go ahead."

"Who on earth suggested that we were?"

I brought my face close to his, unafraid and triumphant. Then I felt my mind go hot and blank.

"But it's obvious," I stammered. "Anyone could see—I mean, our family—your name—"

"I'm *curious*, that's all," he said, lowering his feet to the floor. "I've certainly never implied that we were fellow travelers—far from it!—and you've gone to great pains to assure me our kinship means nothing. Your father and mother, to judge by your memoirs, kept my existence a secret; and those matzo-chewing aunts of yours—may Jehovah preserve them!—seem to have viewed you as a guinea pig for their sad little experiments, which most assuredly is not how they saw *me*. All of which raises the question"—here he smiled and draped an arm around me—"who was it, Waldy Junior, who planted the half-baked notion of our spiritual and moral equivalence in your antsy little brain?" He brought his body weightlessly against my own. "I'll tell you what I think. I think it came from no one but yourself. You sense our connection with the sureness of instinct. You feel it in your muscles and your bones."

"You're here to drive me insane," I said, hiding my face in my hands. "I understand that now."

"There's something else you'd like to ask. Why don't you ask it?"

"I don't want anything from you."

"I disagree, *Nefflein*. I think that you do."

I steeled myself, expecting some new jeer—but his expression was solemn.

"Can you get me out of here?" I heard myself whisper.

"I thought you'd never ask!" he said. "I can't."

"Why can't you?"

"Because I'm not the person who *did* this to you, Waldy." He regarded me sadly. "I'm not the reason you're here."

"You're lying. Who else could possibly have done this?"

He shook his head. "It's no use. You're not listening."

"Go away," I said, starting to weep.

I sank to the floor and pressed my forehead to my knees. I should have felt shame for breaking down in front of him—for allowing him to see me at my weakest—but I felt none at all. Why was that?

I heard him curse under his breath as he arranged himself beside me.

"I want to get out of this place," I said.

"I don't believe you."

I looked up at him. "What do you mean by that?"

He shook his head a second time, regretfully and slowly.

That jarred something loose inside me, Mrs. Haven. I spun around and caught him by the shoulder. There was no electric charge now, no tingling, no phantom chill. He felt almost as real to me as my own body.

"You come and go," I said. "Tell me how."

"I got here the same way you did, Waldy. There's no difference between us."

I wanted to strangle him by his antiquated collar, to shake him until the truth came tumbling out; instead I asked him again, as calmly as I could, to explain how I'd been exiled to this place.

"Waldy!" he said, raising his eyebrows. "Can it be you really don't recall?"

My mind gave a twitch as I tried to reply. It was *there*, Mrs. Haven, at the edge of the light: the memory of my final instants in the timestream. It was there but it refused to show itself. I shut my eyes and held my breath and waited.

"It's no use," I said finally. "I can't remember."

"Let me ask you this," he said softly. "Have you tried simply getting up and walking out the door?"

His face began to blur as he said this, to lose definition—but his expression was sincere, almost beseeching. He was right, Mrs. Haven. I'd never once attempted to escape. I pictured my aunts' massive door, long since dropped from its hinges, cobbled together out of trash-can lids and drywall studs and casement frames from gutted Harlem brownstones. What need could they have had for such a barrier? What forces had it been constructed to withstand? Was the chronoverse in suspension on the landing outside, sucking against the door like space against an air lock, waiting silently to readmit me?

I pushed past Waldemar into the Archive. Its length seemed greater than I remembered—immeasurably greater—but I was used to the apartment's tricks by then. I noticed in passing a ream of UCS stationery, a book of Czech folktales, and a balsa-and-playing-card model of the General Lee. When I came to the door I drew myself up, pulled in a steadying breath, and reached for the first bolt.

∞

"Nefflein," my great-uncle said gently. "Answer me, *Nefflein.* Do you hear my voice?"

I placed myself by smell before my eyes came open. I was flat on my back on my aunts' immense bed, the one with the strangely carved headboard and discolored sheets. It was morning outside, to judge by the brightness, and I wondered—as I so often had before—how the light of chronologic day could reach me. This time, however, I remembered a joke Orson had once told me about singularities. It's no problem at all, physics-wise, to enter a black hole: an event horizon is an easy thing to cross. Problems only arise if you should reconsider.

"What am I doing on this bed?"

"I brought you here, *Nefflein*. You had an accident."

I watched the dust roll and coagulate above me. "It's possible I'm going to be sick."

"That might be for the best."

I waited for the nausea to pass. It took a while.

"What happened to me?"

"I found you facedown at the door to the apartment. Your idea must have been to open it. Apparently you had second thoughts."

"Second thoughts? I collapsed on the floor!"

"That's right," he said, snuffling. "This concludes your lesson for today."

"What lesson, for God's sake?"

He gave me an affectionate pat on the shoulder. "I *told* you that you didn't want to leave."

XXIII

GIVEN WHAT YOU KNOW about my two earlier visits to the General Lee, Mrs. Haven, you can probably guess that my feelings the third time—a month after my father's *Timestrider*-induced coronary—were mixed. Orson had ranted less than usual on the drive down, speaking mostly in grunts, so I'd had plenty of time to sort through my memories of my aunts' apartment, and the wonders—or *alleged* wonders—that had transpired there. The difference between ages seven and thirteen is enormous (the difference, really, between an overgrown toddler and a miniature taxpaying citizen) and I viewed my younger self with prim disdain. Five years after the episode in the dark at the bend in the hallway, it was my informed thirteen-year-old opinion that I'd dreamed the best parts of it up.

They'd found me facedown on the floor, after all, blubbering and shivering with fever. I'd barely recognized Orson, who'd fed me some aspirin and rushed me straight home. My aunts had failed to prevent our departure: there'd been no sorcery, no kidnapping, no human sacrifice. If my father displayed any emotion at all on the drive back to Buffalo—as far as I can recall—it was boredom. The status quo had reasserted itself so unconditionally that I'd found myself doubting, as the months and years passed, that we'd driven down to see my aunts at all.

But none of my considered thirteen-year-old opinions, however blasé, could stave off a spasm of anxiety as we rang the General Lee's epileptic buzzer, or an equal and opposite thrill of excitement as the lobby lamps sputtered to life. There remained zones of magic in the world, apparently, and 109th Street was one. (It didn't hurt that enchantments in folktales, both benign and horrific, have a habit of coming in threes.) Orson kicked the lobby door open without waiting to be buzzed in, shot me a look that I couldn't account for, then steered me upstairs, gripping me by the shoulder, as though afraid that I might try to run away. *He's reconsidered their offer*, I found myself thinking. *He's going to sacrifice me after all.*

∞

This might be as good a place as any, Mrs. Haven, for a caplet-sized history of the United Church of Synchronology, from 1970—the year of both my own and the Church's conception—to the moment my father rang his sisters' bell. You know some of what follows, of course, but I'm betting you don't know it all. You always insisted that the Husband kept you at a remove from the Church, and I still believe that, in spite of everything I've found out since. I refuse to indulge the suspicion (clamorous though it sometimes gets) that you were a willing party to his machinations. I could never have fallen in love with one of Haven's automata.

If my father hadn't learned of his wife's pregnancy moments before the First Listener and his sidekicks had appeared on his stoop, he might have taken the "Three Fuzzy Fruits," as he took to calling them, more seriously—but I can't say for certain. Orson was a celebrity at the time, however priggish and conflicted, and Haven and Co. had by no means been the only pilgrims to Pine Ridge Road. Like some solitary king under a spell—one who never leaves his throne room, and eventually comes to doubt the existence of the world outside—Orson rarely engaged with anyone anymore, his wife and son included, and the more isolated he became from his so-called generation, the more he saw himself as its True Voice. In other words, he was beginning, like so many successful men before and after, to believe that his shit smelled like rosewater. He'd stopped seeing anything funny about *Life*'s portrait of him long before. And if he still ate death biscuits, Mrs. Haven, he ate them in private.

In defiance of Orson's rejection of the world, however, the world continued to exist, and it was growing fuzzier and fruitier by the day. The sixties may be the decade we tend to associate with communes and dropouts and thousand-yard stares, but it was in the seventies that things got seriously weird. There were never more quasi-religious organizations on the FBI's watchlist than in 1979: the number of cults in North America was estimated at 108, not counting Mormons, vegetarians, or the Daughters of the American Revolution. A house just up the street from ours had a sign on its lawn with a quotation from the Reverend Sun Myung Moon—GOD WILL TAKE THE WORLD BY LOVE—and though the people who lived there looked more like candidates for a mass divorce than a mass wedding, there was never a shortage of tenants. If Orson didn't see why the Fuzzy Fruits were worth his time, Mrs. Haven, who can blame him? He'd set his sights on withdrawing from the world, after all, in the classic Toula/Tolliver tradition: not for his father's reasons—or his mad uncle's, either—but because it suited his vocation as a prophet.

Missives from the faithful arrived in our mailbox regardless. It was my job, once I was old enough, to bring in the mail, and I used to dread finding those letters: somehow I'd intuited that they were dangerous. The first were from the Listener himself, with the return address scrawled clumsily in cursive; then from Menügayan, typewritten; then from people we had never heard of, on corporate-looking UCS stationery. Orson passed them along, unread, to Ursula, who rolled them into tight little joints that she used to light the burners on our stove.

For a while near the close of the decade, the doorbell would ring at odd hours—most often between seven and eight in the morning—and Ursula would discover progressively more desperate "Iterants" (as UCS members had taken to calling themselves), always in groups of three, petitioning for an audience with the Prime Mover. Eventually Ursula took to calling the cops, and a court injunction was obtained, much to my parents' and the neighborhood's (and quite possibly the Iterants' own) relief. All of which explains how it was possible for my father to go a full ten years without realizing that the UCS had become—both figuratively and by official church decree—the cult to end *all* cults, along with organized religion, Western philosophy, and the Internal Revenue Service. He had no one to blame for the shock but himself, needless to say—which didn't make it any easier to stomach.

It had been a busy decade for the Church of Synchronology. They'd had a wobbly start, unsure how to market the G.S.M. (Gospel of the Scientific Method)—let alone the B.E.C.T. (Benefits of Emancipation from Chronologic Time)—to the general public, but their eyes had ultimately been opened, after a series of setbacks, to a wonderfully liberating truth: the general public was not their target demographic. The meek and the down trodden and the underinformed were the stuff all great religions had grown fat on, and the fact that Religion with a capital *r* was the single greatest fraud ever perpetrated on humankind (aside from the persistent illusion, fostered by said Religion, that the arc of time tended from Present to Past) was no reason to reject its business model. What was an "empiricist," after all, but someone who analyzed cause and effect, and adapted his theories accordingly?

Once this point was cleared up—by Haven himself, in the late spring of '77—the path lay clear for global domination.

∞

The first Theater of Simultaneity was consecrated in Tempe, Arizona, on September 17 of the following year. The entire UCS membership to date— all thirty-seven dues-paying members, not counting dependents—turned out for the groundbreaking ceremony, which was presided over by Archchronoclast Johnson, who dressed for the occasion in a tuxedo T-shirt and frayed dungarees. (The faithful, in those early days, looked more or less indistinguishable from graduate students in the humanities.) The appendix to *The Excuse*—dubbed "The Ω" by the UCS, and elevated to a sacred text in its own right—was read from aloud, after which the congregation traveled 6.5 seconds into the future. The "chronologic boom" this occasioned went unnoticed by the neighborhood's residents, just as the First Listener had predicted it would. *For those with ears to hear, let them hear*, as a noted proto-chronoclast had put it.

The scene of this first—and admittedly modest—mass chrononavigation was a narrow dirt lot in a residential development on Tempe's southwestern perimeter, occupied for the most part by lower- to middle-income retirees. Haven gave a brief speech, in which he cautioned the faithful that it might well take a decade, given scarcity of funds, for the Theater of Simultaneity to be completed. "Which span may have meaning for *them*," he said, waving a hand to indicate the neighboring condos. "Not so much for the chrono-enlightened. For *us*," he said genially, opening an imaginary door, "the temple is already finished. Won't you come in?"

History teaches us, Mrs. Haven, that every great movement—however corrupt its eventual result—is launched in a fireball of idealism and brotherly feeling, which lasts exactly as long as the movement in question has nothing to lose. Even the Methodists were revolutionaries once, much as they'd like to deny it: they preached against slavery and patriarchy and private property, and had nearly as many women as men in the ranks of their preachers. So it only stands to reason that there must have been an era (or a moment, let's say) when Synchronology was a genuine philosophy: fruit of the idea that *The Excuse*'s description of "timespin"—which itself was just a mongrelized version of Waldemar's "rotary time"—might be taken as the model for a different way of life. I have a hard time picturing this age of innocence, Mrs. Haven, but I'm willing to accept that it existed. If nothing else, it helps to explain the UCS's meteoric rise.

Within a few years of that seminal afternoon on the outskirts of Tempe, the United Church of Synchronology had become the largest nonaccredited religious organization in America, with Theaters of Simultaneity in forty-seven cities nationwide. The IRS—which had long since revealed its Hidden Agenda by refusing to grant the UCS tax-exempt status as a recognized spiritual entity (code 501(c)(3))—had finally buckled the tax year before, in the face of a wave of lawsuits (and a tsunami of threatened lawsuits) by the faithful. This spot of legal reshuffling had the result of making Haven's little movement—which had been doing perfectly well already, thank you very much—wealthier than many midsized corporations.

Like any booming enterprise, the Church was faced with the problem of how to reinvest its profits, and—like any sober, well-counseled investor—it opted to diversify. Investments were made in everything from pharmaceuticals to coffee beans to LCD technology to Hollywood. Archchronoclast Menügayan, who'd overseen media and public relations for the UCS since the autumn of '73, had been developing a film concept for quite some time, loosely based on book III of the Codex; she was a fervent devotee of *The Excuse*—perhaps the most fervent—so it's no wonder that much of the text found its way into the shooting script verbatim. Church dogma has it that Haven himself came up with the title, though a competing account attributes it to Don Harvey Mueck, the goateed man-child director who hogged most of the credit for the movie's success. And *Timestrider: Clash of the Aeons* was very successful indeed.

∞

It was more than free-floating suspicion that brought us to Harlem that third time. I'd seen something else in the *Timestrider* credits: in considerably more modest type than BROUGHT TO YOU BY THE UNITED CHURCH OF SYNCHRONOLOGY, midway through a column of miscellaneous titles (cicada wrangler, acupuncturist, defribrillator) I'd spied the names of my aunts listed under "technical advisement." Orson scoffed when he heard that, but I could tell that the news shook him; it had shaken me almost as badly. The adult world may never have made much sense to me, Mrs. Haven, but the filament connecting the General Lee to the Paramount backlot was beyond my capability to trace.

This time my father's knuckles had barely brushed the doorframe before a strident voice—Gentian's, I thought, though I couldn't be sure—announced there was no need to raise a ruckus. The door was in even worse shape than I remembered (it was as battered as a road sign on an Indian reservation, with three disquietingly rat-sized holes along the bottom) and open just enough for me to see inside. It was Enzian who received us, not her sister. I could tell by the way she scrutinized Orson—nervously and defiantly at once—that she'd guessed the reason for our sudden visit. Her expression wasn't lost on Orson, either.

"Let me in, Enzie. You know why I'm here."

"Hello, Waldemar," Enzian said to me, ignoring him completely. I'd never seen her smile before, and I can't honestly say I liked the look of it. I did my best to smile politely back.

"Hello, Aunt Enzie. Nice to, um, see you again."

"Marvelous boy! *Enchanting* boy!" came a voice from inside. I squinted past Enzian into the shadows of the Archive, but couldn't make anything out but a stack of microwaves and fax machines.

"*Lass mich sehen!*" the voice protested. "Let me see!"

"This is ridiculous," said Orson. "Let us in."

"There's no room."

"*Lass mich sehen,*" the voice repeated. "Waldemar?"

"There's no room."

"For crying out loud, Enzie—"

Before Orson could finish there came a skittering sound—like a puppy's toenails clattering over tile—and Enzian stepped out quickly onto the landing. "Go in, Waldemar. There's room for you now. Go in and say hello to your aunt Genny."

I hesitated, unsure how to behave; then I caught my father's eye and saw that he was no better off than I was, and that Enzian was worse off than either of us. Her hair had gone gray since I'd last seen her, and her dress—the same one as last time, it seemed, though I couldn't be sure—hung mournfully from her diminished body. Orson looked like a trained bear beside her. I left the two of them out on the landing, making a big show of not looking at each other, and slipped tentatively inside.

Although it was the same twilit entryway I remembered—the same chipped parquet, the same tang of mildew—I barely recognized the place. The sky-blue ceiling I'd admired at age seven was visible only in patches now, like breaks in a fog in the mountains; which isn't as far-fetched as it sounds, Mrs. Haven, because what I'd stepped into looked more like a Himalayan col than a New York apartment. Great sloping drifts of every conceivable type of object—from telephone directories to Persian rugs to lengths of oxidizing copper pipe—rose steeply to either side, leaving barely enough space for a body to wriggle between; Enzian hadn't been exaggerating when she'd warned us that there was no room. The trompe l'oeil effect that had once made the hallway seem endless had been superseded, at some long-ago juncture, by a crevasse that had no quality of height or depth at all. As I worked my way deeper, however, the chaos gradually resolved itself into a kind of order. *Classes* of object were grouped together, I realized, according to function: telephone books might not look much like eight-track cassettes, but they were both reference materials, of a kind, and they both transmitted information, as did the coils of fiber-optic wire they sat on. I have no idea how I intuited this, Mrs. Haven, but it came to me all in a rush. Nothing had changed since my last visit, at least not in principle. The Archive had expanded, that was all. Just as Genny had predicted that it would.

I heard my aunt's voice before I saw her. She was whistling—some half-remembered Tin Pan Alley air she'd probably learned from Buffalo Bill—and I followed the sound back to its source. I found Genny on a cowhide settee in what I guessed to be the parlor's southeast corner, one bandaged foot propped on a stack of board games (Battleship was topmost, I remember, followed by Mastermind and Stratego and Risk), and holding a tray of powdered doughnuts in her lap.

"There you are, dear," she said. "I'd have come to the door, but I'm a *gottverdammter* cripple, as you see."

It took me a moment to answer—a long, fretful moment—because of how greatly she'd changed. Enzie had also struck me as aged, of course, but Genny seemed a different person altogether. She was gray-faced and frail, half the size that she'd been, with the papery look that people in their dotage tend to get. Her bandaged foot was preposterously large, like the leg of a mummy, and its swaddling looked less than clean. I had a vision of gangrene and suppressed it at once.

"First things first!" said Genny. "Have a doughnut."

I took one, then another, eager to hide my discomfort. "These are delicious, Aunt Genny," I said, and I meant it. They had a peppery flavor I'd never encountered before.

"I'm glad you like them, Waldy. Have another."

"Thanks, Aunt Genny." I chewed for a while. "The Archive sure has, um, expanded."

"*Hasn't* it?" she said. "I'm so pleased you noticed."

I stood awkwardly beside the settee as I ate, looking everywhere but at that leg of hers. I was standing, Mrs. Haven, because there seemed to be nowhere to sit. I'd been tempted by a milk crate near the newsprint-covered window, but I wasn't sure whether it was furniture or an exhibit of some kind. I still had a lot to learn about the Archive.

"Bring that crate over here," my aunt said abruptly. "Let's have a nice long look at you." She waited for me to sit, then added, more quietly: "I have a confession to make, Waldemar. Your aunt Enzie and I think about you every day."

We sat in total silence while I thought of a reply. I wondered—not for the first time—what importance I could possibly have for two elderly shut-ins who'd seen me only twice since I was born. It seemed more than a strictly auntly sort of interest.

"Did you make these doughnuts yourself?" I said finally.

"What! Those things?" Genny said, chuckling. "I found them in a paper bag at Park and Ninety-Seventh."

Even all these years later, Mrs. Haven, I feel proud of my reaction. I gave a businesslike nod, forced myself to keep chewing, then slid the uneaten portion of the doughnut into the pocket of my parka. If Genny noticed this maneuver, she didn't let on.

"What happened to your foot, Aunt Genny?"

"You're sweet to be concerned, dear. An occupational hazard. A minor landslide in the beaux arts section."

"Who does the shopping now?"

"Why, *I* do, of course. Enzie could never manage by herself."

"But how do you make it outside?"

She settled back comfortably on the settee. "If you don't like the place where you find yourself, Waldemar, it pays to remember that you'll be somewhere else in just a moment. The place itself will *be* a different place." She gave a catlike grin. "There's always more than one way out. Remember that."

I was about to ask what she meant when Enzie appeared with my father trailing after, looking as though he'd spent the intervening minutes sucking on a lime.

"Enzie tells me it was your idea," he snarled.

"They came to *us*, Peanut," Genny replied equably. "They came here, to One Hundred and Ninth Street, and they asked us nicely. That's more than you ever did."

"Fuck you," said my father. "Fuck you both."

I'd expected a showdown of some kind, of course, but not this kind of showdown. I tried to blend in with the wall behind me.

"You're upset, Orson," Enzie said, making no attempt to hide her satisfaction. "It sits poorly with you that we persist in our work, after you've so bravely washed your hands of it in public. It sits poorly with you, after you've repeatedly refused to advocate for the Accidents—the vocation you were born to, and trained in, and which brought you your fame—that we should accept assistance from another quarter. We can understand your feelings very well."

"You've been used," wheezed my father. "They couldn't get my endorsement, so they settled for yours."

"That's true, Peanut!" said Genny. "They used us—and we used them in return. Isn't that quite the best way?"

"They're a *cult*, for fuck's sake!"

"That's right, Orson," said Enzie. "And an effective one, as far as we can gather."

He closed his eyes. "That movie is a steaming pile of—"

"We'll have to disagree on that point, I'm afraid. Genny and I went through the screenplay very carefully. The plot may be a little *kindisch*, but the words are all in order."

My father's answer was so extravagantly filthy that it made my eyes water.

"It was that woman who wrote the screenplay, Peanut. We just made sure that the science was correct."

"Science?" he bellowed. "You call that *drivel* science?"

A hush fell instantly. Even Orson seemed to know he'd said too much. For all his contempt for my aunts' theories, for all the fierceness of his opposition, I noticed again that he was wary of upsetting them too deeply. What's he afraid of? I wondered. What have they got on him?

It was fascinating to sit quietly in that devastated room, looking from face to face, waiting for hostilities to resume. These three people grew up in the same house, I found myself thinking. These three people were once dear to one another.

"It's what we *believe*, Peanut," Genny murmured at last. "It's what Enzie and I believe to be the truth. What else could we possibly call it?"

"Have either of you seen the movie?" Orson gave a dull laugh. "What a stupid thing to ask. Of course you haven't."

My aunts exchanged a puzzled look. "Why would *we* need to see it, Orson? We already know about the Accidents."

"What are the Accidents?" I said.

All heads turned. Genny began to speak, then stopped herself; Enzie did the same. I couldn't tell, at the time, whether the look on my father's face was one of anger or bemusement or concern. Now I think that it was all of the above.

"What are the Accidents?" I asked again.

One by one they sighed and looked away. I'd posed the question, in all innocence, that defined them. Even my father's rebellion, his duration-long evasion of his legacy, was no more than a way of restating the problem. Whatever the term may have meant in Ottokar's brining room in Moravia in 1903, it had become synonymous, by the end of the century, with the dilemma of existence itself.

∞

We pitched camp in the parlor that night, Orson and I, on a mattress made of bubble wrap and twine. I'd never slept in the same room as my father, much less under the same packing sheet. The experience was not a pleasant one.

"Laugh and the world laughs with you," he said as he blew out the candle. "Snore, son, and you sleep alone."

I didn't appreciate the finer points of this joke—it seemed like standard-issue Tolliver cornpone to me—until he drifted off. The sounds he emitted over the next seven hours, Mrs. Haven, are impossible to render in prose. At least every ten minutes he seemed to suffer some sort of attack, and I was sure he was about to suffocate; the rest of the time he panted sadly—defeatedly, even—like an unfulfilled pervert. I found myself wondering what my father was dreaming about, which is never a good thing for a son to wonder. And as if all of that wasn't bad enough, he kicked.

It was after midnight when I gave up on sleep. I wasted a huge amount of effort getting out of bed with as little noise as possible—Orson would have slept through a putsch—and groped my way back out into the Archive. I rounded a corner, then a second, then a third. The tunnel straightened for five or six steps, then made an even sharper turning. I had no clear objective—I was too drowsy for that—but I must have had some expectation as to what I might find, because what I saw next somehow came as no surprise. I saw the outline of a door—high and narrow, with a beveled glass knob, a simulacrum of the doors at Pine Ridge Road—silhouetted by a thread of yellow lamplight. *Most likely the kitchen*, I said to myself. I pushed the door open.

"Hello, Waldemar. Can't you sleep?"

"Hi, Aunt Enzie," I said, shading my eyes against the sudden glare.

She was sitting straight-backed at her desk with a look of calm forbearance on her face, a willingness to interrupt important work, if only for a moment. A pair of reading glasses rode low on her long equine nose, making her seem more like a mad scientist than ever. She had on a Pendleton shirt—an aubergine-and-yellow "shadow plaid"—with the sleeves rolled up high. Her colorless eyes were unblinking as ever. Her feet made fan-shaped dust marks on the floor.

"What are you doing?" I asked.

"I'm working," she said. "Come on in, Waldemar. I could do with some company."

I approached the desk cautiously. The papers spread out before her were covered in formulas and algebraic proofs and phrases in a language that might have been Sanskrit.

"Why are you still working, Aunt Enzie? It's the middle of the night."

"*Ach!* The hour makes no difference here. It takes me a great deal of effort, *Nefflein*, to hunker down and set my mind to thinking. I need quiet and dark." She closed her eyes for a moment, then smiled to herself. "I'll tell you a secret, Waldy—I have a tendency to put things off. I like to watch the hands of the clock go round. I'm addicted, you might say, to the passage of time."

"So am I," I said, mostly out of politeness. But I realized, as I said it, that the statement was true. It gave me pleasure to feel wasted minutes pass.

Enzian's smile widened. "You're a Tolliver, *Nefflein*. Time is our shared disorder."

"My father says it's our fetish." I hesitated. "Your fetish, I mean."

"Your father ought to know." She turned back to her papers. "Do you happen to know what a 'fetish' is?"

I watched her for a moment. "Something bad."

"Not necessarily. Something important." She gathered up the papers and flipped them over one by one, precisely and smoothly, like a dealer at a black-jack table. I noticed an actual deck of cards at her elbow, warped and discolored with age. Then my eyes fell on the object in the center of the room.

"What's *that*?"

"Hmm?" she said without turning.

I raised my arm and pointed.

"Why don't you go and see?"

I rallied my courage and stepped past the desk. The blankness of the thing had somehow kept it hidden. It looked like a steamer trunk, or a re-frigerator box, or a crudely made and freshly whitewashed casket. There were no knobs or buttons that I could detect: no hinges, no levers, no markings on the outside at all. The hair stood up on my forearms when I went to touch it, as if the air around it were electrified. I felt younger than thirteen now—much younger. I felt about six.

"Go on, Waldemar," said Enzie. "It won't bite."

I ran my hand along a corner of the thing—it sat on sawhorses, and came up to my armpits exactly—then drummed against it lightly with my thumb. A dusting of whitewash came off on my skin. It dawned on me that Enzie had built it herself, and that it was connected to the "research" she was doing. The embarrassment I felt on her behalf came close to pity.

"Isn't it lovely?" she said, rising from the desk and joining me.

"What is it?"

She took in a breath. "It's an exclusion bin."

"I'm not sure what that means."

"There's no shame in that, Waldemar." She nodded. "You might say it's a kind of time machine."

Given everything I knew about my aunts, of course, this was no more than I ought to have expected. At regular intervals throughout my childhood I'd pictured them at work on some vast contraption, a vaguely starship-shaped confusion of wires and transistors and throbbing Tesla coils; I'd abandoned this daydream a few years before, around the time I'd stopped believing in centaurs and alien abduction. But now I'd have to reconsider everything. I was standing next to Enzie in her workshop in the middle of the night in Spanish Harlem, resting my right hand on an impossibility.

It looked nothing like the machine that I'd envisioned—nothing at all—which was precisely what convinced me it was real. I'd have been skeptical of flashing lights and pulsing panels, but I didn't question this. There was nothing to question. My aunt undid a hidden catch and its top swung creakingly upward, like the hood of a go-kart. There was nothing—or next to nothing—inside: just a graphite-colored layer of some spongy material that might have been Nerf, enclosing what looked to be (and in fact, on closer inspection, actually turned out to be) a reclinable Naugahyde seat. There was no denying what I was looking at any longer. Enzie's "exclusion bin" was a white plywood crate, roughly three feet by seven, with a second-hand car seat inside it.

"I'm going to ask you to do me a kindness," Enzie said into my ear. "I'm going to ask you to get inside this apparatus. Will you do that for me?"

I should have countered her question, Mrs. Haven, with a few of my own. I should have asked *why* she wanted me to climb inside the "apparatus," and what might happen to me if I did. Instead I nodded gravely, like a prizefighter about to be pushed out of his corner, and did as she asked.

The interior smelled of Windex and vinyl and—faintly—of something like cloves. It smelled, in other words, like a used car. The seat was too big for me, squeaky and cool, and the blood rushed to my head as I lay back.

"No cause for alarm," Enzie said, resting her palm on the crown of my head. "It's likely that nothing will happen."

"Where am I going?" I heard myself croak.

"Nowhere at all. This isn't a rocket ship, as you can see. The first task of the scientist, Waldemar, is to ask the appropriate question."

I sank into the seat—it was cracked at the corners, I noticed, and oddly deflated—and watched as she lowered the lid. The appropriate question arrived half a second too late.

"When?" I said, just as the light disappeared.

I remember a sharp rush of panic, then a sudden, inexplicable calm; I remember how absolute the blackness was, and how remarkably little this scared me. Incredibly, the silence was as total as the darkness. Touch remained, but without hearing or sight it seemed stripped of its context, a vestigial trait, an x coordinate without a y or z. I'd been cautioned to expect "nothing"—and I should have been prepared for it, science fiction addict that I was—but the nothing I'd imagined was a vastly different animal than the *nothing* I was being swallowed by.

I say "animal," Mrs. Haven, because it soon became a living thing to me. I felt its weight against my open eyes; I inhaled its musk; with time I even came to hear it breathing. The silence was so consummate that my brain began to manufacture sounds. They came on mildly enough, as a hubbub of faraway squeaks; soon, however, they built—gently but irresistibly—to a thundering wall of antic background hiss. From time to time it was possible to make out voices, though what they said was gibberish, like the voices one hears before falling asleep.

That was all, Mrs. Haven, for the first long, lightless stretch of nothingness. Then the images came.

Like the noises, they started as liminal blips, imagined as much as perceived, then gradually took on form and definition. Those first abstract
shapes and color fields bore little or no relation to my state of mind, as far as
I could tell—my sense of self, in fact, seemed to have been expunged. But if
I was as blank as the darkness around me, as empty of thought or intention, I was also just as charged with possibility.

When the first of these vague shapes was brought into focus, I felt a
cold jolt of excitement; my excitement, however, was brief. The image before my mind's eye was of a pair of pocket nail clippers, the kind designed
to double as a key chain, missing its nail-file attachment. As visions go, this
was about as thrilling as a balled-up Kleenex—which turned out to be the
next thing that I saw. The Kleenex was followed by a pellet of crumpled
silver foil, which was followed, after a brief delay, by a capless ballpoint pen.
I could have seen as much in Orson's glove compartment.

My sight went black after that, then violet, then green, then bluish white;
then dim and flat and colorless again. Awareness returned to me slowly,
and a sense of confinement that seemed independent of sight or touch or
any sense at all. My scalp and feet and tongue began to tingle. I could feel
claustrophobia sweeping toward me through the dark, and had just taken
in air to yell when the catches were thrown and the lid was pulled up and
Enzie's shining eyes peered into mine.

"What was it, Waldemar? What did you see?"

"I'm not sure. I mean, I don't really have—"

"Describe it to me."

I blinked at her. "Nothing, I guess."

"Of *course* you saw nothing," she said impatiently. "It's an exclusion bin.
But what did you see after that?"

I took a long time to answer. I was groggy and anxious and deeply confused, and what I'd seen seemed far too trivial to mention. "Not much," I
mumbled.

She stared hard at me. "You *are* Waldemar Tolliver, son of Orson, son
of Kaspar, son of Ottokar Gottfriedens Toula?"

I looked away from her and shrugged.

"I fail to understand," she said, apparently to herself. Then, in a kindlier voice: "Perhaps it's too soon yet. You're still a child."

"Okay," I said, still dodging her questioning look. "Sorry." Now that the whole thing was over I felt the same embarrassment I'd felt before. What had she been expecting—flying saucers and mushroom clouds and backward-running clocks? What had she needed *me* for anyhow? I climbed out of the bin and looked around me with a sinking heart. The room was better lit than I recalled: brighter and smaller and more full of junk. It looked less like a mad scientist's laboratory, suddenly, than the basement workshop of a pensioner.

"Genny will fix you breakfast," said my aunt. "You've lost some sleep, of course, but you'll catch up. You can sleep in the back of the car on your way home."

I was about to point out that Orson and I weren't likely to be leaving right then, not at two in the morning, when I realized why everything seemed changed. There was a skylight above us—a peaked gray rabbit hutch of wood and chicken wire and frosted glass—and the first pale light of day was seeping through it.

"What time is it, Aunt Enzie?"

She gave me no answer. A sense of unreality broke over me: I held my hands up to my eyes, half expecting to be able to see through them. I'd have estimated my time in the exclusion bin at less than twenty minutes, half an hour at the most. It should have been the middle of the night.

"What time is it?" I said again. "How long was I in there?"

For the space of a breath my aunt stayed as she was, smiling an odd little unamused smile. Then she took up a ledger and ran her finger down a row of scribbled entries. It was only then, seeing the obvious pleasure my bewilderment gave her, that I remembered Orson's jokes about her lack of human feeling. But there was nothing flat or robotic in my aunt's expression now. If anything there was too much feeling in it.

"Three hours, forty-one minutes, and thirty-seven seconds," she announced. "That's an awful lot of *not much*, Waldemar."

∞

We found Orson awake in the parlor, sitting on a corner of our little make-shift bed, the packing blanket draped across his shoulders. I could see right away that he'd guessed what had happened. He looked at me as though we'd never met.

"There you are, Waldy," he said. "I'd been wondering."

"Waldy and I have been up to no good," Enzie said with a wink.

"Is that so."

"You were snoring," I told him. "Snore and you sleep alone. *You* told me that."

My father said nothing. Genny appeared in the doorway with a mug of green tea—her bum leg had mysteriously improved—and he took it from her and slurped from it morosely. My aunts beamed at each other as though they'd just won the Heisenberg Prize.

We said our goodbyes not long after, the Buick idling feebly in the smoky Harlem dawn. My aunts smiled down at us from their tattered whorehouse curtains while we waited in the cold, expecting the engine to die each time it stuttered. Orson didn't glance up at them once. Some point of honor had been settled—apparently in Enzie's favor—and from the look of things I'd been the catalyst. But what had I actually done? I'd let her lock me up in a box, then drifted off for a time, as anyone might have. Where was the betrayal in that?

"Have fun in high school, Waldy!" Genny shouted as we pulled away. "Kiss the little girls and make them cry!"

∞

The next two hours with Orson passed in a kind of mutual brain-squeamishness, both of us circling the same unmentionable event, like diplomats on the morning of a coup. I was grateful for the city's drab distractions, its freeways leading to bridges leading to gridlocked toll plazas leading—eventually, as if against their better judgment—to the traffic-choked interstate. After batting us around for a while, the city abruptly grew bored, and its sprawl gave way to cinder-colored scrub. Orson wanted to talk, I could tell, but I was too worn out to do his talking for him. I was fiddling with the handle of the glove compartment—which had been broken since I could remember—when he suddenly sat up and cleared his throat.

"I want to talk to you about your aunts, Waldy. As you've probably noticed—"

"Aunt Enzie says she named me. Is that true?"

I expected him to deny it, but he did no such thing. "Not just Enzie. The two of them together."

"Why did you let them do that?"

"I don't know." Orson adjusted the rearview mirror, squinted over his shoulder, made a sour face, then nudged the mirror back. "I owed them something, I guess. And I like the thought of things moving in circles." He shook his head slowly. "I'm my sisters' brother, Waldy, sad to say."

"Moving in circles? What is that supposed to—"

"See that van behind us?"

"Huh?"

"That white van back there. I don't care for the cut of its jib."

I sized up the vehicle in question: a shabby Econoline two-door, no different than a dozen others we'd passed on the highway that morning. I was old enough to know when my father was stalling, but there was no rush: we had hundreds of miles left to drive. I slouched down in my seat and let him stall.

"I want to talk to you about your aunts," he repeated.

"Okay, Orson. I'm listening."

This time there was no hesitation. He wanted me to keep "a healthy degree of distance" from his sisters in the future, for reasons he assumed I understood. He made no explicit mention of Enzie's mental state, or of Genny's peculiarities, or even of the condition of the apartment; he made no mention—needless to say—of reconnaissance missions in the chronosphere. It struck me then, watching him squirm and fidget, how much that brief visit had changed him. Leaving Buffalo, he'd been as righteous and judgmental as a prophet; now, for better or worse, all his passion was spent. For the first time in my duration, Mrs. Haven, I thought of my father as old.

It therefore came as a relief—or at least as a welcome distraction—when the Econoline van made its move.

I saw it coming before he did, but I couldn't bring myself to say a word. There was a precision to the Econoline's gambit—a purposeful, tactical smoothness—that held me mesmerized. By the time I'd grasped what was happening it had pulled alongside us.

"Don't look at them, Waldy," Orson hissed through his teeth.

The oddest thing about the people in the van, I remember, was the absence of expression on their faces. Even as they leaned toward us, drawing complex sets of symbols in the air, there was a kind of dazed indifference about them. The woman especially—the only one of the three who wasn't wearing a Red Sox cap—had a face as dead as a receptionist's.

"What are they doing?" said Orson, eyes fixed on the road.

"Moving their hands, mostly. I think they're trying to cast some sort of spell."

"They want us to pull over."

"How do you know?"

He returned my look wearily. "Because this has happened before."

For the next fifteen minutes the van baited us, sometimes pulling ahead, sometimes letting us pass, but never dropping out of sight completely. Then, at exit 23 (Albany/Delmar) it braked, smooth and deliberate as ever, and curved away from us into the trees. It hadn't been a Hollywood car chase, exactly—we'd only broken the speed limit twice, and not by much—but it had been *something*. A warning, I decided. I felt curiously calm, all things considered. I understood that what had happened was unusual, even bizarre; but it seemed no weirder to me, on that particular morning, than any other feature of the grown-up world.

"Those were Iterants, huh?"

Orson gave a slight start, as though he'd forgotten I was in the car. "Of course."

"Why didn't they *do* anything?"

"They did all sorts of things. They did plenty."

"I saw the woman flapping her hands, and the guys with the caps—"

"They were orbiting us."

"What?"

"They were *orbiting* us. Each time they passed our car, then switched to the right lane, then slowed down and passed us again, they completed one circuit. They were interfering with the linearity of our progress—calling attention to the bias inherent in our perceptions of spacetime. Done well, this can lead to a kind of short-term temporal confusion."

I couldn't help but notice, as my father held forth, that he sounded like an Iterant himself. "How do you know all this?"

He smiled. "I guess you could say I've read the literature."

"What literature?" He was worrying me now. "I've never seen you—"

"The technique I just described," said my father, "is from the opening paragraph of 'The Emperor of If.' The term I coined for it is 'chronojamming.' It was the last thing I wrote that my sisters approved of." He let out a sigh. "They're close readers, those Fuzzy Fruits. I'll give them that."

I pondered this for a minute. "What did Enzie and Genny do for them? For the Iterants, I mean. Why were their names in the *Timestrider* credits?"

"Haven and his goons dropped in on them about a year ago. They talked about my books, then asked all sorts of other questions, though they never made it farther than the coatrack." He shook his head. "God knows how they got Enzie to spill about her research, but they did. That's what worries me most."

"But why should *that* worry you? I thought you said that Enzie was a—"

"A crackpot. That she is, without a doubt."

"Then what difference does it make what she told them?"

He frowned and said nothing. I fiddled with the handle of the glove compartment while I waited for his answer. The look in his eyes was one I seemed to recognize.

"Do you need to stop at a rest area, Orson?"

"What I'm about to tell you, Waldy, is probably going to sound a bit outré. I want you to promise that you won't pass it on to your mother. Will you promise me that?"

"Sure."

He nodded to himself for a while, exactly like Ben the Seer in the scene in *Timestrider II* when the Timestrider finds out that he's secretly a prince. I concentrated on the little plastic handle.

"I'm not a physicist, thank Christ. I'm just a writer. I have no use for Enzie's quote-unquote 'work,' and I don't subscribe to her ideas about the timestream." He chewed on his lip. "But that doesn't make my sisters any less dangerous—especially for you."

"For me?" I said, feeling more like the Timestrider than ever. My fingers closed on something cool and metallic in the glove compartment.

"Listen to me, Waldy. There's a reason why we've been to Harlem so few times in all these years. When you were first born, we took you down to your aunts—"

I brought the object in my hand up to the light. It was a pair of nail clippers, the kind designed to double as a key chain, missing its nail-file attachment.

"—and Enzie said she had the perfect name for you. I asked her what she'd come up with, and she smiled at me for the first time since I'd run away from home. Then, when she told me what the damn name *was*—"

I reached into the glove compartment a second time and retrieved a balled-up Kleenex. I turned it this way and that, noting every detail, looking down at it as if from a great height. I dropped it into the molded plastic pocket of the door, where it came to rest between a scrap of tinfoil and a capless ballpoint pen.

"—I protested, of course. The Kraut raised no objection—keeping the peace, as always—but I wanted at least to know why. 'Tradition,' Enzie said. 'It's a family name.' But that didn't cut it with me. 'Why him and not someone else?' I demanded. 'Why call *him* Waldemar and not me?'"

"Orson—"

"I'll tell you what she said to that, Waldy. It gives me the creeps, but I'll tell you."

"It doesn't matter anymore. Please don't get—"

"Enzie looked into my eyes with real regret. 'We *couldn't* name you Waldemar,' she told me. 'We'd have liked to so much, Orson, but we couldn't. It wasn't up to you to close the circle.'"

I could barely make out my father's voice now, or the rumble of the road, or anything but a deep, hydraulic hiss—the sound I'd heard inside the whitewashed box. Things around me went black but their outlines stayed bright, the way the sun looks at the height of an eclipse. The sensation was a new one to me, without precedent in my experience, but I never doubted what was happening. It was up to me, and no one else, to close the circle. I was remembering what was going to happen next.

Monday, 09:05 EST

"What does it feel like?" I asked the Timekeeper.

"What does *what* feel like, Waldy?"

I watched him as he lay on the bed, popping sprouts into his mouth as if they were gumdrops, smacking his dewy lips with satisfaction. He genuinely seemed to find the things delicious.

"Chrononavigation," I got out finally.

"That's an awfully big word. Did those Jewy aunts of yours teach you that?"

"Time travel," I said, biting back my disgust.

"Ah!" He worked himself upright, keeping his glaucoma-clouded eyes on mine. "I was wondering when you'd think to ask me that." He bobbed his head, leering in just the way I'd been afraid of. "Are you certain you won't have a sprout?"

If he were a product of my own mind, I thought, *I should be able to make him put those things away. If this were a dream—if I knew I was dreaming—I ought to be able to do it.*

"All right, then." He set the container aside. "I'll tell you, *Nefflein*, if you ask me nicely."

I steadied myself. "What does it feel like, Uncle?"

"Excellent question!" He frowned and pressed his fingertips together. "You feel nothing at all, strange to say, while it's happening. Your eyes and ears and ganglia are still open to stimulus, of course, but it takes time— however minuscule a span—to communicate sense impressions to the brain, and you've *excused* yourself from time, for the time being." He snuffled.

"Go on."

"When you arrive at the transfer point—the interzone, the place of exchange—*that's* when your sense impressions catch up. You sit stricken and dumb for the length of time it takes to process them. Every inch of skin, exposed or not, has been chapped and burned with interdimensional cold— the coldest cold, *Nefflein*, that you can possibly imagine. You thank chance and fate and Providence for the transfer point's existence, for its warmth and its calm. I can promise you that." He sighed. "Then you take your bearings, select an entry point, and start again."

I considered what he'd told me. "Tell me more about that place."

"The transfer point? Ah. Well." He closed his eyes. "The transfer point is marvelous. I don't quite know how to describe it. Nothing ever happens there—time doesn't appear to be passing—but there *is* time, of a certain kind. Transfer Time, I like to call it. You can breathe and see and think, but nothing happens."

"Nothing happens," I murmured. "Just like where we are now."

He nodded. "You can stay there as long as you like, and you won't age a day. Entry points are all around, evenly and conveniently spaced, waiting on your pleasure and convenience. To me it's always seemed like the depths of a wood, mild and peaceful and quiet, with shallow, perfect pools between the trees. It takes a while to recover your senses, as though you're gradually rising out of sleep, and you never manage to wake up completely. The temptation is great to remain there, in that beautiful limbo, forever."

I stared at him when he'd finished. He returned my look affably.

"A peaceful patch of woods," I said. "With little pools inside it."

He shrugged.

"Can I ask something else?"

"I shall answer with pleasure."

"How do you reenter the timestream?"

"Nothing's simpler than that. You lower yourself into one of the pools. You'll come out in some other world, some other universe, some other time."

"*The Magician's Nephew.*"

"Beg pardon?"

"*The Magician's Nephew*," I repeated through clenched teeth. "My favorite book when I was ten years old. You're describing a place in chapter seven called the Wood Between the Worlds. You're describing it exactly, down to the slightest detail."

"Right you are, *Nefflein!*" He snuffled again. "You'll have to allow me my fun. I like to tell you what you want to hear."

"Is anything you've told me true? Have you ever time-traveled at all?" I stood over him now. "Answer me, Uncle! Do you even exist?"

He grew thoughtful at that, and his eyes lost the last of their light.

"It's painful," he said.

"What does that mean? What's painful?"

"It's a *leave-taking* from things," he went on, as if I hadn't spoken. "The pain comes beforehand, of course—but especially after. While it's happening you feel nothing at all."

The mischief drained out of his features as he spoke, and I saw how time-ravaged he was. He looked ready to crumble into a pile of ash, like a Hollywood vampire in the first ray of dawn.

"The pain is more than anyone deserves," he said in a whisper. "Like the pain of ordinary loss, but compacted—accordioned together. There's just one thing that makes it bearable."

I kept my eyes trained on his face, searching for any hint of deceit. I couldn't help it, Mrs. Haven. I believed him.

"What is it, Uncle? What is that one thing?"

"You forget, *Nefflein*," he said, bowing his head. "You forget."

XXIV

MY HIGH SCHOOL YEARS, Mrs. Haven, are another period I'd rather skip. I was bullied no more than any other ectomorphic stammerer with a time-travel obsession would have been, I'm assuming, but the comfort this brought me was slim. My first and only pre-collegiate experience with girls— a few hours spent guzzling Schlitz and watching *The Day the Earth Stood Still* with my next-door neighbor Esther Fletcher-Suarez—was a defeat on par with the destruction of the United States Marines by Klaatu's giant robot. When I asked if I could kiss her, Esther—whose pecan-brown face was covered in colorless down, soft and nearly invisible, like the rind of a kissable kiwi—excused herself politely, covered her entire face in lipstick (ears included), and locked herself in the bathroom until I'd left the house.

Orson was in the TV room when I got home, eating Wheat Thins and watching the NBA draft. I'd always assumed that my father possessed privileged, hard-won knowledge of the opposite sex, and I decided to ask him where I'd gone awry. He had opinions about every other aspect of "the Human Experiment," as he liked to call it. Why not about this?

"That sounds like quite a life event, Waldy," he said when I'd finished. "I'm happy you had a nice time."

"You're happy I what?"

"Want my opinion? You ought to feel honored. It's probably not every guy she puts on lipstick for."

"You're right," I said. "The other guys she probably makes out with."

"It was a courtship display, that's all. A little conjugal theater." He turned the sound back up on the TV. "Try to put the experience in per-spective. It's not like she's your first sexual partner."

"That's true, Orson," I said, feeling farther from him than I'd ever felt. "She's definitely not that."

We watched the draft for a while. A man named Crumbs had just been drafted by the Heat. The Kraut was doing some late-evening baking in the kitchen: a strudel, to judge by the smell. This usually meant that there had been a fight.

"Mom's making a strudel," I said. "What's that about?"

"No idea." Orson sighed and hit the mute. "That reminds me. We've got some guests coming this weekend."

"Guests," I said. "Of course." We never had guests.

"All right then, son. Glad we had this little mano a mano."

I kept my gaze trained on the side of his head, telepathically command-ing him to turn and meet my eye. He picked his nose and grimaced at the screen.

"Who are the guests, Orson?"

"Haven and some of his people."

This was said in a casual tone, as though they came to dinner every weekend.

"Haven and some of his people," I repeated. "The Iterants. The Fuzzy Fruits."

"Correct."

I stared at him in dumbstruck silence.

"Don't give me shit, Waldy. The Kraut's already run me through the grinder."

I settled back into the couch, feeling the beer in my bloodstream reas-sert itself. The sounds from the kitchen were louder now, the aroma more sweet: cinnamon and filo dough and apples. I wanted to lay my head in the Kraut's floury, buttery lap.

"I don't get it," I said. "What's Haven after?"

"My name," answered Orson, puffing his chest out involuntarily. "My name and endorsement."

"Why?"

"As you no doubt recall, my writings form the template—"

"That's not what I meant. Why would you *give* it to him?"

"You know that, too," he said, though with slightly less bluster. "Because of my sisters." He avoided my look. "He's promised to leave them alone."

∞

In the handful of years since we'd last seen my aunts, my father and I had discussed that momentous night exactly once, and then only because the Kraut had forced us to. Orson steered clear of the topic for classically Orson-ish reasons, ranging from denial to peevishness to injured pride; I avoided it because it creeped me out. Each time I tried to make sense of what had happened, both in Enzie's "exclusion bin" and after, I felt an abyss open under my feet. I was too young to be asked to do the things my aunt had asked of me. Odd as my childhood had been—and eccentric, God knows, as my family remained—I'd been raised in a rational household, one in which the laws of science ruled. But my childhood had ended with that trip to Harlem. There are more things in heaven and on earth than reason accedes to, Mrs. Haven, and there was no forgetting what I'd experienced at the General Lee.

I'd heard the story of the Fuzzy Fruits' first visit a hundred times by then, and I'd seen the First Listener's tense, athletic face in magazines; even once—extremely briefly—on the news. It was a face better suited to torch-lit trials in some hidden star chamber than to the exigencies of modern-day PR, and no amount of styling gel or cosmetic dentistry could change that. Regardless of what he was doing, no matter how candid or innocuous the photo, Haven always looked as though he'd just stopped screaming. But it wasn't his inquisitor's face that disturbed me most deeply, or his army of ghoulish true believers, either. It was the fact that I didn't have a clue what he wanted—what he wanted from *us*, from my family—and the further fact that Orson seemed to know, but wouldn't say.

He changed the subject whenever I asked, or turned up the volume on the TV, or glowered at something just over my shoulder, as though a cicada-sized Haven were hovering there. I didn't buy any of his jabber about the Iterants needing his "endorsement": Synchronology was the fastest-growing religion in the United States, bar none, and it wasn't shy about it. Orson was more useful shut away in Cheektowaga than he would have been in any kind of spotlight. The most profitable prophet is a dead one, Mrs. Haven, ecclesiastically speaking. Those who overstay their welcome start to stink.

∞

It was the Kraut who answered the door that fateful Saturday—not out of any sense of wifely decorum, but because Orson refused to come up from the basement. I was mature enough, at fifteen, to be disgusted by his prima donna act: I pictured him skulking down there in his "Myth Creation Station" (as he insisted on calling his office) with a glass of lukewarm rosé in his fist, listening to every move we made upstairs. What I wasn't old enough to consider, I now realize, was that he might have been as terrified as I was.

The only one who wasn't terrified—not even remotely—was the Kraut. The bell had barely rung before she'd thrown the door open and advised our callers that Mr. Tolliver would be up presently; in the meantime there was coffee in the den. I took all this in from my post at the top of the stairs.

"Come down here, Waldy," the Kraut said without turning. "Kindly show our visitors where they can put themselves."

I'd never heard her use that tone of voice before: it was flat and metallic and brooked no objection. I came downstairs at once. She turned on her toes and marched off to the kitchen, leaving me alone with our guests, none of whom had so far said a word.

There were three of them in the foyer, just as there had been in the Econoline, just as there had been almost sixteen years earlier, the first time they'd come to the house. Two were wearing white leather sneakers with baby-blue treads; one of them—the one in the center—had on a pair of yellow calfskin loafers. All three wore matching wide-wale corduroys, and I realized to my horror—in the precise instant, as C*F*P would have it, that my eyes and *his* eyes met—that I was wearing wide-wale corduroys myself.

"Hello, pal," the First Listener said. "I like your cords."

He said it softly, I remember, as though we were alone. His crimped hair was subtly frosted, making him look like a preacher in some California church—the kind with acoustic guitars and headset microphones and not much use for the actual Bible. He looked exactly the way he would look eight years later, standing over me in a sunlit Moravian alley, grinning and wiping the blood from his lips.

"My dad's in the basement," I heard myself say.

"We have a 'thing' for corduroy, too, as you can see. Can you guess why that is?"

I shook my head woodenly.

"Corduroy, being a material composed of a grouping of parallel lines, performs two services for its wearer simultaneously." He held up two fingers. "The first is the practical service of keeping him (or her) warm, and shielding him (or her) from the elements, if inclement. The second is an ideological service, if you'll pardon the expression. It reminds him (or her) of the multiplicity of timestreams running parallel to our own, and of the possibility of congruence between them."

I blinked at him. "I hadn't thought of that."

"Of course you hadn't." He patted my shoulder and slipped gracefully past me. "There are many things you haven't thought of, Waldemar—not yet. You're still early in your cycle, after all. But you'll find yourself considering them soon."

"What do you mean?"

"The den is just through here, as I recall."

My instinct was to stop him—to catch him by the scruff of his neck or the collar of his Eddie Bauer blazer (corduroy, of course)—but he was only doing as my mother had suggested. I followed him sullenly into the den.

Haven draped himself across my father's leopard-print armchair as though he dropped in all the time, while his escort (after a kind of ritual pause, during which I could actually see them counting under their breath) dropped synchronously onto the couch. I knew with absolute certainty, without being able to say *how* I knew, that the configuration was exactly the same as it had been in 1970, when the Fuzzy Fruits had made their shy debut. The only available seat was between the two mouth-breathers on the sofa, so I decided to stay on my feet. Haven wasn't the least put out by this, as far as I could tell. It's possible he took it as a gesture of respect.

"Are you a *Timestrider* fan, pal? I'm guessing you are."

"I couldn't care less about it."

"Is that right."

Silence fell. Haven let out a contented sigh every so often, smiling blandly at the walls and at the ceiling and at me. It was a victory lap for him, this visit; that much was clear.

"Where's your father, Waldy?"

"My family calls me Waldy."

"I know that, pal. Where's your—"

"You're not my family."

This was unquestionably the boldest thing I'd said in my duration thus far, but it didn't have the effect that I'd intended. Haven grinned at the mouth-breathers, showing his teeth; they tittered and nodded, as if I'd just stood up on my hind legs and barked.

"Right you are, pal," said Haven. "Nicely put."

He closed his eyes and gave a happy shiver. When he looked at me again I had the sense that something about his face had changed—that his jaw was slightly heavier, or that his eyes had taken on a different tint. I wondered where the hell my father was.

"It doesn't really matter where the Prime Mover is," said Haven, as if I'd been speaking aloud. "We didn't come to see him, after all."

"What are you talking about?" I said, cursing the quaver in my voice. "Of course you came to see the Prime—of *course* you came to see Orson. My father, I mean."

Haven shook his head. "That's the funny thing, Waldy—we didn't. We came to see you."

The Kraut rematerialized at that instant, for some reason holding a Warranted Tolliver egg timer, and announced that my father would be receiving his callers downstairs. Haven thanked her politely and got to his feet. I kept perfectly still, staring fixedly down at the sphincterish spots on the leopard-print armchair, watching the imprint of the First Listener's backside gradually disappear. By the time I'd recovered my composure he was gone.

L ESS THAN AN HOUR after the Kraut's whispered warning, I was sitting in an open second-class car of the Václav Divis Regional from
Vienna to Brno, looking past your freckled shoulder at the men
across the aisle. Both of them were wearing trench coats, I noticed, and
expensive-looking leather driving gloves. The Kraut was right: everyone in
this part of Europe looked like a member of the Gestapo.

But no sooner had I had this thought, Mrs. Haven, than the various
doubts I'd been suppressing wriggled up into the light. Could that really
have been what the Kraut had said? It wasn't true, of course—the only
people who looked like members of the Gestapo were the trench-coat-
wearing men across the aisle. My mother was a rational woman, as far
as I knew: the single levelheaded member of our family. Why on earth
would she have told me that you, of all people, "wished me ill"? Either
her brain chemistry had shifted radically or I'd made a grievous error—
the most grievous one, by far, of my duration. I could think of no other
hypothesis.

To calm myself, I brought out the postcard of Znojmo and studied it,
imagining the two of us already there. I recited its doggerel under my
breath like a charm:

> *"A gherkin from the land of Znaim*
> *Is mightier than the Hand of Time;*
> *Its savory brine, at first so sour*
> *Grows sweeter with each Passing Hour."*

I glanced at you when I was done, to see whether the spell was having any effect—but you looked lost to the world, Mrs. Haven, or at least lost to me. Some flywheel had shifted; some cog had been thrown. You didn't seem to see the men in the trench coats, or perhaps you were making an elaborate show of not seeing them. Maybe that in itself was proof of some sort of conspiracy. But you'd never looked more beautiful to me.

"What are you thinking about, Mrs. Haven?"

Slowly—unwillingly, it seemed—your eyes met mine. "If you really want to know, Walter, I'm not feeling so great about myself."

"He doesn't need you. You told me that, remember? He'll barely even notice that you're gone."

You smiled abstractedly and shrugged your shoulders. "I wasn't thinking about him."

"Is it me, then? Were you thinking about me?"

A blank moment passed. "Of course not," you said. But I'd already gotten my answer.

"Listen to me, Mrs. Haven. I know you think I'm leading you on some kind of goose chase across Central Europe—maybe even that I've lost my mind—but I've got to get my family behind me. Can you understand that? I want the past to be *past*: to stop spinning in circles, to stop sucking me in, to let me make my own goddamn decisions. I'm in love with you, Mrs. Haven, and I want to start over." I took in a breath. "For the first time that I can remember, I have a feeling that the future might be—"

"I don't want to *talk* right now," you said, pressing your hands to your face. "Not about your family, not about your goose chase, and most of all—for God's sake!—not about the future." You let your hands fall and turned to the window. "Could you leave me alone until dinner?"

I bobbed my head jerkily, digging my nails into the armrests of my seat. "Of course I can do that."

"Thank you, Walter."

It was cold in the car, cold enough to see your breath, and your woolen skirt crackled like a Tesla coil each time you rearranged your legs. You rearranged your legs often—for my benefit, perhaps, or for the benefit of the men across the aisle—and the counterclockwise spirals on your vintage patterned stockings emphasized your haunches in a way that made my forehead start to cramp. You steadfastly refused to meet my eye. The trees outside the window blurred and bowed.

"Gentlemens and ladies!" the intercom warbled. "We regret to inform you the restaurant car is now open."

"At least they're honest about it," you said, getting up.

∞

The restaurant car was populated by hollow-eyed businessmen and little old ladies who looked pickled in aspic and spleen. The men in trench coats were there, hunched together at the starboard center table; we seated ourselves hard to port. I tried to commit their features to memory—in the event of a future investigation by Interpol—while you squinted down at the greasy plastic menu as if you could make it appetizing by sheer force of will. You must have succeeded, because you ordered a bowl of *česnečka*— Czech garlic soup—for each of us.

"*Česnečka,*" I said after a time. "I wouldn't have thought—"

"They don't seem to have any bourbon. How do you say 'bourbon' in Czech?"

The last time you'd ordered a bourbon had been on the airplane, after I'd explained the details of my plan. I knew what bourbon signified.

"Mrs. Haven," I said, attempting to keep my voice steady. "Are you starting to have second thoughts?"

You smiled at me and took my hand in yours. "I had second thoughts the moment we met, Walter. That's how I ended up here."

If the happiness this gave me was short-lived, Mrs. Haven, it was also very close to absolute. I reminded myself that you'd abandoned home and country—not to mention your personal safety—to be sitting with me in that joyless dining car. As always when I considered this fact, I felt that a mistake had been made: the most glorious and historic mistake since our ancestors descended from the trees.

Our soup came and we ate it dutifully. It tasted of cabbage and socks.

"This is the slowest train I've ever been on," you said between spoonfuls. "The Sensational Gatsby would have loved it."

"I didn't realize the Husband was a train buff," I said, with what I hoped was a nonchalant air. "I'd have thought jet packs and hovercraft were more his thing."

"He has a set of guidelines that he follows," you said, watching the farmhouses and wheat fields gliding by. "He believes that time passes faster when you're having fun."

I hesitated, trying and failing to read your expression. You gazed out the window impassively.

"Most people think that," I said. "About time passing, I mean."

"They *think* it, maybe. But they don't arrange their lives around the concept."

"What's that supposed to mean?"

"Richard is trying to decelerate time, Walter, by any means at his disposal." You set down your spoon. "The most effective method he's found, so far, is what he calls 'autosuggestive psychostasis.'"

"I'm not familiar with that term."

"He spends his days trying to achieve total boredom."

I gave an awkward half smile at that, certain now that you were pulling my leg. Even as I did so, however, I remembered those static, empty days before I'd won you back, and how the hours had advanced with sublime, psychotropic precision.

"Correct me if I'm wrong, Mrs. Haven—"

"I'd be happy to."

"—but your husband buys and sells companies and cuts ribbons at galas and zips around the planet in a private jet. If he's trying to live a boring life, he's doing a piss-poor job of it."

That made you smile a little, and I allowed myself to feel I'd won a modest victory; but the smile you gave seemed meant for someone else.

"The jet's a time-share, Walter. But you're right about one thing. This trip of ours would do the trick much better."

∞

Znojmo was damp and gray and alcoholic-looking when we pulled in, the way towns look in Czech New Wave films from the sixties. The Himmler twins stayed put in the restaurant car, sipping somnolently from steins of

Pilsner Urquell; I watched them as the Divis rolled away. Time was moving slowly on that train indeed.

The platform, by contrast, seemed to empty instantaneously. The only person in sight by the time we'd gotten our bearings was a stooped teenager with a gigantic Saint Bernard in a seeing-eye harness. The dog was circling the boy—counterclockwise, of course—and the boy had no choice but to follow suit.

"Look at that kid, Mrs. Haven." I didn't know whether to laugh or burst out crying. You were halfway along the platform already, tilting your head to look up at the sky. "Come on, Walter!" you called. "It's beginning to rain." And it was.

We spent that next week in the Hotel Zrada on Republiky Square, living in high style on the UCS's dime, littering the honeymoon suite with room-service trays and bottles of prosecco and sundry other forms of recreational debris, any of which would have looked right at home in Genny's Archive. Our sideboard was soon populated by sweating mason jars of local gherkins: the riddle of my great-grandfather's brining-room discovery couldn't have interested you less, as far as I could tell, but brining itself seemed to fascinate you. While I dithered around town with a dated Czech phrase book and a list of addresses scavenged from century-old journals, you devoted yourself to the history of the pickle trade, spending hours in the kitchens of button-eyed *babičkas*, lamenting the post–Cold War rise of the Polish *okurka* and parsing the mysteries of dill. You got around your lack of Czech in a way I never would have thought of: by refusing to acknowledge its existence. Within the week you were friends with half the grandmothers in town, it seemed, while I was no further along than I'd been in New York. I won't deny it, Mrs. Haven—I was envious. There's only so much *Znojemské okurky* a person can eat, no matter how his forebears made their living.

It was your interest in pickling, appropriately enough, that led us to Ottokar's secret. After eight days of begging admission to every storehouse and factory and cellar my family had owned, I was ready to consign both my quest and my history—and even the Accidents themselves—to the far side of their own event horizon. Our suite at the Zrada was a pigsty by then: you'd hung the provided DO NOT MOLEST sign on the door handle when we checked in ("Present company excluded," you'd whispered into my ear) and the cleaning staff had heeded it devoutly. It smelled of sex in those rooms for the first several days; later in the week, when things had soured between us, it smelled of old sex; finally even that faded, and it smelled of dirty sheets and pickled cabbage. A feeling of stagnation had set in between us, of fidgety pseudocalm, that scared me worse than any squabble could have done. Never before had we had so much time to observe each other, carbuncles and all, and I think we were both surprised by what we found. You had a way of running your tongue over your back teeth, for example, as though searching for food, and you tended to sulk over trifles. Worse yet, I found myself—especially since our disastrous audience with the Kraut—progressively less able to amuse you. Not to say that you seemed bored, Mrs. Haven: you were conspicuously, demonstratively chipper. But I began to pack my suitcase anyway.

"You want to leave already, Walter? We're just getting settled."

"I've done everything I can here. I give up."

What I didn't tell you—due to some obscure suspicion, perhaps, but more likely simply out of injured pride—was that I was beginning to have doubts about my mission. Even if I somehow managed to get my hands on Ottokar's notes, what would they help me accomplish? How exactly would they enable me to find the Timekeeper, and what did I suppose would happen if I did? He was a mass murderer, after all, and I was a caretaker at an old folks' home. I was dangerously out of my depth. Sobriety, if you want to call it that, was returning to my overheated brain.

If we'd left Znojmo then—right away, that same night—I might even have made a full recovery.

"It's been a bad week, Walter." You nodded to yourself. "I've been up all night thinking about it. Maybe coming here was a mistake."

"Coming where? To Znojmo?"

"To Europe."

I stared down into my suitcase, unable to speak. The problem, of course, was that a part of me agreed. You saw as much and smiled at me forlornly.

"Do you remember *euphasia*, that word we invented? The feeling you get, coming out of a theater, that the movie you've been watching is still going on—still playing everywhere around you—even though it's actually over?" You nodded to yourself. "I think we might both have *euphasia* now."

I set down the shirt I was folding. "Mrs. Haven—"

"But here's the problem. I've staked my future on you, Walter, maybe even my life. And there's no going back from that. Not ever." You bit your lip for a moment. "I still don't understand what you came here to find—"

Just then, so fleetingly it barely registered, I felt a slight twinge of suspicion. You were playing the part of the innocent so well—a thousand times better than I could have managed. The performance called attention to itself.

"I've told you," I said. "The missing pages to my great-grandfather's notebook. The ones that explain—that I hope will explain—what he meant by the Lost Time Accidents. But I'm starting to doubt—"

"If *that's* what you're after, why waste time with the Toulas? You told me his mistress was the last one to see him alive. Marta Svoboda, wasn't it? The wife of the butcher?"

I rolled my eyes in frustration. "I've been to see all the Svobodas in Znojmo, Mrs. Haven. No one knows what I'm talking about."

"Is that all?" You cocked your head at me. "You can't find any of Marta's relatives?"

"That's all. And since I can't find her relatives, I'm sure you'll agree—"

"Your mistake was looking for *Svobodas*," you said matter-of-factly. "Marta only had one child—a daughter. That daughter married into the Hargovas, who own the electronics shop on Kollárova Street. Their son is the custodian of the Václav Prokop Divis house. Does that name ring a bell?"

I said nothing for at least half a minute. "Václav Prokop—"

"That poor cross-eyed priest who invented the lightning rod. The train we came here on was named after him."

"I know who he *was*, Mrs. Haven. What I don't understand—"

"Adéla Hargova is the sweet old granny who gave me those boiled eggs in vinegar." You pointed at a jar on the sideboard. "The one with the limp and the little mustache. She also happens to be Marta Svoboda's granddaughter."

I let out a slow breath. "Have you told her about me? About what I'm here for?"

"I've told everybody what you're here for. How else could I have found all this out?"

"Could you take—" I was stammering again. "Could you take me to her?"

The smile you gave me was so conspiratorial, so self-understood, that I sensed there might be some hope for us yet.

∞

Adéla Hargova lived in a bright, dreary flat that smelled faintly of beer, on the third floor of a housing complex that must already have looked decrepit the year it was built. Everything about the place was defiantly Soviet bloc, including Boromir, the man of the house. He ignored us completely— some arcane, ultraviolent sporting event was on TV—which was probably all for the best. We sat with Adéla in her curtainless kitchen, sipping wonderfully peppery oolong tea, eating *okurky* and fresh-baked bread with raisins in it. Our hostess scrutinized me darkly.

"You are Toula?"

"Not exactly, Mrs. Hargova." I smiled. "But *dost blízko*. Close enough."

"Who are you?"

Her expression was scornful, inclining toward anger, but for once in my duration I was ready. I laid three photographs on the table: a playing-card-sized daguerreotype of my great-grandfather, a snapshot of Kaspar and Waldemar at Belvedere Palace in Vienna, and a Polaroid of Orson dandling me on his knee. She glared at each in turn, then back at me. The look on her face remained grim.

"You are *Toula*?" she repeated.

"Yes, Mrs. Hargova," you cut in, taking her hand. "Waldemar Tolliver, son of Orson, son of Kaspar, son of Ottokar. *Syn* Ottokar Gottfriedens Toula."

"I know the man," she said. "All of us know. Passport, *prosím*."

I gave her my passport—thanking chance and fate and Providence that I'd remembered to bring it along—and she inspected it as thoroughly as any border guard. Then she leaned back in her threadbare, potato-shaped armchair and knocked twice on the flimsy wall behind her.

"Coming out for our guests, Artur," she singsonged. "Bringing also the box."

A chair was pushed back on the far side of the wall, a pocket door opened, and the blind boy from the station shuffled out. You looked as startled to see him as I was.

"This is Artur," Adéla announced. "Artur is *historik* in our home."

Artur squinted at us through his chalk-pebble eyes. He was a handsome-enough boy, if a little dough-faced; but there was something pinched about him, even sly. Though we were unrelated, as far as I knew, I saw a hint of Waldemar in his elegant, affectless features. I held tightly to the creaking stool beneath me. I was within grasping distance of the Accidents: closer than any Toula had been in more than eighty years. I could feel it, Mrs. Haven, in my fingers and my teeth. The conclusion of our long, recursive quest was close at hand.

"You're here for the papers, I expect," Artur said, in English far more polished than his mother's.

"That's right, Artur," I heard you reply. "Thank you for preserving them for us."

"We did nothing for *you*," he said quickly. "We did this for the family—our family." His grip on the box tightened. "We did this for history."

"Artur says to me—always—these are *science* pages," his mother put in. "Scientists will come to ask, he says. Technicians. I am always thinking these are *poems*." She beamed at him, then glowered back at us. She really was a wonderful old biddy.

"Which is the scientist?" Artur demanded.

"Walter is, of course. Just look at him!" You gripped my knee under the table.

"What will happen with these pages, Mr. Walter? You are meaning to employ them for research? To publish? To win the Nobel?"

I looked from the son to the mother. The air in the kitchen had gone thick and damp. The question had never been put to me before—not so directly—but it was easy to answer. I had only one answer to give.

"I'm not looking to *use* them at all, Artur—not in the way that you mean. The contents of that box are an end for me, not a beginning. That's what an answer is, isn't it? The end of a question?" I coughed into my fist, stalling for time, aware of the micrometer-thin ice I was skating on. "If those pages have a purpose at all, it's to put the past behind me. To put a hundred-year-old ghost—a *starověký fantóm*—to rest."

Silence fell for a moment.

"The end?" Artur said.

I nodded.

"All right, then—the end." He broke into a grin, as though I'd delivered some password, and held the box toward me. "I wish you luck with this."

I mumbled my thanks in Czech—the phrase book was coming in handy at last—and took the box from him. Its lightness surprised me. I seemed to feel a faint subsonic thrum.

"Go *on*, Walter," you said. "Open it."

It was a typical teenage boy's treasure chest—crows' feathers, spent shotgun cartridges, dated Czechoslovakian coins—except for three sheets of foolscap at the very bottom, slightly too wide for the box, covered in precise *courant* script. The first two pages were journal entries; the third looked to be a single formula, so dense as to be almost indecipherable. I'd have to find a mathematician to make sense of it, I realized, and possibly a handwriting specialist. I was getting ahead of myself, Mrs. Haven, but I couldn't help that. It was all that I could do to keep from shouting.

"It was wonderful of you—both of you—to have guarded these papers," I murmured. "My family has been searching for my great-grandfather's notes since the day of his death. We thought that they'd vanished forever."

"*He* told Marta—our Marta—that men would be coming," Adéla Hargova said. "Coming after the papers. He told her not to give them." She grew suddenly shy. "That is the story I know."

"And she hid them. Bless her for that. She knew they were important."

"Ah! I'm not sure about *that*."

"What do you mean, Mrs. Hargova?"

"He told her to burn them," Artur said, smiling strangely.

"Burn them?"

He nodded. "Or throw them away."

∞

As soon as we stepped outside I saw the mover. He was standing at the entrance to Masarykovo Square, dressed in a well-cut gray suit, holding his hands out, palms upward, as if checking for rain. It was the man who'd been carrying the clipboard in my cousin's apartment, the one the other movers deferred to: the man they all called Little Brother. The square was unusually crowded—it was Saturday, a market day—but he stood out as if he were spotlit. I felt surprise, I remember, but only a flutter. It was as if I'd agreed to meet him there, at that particular juncture of spacetime, then forgotten we had an appointment. He of course showed no surprise at all.

I waited until we were halfway across the square to tell you. You took my hand and gripped it.

"You were right, Walter. We should have left yesterday."

"Do you recognize him?"

"It's you they're here for—you and Ottokar's papers. Not me." You let go of my hand. "It's all right. We can lose him."

"Lose him? How would we—"

"There's just one of him—at least so far—and two of us. We'll have to split up."

"What if you're wrong? What if it's you they want?"

You shook your head. "They've been waiting for this to happen, Walter. Waiting for you to come here for those notes."

I stopped short and turned you to face me. We were at the edge of the square, screened from view by a row of stalls selling iridescent raincoats; I couldn't see Little Brother, but I knew he was close. The sun came out then, shining into your eyes, and I watched your pupils narrow into pinpricks.

"How long have you known about this, Mrs. Haven?"

"There's no time for that, Walter—do you understand? Meet me in an hour at the Václav Prokop Divis house. I'll get us a car."

You spun on your heels—your square, well-calloused heels that fit so perfectly into my palms—and hurried off down Kollárova Street. Just that morning you'd treated my search for my great-grandfather's papers with amused condescension; now you'd told me with perfect matter-of-factness that your husband's goons had followed us to Europe for no other reason. You'd looked pained to have to say it, even angry. But that may have been due to the sun.

"Mrs. Haven!"

"Yes, Walter? What is it?"

You came back to me eagerly, as though you knew we'd never meet again, and wanted one last look, however ill-advised, to recollect me by. I still choose to believe that was the reason.

"Take the notes, Hildy."

"The notes?" you said, frowning. "I don't understand."

"If that man follows me, it's the notes that he wants. But if he follows *you*—if you're the reason he's here—then the notes aren't important. And either way they're safer in your hands."

You made as if to say something, then closed your eyes and gave the slightest nod. I undid the top two buttons of the jacket you'd bought in Vienna and slid the pages inside, then pulled your body close to mine and kissed you. It was my best attempt at a heroic gesture, my last turn in the spotlight, and I'm proud to say I took my time about it. That kiss enabled me to recover my nerve, Mrs. Haven, the way an overdone flourish helps a second-rate actor remember his line. By the time you'd disappeared around the corner of Kollárova Street I was ready for the worst that might befall.

I slipped out past the raincoats, back into the open, and waited calmly there for Little Brother. He came into view almost instantly, no longer feigning indifference, fixing his creased pink smoker's eyes on mine. He was moving like an old man, silently and smoothly, in that terrible, deliberate tai chi way of his. He could have moved faster, I'm sure, but he chose to go slowly. He was giving me a sporting shot—the chance to make my break—and I didn't wait around to ask him why.

You'd taken Kollárova Street south, so I headed due west, down Lazebnická Street toward the river. You'd been right, Mrs. Haven. It was me he was after. The thing to do now was give him the slip and get to the Divis house without attracting notice. I forced myself to think. We bought our breakfast *houskas* from a baker on Antonínská Street, less than half a block away. If I ducked into his shop before Little Brother rounded the corner, and begged him, as a loyal customer, to let me through into the courtyard—

"Hello, Waldy."

I recognized that honeyed voice at once. It belonged to a man in a corduroy blazer and cheap-looking loafers, leaning against a pockmarked stucco wall, leafing casually through the local paper. Which had to mean that he'd known, well before I knew myself, that I'd come running up the street at just that hour.

He studied me at his leisure, paying particular attention to my eyes, as though taking note of how the years had changed me. I could find no anger or ill will in his expression—I could locate no emotion there at all. I remembered what you'd told me on the train up from Vienna: your husband cultivated boredom to impede his sense of time. And I became aware, as I stood frozen in place—excruciatingly aware, but in a far-off sort of way—that panic seemed to have the same effect.

"No cause for alarm, pal," he said sleepily. "I'm not going to cut your cock off with a rusty pair of scissors. I'm not even going to punch you in the nose."

I took a half step backward, slipping slightly on the cobblestones, and asked him why not.

"Do you need me to say it?" He raised his eyebrows. "Because you've rendered me—and the Church of Synchronology, and the entire human race—an invaluable service. A service that only you, Waldemar Gottfriedens Tolliver, son of Orson, grandson of Kaspar, great-grandson of Ottokar, could have performed. We've been trying to get our hands on that theorem for years."

I mumbled something to the effect that I thought he'd put his Iterant days behind him—that he was a financier now. He smiled wistfully.

"It's a fallen world, Waldy. I've had to adapt. The public respects a businessman considerably more than a philosopher in the current age, never mind a prophet." He folded his newspaper neatly down the middle. "But thanks to you, pal, public opinion is going to matter less to us—*much* less—than it has previously. We'll have other means of bringing folks around."

"By traveling into the past and changing things, you mean. By manipulating history."

He gave a tuneless whistle.

"Listen to me, Haven. I'm sure you don't need me to explain to you about the grandmother—"

"Let's not *presume*, Waldy. Let's not get impatient. We'll have to review those calculations first."

"Why not use Enzie's exclusion bin? That's what you've been after all along, isn't it?"

His smile tightened slightly. "We overestimated your aunt's abilities,

I'm afraid. She may not have chosen to share this with you, Waldy, but that contraption of hers never worked. Not even a little."

"Is that right?" I said, thinking of the hours I'd spent in that dark nowhere place and of the series of visions I'd seen. Enzie had told Haven one lie, at least. There was reason for hope.

Haven shook his head. "You saw for yourself that Enzian's 'bin' was no more than a painted packing crate. We've since determined that anything—any confined space at all—can be used, if it falls within certain parameters." He grinned at that, as if he'd made a joke. "What *exactly* those parameters might be—the ideal, specific ratio—has eluded all of us so far, your daffy aunts included. But it didn't elude old Ottokar." He let out a sigh. "What an extraordinary man he must have been."

"It *didn't* elude him? How could you know that?"

The slyness crept back into Haven's face. "Your great-grandfather made one successful jump forward, remained for three-quarters of an hour, then returned to the instant and location of his death. We have reason to believe that he manifested himself at this very corner, in fact, at twelve forty-seven CET on June eighth, 1970."

My head felt hot and light and full of noise. "What 'reason to believe' could you possibly have?"

"Enzian told us. She was very clear-cut."

"But how could *she* have known?"

"Isn't that obvious, Waldy? Because she was there."

I said nothing to that.

Haven regarded me fondly. "See if you can follow me, pal. Ottokar was walking home from his mistress's house—in a postcoital daze, I'm assuming—when a man who could have been his doppelgänger passed him on the street. Seconds later, before he could act, he saw this same man run down by a car. Your great-grandfather slipped in among the crowd that had formed around the accident, and realized, to his amazement, that the man on the ground was himself. Not only that, but the victim was dressed in the clothes that he himself had on, with an identical mustard stain on the lapel. Ottokar realized at once what this event signified. It meant that he had, as he'd suspected and hoped, hit on the secret of chrononavigation that very morning in his workshop. But far more than that: it proved that he would manage to break free of the chronostream, not at

some point in the future, but *on that very day.* How else could his body occupy the same *t*-coordinate twice, in precisely the same suit of clothes?"

"Hold on a second. I don't see how—"

"Ottokar rushed back to his cellar and lost no time in putting what
he'd learned into practice, first using his sons' pet cicada as a trial subject,
then experimenting directly on himself. He was not as astonished by his
rapid success as he might otherwise have been: he'd seen the proof with his
own eyes, after all, less than an hour before. When the moment came—
and it came quickly—to put his discovery to the ultimate test, he boldly cut
the chronologic ties that bound him. Thus began an extended, random
odyssey through the chronosphere: not unlike that of the protagonist of
'Everywhen,' my personal favorite among your father's works."

"A hack job," I managed to stammer. Haven shrugged and continued.

"Your great-grandfather must have known, when he finally returned to
Masarykovo Square at thirteen hundred CET on the day of his departure,
that his duration was about to conclude. But I choose to believe, as he saw
Herr Bachling's Daimler bearing down on him, that he found solace in
two certainties." Haven held up two fingers. "Firstly, that his discovery had
been borne out by his own direct experience; and secondly, that his legacy was assured. Half his notes—the three most precious pages—were
still in his mistress's possession; and he'd entrusted the rest to his twin
granddaughters, with his very own hands, on June eighth, 1970, at twelve
forty-seven, Central European Time, at the very spot where you and I
now stand."

I thought hard for a moment after Haven had finished. He reclined
against the wall and indulged me. Everything I did that day seemed to delight him.

"What you've just told me makes no sense at all," I said.

"'Sense' is a quality of human consciousness, pal. 'Time' is a quality of
the physical universe, as our consciousness perceives it. To make any true
progress—to attain the slightest degree of freedom—one has to be willing
to part ways with both." He snuffled. "I'm disappointed in you, Waldy.
Saint Augustine knew as much in 397 C.E."

Even as I scoffed at this—even as my mind fought to reject his account as impossible—I recalled the trip Enzie and Genny had taken to
Znojmo. It was suddenly clear to me that the beginning of the change in

my father—his withdrawal from the world, his growing fear of his sisters, and even his mental decline—could be dated from my aunts' return from Europe. If they'd told Orson what Haven was telling me now—and if he'd swallowed it whole, as he may well have done—what chance did *I* have to resist?

But at the same time, Mrs. Haven—in some neglected, underventilated shaftway of my brain—I was having none of it. It was Waldemar, in his sick and wounded egotism, who'd first thought of warping the chronoverse; his father may have lusted after knowledge of time, but never after influence over its course. I already knew that my aunts had told Haven one lie. Who was to say they hadn't told a second?

"I'm going to point something out to you, Waldy, and you aren't going to like it." Haven set aside his paper. "We're not so very different, you and I."

I took another step backward. "Your wife said something like that to me once."

"Ah," he said slowly. "My wife."

"You've missed her."

"What's that, pal?"

"You've missed her," I repeated. "She's halfway to Vienna by now."

His lips gave a barely perceptible twitch. "My wife is in the honeymoon suite of the Hotel Zrada at present, in the company of certain men in my employ."

I let out a small, sharp cough and doubled over.

"How are you feeling, pal? Would you like to sit down?"

I shook my head.

"Good boy. Now here's what's going to happen next." He gestured to Little Brother, who stood just a few steps behind me, breathing musically through his nose. "My colleague and I are going to search you, right here on the street, and you're going to cooperate fully. Then we'll return to the Zrada to collect my dear Hildy and the papers you entrusted to her care. At that point, we—my wife, my associates and myself; not you, of course—are going to get on a plane." He smiled at me and shrugged his boyish shoulders. "Where we go in that plane—*how* we go, for that matter, and when—will depend on what those documents contain."

"Those 'documents,' if you want to call them that, were written in 1903. What are you expecting to find in them, Haven? A set of directions?"

I'd meant this mockingly, of course, but his smile only sharpened. A set of directions was exactly what he was hoping to find. I felt a powerful urge to lie down in the street.

"Can I ask one last favor?"

"I'd say that depends."

Little Brother frisked me in silence and brought my arms together behind me. It took less than ten seconds. No one looked out their windows or opened their doors.

"It's about your wife," I said.

"I suspected it might be."

"Don't be too hard on her."

"Hard on her, pal?" Haven looked at me blankly. "Why on earth would I be *hard* on her?"

I was confused for an instant; no longer than that. He watched the understanding hit and didn't say a word. I have no idea how my face looked to him, Mrs. Haven, but what he saw there seemed to gratify him deeply.

"Hildegard asked me to pass a message along to you, Waldy, before we let you go. Would you like to hear it?"

"Go to hell."

"It's easy to remember, luckily, because it rhymes." He cleared his throat and leaned in close to me. When he spoke again his voice was high and dainty.

> *"Here lie I, Melvin Elginbrodde:—*
> *Have Mercy on my Soul, Lord God,*
> *As I would do, if I were God*
> *And Ye were Melvin Elginbrodde."*

Little Brother had me in a full nelson now, with my chin driven into my chest, so that all I could see of Haven were his loafers. The cuffs of his corduroys were perfectly creased, like the brim of a child's paper hat; his socks were red and white and blue, like barber poles. I'd seen those socks before, Mrs. Haven, though I couldn't think where. And then it came to me.

"You were standing right there. You heard every last word."

"You'll have to explain that one, pal. Where and when was I standing?"

"In the kitchen at Van's party." My mouth had trouble forming the words. "Hildy knew you were there—she had to have known—but it made no difference."

"I'll need you to repeat that last bit. Couldn't quite make it out."

"It made no difference," I said. "Because she had your blessing."

Haven leaned in closer still—so close to me that I could feel his breath. It smelled rich and slightly sour, like buttermilk.

"That hurts my *feelings*, pal. If you were right, I'd be no better than a pimp."

A white van was rounding the corner from Antonínská Street as I kicked away from Little Brother and brought my forehead down against your husband's face. If he screamed or gasped or cursed I didn't hear him. Little Brother yanked me back with all his might, nearly wrenching my arms out of their sockets. Blood was running from your husband's nose and mouth, dripping from his dimpled chin onto his shirtfront.

"Goodbye, Waldemar," he said serenely, passing the back of his hand across his bloodied lips. "I wish you an endurable completion of your term." He wavered on his feet for a moment, then gave me a jaunty salute. "The Timekeeper sends his regards."

∞

No sooner had he said those words, Mrs. Haven, than I chrono-jumped into the future. The world went red and gold and green, then inky black; when I opened my eyes, Lazebnická Street was empty. I lay there quietly, lazily, my right cheek flush with the curbstone, until I heard the bell of Paměť Cathedral toll the hour. It was one o'clock, CET, presumably of that same afternoon. I'd traveled forward by exactly eighteen minutes.

I raised my head carefully, an inch at a time, and felt my jaw click back into alignment. A tooth sat glistening on the curb beside my cheek: a well-maintained molar, slightly yellowed at the crown. The sky was low and packed with marrow-colored clouds. I took a breath, leaned to one side, and vomited onto the pavement. Then I stood up and walked back to the hotel.

The door to our suite was open when I got there but the room beyond was dark. You were gone, Mrs. Haven, and so were your bags. The jars of pickles remained: I could smell their tang around me in the gloom. Somehow this drove the truth home better than anything else could have done. You'd left those precious jars behind, although you'd collected them so eagerly, because they served no purpose for you any longer. Even those reeking *okurky*—and the prune-faced grandmothers you'd gotten them from— had been no more than a means to an end.

I switched on a light and discovered a note, on Zrada stationery, crumpled up at the foot of the bed. It looked to have been written in a rush.

> *Im writing this to get things clear between us. Ive been told to write/ say nothing but I want to get things clear.*
>
> *The things that happened to us didnt happen. Thats the best way to see it. We never met at Markhams party. I never came to your apartment. No Vienna no Znojmo. We have no history the two of us. You never talked to me or heard my name.*
>
> *Do you understand Walter? Youre alive right now because you do not matter. Theyd have killed you but this way was easier. Dont mistake it for kindness. Dont mistake this note either. You have your passport and your ticket. Go back home.*
>
> *Im forgetting you Walter. Im erasing the file now and you do the same. Dont try*

I set the note down with care, using both of my hands. I'd always struggled to trust in the favor you showed me. You'd complained more than once about my lack of faith, and maybe you were right to complain. But I must have had some faith in you, at least in our last weeks, because now that I was confronted with evidence to the contrary I temporarily lost direction of my body. My legs pitched me sideways, upsetting the sideboard and the jars arranged across it, and as the carpet surged upward a gurgling informed me, in a way no words could, that the term of our romance was at an end. The gurgling was coming from my own throat, I realized. It was the sound of hope escaping through my teeth.

"Mr. Walter?"

I kept still as long as I could. Then I rolled onto my knees, forced my bruised lips to close, and compelled myself back up onto my feet. I found Artur sitting on an empty luggage rack inside the bathroom.

"I hope, sir, that you will excuse—"

"This is not a good time, Artur."

"I'm sorry to have entered here, Mr. Walter, into your private boudoir. But under the circumstances—"

"Just tell me what you want."

"I had to come here. At home I could not say this. My family was there—and also that woman." He lowered his voice. "I do not care for that woman."

"You can rest easy on that score. That woman is gone."

He nodded. "Two items."

"I'm listening."

He held up a finger. "First item: Marta's daybook. She kept one, Mr. Walter, and I have it here."

"Okay. Leave it on the coffee table, and when I get a chance—"

"The *ztracené čas nehody*," Artur cut in sharply. "The mistakes of lost time. You said to me this was important."

Even then, in that hour—the lowest of my duration—that phrase retained some shadow of its power. "I did say that, yes. But right now, as you might have noticed—"

"I'm not blind, in fact. With a magnifying glass, I can read."

"I'm happy to hear that. That's fabulous news. I need you to leave."

"I have a theory about Ottokar's discovery. You'd be interested, I am sure, to hear it?"

I cursed him under my breath. "Weren't you listening to what I told you in your mother's kitchen, Artur? *Everyone* has a theory about the Lost Time Accidents. Every fool who's ever heard the phrase. Even I, idiot that I am, with my total lack of scientific—"

"That thing is a *vtip*, Mr. Walter. A little joke."

"What thing?" I felt my stomach twist. "The Accidents, you mean?"

He nodded. "It was nothing, Mr. Walter. No discovery, no breakthrough. He was ending with science, your grand-grandfather. He was tired of researching. Look in here, in Marta's daybook. She writes down that this makes her very glad."

It grew as quiet in that bathroom as in an exclusion bin.

"That's impossible, Artur," I heard myself answer. "Ottokar said so himself in his letter: *Today it has happened*." I gripped the sink for support. "*The Lost Time Accidents*, he says. Not once but three times. What kind of joke is that? Both of his sons were convinced, not to mention his—"

"It was a comedy, that's all. A kind of game." He pulled a battered notebook from his pocket. "Marta liked to hear nonsense. She says in this book, in this journal, that he read poems to her at their tête-à-têtes—smallish comedies, with simple puzzles in them. On this day he was late, so he took a special effort to please her. The puzzle, in this case, was one of repeated first letters. How do you say this? The first letter of each of the words?"

I stared at him a moment. "Alliteration? Is that what you mean?"

"Yes! I mean this exactly! Go and look at his note. For each 'literation,' count the number of alphabet stops from the repeated letter. *Bim bam boom*, for example, would be three stops—B to C to D—do you see?—so D would be the beginning of the message. And so on, Mr. Walter, getting one letter for each grouping."

"That's a parlor trick, Artur." My head felt light again. "That's a game that you'd play with a child."

He grinned to himself in his unseeing way. "The message to Marta was one single word. Can you guess which it was?"

I shook my head slowly. He sat up with a triumphant little snort.

"*Fenchelwurst*, Mr. Walter. From the Germanic language. It means, I think, a kind of fennel sausage."

"No," I said, shaking my head. "No, Artur."

"Take this book, Mr. Toula!"

I swatted the book from his hands. "Why are you telling me this? What do you want from me? Why did you follow me here?"

"To be honest," he mumbled, "I did a bad thing."

But by that point, Mrs. Haven, I was barely listening. I couldn't accept what I was hearing—not on that day, in the state I was in. It took all my self-control to keep from hitting him.

"It may have some kind of code in it," I said. "That may be true. But there are other sentences, aren't there? There are whole passages with no alliteration. Those passages *must* have some other meaning—they wouldn't be in there otherwise." I looked at him. "Would they?"

"I don't know, Mr. Walter," Artur said quietly. A look of something like compassion crossed his face.

"You have to realize, Artur, that my family has been trying to make sense of this 'comedy,' as you call it, for the last hundred years. The last *hundred* years, do you understand me? People have wasted entire life spans trying to extract meaning from it. Crimes have been committed, Artur. All to answer this one riddle."

Artur scratched his nose, considering what I'd told him.

"But why?"

In place of a reply, my tongue found the hollow where my molar had been. I thought of you, Mrs. Haven, and of your husband, and of his airplane, and of the whole belief system that had sprung, however crookedly, from a few words scribbled on a sheet of paper.

"What about the mathematics?" I said, sinking down onto the tiles. "What about the algebra—the third page, that proof? Are you going to tell me that was nonsense, too?"

"No," Artur said, looking suddenly frightened. "No. That proof was not a portion of the *vtip*."

"Then even if you're telling me the truth—even if the letter is gibberish, a meaningless joke—that still leaves the math. And don't tell me Ottokar wrote *that* for his mistress."

Artur bowed his head. "That's the second thing I have to tell. That leaves the math, as you say. But I made certain changes."

I'll confess to you, Mrs. Haven, that I could have killed him then. I sat on my hands to keep them from closing around his dumpling-colored neck.

"Certain changes?" I said.

He bobbed his head quickly. "Before I brought the box—when I was listening to you through the wall. I stood the ∞s up straight—all of them. I turned them into eights."

"Why did you do that, Artur?"

He made a sound that might have been a laugh. "I told you," he said. "I did not care for that woman."

Monday, 09:05 EST

It's been seven sleep cycles since I saw the Timekeeper. I've been making regular expeditions to the bedroom and the kitchen, his usual haunts—but the contents of the fridge remain constant, and there's been no change in his imprint on the bed.

Chances are good, Mrs. Haven, that he'll never come back. With every iteration he's looked more spent, less recognizable, like a joke that grows more garbled with each telling. His travels through the chronosphere seem to be distorting his body, buckling and inflating it grotesquely; or maybe it's my perception that's distorting. There seems to be no way for me to tell.

By now, I'm guessing, you've decided that I've imagined Waldemar, called him into being as a tonic for my loneliness and lust for resolution: that the distortions I'm seeing are caused by my imperfect memory, forced to recall his features time and time again, like the dubbing and redubbing of some overplayed cassette. It's the likeliest explanation, I can't deny that— but its likelihood no longer troubles me. After all, Mrs. Haven, I called you into being the same way.

If there's one thing I've learned about my family by setting down this history, it's that the zone of so-called objectivity—whatever, and wherever, and whenever that may be—has always been a foreign country to us. But the great compensation of madness, as every madman knows, is that it keeps its victim company. If my own brain gave birth to the Timekeeper, in other words, why should I scorn him for it? Who's to say that it makes him less true?

XXV

AT LONG LAST, MRS. HAVEN, college happened.

Back in Orson's day—as he never tired of reminding me—a towheaded American youth of no particular ambition could sidestep higher education altogether and still be regarded as sentient; by the time I left for college, even aspiring pheromone dealers were expected to earn their BAs. This was less for educational purposes, according to my father, than as a means of establishing credit: in late twentieth-century America, he argued, you existed in proportion to your debt.

My freshman-year roommate, Karl Hornbanger, carried Orson's argument to its logical extreme, proposing to the registrar that he assume debt directly in exchange for his diploma, dispensing with his coursework altogether. "They call them 'credits' for a reason, Tolliver," he used to say, as we were falling asleep on our rubberized sanitarium-surplus mattresses. "The truth is right there in the open, beating the air with its giant batwings, for anyone with the soup-and-nuts to look." Hornbanger dropped out of school eighteen months later (which didn't surprise anyone) to work in foreclosures in Miami-Dade. By all accounts he leads a happy life.

∞

Ogilvy College ("The Sorbonne of Butternut Country") played its own modest role in the aforementioned grift, gamely parting its gates to those spurned by the Ivy League for their lack of ambition or pedigree. It had once been the Lake Erie terminus of a branch of the underground railroad, and thus had a time-honored tradition of comforting the wretched, which I'm not ashamed to say included me. I was foaming at the mouth when I arrived, in a fever to get my puberty behind me, to relinquish all rights and privileges pertaining to my Cheektowaga self. By my third semester I had clavicle-length hair and a "math rock" band that I played "tape loops" in (The Educated Consumers) and an elementary grasp of the principles of cause and effect—which came in handy, Mrs. Haven, because I'd also found a girl.

Every male of the species, I'm fairly sure, is flabbergasted by the first woman who doesn't run from him in bug-eyed horror, and goes on to suffer a kind of blissful PTSD for months thereafter—but even after adjusting for my near-total lack of sexual intelligence (not to mention my overall state of shock), Tabitha Guy was inexplicable. She was ferally at ease in her own body, as if she'd never heard of either Testament; she was pale and plump and up for almost anything. She had hair in her armpits the color of honey. She was a black studies major. And out of some occult motive—some faux-political agenda, some inscrutable kink—she was willing to lower her overalls for me (her *corduroy* overalls!) in the lockable single-stall bathroom on the fourth floor of the Clay Undergraduate Library, less than an hour before I caught the bus home for Thanksgiving.

"You can give thanks for *that*, Tolliver," she announced when it was over. "Waldy? Look at me, Waldy. How soon are you going to be sick?"

The loss of my virginity enlightened me on a number of points that everyone else seemed to know already, such as the fact that it's possible, for short periods of time, to go agreeably insane. Thanksgiving break that year was an extended hallucinogenic odyssey for which all the necessary psychoactive compounds were produced by my own stunned metabolism. I remember only three things about it with any clarity: Orson's forced-seeming cheer, the Kraut's puzzling remoteness, and a letter to me from my aunts—the first one in years—that I used as a bookmark instead of opening. I might as well have spent that week inside of Enzie's plywood crate.

Tabitha's surrender stood as the defining singularity of my duration—at least until spring term started, when it practically became an hourly event. She surrendered to me on the futon of her "divided double" in the all-girls wing of Jodorowsky Hall; she surrendered in the coed showers of my dorm, cool and arch-backed and sudsy, like a hooker in a made-for-cable movie; she surrendered pretty much anywhere, in private and in public, without even considering it surrender. For my part, I partook ravenously, hysterically, certain that my luck was temporary. I was availing myself of some providential oversight, some dimple in the cosmic status quo, and I knew that a correction would be made before too long.

What I didn't suspect, Mrs. Haven—not even in my wildest fits of adolescent mania—was that I would make the correction myself.

I can't say when I first got wind of the Ogilvy Synchronology Society, known unofficially around campus—for appropriately cryptic reasons—as the Stuttering Few. No one took the SFs seriously except the SFs themselves, who took their society so excruciatingly seriously that they never spoke its name aloud or publicized their meetings. This was rote cult behavior, of course, but it also made practical sense: self-promotion was risky at Ogilvy, especially if you were into something geeky. The Ogilvy Middle-Earth Collective (the "Elfdiddlers," in Ogilvy-speak) had learned this the hard way the previous spring. In the hope of attracting fresh blood to their weekly Helm's Deep reenactments in the college arboretum, they'd plastered the campus in Celtic-lettered flyers:

HEAR YE! HEAR YE!
ALL YE STEADFAST OF BROADSWORD
AND NIMBLE OF BOW!
ALL YE *YEOMEN* OF VIRTUE!
THE HOUR IS AT HAND.
COME DO BATTLE WITH *ORKS* IN THE ARB.

All it had taken to undo their good work was one unbeliever with a Sharpie, a few idle hours, and the idea of prefacing *ORKS* with an uppercase *D*. The Elfdiddlers never recovered.

I'd have managed to ignore the Ogilvy Synchronology Society altogether, I think, if it hadn't been for Tabitha Guy. It happened by the ruthless whim of C*F*P: as Tabitha and I reclined on her mattress one midwinter evening, both of us smug and sweat-soaked and (temporarily) immortal, I noticed a dog-eared pamphlet on the floor. Its bottom half was wedged under the bedframe, and the author's name—in a Celtic-looking font, if I remember correctly—was badly smudged, but its title was plain, even in the lava lamp's slithering light:

THE HOUR IS AT HAND.
THE HOUR ***ALWAYS*** IS AT HAND.
& SO CAN YOU!

The jumbled-clock symbol of the UCS was stamped underneath, not quite centered on the page, but I didn't need to see it. I could smell an Iterant a mile away by then, Mrs. Haven, if the wind was blowing right. Or so I'd always let myself believe.

"What's this?" I said to Tabitha, as nonchalantly as I could. She scratched one honey-colored armpit and emitted a coo.

"Tabitha. Hey."

"I'm trying to sleep, bunny. What do you want?"

I jerked the pamphlet free of the mattress, biting back my paranoia, and laid it across the humid sheet between us. "I asked you about this—" I hesitated, not sure what to call the thing. "This *literature.*"

"Oh! That," she said, yawning. Her yawn struck me as false: it seemed too athletic, too studied. "I've been meaning to show that to you, actually. There's some trippy shit in there."

I'd told Tabitha nothing about my history with the Iterants. This wasn't because I distrusted her, necessarily, but because of the vow I'd sworn to bury the teenaged iteration of Waldy Tolliver alive, along with his retainer and his collection of *Timestrider* memorabilia and the green knickerbockers his parents had dressed him up in before he was old enough to reason for himself. I was less a "new man" at college, psychosocially speaking, than a man who'd demolished his identity and reassembled the rubble along wildly incongruous lines, thereby becoming both his own executioner and his own parent. (Unlikely as this sounds, the Church of Synchronology preaches that just such a wonder is possible, once the time-consuming— and costly—Seventeenth Level of Iteration has been reached.) But we tamper with the weft of the universe at our peril, Mrs. Haven, as I was about to discover. I was beginning to suspect that the Tolliver/Toulas had had things backward from the very beginning: we'd brought our combined wills to

bear on escaping our past, when the future was the thing we should have
run from.

∞

I didn't tell Tabitha about the Iterants the night I found that pamphlet, either,
though it would have been the perfect occasion. I didn't tell her over the
course of that next week, during which period I grew steadily more guarded
and suspicious; and I didn't tell her that following Saturday—exactly seven
days from our first and only conversation about the UCS—when I suggested that we "spend some time apart."

I felt sick to my stomach as I watched the meaning of that hateful
phrase register on her lovely face; but I also felt jaded and cosmopolitan,
master of my emotions—the tragic, stiff-lipped, self-denying hero. This is
what adults do, I assured myself coolly. In reality I was terrified, hopelessly
out of my depth, gnawed to ribbons by a frantic, all-purpose jealousy that
had no fixed target and therefore applied to everything I saw. Tabitha Guy
had been an Iterant all along: I saw that clearly now. Why else would someone so exquisite have allowed my piggish fingers to besmirch her?

∞

Right or wrong, Mrs. Haven, the rest of sophomore year confirmed this
theory nicely. Girls recoiled from me as if I still had green knickerbockers
on, or my entire face were covered in lipstick, or I'd invited them to fight
dorks in the Arb. Friends ran out of patience with my customized blend of
paranoia and self-pity almost instantly—with the exception of Hornbanger,
who never listened to me very closely—and before long I was spending my
nights in the periodicals reading room on the third floor of Clay, combing
back issues of *Galaxy Science Fiction* for mentions of my father and trying
not to think about the lockable single-stall bathroom one flight up. *Galaxy*
loathed the works of Orson Card Tolliver—it hated all of his books, soft-
and hard-core alike—with a dedication I found oddly soothing. (Sample
quote: "Mr. Tolliver writes his novels for the ages. The ages between five
and eleven.") After a couple of weeks, however, even the periodicals reading room began to lose its charm.

TV helped for a while, until it suddenly didn't; and the same with Advanced Dungeons & Dragons and pornography and pot. Within a month I was gripped by the life-or-death need, well known to junkies and AA members (and regular garden-variety obsessives), for something louder than the whinging of my brain. Which is how I came to be sitting cross-legged on the floor of my dorm room one Saturday night—moderately high and bored out of my skull, but too afraid of my own thoughts to fall asleep— staring down at the unopened letter from Enzie and Genny that I'd been using as a bookmark. I opened it, Mrs. Haven, and it worked right away. By the second time through I wasn't even stoned.

> *Dearest Waldemar!*
>
> *Nearly six years have passed since your visit to Harlem: enough time to do a bit of growing up. How much you've grown since that time? this is what we've been wondering. Your father has sent us ~~pictures~~ one small picture of you, unfortunately something out of focus. You look, as far as we can tell, like an American adult—meaning rather too "fleischig." Remember to keep fit for the little girls!*
>
> *But we're interested in other manner of changes, your aunt Enzie and I. Can you think for yourself yet, Waldemar, or are you still your father's "schlemiel"? This is one thing we are curious about. For this reason we include a little "Märchen."*
>
> *An old man goes to sleep one night and has a funny dream.*
>
> *He dreams that he arrives at his workplace, ready to begin the day's business, and finds his desktop strewn with cherry pits. There are pits in the drawers, on the floor, even under his heels.*
>
> *Once the desk has been cleared, the old man's work goes well. It goes so well, in fact, that after only a few hours he gives himself a holiday. He takes his lunch as usual, savoring every bite, then goes for a walk along a cobbled street, congratulating himself on his success.*
>
> *A car surprises him in the dream, and he wakes up.*
>
> *A few hours after waking, the man arrives at his workplace and finds his desktop strewn with cherry pits. One of his assistants (a teenaged boy!) has left them there.*
>
> *Another man might prefer to dismiss these events—to attribute*

them to happenstance, or to an attack of nerves, or even to mystical sight. This old man does none of these things. He approaches the problem as a man of science would. There is meaning hidden here, and he will find it.

He has had such dreams before, he begins to recall. He has always chosen to dismiss them, as everyone else does, since such dreams are offensive to Reason. But this time the old man has a different idea. What if—he asks himself—this thing that has happened is not, in fact, odd or uncommon at all? What if it's not a freakish occurrence, but an everyday one? What if it happens to all of us, virtually every night, while we're asleep?

What if the Universe is, as other men of science have conjectured, spread out across <u>Time</u> as well as Space? What if the partial view we have—a view with the Future mysteriously missing, kept from the ever-expanding Past by the rolling windowpane we call the Present—is the effect of a <u>mentally imposed barrier</u>, one that functions only while we are awake?

This might explain the dream of the cherry pits, the old man thinks. He was seeing into the Future while he dreamt, as the driver of an automobile looks across a bridge that he has yet to cross.

Applying the principle of Occam's razor, he now pares his theory down to its essentials. If, in fact, the Universe is—as some scientists claim—composed of at least <u>four</u> dimensions, why can we fully perceive only three? What if the Attention of the dreamer, obeying no rules but the rules of association and chance, travels back and forth across the Present/Past membrane at will?

The longer he considers this point, the more absurd it seems that our movement should be restricted in this so-called Fourth Dimension, when we enjoy such freedom in the others. If we travel with the prevailing wind through Time, like children adrift in the hold of a pilotless yacht, it can only be, he decides, because we haven't learned to take our bearings yet. The sea, after all, looks the same in every direction—it's easy to find oneself sailing in circles. Why should our voyages through the chronosphere be any different?

The old man is taking his afternoon stroll when this idea arrives, and its significance is clear to him at once. It represents the summit of his rational duration. His discovery will shake the scientific world to its foundations.

He is ambling over the cobblestones, congratulating himself on this stroke of good fortune, when a car comes rolling up the street and kills him.

If you understand this much, Waldemar, you might be old enough. Are you old enough, finally? If you are then come along and see us.

ET & GT

XXVI

IN THE FALL of my third year at Ogilvy, Mrs. Haven, my father joined the Church of Synchronology. We didn't find out until later, the Kraut and myself, because he didn't stick around to clue us in. My mother had gone down to the basement one wet November afternoon, to check for flooding in the boiler room, and also to bring Orson the weird red South African tea (Redbush? Roy's Bus? *Rouge-Bouche?*) that he always insisted on drinking, only to find the door of his office wide open and its floor and bookshelves in a shocking state. The shelves were dust-free and immaculate, the drafting table had been neatly clapped together, and the purple shag rug with the Möbius-strip pattern actually looked as if it might have been shampooed. The man she was married to would have been appalled. She stood transfixed in the doorway with her mouth hanging open, swaying lightly in place, like a scientist who's had a sudden breakthrough. She felt sure, in that moment, that she'd never see Orson again.

In later years, the Kraut would come to wonder how her husband could have vanished so utterly, with a roomful of books and papers and typewriters, in the course of a day she'd spent almost entirely at home; but at the time the question barely crossed her mind. She called the police but hung up as soon as the dispatcher answered, feeling ashamed without quite knowing why. She called me at Ogilvy and left a rambling message, full of cleaning tips and Cheektowaga gossip, that made no mention of my father's disappearance. What surprised her most, she told me afterward, was her relative composure. Being a woman of science, she put this down to denial, and braced herself for the inevitable hair-tearing, teeth-gnashing hysterics.

She was still waiting, two and a half weeks later, when I arrived home for Thanksgiving.

I found her at the kitchen counter, the picture of bland domesticity, peeling a heap of fingerling potatoes. "*There* you are, Waldy," she said. "Orson's gone."

Somehow I understood her instantly. "To Znojmo?" (A visit to his father's birthplace—followed, if all went well, by application for political asylum in the Czech Republic—had been a hobbyhorse of Orson's recently.)

She smiled to herself and kept peeling. "I doubt it."

"Where to, then? To Harlem?"

"I've spoken to your aunts—both of them. They haven't heard from him in months." Her smile stiffened slightly. "They suggested I might try the Fuzzy Fruits."

"That can't be true," I said. "I don't believe it."

The Kraut didn't answer. She was still, at just past forty, a singularly beautiful woman, at least to me. It was painful to see her so chastened.

"Why the hell would he want to go *there*? Why to the Iterants, in the name of all that's holy?"

"In the name of all that's holy," the Kraut repeated. She gave an airless little laugh. "What a funny choice of words. That must be it."

"What do you mean?"

"They've been calling your father a prophet for years. What middle-aged man wouldn't like the sound of that?"

Neither of us spoke for a time.

"Is there gas in your car?" she said, setting her knife down abruptly. When the Kraut decided a subject was finished, Mrs. Haven, she wrung its neck without remorse and tossed it in the river. There was no going back for her, only ahead. She was like the nineteenth-century chronoverse that way.

I nodded. "Half a tank."

"Excellent! We need to buy a turkey."

∞

For reasons I can't entirely describe, Mrs. Haven, those four days with the Kraut were as pleasant as any I'd passed in that house. For the first time since I'd been a toddler, the two of us had the place entirely to ourselves, an extended weekend's worth of idle hours, and an almost mystical ability to see each other as we were. The quirks that had driven me bonkers for years—her way of looking past you when she spoke, her sitcom-Nazi accent, her earsplitting, glass-cutting laugh—now somehow had the opposite effect. I'd taken her for granted as a child, the way spoiled children will— she was so constant, so effective, so *elemental* that she was often hard to see. Orson had always been sharply in focus, never anywhere but front and center, the cardinal or potentate or dragon in the foreground of the painting; my mother, by contrast, was the fortress in the distance, or the range of sky-blue mountains, or the gauzy blue dome of the sky itself.

The chicken-sized turkey we ended up buying was our single concession to the holiday spirit. We ate it from sheets of tinfoil spread out on the counter, along with Triscuits and cans of Genessee Cream Ale.

"So what happens now?" I asked her, feeling worldly and urbane. "Will you guys get divorced?"

She laughed. "He hasn't left me for a woman, Waldy. He's left me for himself."

"Does he really believe all that UCS horseshit?"

"I hope so, for his sake. Otherwise it won't be very fun."

"Maybe he's trying to infiltrate the Iterants, to figure them out—to study them from the inside." My voice had gone childish. "Maybe this is about the Accidents."

"The Accidents?" She looked at me sharply. "Who's been talking to you about that?"

"There's a mystery about them—Orson told me that much. I know they're supposed to be some kind of code, but no one understands what for. I know they're why my great-grandfather died."

The Kraut heaved a sigh. "If they're code for anything at all, sweetheart, it's self-delusion. For all the good that ridiculous phrase has done this family, it might as well have been written by a chimpanzee on a banana peel."

"But don't you think there's a chance—"

"I'd rather talk about something else." She pursed her lips. "Your future, for example."

"Groan."

"You'll have to declare a major soon, and—"

"I've already declared a major."

That surprised her. "What is it?"

"History."

"History?"

I gave a solemn nod.

"History!" the Kraut repeated. "I'll be damned."

The relief in her voice was unmistakable. I hadn't said writing or panhandling or gunrunning or—God forbid!—physics. I'd said the first thing that had popped into my head, Mrs. Haven, to tell you the truth. But I liked the sound of it.

"You'll have to write some kind of thesis, won't you?" the Kraut said, once she'd recovered her bearings. "The challenge of history, I've always thought, is that the field is so big. You've got millennia of stupidity and hysteria to choose from."

"I've thought about that, too," I told her. "I'm going to stick to the hysteria I know."

"Very good," she said, taking a thoughtful sip of her beer. "Write what you know."

She was wondering what the hell that meant, of course, and so was I.

Looking back, it's clear to me that I had this chronicle in mind already, though neither of us knew it at the time—at least not consciously. This was part of what made that weekend so extraordinary: we were able to chatter on about the future happily, to treat it as a glowing white unknown, free of any fear of its petrifying blankness. We had no need of tarock cards or exclusion bins. The one thing we knew about the future was that it was likely to be—that it *had* to be—different from the past. That was all we knew, Mrs. Haven, but it was enough.

It dawned on me gradually, as the hours and days passed, that my mother had plans of her own, and that some of them were intricately plotted; which could only mean she'd seen the end approaching. She wanted—after a twenty-year hiatus—to finish her doctorate, if possible at the

University of Vienna. I bluffed my way through these conversations, nodding and frowning as if deep in thought, doing my best to hide my wonderment. The Kraut would be returning to Europe, she told me, and possibly not coming back. It occurred to me at one point—I think it was late Sunday morning, eating apricot *palatschinken* in the kitchen—that I'd never before seen her so happy.

"It's for the best that he left, then," I said tentatively. "I can't see Orson moving to Vienna."

The Kraut didn't answer.

"He was a good father, basically," I continued. "I know he meant well. But sometimes days would go by—more than days—when I didn't understand a single word he said. He's like—" I hesitated. "I don't really know what. I guess he's like Enzie and Genny."

"You're right," said the Kraut. "He's *exactly* like them."

"That's what I can't figure out. Why is it that no one's like Orson but Enzie and Genny, and no one's like Enzie and Genny but him?"

She said nothing to that. But she looked as though she wanted to say something.

"You must have thought about this, Ursula. It must have occurred to you, some time or other, that there was—I mean, that there was kind of an unusual—"

The Kraut took my hand in both of hers and stared at me. "You're too close to see it," she said. "How *could* you see it? It's all you've ever known."

I didn't like the way she was looking at me. "What is it," I said carefully, "that I'm too close to see?"

"Don't you understand yet, Waldy, that your family is mentally ill?"

∞

I arrived back at Ogilvy flush with high-minded purpose, having managed to convince myself on the three-hour drive back from Buffalo that I was a budding connoisseur of human history. Tabitha and pot and social paranoia, not to mention the UCS in all its forms and guises, were the stuff of my personal past. I was determined to call my own bluff, to focus my fractured attention into a photon beam of sober inquiry: to get to work on my thesis immediately, or at least to start going to class.

All of which might actually have happened, Mrs. Haven, if C*F*P had only looked the other way.

I was six weeks into the kind of kitchen-sink cinema studies course (The Scl/erotic Muse: Introduction to Postwar European Cinema, 1944–78) that undergrads laboring under delusions of profundity generally take, when the answer to the riddle of my great-uncle's disappearance—or a maddening complication of that riddle, depending on your point of view—was dropped into my lap as I sat in my dorm's "media lounge," sulking my way through yet another loveless Friday night. Hornbanger and I were halfway through *The Damned*, Luchino Visconti's '69 Nazisploitation campfest; he thought it "shredded", my feelings were mixed. Hornbanger (who was about to drop out, had his bags packed already, was only waiting for his stipend check to clear) had just done two bumps of a flesh-colored powder that he claimed to have stolen from a birth-control clinic; I was brutally sober. My attention was starting to drift when a heavyset man with a passing resemblance to Reichsmarschall Goering shuffled grouchily across the mise-en-scène, scratching his back with the butt of his Luger. I sat up at once. The Goering look-alike, who appeared to be in early middle age, blinked nearsightedly into the camera for a second or two; then he adjusted his gun belt, which looked too small for him, and gave a half-hearted "Sieg Heil."

"That is one chubby Nazi," Hornbanger observed.

"That's my great-uncle Waldemar Toula."

"Say huh?"

I'd never seen Waldemar in the flesh, needless to say, but I'd spent hours examining the pictures of him reproduced in various histories of the Third Reich, and I'd identified him in a sepia-tinted portrait of the family in Znojmo. This portrait, in turn, had led to my greatest discovery: a photograph of my grandfather and his brother from their student days in Vienna—in front of the Schloss Belvedere, of all places—gawping into the camera like the starry-eyed yokels they were. Waldemar is a sight to behold in the snapshot, assured in his new-minted manhood—worlds more handsome than his elder brother, in spite of their identical shit-eating grins. His smile doesn't quite reach his eyes, however, which seem unaccountably tired. I might not have recognized the world-weary Nazi in Visconti's film if not for that photograph, liberated from a shoe box in our terminally cluttered garage. But knowing it as well as I did—having scrutinized it over and over, until it was rotogravured into my memory—there was no chance of mistaking the resemblance. Those flat eyes could belong to no one else.

∞

I left school two weeks later, on the same day as Hornbanger. I didn't drop out officially, didn't make a show of it the way he did—I just left. My ancient Subaru refused to start, so I bummed a ride from him as far as Pittsburgh. You wouldn't have known from Hornbanger's looks that he was a metalhead, necessarily, but his driving style expressed it eloquently. He got us out of Ohio without switching lanes once, jerking his flat-topped head along to Cannibal Corpse and Deicide and Morbid Angel, running his dad's late-model Taurus up the backsides of trucks like a heifer in heat. He dropped me off at a truck stop that featured a Taco Bell and a Dunkin' Donuts grafted together into a two-headed hydra of dining convenience, still a novelty in the early nineties. It seemed as good a place to hitch a lift as any.

"So long, Tolliver. Good luck finding your pops."

"I already know where to find him, Karl. But thanks."

"I know where to find mine, too," Hornbanger said, gunning his engine. "At the Seminole Rez in Tampa, playing slots. If things don't work out on your mission, maybe you could liberate my dad instead. But I'm not holding my breath or anything."

I didn't know what to say to that, so I gave him a thumbs-up and stepped back from the car. It was late afternoon and the parking lot was hot and bluish gray and weirdly empty. Hornbanger did a few doughnuts, flashed me the devil horns, then rolled off at a surprisingly moderate speed. He had no one to impress anymore, Mrs. Haven, and neither did I.

I'd left school for the usual reasons, I suppose, but also for some I considered distinctive. I knew plenty of kids at Ogilvy whose mothers were naturalized U.S. citizens, for example, but I'd never heard of any of them choosing to reverse the procedure, and if anybody else's father had been spirited away by a cult of long-haired, corduroy-sporting time fetishists, word of it had somehow passed me by. The clincher, however, was this: I'd become convinced, since seeing him waddle across that Cinecittà soundstage, that the Black Timekeeper of Czas had escaped the destruction of the

Äschenwald camp, just as the conspiracy-theorists had claimed. But I went all those nutjobs one better, Mrs. Haven. I'd decided that he was still alive—here and now, at the complacent, listless end of the twentieth century—and that it was up to me, and only me, to hunt him down.

∞

Three days later, at 10:43 EST, I found myself standing at an ivy-choked gate on a quaint country lane, debating whether or not to ring its fat brass bell. Above the bell hung a plate, even brassier and more expensive-looking:

THE UNITED CHURCH OF SYNCHRONOLOGY
∞
VILLA OUSPENSKY

I studied my reflection in the plate, adjusting my posture, taking deep breaths and stalling for time; time obliged, for once, and moved with tidal slowness. The gate was almost imperceptibly ajar. Beyond it, up a violet-green lawn—a color I'd never seen before in nature—stood a gingerbread house, in full view of the road. I passed through the gate without ringing the bell.

I had no burning desire to see my father, Mrs. Haven, least of all in that place, but I needed his help. I needed a hint of some kind, however grudging or clumsy—some small clue as to where to begin. Not that I felt pessimistic about my quest, strange to say: I felt pessimistic about everything else—as any self-respecting college dropout and/or child of a broken home should—but not that. I knew from the start that I'd find Waldemar. In a sense I'd always carried him within me.

No one met me on the lawn, or on the ∞-shaped drive, or even on the stoop of the villa, though I felt myself being observed. They let me ring the doorbell—fatter and brighter and brassier still—and made me wait just long enough to weaken my morale. Eventually an intercom sputtered and a woman's voice asked me, somewhat frostily, to state my name and business.

"Waldemar Tolliver. I'm here to see my father."

"Your father?" A southern accent, I decided, or possibly English. "And who might that be?"

"You know damn well who my father is."

No response came. Everything seemed to hold still, from the sparrows in the bushes to the clouds above the trees. I'd just begun to ask myself whether I'd picked the wrong UCS outpost—whether the Kraut might have had bad intel about Orson, or I'd misunderstood—when the lacquered door swung inward with a smooth, hydraulic sigh, like the hatch of a spaceship, and a beautiful dark-eyed woman with hands of polished wax pulled me inside.

She was the whitest and most elegant woman I'd ever seen, Mrs. Haven, including the Kraut, who (as you know yourself) was as pale as a fish. Somehow she even gripped me elegantly. Her hands weren't really made of wax, of course, although they looked—and even felt—as if they were. She seized me by the elbow and jerked me hard across the threshold, then receded holographically down a tastefully furnished hall, as if my presence there were no concern of hers. Her bare feet made no sound on the cream-colored runner. Before the latch had closed behind me she was gone.

I took a moment to steady myself. The experience had been appropriately cultish so far, which pleased me on some adolescent level. The air in the corridor seemed to hum very slightly, and I could feel the floor vibrating through the soles of my sneakers, although this might have been a trick of my nerves. The walls were smooth and bare and starkly lit. No one else was in sight. I took off my shoes for some reason—decorum, perhaps—and began creeping forward. The length of the hallway proved tricky to gauge in the flat, bloodless light. I expected to catch sight of the woman when I turned the first corner, but I found only a second length of hallway, as bare as the first, ending in another left-hand turn. It reminded me of something.

It reminded me of the corridor in Enzie and Genny's apartment.

I pulled back around the corner and rested my head against the wall, breathing in stuttering sucks. All my false courage left me. I wanted to get out of there, Mrs. Haven. I'd made a terrible mistake. The floor *was* vibrating—I was sure of it now. It occurred to me then—how could I have overlooked it?—that there were no doors or windows in sight. The wall was shuddering behind me: I could feel it in my shoulders and my spine. I tried to recall what I'd just glimpsed around the corner. There might have been a sort of door—a small one, maybe six feet past the turning. But I was too unnerved to take another look.

It meant something—it had to—that the interior of the Iterants' headquarters was laid out like the Archive, but *what* it meant was beyond me. I knew no more than this: that the arrangement of Enzie and Genny's rooms was connected to something secret, or was possibly the *expression* of that secret; and that this secret was a vital and ominous one, at least in relation to me. If Haven had discovered what that secret was—or had access to someone who did, such as Orson—but I stopped myself there. It was better not to attempt to guess what that might mean.

When I forced myself to round the corner a second time, still shaken and woozy, the white lady was waiting. There *had* been a door—narrow and knobless and low—and we passed through it, into a kind of winter garden. Its ceiling was of glass, like the roof of a greenhouse, and the space itself was small and shadowless. There were couches arranged in a ring— she led me to one of them, and sat down beside me—but I took in almost nothing, in those first dazed moments, but the mural covering the room's eight walls.

"Well, Mr. Tolliver? How do you like the decor?"

I opened my mouth and gave a sort of peep. The mural was done in thin washes of paint—so thin that the plaster's imperfections showed through—with the most delicate of brushes. Running counterclockwise, it depicted all the great theorists of time, from Herodotus to Newton to Stephen J. Hawking. The entire hall of fame and infamy stood assembled on those walls: everyone I'd ever heard Orson disparage or praise. The figures were rendered in one-to-one scale, precise as Audubon engravings, their hands and faces more alive than any photo could have been. They looked so human, in fact, that it took me a moment to see what was wrong about them.

Each figure had the head and the limbs of a man—or a woman, in a handful of cases—and the glossy, reddish body of an insect.

"What is this place?"

"This is the Listening Room. Mr. Haven's personal retreat."

"Oh."

We gazed up at the mural for a time.

"Quite a feast for the eyes, isn't it? Most people who see it—not that there are many of them, mind you—tend to be rather impressed." She parted her pale lips and stared at my own, as if in expectation of a kiss. "Are *you* impressed, Mr. Tolliver?"

"Can I see my father now?"

"Let me ask you a question. *Why* do you want to see him?"

"I'm his son."

She patted my knee. "Sons like to visit their fathers now and again. That's perfectly in order." She turned back to the mural. "I should tell you, however, that the Prime Mover hasn't received any visitors in quite some time."

"If you're trying to stop me—"

"I have no intention of trying to stop you, Mr. Tolliver."

She led me back out of the room, moving with a dreamlike lack of effort, and I seemed to follow her in the same way. There were people in the corridor now: young men and women in tweeds and pastels, carrying clipboards and padded manila envelopes and sheaves of yellow paper. We went up a steep flight of stairs, then another, then another, and arrived at a low attic room. The man I found there, reclining in a La-Z-Boy beside a dormer window, bore a remarkable resemblance to my father. He waited for the woman to go, then smiled at me and asked me how I was. I said I was doing okay.

"I knew you'd be coming, Waldy. And now here you are!"

He placed a sly sort of emphasis on the word *knew*, I remember, as if he'd been informed of my approach by a network of spies, or predicted it by means of calculus, or seen it reflected in a mystic pool.

"My name isn't Waldy," I heard myself answer. "I changed it after you ditched us." I racked my brain for a moment. "It's Jack."

His only response was a shrug. He had my father's blunt features, he smelled like my father, and he was wearing a shirt I must have seen a thousand times—but something was off. He wasn't as *Orson*-ish, for want of a better word, as he ought to have been. He sat there so passively, utterly sapped of authority, like a codger in some cut-rate nursing home. He looked a decade older than he was.

"What do you do in this place all day long?"

"Glad you asked, Jack! The answer is simple. Whatever I want."

I nodded, taking in the dank, untidy room. "What did you do today?"

"That's easy! I've been looking out this window at the trees."

"At the trees. Okay."

He heaved a drawn-out sigh and rubbed his belly.

"Okay," I repeated. "I'm glad that you have—that you're happy, I mean."
I hesitated. "I wanted to ask—"

"I had a thought!" he announced. "It hit while I was looking at the
trees. I'd like to lay it on you, Jack. I'd like to hear *your* take."

I said nothing to that. My father cleared his throat and pointed out the
window.

"In contemplating the natural world, Jack, we tend to distinguish between objects in motion—squirrels, let's say, or sparrows—and things that
are fixed: flower beds and ginkgo trees and such. It's *simpler* that way, and
it seems to make sense." He belched gently into his fist. "But that's just one
way, among many, of perceiving the world. Outside this window right now,
the grass is extending itself upward, and the ginkgos and dogwoods are
doing the same. The flowers in that bed there—right there, along the patio—
are revolving to follow the path of the sun. You get what I'm saying? All
this stuff is *in motion*. Our senses are cued to a rate set at random—one
speed out of an infinitude—and we mistake it for the only speed there is."

I said nothing to this, either. I never should have come. I realized that
now.

Orson squinted at me. "Why'd you come here, Jack? Is there something
you want?"

"I'm not sure."

"Don't shit a shitter."

"I'm not—" I stopped myself. "To be honest, I need your advice."

"I suspected as much." He grabbed a lever on his armrest and winched
himself upright. He seemed like Orson to me now, or close enough. "What's
the nature of the problem? Is it money? Is it girls?"

"Neither, actually. I wanted—"

"It *isn't* girls? Why the hell not?"

"What I really—"

"You're not an *enculeur*, are you? A French pastry baker? A swish?"

"Orson, I'm not even sure what that means."

"Never mind." He tugged at his beard. "How's this for a potential course of action. Why don't you tell me what the fuck you want."

"I want to talk about the Timekeeper."

"The which?"

"Waldemar Gottfriedens von Toula, the Black Timekeeper of Czas." I waited until his bleary eyes met mine. "I've got a feeling that he might still be alive."

"A *feeling*, eh?"

Something in his sidelong glance encouraged me. I told him, as quickly as I could, about my revelation in the media lounge at Ogilvy. Hearing the words as I spoke them, I realized they sounded absurd, even childish; but Orson, for once, gave me his full attention. When I'd finished, he wiped his nose and turned back to the window.

"Well, Orson?" I said. "What do you think?"

"I think it's ridiculous."

He was right, of course—it *was* ridiculous. I practically laughed with relief. "You really do?"

"Of course I do." He shook his head. "I said the same thing to the First Listener yesterday."

I bit down on my thumb to keep from shouting. Orson stared imperturbably out through the glass.

"Come on over here, Jack. I'll show you where I get *my* feelings from."

I joined him at the window. On the lawn behind the villa, in diaphanous dresses that managed to look ethereal and uncomfortable at once, two stoned-looking redheads with sixties-style beehives were pulling up weeds. Their trim, sweating haunches made twin egg-shaped prints through the cloth.

"Orson," I said, taking hold of his arm. "Look at me for a second. I know you have no reason to help me with this, other than the fact that I'm your son—"

"My *alleged* son."

"—but I need to know what Haven said to you about the Timekeeper. If the Iterants have hit on the same idea, then there has to be a reason, don't you see? Waldemar had carte blanche in that camp of his, and all the room and resources he needed. If it's true that he escaped, when the Soviets came, by slipping out through a hole in the fabric of—"

"Haven's a cult leader, Waldy. A *cult leader*. Don't you get what that means?"

"I know what he is. But if—let's say *if*—we track Waldemar down, we could finally put an end to all of this. To everything that's gone wrong with us—as a family, I mean—for the last hundred years. We'd be doing humanity—"

"Ah!" my father said. "Of course. *Humanity*."

I took hold of his arm. "I'll tell you what I think, Orson. I think our curse doesn't have anything to do with the Lost Time Accidents at all. Our troubles began with Waldemar—not with his father or the Patent Clerk or anybody else. We've been ashamed for generations now, ashamed and paranoid and isolated, and *not* because we can't figure out some non-sense scribbled in a notebook. All your grandfather did, really, was get hit by a car. But his son—your own uncle, Orson—killed hundreds of people, possibly even thousands. Our curse is that we've looked the other way."

Orson shifted in his armchair and said nothing.

"But if we can catch him—are you listening?—we could finally start over." I let go of his arm. "I need your help, Orson. I think he's somewhere in the present, in the *now*. Maybe somewhere close by."

He was looking at me again, not at the jailbait out on the lawn. His eyes were wider than I'd ever seen them.

"It's in you," he murmured. "It skipped a generation—thank God!— but now you're infected." He gripped the peeling arms of his recliner. "I can see it on you, Waldy, and I can hear it in your voice. I can practically *smell* it coming off you."

"What are you talking about?" I murmured, though of course I knew perfectly well.

My father covered his eyes. "In spite of everything—everything I did, since you were small, to keep you safe—the Accidents have got you." A muffled sob escaped him. "Enzie told me, the first time I brought you to see her. She *knew*. 'There's nothing to be done,' she said to me. 'It's in the genes.'"

"The Kraut told me the same thing," I said. "She thinks our whole family is mentally ill."

"Smart lady, your mother. She's right—I'm the only exception."

"She doesn't quite see it that way."

For an instant he looked genuinely pained. "I can't help what she thinks. Not anymore."

Looking down at my father then, swaddled in his seedy recliner like the ailing, aging pervert that he was, it struck me that I finally understood him. He'd been abused in his time, disparaged and manipulated and underpaid, and even—once the Fuzzy Fruits had gotten to him—hounded; but until recently he'd never been ignored. His heart attack had been a sign to him, a harbinger, a marker of the passing of his prime. Each new novel had sold slightly worse than the last; *starporn* was a dated term now, rarely made use of even as a slight; the Kraut's attention had migrated back to her work, and his son seemed to have checked out altogether. Greater men than Orson Card Tolliver have converted late in life—most, I'm guessing, for similar reasons. At least my father was converting to a religion he'd invented.

"What did you think of the mural?" he said, cheerful again. "I'm assuming you've seen it. They show everybody."

"I meant to ask about that, actually. The faces are human, but the bodies look like—"

"You'll have to ask Miss Greer. She painted it."

"Miss Greer?" This took me a few seconds to process. "Do you mean that lady downstairs?"

Orson nodded.

"What is Miss Greer, exactly? Is she some kind of church administrator, or—"

"Miss Greer is a synthetic human being."

"What?"

He eased his La-Z-Boy backward and puffed out his chest. "Miss Greer is an android—*Auto sapiens*, to use the industry term—created for my pleasure and relief."

As I recall it, Mrs. Haven, right here was where my tolerance reached its limit. If my father was playing a game of some kind, I wanted no part of it; and the other possibility—that he was demented, or high, or insane, as the Kraut seemed to think—was more than I was willing to accept. I'd come to the Villa Ouspensky with some underbaked notion of bringing him home—even freeing him by force, if necessary—but now I saw this for the pipe dream that it was. There was nothing more that I could do for him.

"I'm going to ask you one last thing, if you don't mind."

"Go ahead, Jack! Fire away." He made six-shooter gestures at me with both hands.

"What made you leave the Kraut like that?"

He frowned. "Like what, exactly?"

"Like a coward."

The Orson I'd known would have blown his stack at this, rightly or wrongly; the current Orson heaved a wistful sigh. "She's a tough one, your mother—you know that yourself. She'd have demanded to know *why* I was going away, and I'd have had no answer for her." He took my shoulder and squeezed it. "None that wouldn't have caused her distress."

Something snapped in me then, Mrs. Haven. Strung out and/or senile though my father may have been, I wanted to kick his nicotine-stained teeth down the back of his throat.

"You know something, Orson? That's not a good enough reason. Not even close. As a matter of fact, it's a goddamn—"

"Also, there were extenuating circumstances," he cut in, as though the notion had only just occurred to him. "I'd learned, on the previous morning, that my current iteration has come due."

"Spare me the cult-speak. What I want from you is a straight-forward—"

"Cancer of the small intestine. Stage three, whatever that means." He beamed up at me. "That straightforward enough?"

A particle of dust turned in the sunlit air between us. The wallpaper, which was coming loose around the soot-grimed window, was patterned with tiny, shabby-looking fleurs-de-lis. Everything in that awful room was shabby, my father included, and everything outside was clear and bright.

"So that's it?" I croaked, my throat thick, my voice breaking. "So that's it, Dad? You're going to die?"

"That appears to be the general consensus." He shifted in his chair and closed his eyes. "I've never been all that troubled by dying, to tell you the truth. Must be my natural aversion to cliché."

∞

I'd expected the Iterants to hold me prisoner in the villa, or at least to de-tain me until Haven arrived, but they did no such thing. The house seemed deserted when I left Orson's room, the way it had seemed when I'd first been let in, and I sat on the second-floor landing with my head in my hands for what felt like a very long time. Our talk had left me hollow and weak, as if my organs had been harvested—discreetly and painlessly—while my father rambled and evaded my questions.

When my nausea had passed I continued downstairs without caring who saw me. I was reaching for the front door when an elegant white hand closed around my wrist.

"One moment, Mr. Tolliver."

I turned to face her, prepared for the worst, and saw to my surprise that she looked frightened. She smelled—faintly but unmistakably—of hair-spray and coffee and sweat. So much for the "synthetic human" theory.

"Let go of me, Miss Greer. I'm not my father."

"Let's suppose, Mr. Tolliver, that there's a tiny grain of truth to your idea. Not an *enormous* grain, mind you, but just enough. There would likely be people—individuals, or even entire groups—who'd have an in-terest in keeping that truth to themselves." Her voice dropped so low that I could barely hear her. "Don't go to the General Lee. It's being watched."

"What do you mean?" I said, feeling queasy again. "Who's watching it?"

"You don't need to go to Harlem, Waldy. Use your head a little. You're a history major. You ought to *know* where to go next."

"I'm trying to come up with a reason to trust you, Miss Greer."

"Do you think you're the only one—you and the rest of your family—with an interest in turning back time?"

She glanced quickly over her shoulder, then unlocked the door and pulled it smoothly open. I stepped out onto the stoop, feeling as though anything in the world might happen next. It ought to have been a good feeling, Mrs. Haven, but it wasn't.

"Can I ask you why you're telling me all this?"

She gave a clipped laugh. "I'm in love with your father. Is that so hard to imagine?"

"It is, actually. What's in it for you?"

"I had no choice in the matter—I thought you'd been informed. I'm an autobot, created for his pleasure and relief."

She gave another, harsher laugh and shut the door.

Monday, 09:05 EST

I was on my way back from the bathroom, Mrs. Haven, when I saw him.
He lay spread-eagled in the Archive, around a slight crook in the tunnel,
and only the heels of his wingtips were visible. His eyes came open when I
reached him, identified me, then fell closed again. His face was not a face I
recognized. If not for his shoes and his tattered green satchel I might not
have known him at all.

"There you are, *Nefflein*," he managed to rasp. "I've been eavesdrop-
ping again, as you can see."

He gestured at his lap, wincing from even that small effort, and I saw
my latest pages scattered there. The top few were coated with a fine, slate-
gray dust, as though they'd traveled with him a great distance. Some of
them were dog-eared at the corners: passages, presumably, that he took issue with. He asked if he might have a drink of water.

When I returned with the water he was sitting upright, or as near as he
could manage, and my manuscript lay neatly stacked beside him. He took
the glass from me and drained it, then let out a sigh—long and damp and
contented—and sucked in enough air to speak.

"Judging by the look on your face, *Nefflein*, you're asking yourself why
I make these visits."

"You come because of me. I understand that now."

He nodded. "And because of the book."

I took the manuscript and leafed through it, fingering the occasional
dog-eared corner. "It looks as though you've found some more errata."

"Not at all," he said, smiling a little. "Those are places where you've gotten something right."

It was the first joke we'd shared, and it seemed to ease his pain, or at least to distract him a little. I refilled his glass and let him drink, in no hurry to ask my next question. I had very few left.

"Tell me what happened at Äschenwald."

His smile was gone before I'd finished speaking. "No use talking about *that*. I set everything down, clear as day, in my protocols." His voice cracked. "If you care to consult—"

"Your protocols describe how you did what you did. That doesn't interest me, Uncle. I want to know why."

"I've told you already."

"Tell me again."

He seemed to pull back into the wall of trash behind him. "Why do you persist in the delusion that my crimes are your concern? If our positions were reversed, *Nefflein*, I'd feel no such responsibility—I can assure you of that."

"That's the difference between us," I heard myself say, and I felt the Archive tremble as I spoke. "That's the difference between us," I told him again. "That's why you and I are not the same."

I had my answer at last, Mrs. Haven, and the Timekeeper knew it.

"Are you satisfied?" he wheezed, his voice heavy with defeat. "Will you leave me in peace?"

"Not just yet. Tell me what happened when the Red Army came. Tell me how you escaped."

His face grew distant and set, and for a moment it seemed as if he might refuse. But he was only remembering—or attempting to remember. Eventually he coughed and sat upright.

∞

"It was the crowning act of my duration, of course, but it was done in the blink of an eye. I'd always conceived of time travel as a matter of *addition*, if you understand me: of creating a machine, or an approach, or a propensity. In fact, as I discovered quite by accident, it proved a simple matter of subtraction. It happened naturally, effortlessly, as a function—in perfect accordance with my theory—of environmental stress. The Red Army had just overrun the compound. My intention was simply to excise myself from the timestream; I never thought of it as an escape. I'd calculated that the event would be immediate—that the extrachronological ether would reject me as an alien object, like a body attacking a virus—and that I'd return to the instant I'd left. At that point the Russians would find me, and I'd attempt to negotiate terms; or the partisans would find me, and beat me to death with their rifles. I was reconciled, by necessity, to either of these outcomes. It would have been irrational to hope for any other.

"Instead I found myself cut free absolutely, expending my duration in haphazard snatches of time, with no control over the direction of each 'translation.' Eventually, in the course of my wanderings, two constants became evident. The span of each chrononavigatory leap was a factor of seven solar years—not unlike the life cycle of a cicada, fittingly enough—and my spatial coordinates were never affected. No matter *when* I found myself, in other words, I found myself exactly where I'd been.

"The first of these translations—which seemed instantaneous, just as I'd predicted—deposited me in the depths of a forest, among a landscape of overgrown, box-shaped depressions which I recognized, with no small amazement, as the ruins of the Äschenwald camp. I had no guess as to the year—it might have been seven years into the future, or forty-nine, or seven hundred—but I began walking toward the sun, which was setting, as soon as I'd recovered from my shock. I felt surprisingly little sorrow as I stumbled through that dense, unpeopled forest, and even less regret: there can be no greater joy, for a scientist, than the thrill of complete vindication. My crimes seemed trifling to me, the actions of some vague acquaintance, some half-forgotten relative. My biography had been reduced to a single entry. I'd made a guess—the greatest guess since Galileo's marble—and I'd been proven right.

"The next translation happened just before the sun went down. It dropped me without warning onto a field of steaming tarmac: the parking area for a Soviet-administered *sovkhoz* the forest had been flattened to make room for. The year, I would soon learn, was 1959. I got my bearings quickly: fifties Poland, in certain respects, was not so different from the German Reich. I made my way to Warszawa in the guise of a Czech day laborer, hitching rides and doing odd jobs for my fare. The skills I'd learned in Budapest came back to me readily, and I made my living in the capital—once I finally arrived there—as a thief. My plan was to bribe my way over the border, and I was saving my *złoty* to that end when the next breach in the chronosphere occurred: forty-nine years backward, to June sixteenth, 1910. This was a considerable frustration, I have to confess. Crossing the border was no longer a problem—there wasn't any border to speak of—but the money I'd saved was now worthless. I was thrown back, yet again, onto the kindness of strangers.

"It took me seven grueling weeks to reach Vienna. My idea had originally been to find my father and disclose myself to him, as the ultimate proof of his theory; or, barring that, to locate my twenty-one-year-old self and do the same. By the time I crossed into Moravia, however, my objective had changed. I had no memory, after all, of an encounter with my future self, and the dangers of tampering with so-called past events remained unknown. I decided to track Kaspar down instead—if possible at some point *after* our encounter at Trattner's, in 1938. This was a great deal harder than you might suppose. I knew he would leave for America, of course; but I was a prisoner of 1908, remember, with no access, temporal or spatial, to his destination there.

"I'd been in Vienna less than three months, however—all praise to chance and fate and Providence!—when my predicament was rendered null and void. I was strolling along the Ringstrasse on a glorious late-October morning, dressed in a suit of saffron-colored twill, when a colorless curtain fell over the sun and the gravel beneath my wingtips turned to tar. No sooner had this occurred than a girl on a bicycle—a student at the university, wearing clothes that would have gotten her institutionalized, frankly, in 1908—clipped me with her handlebars and sent me flying. My twill suit was torn at the crotch and the shoulder; the girl was only slightly harmed in body—poor darling!—but thoroughly shaken in spirit. And her alarm only deepened, needless to say, when I asked politely what the year might be.

"'Nineteen seventy-three,' the girl stammered, then spent the better part of an hour trying to coax me to the hospital to test for a concussion. She gave up eventually, but only after I'd allowed her to buy me a new pair of trousers—the very ones I'm wearing now, in fact.

"I'd arrived at the ideal time and place to continue my search, and I went to the municipal archives that same afternoon. I was quickly able to establish that Kaspar had left Europe by a packet steamer, the *Comtesse Celeste*, bound for New York from Genoa by way of Spain. Sentimental numbskull though he was, I'd nevertheless expected my brother to have made a name for himself in the New World; imagine my surprise and dismay, if you can, when I found no mention of him in any of the papers. I cursed his lack of ambition, *Nefflein*, I can tell you. There was nothing for it, at that juncture, but to become an immigrant myself.

"I made my way by train to Naples, where the cheapest New York–bound steamers had once docked, and resolved to wait there to be knocked back to the first years of the century, when emigration to America was as simple as paying one's fare. This took far longer than I'd anticipated: nearly seven years of my innate duration, during which span I completed no fewer than eighty translations. I saw Naples in ruins in 1945, after the brunt of the Allied invasion; I saw it forty-two years later, during a garbage crisis so extreme that it was agony to breathe. I grew to feel more at home in that great city than I had in any other, and would gladly have passed my whole duration there; but when my chance finally came—on May seventeenth, 1903—I seized it at once.

"I made the Atlantic crossing without a single breach—which was fortunate, *Nefflein*, considering that I was in the middle of the ocean—but I'd no sooner set foot on the pier at South Street than the air cleared of coke dust and a roar smote my ears and the sun disappeared behind a wall of steel and cinder block and glass. Never before had a translation struck so violently: it was as if a cliff had been thrown skyward by an earthquake. I wandered westward from the river in bewilderment, sporting clothing generations out of date. Luckily for me, this was Manhattan at the close of the twentieth century, and no one on the street looked at me twice.

"Somewhere in Chinatown I picked a drunk's pocket and took the money into a corner shop—a bodega, I should say—for something to eat. My first meal in the United States, I'm pleased to report, was a chicken cutlet sandwich on a roll. I examined that morning's edition of *The New York Times* as I ate, and found that I could follow most of the pieces, especially those that dealt with civic matters. The date was still the seventeenth of May—my birth month, as you may recall—which struck me, for some reason, as auspicious. And in this I was not disappointed.

"On page one of the Metro section—page B1 of the paper in toto—I came across an article that led me here, to this very apartment. I remember its headline, *Nefflein*, word for word. Can you guess what it was?"

∞

"Can you guess what it was?" my great-uncle repeated.

I sat forward, blinking and rubbing my eyes, as though I'd just been jolted from a trance. "I have no idea."

He privileged me with an indulgent smile. "Enzian Tolliver, Harlem Recluse, Found Dead at Sixty-Two."

"So that's how you got here? The *Times* gave you the address?" The blood rushed to my head. "Are you telling me you walked up here from South Street?"

"Not at all. I took the M4 bus."

I stared into his face to see if he was joking. It was no help at all. It was barely a face.

"You never found your brother, then. My grandfather, I mean."

"On the contrary! I saw him just two weeks ago, innately speaking. And those potty aunts of yours. And your father, of course. And our friend Richard Haven."

"You're lying again. How could you have been to all those times, not to mention those places? You'd have been found out by now. You'd have been—"

"There *was* some danger of that, admittedly." The smile crept back into his features. "I had to choose my confidants with care."

"Your *confidants*? What do you—"

"I haven't devoted the last two innate decades of my existence to the pursuit of this family through the chronosphere, *Nefflein*, for recreational purposes. There remained important work to be done—groundbreaking work." His voice dropped to a whisper. "There still does."

"What sort of work?"

He looked up at me fondly. "Even the greatest experiment, as any researcher can tell you, is of value only if its results are *reproducible*. It had to happen a second time, Waldy. Another excision." He sighed and took my shaking hand in his. "I had need—to put it bluntly—of an heir."

"A test subject, you mean. A guinea pig."

"Call it by whatever name you like."

My hand prickled strangely in his grip, like a dead limb returning to life, and the tunnel began revolving counterclockwise. He tightened his grip. "You've done wonderfully, *Nefflein*—better than I dared to hope. We're all of us so very proud of you."

"More lies," I managed to sputter. "How could you have found all those people? How could you have known where to go, never mind *when* to go there? No hall of records could have told you that."

This question pleased him better, Mrs. Haven, than anything I'd thought to ask him yet.

"Why would I need a hall of records, *Nefflein*, when I have your book?"

"My book?"

He nodded. The Archive around us was starting to blur. I freed my hand from his and pressed it to the floor.

"So that's why you come here." I shook my head slowly. "To read the next installment of the story."

"And to see *you*, of course, Waldy. You're the most important Tolliver of all."

"Don't say that to me, Uncle. I'm nothing. I'm a failure."

"A *failure*, my boy? You're a triumph! Didn't you set down this history— this testament—now virtually complete? Didn't you emancipate yourself from the chronosphere, using nothing but tenacity of will? Aren't you the last of us, the best of us, the one whose role it was to close the circle? Without you to remember us—to *invoke* us—how could we continue to exist?"

Strange to say, Mrs. Haven, I believed what he said. I felt no anger toward him any longer—he was too diminished, too ruined, and I was too drunk on the answers he was giving. There was no further use in denial: the writing of this narrative has been my reason for existing. Despite my love for you, regardless of the anguish it has caused me, I never truly had another. I needed an audience, a receiver, and I found one in you. If you exploited me, Mrs. Haven—if you used me, ruthlessly, for your own ends— the truth is that I used you in return.

The Timekeeper coughed and sighed and licked his tattered lips. I wondered if he'd been as outspoken with Enzie, or with Kaspar, or with my poor father.

"Who else did you visit? Who among them knew that you were there?"

"Only your aunts, when they were little girls." He snuffled. "And Haven, of course."

"Why *Haven*, for God's sake? What did you tell him?"

"Whatever nonsense came into my head."

I thought for a moment, then gave a weak laugh. "I suppose that explains a few things."

"I did what was necessary, *Nefflein*. No more and no less. To be frank, he was beginning to intrude."

I wasn't sure what this meant, Mrs. Haven, and I didn't ask. The spinning of the Archive seemed to lessen.

"How is it coming?" he said, his voice suddenly shy. "Your history, I mean. Have you made any progress?"

"Just a chapter about Enzie and Genny. I doubt you'll find it useful."

He gave a wolfish grin and pinched my cheek. "Why don't you let *me* be the judge of that?"

XXVII

I LEFT THE VILLA OUSPENSKY in worse shape, Mrs. Haven, than when I'd gone in. The fact of Orson in that place, surrounded by a swarm of bee-hived, pastel-skirted zombies, was destabilizing enough; but Miss Greer's whispered warning had thrown me completely. I'd shown up with a theory—an absurd one at best—and she'd done the one thing I'd been unprepared for. She'd confirmed it.

For the whole of my childhood, I'd pictured the timestream as a flickering tunnel we all move through together—everyone who's ever lived, or ever will—like passengers on a fairground logjam ride. After that last trip to Harlem, try as I might to repress it, I'd come to view the timestream as a magical streetcar of sorts, one that could move either forward or back. And now the revelation about my great-uncle—the possibility that he was traveling through both time *and* space at whim, in lines both straight and crooked, like a bishop or a knight around a chessboard—had transformed the timestream into a vast and roadless thicket, shadowy and dense in all directions, full of numberless places to hide. Even the term *timestream* now expressed a dated concept: an infinite array of streams flowed outward in every conceivable direction, it seemed, from any given moment. And Waldemar had access to them all.

The Timekeeper wasn't likely to take kindly to my meddling, family ties notwithstanding—but that wasn't my greatest fear. The concept itself was what frightened me most: the concept and all it implied. It gnawed at the margins of my well-being over the next few days, especially at night. At times it seemed a modest notion, almost trifling; at others it swelled to the dimensions of a nightmare. If there was suddenly more than one set of rails to move along—if the logjam ride of my childhood was in fact some universal junction, with countless radiating tracks—once I changed course, what was there to bring me back?

Though I believed what Orson's nurse/lover/jailer had told me, Mrs. Haven, I chose to ignore her advice. My next move was clear: to determine the nearest point in the future the Timekeeper was likely to visit—both its temporal coordinates and its spatial ones—then go to that $x/y/z/t$ intersection and kill him. Of all the innumerable descendants of SS war criminals, I alone still had the chance to bring my forebear to the ultimate account. I didn't need to comb the chronosphere to accomplish my objective, either: the flow of what Orson liked to call "consensus time" would lead me to him. One hurdle remained, though, and it was a big one. I had to learn enough about my great-uncle, a man I knew next to nothing about, to predict both when and where he'd turn up next.

There was no way around it: I had to see Enzie and Genny.

I'd kept clear of my aunts for as long as I could—out of loyalty to Orson, I suppose, and possibly some sense of self-protection—but Orson's power over me was at an end. My grandfather had turned his back on the role he'd been given—and so, in his way, had my father—but I had no intention of repeating their mistakes. If there was one quality that separated the Timekeeper and the Iterants (and the Patent Clerk himself, for that matter) from the wretched of the earth, it was this: they acted, Mrs. Haven, and the rest of us sad, frightened bumblers were acted upon.

Not me, I swore to myself. Not anymore. I was through pretending not to be a Tolliver.

∞

Manhattan was in the grip of a cold snap the day I arrived, the iciest first of May on record, and the Boathouse and Nutter's Battery lay fixed under a scrim of frozen rain. I sat on the stone wall of the park for a while, watching the trees flash and rustle, putting off my next move as long as I could. There was no sign of anything suspicious across the way: just a steady stream of grim, time-mired locals. I was shivering and my legs were going numb. It was time to cross the street and ring the buzzer.

Before I could do that, however—before I'd even crossed Fifth Avenue—
I was treated to a piece of vaudeville. A silhouette caught my eye through
the General Lee's doors, then a flurry of movement; a few seconds later,
just as I reached the curb, a hobo shuffled out onto the pavement. I use the
term *hobo*, Mrs. Haven, because no other word suits the case. His toes jutted out from the tips of his boots and his pants were held up by duct-tape
suspenders and his five o'clock shadow had the sheen of burnt cork. He
turned toward me in a kind of dust-bowl soft-shoe, the steely glint of hard-
ship in his eye. I expected him to cuss at me, or dance a jig, or possibly to hit
me up for change. Instead he asked if I could hold the door.

There were two more drifters in the lobby, it turned out, standing on
either side of what looked to be a refrigerator wrapped in a tarp. They were
more presentable than their friend, but only barely. The three of them
hoisted the thing without the least sign of effort and steered it neatly out
onto the curb. The man in the suspenders thanked me and slipped me a
dollar. I left them on the ice-encrusted stoop, apparently waiting for their
ride, which I could only assume was a Model T Ford.

Hobos and refrigerator boxes aside, something was different about the
General Lee—I sensed it as a tightness in the hollow of my chest. Had I
been an older man, I might have put this down to hypertension; if I'd been a
paranoiac, to airborne pathogens or smog or cosmic rays. As it was, I chose
to blame it on anxiety, and urged my body up the darkened stairwell. But
something was different.

My nerve failed me again when I reached my aunts' door. Orson and I
had stood on that same water-stained landing nearly a decade earlier, I remembered, on the night that had ended my childhood. We'd hesitated
then, too, and with good reason. I remembered Orson's obvious discomfort, and his clumsy attempts to conceal it—I'd seen him embarrassed so
rarely. He'd been afraid on that visit, I realized now: that had been the
source of his embarrassment. That I might look at him and recognize
his fear.

The door swung loudly open before I could touch it. What I saw next
stopped all speculation cold: dozens of bustling strangers, coming and going through those once-majestic rooms, burrowing like moles or dwarves
or termites through my aunts' beloved Archive. Enzie and Genny—who'd
let virtually no one cross their threshold since the Nixon administration,

who'd set booby traps and cut all ties to keep the world at bay—suddenly had a house full of guests.

It was Genny, smiling tightly, who received me at the door.

"You certainly took your time," she snapped, before I could say a word.

"What do you—"

"Enzie!" she called over her shoulder, standing squarely in the doorway, as if I'd come to repossess the sofa. "Enzie! That *person* is here."

I couldn't see much over Genny's white, Andy Warhol–ish bob, but what I managed to glimpse struck me speechless. Shabby young men and women with clipboards and archivists' gloves were jostling and whispering to one another in the hallway behind her, scribbling notes with thick, expensive-looking pens. The theatrical decrepitude of their outfits clashed wildly with the businesslike air of the proceedings, not to mention their Mormon-ish hairstyles, and instantly put me in mind of the hobo downstairs. It was obvious that he'd been coming from my aunts' apartment—but what could he have wanted with poor Genny's fridge? And why was everyone dressed like extras in some dust-bowl reenactment?

"*There* you are," said Enzie, squeezing out into the hall. Her tone was peculiar, self-conscious and stilted, as though put on for the benefit of someone on the far side of the door.

"I'm sorry," I heard myself mumble. "I didn't know—"

"We called at *eight* this morning, and again at half past ten. Anyone would think you didn't care for our business." She held a package in her arms, I now saw: a padded manila envelope, like those I'd seen at the Villa Ouspensky, on which *UPS* had been written in block letters with a Sharpie. She thrust it hurriedly into my hands. The look on her face, severe at the best of times, was nothing short of marrow-chilling now.

"I *do* want it," I got out at last. "Your business, I mean. As a matter of fact—"

"Run along, then," hissed Enzie. "And be careful. It's a family heirloom."

"I will, ma'am—of course."

"Good. Now you'll have to excuse us." She scuttled back inside and shut the door.

I stood motionless on the landing, barely breathing, until I was sure she wasn't coming out again; then I leaned against the wall and tried to think.

Enzie and Genny were too otherworldly, somehow, for me to fear much for their safety, but the thought that we'd never spent a single moment together under anything approaching normal circumstances—that we'd never sat around a dinner table, or watched a movie, or compared notes about Orson and the Kraut—suddenly filled me with remorse. Why it hit me then and there, I couldn't say; it wasn't the ideal time or place, to put it mildly. Perhaps I sensed my chance had come and gone.

It was only after I'd snapped out of it and made my getaway, slinking off into the icebound afternoon, that it occured to me that the fridge-like object in the tarp had been the size and shape of the exclusion bin.

∞

It might be overstating the case, Mrs. Haven, to say that my aunts' envelope contained the whole of this account in capsule form; but it wouldn't be overstating it by much. I took it straight to the Forty-Second Street Library—the beautiful main branch, the one with the lions—where I tore it open with the key to my Ogilvy dorm room. I'd barely made myself comfortable at one of the Rose Reading Room's gargantuan tables before I saw that I'd been slipped a century.

Kaspar's journals—eleven pocket notebooks crammed with dense, schoolboyish cursive—were first out of the envelope; then a copy of the Gottfriedens Protocols; then Enzian's crude account of her grandfather's work, written when she and Genny were still in their teens. Some juvenilia of my father's—along with his second-to-last novel, *Salivation Is Yours!*—distracted me so completely that I overlooked the scrap of rag paper at the bottom of the pile until a few minutes before the building closed. By the time I came up for air it was a quarter past six, all the tables were empty, and a security guard with a sad yellow mustache was tugging at the collar of my coat.

The scrap of paper in question was a copy of Ottokar's seminal riddle: the half page of alliterative, semiliterate gibberish that had started it all, written out in pencil in the Timekeeper's precise, archaic hand.

The next thing I knew I was out on the street, blinking through thin, stinging rain at a power plant on the far side of the river, alive with a sense of consequence I'd never felt before. I was Waldemar Gottfriedens Tolliver, after all. I'd been given those names for a reason—Enzian and Orson (and even the Kraut herself) had told me so. It was my burden and birthright to close the great circle, to restore the Toula/Tollivers to what we'd been before Ottokar's breakthrough: a family of inconsequential picklers. And I would do it, Mrs. Haven, if it killed me.

But first I had to find a place to sleep.

∞

I knew only one person in the city aside from my aunts, and I called him from the first working pay phone I found. Van Markham was Buffalo Bill's half sister's grandson, and therefore some species of cousin to me, though I'd never really thought of him as family. But I was too hungry and wet, at that moment, to recollect exactly why this was.

"Equus Special Blend and Affiliated Products. Markham speaking."

"Cousin Van! It's Waldy Tolliver. I'm not sure if you remember, the month before last—"

"I remember you, Waldy. How did you get this number?"

"You gave it to me."

The line went silent for a moment. "That sounds plausible."

"What's Equus Special Blend?"

"Let me answer your question with a question. What do you want?"

For once I felt grateful for Van's bluntness. "I'm here in New York. I just dropped out of college."

"Congratulations, cousin. *Willkommen* to actual life."

"What I mean is, I don't have a place to stay." When he said nothing, I continued: "You're the only person in town that I know."

"Aside from the Sisters Frankenstein, you mean." I could picture him pursing his lips in distaste. "*They've* got a big-enough cave up in Harlem, don't they? Or have they filled it with junk mail and cat food by now? On second thought, don't answer that."

"Something's happened to them, actually. That's why I'm calling. They wouldn't let me into their apartment."

"People/Feelings," said Van.

People/Feelings was a phrase Van had coined, sometime before dropping out of college himself, to stand for all the things in life that bored him.

It freed him to focus on matters of genuine import, i.e., his personal business ventures and sex. His term for himself, when actively engaged in these latter pursuits—which was practically his every waking hour—was Randy the Robot. Randy didn't go in much for sentiment.

"I need you to put me up for a week," I told him. "Ten days at the most."

"Starting when?"

"Starting now."

The silence that followed was cosmic. A ghostly interference came across the line: a faint, mournful crackle that could have been caused by gamma radiation or dark-matter accretion or the frantic buzzing of my cousin's brain. I wasn't bothered by the delay, particularly. The algorithm Van used in situations of this nature was complex.

"I've got a studio in midtown," he said eventually. "I'm looking to rent it on a fixed semiannual plan, with a subsidiary lease, but there's a problem with the bylaws of the building re: sublets. I could let you have it on a binightly basis, I suppose, seeing as how you're flesh of my flesh."

"A binightly basis," I repeated. "Sounds great."

"Since you're family," Van said, after a slight hesitation, "I won't require a security deposit." He didn't seem to expect a reply. "Sixty-eight West Forty-Fourth. Meet me there in an hour."

I asked him what the binightly rent might be, in dollar terms. My only answer was the solar wind.

∞

"Ask me how things are going," said Van. We were sitting in a Popeye's Chicken and Biscuits across the street from the apartment I was going to be renting, at forty dollars a night, to be paid in binightly installments. He hadn't explained why I'd be paying him on a forty-eight-hour cycle—in person, in cash, preferably in ATM-fresh twenties—and I was too thankful and exhausted to object.

"Go ahead, Waldy. Ask me. I can tell that you're dying to know."

I pulled myself together. "Okay. How are things—"

"Gangbangers."

"Gangbusters, I think you mean."

"Gang*bangers*," my cousin repeated, with emphasis. "What do you think of that for a name?"

"That depends. What exactly are you selling?"

"Satisfaction," Van said, smacking his lips.

"Unless the kind of satisfaction you're talking about involves Glocks, secret handshakes, and drug deals gone wrong—"

"It does, in a way." He narrowed his eyes. "And I'll tell you another thing, cousin, though this is strictly classified. I've already found myself a backer."

"That's fantastic, Van. Congratulations. Now if you wouldn't mind—"

"I'm telling you this for a *reason*, you jackass. Do you think I like to listen to myself talk?"

He seemed to view the question as hypothetical, so I let my attention drift—nodding amiably all the while—to take in the self-importantly stoned teens at the counter, the rain against the scratched and oily window, and a Möbius-strip-shaped dab of mayonnaise on the tabletop between us. I'd almost managed to forget where I was when my cousin dropped a name that ruined everything.

"What did you just say?"

He let out a titter. "Funny how things loop together, isn't it? Who'd have thought the Iterants would want to horn in on the sensuality-enhancement industry?" He sighed happily. "But they've got to invest their cash the same as anybody else, I reckon."

"How did they—" I took in a breath and counted slowly down from ten. "Who from the UCS contacted you?"

"What makes you think it wasn't me doing the contacting?"

"They think you're one of *us*, Van," I said, fighting the urge to slap his smirking face. "That's the reason they're backing you—not that tarted-up horse piss you're selling. There's not a branch of this family they haven't gotten their hooks into. First Enzie and Genny, then Orson, now you." I clung white-knuckled to the edge of the table. "They haven't hooked me, though—not yet. That's why I need your help. I've got to—"

I cut my rant short when I noticed his expression. "You don't believe me," I muttered. "You're not even listening."

"I'm worried about you, Waldy." He cleared his throat primly. "You can stay in my place for as long as you want—we'll figure the payments out later. Get some rest. Watch some cable. Thirty-six is the vanilla porn channel, if memory serves. Thirty-seven is predominantly anal."

I blinked at him, then at the keys he'd set down on the table. "You're just like the others," I said. "You think I've gone crazy."

"Not at all," Van assured me—but the look in his twitchy, bloodshot eyes said otherwise. "I'm leaving now, Waldy. Promise me you'll get some fucking sleep."

I watched him dart in his couture trench coat across the rain-slick pavement, relieved to have our rendezvous behind him, already intent on the next item of business. I envied him in that moment, Mrs. Haven, I have to admit. He nodded to his doorman, ducked briefly inside, then came back out with a package in his hands. His aviator glasses—mirrored, of course—matched his trench coat and expression perfectly. *Only my cousin*, I said to myself, *would wear aviator glasses in a downpour.* Then I looked at the package more closely.

It was a padded mailing envelope, crisp and marzipan-colored, identical to those I'd seen at the Villa Ouspensky. Van was cradling it as if it held a bomb.

∞

Those next seven days passed like a dream, Mrs. Haven—or like a short, bumpy ride in the back of a van with packing tape covering its windows, driven by strangers wearing hazmat suits and Albert Einstein masks. I spent the week with the blinds drawn and the door double-locked and the telephone disconnected from the wall, living on stale ramen noodles and lukewarm tap water and cheese. I needed time with the package that Enzie had slipped me: time to ravel the threads and wires and light rays back into some kind of fabric, to reverse-engineer my family's cataclysmic century. Things went on happening out in the world—horrendous things, mostly—and I was the last to find out. It was Heisenberg's principle in all its dark glory: the observer affects the events he's observing, no matter how many deadbolts he has on his door. I was changing, Mrs. Haven, and the chronosphere was changing with me.

I spread the contents of the package out in fan-shaped symmetry across the floor—like Ozymandias with his cards in *The Excuse*—and spent the first day sitting Indian-style on a cushion pulled down from the mildewy, beer-smelling couch, waiting for the universal Answer to arrive. It was inevitable, I suppose—or at the very least par for the course—that questions started pelting me instead.

They came slowly at first, almost bashfully; then faster and harder with each passing minute, until the floor and the sofa and the countertop were littered with scribblings on torn scraps of paper, feverish demands on one part of my brain by another. Enzie and Genny had clearly been trying to protect me at the General Lee, to keep my identity a secret from the Iterants; but what had the Iterants been doing there in the first place? What sort of a deal had been struck, and to whose benefit?

I was reading the entry in Kaspar's diary—rereading it, to be accurate, for the seventeenth time—describing that horrific afternoon on which he'd discovered his brother in the Brown Widow's attic, when a line suddenly stood out from the text surrounding it, like the wing of a butterfly caught in a stray beam of light:

> *You look funny down there, he called to me from the top of the wardrobe. You look like a cicada in a jar.*

A cicada in a jar, I thought, turning the phrase over in my mind. It was then that I recalled a further point in the series, not in the diary but in my own experience, in the immediate past, so recent that the memory was still damp. The mural in Haven's sanctum in the Villa Ouspensky: the one Miss Greer had allegedly painted. Those insects had been *cicadas*, not grasshoppers or cockroaches or ants. I hadn't made the connection at the time—I hadn't been sure—but I was sure of it now. And with that first modest link, that initial line drawn between a casual turn of phrase and its most extravagant, fantastic expression, I was suddenly attuned to other points in the sequence, other appearances, both in the documents littering the floor of Van's apartment and in my own memory. It was a cicada that my great-uncle had been mesmerized by as a boy; it was a cicada I'd seen trapped under a glass at age ten, when Genny had shown me the Archive; and what else could the "little flying thing" have been that the twins had communed with as children? It had visited them every seven years, after all—in between, it had been "no-where and no-when," as Enzie had put it in her diary. No wonder they'd given it Ottokar's name.

I lowered my throbbing head onto the couch. Was the cicada some-how significant to Waldemar's argument for rotary time—as a symbol of the overlooked, perhaps, or of the meandering, or of the cyclical? Or was it simply the Timekeeper's totem, a fetish he left behind him at every point of the chronosphere he visited, like a dirty drawing on a bathroom stall?

I'd taken the critical step, Mrs. Haven: the leap from the rational to the occult. But none of the above, beguiling though it was, brought me nearer to cracking the fundamental conundrum, the one from which all the oth-ers arose, and without which they subsided into nothing. Physical time travel, especially into the past, has long been regarded as an impossibility. How had Waldemar—indigent, paranoid Waldemar, embittered and em-battled and patently mad—succeeded where so many better men had failed? What sliver of his grotesque, rabid, mystical pseudotheory had ulti-mately turned out to be true?

Dreams had something to do with it, according to my aunts: dreams and subjectivity, and the inexorable influence of the observer. The secret of Enzie's homemade time machine, in other words. What was an "exclusion bin," in effect, but an objectivity filter? I'd seen into the future myself, after all, using nothing but a whitewashed plywood box. Was it possible that Waldemar's madness, far from being a hindrance, had brought him some sort of advantage? Could the breach of consensus reality be a preliminary step—perhaps even a *precondition*—to escaping from consensus time?

I reached this inductive toehold again and again in the course of that week, in relative psychological comfort; but whenever I tried to move past it, to find the next step, my brain would begin to feel greasy and hot and penned in by my skull, like a tin of pâté left out in the sun. Orson had tried to shield me from this punishing, frightening, hazardous mental state for the bulk of my childhood—he'd told me as much at the Villa Ouspensky. But it was too late, Mrs. Haven. It had been too late forever.

∞

Time is a nightmare, wrote Theodore Sturgeon—hero of West Village coffee-shop Orson—*that madmen have always felt themselves at home in.* The problem with time, Sturgeon argues, is that it's too boundless a concept—too fever-dream nightmarish, too all-pervasive, too sublime—for us to wrap our feeble primate brains around. Saint Augustine struggled with time all his life; Newton, in his arrogance, reduced it to a constant; Nietzsche tied it into pretzel knots to make it submit to his mania, then ultimately scrapped it altogether. And the harder I tried, in the course of that week, to distill the contents of my aunts' package into a single explicable truth, the more inclined I was to follow his example.

What then, is time? writes Augustine. *If no one asks of me, I know; if I wish to explain to him who asks, I know not.*

What confounded me most about the Accidents was the lack of unanimity about them. Everyone who'd tried to crack the rebus of Ottokar's discovery had come up with his or her own inimitable answer, often contradicting all the rest. My namesake had discovered impunity there: a sovereign solution, accountable only to itself, that could be warped to accommodate every possible question, to rationalize every crime. My grandfather, understandably enough, had come to view them as a conduit to madness. And to Enzie and Genny, after their mother's death, the puzzle of the Accidents became nothing less than the window frame—the only one they didn't fill in, or brick up, or shutter over—through which they watched and understood the world. For my part, Mrs. Haven, I was tempted to view my greatgrandfather's legacy as a window, as well: a blank pane of glass—sometimes letting light through, sometimes throwing it back—in which we'd discovered nothing but our own monkey-like reflections.

The glass-pane notion was a seductive one, for obvious reasons: it would have allowed me to dismiss the whole mess and head back to Ogilvy, or to Cheektowaga, or to some cottage in the country, as Nietzsche had done, and spend the rest of my duration shaving horses. There was only one catch, Mrs. Haven. My projection theory might have explained Enzie and Genny and Kaspar, and even, with a bit of fiddling, Ottokar himself; but Waldemar had actually succeeded. Waldemar, the worst of all of us, had broken free.

If no one asks of me, said Augustine, *I know.*

∞

By the end of the sixth day I was out of ramen noodles, and the only cheese I had left—"Processed Manchego," according to the packaging; exactly the sort of thing Van would eat—was making the roof of my mouth itch. I was sick to death of sifting through the ashes of my paternal lineage in search of the keys to the chronoverse. What I needed had been clear to me since I'd woken up that morning, bug-eyed and antsy, at 07:45 EST.

I needed a bucket of Popeye's.

I made it through the building's faux-Soviet lobby and across Forty-Fourth Street without incident, unless you count one near-collision with a taxi, one actual collision with a UPS dolly, and some dubious looks from the doorman, a red-bearded Sikh. I ducked into Popeye's, placed my order politely, then hit the ATM next door to liquidate the next installment of my college fund. I'd come to a decision the previous night: I'd figured out my next move, and it was a doozy. The plane ticket alone, according to my calculations, would cost all I had left in the bank.

I was still standing at the ATM ten minutes later, my arms outstretched as if in supplication. Its screen had just informed me, in no uncertain terms, that not a dime of Orson's cash would be forthcoming. It had informed me of this sixteen times in a row, and the people behind me—eight of them, the last time I'd checked—were starting to run low on Christian feeling. When the machine finally opted to swallow my card, leaving me with nothing but my driver's license and my Ogilvy ID, the woman behind me nudged me with her purse. "Here's a dollar," she whispered. "Go buy yourself a Snickers. Then get yourself a motherfucking job."

For want of any other option, Mrs. Haven, I took her advice. I went back into Popeye's and canceled my order and brought her dollar to a bodega at the corner of Forty-Fourth and Sixth. I spent it on a Mars bar, not a Snickers, and ate it while I browsed morosely through the *Times*. Which is how, within fifteen minutes of reconnecting with the outside world, I found out that Enzie was gone.

ENZIAN TOLLIVER, HARLEM RECLUSE, FOUND DEAD AT 62

Police Require Two Hours to Break into 5th Ave. Home, Booby-Trapped with Junk

SISTER FAILS TO APPEAR

BY WILLIAM HALL

Enzian Tolliver was found dead yesterday in her decaying tenement apartment at 2078 Fifth Avenue, but the legend of the reclusive Tolliver twins persists.

Her sister, Gentian, devoted to the frail and aging Enzian, may still be in the seven-room apartment, her home since 1969, although it is now boarded shut. There was no sign of her yesterday, despite the police activity at her home.

The circumstances surrounding the death of 62-year-old Enzian, rarefied as the flower both she and her sister were named for, are as mysterious as the life the two eccentric sisters lived on the unfashionable upper reaches of Fifth Avenue, at the Harlem terminus of Central Park.

UNKNOWN MALE CALLER GAVE TIP

A mysterious telephone call to Police Headquarters yesterday morning reported that there was a dead woman at 2078 Fifth Avenue. The caller gave his name as Waldemar Toula, a deceased uncle of the sisters. Police believe that it

may in fact have been Waldemar "Jack" Tolliver, the sisters' nephew, who reportedly is visiting the city.

I stopped there a moment, punch-drunk with shock. The shopkeeper
said something to me but I ignored him.

Police Emergency Squad 6 used crowbars and
axes in trying to force their way into the apartment, but the reinforced door proved impass-
able. It was 12:10 P.M. before Patrolman
LaMont Barker forced his way through the picture window at the fourth-story front.

He disappeared from view for several moments, then returned and called down, "There's
a D.O.A. (Dead on Arrival) here." Detective
Ali Lateef climbed the ladder to inspect the
body. He reported that the dead woman was in
a sitting position, dressed only in a Pendleton
shirt. The emaciated body was tentatively identified as Enzian by Willis James Buckram, a
neighbor. At 3:45 P.M. Medical Examiner
Roger C. Erfect reported that the woman had
been dead for fourteen hours.

There was no sign of Gentian Tolliver in
the building, no indication of how she entered
or left the apartment on her heretofore regular
shopping trips to buy food and medication for
her sister. The entire foyer of the apartment, to
a distance of sixteen feet from the door's interior side, was packed with bundled newsprint
from ceiling to floor, to a total weight of seventeen and one-half tons.

"NEPHEW" SOUGHT FOR QUESTIONING

A search has been initiated in all five boroughs for Waldemar Tolliver, the sisters' nephew, who was last seen at 2078 Fifth Avenue one week ago. He is believed to remain at large in New York City.

There was more—an attempt to catalog the apartment's astonishing contents, interviews with the neighbors, disgustingly explicit (and grossly exaggerated) forensic details—but I'll do both of us a favor, Mrs. Haven, and skip all of that. Once I'd gotten over my panic at the thought of being wanted by the NYPD, I found myself more intrigued by what the article omitted than by the few anemic facts that it contained. What had the medical examiner (the suspiciously named Roger C. Erfect) determined to be the cause of death? Why was no mention made of the army of Iterants I'd seen on my last visit, but such elaborate mention made of me? Why, come to think of it, was "nephew" in quotation marks? And where on earth had Genny disappeared to?

The answer to the last of these mysteries wasn't long in coming, Mrs. Haven, though it raised more questions than it laid to rest.

"What you got there's from yesterday," the shopkeeper said. "I won't charge you for that." He handed me a newer, fatter paper from a stack beside the register.

BODY OF GENTIAN TOLLIVER FOUND

Eight-Hour Search of Junk-Filled Home Believed Fruitless—Then a Puzzling Discovery

---

CROWD GATHERS IN STREET

The police searched the junk-filled home of the Tolliver sisters at 2078 Fifth Avenue for eight hours yesterday, but found no trace of Gentian Tolliver, missing since Thursday. Just as the apartment was being sealed, however, her body was found, in a location that had been inspected repeatedly in the course of the day.

"It (Tolliver's body) was just inside the door of the library, the first room to the right off the hall, under a writing desk," said Detective Ali Lateef of the 23rd Precinct. "It was covered by newspapers, but it should have been obvious," said another member of the force, who spoke on condition of anonymity. "This was a room we'd covered twice. The second time was just two hours earlier."

Neither officer volunteered an explanation for the oversight.

I went up to Harlem that same day, in spite of the risk, for reasons I still don't fully comprehend. The frost of the week before had thawed, leaving the park looking the way I imagined the forest around Czas must have looked after the Wehrmacht and the Soviets had left: muddied and broken and bereft, with bits of garbage strewn about like evidence of some lost civilization. There were still a few bored-looking loiterers outside my aunts' building, but the crowd had dwindled to a morbid handful. The show had already moved on.

One man, who claimed to be a researcher for 1010 WINS news radio, was summarizing the events of the day in a high, nasal voice, but nobody seemed to be listening. If there were cops around, I couldn't pick them out. The windows on my aunts' floor seemed blocked from the inside, except for the sixth from the left—the bathroom window, I was guessing—which was open in spite of the damp. I was gripped by the urge to duck under the POLICE LINE: DO NOT CROSS tape—I could say I was a tenant, if anyone asked—but I had the good sense to resist it. The 1010 WINS guy was the only one who noticed.

"Too late, buddy," he said, grinning at me in a way that made me want to kick him in the shins. "Everything worth taking's already gone."

∞

The annals of art and science, writes Kubler, *like those of bravery, record only a handful of the many great moments that have occurred. When we consider the class of these great moments, we are usually confronted with dead stars. Even their light has ceased to reach us. We know of their existence only indirectly, by their perturbations, and by the immense detritus of derivative stuff left in their wakes.*

As I walked the sixty-odd blocks from Harlem to midtown, it seemed that a flickering beam of my aunts' light still reached me; but though I could feel it on the back of my neck and the palms of my hands—especially when my eyes were closed—it illuminated nothing. The mess they'd left behind them would have delighted Professor Kubler, no doubt, but I had little hope of finding meaning there. There was too much of everything, Mrs. Haven, and not enough of me.

∞

I made it back to Forty-Fourth Street a few minutes before midnight, knock-kneed and dizzy with hunger, my mind a humid, hypothermic blank. I'd meant to call the Kraut as soon as I got in—even to contact Orson, if I could—but I ended up facedown on the couch. I fell asleep instantly, without the slightest preamble, and started awake just as the sun came up. The phone was ringing in the kitchen, reverberating cruelly off the tilework, and a man was sitting on my windowsill.

"I'm dreaming," I said to the man.

"You might want to get that," he answered, in an accent I couldn't pin down.

I rolled off the sofa and got to my feet. The ringing was becoming unendurable. My visitor wore a threadbare tweed jacket, a dented gray homburg, and greasy-looking yellow calfskin gloves. The overall effect, Mrs. Haven, was seedy. He looked only vaguely like Waldemar Toula—he was too young, for one thing, and his face was unnaturally wide—but I knew he could be no one else. He was waiting to kill me, or to answer my questions, or to take me with him to eternity. But first I had to stop the phone from ringing.

I lurched into the kitchen and grabbed the receiver. I'd meant to hang up right away, but something happened.

"Collect call from the year 2718. Will you accept the charges?"

"What do you want, Van? It's late—"

"It's early," the man in the living room told me.

"It's *early*, you mean," Van said, stifling a yawn. "But I'm awake, for some reason, so I thought I'd check in. How did you spend your summer vacation?"

It took me a moment to answer. "I have to tell you something, Van. Something terrible. Enzie and Genny are dead."

"I know that, Waldy. That's why I called. You're not the only one who reads the paper."

"How stupid of me. Of course not. Now if you'll excuse me, I have—"

"You have *what*, exactly? A job? A date? An uninvited guest?"

I glanced involuntarily over my shoulder. "Actually—"

"There's a reason I'm calling, believe it or not. I won't take up much of your time."

"Listen," I said, passing a hand over my face. "I can't—"

"Normally, Waldy, this would be People/Feelings territory. But nothing about what happened to those aunts of yours was normal. Therefore—"

"They were *your* aunts, too, the last time I checked."

"Once removed," Van said tartly. "Don't go changing the subject. It's been bothering me all week, what to do about you."

"About me? I don't—"

"You're depressed," Van declared. "And why wouldn't you be? Your parents have split, you've just dropped out of college, and the bodies of your father's only sisters, the people you'd come all the way from Ohio to visit—for *Christ* knows what reason—have just been dug out from under seventeen tons of—"

"Enough!" I said, turning to check on my visitor, who suddenly was nowhere to be seen. "What's the answer, Van? What's your brilliant solution? What are you going to do about me?"

"I thought you'd never *ask*." He paused for dramatic effect. "I'm going to throw you a party."

Monday, 09:05 EST.

The Timekeeper just left, Mrs. Haven, for the very last time. We've gotten what we hoped for from each other. He doesn't need me any longer, because I've helped him to see how this history ends—and I don't need him, either. I've finally remembered for myself.

I was sitting at my usual station, revising my next-to-last chapter, when the air heaved a sigh and pulled soundlessly back, disclosing the crown of my great-uncle's head. He was pushed through the skin of this world, Mrs. Haven, like a baby pushed out of a birth canal. He dropped onto the floor with a damp, muted thump, barely clearing the table, then lay face-down on the parquet. The coat he was wearing hung off of him strangely. I got up and went to him and turned him over.

I should have been prepared, Mrs. Haven, for what I saw next. He was coming apart, warping and buckling, like a plastic plate held over a fire. It seemed impossible that he could speak, but he did speak. He forced his lips apart and spoke my name.

"What is it, Waldemar?" I said. "What can I do?"

He asked me to help him raise his head and I obliged. I could feel his deformities through the jacket's threadbare tweed, and what I felt there made my stomach twist.

"Where are you coming from, Uncle?" I pulled him up by the shoulders. "The Forty-Fourth Street apartment?"

He moved his head in what I took to be a nod.

"What were you there for? Did you have something to tell me? Was it something important?"

His head jerked again, downward and to the left. I was suddenly less sure that he was nodding. It might have been a gesture of denial, or of help-lessness, or simply a spasm of pain.

"Tell me what I can do. Can I bring you some water?"

His head lolled forward and he took my arm and gripped it. I was sur-prised by the strength in his hands. His ruined mouth twitched and came open.

"What was that, Uncle? I didn't quite hear."

He pulled me closer, slowly and irresistibly, until I was within a hair's breadth of his face. It took all my self-control to keep from retching. His breath smelled of dust and old newsprint: the dead, airless smell of the Archive.

"Read me the last one, *Nefflein*. Close the loop."

I went back to my armchair, relieved to get away from him, grateful to have been asked a thing that lay within my power. I read the last chapter to him, taking care to enunciate clearly, unsure whether his ravaged ears could hear me. You'll say he deserved what he got, Mrs. Haven, and most likely you're right—but still it was a grievous thing to watch him suffer. The chapter was a long one and I read it slowly. His name was mentioned more than once, in the most damning of terms, which seemed to give him some small satisfaction. When I'd finished he forced his eyes open as best he could, turned his head in my direction and beckoned me to him. He was saying something almost inaudibly, repeating it with each exhalation, and I knelt down next to him to make it out. It was a request, Mrs. Haven—the last request he'd ever make of me. I let him say it a dozen times, then as many times again, to make sure there was no misunderstanding. Then I squatted beside his right shoulder, braced a knee against his collarbone, and brought my hands together at his neck.

Disfigured though he was, Mrs. Haven, his life took a long time to leave him. He put up no resistance, even lifted his chin to help my hands find purchase, but the force that had deformed him had tautened his skin, and it took all my strength to press his windpipe shut. The live-wire sensation returned to my palms, and my own throat seemed to close along with his, but I didn't let go until the thing was done. I'd foreseen this, after all, and I knew how it ended. Waldemar had said it himself long before, in his last conversation with Sonja. The ultimate Lost Time Accident is death.

It was at this instant, watching the Timekeeper's body resolve itself into its component particles, that I remembered how I'd fallen out of time. I hadn't fallen at all, Mrs. Haven. I'd jumped.

I T WAS MENÜGAYAN, fittingly enough, who broke the news about your disappearance. After a week in Vienna being ministered to by the Kraut (who'd managed, by a heroic effort of will, to conceal her relief at how things had turned out) I got a standby seat on a direct flight to Newark, rode a series of progressively more malodorous buses into Manhattan, and found a hostel in Chelsea that I could just barely afford. I kept away from West Tenth Street, for obvious reasons, but eventually I dialed your neighbor's number. I could tell right away, by her grunted "Who's *this?*" that she was even more depressed than usual. I assumed the reason must be Haven's triumph.

"I need to see you, Julia. I need to ask—"

"Tolliver?"

"Of course it's me. I've come back."

No response.

"What is it?" My throat went tight at once. "Is this line not safe?"

"Don't be an idiot. What do you want?"

"To see you, that's all." When no answer came, I said, "I shouldn't have run away, Julia. I should have listened to you. I should have trusted in your plan, even though you never told me what it was. Now something terrible has happened, the worst possible thing, and I need your advice. Can I meet you somewhere?"

Her breath came through the line in a low, toneless whistle, as if she were falling asleep.

"All right, Tolliver," she said finally. "Come on over."

"Over *there*? Are you crazy? The last time I saw Haven—"

To my bewilderment she gave a stony laugh. "Shut up and get over here, Tolliver. It's never been safer."

"Listen to me, Julia. I don't think—"

She set down the receiver with a bang.

∞

I knew your brownstone was vacant as soon as I saw it. No one had been home for weeks and the place had been gutted. Menügayan confirmed this when I asked her.

"I grokked that something *pesado* had gone down as soon as those movers showed up. They didn't leave beans behind, either—just some Klimt posters down in the basement." She shuddered. "Piles of them, actually. Hideous stuff."

I told her about our meeting at the post office, about our elopement, about our time in Vienna and Znojmo—I told her everything, Mrs. Haven, down to the most piddling detail. She was the only person I could tell it to, the whole hopeless fiasco, and it felt good to tell it. She sat there like a pile of rocks and let me ramble on.

"You see, Julia? That's why Haven has shifted his base of operations. He's finally got what he needs: he can chrono-jump now, or so he believes. He doesn't know about the changes Artur made, apparently, or he doesn't care. My guess is that he's relocating upstate, to that villa of his, to work on a new type of exclusion bin, or some other device we don't know about yet. Which means that if I want to find her—to find Hildy, I mean—all that I have to do—"

"Why the hell would you *want* to find her, Tolliver, after what she's done to you? Is this some kink of yours—some glutton-for-humiliation type of deal? Is it penance for your Nazi uncle, or for your father, or for your whole pathetic family? Taking one for the team, are you, Tolliver? I'm just curious. Because the last time I checked you didn't *have* one. No team. No friends. No family to speak of. You're on your own, little man, just like everyone else. It's time you made a fucking note of that."

The above speech was delivered in a lifeless monotone, barely loud enough to hear, but it had the effect she intended. By the end of it I was shivering with rage.

"I need to see her," I said. "I need to hear what happened in Znojmo from Hildy's own mouth—not from Haven or his army of cyborgs, and definitely not from you." I got to my feet. "I'll go up to that compound of theirs, if I have to, and pound on the door until they let me in." I wavered for a moment, breathing hard. "I'll leave right now, in fact. I'll go today."

Menügayan watched me with a look of bleak amusement. "I forgot," she said. "You haven't heard the news."

"What news?"

"Forget Hildegard, Waldy. Forget both of them." She shut her eyes. "That's what I hope to do."

The sorrow in her expression gave me pause. "I apologize for losing my temper, Julia. I'll admit that things look pretty bad right now, but if we put our heads together—"

"Haven's jet disappeared eleven days ago over the Atlantic, a few miles southeast of the English coast. One minute they were clear on the radar, the next they were gone. There hasn't been a whisper from them since."

A curious thing happened as Menügayan spoke. The cluttered slate-gray walls that had always made the room seem like a props closet in some defunct third-string theater began to fall away, to move steadily outward in all four directions, until the couches were the only solid objects, twin parenthesis-shaped atolls in a depthless, twilit sea. Menügayan was still there, and so was I; but everything else had lapsed into the shadows. This all took place without the slightest sound.

Free of the room's distractions, I was able to bring my full attention to bear on Menügayan herself, and to see how profoundly she'd changed. There had always been a power to her sullenness, or at least a kind of adolescent menace; now there was only exhaustion. Her neck was wedged into a horseshoe-shaped velveteen pillow, the kind tourists carry on overnight flights. All the vengefulness and guile had been sucked out of her.

"There's only one explanation," I murmured. "The two of us will have to face the truth."

"You're right about that," she said, gentler now. "It won't be easy at first, but—"

"They disappeared just south of England, you said? Off the south-eastern coast?"

"Does it matter?"

"It matters, Julia." I nodded. "GMT."

"What the hell is *that* supposed to—"

"Zero degrees longitude. The prime meridian. The Royal Observatory at Greenwich."

Her eyes went wide and glassy. "Jesus, Tolliver."

"They've made the jump already," I said, pulling on my coat. "Ottokar's calculations were right, somehow, in spite of the alterations Artur made. *Any* confined space can be used, if it falls within certain parameters— Haven told me so in Znojmo. You see what this means, don't you?"

"I'm not—"

"They've used his jet as their exclusion bin."

∞

I left Menügayan's brownstone soon after, feeling restless and confined by my own skin. There was no point in heading upstate—not yet, at least—so I drifted across town, in the approximate direction of my hostel, going over everything I'd learned. I'd attempted to talk the implications through with Menügayan; I'd expected her to brighten at the news of a genuine jump, if only because it meant that you were still alive. Instead she'd pulled back into herself like a barnacle, going saucer-eyed and quiet. It was obvious she thought I'd lost my mind.

This disappointed me, Mrs. Haven, I have to admit. Maybe Enzie and Genny had been right, after all: maybe you had to be a Tolliver to play cards against the chronoverse and win. But as I was crossing Union Square, to my own astonishment, I realized I didn't give a damn. If the rest of humankind saw no worth in our theories, whose problem was that, in the final accounting—ours, or the rest of humankind's?

I got to the hostel at midnight, worn out and giddy from thinking, but the good times there were only getting started. Chicken vindaloo was bubbling in the kitchen, merengue was squawking from somebody's laptop, and the TV in the 1-Love Lounge was tuned to the Sri Lankan lawn bowling championships, although no one in that sticky, smoke-filled room was watching. They were playing a game on the floor with what looked like a lopsided clog; someone explained it was like spin the bottle, but Swiss. The lounge smelled of hashish and muesli and socks. My bunkmate looked disappointed that I didn't join in: he'd taken a shine to me, God bless him, and wanted me to meet his lady friend. He was one of those suntanned, straw-haired, ice-cube-eyed Australians who look like a member of the Aryan Nation on holiday. "Get a big black *dog* up yar," he growled when I turned in, which I'm guessing is Australian for good night.

My night was not good, Mrs. Haven—not even remotely. Unmentionable acts were transpiring less than three feet below me, in a half-dozen languages, until past 04:00 EST; but it wasn't just that. The brave face I'd put on in Menügayan's parlor wasn't nearly as convincing in the dark, and doubts began to infiltrate my dreams. I saw you lounging in a *kif* house in the souk of ancient Alexandria, then riding bareback on a cantering mastodon, then attending a gala in New Singapore in the twenty-fifth century, dressed in a ball gown of pulsing, intelligent gas. You'd never be bored again, Mrs. Haven. The Sensational Gatsby had cured you at last.

"One man's *now*," the Patent Clerk famously declared, "is another man's *then*." He was talking about relativity, of course—and about its knock-kneed little mascot, "the observer," the puppet who had to jump through all of its hoops, no matter how they danced and jiggled, for the amazement and amusement of the public—but I couldn't help recalling it that night, tossing and groaning in that overheated room, whenever I imagined the Husband beside you. The second law of thermodynamics, the most bitter in physics, states that the sum of entropy in the universe must always increase: no matter how madly we fight to create systems and structures and vital connections, the result of all our striving yields the opposite. "Now I am become Death," said Oppenheimer. "The destroyer of worlds." The rush he felt at the Trinity site that fateful day was less professional or political, I now realized, than cosmic. He was finally batting for the winning team.

It was growing light in the room when I had this last thought. My bunkmate and his Sri Lankan clog-spinner had fallen asleep, having spent a fair part of the night attempting to create order (i.e., a new human being) while contributing inescapably to disorder (expended thermal energy, bodily fluids, time). But no sooner had I tried to flush the second law of

thermodynamics from my brain than a memory rushed in to fill the vacuum: something Genny had told me when I'd first seen the Archive.

"The *past* of X is thought of by most people, if they consider it at all, as
the set of all events that can affect what happens *at* X. But most people—
how shall I put this, Waldemar?—are fools."

I'd asked her what she meant by that, and she'd smiled down at me in
her daft, sunny, Genny-ish way. "Let me put it differently, *Schätzchen*. Entropy increases with time, people say. Fair enough. But there's one point—
one minor detail—they forget to consider. Entropy increases with time for
a reason. Can you guess what it is?"

I'd thought hard for a while, then confessed that I couldn't.

"Because we choose to measure time in the direction in which entropy
increases. Now run along and tell Enzie her coffee is ready."

I sat up in my bunk, banging my head against the flaking ceiling. I'd
had an idea, Mrs. Haven, and it couldn't wait. I climbed out of bed and
struggled into my jeans and dug the envelope Enzie had given me out of
my suitcase. The key to my aunts' apartment was inside, wedged down in
the bottom left-hand corner. The Husband's goons had taken most of the
rest, but that no longer mattered. The key itself was all I needed.

The sun was still low when I got to the General Lee. The only person
on the street was a man in an electric wheelchair and a peach-colored fe-
dora, running slalom around two yellowing ginkgos—first the one, then
the other—in tribute to the symbol for infinity. I gave him the last dollar
in my wallet, and he looked up at me with watery, grandfatherly concern. "You take *care* now," he said. Something about me must have worried him.

"I'll see you tomorrow," he said, taking me by the wrist. "I'll see you
tomorrow, you hear?"

Police tape still barred my aunts' door, but it was sagging and dusty,
like the velvet rope to an abandoned club. It took me a few tries to inveigle
the key into the lock, and another half-dozen to coax the corroded deadbolt
into sliding. The door jammed after less than half a foot: I could work my
way in sideways, but my suitcase had to stay out on the landing. I took out
what I needed—a few books, my toothbrush, the notes for my history, the
manuscript itself, a refillable tortoiseshell pen that I'd bought on the flight
from Vienna—and left all the rest. It was daylight by then, a clear autumn

morning, and the clatter of cooking carried brightly up the stairwell. It was strange to imagine the neighbors at breakfast, to picture them nestled in their dining nooks, complacent in their chronologic serfdom. I pitied them, Mrs. Haven, but I envied them more. The apartment before me was dark as a tomb.

∞

Within four steps I was forced into a crouch, plowing headfirst through the ruined Archive, and in no time I was on my hands and knees. The reek of mold and rot was overpowering. And there was another smell underneath, thicker and more pungent the farther I crawled, but never strong enough for me to guess its source: a heavy smell, fetid and sour, like the musk of an animal's cage.

Gradually my eyes adjusted to the gloom. I thought at first that the roof had fallen in, or one of the load-bearing walls; then I recalled what I'd read in the *Times*. They'd found Genny under a landslide of newsprint, immobilized but not crushed, a wire looped around her bare left foot. She'd tripped it by accident, the police speculated: she'd forgotten, in a moment of absentmindedness or panic, the location of one of her traps. Enzie had been less than ten feet away when the landslide was triggered—dead already, most likely, though possibly not. The chronology was hazy, forensically speaking, which would of course have pleased my aunts no end. Rats and cockroaches had gotten to them both.

I was slithering forward now like some prehistoric fish, both arms pressed against my sides. *Just as beauty lies in the eye of the beholder*, the Patent Clerk wrote, *so does each man carry with him his own space and his own time.* The garbage bearing down on me grew heavier, denser, expelling the breath from my body. My mouth and windpipe were becoming furred-over with dust. *It's dizzying to think of seeing into the future, Walter*, you said to me once. *Why isn't it dizzying to see into the past?*

The question made me light-headed, Mrs. Haven, and I welcomed the feeling. I gave up struggling, gave up breathing altogether, let gravity have its sluggish way with me. I was being pushed through the tunnel peristaltically now, like a morsel through the bowels of some great snake. There was no point in resisting. There was no need to use my arms or legs at all.

∞

I found myself in a low, dome-shaped chamber, its roof tapering upward like the impression left by an enormous bell. The walls looked cut from a solid mass of envelopes and photocopies and Styrofoam bricks, like a hidden money pocket in a book; light came through one of three small openings at the level of my knees. The floor to my right was exposed, inexplicably dustless, and I could just make out the bottom of a green enameled door. My aunts' bathroom door had been green, I remembered. The opening to my left—the one a weak gray light was coming through—must lead to what had once been Genny's parlor. That left the third one unaccounted for.

I examined it carefully, unsure how to proceed. Four books had been removed from a row of *Encyclopedia Americana*, volumes 22 (Photography to Pumpkin) through 37 (Trance to Venial Sin), leaving a gap the size of a post office box. A single book set crosswise kept the portal from collapsing: a hardcover copy of *Plotinus' Ladder* by Orson Card Tolliver, cheaply bound in imitation suede. I spun in a deliberate circle, straining to see in the feeble light, then turned to face my father's book again. Of the countless things embedded in those walls, Mrs. Haven, it alone looked placed there by design.

As the soul grows toward eternal life, wrote Plotinus, *we remember less and less*.

I gripped its spine, took in a wheezing breath, and pulled it free.

Once the dust had cleared and my fit of hacking had subsided and I'd worked myself out from under the avalanche that pinned me, I saw that half the dome had fallen in. There was barely enough space to sit upright, and the tunnels to either side had disappeared; the way ahead of me, however, was open and clear. It was darker than the tunnel I'd come through, but it was wider as well, and high enough that I could walk upright. Soon, I was guessing, I would reach the turning in the corridor: the one I'd found by accident at seven years of age. It had been that corridor I'd thought of a few hours before, half-asleep in my bunk at the hostel. I'd remembered its darkness, so unlike the darkness of night—as different from night as Enzie and Genny had been different from other human beings.

And something else had come to me, Mrs. Haven, as I made my way up to Harlem through the cold.

There had been no mention of that corridor in any of the papers.

∞

I'd guessed correctly, of course—my father's book had not been placed at random. It marked the event horizon of this history, the point of no return, and as soon as I passed it I felt C*F*P guiding me in. The tunnel veered leftward, then upward, then plummeted down—or so it seemed in the blackness—then upward and leftward again. I should have been afraid, Mrs. Haven, but what I felt was an ecstatic helplessness. I ended up in the library, or in the place the library had been. The walls fell away from my fingers and the ceiling receded and the air became less thick with dust. The darkness was immaculate, almost viscous to the touch. I knelt and ran my fingertips across the warped parquet: the first thing they encountered was a socket in the floor, and the second was a snarled electric cord. I plugged it in without the slightest hesitation.

A standing lamp next to me stuttered to life, which I'd have wondered at if I'd had any wonder left. I was in another bell-shaped chamber, twice the size of the first, with more than enough space for the armchair and the table it contained. A stack of books sat nearby, though I couldn't read their spines from where I stood. A length of copper wire curled downward from the ceiling to the chair, ending in a graceful, thumb-sized loop. Even before I'd opened the letter I found on the table, before my eyesight had adjusted to the sudden crush of light, I'd realized what the bell-shaped room was for. It was for me, Mrs. Haven. It was time to bring this history to a close.

DEAREST WALDEMAR! NOW YOUVE ARRIVED.

*NOW YOUVE ARRIVED & WE CANT CALL YOU "WALDY"
ANY LONGER. ENZIE & I AGREE. YOURE ONE OF US NOW.
YOURE NO MORE ONE OF "THEM" FOREVER AFTER.
YOU MIGHT THINK IT CRUEL THAT WE SENT YOU
TO ZNOJMO WHEN WE HAD WHAT WE NEEDED RIGHT
HERE. PERHAPS IT WAS CRUEL. BUT YOU HAD TO FIND*

SOMETHING WALDEMAR—TO FIND SOMETHING & LOSE ALL THE REST. THIS WAS VERY IMPORTANT. IF YOU HADNT <u>LOST</u> SOMETHING—EVERYTHING YOU MIGHT SAY—YOU WOULD NEVER HAVE COME.

TO COME <u>HERE</u> WALDEMAR YOU MUST LEAVE YOUR DURATION BEHIND.

WHAT TO DO NEXT IS SIMPLE. YOUVE JUMPED ONCE BEFORE AFTER ALL. REMEMBER HOW YOU DID IT THEN. REMEMBER CLIMBING INTO THE BIN. REMEMBER THE QUIET & THE DARK & THE THINGS THAT CAME AFTER. REMEMBER EVERYTHING FALLING AWAY. FRIGHTENING YES! BUT A JUMP ALWAYS IS. SIT RIGHT HERE AT THIS TABLE & MAKE YOURSELF EASY. THEN CLOSE YOUR EYES. THEN LET IT COME DOWN.

PLEASE TO FORGIVE US WALDEMAR. & PLEASE TO UNDERSTAND. ALL YOU EVER HAD TO DO WAS THIS. TO CLOSE YOUR EYES.

There was no signature, no closing endearment. The words ended where the sheet of paper did. I set it down carefully, as if the letter itself might be a kind of trip wire, and looked around me with enlightened eyes.

My mistake, Mrs. Haven, had been to think of Enzie's work in terms of science. I'd always viewed that apartment, and even its contents, as a kind of protective exoskeleton around her research—and I'd both been right and missed the point completely. The truth of that non-place was sad and uncanny and beautiful to the exact degree that my aunts' lives had been.

A fragment of the *"Märchen"* they'd once sent me came to mind:

> *What if the Attention of the dreamer, obeying no rules but the rules of association and chance, travels back and forth across the Present/Past membrane at will?*

Its meaning was clear to me at last, or clear enough. By tunneling through those rooms in a counterclockwise spiral—the form of certain pharaonic crypts, of the game of tarock, of Oppenheimer's famous fallout shelter blueprint—and packing them with light-and-sound-absorbing trash, my aunts had created a sensory and symbolic dead zone as effective as any deprivation chamber: an amplification corridor for travels back and forth across the Barrier, a particle accelerator of dreams. The Archive wasn't simply some whimsy of Genny's, or a fortress to sequester Enzie's work: it was the work itself. Which was why, when Haven and his Iterants stole Enzie's exclusion bin, it did so little for them. They'd taken a potted plant and missed the forest.

∞

It was 08:17 EST when I dialed Menügayan's number—not an hour when she was generally awake—and the phone rang sixteen times before she answered. Before she could say a word I told her everything. It was important to me that someone understand.

"Do you understand, Julia? My father had it right when he wrote *The Excuse*. Your consciousness is all the time machine you need. All that other nonsense—the notes, the calculations, even the exclusion bin—was a heap of pseudoscientific clutter. How on earth could I have missed it all this time?"

"Tolliver," said Menügayan, "don't call me again."

"Don't you see what this means? I have something to offer—something even Haven himself, with all his money and pull—"

"Is that right, Tolliver? You have something to offer? And what might that be?"

"I've just *told* you," I said, struggling to keep the exasperation out of my voice. "I've figured out my aunts' secret. I made a kind of half jump myself, it turns out, back when I was twelve. It's the simplest thing, really. Now I need to tell Hildy. She asked me for a time machine once, but—idiot that I was—I thought she was joking. I just need to explain—"

"They were found this morning. Their jet was, I mean. It's all over the news."

"Where?" I stammered, so excited I nearly dropped the receiver.

"Different places."

"Julia, just this once, I'd appreciate a simple—"

"Parts off of the coast of Dorset. Other parts near the Isle of Wight."

"Not true," I said. "You're lying. That's a lie."

"Suit yourself."

I'd been standing beside my aunts' toilet—the only place in the apartment where their ancient cordless phone still got reception—and now I came to rest against its cushioned seat. I found myself staring at the watch on my wrist, a Warranted Tolliver Navigator, rated to a depth of fifteen fathoms. It showed 08:21 EST. I took it off and laid it on the floor.

"You're not the only one who loved her," said a faraway voice.

"She's not dead, Julia. Not in any real sense. It's a mistake, mathematically speaking, to think of the past—"

"Goodbye, Tolliver, you poor misguided nutter. It's over, do you hear me? You're excused."

∞

It was the Timekeeper, of all people, who came to my mind in those ultimate seconds of consensus time, and I'm not ashamed to say I thought of him with sympathy. As I laid out the few things I'd brought from my suitcase—a bottle of Foster's the Australian had given me; your silver-bound edition of *Strange Customs of Courtship and Marriage*; Genny's copy of *The Shape of Time*; the manuscript of this history, nearly finished—I thought of Waldemar in his bunker in Czas, hearing the sound of Soviet gunfire in the surrounding woods, taking his leave from a world in which his passions and ambitions had no future. I would never find out how he'd managed his jump, or what had happened to the body he'd abandoned—the Russians had taken it, most likely, and done things to it that had brought them some small sense of reparation. I was reasonably sure now that I'd been wrong about his cameo in Visconti's *The Damned*, but I'd have liked to know at least that much for certain. I'd have asked him these questions, and plenty of others, if I'd succeeded in tracking him down—we'd have had a nice long chat, the two of us. But I wouldn't have asked where he'd found the nerve to excise himself from time so brutally, or why he'd chosen such an absolute escape. I wouldn't have had to ask, because I knew.

I drank a toast to him, Mrs. Haven, before I sat down in this chair and tripped the wire. There was no moral high ground where I was going—no agency, no consequence, no cause or effect. And still I hoped that I would find you there.

Monday, 08:47 EST

I dreamed that time was moving backward, Mrs. Haven. The universe had reached its point of maximum expansion and tipped back toward collapse, reversing direction from redshift to blueshift, from future to past, and the thermodynamic arrow shifted with it. Order increased with each instant, as certain renegade physicists have predicted it will, and in time those same physicists, long dead and forgotten, duly rose from their graves and reconstituted themselves and moved through life end-to-front, smoothly and effortlessly, like tourists sitting backward on a train.

Everything happened, Mrs. Haven, that had happened before. Rivers flowed uphill and trees shrank to seedlings and the overheated earth began to cool. Sounds gradually took form out of nothing and were cut off at the apex of their curves. Eggs returned to their chickens, bombs returned to their bombers, and effects flew home like bullets to their causes. The last became first and the first became last, though no one profited by the exchange. But I was grateful all the same—grateful even for that awful certainty—because I knew that you were coming back to me.

I sat on the same train as everyone else, fighting my fear of all the black, empty aeons before I was born. The farther I traveled the younger I grew, and the younger I grew the less I could remember. The universe was contracting to a pinprick, the first singularity, a videotaped explosion playing coolly in reverse. I returned to you, Mrs. Haven, as I'd known that I would, and there was nothing either of us could do to stop it. Pain compressed to a spike, no differently than light or sound or thought, and vanished just as it became too much to bear.

We backed into each other on Masarykovo Square, returned the pages to Artur and regressed to Vienna, growing more confident and loving by the hour. I knew each event of my duration before it occurred—I saw it ever more clearly as it came hurtling toward me—but as soon as it happened my mind was flushed clean. Haven didn't matter, Menügayan didn't matter, because soon they'd be erased from the record, swept clear of the field, exactly as if they had never been. I drifted through Manhattan alone, just as desperate and dejected as before, though I knew our separate time lines were converging. It was terrible, Mrs. Haven, to have such definite knowledge, and to have it confirmed with each recurring scene. You were with me at the Xanthia, in the James A. Farley Post Office, at West Tenth Street and in my own bed. The silver book returned itself to sender and I followed it down to your basement apartment. I helped you put your clothes on, Mrs. Haven, growing more nervous with each button I did up. You pursued me back uptown to Union Square, never once turning your head to see where you were going. People fled from you on University, smiling and deferential, happy just to see you pass them by.

There was no stopping any of it, Mrs. Haven—no stopping it or altering its course. You were gone from me for a cloudy, leaden month, then you were mine: as close to mine as you would ever be. You lay down with me on the corkwood floor of Van's bedroom and your backside chased me down his spiral stairs. We reached the kitchen door and slipped under the counter. You let go of my hand. The smile left your face as I left you behind. You covered your upper lip with your ring finger. Then all trace of you was gone, even from my memory, and I was free.

Time passed more slowly the farther I traveled. The music of the spheres grew louder by the day, by the hour, by the second, though like everyone else on earth I barely heard it. I was a man, then a teen, then a child, then a fertilized egg. That vast sepulchral symphony was all there ever was.

Then it ended, Mrs. Haven, because I'd come to the beginning of my dream.

Dear Mrs. Haven—

This morning, at 08:47 EST, I woke up to find myself excused from time.

I can picture you perfectly, reading this letter. You'll be telling yourself I've gone stupid with grief, or that I've lost my mind—but my thinking has never been clearer. Believe me, Mrs. Haven, when I tell you that this is no joke. Time moves freely around me, gurgling like a whirlpool, fluxing like a quantum field, spinning like a galaxy around its focal hub—at the hub, however, everything is quiet.

ACKNOWLEDGMENTS

Kathleen Alcott, Jin Auh, Francis Bickmore, Charles Buchan, Eric Chinski, Ronald W. Clark, Brooke Costello, Elizabeth Costello, Kathy Daneman, Doug Dibbern, Joanna Dingley, Matt Dojny, J. W. Dunne, Marion Duvert, Nathan Englander, Alexander Fest, Adam Foulds, Jessica Friedman, Laird Gallagher, J. Richard Gott, Sophie Gudenus, Bill Hall, Barbara W. Henderson, Edward Henderson, Corin Hewitt, Heinrich Höhne, Allan S. Janik, James Jeans, Christy-Claire Katien, Kirsten Kearse, Frank Kendig, Ursula LeGuin, Haruki Murakami, Vladimir Ouspensky, Gary Panter, Sara Poirier, Sarah Sarchin, Akhil Sharma, Adrian Tomine, Thomas Überhoff, Jared Whitham, Nicolas Williams, Anni Wünschmann, Peter Wünschmann, Andrew Wylie.

The author wishes to express his gratitude to the John Simon Guggenheim Memorial Foundation, the Dorothy and Lewis B. Cullman Center for Scholars and Writers, the American Academy in Berlin, the Civitella Ranieri Foundation, and the Santa Maddalena Foundation for invaluable assistance in the completion of this book.